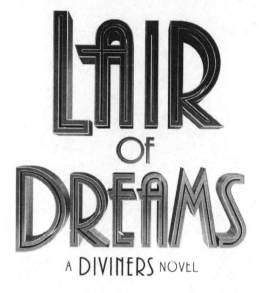

LAIR OF DREAMS

A DIVINERS NOVEL

LAIR OF DREAMS

OF

DREAMS

A DIVINERS NOVEL

LIBBA BRAY

(L B)

LITTLE, BROWN AND COMPANY

NEW YORK   BOSTON

Copyright © 2015 by Martha E. Bray

Photograph on pages ii–iii and pages vi–vii courtesy of the Library of Congress, Prints & Photographs Division, HAER NY, 31-NEYO, 86—99

Little, Brown and Company

Hachette Book Group
1290 Avenue of the Americas, New York, NY 10104
Visit us at lb-teens.com

Little, Brown and Company is a division of Hachette Book Group, Inc.
The Little, Brown name and logo are trademarks of Hachette Book Group, Inc.

The publisher is not responsible for websites (or their content) that are not owned by the publisher.

First Edition: August 2015
First International Edition: August 2015

Library of Congress Cataloging-in-Publication Data

Bray, Libba.
    Lair of dreams : a Diviners novel / Libba Bray.—First edition.
        pages cm
    Summary: "After a supernatural showdown with a serial killer, Evie O'Neill has outed herself as a Diviner and has become a media darling. In the meantime, a mysterious sleeping sickness has hit New York City, and the Diviners must band together to find the cause and the cure"— Provided by publisher.
    ISBN 978-0-316-12604-5 (hardback) — ISBN 978-0-316-28645-9 (international) — 978-0-316-36488-1 (ebook) — ISBN 978-0-316-36487-4 (library edition ebook) [1. Psychic ability—Fiction. 2. Supernatural—Fiction. 3. Sleep—Fiction. 4. Dreams—Fiction. 5. New York (N.Y.)—History—1898–1951—Fiction. 6. Mystery and detective stories.] I. Title.
    PZ7.B7386Lai 2015
    [Fic]—dc23
                                                                                2015010856

10 9 8 7 6 5 4 3 2 1

RRD-C

Printed in the United States of America

For Alvina & Greg

True love is the best thing in the world, except for cough drops.
Everybody knows that.
—William Goldman, *The Princess Bride*

And for Alex Hillian
1970–2013

Sweet dreams, Senator.

I cannot be awake for nothing looks to me as it did before,
Or else I am awake for the first time, and all before has
been a mean sleep.

    —Walt Whitman

To believe in one's dreams is to spend all one's life asleep.

    —Chinese proverb

PART ONE

DAY ONE

THE CITY UNDER THE CITY

New York City, 1927

Every city is a ghost.

New buildings rise upon the bones of the old so that each shiny steel beam, each tower of brick carries within it the memories of what has gone before, an architectural haunting. Sometimes you can catch a glimpse of these former incarnations in the awkward angle of a street or a filigreed gate, an old oak door peeking out from a new facade, the plaque commemorating the spot that was once a battleground, which became a saloon and is now a park.

Underground, it's no different.

Beneath the streets, this city grows. Tracks push farther out into Brooklyn, Queens, and the Bronx. Tunnels connect one place to another, closing the distance between impossible and possible. So many people to move. The city's aspirations do not stop at ground level. The whine of the drill and the clank of the pickax serenade the workers as they clear out rock for a new subway tunnel. Sweat binds layers of dust to the men till it's hard to tell where they leave off and the gloom begins. The drill bites away bedrock in small mouthfuls. It's hard, tedious work. And then suddenly, they're breaking through the rock too fast.

"Watch it! Watch it, now!"

A wall of earth drops away. The men cough and cough, choking on the thick air. One of them, an Irish immigrant named Padraic, wipes a dirty forearm across his sweaty brow and peers into the large hole the drill has made. On the other side is a tall wrought-iron gate gone to rust, one of those ghosts of an earlier time. Padraic shines his flashlight through the gate's bars, and the rusty coating brightens like the dried blood of an old wound.

"I'll be," he says and grins at the others. "Might be somet'ing worth havin' inside."

He tugs and the rusted gate shrieks open, and then the men are inside the dust-choked hole of a forgotten part of the city's past. The Irishman whistles as his beam bounces around the tomblike room, revealing wooden panels grayed with cobwebs, tile mosaics obscured by layers of grime, a light fixture dangling precariously from a broken chain. A train car sits half-buried under a mountain of fallen dirt. Its wheels are silenced, but in the darkness, it's almost as if the workers can hear the faint whine of metal on metal lingering in the preserved air. Padraic's flashlight beam shines across the tracks, tracing them backward to a dead tunnel. The men move close and peer into the murkiness. It's like looking into hell's gaping mouth, tracks for tongue. The tunnel seems to go on forever, but that's just the dark talking.

"What's in here, then?" Padraic asks.

"A speakeasy," says another man, Michael, chuckling.

"Grand. I could use a drink," Padraic jokes as he heads inside, still hopeful of some lost treasure. The workers follow. These men are the unseen builders of the city, like ghosts themselves, and they've no need to fear the dark.

Only Sun Yu hesitates. He hates the dark, actually, but he needs the job, and jobs are hard to come by when you're Chinese. As it is, he only got the job because he shares a cold-water flat with Padraic and several others in Chinatown, and the Irishman put in a word for him with the boss. It wouldn't do to make waves. So he, too, follows. As Sun Yu navigates the mounds of fallen dirt and brick on the tracks, he stumbles over something. Padraic swings his flashlight beam over the tracks again and finds a pretty little music box with a hand crank on top. Padraic lifts the music box, admiring the workmanship. They don't make them like that anymore. He turns the crank on the cylinder. A song plinks out note by note. It's one he's heard before, an old song, but he can't really remember it.

He considers taking the music box but puts it back. "Let's see what other treasures are down here."

Padraic swings the flashlight. The beam finds a skeletal foot. At the base of the curved wall is a mummified corpse mostly eaten away by rot and rats and time. The men fall quiet. They stare at the tufts of hair gone as thin as candy floss, and at the mouth, which is open as if in a final scream. A few of the men cross themselves. They left a lot behind to come to this country, but not their superstitions.

Sun Yu is uneasy, but he doesn't have the words in English to communicate his feelings. This woman met a very bad end. If he were back in China, he'd see to the proper prayers and burial. For everyone knows a spirit can't rest without that. But this is America. Things are different here.

"Bad luck," he says at last, and no one disagrees.

"Right. We best be back at it, lads," Padraic says with a heavy sigh.

The men pile out of the hole. As Padraic closes the gate, he regards the unearthed station with pity. It'll be gone soon enough, knocked out to make way for new subway lines for the growing city. Progress keeps progressing.

"Shame," he says.

Moments later, the high-pitched hum of the workers' jackhammers melds with the constant rattle of the subway trains; the city's song reverberates in the tunnels. Suddenly, the work lights dim. The men pause. Wind wafts down the tunnel and caresses their sweaty faces. It carries the faint sound of crying, and then it's gone. The lights brighten again. The men shrug—just one of those odd things that happen in the city under the city. They start in again; their machines turn up the earth, burying history in their wake.

Later, the exhausted workers return to Chinatown and climb the stairs to their shared room. They fall into their beds, the dirt of the city still caked under their ragged nails. They're too tired for bathing, but they're not too tired for dreams. For dreams, too, are ghosts, desires chased in sleep, gone by morning. The longing of dreams draws the dead, and this city holds many dreams.

The men dream of the music box and its song, a relic from a time long ago.

"Beautiful dreamer, wake unto me / Starlight and dewdrops are waiting for thee. . . ."

The song calls to their blood, ferries them into the best dreams they've ever had—dreams in which they are aboveground, men of fortune and renown, owners in a country that smiles on owning. Michael dreams of overseeing his own construction company. Padraic dreams of a farm upstate filled with horses. Sun Yu dreams of returning to his village as a prosperous man, and of the pride in his parents' faces as he brings them to America, along with a wife for himself. Yes, a wife to share the burdens and joys of life here. He can see her smiling at him. Such a sweet face! And are those his children beside her? They are! Happy sons and daughters welcoming him home at the end of the day with his slippers and pipe and happy cries of "Baba!" as they beg for a story.

Sun Yu reaches for his youngest child, and the dream fades to embers. There is only the dark of the tunnel they found earlier in the day. Sun Yu calls out for his children and hears soft crying. It breaks his heart to hear it.

"Don't cry," he soothes.

In the gloom, there's a sudden spark. For a few seconds, his longed-for family life comes alive again, as if Sun Yu were looking through a keyhole at happiness. One of the children crooks a finger, smiles.

"Dream with me . . ." he whispers.

Yes. I will, Sun Yu thinks. He opens the door and steps across the threshold.

It's cold inside, so cold Sun Yu can feel it even in his sleep. The stove isn't lit. That's the trouble. Sun Yu moves forward and notices that the stove isn't really a stove at all. It wobbles, and underneath that image, he can make out old bricks gone to rot and ruin. Out of the corner of his eye, he spies a rat. It stops to sniff a pile of bones.

Alarmed, Sun Yu turns to his family. The children are no longer smiling. They're lined up, staring at him.

"*Dreamwithusdreamweneedyoutodream*..." the children chorus, his wife looking on, her teeth sharp and her eyes like coals.

Sun Yu's heartbeat begins to double, an autonomic response. Fight or flight. Even in sleep, it works. Sun Yu wants to wake up, but the dream won't let him. It's angry that he's trying to escape. When he runs for the door, it slams shut.

"*You promised*," the dream growls in a voice as thick as a choir of demons.

The music-box song plays. The last of the pretty facade peels away. The dark moves in.

One by one, the other men sense the danger lurking beneath the beauty. It's a trap, this dreaming. In sleep, their fingers stiffen as they try to fight back against the terror invading their minds. For the dream knows their fears as well as their desires. It can make them see anything. Unspeakable nightmares surround the men now. They would scream if they could. It's no use. The dream has them, and it will not relinquish its hold. Ever.

Back in their beds on Mott Street, the men's bodies go limp. But behind their closed lids, their eyes move frantically as, one by one, they are pulled deeper and deeper into a nightmare from which they will never, ever wake.

DAY SIX

SPEAKING TO THE DEAD

A gust of winter wind battered the colorful paper lanterns hanging from the eaves of the Tea House restaurant on Doyers Street. Only a few diners remained, lingering over plates scraped clean of food and cups of tea whose warmth they were reluctant to leave. Cooks and waiters bustled about, eager to end their shifts so that they could unwind with cigars and a few games of mah-jongg.

At the back of her father's restaurant, Ling Chan, seventeen, glared through the carved slivers of a teak screen at the lollygagging patrons as if her stare alone could compel them to pay up and leave.

"This night will never end," George Huang said, suddenly beside Ling with yet another pot of tea from the kitchen. He was Ling's age and as skinny as a greyhound.

"You could always lock the door," Ling said.

"And have your father fire me?" George shook his head and poured Ling a cup of tea.

"Thank you," Ling said.

George gave a half smile and a shrug. "You need to keep your strength up."

The door opened, and a trio of girls entered the restaurant, their cold breath trailing misty white tails.

"Is that Lee Fan Lin?" George said, staring at the prettiest, a girl with red lips and a Marcel Wave bob. Quickly, George put down the teapot and smoothed a hand through his hair.

"George. Don't—" Ling started, but George was already waving Lee Fan over.

Quietly, Ling swore an oath as Lee Fan broke from the group and glided past the lacquered tables and potted ferns toward the back, the panels of her beaded dress swishing from side to side. Lee Fan ran with what Ling's mother called "a fast crowd." Her mother did not say it admiringly.

"Hello, Georgie. Ling!" Lee Fan said, taking a seat.

George grabbed a cup from a tray. "Would you care for tea, Lee Fan?"

Lee Fan laughed. "Oh, Georgie. Call me Lulu, won't you?"

Lee Fan had taken to calling herself that after Louise Brooks, a crime of affectation that Ling placed on a par with people who hugged in greeting. Ling did not hug. George stole glances at Lee Fan as he poured her tea. Ling knew for a fact that Lee Fan could have her pick of beaus, and her pick would not be gangly, studious George Huang. Boys could be so stupid sometimes, and George was no exception.

Lee Fan pretended to be interested in Ling's stack of library books. "What are you reading now?"

"Ways to poison without detection," Ling muttered.

Lee Fan examined the books one by one: *Physics for Students. The ABC of Atoms. Atoms and Rays.* "Oooh, *Jake Marlowe, the Great American*," she said, holding up the last one.

"Ling's hero. She wants to work for him someday." George tried for a laugh but snorted instead. Ling wanted to tell him that snorting was not the way to win any girl's heart.

"What did you want, Lee Fan?" Ling asked.

Lee Fan leaned in. "I need your help. My blue dress is missing."

Ling raised an eyebrow and waited for the words that might make her care.

"My aunt and uncle had it made for me in Shanghai. It's my best dress," Lee Fan said.

Ling managed a patient face. "Do you think you lost it in a dream?"

"Of course not!" Lee Fan snapped. She glanced back at the girls standing up front, waiting for her like good little followers. "But just the other day, Gracie was over to listen to my jazz records, and you know how the old girl is, always asking to borrow my things. I saw her eyeing my dress, which was certainly too small for her, what with those big shoulders of hers. Anyway, that night, when I went to look for it, it was gone," Lee Fan said, adjusting her scarf as if its asymmetry were her greatest concern. "Naturally, Gracie claims she doesn't have it, but I'm sure she took it."

Up front, big-shouldered Gracie Leung examined her fingernails, none the wiser.

"What do you want me to do about it?" Ling asked.

"I want you to speak to my grandmother in one of your little dream walks. I want to know the truth."

"You want me to try to reach your grandmother to find your dress?" Ling said slowly.

"It's very expensive," Lee Fan insisted.

"Very well," Ling said, resisting the urge to roll her eyes. "But you should know that the dead don't always want to talk to you. I can only try. Second, they don't know everything, and their answers can be vague at best. Do you accept the terms?"

Lee Fan waved away Ling's admonitions. "Yes, fine, fine."

"That will be five dollars."

Lee Fan's mouth rounded in shock. "That's outrageous!"

It was, of course. But Ling always started the bargaining high— and even higher if the request was downright stupid, which Lee Fan's was. Ling shrugged once more. "You'd spend that for a night at the Fallen Angel."

"At least with the Fallen Angel, I know what I'm getting," Lee Fan snarled.

Ling concentrated on creasing a napkin seam long and slow with a thumbnail. "Suit yourself."

"The dead don't come cheap," George said, trying for a joke.

Lee Fan glared at Ling. "You probably make it all up just to get attention."

"If you believe it, it will be. If you do not, it won't," Ling said.

Lee Fan slid a dollar across the table. Ling let it sit.

"I have to cover my expenses. Make the proper prayers. I could never forgive myself if I brought bad luck on you, Lee Fan." Ling managed a quarter smile that she hoped passed for sincere.

Lee Fan peeled off another bill. "Two dollars. My final offer."

Ling pocketed the money. "I'll need something of your grandmother's to locate her in the dream world."

"Why?"

"It's like a bloodhound with scent. It helps me find her spirit."

With a drawn-out sigh, Lee Fan twisted a gold ring from her finger and scooted it toward Ling. "Don't lose it."

"I'm not the one who seems to be losing things," Ling muttered.

Lee Fan rose. She glanced down at her coat, then at George, who jumped to help her with it. "Careful, Georgie," she stage-whispered, nodding toward Ling. "She might curse you. For all you know, she'll give you the sleeping sickness."

George's smile vanished. "Don't joke about that."

"Why not?"

"It's bad luck."

"It's superstition. We're Americans now." Lee Fan marched through the restaurant, slowing to allow everyone to watch her. Through the holes in the screen, Ling watched Lee Fan and her acolytes walking easily into the winter's night. She wished she could tell them the truth: The dead were easy to talk to; it was the living she didn't like.

⁂

The cold wind whistling around the curve of Doyers Street made Ling's teeth chatter as she and George walked home toward Mulberry Street. The laundries, jewelers, groceries, and import shops were closed, but the various social clubs were open, their cigarette smoke–drenched

16

back rooms filled with businessmen, old-timers, newcomers, and restless young bachelors all playing dominoes and Fan-Tan, trading stories and jokes, money and ambition. Across the rooftops, the Church of the Transfiguration's steeple loomed at the edge of the neighborhood, a silent judge. A trio of slightly drunk tourists stumbled out of a restaurant talking loudly of heading over to the Bowery and the illicit delights to be found there in the deep shadows beneath the Third Avenue El.

Beside Ling, George jogged up and back, up and back, in little bursts like the track star he was. For a slight boy, he was surprisingly strong. Ling had seen him carry heavy trays without much trouble at all, and he could run for miles. She envied him that.

"You charge too much money. That's your trouble. Other Diviners charge less," George said, panting.

"Then let Lee Fan go to one of them. Let her go to that idiot on the radio, the Sweetheart Seer," Ling said. Lee Fan might live it up in nightclubs uptown, but Ling knew she wouldn't go outside the neighborhood for fortune-telling.

"What are you saving money for, anyway?" George asked.

"College."

"Why do you need college?"

"Why do you let Lee Fan run you like a dog?" Ling shot back, her patience at an end.

"She doesn't run me," George said, sulking.

Ling rebuked him with a guttural "ack" of disappointment. Once upon a time, Ling and George had been close. She'd been his protector of sorts. When the Italian boys from Mulberry Street harassed George on the way to school, it was Ling who had told them she was a *strega* who would curse them if they didn't leave George alone, and whether they believed her or not, they didn't bother him after that. George had thanked Ling with a prune hamantasch from Gertie's Bakery on Ludlow, the two of them laughing as they picked the tiny seeds from their teeth. But over the past year, Ling had watched George grow moody and restless, chasing after things he couldn't have—tagging along with Lee Fan's set as they went to the pictures at the Strand, sitting in on picnics arranged by a local church, or squeezed in the backseat during Sunday drives in Tom Kee's car, one foot in Chinatown and the other outside, angling for a spot they thought was better, a spot that didn't include Ling.

"She's changed you," Ling said.

"She has not! You're the one who's changed. You used to be fun, before—"

George cut himself off abruptly, but Ling could fill in the rest of his sentence for him. She looked away.

"I'm sorry," he said, chagrined. "I didn't mean it."

"I know."

"I'm just tired. I didn't sleep well last night."

Ling drew in a sharp breath.

"I don't have the sleeping sickness!" George said quickly. He held out his hands. "Look: No burns. No blisters."

"So what's the trouble, then?"

"I had the oddest dream."

"Probably because you're odd."

"Do you want to hear this?"

"Go on."

"It was incredible!" George said, his voice hinting at wonder. "I was at one of those mansions like the millionaires have out on Long Island, only it was my house and my party. I was rich and important. People looked at me with respect, Ling. Not like here. And Lee Fan was there, too," George said shyly.

"I didn't realize it was a nightmare," Ling muttered.

George ignored her. "It all seemed so real. Like it was right there for the taking."

Ling kept her eyes on the uneven edges of the bricks. "Lots of things seem real in dreams. And then you wake up."

"Not like this. Maybe it has something to do with the New Year? Maybe it's good luck?"

"How should I know?"

"Because you know about dreams!" George said, jogging in front of her. "You can walk around inside them. Come on—it has to mean something, doesn't it?"

He was practically begging her to say it was so, and in that moment, she hated George a little bit for being so naive, for thinking that a good dream could mean anything other than a night's escape from reality until the morning came. For thinking that wanting something so badly was enough to make it come true.

"I'll tell you what it means: It means that you're a fool if you believe Lee Fan will give you the time of day once Tom Kee comes back from Chicago. You can keep throwing yourself at her, but she's never going to choose you, George. Never."

George stood perfectly still. His wounded expression told her that the words had hurt. She hadn't meant to be cruel, only truthful.

George's eyes went mean. "I pity the poor soul who takes you for a wife, Ling. No man wants to have the dead in his bed every night," he said, and then he marched away, leaving Ling just short of her building.

Ling tried not to take the words inside, but they'd already settled there. Why couldn't she have just left George alone? For a moment, she had half a mind to call him back, tell him she was sorry. But she knew George was too angry to hear it now. Tomorrow she'd apologize. For now, she had Lee Fan's money in her pocket and a job to do. Ling moved slowly toward her building, feeling each bump and brick up her spine. Above her, yellow-warmed windows dotted the building facades, forming urban constellations. Other windows were dark. People were asleep. Asleep and dreaming, hopeful that they'd wake in the morning.

For all you know, she'll give you the sleeping sickness.

It had started with a group of diggers who shared a room on Mott Street. For several days, the three men lay in their beds, sleeping. Doctors had tried slapping the men, dousing them with cold water, striking the soles of their feet. Nothing worked. The men would not wake. Blisters and weeping red patches appeared all over their bodies, as if they were being consumed from the inside. And then they were dead. The doctors were baffled—and worried. Already the "sleeping sickness" had claimed five more people in Chinatown. And just that morning, they'd heard there were new cases in the Italian section of Mulberry Street and in the Jewish quarter between Orchard and Ludlow.

A group of bright young things marched arm in arm down the street, laughing and carefree, and Ling was reminded of a dream walk she'd taken a few months ago. In it, she'd suddenly found herself face-to-face with a blond flapper. The girl was clearly asleep, but she also seemed aware of Ling, and Ling had felt both drawn to and afraid of this girl, as if they were long-lost relatives having a chance meeting.

"You shouldn't be here! Wake up!" Ling had yelled. And then, suddenly, Ling had tumbled down through dream space until she came to rest in a forest where ghostly soldiers shimmered in the spaces between the trees. On their sleeves, they wore a strange symbol: a golden sun of an eye shedding a jagged lightning-bolt tear. Ling often spoke to the dead in dreams, but these men weren't like any dead she had known.

"What do you want?" she'd asked them, afraid.

"Help us," they said, and then the sky exploded with light.

Since then, Ling had dreamed of that symbol a few times. She didn't know what it meant. But she now knew who the blond girl was. Everyone in New York did: the Sweetheart Seer.

Feeling a mixture of envy and resentment, she watched the laughing partygoers walk away, then let herself into her building. Ling stole into her room and deposited Lee Fan's two dollars into the cigar-box college fund she kept hidden in a drawer under her slips. The two dollars joined the one hundred twenty-five she'd already collected.

In the parlor, Ling's uncle Eddie was asleep in his favorite chair. One of his Chinese opera records had come to the end on the phonograph. Ling lifted the needle and covered her uncle with a blanket. Her mother was still at a church quilting bee, and her father would be another hour at the restaurant. This meant Ling finally had control of the radio. Soon, the comforting hum of the Philco warming up chased away Ling's unease. An announcer's voice burbled through the speakers, growing louder.

"Good evening, ladies and gentlemen of our listening audience. It's precisely nine o'clock and time for the Pears Soap Hour featuring that fabulous Flapper of Fate, the Sweetheart Seer—Miss Evie O'Neill...."

THE SWEETHEART SEER

"...Miss Evie O'Neill!"

The announcer, a tall man with a thin mustache, lowered his script. Behind the glass of the control booth, an engineer pointed to a quartet of male singers back in the studio, who crooned into their microphone:

> "She's the apple of the Big Apple's eye.
> She's finer—Diviner—and we know why.
> She's the Sweetheart Seer of W...G...I!"

"Yes, gifted with talents from beyond," the announcer purred over the soft hum of the quartet. "A Diviner, she calls herself, like those soothsayers of old, but a modern girl, through and through. Who knew that such gifts lived in the heart of Manhattan—and in the heavenly form of a pretty pixie of a girl?"

> "Oh, Evie, won't you tell us true?
> What would fate have us do?
> Whether watch or hat or band,
> You hold our secrets in your hand.
> Revealing mysteries pulled from the sky!
> You're the Sweetheart Seer of W...G...I!"

The orchestra rested. Script in hand, Evie stepped up to her microphone and chirped into it: "Hello, everyone. This is Evie O'Neill, the Sweetheart Seer, ready to gaze into the great beyond and tell you your deepest secrets. So I certainly hope you've got something pos-i-tute-ly scandalous for me tonight!"

"Why, Miss O'Neill!" the announcer sputtered.

The audience chuckled, covering the sound of Evie and Mr. Forman turning the pages of their scripts.

"Oh, now, don't you cast a kitten, Mr. Forman," Evie reassured him in her upbeat tone. "For if anything can clear away the dirt of scandal, it's Pears soap. Why, no soap on earth is finer for cleaning up a mess than Pears!"

"On that we can agree, Miss O'Neill. If you value your complexion, Pears soap is the only soap you will ever need. It's—"

"Gee, are you going to talk all night, Mr. Forman? Or can I do a little divining for these fine folks?" Evie teased.

The audience chuckled again, right on cue.

"Very well, Miss O'Neill. Let's take our first guest, shall we? Mrs. Charles Rutherford, I believe you have something you wish to share?"

"Yes, I do!" Mrs. Rutherford rose from her seat, smoothing her dress on her way to Evie, though there was no one to see it beyond those in the small room. "I've brought this money clip."

"Welcome, Mrs. Rutherford. Thank you for coming on the Pears Soap Hour with the Sweetheart Seer—Pears, the soap of purity. Now, Mrs. Rutherford, tell Miss O'Neill nothing of your object. She will divine your secrets using her talents from beyond the veil."

"So if there's anything you haven't told Mr. Rutherford, you might want to let him know now," Evie joked. It was a little naughty, but naughty kept people listening.

"Oh, dear," Mrs. Rutherford tittered.

"And to whom does that money clip belong?" Evie asked.

Mrs. Rutherford blushed. "This... well, it... it's my husband's."

Evie didn't have to be a Diviner to know that. Married women almost always wanted to know about their husbands and whether they were stepping out.

"Now, Mrs. Rutherford, one doll to another: What's the story?"

"Well, you see, Charles has been so very busy lately, at the office every night with only his secretary for company, and I, I worry that..."

Evie nodded sympathetically. "Don't you worry, Mrs. Rutherford. We'll soon get to the bottom of this. If you would place the object in the center of my right palm, please. Thank you." With a magician's flair, Evie placed her left hand on top of her right and pressed down, allowing the money clip to yield its secrets to her.

"Oh, dear me," Evie said, coming out of her light trance.

"What is it? What do you see?" Mrs. Rutherford fretted.

"I don't know if I should say, Mrs. Rutherford," Evie said, drawing out the tension for the radio audience.

"Please, Miss O'Neill, if there's something I should know..."

"Well..." Evie's tone was grave. "You do know that the objects never lie."

An anticipatory murmur spread through the studio audience. *I've got them!* Evie thought. She lowered her head as if she were a doctor delivering grim news. "Your husband and his secretary are in cahoots, all right...." Head still bowed, Evie waited, counting off silently—*two, three*—and then she looked up, grinning triumphantly. "To plan your birthday party!"

The audience responded with relieved laughter and thunderous applause.

"Now it won't be a surprise any longer, I'm afraid," Evie said. "You'll have to act like a Dumb Dora about it. And that goes for all of you folks listening in, too!"

"Thank you! Oh, thank you, Miss O'Neill!"

The announcer stepped up to his microphone again as Mrs. Rutherford was escorted back to her seat. "Let's give a warm round of applause to the brave Mrs. Rutherford."

When the noise died down, Evie welcomed her second guest. When she'd finished with him, telling him where to find a cache of old war bonds his grandfather had hidden in the house, Evie waited for the Seer Singers to croon the Pears soap jingle, then stepped again to the microphone, the studio lights blazing in her eyes. Even though the home audience couldn't see her, she knew from her daily elocution lessons that a smile could be communicated through the wires, so she kept hers bright.

"Ladies and gentlemen, when I finish my radio show, I love nothing more than to relax with a nice hot bath. But when I bathe, I'm not alone."

"You're not?" the announcer shot back, shock in his tone.

"Oh, no! I have company in my tub."

"Why, Miss O'Neill!"

"Dear me, Mr. Forman! It's Pears soap, of course! Pears keeps a girl's complexion smooth and lovely even when the winter winds are howling like a jazz band. Why, it's so pure, even *I* can't see anything in it!"

"That's pure, indeed! Choose Pears—the modern choice for you and your loved ones. Now, Miss O'Neill, before we say good night, can you tell the fine members of our listening audience what you see?"

"I'd be happy to." Evie let her voice take on a faraway tone. "Yes... I can see into the future and I see"—she let the silence hang for a count of three—"that it's going to be a swell evening here on WGI, so don't dream of touching that dial! This is Evie O'Neill, America's Sweetheart Seer, saying thank you and good night, and may all your secrets be happy ones!"

❀

As Evie passed down the long Art Deco hallway of the radio station, people called out their congratulations: "Swell show, Evie!" "Gee, that was terrific!" "You're the berries, kid!"

Evie drank up their praise like a champagne cocktail. She stopped for a second in the foyer of a large, wood-paneled office with gleaming black-and-gold marble floors. A secretary waved to her from behind a desk.

"Great show, Evie."

"Thanks, Kaye!" Evie said, preening.

There were only two rules she followed on her show: One, she never went in too deep. That was what kept the headaches manageable. And two, no bad news. Evie only told the object holder what he or she wanted to hear. People wanted entertainment, yes, but mostly they wanted hope: *Tell me he still loves me. Tell me I'm not a failure. Tell me I did right by my dead mother, whom I never visited, even when she called my name at the end. Tell me it'll be okay.*

"Loved the way you played with the money clip," the secretary continued. "I sure was nervous for that Mrs. Rutherford."

Evie strained to see into the office just beyond the secretary, but the burnished gold doors were shut. "Did…did Mr. Phillips like it?"

The secretary smiled sympathetically. "Gee, honey, you know how the Big Cheese is: He only shows up for the biggest names. Oh!" she said, catching herself. "Gee, I didn't mean it like that, Evie. Your show's very popular."

Just not popular enough to get the full attention of WGI's owner. Evie tried not to dwell on that fact as she grabbed her new raccoon coat and gray wool cloche from the coat-check girl and headed out front, where a small but enthusiastic crowd waited in the January drizzle. When Evie opened the door, they surged forward, their umbrellas like fat black petals of the same straining flower.

"Miss O'Neill! Miss O'Neill!"

Slips of paper and autograph books were waved at her. She signed each with a flourish before dashing down the alley toward a waiting taxicab.

"Where to, Miss?" the cabbie asked.

"The Grant Hotel, please."

The rain was coming down; the taxi's windshield wipers beat in time to some unseen metronome as they cleared the fogging glass. Evie peered out the taxi window at the study in smoke, fog, snow, and neon that was Manhattan's Theater District at this late hour. A lightbulb-ringed theater bill featured an illustration of a tuxedoed man in a turban holding out his hands like a soothsayer while comely chorines danced under his enchanting sway. A sash at the top read COMING SOON—THE ZIEGFELD FOLLIES IN *DIVINERS FEVER!* A MAGICAL, MUSICAL REVUE!

Diviners were big and getting bigger, but so far, no Diviner was bigger than Evie O'Neill. If only James were around to see her now. Evie traced the empty space at her neck where the half-dollar pendant from her brother used to rest, a reflex.

A billboard for Marlowe Industries loomed above the jostling cab as they waited for the light to change. The billboard showed a silhouette of the great man himself, his arm gesturing to some nebulous future defined only by rays of sunshine. Marlowe Industries. The future of America.

"He's coming to town soon, you know," the taxi driver said.

Evie rubbed her temples to keep the headache at bay. "Who?"

"Mr. Marlowe."

"You don't say."

"I do say! He's breaking ground out in Queens for that whatchamacallit—that exhibition he's planning. Traffic'll be murder that day. I tell ya, he's already given us the good life—automobiles, aeroplanes, medicine, and who knows what else. Now, that's a great American." The cabbie cleared his throat. "Say, uh, ain't you the Sweetheart Seer?"

Evie sat up, thrilled to be recognized. "Guilty as charged."

"I thought so! My wife loves your radio show! Wait'll I tell her I drove you in my cab. She'll have kittens!"

"Jeepers, I hope not. I'm all out of cigars."

The light changed and the cab turned left off the arterial throughway of Broadway, following the narrow tributary of Forty-seventh Street east toward Beekman Place and the Grant.

"You're the little lady who helped the cops catch the Pentacle Killer." The cabbie whistled. "The way he butchered all those people.

Taking that poor girl's eyes? Stringing that fella up in Trinity Cemetery with his tongue cut out? Skinning that chorus girl and—"

"Yes, I remember," Evie interrupted, hoping he would take the hint.

"What kind of person does that? What's this world coming to?" The cabbie shook his head. "It's these foreigners coming over, bringing trouble. And disease. You hear there's some kinda sleeping sickness now? Already got about ten people with new cases every day. Heard it started in Chinatown and spread to the Italians and Jews." He shook his head. "Foreigners. Oughta t'row 'em all out, you want my opinion."

I don't, Evie thought.

"There's talk the killer—that John Hobbes fella—wasn't even human. That he was some kinda ghost." The cabbie's eyes met hers in the rearview mirror for a moment, seeking either confirmation or dismissal.

Evie wondered what the cabbie would say if she told him the truth—that John Hobbes was most definitely not of this earth. He was worse than any demon imaginable, and she'd barely escaped with her life.

Evie looked away. "People say all sorts of things, don't they? Oh, look. Here we are!"

The driver pulled up to the monolithic splendor that was the Grant Hotel. Through the cab window, Evie spied a scrum of reporters staked out on the hotel steps, smoking and trading gossip. As she exited the cab, they dropped their cigarettes along with whatever gossip du jour held their fickle interest and surged forward to greet her, shouting over one another: "Miss O'Neill! Miss O'Neill! Evie, be a real sweetheart and look this way!"

Evie obliged them, posing with a smile.

"How was the show tonight, Miss O'Neill?" one asked.

"You tell me, Daddy."

"Find out anything interesting?"

"Oh, lots of things. But a lady never tells—unless it's on the radio for money," Evie said, making them laugh.

One smirking reporter leaning against the side of the hotel called out to Evie: "Whaddaya think about all these Diviners coming forward now that you let the cat out of the bag on your own talents?"

Evie gave the reporter a tight smile. "I think it's swell, Mr. Woodhouse."

T. S. Woodhouse raised an eyebrow. "Do you?"

Evie fixed him with a stare. "Sure. Perhaps we'll start our own nightclub—hoofers and hocus-pocus. If you're nice, we'll even let you in."

"Maybe you'll have your own union," another reporter joked.

"There are some folks who say the Diviners are no better than circus freaks. That they're dangerous. Un-American," T. S. Woodhouse pressed.

"I'm as American as apple pie and bribery," Evie cooed to more laughter.

"Love this Sheba," the second reporter murmured, jotting it down. "She makes my job easy."

Woodhouse wasn't giving up. "Sarah Snow, who shares the radio with you, called Diviners 'a symptom of a nation that's turned away from God and American values.' What do you say to that, Miss O'Neill?"

Sarah Snow. That small-time, Blue Nose pain in the neck, always looking down at Diviners in general and Evie in particular. She'd like to give that two-bit Bible thumper a kick in the backside. But that kind of publicity Evie didn't need. And she wasn't about to give it to Sarah Snow for free by starting a war.

"Oh, does Sarah Snow have a radio show? I hadn't noticed," Evie said, batting her lashes. "Come to think of it, no one else has, either."

As Evie bounded up the steps, T. S. Woodhouse sidled up next to her. "You went after me a little hard there, Woody," Evie sniffed.

"Keeps things interesting, Sheba. Also keeps anybody from suspecting our arrangement. Speaking of, my wallet's feeling a little light these days, if you catch my drift."

With a careful glance at the other reporters, Evie slipped Woodhouse a dollar. Woodhouse held the bill up to the light.

"Just making sure you're not printing your own these days," he said. Satisfied, he pocketed the bill and tipped his hat. "Pleasure doing business with you, Sweetheart Seer."

"Be a good boy, Woody, and go type something swell about me, will ya?" Evie said.

With a little backward wave, she flitted past, letting the bellhop open the gilded door for her while the reporters continued to shout her name.

THE TIPPY-TOP OF THE WORLD

The lobby of the Grant Hotel was festive chaos. Partygoers of all sorts—flappers, hoofers, gold diggers, Wall Street boys, and aspiring movie stars—draped themselves over every available inch of furniture while baffled hotel guests wondered if they'd wandered into a traveling circus by mistake. On the far side of the lobby, the angry hotel manager wiggled his fingers up high, trying to get Evie's attention.

"Horsefeathers!" Evie hissed. Turning the other way, she squeezed through the tourniquet of revelers on her way toward the Overland Room, where she spied Henry and Theta in a corner. As she shimmied sideways through the swells, past a sad-eyed accordion player singing something doleful in Italian, people turned and pressed closer to her.

"Say, I've got to talk with you, sweetheart," a good-looking boy in a cowboy hat purred. "See, there's a little interest in an oil speculation out in Oklahoma, and I want to know if it's going to pay off...."

"I can't see the future, only the past," Evie demurred, pushing on.

"Evie, DAAAARLING!" drawled a redhead in a long silver cape trimmed in peacock feathers. Evie had never seen the woman before in her life. "We simply MUST talk! It's URGENT, my dove."

"Why, then, I'd best go put on my urgent shoes," Evie called back without stopping, bumping headlong into someone. "Pardon me, I..." Evie's eyes narrowed. "Sam Lloyd."

"Hiya, Baby Vamp," he said, ever-ready smirk in place. "Miss me?"

Evie put her hands on her hips. "What crime have I committed that has landed you on my doorstep?"

"Just lucky, I guess." He stole a canape from a passing waiter's tray and shoved it in his mouth, rolling his eyes in rapture. "Caviar. Boy, do I love caviar."

Evie tried to go around Sam, but he moved with her.

"Could you step aside, please?" she asked.

"Aww, doll. Are you still sore because I told the *Daily News* that my sleuthing helped you catch the Pentacle Killer and that the reason you never come to the Creepy Crawly is that you're so crazy about me you have to stay away?"

Evie put her hands on her hips. "Yes, Sam. I *am* sore about that."

Sam spread his arms wide in a gesture of apology. "It was a charitable act!"

Evie raised an eyebrow.

"The museum needed the press, and that story gave us a little razzle-dazzle. It also got me a date with a chorus girl. A blond named Sylvia. You would not believe what that girl can do with—"

"Good-bye, Sam." Evie tried to push her way through the crowd but got stuck again. Sam followed her.

"Aww, c'mon, doll. Let's let bygones be bygones. Did I get mad when you told them I was...how'd ya put it again?"

"A liar, a cheat, and the sort of scum the other pond scum try to swim away from?"

"That was it." Sam looked at her with big peepers. "Great to see you again, Sheba. Say, why don't we find some little corner and catch up over a sloe gin fizz?"

"Holy smokes!" Eyes wide, Evie pointed across the room. "Is that Buster Keaton?"

Sam whirled around. "Where?"

Quickly, Evie ducked past him and pressed through the throng. Behind her, she could hear Sam calling: "Was that nice?"

At last, Evie collapsed into a seat beside Theta, who blew smoke from a cigarette perched at the end of a long ebony holder. "Well, if it isn't the Sweetheart Seer herself. Was that Sam?" Theta asked.

"Yes. Every time I run into him, I have to remind myself that murder is a crime."

"I don't know, Evil. He sure is handsome," Henry teased.

Evie glowered. "He's trouble. And he still owes me twenty clams."

"Say," Henry asked, "how about that party you went to last week at the Egyptian Palace Room? On the level: Do they really have live seals in the lobby fountain?"

"Occasionally. When the residents don't steal them for their own bathtubs. Oh, *daaarlings*, next time there's a party there, you must come!"

"Daaahlings, you maahhst cahhhme," Theta mimicked. "Those elocution lessons are turning you into a regular princess, Evil."

Evie bristled. "Well, I can't very well be on the radio sounding like a hick from Ohio."

"Don't get sore, Evil. I'd like you even if it sounded like you'd swallowed a whole bag of marbles. Just don't forget who your friends are."

Evie put her hand on Theta's. "Never."

There was a loud crash as a monkey trailing a leash knocked a vase off a table. It leaped from the bald head of a very surprised man and onto a drapery panel, where it now clung, screeching. A girl wearing a puffy feather boa pleaded with the monkey, but it would not be wooed. The animal held tight, squawking and hissing at the crowd.

"Where'd they come from?" Henry asked.

Evie shot her eyes heavenward, trying to remember. "I think they're with a circus from Budapest. I met them in Times Square and invited them along. Say, did you hear what Sarah Snow said about Diviners?"

"Who's Sarah Snow?" Theta said on a stream of cigarette smoke.

"Exactly my point," Evie said, triumphant. "Well, anyway, she said Diviners were un-American is what."

"I wouldn't let it bother you, darlin'," Henry said. "You've got bigger problems."

"What do you mean?"

Henry jerked his head in the direction of the scowling hotel manager walking briskly toward their table.

Quickly, Evie slipped her flask into her garter. "Oh, applesauce. Here comes Mr. Killjoy."

"Miss O'Neill! What is going on here?" the hotel manager thundered.

Evie smiled brightly. "Don't you just adore parties?"

The manager's lip twitched. "Miss O'Neill, as the manager of the Grant Hotel, what I adore—nay, demand—is an end to this nightly chaos. You have made a mockery of a venerable New York institution, Miss O'Neill. There are reporters camped outside the premises every night just to see what fresh madness will erupt—"

"Isn't it mahhh-velous?" Evie drew the word out. "Think of how much publicity the hotel's getting for free!"

"This is not the sort of notoriety the Grant wants, Miss O'Neill. This behavior is intolerable. The party in the Overland Room, as well as the one currently occupying the lobby, is now over. Do I make myself clear?"

Brows knitted together in concern, Evie nodded. "Perfectly." She positioned two fingers between her teeth and let loose a piercing whistle. "Dolls, the lobby's become abso-tive-ly murder. We can't stay here any longer, I'm afraid."

The hotel manager nodded curtly in appreciation.

"So everybody up to my room!" Evie shouted, and the stampede began. The Hungarian girl in the feather boa handed the monkey's leash to the hapless hotel manager, who stood paralyzed as the partygoers swarmed the elevators and stairs.

"You looking to get evicted again, Evil?" Theta asked as they dashed up the gleaming wooden staircase. "What is this, hotel number two?"

"Three, but who's counting? Besides, they won't evict me. They love me here!"

Theta looked back down at the hotel manager, who was shouting at a bellhop who was trying to distract the screeching beast with a broom while a telephone operator frantically connected cables in search of someone, anyone, who could remove a monkey from the Grant Hotel.

Theta shook her head. "I've seen that look before. It ain't love, kid."

Evie's room was so thick with people that they spilled out into the elegant damask-papered hallways of the Grant's third floor. Evie, Theta, and Henry took refuge in the bathroom's claw-foot tub, leaning their backs against one side of it and resting their legs across the other. In the room just beyond, the accordionist launched into the same doleful number he'd played twice before.

"Not again!" Evie growled and drank from her flask. "We should get him to play one of your songs, Henry. You should write for the accordion. An entire accordion revue! It'll be a sensation."

"Gee, why didn't I think of that before? *Henry DuBois's Accordion Follies! The Ins and Outs of Love…*" Henry sighed. "That's almost bad enough to be a Herbert Allen song."

"Herbert Allen! I've heard his songs on the radio!" Evie said. "I like the one that goes, '*I love your hair / I love your nose / I love you from your head to toes, My daaaaarling girl!*' Or the one that goes, '*Daaarling, you're top banana / Baaaby, you're my peaches and cream / Orange you gonna be my Sherbet—*'"

"For the love of Pete, please stop," Henry groaned, cradling his head in his hands.

Theta poured the rest of her booze into Henry's glass. "Herbert keeps getting his rotten songs in the show over Henry's just because he's published," she explained. "It's all the same song. The same horrible song."

"Gee, they do sort of sound alike, now that you mention it," Evie said, thinking it over.

"Every time I play something for Wally, Herbert finds a way to sabotage it," Henry said, picking up his drink again. "I tell you, if Herbie Allen fell off an apple truck tomorrow, I wouldn't cry."

"Well, then we hate Herbert Allen," Evie said. "I'm sure whatever you write will be dreamy, Hen. And then we'll all be singing your songs in hotel bathrooms."

Theta appraised Evie coolly through her cigarette haze. "Jericho asked after you."

"Oh? And how is dear old Jericho?" Evie kept her voice even, though her heart beat faster.

"Tall. Blond. Serious," Theta said. "If I didn't know better, I'd swear that big lug is sweet on you. And you on him."

"You don't know better!" Evie mumbled. "You don't know at all."

"You can't stay away from the Bennington forever, Evil."

"I can so! May I remind you that Uncle Will wanted me to keep my talent under lock and key? Why, if I'd listened to him, I wouldn't have any of this," she said, throwing her arms wide and nearly knocking Henry's drink from his hands.

"We're in a bathtub, Evil," Theta said.

"And snug. As. Bugs." Evie knocked back more gin. A warm buzz was starting to take the edge off the headache from her object reading and she wanted it to stay that way. "I refuse to become morose! This is a party. Tell me something happy."

"Flo's calling a press conference next week announcing our new act and letting me give my first interview as Theta St. Petersburg-ski, smuggled into this country by loyal servants during Revolution," Theta said, in an exaggerated Russian accent. She scoffed. "What a load of bunk. And I gotta sell that act to those tabloid jackals."

"Well, it's not like they can prove otherwise. For all you know, you could be a Russian aristocrat. Right, Henry?"

"Right," Henry said, staring at his drink.

Evie squinted at Henry. It wasn't like him to be so solemn. "Henry, you're very quiet this evening." She put her face up to his. "Is it because you're an artiste? Is this what artistes do? Get sad and quiet in party bathtubs?"

"Mostly, we take baths in bathtubs."

"You *are* sad. Is it because of this Herbert Sherbet fellow?"

Henry pasted on a smile. "Just beat."

A girl and her fella stumbled into the bathroom. "When will these accommodations be available?" the girl slurred. Her date held her up. "I should like to make a resh . . . reservation."

"I'm afraid this booth has been reserved indefinitely," Henry said with an apologetic bow of his head.

The girl peered at him through smeary eyes. "Huh?"

"Scram!" Theta yelled.

The girl pulled up the strap of her gown with as much dignity as she could muster. "I shall complain to the management," she said and slammed the door behind her.

"I think that's my cue," Henry said, pushing out of the bathtub. "Thanks for a swell party, Evie."

"Oh, Henry! You're not leaving yet, are you?"

"Forgive me, darlin'. I have a pressing engagement. With sleep."

"Henry," Theta said. Her voice carried a hint of warning. "Not too long."

"Don't worry."

"Don't worry about what?" Evie asked, swiveling her head from Henry to Theta and back again.

"Anything," Henry said, giving a courtly bow. "Ladies, I'll see you in my dreams."

"What was that about?" Evie asked once Henry had gone.

"It's nothing," Theta answered.

"Uh-oh. I know that face. That isn't a happy Theta face," Evie said, sitting up so suddenly she sloshed the contents of her flask onto her dress. Theta took the flask away.

"That's not fair," Evie groused. "I shall report you to the authorities for the crime of gin-napping!"

"You can have it back in a sec. I got something I wanna talk about."

Evie rolled her head left toward Theta and sighed heavily. "Oh, all right."

"I wanna talk about what happened to us. I wanna talk about the Pentacle Killer."

Evie pouted. "That is pos-i-tute-ly the last topic I wish to discuss."

"You say that every time I bring it up. I know you told the papers that John Hobbes was a crazed madman. But you and me, we both know that ain't the truth. That night, when I was trapped with Hobbes in the theater, I felt something I'd never felt before."

"What was that?"

Theta took a deep breath and let it out. "Evil."

"Yes?"

"Not you. I meant I felt the presence of evil."

"Well. It's over now," Evie said, hoping Theta would take the hint.

"Is it?"

"Well, sure. He's gone," Evie said a little defiantly. "It's all going to be the berries from now on. Nothing but blue skies. Just like the song."

"I don't know about that," Theta said, leaning her head back against the cool bathroom tiles. "You still dreaming about that eye symbol?"

"No. I'm not. My dreams are pos-i-tute-ly the swellest," Evie said, but she didn't look at Theta when she said it.

"It just seems like something's bubbling up. Something bad."

Evie slung an arm around her pal's shoulders. "Darling Theta. There's no need to worry," Evie said, expertly stealing her flask back from Theta. "Do you know, in the taxi on the way here, I saw a billboard for Marlowe Industries. It said 'The future of America.' The future is now, and we're on the tippy-top of the world. Our best lives are waiting for us around that next bend. We just have to reach for them. Forget bad dreams. They're just dreams. Let's drink to the future of America. The future of us. Long may we both reign."

Evie clinked her flask against Theta's glass. The bathroom blurred a bit, giving it a soft glow. Evie liked it blurry.

"There's something else I gotta ask you," Theta said softly. "It's about this whole Diviners business—"

"Most of them hocus-pocus phonies," Evie warned, holding up a finger.

"What I wanna know is, you ever hear of somebody who had a power that was dangerous?"

"Whaddaya mean?" Evie asked. "Dangerous how?"

They were interrupted by a sharp pounding on the hotel room's door, followed by a gruff voice calling, "Open up. Police."

"Horsefeathers!" Evie launched herself from the tub, poured her gin into the mouthwash tumbler, and stumbled woozily across the room, exhorting everyone to hide their booze. She spied Sam in the corner avidly kissing the Hungarian circus performer.

"No class a'tall," Evie tutted on her way past.

She threw open the door. Two policemen flanked the hotel manager. Evie managed a big smile even though her head ached. "Oh, hello! I hope you've brought ice. We've run out."

The manager muscled his way in. "The party is over, Miss O'Neill," he said with barely suppressed fury. "Everyone out! Now! Or I'll have you all thrown in jail."

A boozy exhale escaped Evie's lips, momentarily lifting a curl that immediately fell into her eyes again. "You heard Papa. Better get a wiggle on, everybody."

Drunken party guests gathered misshapen hats, loose shoes, bow ties, and stockings, and shuffled through the door after the police. Sam left with the Hungarian circus girl in tow.

"She's too tall for you," Evie hissed.

"I'll bet she can bend," Sam shot back with a grin.

Evie kicked him in the behind.

The manager handed Evie a folded note.

"What's this?" she asked.

"An eviction notice, Miss O'Neill. You have until eleven o'clock tomorrow morning to vacate these premises permanently."

"Eleven o'clock? Gee. But that's before noon!"

"I weep," the manager said, turning on his heel. "Sleep tight, Miss O'Neill."

Theta grabbed her wrap and headed for the door, shaking her head. "Don't worry, pal, she's well on her way to being tight."

At the door, Evie grabbed Theta's arm. "Say, Theta, what were you telling me before the cops came?"

Theta's big brown eyes showed worry for just a second. Then she let the tough-girl mask slide back into place. "Nothing, Evil. Just hot air. Get some sleep. I'll tell Jericho you say hello."

When the last guest had cleared out, Evie stumbled to the window and opened it, breathing in the cold night air as she stared at the neat window squares of light and thought of all the lives taking place behind them.

Why did Theta have to mention Jericho?

Evie had petted with lots of boys. Her world was good times. It spun like a roulette wheel. Boys were fun. Boys were playtime. Boys were distractions. Jericho was not a boy.

Just now, with the room emptied of revelers and the prospect of the long, hollow night looming, Evie craved the comfort of another human being. It wouldn't hurt to talk to him, would it? she reasoned as she fumbled the hotel phone from its cradle.

"Good eee-ve-ning," she said to the operator, the alcohol suddenly thickening her tongue so that she had to work to sober up her speech. "I'd liiike to place a caaall to Bradford...eight-ohhh-five-niiine, pleeease."

Evie wrapped the telephone cord around her index finger as the operator made the connection. Probably Jericho was sleeping, or perhaps he was out with another girl having the time of his life, not thinking about her at all. What if Uncle Will answered the phone?

What was she doing?

Evie slurred into the receiver, "Nev'r mind, op'rator. Cancel this call, please," and quickly hung up.

A collection of spent bootleg bottles, half-spilled cups, and overflowing ashtrays covered the top of the bed. Evie was too tired to clean it up. Instead, she grabbed the silk coverlet from the chaise and curled up on the floor like a child. She'd lied to Theta about the dreams. They still came, bewildering, stained in horror. The soldiers. The explosions. The strange eye symbol. And on the worst nights, Evie dreamed she was still trapped in that house of horrors with John Hobbes whistling down the stairs while the wraiths of the Brethren poured from the walls.

"Ghosts. Hate ghosts. They are terrible...terrible people," Evie mumbled sleepily, her head spinning as it rested on the rug. For a moment, her hand strayed to her neck again, searching for a comfort that was no longer there.

BAD DREAMS

After leaving the Grant, Henry had found a little club, where he played piano until the wee hours. It was inching toward three by the time Henry let himself into the tiny flat he shared with Theta at the Bennington Apartments. He peeked through the crack in Theta's bedroom door and saw that she was fast asleep with her silk mask over her eyes to block out the haze of city bright that crept through the windows despite the shades. Henry shut her door and made his way to the small card table awash in onionskin sheet music filled with his blotchy notations and unfinished lyrics. In the center of the table was an old coffee can marked HENRY'S PIANO FUND. For well over a year, Theta had been stuffing it with every dollar and bit of change she could spare to pay Henry back for taking care of her when she had needed it most. He stared at the song he'd been trying to get right for the better part of a week, then slumped into his chair.

"This is a sorry affair," he grumbled, crumpling the page and tossing it onto the floor, which was already littered with his previous attempts.

Back in New Orleans, on the riverboat, when someone played a wrong note, Louis would grin and say, "What that cat ever do to you, you gotta make it cry like that?"

Louis.

Henry pushed aside the music and set a metronome in the center of the table. Then he wound the arm of his alarm clock and placed the clock on the windowsill, dangerously close to the edge. Henry released the metronome's pendulum and settled his lanky frame into a worn chair beside a hissing radiator. For comfort, he put his straw boater on his head. The metronome's steady ticking grew louder, drowning out the soft bleating of New York City street life, lulling Henry into a hypnotic state. His eyelids fluttered—once, twice.

"Please," he said softly. And then he was under.

Henry came alive inside the dream world with a choking gasp, as if he'd been holding his breath underwater. For the first few seconds, there was only panic as his confused brain sought to make sense of what was happening. Slowly, his heartbeat settled. His breathing relaxed. Henry blinked, allowing his eyes time to adjust to the dream light. Sharp and unforgiving, it rendered ordinary objects— a haystack, a wagon, a face—starkly beautiful or, at times, slightly ghoulish.

Right now, that strange brightness caught the faces of a herd of buffalo whose deep, dark eyes watched Henry impassively.

"Hello," Henry said to the majestic beasts. The buffalo opened their mouths, and music poured out as from a radio.

Henry grinned. "Shall we dance? No? Next time."

Stretching behind Henry was a tall, snowy hillside whose top disappeared into a cloud bank. Theta sat on a rock nearby, watching the village below, where ropes of smoke twisted up from a row of floating, houseless chimneys.

"Hey, darlin'," Henry said, standing beside her. The brightness of the dream gave her cheekbones a cliff's-edge sharpness, like a German film star. She seemed agitated. "Bad dream?"

"Yes," Theta said in an eerily flat voice. "I don't like the looks of those red flowers over there."

Henry followed Theta's gaze. Where the buffalo had been was now a field of poppies. As he watched, the flowers trembled into flames and melted into thick red pools. Theta's breathing quickened, signaling the descent into nightmare.

43

Henry's voice was soothing. "Listen, Theta, why don't you have another dream? How about the circus? You like the circus, don't you?"

"Sure," Theta said, smiling slightly. When Henry looked again, the flames had been transformed into a funny little juggler who kept dropping his pins on purpose.

"I gotta look for Louis now, Theta."

"Sure, Hen," she said, and then Theta was gone.

Majestic pines shot up from the ground. Their gray shadows spilled boldly across the white floor of the forest. On a tree stump, the needle of an old Victrola caught again and again on the damaged grooves of a slightly warped record, distorting the song: "Pa-uu-ck up your trou-u-u-u-bles in your o-oold kit b-u-ag and s-uu-mile, smile, smi-i-ile. . . ."

Beside the Victrola, a soldier mimed the words as he danced a little soft shoe. His smile was unnerving. Nearby, a group of soldiers sat at a table, playing cards. The cards all carried the same painted image of a macabre man in a long, dark coat and a stovepipe hat. The man's black eyes were bottomless.

"We're about to get started, old boy. You'll want to take cover," one of the soldiers said before securing his gas mask, the side of which had been stamped with an eye and a lightning bolt. That same symbol shimmered on the foreheads of the soldiers, a ghostly tattoo.

"The time is now!" a sergeant barked.

The soldiers quickly fell into position. The phonograph's needle skipped: "Pa-uu-ck up your troubles . . . troubles . . . trou-u-u-bles . . . troubles. . . ." The smiling, dancing soldier faced Henry once more, but this time half of his face had been eaten away. Flies swarmed the rotting flesh along his jaw.

With a gasp, Henry stumbled backward, scrambling up the hill and into the forest, away from the camp. Beneath his feet, the snow vanished like a tablecloth snatched from under a place setting by a skilled magician's hands. Now he stood on a weather-cracked road that stretched out toward a horizon line so sharp it seemed painted. Wheat fields lay on either side. The sky churned with storm clouds.

On the windswept prairie, his mother sat in an enormous red

velvet chair. The wind whipped her silver-threaded hair across her delicate face. Henry couldn't feel the wind or smell the dust—he never could on a dream walk, just as he couldn't touch people or objects—but he was aware of the idea of both. Henry's father stood behind his wife, one hand on her shoulder as if to keep her from flying away. His father's face was stern, disapproving.

"Saint Barnabas told me the truth," his mother said, wide-eyed. "It was the vitamins. The vitamins did this to you. I should never have taken them." His mother began to cry. "Oh, why did you leave me, Bird?"

"Please don't cry, Maman," Henry pleaded, his heart sinking. Even in dreams, a fellow wasn't safe.

"What is this filth?" his father's voice boomed. In one hand he held a letter, which grew so big it blocked out the sun. Henry's heart pounded against his ribs.

"It was the vitamins," his mother said again, and she held out her bleeding wrists. "I'm sorry. I'm sorry."

"Stop. Please," Henry said. He shut his eyes and tried to seize control of the runaway dream. Why could he change dreams for others, but never for himself?

"Louis! Louis, where are you?"

The wind kicked up dust on the road, and in the dust, Henry could make out faint figures, as transparent as Irish lace at a sunstruck windowpane. Leading them was the man he'd seen on the tarot cards—the thin man in the tall black hat. Henry started toward them, but a crow darted in front of him with a great flapping of feathers, as if urging him away from this place, ahead of the dust and the things moving inside it.

And so Henry ran after it, deeper into the wheat field.

※

Ling's eyes fluttered open inside the dream to a flurry of pink-white petals falling down around her. Sitting up, she found herself in a garden of cherry trees in full bloom. The place had no meaning for Ling,

45

so she surmised that it must have had meaning for Lee Fan's grandmother. Often when she conjured the dead, they returned to a place they'd loved in life—or a place of trouble they revisited in order to put that trouble to rest.

Before sleep, Ling had offered prayers and joss money out of respect. She'd put Mrs. Lin's ring on the index finger of her right hand. Now, as respectfully as possible, she called for Mrs. Lin and waited. Ling didn't know why she had the power to manifest the spirits of the dead inside dreams. They didn't come for long—usually just long enough to answer the question posed to them, and then they were gone, back to wherever their energy was scattered.

Another person might've seen the power to dream walk and speak to the dead as a spiritual gift. Ling had no such sentimentality. To her, it was a scientific puzzle, a great "Eureka!" moment waiting to be explored, examined, quantified. Was a visit from the dead proof that time was merely an illusion? Was there something about Ling observing the dead that made it happen, as if the dead needed her consciousness in order to take form? Where did the dead come from? Where did their energy go afterward? *What* was that energy? Did the existence of ghosts mean that there might be more than one universe, and dreams were the beginning of a way into them? With every dream walk, Ling searched for clues.

Soon, Lee Fan's grandmother appeared. A subtle, shimmery aura fuzzed the edges of her. This was how Ling knew the dead. She paid attention to the golden glow, making mental notes like a scientist would: Was Mrs. Lin's aura stronger? Brighter? Did it waver or hold other colors? Did she appear more like a solid or a wave? Did any event precede her appearance?

"Why do you disturb my rest?" Mrs. Lin demanded, snapping Ling back to the task at hand.

"Auntie, I've come with a request from your granddaughter, Lee Fan. She can't find the blue dress made for her in Shanghai and wondered if you might help her find it. She's afraid of offending her aunt and uncle, and wishes—"

"She isn't afraid of offending anyone," Mrs. Lin interrupted sharply.

"Tell my granddaughter that I am not to be summoned for such trivial concerns and that if she cannot keep up with her things, I don't know why she expects me to do so from beyond the grave."

Ling suppressed a smile. "Yes, Auntie. I will tell her."

"She is a foolish girl who—" Mrs. Lin cut off abruptly, her expression shifting from irritation to fear. "It isn't safe," she whispered, making Ling's pulse quicken.

"What do you mean, Auntie?" Ling asked. Already she was losing her connection to Lee Fan's grandmother, who began to fade.

The unseen machinery of the dreamscape lurched into motion, and Ling felt herself falling. She landed on a dirt road that seemed to stretch on forever. To her left, a swath of ripe wheat rippled like a burnished sea under a daytime sky. To her right stretched the long twilight expanse of the city, heavy with smoke and fog.

"Hey! You there!"

A sandy-haired boy wearing an old straw boater hat waved to Ling from the edge of the wheat field. Ling was so startled she couldn't speak. This boy wasn't a part of the dream.

This boy saw her.

He was awake—awake and walking, just like Ling. All of Ling's scientific curiosity left her. For the first time on a walk, she was afraid.

"Hey!" the boy shouted and moved toward her. And all Ling could hear in her head were the words of Lee Fan's dead grandmother: *It isn't safe.*

Ling turned and ran as fast as she could toward the city.

☀

"Wait!" Henry called, but the girl was swift. She folded into the fog of the city. Another walker! Henry had never come across anyone who could do what he did. He needed to catch up to this girl. He had to talk to her. Maybe she could help him find Louis somehow. Buildings appeared like dark handprints of paint against a primed canvas: apartment buildings, shops, and restaurants. The distant scaffolding of the elevated train. Banners lettered with Chinese characters rippled in the breeze. Henry knew this place. He was in Chinatown.

He spied the girl standing in front of a restaurant with an upper balcony that reminded him a little of the houses on Bourbon Street. A neon sign blinked out THE TEA HOUSE.

"Wait! Please!" Henry called as she again took off running, this time down an alley thick with fog.

On the other side of the alley, the fog thinned. Henry whirled around, trying to get his bearings. He could just make out a line of ramshackle buildings hiding in the gloom. He didn't see the other dream walker, nor did he see Louis.

Henry was so frustrated he wanted to punch something. "Louis!" he screamed. "Where are you?"

"What are you doing?"

It was the girl, shouting at him. She was close enough that he could see the green of her eyes. She seemed both angry and frightened.

"Get out of my dream! I don't want you here!"

"*Your* dream? Now, wait just a minute—" Henry moved toward the girl and she stumbled backward. On instinct, Henry grabbed hold of her arm to keep her from falling and was shocked when he made contact. Electrical sparks danced along their skin. With a yelp, Henry yanked his hand away, shaking it out. The air smelled strongly of ozone.

Pop-pop-pop!

Fireworks exploded over the rooftops, faint sketches of light. Sounds echoed on the cobblestone streets: The *clip-clop* of horses. The squeak of wooden wheels. Angry shouts and raucous laughter. Crowd noises. Ghostly figures moved inside the fog, too. It was as if the dream itself had been sleeping and now it was coming to life. And then, faintly, Henry heard fiddle music. It was a song so familiar his body knew it before his brain—"Rivière Rouge," an old Cajun song, Louis's favorite. Whoever was playing the song played it exactly the same way Louis did, jazzed up, Delta style.

"Louis," Henry whispered. He whirled around, searching for the source of the music. It seemed to be coming from behind the facade of an old limestone building with the words DEVLIN'S CLOTHING STORE whiskered across the front.

"Louis!" Henry called, running for the building.

"Wait!" the girl called, startling.

A woman's shriek pierced the dream: "Murder! Murder! Oh, murder!" Something was moving in the fog, coming closer.

A church bell tolled, growing louder and louder. Suddenly, the distant roofs of Chinatown, the impressionistic streets of the old city, the limestone building—all of it curled up as if the dream been thrown into the fire.

"No! Not yet!" Henry cried, but it was too late. The last thing he saw was the girl dream walker's bright green eyes, and then he woke to the clang of his alarm clock as it tumbled from the windowsill and landed on the floor with a clatter. On the table, the metronome ticked away. His watch showed one minute till four. He'd been under for fifty-nine minutes.

"Horsefeathers, Henry!" Theta marched into the room with her sleep mask pushed up over her short dark bangs and shut off the alarm.

"S-sorry, Theta."

Sighing, Theta silenced the metronome. "You went looking again?"

"Theta, I think I found him."

"You did? Oh, Hen!" Theta covered the shivering Henry with a blanket and pulled a chair for herself next to his. "Go on. Spill."

Henry told Theta about hearing Louis's fiddle. "Maybe he's trying to find me, too."

"Gee, that's swell news. Hen," Theta said, sounding worried, "can you move yet?"

For at least five minutes after a dream walk, Henry remained paralyzed, as if his body were still in that other world. With effort, he lifted his arm a fraction, wincing as he worked movement back into the muscles. "See? Good as new."

"You know it scares me when you do this. What if one time you can't move? What if you don't come back?"

"Don't worry, darlin'. I don't overdo it."

"Only one night a week," Theta reminded him. "Only for an hour."

"Yes, ma'am," Henry said. "I haven't even told you the strangest part: I wasn't the only one walking around tonight."

"There's somebody else like you?"

"Yes! A girl. When she showed up, I heard the song. Maybe she knows something about Louis. Maybe she can help me find him, Theta."

"Well, did you get anything from her? A name?"

"No," Henry said mournfully. "But it's the first bit of luck I've had."

"We'd better get some sleep or we'll be dragging through rehearsal tomorrow."

Henry rolled his eyes. "Florenz Ziegfeld presents: *Hocus-Pocus Hotcha!* An all-new Diviners revue filled with magic and mysticism in song and dance!"

"So it's a lousy show. We'll make it better. It's the one that's gonna take us to the top, kid."

"Take *you* to the top, you mean. You're the one Flo's grooming to be a star."

"We're a team. You take one, you gotta take the other."

"Who's my best girl?" Henry asked.

"I am. And don't you forget it."

Theta let out a long sigh and snuggled next to her best friend, resting her head on his chest. Her sleek dark bob still smelled like cigarette smoke. "Maybe we're all going crazy."

"Maybe." Henry kissed the top of Theta's head, and she put her arm across his stomach.

"Hen?"

"Yeah, darlin'?"

"Can I sleep in your bed with you?"

"If you can get me there."

Theta helped Henry to his feet and then to his room, where the two of them fell asleep side by side, arms entwined like two halves of the same whole.

RED DRESS

In his dream, George Huang stood under the hazy sun at a late-afternoon party wearing a cream-colored suit and a striped silk shirt with fancy French cuffs of the sort he'd stared at in shop windows where they didn't welcome people like him. The bright, fast rhythms of a jazz band echoed through the dream. Up on the hill, a sprawling white house loomed, casting sharp blades of shadow across the summer-green lawn.

George smiled, ecstatic. His good dream! Somehow, he'd made it back here.

Men nodded solemnly as George walked by. He was important here. Respected. Photographers took his picture for the papers. As George smiled and posed, he saw the boys who'd bullied him and the customers who ordered him around as if he were barely human huddled together on the other side of a tall picket fence, watching, envying. George raised his champagne glass. *How do you like me now?* he thought.

"Georgie! Over here! Hey!" Several pretty girls waved to him as they peeled off their stockings and jumped into a champagne fountain, giggling and splashing with abandon. George threw his head back and laughed. Oh, this was the best dream in the world! He never wanted to wake up.

On the edge of the lawn, Lee Fan appeared wearing a red cheongsam, the wind whipping her hair across her rouged cheeks.

"*Dream with me . . .*" she whispered. She turned and walked inside the tall white house.

That whisper ignited a new fire in George. He'd never wanted anyone or anything so desperately. His ancestors shimmered on the edges of the party like images fading from a photograph. Some of them seemed to be reaching out, as if they could grab hold of him, as if they wanted to tell him something important, but George didn't want to lose sight of his dream. So he raced ahead, leaving them behind. He ran past the fountain, where the dripping girls eyed him hungrily. Their voices swirled, a seductive, whispering chorus: "*Dream with us, dream with us, us, us, the dream wants you wants you wants you to dream to dream to dream with us.*"

Lee Fan stood just inside the darkened doorway of the house in her red dress. She waved her arm, and behind her the dark lit up like a movie screen, showing a film in which the two of them danced close while an orchestra played and a girl singer crooned, "*Beautiful dreamer, wake unto me. Starlight and dewdrops are waiting for thee. . . .*"

On-screen, Lee Fan angled her face toward George's for a kiss, and his heart fluttered. But just before the actual kiss, it all went dark again, like a nickelodeon cutting out at the good part so you'd keep putting in nickels. In the doorway, Lee Fan crooked a finger, beckoning George as she backed in, letting the gloom swallow her whole. Everything George wanted was waiting there in the dark, so he went inside.

Above him, the ceiling winked with a soft phosphorescence. The shivery coolness was an unwelcome surprise, though. And there were sounds—low growls and scratchings that gave him pause. He glanced back through the open door at the sliver of sunshine he'd left behind, then pressed on, walking deeper into darkness.

"Lee Fan?" he called.

No answer.

Shadows moved across George's hands, and he looked up toward the flickering ceiling.

No, not flickering.

Moving.

The low growls he'd heard swelled into a bone-chilling chorus, and George had only one thought: *Wake up NOW.* He ran back toward the hazy circle of daylight. Back to where everything was good. But every time he got close, the sunlight drew farther away.

At last, George pushed free, tumbling down onto the lawn. The summer grass had gone brittle; it twisted with snakes. The champagne fountain ran red with blood. The half-dressed girls slurped up handfuls of the stuff, and when they opened their rotting mouths, they had teeth as sharp as a razor's edge. "More!" they cried. "More!"

"*Promise . . .*" the dream demanded.

"Wake up. Wake up wake up wake up," George whispered to himself. He shut his eyes, but it didn't matter; the dream pushed further and further into his mind until his head was filled with the most terrible images: demons eating his entrails, tearing at his neck with their teeth. He couldn't take another second.

"I promise!" he cried, opening his eyes again.

There was a sharp prick of pain, then an icy cold spreading through him. Far off, Lee Fan waved to him. He could not reach her. He would never reach her.

His lips opened to let out one last cry for help.

But it never came.

DAY SEVEN

THE MORNING SUN

The dull gray morning parceled out a meager portion of winter sun to the immigrant neighborhoods of Manhattan's Lower East Side. Merchants rolled up window shades for another day of business. Tailors who'd escaped pogroms in the Pale readied their sewing machines on Ludlow and Hester Streets while steam rose from the basement grates of the Chinese-run laundries lining Pell and Bayard. The Italian bakeries on Mulberry Street stocked their front windows with golden loaves of bread; the yeast scented the winter air, mixing with the savory tang of chow fan, the tart brine from the pickle barrels, and the cinnamon sweetness of rugelach, a true melting pot of smells. Wind whipped over synagogues, churches, and temples and clanged through the zigzag of metal fire escapes, but it was no competition for the rumble and squeal of the Third Avenue El on the Bowery, the towering dividing line between the Lower East Side and the rest of New York City.

From her bed, Ling peered out at the gray-wool clouds threatening to muzzle the paltry sun above Chinatown and made a growl of contempt low in her throat, as if the winter sky were out to get her personally. Fiery spasms rippled across the nerve endings of her legs, and Ling bit down against the pain just as her mother's voice sounded on the other side of the door: "Rise and shine, Ling!"

Her mother poked her freckled face in, frowning. "You're not even dressed, my girl. What's the matter? Are you feeling all right?"

"I'm fine, Mama," Ling managed to say.

"Here. Let me help you."

"I can do it," Ling said, trying to conceal both her pain and her irritation.

Her mother hovered in the doorway. "I laid out your slip and dress for you last night. And the wool stockings—it's terrible cold out."

Ling flicked her eyes toward the end of the bed. Her mother had chosen the peach dress Ling hated, the one that made her look like a sad fruit salad. "Thank you, Mama."

"Well," her mother said at last, "don't dally. Breakfast will get cold, and I won't be hearing a word about that."

Only when the door had closed did Ling let out the grunt she'd held back as the tightness loosened its grip on her legs. She lay in bed a moment longer, mulling over last night's strange dream walk. She'd never met anyone else who could do what she could, which was how she liked it. Her nighttime wanderings were private. Sacred. *But that spark . . .*

Ling sat up. With a sigh, she reached for the metal braces propped against her nightstand and slid them on over the useless muscles of her calves, cinching the buckles of the leather straps just below and above her knees. Using both hands, she swung her caged legs over the side of the bed, grabbed her crutches, and shuffled stiffly to her cupboard, tugging on a dark blue dress that didn't make her feel as if she were an item on a summer picnic table. She tied the laces on her black ortho-pedic shoes. In the mirror, Ling took a last look at herself. What she saw was metal, buckles, and ugly black shoes.

"Ling!" Her mother's voice again.

"Coming, Mama!"

She squinted at her reflection until she was nothing but a blue blur.

In the dining room, the radio played a Sunday-morning program of hymns while her mother poured tea into delicate china cups. Ling took her silent place at the table beside her father and examined the spread before her: fried eggs, bacon, noodles with pork fat, shrimp dumplings, porridge, and toast. The eggs, she knew, would be slightly slimy—her

58

father was the real cook, not her mother—and the porridge was out of the question, so she settled for the toast.

"That isn't all you mean to eat," her mother said with a *tsk*.

Her father maneuvered a dumpling onto Ling's plate. Ling scowled at it.

"You've got to keep your strength up, my girl," her mother said.

"Your mother is right," her father agreed automatically.

Ling turned toward her great-uncle. He was the eldest; his opinion mattered most.

"If she wants to eat, she'll eat," he said, smiling at her, and Ling could've hugged him.

If she'd been the hugging sort.

"At least have some tea." Ling's mother placed the steaming cup down at Ling's plate. She poured tea for Ling's father, too, and laid a comforting hand on his shoulder. Mr. Chan smiled up at his wife. Twenty years ago, when both of them had newly emigrated—her father from China and her mother from Ireland—her parents had met at a church social. They'd married six months later, and sometimes they still looked at each other like shy, smitten kids at their first dance. Ling found it hideously embarrassing, so she angled her head away from them and toward the newspaper tucked against her father's plate. An article bore the headline JAKE MARLOWE ANNOUNCES FUTURE OF AMERICA EXHIBITION.

"It might be easier to read this way," her father said. He smiled as he handed the newspaper to her.

"Thank you, Baba."

"Read while you eat," her mother pleaded. "Or we'll be late for Mass."

Ling nibbled a corner of her toast as she skimmed the article:

> Jake Marlowe to break ground in Queens, New York, for his Future of America Exhibition. Celebrating "The Brave New Age of the Exceptional American," the fair will highlight America's best and brightest, showcasing achievements and advances in the

sciences, agriculture, mathematics, eugenics, robotics, aviation, and medicine.

"I suppose you'll want to go," her father said, his eyes twinkling.

Ling knew it was a long shot. Life in the restaurant was all-consuming. For her parents to drive her out to Queens for the groundbreaking ceremony would be precious time away.

"Could I, Baba?"

"We'll see what we can do."

Ling gave a half smile. Another, smaller headline caught her attention, and the smile was replaced by a frown.

MYSTERIOUS SLEEPING SICKNESS BAFFLES HEALTH OFFICIALS

The sleeping sickness that has bedeviled the residents of Chinatown is now the scourge of other New York City neighborhoods. Four new cases have been reported on the Lower East Side, and one case has been documented as far north as Fourteenth Street. Health officials who remember all too well the devastation of the Spanish Influenza Pandemic in 1918 assure the public that they are investigating with rigor and will ensure the safety of all New Yorkers.

"I heard there's a new case on Mulberry, an Italian girl. And possibly another on Hester Street," Uncle Eddie said. "You know they're calling it the Chinese Sleeping Sickness."

Ling's father continued sipping his coffee, but she could see from the set of his jaw that the illness's name registered.

"But this sleeping sickness isn't just here in Chinatown," Mrs. Chan said, wiping her pink, freckled hands on her apron.

"All it takes is someone to say it started here and we're to blame.

I hear the city might even cancel our New Year's celebrations," Uncle Eddie said.

"Baba, would they really?" Ling asked. The Year of the Rabbit was only a few weeks away.

"Don't worry. The Association will make certain the celebrations go on as planned," Ling's father said.

"Not if they don't stop this sickness soon." Uncle Eddie sighed. "Already business is down. Fewer tourists come every day."

"It will be fine," Mr. Chan said.

Uncle Eddie shook his head and turned to Ling. "Your father. Ever the optimist."

"And what's the matter with that?" Mrs. Chan tutted.

"If you believe it, it will be," Mr. Chan said. "If you do not…"

"It will not," Ling finished. She bit down as another spasm gripped her left leg.

"Ling! Are you all right?"

"Yes, Mama," Ling managed to say.

"Perhaps you oughtn't go to Mass this morning."

"I'm fine," Ling said. It wasn't so much that she wanted to go to church as it was that she was desperate to get out of the house. If her mother thought the spasms weren't improving, she'd make her stay in bed. Ling felt guilty enough that she wasn't pulling her weight at the restaurant, and Sunday was the busiest day of the week at the Tea House.

Her mother sighed. "All right, my stubborn lass. I can't fight you on everything. Put your coat on."

Church bells sang a Sunday-morning city hymn as Ling and her parents strolled past the pushcart vendors, the greengrocers, and the fish sellers setting up for another day. The occasional automobile honked its way up the narrow street, threading around people dressed in their Sunday best and people dressed for work. As they walked, Ling's mother nodded and smiled and chatted with neighbors who averted their eyes at the sight of Ling's braces, as if she only existed from the waist up, as if they could catch the bad luck of her illness simply by looking. Ling would have to force a smile and feign interest in what was being said while thinking, *If only I were asleep. If only I were dreaming.* Everyone fell silent as they passed an apartment building where a yellow sign had been pasted across the front doors: CITY OF NEW YORK DEPARTMENT OF HEALTH. THESE PREMISES ARE UNDER STATE QUARANTINE REGULATIONS. SLEEPING SICKNESS: KEEP OUT.

The streets of Chinatown seemed charged, the scent of iron before the storm.

The doors to the quarantined building opened. Masked members of the Chinese Benevolent Association dragged infected bedding into a nearby alley, where other men waited with pails of water. They set the bedding alight. Everyone stopped to watch it burn. The wind blew soot into Ling's eyes. She turned her head away from the flames and gritty air and, for a second, she saw George, chalk-pale, without a coat, standing just beyond the crowd on the edge of Columbus Park. Ling rubbed at her tearing eyes, and when she opened them again, there was no sign of George anywhere.

"It's terrible, isn't it?" Lee Fan had sidled up next to Ling. They watched as the men in masks doused the fire with the pails of water.

"Yes," Ling said, trying not to cough at the acrid air.

Lee Fan smiled at Ling's mother. "I'll walk Ling to church, Mrs. Chan. She and I have so much to catch up on!"

Mrs. Chan smiled. "Well, that's awfully nice of you, Lee Fan. You've a good soul."

You are leaving me with the Devil! Ling wanted to shout after her mother.

Lee Fan waited until Ling's mother had moved several paces ahead. She looked around to make sure no one was eavesdropping. "Did you speak to my grandmother?"

Lee Fan could call herself Lulu and dress like a flapper, but Ling knew that, deep inside, Lee Fan carried the same superstitions, the same fears about offending ancestors, as those around her. It was a thread of obligation sewn into the lining of all of them. It bound them tight.

Ling nodded, and Lee Fan's face lit up. "Well, what did she say? Does she know what happened to my dress? Or did she have something even more important to tell me? Did she mention Tom Kee or a wedding date? Did she have any advice for me at all?"

"Yes" was all Ling said. She'd decided to make "Lulu" work for it.

"Well? What was it?" Lee Fan demanded.

Ling could've told her anything: Shave your head and live as a nun. Give me the blue dress. Every morning at dawn, you are to leave three shelled walnuts on a linen napkin for the squirrels of Columbus Park.

"She said you were a foolish girl and to stop bothering her rest," Ling said.

For a split second, Lee Fan was too shocked to say anything. But then her mouth tightened as she spat the words out: "You're a liar! My grandmother would never say such a thing. I'll bet you can't walk in dreams or talk to the dead at all. You're just a pathetic little fool trying to get attention. I want my two dollars back!"

"We had a deal. Are you going back on your word?"

"How do I know if you even spoke to my grandmother? There's no proof! You're not even fully Chinese," Lee Fan scoffed. "Why would any of our ancestors want to talk to you?"

Some of Lee Fan's crowd had gathered to watch the spectacle. No doubt they'd be whispering about this for days to come. Ling's cheeks burned.

"To think I used to feel sorry for you about what happened." Lee Fan glanced quickly at Ling's leg braces. The girls were all staring now, gossiping and gawking, and Ling wanted nothing more than to turn and walk back toward home, to go to sleep and slip into a dream where she could do anything she wanted—where she could run far away.

In a wail of sirens, an ambulance roared past. The street was abuzz with nervous speculation. A moment later, Gracie Leung was hurrying toward the girls, calling Lee Fan's name.

"What is it? What's happened?" Lee Fan asked.

Gracie was breathless and her eyes brimmed with tears. "Did you hear? Did you hear?"

"Hear what?" Lee Fan said, exasperated.

"Oh, it's too awful!" Gracie mewled.

"Honestly, Gracie Leung, if you don't tell me right this instant—"

"It's George Huang!"

"What about George?" Ling cut in.

Gracie seemed to register Ling's presence for the first time. "His mother went to wake him this morning and she couldn't. She tried and tried. They brought in Dr. Hsu." Gracie took a deep breath. "They think George has the sleeping sickness!"

The noise in the street crescendoed. The news was spreading quickly from person to person, an infection of gossip.

It felt as if a hole had opened in Ling's stomach. *But I just saw him.*

"Ling! Ling!" Her mother was suddenly at her side, a protective arm wrapped around her daughter's shoulders, as if she could keep her safe forever. For once, Ling didn't want to push her away. She let her mother hold on tightly, but her eyes searched Pell Street frantically. Yes, the sun had been strong. Yes, there'd been grit in her eyes. But she could've sworn that for just a few seconds, it had been George she'd seen standing at the edge of the crowd under a winter sky, shimmering ever-so-faintly around the edges like the dead, his mouth opening and closing in a silent scream.

WE MAKE OUR OWN LUCK

Dr. William Fitzgerald entered the Museum of American Folklore, Superstition, and the Occult, walking briskly toward the museum's library. As he passed the collections room, his assistant, Jericho Jones, called after him, but Will did not break stride, forcing Jericho to catch up.

"A club on Long Island, the Spiritual Divine, has asked you to speak at its hall in two weeks. And the Ladies Ghostly Sunday Supper Club has also requested an appearance."

"No and no," Will said.

"You've also received a request to entertain at little Teddy Sanderson's tenth birthday party in Brooklyn."

Will stopped short, his eyes narrowing behind his spectacles. "A *child's* birthday party? I'm a *curator*, for heaven's sake, not a performing circus clown."

Jericho shrugged. "They were offering five dollars."

"Tell them no."

"Of course. Oh, and Miss Walker called. She said to tell you that she'll come for you at two o'clock sharp tomorrow and not to be late. She said, and I quote, 'Tell Dr. Fitzgerald that we'll be taking my car, as I refuse to ride in that ancient, death-trap Tin Lizzie of his.'"

Will's face registered nothing. "Thank you. Anything else?"

Jericho winced. "Your lecture group is waiting for you in the library. The Mystical Mediums for Peace Between the Dead and the Living?"

Will's shoulders sagged. He let out a long sigh. "It's official. I *am* a circus clown."

With Jericho keeping pace, Will marched into the library, where the ten "Mystical Mediums" sat in a neat row wearing identical headbands featuring a third eye emblem affixed to the front.

Will gestured vaguely to the headband. "What is, um…that for?"

A woman in a beaded turban smiled knowingly. "It increases our contact with the spiritual plane!"

Will shot a withering glance at Jericho, who waved all five of his fingers—*five dollars*—and retreated to the second floor, hiding out in the rows of bookshelves as Will's voice floated up from below: "Good afternoon. I'm Dr. William Fitzgerald, curator of this museum. Let's begin, shall we? The history of Diviners is aligned with the history of our country, starting with the indigenous population.…"

Up in the stacks, Jericho whispered to Sam, "He can't keep giving these lectures."

"He can if he wants to keep heating the museum," Sam answered. "Did you ask him about you-know-what?"

"Not yet."

"Aww, c'mon, Freddy! That was s'posed to be your job."

"He'll say no."

"Then we gotta convince him," Sam said.

Down below, one of the Mystical Mediums had interrupted Will. "Dr. Fitzgerald, what with all these reports of Diviners these days, wouldn't you say, then, that it is proof that God Almighty has singled out America as a place for the Divine? For the exceptional, just like Jake Marlowe says?"

"I suppose that depends upon your definition of *exceptional*."

"I mean exceptional, sir! The exceptional nation built upon ideals of peace, fairness, and the promise of prosperity."

Will glanced up at the ceiling mural of beautiful hills, the railroad crisscrossing the verdant nation, the rivers with their original names long forgotten.

"I would argue that every country is built upon dreams and violence. Both leave scars. America is certainly no exception to this."

66

"That doesn't sound very patriotic to me," a woman grumbled to her seatmate.

"Dr. Fitzgerald, what do you think of your niece's radio show?" a man asked, and everyone fell into excited whispers. "Did you know she was a Diviner all along? How, exactly, were her talents employed to catch the Pentacle Killer?"

"Yes, tell us about the Pentacle Killer!" the Mystical Mediums begged.

"I'm afraid that's all for today," Will said abruptly and walked out.

"Uh-oh," Sam said. "Not again."

"Go!" Jericho hissed, practically pushing Sam ahead of him on the spiral staircase.

"I thought the lecture was an hour," a tweedy gentleman protested. "We paid for an hour!"

"Careful there, pal," Sam said. "You don't wanna make your third eye all weepy. Listen, how would you folks like an exclusive look at the diary of Liberty Anne Rathbone, the fabled Diviner sister of the great Cornelius Rathbone, huh? If you would kindly follow me to the collections room. This way, please."

While Sam tended to the tour, Jericho let himself into Will's office. Will stood facing one of the tall windows, staring out at the wintry street.

Jericho cleared his throat. "Will, they paid in advance."

"I know." Will pinched the bridge of his nose. "Give them a free tour or something."

"Sam's doing just that."

"I am indebted to you both," Will said, turning toward Jericho. "Do you have those articles I asked for?"

Jericho tapped the folder on Will's desk. "Everything from the past week regarding supernatural sightings, along with today's newspapers." He took a deep breath. "And this came for you as well."

He handed an official-looking envelope to Will, who glanced at the return address—New York State Office of Taxation—with its large red letters stamping out FINAL NOTICE, and put it aside.

"Ah. Thank you, Jericho. Well. Let's see what we have today...."
Will took a seat at his desk, wiped his spectacles clean, hooked them
over his ears again, and dove into the clippings. From the pile he selected
four that caught his attention. Next he gave a cursory glance to the day's
headlines, flipping through the pages till he came to a picture of Evie
smiling out from under a fashionable hat.

SWEETHEART SEER HOSTS WILD PARTY AT GRANT HOTEL

Nothing could be "DIVINER" than a night with Evie O'Neill

BY T. S. WOODHOUSE

"It's a nice picture," Jericho said, standing beside Will.

Will peered up at him. "Didn't anyone ever tell you it's rude to
read over someone's shoulder?"

Jericho's face remained impassive. "Didn't anyone ever tell you it's
rude to be rude?"

"Sorry," Will said, chastened. "I'm sorry, Jericho."

"It's all right." Jericho tapped the clippings Will had put aside.
"Why these?"

"They're all upstate, within a hundred-mile radius of one another."

"Brethren isn't too far from that path," Jericho noted.

"Mmm."

"That night, when you—when I was shot and you had to admin-
ister so much serum at once, was my behavior...what I mean is..."
God, what was the matter with him? He could barely get the words
out. "Did I frighten Evie?"

"Pardon?"

"Evie. Was she frightened, seeing me like that, with all those tubes
and gears inside, knowing what I am?"

"It wasn't the only unusual circumstance she's faced in the past few months. She appeared none the worse for it."

Jericho nodded, letting his breath out slowly. Maybe there was hope after all.

"None the worse for what?" Sam said, pushing through Will's office door.

"Nothing," Jericho said, his brows sharpening. "Where are the Mystical Mediums?"

"The Third Eyes? I left 'em to play with the tarot cards."

"You *what?*" Jericho said.

"Relax, Freddy. I told 'em the tarot cards can only be read by special people with special powers. Naturally, they think that's them. Trust me: They're as happy as clams."

"That's a ridiculous analogy. As if someone could gauge the happiness of a mollusk," Will grumbled, pawing at his messy desk till he found his cigarettes.

What's eating him? Sam mouthed to Jericho. Jericho slid out the ominous tax letter, and Sam acknowledged it with a curt nod.

During the Pentacle Murders, the Museum of American Folklore, Superstition, and the Occult had drawn sizable crowds. Everyone wanted a look at the professor of the supernatural who was helping the police hunt down the gruesome, occult-obsessed killer. But then the murders stopped. Manhattan's frenzied pulse beat for other crimes and scandals, and now, once again, the museum had been forgotten by most everyone except the taxman.

Sam cleared his throat. "Professor, if you don't mind my two cents..."

"I'm fairly sure that I will," Will said, his eyes on his papers.

Jericho gave Sam a *Let it go* look, but Sam ignored his warning.

"We're barely hanging on. A lecture here, a group of self-appointed mystics there. A coupla curious tourists. It's not enough to keep us off the auction block."

"We've always managed to pull through."

"Not this time, Professor. That's a final notice. We need a surefire moneymaker. What's the biggest thing to hit the city since Chock full o'Nuts started roasting peanuts?"

Will looked up, perplexed. "Chock...full—"

"Diviners! You can't pick up a newspaper, turn on the radio, or see an advertisement for chewing gum without bumping up against Diviners fever. Seems to me we're overlooking an obvious gold mine."

"I'm sorry, Sam. I don't follow."

"We put together a Diviners exhibit. Capitalize on the fever while everybody's feverish. Heck, half the loot in here is about or from Diviners already. Just make sure you add some razzmatazz, and you're in business."

"Will, it's a good idea," Jericho said.

"See? Even the nihilist agrees. And he likes nothing." Sam grinned at Jericho, who rolled his eyes. "And...we could get a big name in to draw a crowd. Somebody people would pay to see."

"Who, pray tell, would that be?"

Sam paused. "Evie."

The muscles along Will's jawline tightened. "No."

"C'mon, Professor. You two can't be on the outs forever. You gotta break the ice sometime. I saw her last night and—"

"Wait a minute: You saw Evie?" Jericho interrupted.

"Yeah, that's what I said. Professor, I'm telling ya, one word from her on the radio and we're made. And if she agrees—"

"Where did you see Evie?"

"The Grant Hotel...If she agrees—"

"But how did—"

"Settle down there, Freddy," Sam said. "Like I was saying, if she agrees to be our special guest for the Diviners exhibit party, everything's jake."

"I'm sure we'll come up with the money for the taxes without having to sully the ideals of this institution," Will said sharply.

"So you won't make nice with her? Not even to save the museum?" Sam held up the notices. "We've only got until March before the city takes this place, Professor."

Will shoved the tax letter beneath the stack of clippings on his desk. "We'll pull through. As for these sightings, there are more of them in the past couple of months, ever since John Hobbes. Have you noticed?" And just like that, the topics of a Diviners exhibit, the party, and Evie were dismissed. Will tapped a fountain pen in a slow rhythm against the desk. "There's something there. Somehow I sense that it's all connected."

"How?" Jericho asked.

Will was up and pacing. "I don't know. Yet. But I don't think I'm going to find out by staying here." Will stopped beside the tall globe stand. He gave the world a spin, trailing a finger over its curved surface. "That's why I'm considering going out into the field, like in the old days when I was a researcher. Do you think the two of you could run the museum while I look into a few of these cases? I'd only be gone for a short while. Ten days. A few weeks at most."

Jericho shook his head. "Will, I don't think—"

Sam stepped on Jericho's foot, cutting him off. "Of course we could! Why, the giant and I are a terrific team!"

"Very well, then. It's settled. I'll leave tomorrow around two o'clock."

Suddenly, Miss Walker's mysterious telephone message made sense to Jericho. Will had decided to leave long before he brought up the idea. This conversation they were having now was strictly a formality.

"Well then," Will said abruptly, "I believe I'll take a walk, if you don't mind."

Sam followed Will down the museum's long hallway. "Don't you worry about a thing, Professor. I've got this all under control."

"That is precisely the statement that makes me worry," Will said, throwing wide the front door. The morning sun had given way to the first warning drops of what surely would become a dismal drizzle. He shook out his umbrella.

"Don't open that in here, Doc," Sam cautioned.

"Why not?"

Sam shrugged. "It's bad luck. Everybody knows that."

"We make our own luck." Will released the black spiderlike canopy, angling its full bonnet through the door like a shield.

※

After seeing the Mystical Mediums out, Sam returned to the library to find Jericho perched at a long table, reading as usual. "I'm back. Did you miss me?" he said, dropping into Will's chair.

Jericho didn't look up from his book. "Like typhoid. By the way, as regards the party, I told you so. And that's Will's chair."

"Yeah. Comfy. I had no idea it was so soft."

"Out."

"C'mon, Freddy. Dad's not home."

"Out."

With a sigh, Sam moved to the Chesterfield. He put his feet up on the table near Jericho's hands just to annoy him. "Pal, we gotta pull off this Diviners exhibit. We can't let Will lose the museum."

Jericho gave Sam a dubious glance as he turned the page. "Since when did you become so invested?"

"I'm a caring fella. Can't a fella want to do a good turn for another?"

"There's gold buried in the walls, isn't there?"

"Look, I got it good here. If the museum goes under, so do I."

"And there we have it."

"It's not just me, pal. You've got a square deal, too. How many jobs out there for fellas who read Nietzsche and catalog gris gris bags? We need a plan if we both want to stay employed. This Diviners exhibit is just the ticket. With the professor on the road, we've got two solid weeks to put this thing together without him interfering."

"He won't like it."

"He won't be around to stop it, and once we put the plan in motion, what's he gonna do? Bold action, Jericho."

Jericho leaned back in his chair, his eyes on Sam. "So what's your brilliant plan to get Evie to host the party? She and Will haven't spoken since she told all of New York that she's a Diviner."

"Oh, I'm sure I can persuade Evie," Sam said, hooking his hands behind his head.

Jericho turned back to his book. "Yeah? Did you discuss that last night at the Grant?"

"You're really put out about that, aren't you?"

"I didn't say that." Jericho flipped the page. "So...how is she? Did she seem happy?"

Sam shrugged. "Sure. It was a party. You know how those things go. Or no, you don't, do you?"

Jericho ignored Sam's jibe. "Do you see each other often?"

Sam could tell Jericho the truth, that Evie had practically kicked him out of her party. But it was more fun to let the giant think otherwise. "Oh, gee. As a gentleman, I probably shouldn't say more than that."

"Fine. Don't tell me." Jericho glanced at the clock. "It's almost time. Go open up."

"*Me?* How come I gotta go? C'mon, Freddy. It's cold out there. If I get sick, half the girls in New York will be crying their eyes out."

"No doubt the other half will volunteer to dig your grave."

"Aww, Freddy. That hurts my heart."

"You don't have a heart. It's your turn. Go."

"But—"

Without looking up, Jericho pointed to the door. "You are banished. I banish you."

"Fine," Sam grunted. "I'll go hang out the 'open' shingle. Not that it matters."

"Now who's the nihilist?"

Jericho waited until Sam had gone. Then he slid the newspaper out from under his book and opened it to the article on Evie. Over the past few months, he'd sent her two letters and composed at least two dozen more that he hadn't sent. The letters were all the same: *Dear*

Evie, I hope you're doing well. I really enjoyed your radio show. The Bennington isn't quite as interesting since you left. But he was fairly certain she could read between the lines: *Dear Evie, I miss you. Do you ever think of me?*

Together, he and Evie had lived through their own small war of a night. No one else truly understood the pure evil they'd faced in that house with John Hobbes. A few days later, as the morning light crept over the city, he'd kissed her for the first time. How often he relived that moment—the taste of Evie's mouth, the feel of her body against his, the comfort of her arms around his back. It had been the best few hours of his life. And then it was over. Evie had come to his room that night, and all he wanted was to kiss her again. *I can't,* she'd said quietly as she pushed his hands away. *It's no good. It's Mabel, you know. She adores you. And she's my dearest friend in this world. I can't, Jericho. I'm sorry.* She'd left him sitting in his room in the dark. But she'd never left his thoughts.

Jericho tore Evie's picture neatly from the paper and slipped it into his pocket even though he'd promised himself he'd stop doing that.

"What a chump," he said—a phrase he'd gotten from Evie. Then he closed the book and set about his work in the empty museum.

☀

Sam peeked his head out the museum's front doors. Nothing. Not a soul. With a sigh, he sauntered down the steps in the light rain and slid open the wooden panel that read CLOSED, exposing the OPEN sign.

He couldn't tell Jericho the real reason he needed to keep the museum alive. Two months ago, he'd asked his informant for a tip about Project Buffalo—a place to start. The contact had written down a name: William Fitzgerald. It had seemed like a joke. What could the professor of the world's dullest museum know about a secret government project during the war that had taken Sam's mother away from him? But it was the only lead he'd gotten in a very long time, and so even though it made him feel like an ungrateful heel, any chance he got he searched every drawer, cabinet, crevice, and corner of the place for clues that might lead him to the truth. So far, his search had yielded bupkes. He couldn't let the museum be sold off until he'd found what he was looking for or proved that his contact had been wrong and that Will was in the clear. At times, he wasn't sure which of those scenarios would be best.

Sam craned his neck, looking for signs of possible visitors. A mother pushing a carriage. A window washer packing up his supplies. Two men in dark suits waiting out the rain in their sedan. And one fellow in a Harvard letter sweater striding up Sixty-eighth Street.

Sam smirked. "Perfect," he said under his breath. He bounded down the steps toward the fella, smiling and waving. "Buckwald? Buck Macy, is that you, you son of a gun?"

"I'm sorry. You must have me confused with someone else—"

"Do I?" Whip-fast, Sam stuck out a hand. "Don't see me," he intoned, and the college boy's eyes glazed over.

Sam reached into the fella's jacket, found his wallet, removed five dollars, and placed the wallet back inside, all in the space of six seconds.

"Nine, ten, eleven, twelve..." Sam counted. When Sam hit fifteen, the man came out of his hypnotic trance, blinking and befuddled. *Not bad*, Sam thought. Fifteen seconds was the longest he'd ever been able to put somebody under.

"Are you all right, pal?" Sam said, all concern. "You got a little woozy there."

"Must've been that party last night at the Harvard Club," the college boy said, still a little dazed.

"Must've been that," Sam agreed. "Sorry that I had you confused with somebody else. A *Yalie*," he whispered.

"Well. It's... I'm fine now. Yes," the fella mumbled. "Thanks, old boy."

"Anytime, old boy," Sam parroted and sent the still-wobbly fella on his way. He kissed the five bucks he'd stolen and shoved it into his pocket.

"The Museum of the Creepy Crawlies thanks you for your generous donation, sir," he said to himself, then hurried up the steps into the museum.

"Did you see that, Mr. Adams?" the driver of the sedan asked, breaking the silence in the car.

The man in the passenger seat retrieved a pistachio from the oil-stained bag in his hand and maneuvered it into his mouth, cracking the shell with his back molars. But he kept his eyes on the museum the whole time.

"I did indeed, Mr. Jefferson," he answered at last.

THE DEVIL'S BUSINESS

The wind whipping down 125th Street in the wake of the zippering trolleys was brisk, and Memphis Campbell blew on his hands for warmth. A tall ladder leaned against the outside of a brownstone where two men hoisted a banner above a second-floor window: MISS CALEDONIA: READER OF OBJECTS, HEALER OF MALADIES, DIVINER EXTRAORDINAIRE. Memphis shook his head. Everywhere he looked, it seemed people were trying to cash in on the Diviners craze.

As he walked with his younger brother, Isaiah, and old Blind Bill Johnson, Memphis counted the signs hanging from doorways or posted in windows up and down the streets of Harlem: FATHER FORTUNE WILL FREE YOU FROM HARM. MYSTICAL MOHAMMED, TELLER OF TRUTHS FROM BEYOND. OBEAH MAN: PALMS READ, FORTUNES TOLD, CURSES LIFTED. Most of them couldn't tell a crystal ball from a bowling ball. And the only fortunes were the ones they were collecting from gullible clients.

None of them had half the stuff Isaiah did, and Memphis knew it galled his little brother not to be lapping up the attention. Ever since Isaiah had gotten sick, their aunt Octavia had kept a watchful eye on him, preaching about "the dangers of the Devil's business."

"You remember what happened? How you lay in that bed for three days?" she'd said, pronouncing each word as if she were spitting it into stone to stand the test of time. "Jesus healed you, so don't you go throwing his blessings away. This family has no business with Obeah men, mambos, houngans, and card readers. And we certainly don't have business with Miss Margaret Walker. Never again."

But it hadn't been Jesus who'd healed Isaiah. It had been Memphis himself.

He'd never told his aunt that he'd gone to his brother's bedside as Isaiah lay in that sleep between life and death. In secret, he'd put his hands on his brother, and the power he'd thought had left him forever the night he tried to cure his dying mother had rushed through him once more, just as it used to do back when he was the Harlem Healer, curing the sick in a storefront church with his mother looking on and praising God. It seemed that Memphis had been given a second chance at his gift. He didn't know why. But he did know that this time, he'd figure it out on his own terms. And no one, except for Theta, would need to know until he was ready.

"You awful quiet back there, Isaiah," Blind Bill said, breaking Memphis out of his reverie.

"I hate this stupid tie," Isaiah grumbled, pulling at his collar, and Memphis knew it wasn't the suit that was bothering him. He put a hand on Isaiah's shoulder, but Isaiah shrugged it off.

"I have powers bigger'n a lotta these fool Diviners making money now. I coulda had a radio show, too!" Isaiah said and kicked a small rock down the street.

"No, you couldn't. Too shrimpy to reach the microphone," Memphis said, hoping to tease Isaiah out of his mood. It didn't take much to set his brother off these days. Not being able to use his clairvoyant gift was like keeping him inside the house when there was a warm, sunny day taunting him on the other side of the window. Lately, he'd been talking in his sleep again. Nightmares.

"I liked going to Sister Walker's house. She was a nice lady. She was good to me," Isaiah grumbled.

"Now, now, now. I can feel you pouting clear over here, little man. Gonna get your face stuck like that," the bluesman said. These days, Bill seemed to be the only one who could calm Isaiah when he was in a mood.

For the past month, Bill had been a boarder in Octavia's house.

"Can't let the man who saved my nephew live in some flea-ridden flophouse," she'd said as she readied the small room off the parlor that wasn't big enough to hold anything other than a cot, but Bill insisted he didn't need more than that, anyway.

"This is like a king's room to me, Miss Octavia," he said, smiling as he patted the cot with a rough, scarred hand.

It seemed like no time at all before Bill was part of their family—sitting in at meals, going to church with them, telling stories about the Louisiana cotton fields, or showing Isaiah how to bend his fingers to make guitar chords. Sometimes it was nice to have Bill around. There was more time for Memphis to write, more time for nights with Theta.

"Come on, little man," Bill said now. "Let's get you something good to drink." The bluesman offered the hand that was not on the cane, and Isaiah came to his side and took it easily, as if they belonged together.

The after-church crowd filled the booths of the Lenox Drugstore soda fountain for a little refreshment and Sunday gossip.

Bill excused himself for a moment. Memphis and Isaiah hopped onto the stools at the counter in the back and ordered two root beers. The brothers sipped their drinks, Isaiah arguing baseball with Mr. Reggie.

"If you ask me, the Homestead Grays are the team to beat. The Giants are finished," Mr. Reggie said, wiping down the counter.

Isaiah took umbrage at the insult to his beloved New York Lincoln Giants. "Si Simmons gonna pitch for the Giants and win it all this year!"

"Suppose we'll have to see about that," Reggie teased.

Memphis pulled out his notebook, scribbling some changes to a poem he'd been working on for the better part of a week. The words didn't feel quite right yet, like he was trying to write in somebody else's clothes, and he wondered when he would know he'd written something that felt true to himself instead of feeling like an impostor with a pencil.

"Hello, Isaiah. Memphis. How are you boys getting along?"

At the sound of Sister Walker's voice, the boys' heads shot up. If Sister Walker was sore that Octavia had forbidden them from seeing her, she didn't show it, offering them one of her warm smiles.

"Fine, ma'am," Isaiah said almost shyly.

"Well, I believe you've grown a foot since I saw you last," Sister Walker said.

Isaiah grinned. "Gonna be as tall as Memphis. Taller, even!"

"Keep telling yourself that, shrimpy," Memphis said. Isaiah socked Memphis in the arm. It barely hurt, but Memphis pretended it was a mortal wound, which pleased his brother greatly.

"And how are you feeling, Isaiah?"

Isaiah's smile faded. "Fine, thank you, ma'am."

"I believe my candy dish misses you," Sister Walker joked.

"I miss it, too. You still got Bit-O-Honeys?"

"A whole mess of them. You're welcome back at my house any-time. I want you to know that." Sister Walker lowered her voice to an urgent whisper. "Memphis, I need to talk to you about something. It's important."

"I don't believe I ought to, Miss Walker. My aunt Octavia—"

"It won't take long, I promise. I'm leaving town for a bit. But before I do, it's very important that we—"

"Well, well, well, is that the Campbell brothers I hear talking to some pretty girl?" Bill called as he tapped his way over to the group.

Memphis made the introductions, and Bill bowed, all charm, making small talk about the weather and the wisdom of the reverend's sermon they'd just heard.

"Do I know you? You look familiar," Sister Walker said quite suddenly.

Bill's mouth worked its way into a smile. "I always look like some-body. Got a familiar face, my mama said."

"You have family in Baltimore?"

"No kin that I know."

"Where are your people from?" Sister Walker pressed.

"Georgia," Bill said, his mouth tense around the word.

"I thought you were from Louisiana," Isaiah said.

Bill placed his hands on Isaiah's shoulders, pressing down slightly. "I'm from everywhere. Been all over this country."

"Memphis! Isaiah!" Aunt Octavia's angry voice announced her arrival. She marched through the drugstore and right up to Sister Walker. Her body had the feel of a slingshot pulled to breaking.

"Afternoon, Octavia," Sister Walker said.

"Don't you 'afternoon' me, Margaret Walker. I know what you were doing with my nephew behind my back. I told you before and I'll tell you for the last time: This is a God-fearing family. You understand?"

Every head in the drugstore had turned in their direction. All chatter had ceased. "Octavia, Isaiah has a gift—a rare gift. It's important that we continue our work—"

"Don't tell me how to raise my sister's children!" Octavia stood a hair's breadth from Sister Walker. "That boy lay in bed near death thanks to you. You're never getting near my family again, you hear me?" Octavia turned sharply to the boys. "Isaiah, Memphis—we are leaving."

Like a scared jackrabbit, Isaiah scrambled down from his stool and, with a backward forlorn glance, said good-bye to Sister Walker before taking Blind Bill's hand and leading him from the drugstore. The after-church crowd made a pretense of moving food around their plates, but they were still watching. Nothing in the preacher's sermon carried the same fire as the scene they'd just witnessed.

Sister Walker laid a hand on Memphis's arm as he walked past. "Please. It's important."

"Memphis John Campbell!" Octavia shouted from the door.

"I have to go," he said.

"Memphis, you don't believe I would harm Isaiah, do you?"

"To be honest, Sister . . . Miss Walker, I don't know what I believe," Memphis said and ran to catch up with his family.

※

While Octavia bustled about the kitchen, preparing Sunday supper, Memphis sat on the front stoop and read over his latest love letter to

Theta one last time before mailing it. But his mind was on the earlier encounter with Sister Walker. What could be so important that she had to speak to him? And if it was that important, why hadn't she brought it up before? Aunt Octavia said that Sister Walker had been in prison—for what, no one seemed to know for certain, though there'd been a rumor floating around church that it had been for sedition during the war. "Can't trust a word what woman says," Octavia declared, and Memphis wished he could be so sure.

"Memphis? You out here?" Bill tapped his way out the door.

"Over here, Mr. Johnson," Memphis said, guiding the old man to a seat on the stoop.

"What you working on out here in the cold?" Bill asked.

Memphis stuffed the letter into his pocket. "Nothing."

"Hmph. Sound like a woman to me," Bill said and laughed.

Memphis grinned. "Might be."

"Sound like a pretty woman."

"Might be that, too," Memphis said, embarrassed.

"Aww, now, I don't mean to be in your business. Mostly, I got to wondering if that Walker woman upset you earlier."

"No, sir," Memphis lied.

Bill fished in his pocket and came out with two sticks of chewing gum and passed one to Memphis. "What she want with you, anyhow?"

"Just to talk," Memphis said, brushing the lint off the gum. It was brittle and stale, so he stuffed it in his pocket.

"And did you?"

"No, sir."

Bill nodded. "You did right, Memphis," he said, like an older, wiser uncle. "You did right to look out for your brother thataway."

Memphis bristled. He wasn't sure that keeping Isaiah from using his gift was the right thing.

"Little man ever talk about what happened to him the day he got sick?" Bill asked, chewing his gum slowly.

"No. He doesn't remember anything."

Bill nodded. "Well, I 'spect that's for the best. We shouldn't bother

82

him none about it. Prob'ly just upset him. Still"—Bill took in a sucking breath—"that sure was a miracle the way he pulled through. Yes, sir, a miracle."

"You sound like Octavia," Memphis said.

"Wasn't you, then, that did the healing?" Bill said, lowering his voice.

Memphis's tone went flat. "Told you, I can't do that anymore."

"Yes, you did. You did tell me that." Bill's laugh came out like soft cat hisses. "Why, I reckon if you had the healing power on you, you'd put those hands on poor old Bill Johnson and heal up his sight, wouldn't you, now?"

Memphis's stomach tightened. He'd never thought about healing Blind Bill. That seemed too great a miracle to attempt. In fact, since healing Isaiah, Memphis hadn't quite worked up the courage to try again. What if he couldn't do it a second time? What if there were limits, like a genie in a bottle granting only three wishes? What if it turned sour, like it had with his mother, and he hurt someone? Memphis needed an opportunity to work in secret, in small ways. Easing a scrape here or a sore throat there wouldn't draw much attention. But giving a blind man back his sight? That wasn't the sort of healing that went unnoticed.

"You would do that for old Bill, wouldn't you?" Blind Bill asked again. The playfulness of his tone had vanished.

"Isaiah, Memphis, wash up for supper now!" Octavia called from inside.

"Yes, ma'am!" Memphis called back, grateful for his aunt's interruption. "Coming, Mr. Johnson?"

"You go on ahead. I'll be in shortly."

When he heard the door close behind him, Bill sat for another minute on the front stoop and tilted his head up toward the sky, which he could only see as a dark, grainy impression.

That would change soon, if it all worked out right.

Somebody had healed Isaiah Campbell as the boy lay in that back bedroom at Octavia's house all those weeks ago. Somebody very powerful. When Bill had put his hands on the boy's head, trying to see into his Diviner mind in the hope of getting another lucky number to ease his gambling debts, he'd felt the energy in the boy's body immediately. It had traveled up Bill's arms and into his own body, till it was too much, and he'd had to let go. That was when he noticed the change in his vision. It was very small—where there had been total darkness he now saw faint, blocky shapes, like looking through several layers of gray gauze. But it had been enough to let him know that it was possible: He could be healed. He could see again. And if he could see again, he could get revenge on the people who'd taken his sight from him in the first place.

Diviners were everywhere these days, it seemed. But Bill was fairly certain there was only one person who had the gift to do that sort of healing, only one person desperate enough to try it. A brother's love was strong, and the Campbell brothers' love was stronger than most. It was clear that Memphis would do anything to protect Isaiah, even lie to Bill about his own abilities. Fine. If Memphis Campbell wanted to play the rabbit and hide in his warren, then Bill would play the fox and wait him out. Memphis would surface in time. And Bill would be right there waiting.

And if not, well, he might have to smoke the rabbit out.

Sometimes a child who'd had one fit suffered another.

It happened all the time.

Nearby, a crow cawed, making Bill jump. "Go on, bird! Git! Shoo!"

It squawked again, passing so close to Bill's head that he gasped at the suddenness of feathers against his cheek like a slap.

TIN PAN ALLEY

Theta waited impatiently for Henry on the corner of Broadway and West Forty-second Street. At last, she saw him sauntering up the street, his beaten boater hat perched on his head. "There you are! Come on, kid. You're gonna be late."

She linked her arm through Henry's, and the two of them hurried as best they could in the bustle of Broadway, past streets housing the many music publishers of Tin Pan Alley, till they came to the address they wanted. Henry stared up at the four-story row house.

"Bertram G. Huffstadler and Company, Music Publishers," he said on a shaky exhale.

"Don't have kittens, Hen. They're gonna love you."

"That's what you said about Mills. And Leo Feist. And Witmark and Sons."

"Witmark and his Sons are a bunch of chumps."

"They're one of the biggest music publishers in the biz."

"And they didn't publish you, so they're chumps."

Henry smiled. "You're my best girl."

"Somebody should be. Hold on, let me fix your tie," Theta said, adjusting the knot. "There. Now. Let's hear your spiel."

With a big razzmatazz smile, Henry stuck out his hand and said, "How do you do? I'm Henry Bartholomew DuBois the Fourth. And I'm the next big thing." He dropped the hand and the smile, pacing nervously in front of the stoop. "I can't say that."

"But you *are* the next big thing."

"I don't feel like the next big thing."

"That's where the acting comes in, kid. You gotta make 'em believe it. Just remember our plan. Now. Who's the one they want?"

"I am," Henry mumbled.

"Very convincing," Theta deadpanned. "You selling 'em your songs or a funeral plan?"

"I am the next big thing!" Henry said a little more forcefully.

"Go get 'em, kid. Ten minutes?"

"Ten minutes."

Henry took the stairs to the second floor, making his way down a narrow hallway of small rooms. Music was everywhere, songs competing with one another till they all sounded as if they were part of the same orchestration. He passed an open doorway where two composers paced a small room, throwing out rhymes to each other. "June, moon, soon, moon—"

"You said *moon* already—"

"So sue me—"

"I can't. It's like suing myself."

In another room, a fella played a verse for a girl who was curled up in a chair with her shoes off and one arm thrown across her eyes.

"What does that make you feel?" the fella asked.

"Suicidal," the girl said.

"Okay. But would you want to make whoopee first?" he shot back, and Henry tried not to laugh.

All of them were selling dreams in rhythm and rhyme. Henry desperately wanted to be one of them. No, he wanted to be the best of them. The ambition burned coal-hot inside him. He hoped today would be his lucky day. If that hack Herbie Allen could sell his terrible songs, why couldn't Henry?

The hallway funneled him into a larger common area at the back. A lanky, dark-haired young man hunched over a typewriter did not look up. The sounds of a treacly, forgettable love ditty competed with

86

the clack of typewriter keys. Of the two, Henry preferred the typing. It was more honest.

"What do you think?"

It took Henry a second to realize that the question was directed at him and that it had come from the typist, who had stopped working and was leaning back in his chair, arms crossed, watching Henry intently.

"About..." Henry gestured toward the room from which the bad song originated.

The typist nodded. Henry wasn't sure what to say. What if this was a test? What if this young man and those composers were the best of friends? What if this was, in fact, Mr. Huffstadler in disguise? The typist seemed too young to be a publisher. In fact, he didn't look much older than Henry. "Well, it's certainly...high-pitched."

The young man grinned. "That's the thing about Simon and Parker—they're nothing but treble."

Henry laughed and stuck out his hand. "Henry DuBois. The Fourth."

"David Cohn. The one and only. Actually, one of about a million. David Cohn is like the John Smith of the Jewish world. You here to see the big man?"

"Indeed I am."

"You any good?"

Theta's voice purred encouragement in his head, but he couldn't bring himself to say those words. "I suppose we'll find out."

"You can go on in," David Cohn said, gesturing with one finger toward a door with a glass window with the name BERTRAM G. HUFF-STADLER fanned out in blocky black-and-gold lettering. "Oh, and don't let the Amazing Reynaldo throw you."

"Who?"

David Cohn smirked as he resumed his typing. "You'll find out. Good luck, Mr. DuBois the Fourth."

Mr. Huffstadler was a small, portly man with a jowly face that seemed to be in a perpetual state of imminent disappointment. He shoved a cigar into his scowling slash of a mouth and gave Henry a dismissive glance.

"Have a seat. What brings you to the Huffstadler Company today?"

I'm the next big thing. "Well, sir, I'd very much like to have my songs published by the great Bertram G. Huffstadler."

"So would a lot of folks. Why should I publish you?"

"Well, sir..." Henry launched into his well-rehearsed patter about his love of music and his passion for songwriting as Mr. Huffstadler shuffled to the door and poked his head out. "Where's Reynaldo?" he shouted.

A moment later, a man in a pinstriped suit and shoes with spats like bat's wings entered. He wore enough aftershave lotion to asphyxiate a busload of people.

"Where you been?" Mr. Huffstadler scolded in what he probably thought passed for a whisper. "I've been looking for you all day."

"The muse must be fed, Mr. Huffstadler. I required sustenance," the other man said with an actor's flair.

"I don't pay you to eat. I pay you to pick hits." The harrumphing Mr. Huffstadler waddled back to his chair. "This is the Amazing Reynaldo. He's a Diviner," the man said with a knowing nod. "Name another publisher who has a Diviner working for him. You can't—I'm the only one. This fella here has the power to communicate with the spirit world and find out which songs stink and which ones will be hits."

Henry felt fairly certain that the "Amazing" Reynaldo's real talent was the ability to detect a sucker and a meal ticket. "Nice to meet you, sir," he said.

The Amazing Reynaldo shook Henry's hand and closed his eyes. "The spirits tell me that you are from the South."

My accent tells you I'm from the South, you faker. "Gee, that is astonishing," Henry said.

Huffstadler smiled around his cigar. "Did I tell you or did I tell you? Okay, kid. You're up. Show the Diviner and me what you've got."

He gestured to the piano in the corner, a cherrywood upright that Henry wished were his. Henry played a portion of his first song, stealing glances at Mr. Huffstadler's face, which was like a stone.

"Reynaldo?" Huffstadler said when Henry had finished.

The Diviner looked heavenward, frowning, then turned to Henry. "Mr. DuBois. May I be frank?"

"I wish you would, Mr. Reynaldo," Henry said, though he wished no such thing.

"I'm afraid your song simply isn't up to the standards of our company. It's too jazzy. Too . . . complicated. The spirits found it odd and displeasing."

"I'm very much influenced by the style of New Orleans, where I was raised."

"Well, this isn't New Orleans, kid. It's the big city. You're competing with George and Ira Gershwin, Irving Berlin, Herbert Allen, and about a thousand other fellas churning out songs folks wanna sing down at the corner dance hall." Mr. Huffstadler spread his hands out as if that gesture were an explanation in and of itself. "We need songs that anybody can sing anywhere. Popular songs. Songs that make money."

"The spirits concur," Reynaldo said, frowning down at his cuticles as if they, and not Henry's future in the music business, hung in the balance. He gave Henry an apologetic smile that was as insincere as his divining. "Alas, it's no Berlin."

Mr. Huffstadler punched the air with the end of his cigar. "Irving Berlin. Didn't have a cent to his name. Didn't even speak English, for Pete's sake. Started his career on the streets of the Lower East Side. Now? He's the biggest songwriter in America—and a millionaire. What you need, my friend, is to make your music sound like Irving Berlin's."

Henry forced a half smile. "Well, sir, we've already got a Mr. Berlin. Seems redundant to have two."

"Kid, if I could have a hundred Irving Berlins, I would. I'm in the business of business. If you write me a song about a disembowelment and it sells, I'm interested."

"*Constipaaation . . .*"

"What's that?"

"Nothing," Henry said quickly.

Right on cue, Theta pushed through the door. "Oh, excuse me! I'm so sorry to interrupt," she said, batting her lashes and doing her "little girl lost" shtick.

"Not at all, Miss . . . ?" Mr. Huffstadler looked her up and down.

Theta got wise immediately and smiled up at him, wide-eyed. "Knight. Theta Knight. And you must be the one and only Mr. Bertram G. Huffstadler," she purred.

The lecherous man laughed. "Guilty in the first degree."

"And I am the Amazing Reynaldo, Seer of Futures, Reader of Thoughts, Diviner and Advisor to great men," Reynaldo said, kissing her hand.

And low-rent music publishers, Henry thought.

Mr. Huffstadler smoothed back his thinning hair. "Now, how can I help you, little lady?"

"Oh, I surely hope you can help me, Mr. Huffstadler. I'm just beside myself," Theta said, baiting the hook. "You see, I work for Mr. Ziegfeld, in the Follies?"

"The Follies?" Reynaldo blurted eagerly before catching himself. "That is, I sensed it."

"No kidding? Golly!" Theta cooed, batting her lashes until Henry had to put a hand over his mouth to keep from laughing out loud. Sometimes Theta's best acting wasn't on the stage. "Well, Flo—Mr. Ziegfeld, that is—he's looking for a new song, and the other night, I was in a little nightclub, and I heard the dreamiest number! But I don't know who wrote it. I was kinda hoping you might know or, gee, bein' as you're such a Big Cheese, maybe you even published it?"

"Well, if we didn't, we oughta!" Mr. Huffstadler winked at Theta. "So what's this dreamy tune called, honey?"

"Jeepers, I don't really know."

"Reynaldo?" Mr. Huffstadler looked to the Diviner, who paled.

"Er . . . the spirits don't see fit to tell me at this time."

"Perhaps if you sang a little of it, Miss," Henry prompted.

"Of course! It went something like this. . . ." Theta launched into the chorus of Henry's song, purposely forgetting some of the words and humming along as if she'd only heard it once.

Henry's eyes widened in mock-surprise. "Why, Miss, that's my song!"

"Your song? You don't say!"

"I do say." Henry picked up the chorus, supplying the right words, and Theta gazed at him with a swoony face. At the end, she applauded enthusiastically. "Oh, that's wonderful! You've gotta come by and play that for Mr. Ziegfeld."

"Of all the luck," Henry said, grinning. "I don't believe it."

"I don't believe it, either." Behind the desk, Mr. Huffstadler scowled. "You kids think I fell off a turnip truck this week? Your song stinks, Mr. DuBois—and so does this phony act. Now get out before I throw you both out."

Theta dropped her smile, along with her breathless voice. "Yeah? You wouldn't know a good song if it came up and bit you in the a—"

"Ascot!" Henry said quickly. "May I escort you out, Miss Knight?"

"I wish you would, Mr. DuBois," Theta said. She leaned in to the Amazing Reynaldo. "And if you're really a reader of thoughts, you oughta be blushing to beat the band if you can read mine right now, ya big phony." She slammed the door behind her for good measure.

At the front desk, David Cohn grinned up at Henry and Theta from behind his typewriter. "Nice try."

"Well, it almost worked." Henry tipped his hat. "It was a pleasure to meet you."

"Likewise." David fiddled with some paper, glancing shyly at Henry. "Hopefully, we'll meet again. Hey!"

"Yeah?" Henry said, turning around.

"For what it's worth, I thought your song was pretty good."

"Good or pretty good?"

"Nothing wrong with your song that a little more heart and a lot of hard work couldn't fix."

"You a Diviner, too?" Henry joked.

David Cohn smiled. "No. Just honest. But nobody pays you for that."

DREAM WITH ME

After saying good-bye to Theta, Henry hopped the El to Chatham Square and made his way through Chinatown in the brisk chill. He moved in and out of shops, pretending to be interested in ceramic bowls and fabric for a new suit, while surreptitiously looking for the girl he'd only met inside a dream.

A commotion erupted in the street. Police were turning out a restaurant, allowing the health inspector passage. The owner protested the disruption to his business mightily: "This is a clean place! No sickness here."

"Do you have your papers?" the policeman asked one of the waiters, who didn't seem to understand. "Your resident permit?"

A translator spoke quickly with the frightened waiter.

"He left it at home," the translator explained to the police. "He'll go get it now."

"Nothing doing, pal. No papers, we take you in." The policeman whistled for his partner, and they loaded the terrified waiter into the back of the wagon.

"Can't he go home and get his papers?" Henry asked innocently.

The policeman scrutinized Henry. "We're just going our job," he said wearily, and Henry was reminded of a time in New Orleans when he and Louis had hidden under the bar while police raided Celeste's, rounding up all the boys dancing together. One of the cops, a fella named Beau, had been seen dancing at Celeste's himself a number of times.

"I'm just doing my job," he'd said to the owner, as if it would be apology enough.

Henry had been powerless that night, and he felt powerless here. He couldn't help this man. He couldn't even find the girl. He was just about to give up and go home when he turned the corner onto Doyers Street and stopped cold. Nestled next to a jeweler's shop was the Tea House restaurant, just as it had been in his dream.

Maybe he wasn't so powerless after all.

Henry ducked inside. He hadn't been hungry before, but it smelled delicious, so he took a seat and ordered a noodle dish, and while he waited, he looked around for any hint of the girl with the green eyes.

"Best chow mein in town," an older man at the next table said in an Eastern European accent. He nodded to the police out on the streets. "The sleeping sickness."

"Oh, yes," Henry said, barely listening. A trio of girls walked past the front windows of the Tea House, but none of them was his mysterious dream walker.

"On my street, Ludlow, there is right now a girl of only twenty, she has been asleep for two days," the old man continued. "Her mother can't wake her up. Her father can't wake her up. Even the rabbi can't wake her up. How do they take ill? Is it in the food or the water? In the air? No one knows."

From somewhere in the restaurant, Henry heard a familiar voice. And then he spied her sitting at a table in the back, partially obscured by a screen.

"Do excuse me," Henry said, walking to the back. He came around the screen and stood beside the girl's table, his shadow falling across her open book. "So you do exist."

The girl looked up at him. Her eyes were a hazel-green, greener in the light. Though she was a slight girl, there was something of the boxer's quality to her, Henry thought; this was someone ready to show

94

knuckles at a moment's notice. Her mouth opened in an O of surprise, and then, just as quickly, she caught herself.

"I'm afraid you have mistaken me for someone else," she said with pointed politeness.

"I don't believe I have. I've seen you in my dreams."

The girl gave him only a disdainful upward glance. "Corny."

"I did see you in my dreams last night. Didn't I? I've never—"

"Shhh!" she whispered, craning her neck to see if anyone was listening. "Sit down. If anyone asks, I know you from school. Do you understand?"

Henry nodded and lowered his voice. "You'll have to forgive my astonishment. It's just that I've never met another dream walker before. Have you?"

"No."

"There must be others, though. Don't you think? What with all these Diviners coming out of the woodwork now. Oh. Forgive my manners. I'm Henry DuBois the Fourth. Pleased to meet you, Miss...?"

"Ling Chan."

"Charmed, Miss Chan."

"I'm not particularly charming," Ling said, without smiling.

"Well, I make it a point never to argue with a lady."

The waiter arrived with Henry's noodle dish and Ling turned suddenly chatty. "As I was saying, the most exciting thing about Mr. Marlowe's exhibition is the science pavilion. I hear they'll have a model of the atom on display...."

As the waiter set Henry's dish down, he gave Ling a curious look. "A friend of yours, Ling?"

"Yes, Lucky," Ling said, without missing a beat. "We were in science club together in school. He's just come to talk about Jake Marlowe's Future of America Exhibition."

"Our Ling is very smart," Lucky said. "As smart as any of the boys."

"The smartest," Henry said, playing along.

"I'd better go. Things are very busy without George," Lucky said before walking away, and Henry saw the girl's face fall.

"Is everything all right?"

"Fine," she snapped.

It clearly wasn't, but Henry had been raised not to pry. "Science club?" he said instead, raising an eyebrow. "I suppose now is a bad time to tell you that I nearly blew up my chemistry lab back at boarding school. It's an amusing story—"

"Why are you here? I assume it's not for the egg rolls."

Henry's easy charm faded, and his smile with it. "I'm looking for someone I lost."

"Lost how? How do you lose a person? Why don't you look in the telephone directory?"

"He doesn't even have a telephone," Henry said. To make Ling understand, he'd have to tell her about the letter, his father, running away from home. He would have to explain what Louis meant to him. But he couldn't do that. Not with a stranger. And she *was* a stranger. Just because they'd shared a dream walk didn't make them friends. "I thought if I could find his dream, I could ask him where he was, or let him know where to find me somehow. Have you ever been able to do that? Locate someone?"

"Only with the dead."

Henry's fork stopped on the way to his mouth. "You see the dead?"

"In dreams I do. Sometimes someone needs to speak to a departed relative. If I take something of theirs, sometimes I can find them."

"How long have you been able to do this?"

"It started a year ago."

"Almost three years ago for me," Henry said. "But it's gotten stronger in the past few months."

"The same for me," Ling said.

"I learned to set an alarm clock to wake me. I found that if I go longer than an hour, I get ill. You?"

Ling shrugged. "I can go longer," she said, and Henry detected a note of pride in it. Ling Chan didn't like to be second, it seemed. "You still haven't said why you're here."

Henry toyed with the noodles on his plate. "Last night, for the first time, I finally came close to finding my friend Louis while we were standing outside that old building. Right after I grabbed hold of your arm, I heard his fiddle. It was Louis's favorite song, played the way he always played it." Henry leaned forward. "I want to go back in tonight and see if it works again. I want us to try to meet in the dream world."

Ling scoffed. "You know how dreams work. They're slippery. We can't control them—we're only observers. Passengers."

"We always have been, but what if we can change that?" Henry said. "Are you at least willing to try? You just said you can locate people. Maybe if I gave you something of mine, you'd be able to find me in the dream world. If that works, we could try to go back to that place where I heard Louis's fiddle."

"And maybe I can become Queen of Romania," Ling said. "There's no promise that we'll find each other or that we'll be able to return to the same dream. It's like a river, constantly moving and changing."

"Please," Henry pleaded. "Won't you help me?"

Ling looked at Henry for an uncomfortable length of time. She didn't want to become involved with this dream walker. But she had to admit she was curious. There had been something interesting about their combined energy last night. What if they could do more together? "All right. It'll cost you. I charge for my services."

"Very well. What's your price?"

"Ten dollars," Ling blurted.

Without a word, Henry removed a crisp ten from his wallet and put it on the table. Ling tried not to let her surprise show. This dream walker was the first person not to haggle over the price. But it wasn't her job to tell him that. Whoever this lost friend of his was, he must be very important.

"I'll need something of yours," she said, pocketing his money quickly. "To find you in the dream."

Henry passed Ling his hat. "Will this do?"

Ling nodded. "What time tonight?"

"It'll have to be late. I play for the Rooftop Revue above the Follies at midnight."

Ling had seen the advertisements for the Rooftop Revue in the newspaper. The girls didn't wear much.

"I'm hoping to get my songs some attention," Henry said sheepishly. "I'm a composer, you see."

"Do I know any of your songs?" Ling asked.

"'You're My Turtle Dove, Coo-E-Coo'? 'September Moon'?"

Ling shook her head. "Never heard of them."

Henry felt vaguely insulted. "It's a tough business."

"Maybe it isn't the business. Maybe your songs aren't that good."

Henry left money for the bill as he rose from the table. "I should be home by three," he said coolly. "Do we have a deal?"

"Three o'clock is fine."

"I suppose we're in business, then." He stuck out his hand for a shake.

Ling didn't take his hand. She looked him straight in the eyes. "It's very brave of you to come down here. Most people are afraid of catching the sleeping sickness."

"I'm not most people," he said, his hand still out.

Ling gave it a quick shake. This time, there was no spark.

"I'll see you in my dreams, Ling Chan."

"I hope your songs aren't as corny as your jokes," she answered.

Henry headed back into the cold city thinking that Ling Chan was possibly the bluntest person he had ever met. But she was going to help him find Louis. It was the first hopeful break he'd had. That hope buoyed Henry's mood as he passed down Chinatown's narrow, winding streets. Above his head, laundry danced from lines stretched between tenement windows like pennants decorating Yankee Stadium, where, come spring, Babe Ruth hoped to swing his way into the record books. He reached the wide sidewalks and winter-stripped trees of Columbus Park, where a man ranted from the steps of the park's steeple-roofed pavilion.

"The Chinaman comes in with Chinese habits—his gambling and his Tong Wars and the opium pipe. He's a secretive sort of fellow. He can't ever be an American. And now he's given us his sickness. I say we should keep America safe for Americans. Send him back to China. Send him back on the next ship."

"Bigot," Henry muttered, and moved on. As he walked through the park, he felt a sudden chill for no reason he could name—a strange feeling of dread.

"You all right, son?" a man in a tweed suit asked. He looked like a judge or a minister.

"Yeah. I mean, yes. Fine, thanks," Henry answered, but the chill remained.

"Here. Have one of these," the man said, shoving a leaflet into Henry's hands: KEEP AMERICA WHITE AND YOU KEEP AMERICA SAFE. THE KNIGHTS OF THE KU KLUX KLAN NEED YOU!

Henry tossed the leaflet in the rubbish can without reading it and wiped his hands on his coat.

On the platform of the City Hall subway station, Henry waited for the train, trying to shake off the odd dread that had come over him in Columbus Park. He thought about all the things he wanted to say to Louis when he saw him again. A young man stumbled down the steps. His suit was rumpled, and he smelled of booze. He muttered to himself as if answering private voices, drawing concerned glances from the other people waiting.

"Where's the damned train?" the man swore. "I need the train!"

"It'll be here soon," a businessman chided. "Settle down, there."

People moved back, keeping a safe distance from the young man as he stalked the platform. "It was so beautiful there. I need to go back. I can't find it. I can't find it!"

Henry flicked a glance down the tunnel and was relieved to see the distant train light moving closer. The troubled man swayed dangerously close to the platform's edge.

"Watch out!" Henry darted forward and yanked him back just as the train screeched into the station.

The young man slumped to the ground, mewling into his hands. "I just want to sleep. I have to get back there! I have to!"

The crowd opened up to allow the police in. One of the officers hoisted the haunted-looking man to his feet. "Come on, pal. We'll get you a nice bed, and you can sleep this one off."

"Dream with me," the man half cried.

He was still muttering the phrase as the police carried him out.

PULLING RABBITS
OUT OF HATS

Evie and her best friend, Mabel Rose, sat in the Bennington's Victorian dining room under the faulty, winking chandelier, drinking cups of hot cocoa to chase away the winter chill. It had been two months since Evie had set foot in her former residence, but Mabel had insisted, and she was surprisingly adept at wearing a girl down. Now that Evie was here, she couldn't help noticing how drab and shabby the place was, especially compared to the modern hotels where she'd been renting rooms. For a moment, she thought she saw Jericho, and her heart skipped a beat. But it wasn't him, and Evie was both relieved and disappointed.

Mabel patted the Gimbels box tied up with blue ribbon. "I can't believe you bought me a dress. It was too expensive," Mabel fretted. "Striking workers could eat for a week on what it cost."

Evie sighed. "Oh, Pie Face, really. Will this be a tragic screed on the dangers of capitalism? Because I must tell you, capitalism makes some darling dresses! Besides, it's my money, not yours."

"It *is* darling," Mabel said.

"Just like you," Evie said, peeping over Mabel's shoulder in the direction of the Bennington's revolving front door.

"What are you looking for? You've been doing that since we left Gimbels."

"I was, um, just making sure Uncle Will wasn't around," Evie lied. "I don't want to run into him. You understand."

Mabel nodded. She broke into a grin. "Gee, this has been swell, hasn't it? The two of us together, just like old times?"

They'd enjoyed a perfect day of ice-skating in Central Park, followed by the shopping trip to Gimbels, where Mabel had burst into giggles as Evie played elevator operator, crying out, "Fourth floor: Hair bonnets and enema bags! Ladies, Gimbels has you covered from top to bottom!" But it all felt so brief and fragile. Mabel missed Evie terribly—they hadn't seen each other in ages—and Mabel worried that Evie's new, exciting friends would eclipse and ultimately replace her. Mabel didn't drink, and frankly, she'd found the one party she'd attended with Evie to be dull and meaningless, populated by shallow people who didn't think much about the rest of the world.

But it didn't stop her from wanting to be included.

"Say! I've got a terrific idea. Why don't you stay over tonight?" Mabel said. "I'm sure my mother won't mind."

Evie raised an eyebrow. "Your mother thinks I'm the Devil."

"She doesn't! Much. Oh, forget about my mother. We could dance to Paul Whiteman records, play Pegity, and eat coffee cake till our stomachs hurt."

"Sorry, Pie Face, but I can't. There's a party at the Whoopee Club. I promised to pop out of the cake at midnight."

"Oh. I see," Mabel said, deflated. There was always a party these days.

"Really. I am sorry."

"What about tomorrow?"

"El-o-cution les-sons," Evie said, drawing out the words in exaggerated fashion. "And *Radio Star* is coming to WGI to take my picture. Well, everybody's picture, but I'm in it, too."

"Sounds...glamorous." Mabel hoped she didn't sound as pathetic and envious as she felt. "I wish I were more glamorous instead of... me."

Evie put her fist on the table. "Nonsense! I won't hear a bad word spoken about Miss Mabel Rose. She's a fine girl. The finest."

Mabel rolled her eyes. "Hip, hip, hooray!"

"You *are* special. You are the only Mabel Rose in existence," Evie insisted.

"I suppose that's why men fall at my feet daily. It's my *fine qualities* that draw them in," Mabel lamented. "If I weren't so ordinary, maybe Operation Jericho wouldn't seem hopeless."

Evie stirred her cocoa intently and hoped that Mabel couldn't see the blush blooming in her cheeks. "Maybe Jericho was carrying a torch for another girl," she said carefully. "Some old flame. And he had to be rid of the ghost of her before he could start courting you."

Mabel perked up. "Do you really think so?"

Evie managed a smile. "I'd bet my new stockings that's it. Do you know what? I don't think you should wait around for Jericho. You should be bold! Show up at the museum and offer assistance. Tell him you've had a message from the spirit world that the two of you are supposed to catalog ghosty things and then go dancing."

"Evie!" Mabel giggled.

"Or you could make him jealous." Evie waggled her eyebrows. "What about that other fellow who gave you his card... Arthur Somebody-or-Other?"

"Arthur Brown," Mabel confirmed. "I haven't seen him since October. Besides, my parents don't like him."

"Why not? Did he vote for Coolidge or something?"

Mabel giggled. "No! Arthur's too radical for them."

Evie put a hand to her forehead. "Stop the presses! Someone is too radical for your parents?"

"They say he's not a union organizer; he's an anarchist. Apparently, he got into some trouble at a rally for the appeal of Sacco and Vanzetti, where those explosions took place? My father said Arthur had to leave town ahead of the feds."

"Golly! A real, live anarchist on one hand, and a boy who spends all his time inside a ghost museum on the other. You sure know how to pick 'em, Mabesie."

The girls broke into fresh laughter. Mabel wiped her eyes. Inside, she felt warm and right with the world. Courageous. It was funny how one afternoon with a best friend could set a girl right. "Gee, I've missed you, Evie. Please, let's do this again soon?"

"Will do, Pie Face," Evie said, giving Mabel's fingers a squeeze before getting up. "I hate to break up a party, but I'd better get a wiggle on. I've got a date with a cake. But before I go, you must model your new dress for me!"

"Now?"

"No. Next Fourth of July. Of course right now! I insist!"

"All right. Let's go upstairs."

Evie shook her head. "Nothing doing. I want the full treatment-ski. Go upstairs and put the glad rags on. Then"—Evie lowered her voice to a husky purr—"I want you to *emerge* from the elevator and drape yourself against the wall like Clara Bow!"

Mabel could feel her ordinariness creeping back. "I am not Clara Bow," she said.

"For Pete's sake, Mabesie! Embrace a little mystery, will you? I'll wait here. Just don't take all day! And put on some lipstick!" Evie called as she shoved Mabel toward the elevator.

"I will return a new woman!" Mabel declared, pointing her finger skyward as the elevator operator slid the gate into place.

"Tick-tock. Party? Cake?" Evie reminded her and dropped into a chair in the lobby to wait. She pushed the heavy velvet drape aside and peered out the front windows. Still no sign of T. S. Woodhouse, the good-for-nothing. Before they'd left Gimbels, Evie had slipped into a phone booth and tipped him off that "Miss Evie O'Neill had been seen escorting her best friend to the Bennington Apartments for the first time since she'd left in November, in case interested parties wanted a story for the papers." It might've been a paltry sum Evie paid Woody to keep her name in the news, but it was still hard-earned money, and he'd better not be spending it in a speakeasy instead of making both of them more famous.

Someone was pushing through the revolving door. *Finally*, Evie thought. She jumped up and posed herself beneath a gilded sconce, turning her best side toward the entrance in case Woodhouse had been clever enough to bring along a photographer. The door swung all the way around. It wasn't Woodhouse who swept into the lobby, but Jericho. He stood for a moment, unwinding his scarf, not seeing her. Evie's stomach gave a carnival-ride flip as the feelings she'd worked to forget came bubbling up. She remembered that morning in the hotel room up in Brethren after Jericho had been shot, the way they'd been with each other, so open, so honest. Evie had never felt so naked with anyone, not even Mabel, as if she could say anything and be understood. It was heady. And dangerous. A girl needed armor to get by in the world, and Jericho had a way of dismantling hers so easily.

Jericho's eyes widened, then his mouth settled into the loveliest smile. "Evie!" he called, walking straight toward her, and her resolve to leave him alone began to erode.

"Hello, Jericho," Evie said softly, and they stood uncertainly in the foyer. People passed by, but Evie was barely aware of them. She'd forgotten the specific handsomeness of Jericho—the severe cheekbones, the sharp blue of his eyes. A long strand of blond hair had been shaken loose, falling across one cheek. He tried to tuck it back, but it fell again, and all Evie wanted to do was cup her hands at the base of his neck. It would be so easy to touch him.

"How are you—" Evie said at the same moment Jericho started to speak. They laughed nervously.

"You first," Evie said.

"I've been listening to your radio show. It's very good. You're a natural."

"Gee. Thanks," Evie said, blushing at the compliment.

An awkward silence descended. Jericho cleared his throat and gestured in the direction of the dining room. "Have you eaten? We could have tea in the dining room. For old times' sake."

Evie glanced toward the elevator. "Oh. I'm actually on my way out. I'm just waiting for Mabel."

Jericho stepped a little closer. He smelled clean and woodsy, as he had that morning on the roof when they'd kissed. "I've missed you," he said in his deep, quiet way.

Evie's breath caught in her chest, a painful ballooning. Her feelings for Jericho had been manageable when he was only a memory. In the whirl of parties and the radio show and, yes, the arms of other, fun-loving boys, thoughts of him could be pushed aside, she'd found. But here in person, it was an entirely different matter. Evie looked up into his eyes. "I..."

"Is that the Sweetheart Seer?"

"Why, it is! It's her!"

Excited burbling filled the front of the lobby as a few of the Bennington residents recognized Evie. She took in a sharp breath and stepped back.

"I...I have to go. I'm late for a cake—I-I mean a party! A party with a cake," Evie said, sounding as dizzy as she felt. "Tell Mabel I said good-bye."

"Wait! Don't go."

Jericho reached for her hand, catching the tips of her fingers just as the elevator doors opened and Mabel flounced out in her new yellow dress like one of Isadora Duncan's dancers.

"Daaaahling! It is I, Mabel BaraSwansonKnightBow...oh."

Quickly, Evie yanked her hand out of Jericho's reach and trotted toward her pal. "Mabesie! You are a vision in that dress!"

"A vision of what?" Mabel joked. Her eyes flicked from Evie to Jericho and back.

"Isn't it funny? Who should I run into but our old friend Jericho," Evie said, far too brightly. She could feel Jericho's gaze on her and she didn't dare meet it.

"Golly. You looked like you were having a very serious conversation. I hope I'm not interrupting anything," Mabel said.

"Just passing the time until you arrived," Evie chirped, her panic mounting. Any minute now, she feared, he'd say something about what had happened, breaking Mabel's heart and scarring their years-old friendship.

The revolving door swung around again as Sam pushed through, talking loudly to Jericho across the lobby. "See, the trouble with

Nietzsche, besides his being a real killjoy, is that he thinks like a spoiled seven-year-old who doesn't want to share his sandbox toys—"

"Sam! Sam, over here!" Evie blurted.

A smirking Sam sauntered over with his hands in his pockets. "Well, if it isn't the Queen of Sheba. Just the girl I'm looking for. Did Freddy tell you the news about our Diviners exhibit? I was thinking that—"

Evie threw her arms around Sam's neck. "Sam, there you are! You're late. Oh, but I don't mind. How handsome you look!"

Sam's brow furrowed. "Forgive me, Miss. I thought you were Evie O'Neill. Clearly I've mistaken you for someone else."

Evie laughed too hard. "Oh, you! Always the comedian." She slipped her arm through Sam's, giving him a small pinch as she did. "Now, I'm late to the Whoopee Club, and I need you to escort me, won't you? So long, Mabesie, darling! Let's do this again soon!" Evie nodded at Jericho. "Lovely to see you again, Jericho."

As she and Sam walked away, Evie chanced a look over her shoulder and saw Jericho watching her, wounded and stoic. It had to be done, even if it felt awful.

Once outside the Bennington, Evie slipped free of Sam's arm. "On second thought, it's too chilly for a walk, and it looks like rain. I'd better grab a taxi here."

Sam smirked. "What? And interrupt our cozy, heartfelt reunion?"

"Yes, I'm all broken up about it, too. But I'm sure I'll recover." Evie signaled to the doorman.

"You remember the day we met in Penn Station?"

"When you stole my twenty dollars? How could I forget?"

"You told me then that you weren't an actress." Sam tilted his head and narrowed his eyes. "I think you pulled my leg on that one."

"I'm sure I don't know what you mean, Sam Lloyd." Evie looked hopefully toward the street, where the doorman stood with his arm raised.

"I'm sure you do. Don't worry—I won't blow your cover. But I need something from you in return."

"Have you given up petty theft in favor of blackmail now?"

"This isn't for me. It's for your uncle. He's gonna lose the museum, Evie, if we don't pull a rabbit out of a hat."

"I don't see how that's any of my concern."

"We need you for the Diviners exhibit. If you mentioned it on that radio show of yours and showed up as the guest of honor, we could guarantee a big opening—maybe enough to pay the tax bill before the collector puts the whole place up on the auction block."

Evie's eyes flashed. "Why should I help Will? I risked my life to help solve the Pentacle Murders, and then he tried to ship me back to Ohio. That was the thanks I got. Maybe it's time to stop pulling rabbits out of hats every month, Sam. Maybe it's time for Will to give up that old museum."

"It's his life's work, Sheba."

"Then he'll find a way to save it, if it means that much to him."

Sam shook his head. "You're a real hard-hearted Hannah, Evie O'Neill."

Evie wished she could tell Sam that if that were true, hers wouldn't ache quite so much. She'd done the right thing by pushing Jericho away and toward Mabel. Hadn't she?

A gentleman in a dark suit sidled up to Evie. "Could you sign this for me, Miss O'Neill? I'm a big fan."

"Of course. To whom shall I make the inscription?" Evie said, taking her elocution-shaped vowels for a walk.

"Just an autograph is fine, if it's not too much trouble."

"No trouble at all," Evie said, pronouncing it "ah tall" and liking the sound of it. She put the last flourish on the inscription. "There you are."

"I can't tell you how much this means to me," the man said, taking it from her, but Evie didn't hear. *It's about time*, Evie thought as she saw T. S. Woodhouse strolling across the street.

"Well, if it isn't the Sweetheart Seer!" he said around a mouthful of chewing gum. He blew a bubble and it was all Evie could do not to pop it.

"How nice to see you *at long last*, Mr. Woodhouse," Evie said.

Woodhouse yawned. "I was rescuing a bunch of nuns from a burning church."

"You probably set the fire to get the story," Evie shot back.

T. S. Woodhouse nodded at the cluster of schoolgirls running toward them across the street, whispering excitedly to one another. "Gee, I wonder who let the cat out of the bag that you were here at the Bennington?" Woodhouse winked.

The bum had delivered after all.

"Miss O'Neill?" one of the girls said. "I adore your show!"

"That's awfully nice of you to say," Evie said in her radio-star voice, and the girls fell into excited squealing. Evie loved being recognized. Every time it happened, she wished she could snap a photograph and send it back to Harold Brodie, Norma Wallingford, and all those provincial Ohio Blue Noses who'd misjudged her. She'd write along the bottom of it, *Having a swell time. Glad you're not here.*

Sam put his arm around Evie as she signed an autograph. "Doesn't she have beautiful penmanship?"

T. S. Woodhouse smirked. "Say, you two look cozy there. Anything the *Daily News* readers should know about? There were those rumors a few months ago that the two of you were an item."

"No. We are not," Evie said firmly.

"Now, that's a fine way to talk to your fiancé, Lamb Chop!"

"Fiancé?" Woodhouse raised an eyebrow.

At this, the girls squealed anew. More people had shown up. A small crowd always drew a larger one. That was the math of fame.

"He's kidding on the square," Evie said.

Sam gave her his best lovelorn look. "Why, I've been crazy about this kid since the day I first saw her in Penn Station."

"Sam—" Evie warned through a tight smile.

"But who wouldn't be? Just look at that face!" He pinched Evie's cheek. She stepped down hard on his foot.

"Gee, that's awfully romantic," one of the girls said with a sigh. A few in the crowd applauded.

"The Sweetheart Seer's got a sweetheart?" a man joked.

"No, he's not—"

"Now, honey blossom. Let's not hide our love. Not anymore."

"I'd like to hide my fist inside your gut," Evie whispered low near his ear.

"You trying to keep the lid on this romance, Miss O'Neill? More important, you holding out on me?" Woodhouse pressed, trying to sniff out a scoop.

"Miss! Your taxi!" The doorman held the taxi door open for Evie.

The first thin, spitting drops of rain hit the sidewalk. Sam practically pushed Evie into the backseat of the waiting automobile. "You run along, sweetheart! Can't have my little radio star catching a cold."

Evie rolled down the back window a smidge. "They'll be dragging the river for your body tomorrow, Sam Lloyd," she hissed just before the taxi lurched down the street.

"Did she just say they'd drag the river for your body?" T. S. Woodhouse asked, his pencil poised above his open notebook.

Sam sighed like a man deeply in love. "She did, the little bearcat. It's the only defense that poor, helpless girl's got against the animal pull of our love. Uh, you can quote me on that."

"Animal…pull…of our…love…" Woodhouse was still scribbling as the skies opened suddenly, unleashing a gully washer.

☀

Down the street, the slim man in the dark suit kept his head down and slipped through the anonymous New York horde as if he had no shadow, angling himself at last into the passenger seat of the unremarkable sedan. He handed the autograph to the driver. "There you are. Don't say I never gave you anything."

The driver glanced at Evie's signature before tucking it into his breast pocket. "Fitzgerald's niece, huh? Interesting."

"The world is an interesting and dangerous place, Mr. Jefferson.

Ghosts and Diviners. People claiming to see a man in a tall hat. Threats from within and without. Security is the cornerstone of our freedom. And we're entrusted with ensuring that security."

"From sea to shining sea, Mr. Adams." The driver started the car. "Is she the real McCoy?"

"Difficult to say," the passenger said, opening a bag of pistachios. "I suppose we'll have to arrange a small test."

A STUPID MISTAKE

Henry sat in his chair waiting for the clock to strike three and thought about the first time he'd laid eyes on Louis Rene Bernard.

It was May 1924. Henry was fifteen and home from his boarding school in New Hampshire. He'd suffered a bout of measles that had frightened everyone, and so his parents had allowed him to spend the summer at home to regain his strength. Henry's father had business that kept him in Atlanta for weeks at a time. His fragile mother spent her days in the family cemetery, offering private prayers to stone saints with painted faces made porous by the relentless New Orleans humidity. For the first time in his life, Henry was free to do as he wished.

He decided to take a day trip on one of the excursion riverboats that churned up and down the muddy Mississippi from New Orleans to St. Paul. Most people came to dance. Henry came to listen. Some of the best bands in New Orleans honed their chops on board the boats; it was a floating master class in Dixieland jazz.

The band aboard the SS *Elysian* was terrific—nearly as good as Fate Marable's. The sweet swoop of a clarinet rose and fell against the suggestive allure of a trumpet while sparkly-eyed passengers bounced shoulder to shoulder on the boat's enormous dance floor under ceiling fans that did little to battle the Delta heat or the mosquitoes. But it was the fiddle player who captured Henry's attention. He'd never seen a boy so beautiful in his life: He had thick, nearly black hair swept back from a face marked by strong brows, dark brown eyes, and a square jaw.

When he smiled, his eyes crinkled into crescents; his eyeteeth were slightly longer than his front teeth, and crooked. And he had a name like a stride piano roll—Louis Rene Bernard. By the end of the third song, Henry was utterly smitten.

Louis had apparently noticed Henry, too. When the *Elysian* docked in New Orleans for the evening, Louis ran after Henry as he disembarked.

"'Scuse me. I believe you may've lost your hat?" Louis said, pointing to the straw boater perched atop his head.

"I'm afraid that isn't mine," Henry said.

"Well, it surely can't be mine. Looks terrible on me."

"Oh, no! I can't agree. It's very…" Too late, Henry realized that Louis was right; the hat was far too small on him. He searched for a word to save the moment. "Boaty."

Louis laughed, and Henry thought that laugh might be the best sound he'd ever heard, better even than the jazz.

"You like beignets?" Louis asked shyly.

"Who doesn't like beignets?"

They went to Cafe Du Monde, where they chased the sugared, fried dough of the beignets with cups of strong chicory coffee. Afterward, they strolled along the riverbank, listening to the gulls and the call-and-response of distant ships. They stood beside each other for some time, waiting until the others had drifted off and they were alone, and then, after several exchanges of sheepish glances, Louis leaned over and kissed Henry softly on the lips. It wasn't Henry's first kiss; that honor had gone to Sinclair Maddington, a school chum back at Phillips Exeter. Their kissing had been awkward and fumbling and a little desperate. It was followed by weeks of mutual avoidance forged by shared shame. There was no shame in Louis's kiss, though; just a sweetness that made Henry's stomach fluttery and his head as buzzy as champagne. He never wanted to stop.

Louis placed the boater on Henry's head. "Suits you better."

"You think so?"

"I know so. That, my friend, is gon' be your lucky hat."

After that, Henry was never without it.

"What is that thing on your head?" Flossie, the cook, asked as Henry swept through the kitchen on his way out, the boater cocked at a rakish angle.

"My lucky hat," Henry said.

She shook her head as she floured the chicken. "If you say so."

That summer was the summer of Henry-and-Louis. Henry learned that Louis was seventeen and as much a part of the river as the fish and the moss-slicked rocks. Before he'd died, too young, Louis's Cajun father had given him a love of music and the gift of a fiddle. His mother had given him an appreciation for self-reliance by leaving him first with distant relatives and then, finally, when he was barely seven, at a Catholic orphanage in New Orleans. Louis had run away when he was twelve, preferring life on the streets, the fishing camps, and the riverboats. A case of tonsillitis had given him a raspy voice that made everything he said, from "Fish are biting" to "Dit mon la verite," sound like a flirtation. He lost money at Bourré and played the sweetest fiddle in the French Quarter. He never stayed in any one place for long, but for now, he was bunking in a hideously hot attic garret above a grocery store on Dauphine. He was crazy about his hound dog, Gaspard, whom he had found abandoned by the river. "Just like me," Louis said, scratching the slobbery pup's fuzzy ears. They took Gaspard with them everywhere. No one in the Quarter seemed to mind, and often there was a bowl of scraps set out for him.

Henry confessed to Louis something he hadn't told anyone else: Ever since he'd been sick, he'd developed a curious habit of lucid dreaming. One night while sick with the measles, he woke gasping for air as if he'd nearly drowned, a terrifying sensation. When he settled, he realized that he hadn't woken. Instead, he was fully conscious inside the dream.

"Did it scare you?" Louis had asked.

"Yes," Henry said, enjoying the feel of his lover's arms around him.

"Could you do whatever you wanted?"

"No," Henry answered.

"If I could dream of any place, I'd dream of a cabin on the bayou," Louis had said at the time. "A little cabin. Fishing boat. A newspaper fulla crawfish ready to eat."

"Would I be there?" Henry asked quietly.

"Wouldn't be a good dream if you weren't."

And just like that, Henry knew what it was to be in love.

That night, he walked in Louis's dream. There was a rustic cabin on a sun-dappled river where ancient live oaks trailed braids of Spanish moss into the water. A hickory rocking chair sat on the front porch, and a fishing boat bobbed nearby. It was a brief walk—the dream shifted, and fight though he did, Henry was unable to stay in that beautiful spot. Still, it made Henry happy to have glimpsed it, even for a few minutes.

In June, they signed on for a stint aboard an excursion boat, playing for their supper. When they'd stop at various sleepy southern towns along the river for the night, Louis and Henry would buy food for the Negro musicians who weren't allowed into the white hotels and restaurants.

"Doesn't seem fair," Henry had said to Louis.

"That's because it ain't fair."

"There's a lot of that," Henry said. He wanted to hold Louis's hand, but he didn't dare out in public, where anybody could see them. Instead, they'd wait until the judging world fell asleep, then they'd sneak away and kiss till their lips, already weary from the southern sun, would make them quit.

July saw hot days of fishing and swimming. Most nights, they'd prowl the nightclubs and speakeasies of the French Quarter, from Joe Cascio's Grocery Store, where all the bohemians came to dance and drink, to Celeste's, where the proprietor, Alphonse, served them bootleg beer in teacups. Sometimes they'd buy a jug of homemade hooch, strongly scented with juniper berries, from an Italian widow who'd taken over the bootlegging business from her late husband. Then they'd take the Canal Street trolley out to the cemeteries to drink, talk, and dream. Surrounded by stone angels and appeals to God's mercy set in marble, a half-drunk Henry would spin out grand plans for them both: "We could go to St. Louis or Chicago, or even New York!"

"What'd we do there?"

"Play music!"

"Same thing we're doing here."

"But no one would know us there. We could be anybody. We could be free."

"You're as free as you decide to be," Louis said.

"Easy for you to say," Henry said, hurt. "You're not a DuBois."

Being a DuBois wasn't a legacy; it was a noose. They were one of the first families of New Orleans society, with a grand antebellum mansion, Bonne Chance, to show for it. White-columned and flanked by strict rows of stately oaks, Bonne Chance had been built by Henry's great-great-grandfather Mr. Xavier DuBois, who'd made a fortune in sugar off the backs of slaves. His heir, the first Henry DuBois, grabbed land from the Choctaw during the Indian Removal Act, and Henry's grandfather had accepted a commission as a colonel in the Confederate Army, marching with General Lee to protect all that stolen land and the stolen people who came with it. Henry often wondered if there had ever been a DuBois who'd done a single noble deed in his life.

The only war Henry's father seemed interested in fighting was the one with his son. It was a bloodless war; his father's infallibility bestowed a certain calm confidence. He never questioned that his edicts would be followed, so there was never any need for him to raise his voice. That was for lesser men.

"Hal, you will not upset your mother."

"Naturally, Hal will matriculate from Ole Miss."

"Law is what you should pursue, Hal. Perhaps a judgeship from there. Music is not a noble profession."

"These jazz and riverboat riffraff are not suitable companions for a young man of your breeding and position, Hal. Remember that you are a DuBois, a reflection on this family's sterling reputation. Comport yourself accordingly."

Henry's delicate, unbalanced mother had long since been worn down by his father's domineering manner. When she'd had her first breakdown, Henry's father refused to send her to the sanitarium for fear of gossip. Instead, the family doctor had prescribed pills, and now his mother wandered the endless halls and rooms of Bonne Chance, a lost bird unable to alight in any one spot for long, until, finally, she'd take refuge in the family cemetery. She'd sit on the weathered bench, staring into the garden, thumbs working the beads of a rosary.

"It was the vitamins. I never should've taken them," she'd say to Henry in a nervous voice. "I was afraid I'd lose another baby. So many lost babies. The doctor said the vitamins would help."

"And they did. Because here I am, Maman," Henry would say.

"She sent me a letter and told me I have to hide the bird," she'd say, worrying the black beads between her frantic fingers.

Flossie would come out and lead Henry's mother back to the big white house. "Come on, now, Miss Catherine. The saints won't mind if you have your lunch."

Henry would sneak away to Louis once more, and the two of them would hop the Smoky Mary out to the West End of Lake Pontchartrain, where they could fish from a pier in Bucktown, take a picnic near Old Spanish Fort, or play music in the Milneburg resorts and camps.

Louis never called him Hal. It was always Henri, said in a drawl as sultry as the air over the Quarter: "Let's get us a mess of crawfish, Henri." "You hear the way he laid out that line, Henri?" "Henri, don't be a slowpoke. Ever'body's waitin' on us down at Celeste's."

And Henry's favorite: *"Moi, je t'aime, Henri."* Henry never wanted the summer to end.

Then, on a terrible, still day in August, Gaspard died. Before Louis could stop him, the sweet hound tore after an alley cat and was struck by the ice man's truck as it rounded the corner of Rampart. There was a screech of wheels and one awful yelp. Louis and Henry pushed their way through the crowd. With a howl of his own, Louis sank to his knees and cradled his dead dog. The driver, a kindly man with a jowly face, removed his hat and patted Louis's shoulder like a father, sorry as could be. "He just come outta nowhere, son. Wadn't time to stop. I'm real sorry. Got three dogs, myself."

Louis was inconsolable. Henry bought a bottle from the Italian widow and they took refuge in the attic garret, Gaspard's body wrapped in a blanket on the bed. Henry held Louis while he cried, feeding him sips of strong drink till Louis was glassy-eyed. Later, Henry borrowed a car from one of the patrons at Celeste's, and they buried Gaspard out in bayou country under a lacy willow tree and marked the grave with a roast bone stolen from Flossie's kitchen.

"She'd kill me if she knew I took her best soup bone," Henry said, taking off his sweat-drenched shirt.

"He was a good dog," Louis said. His eyes were red and puffy.

"The best."

"Why do all the things I love gotta leave me?" Louis whispered.

"I'm not gonna leave you," Henry said.

"How you gonna get your father to let you stay?"

Henry chewed his lip and stared at the freshly tilled earth. "I'll think of something."

"Promise?"

"Promise," Henry said, but he had no idea how.

Late August settled in, bringing a bank of hazy clouds that promised but did not deliver rain. After a day of stifling heat, Henry and Louis sat on a blanket beside a cascading vine of morning glories, their mood tense. There'd been a cable: Henry's father was returning from Atlanta the next day. School would start the week after Labor Day. Henry would be miles away from Louis.

"Why don't you just tell your father you don't want to go?"

Henry laughed bitterly. "No one says no to my father." He yanked a morning glory from the vine and crushed it between his fingers.

"What that plant ever do to you?"

But Henry wouldn't be joked out of his misery. At boarding school, Henry would be stuck in a regimented, colorless life of morning chapel, Latin, bullying upperclassmen, and innuendo about the way Henry walked and talked. There'd be no jazz or crawfish boils or fishing from the pier. There'd be none of the eccentric characters they knew from their haunts in the Quarter, men and women who looked after the two boys as if they were delightful nephews. There would be no Louis. Henry felt it as a physical ache.

In the dirt, Louis scratched a heart. Inside, he wrote L + H. Henry went to erase it before someone saw. Louis stayed his hand. "Don't."

"But—"

"Don't," he said again.

That night, they'd lain together in the narrow bed, listening to the swooshing tide of Lake Pontchartrain eddying about the pilings beneath the cabin. Louis's stubble rubbed Henry's cheeks raw, but he wouldn't have stopped kissing him for anything. There were hands and mouths and tongues. They were sweaty with exploration and pleasure. Afterward, they lay entwined, Henry falling asleep to the soft warmth of Louis's breath on his shoulder, while out on the streets of the West End, the party raged on.

Henry's father returned on a Friday in August as the summer was dwindling to a close. From his chair in the library, he appraised his bronzed and freckled son. "You seem to have recovered your health, Hal."

"Yes, Father," Henry said.

"The school will be pleased to hear it."

Henry's heart beat so quickly he wondered if his father could hear it from across the broad expanse of Persian carpet. "I was thinking that perhaps I could finish school here. In New Orleans."

His father peered around the edge of his open newspaper. "Why?"

"I could help with Mother," he lied.

"We have servants and a doctor for that." The newspaper barrier went back up.

"I'd like to stay," Henry tried. He willed himself not to cry. "Please."

"I've posted the check for your tuition already."

"I'll pay you back."

"Don't be ridiculous."

"I will! I'll take on whatever work I can. I'll—"

"The subject is closed, the matter settled." His father gave him one last, curious look. "Where do you go evenings?"

"I go for a long walk. Dr. Blake advised it. For my health," Henry lied, feeling, for once, power in the secrecy of his other life.

His father had continued squinting at him for only a moment more. "Well," he said, returning to his paper, "I suppose Dr. Blake knows best."

It had been a stupid mistake that trapped them.

Louis had written Henry a letter. A beautiful letter. Henry could almost recite it; he'd read it that many times. He could barely stand to be parted from it, and so he transferred it from pocket to pocket, always keeping it on his person so that he could read it whenever he wanted. But one night, he'd been too tired and had forgotten it in a jacket pocket. The laundress found the note and took it to Henry's father.

Henry got a sick feeling in his stomach as he remembered being summoned to the parlor, their butler, Joseph, closing the doors behind Henry. It was the only time his father's calm had ever threatened to become something else, something violent.

"Do you recognize this?" his father asked, holding up the offending love letter. "What is this filth?"

Henry's fear robbed him of any answer.

"Has this"—his father's mouth struggled to form the word—"boy...compromised you in some way?"

Louis had made him laugh. Louis had kissed him. Loved him. There had been no compromise in any of that.

"Have you thought that he might blackmail our family, tarnish our good name, in pursuit of money?" his father continued. "Do you assume it is only homely heiresses who may fall prey to fortune hunters?"

Henry wanted to tell his father that Louis was kind and good, romantic and gentle. What they shared was real. But telling his father such a thing was impossible. His disapproval was so powerful it para-lyzed Henry, strangled him in shame.

He'd never felt like more of a coward.

"You will not be returning to Exeter," his father announced.

"I won't?" Even in his fear, new hope surged in Henry. He could stay here. With Louis.

"If you are unconcerned with protecting your family's reputation, I shall be forced to do it for you. I've made some calls. At nine o'clock tomorrow morning, there is a train bound for Charleston and the Cit-adel. You will be on that train. Perhaps they can make a man of you where I have failed. You will never speak to this boy again."

As Henry watched, his father tore up the beautiful letter and set the pieces ablaze with a match, tossing them into the fireplace, where they flared and curled into ash.

Henry had been banished to his room, where he found that his suitcase was already packed for him. Military school. If things had been bad at Exeter, the Citadel would be worse. Henry would never survive that. He could save himself, make up a lie: "I had nothing to do with that boy! It's all a misunderstanding!" Then he could do as his father commanded, give up everything he loved, Louis and music, and go back to Exeter, become a lawyer, then a judge. He could marry the right girl and have a Henry Bartholomew DuBois V and see the same people at the same society balls and dinners, all the while knowing that he was still a disappointment to his father, that this would never be forgotten, only denied. Or he could strike out on his own, be his own man. Wasn't that what his father was always telling him to be?

There was a gathering that night of his father's business associ-ates. Henry listened to them downstairs, chuckling with their port and cigars. If that was what "being a man" was, he wanted no part of it. With his father and the servants occupied, Henry knew it was time. He stuffed what he could into a knapsack, climbed out his bed-room window, and shimmied down the tree, sneaking through the cemetery. Henry froze when he came upon his mother sitting with her rosary before a statue of Saint Michael. For a long moment, his mother regarded him, her eyes moving from Henry to his knapsack, then back to his face as if she were trying to memorize it.

"Fly, fly, sweet bird," she whispered and turned back to her saints, letting her son slip away from the prison of Bonne Chance.

Henry had sneaked down to the Quarter, to Louis's attic garret, but he wasn't there. He tried Celeste's next. Louis wasn't there, either.

"I heard him say he might play on the *Elysian*," Alphonse said.

But by the time Henry made it to the docks, the *Elysian* was well upriver. Henry was near tears. He thought about waiting for Louis to get back, but he had no idea how long that would be, and Henry couldn't afford to wait. His father would be out looking for him. Once he got safely settled in his new life, he'd get word to Louis somehow.

Luck had been on Henry's side. A steamer was just about to head up the Mississippi, so Henry talked himself on board, promising to play piano in exchange for a ride to St. Louis. In St. Louis, he posted a letter to Louis care of Celeste's, along with the address for the Western Union office there. No telegram came. None came in Memphis, Richmond, or New York, either. Henry thought about the day they'd buried Gaspard. Louis had extracted a promise from Henry that he wouldn't leave. And what had Henry done but run away? Did Louis hate him for leaving like that, without saying good-bye? Did he think Henry a coward? If only he could find Louis, he could explain what had happened.

Henry didn't give up. He wrote to a few journeymen musicians from the *Elysian*. Only one answered, a cornet player named Jimmy. He said he'd heard from the cousin of a friend that Louis might've left New Orleans and found work with a territory band, but he couldn't remember the name of the outfit. Henry groaned when he heard that—territory bands traveled all over the country. Louis could be anywhere.

That was when he remembered walking in Louis's dream. If this was the only way to make some sort of contact, then so be it. All he had to do was give one suggestion: "Why don't you speak with Henry?

He's waiting for you at the Bennington Apartments in New York City. The Bennington Apartments. Don't forget, now."

But first he had to find him.

Every week for the past year, Henry had tried to do just that. He'd walked through landscapes familiar and odd and sometimes downright frightening, chasing after any clue that would lead him back to the boy he couldn't forget, the boy he'd loved and left. The boy he hoped would forgive him.

Henry checked his wristwatch.

Five minutes until three.

He wound the alarm clock and set the metronome to ticking.

"Please," he said and closed his eyes.

THE LAIR OF DREAMS

Ling's eyes had barely fluttered open inside the dream world when someone tapped her shoulder, and she yelped. She turned to see a startled Henry beside her, his hands up in a gesture of apology.

"Don't ever"—Ling let out a shaking breath—"do that again."

"I'm sorry," Henry said, but he couldn't hold back his grin. "The hat worked! You found me."

"Yes. I did," Ling said in wonder, her mind already at work trying to understand how it had happened. She'd located the living inside a dream. This was a first. "Where are we? Whose dream is this?"

Like magic, the noises began: the *clop-clop* of horses, the distant rattle of an elevated train, the shouts of people hawking wares, and the thin, high squeal of a factory whistle. The bank of fog thinned, revealing the same jumble of worn city streets as in the previous night's dream walk, but now there was action: Two men fell out of a pair of saloon doors, fighting while a crowd egged them on. Half a dozen street urchins pushed after a hoop with a stick. "Anthony Orange Cross..." Their excited shouts lingered after they'd disappeared like wisps of smoke. A ghostly horse-drawn wagon trotted past. "Beware, beware, Paradise Square! The Crying Woman comes!" the driver called just before he was swallowed by the mist.

Pop-pop-pop! Fireworks exploded over the sketchlike rooftops, and a phantasmic man in an old-fashioned vest and coat flickered against the haze as if he were a motion-picture projection.

"Ladies and gentlemen!" the apparition called. "Come one! Come all for a ride on Alfred Beach's pneumatic train. See this marvel for yourselves and be amazed—the future of travel, beneath these very streets!" The apparition gestured to his right, and the limestone building appeared.

"Devlin's! That's the spot where I heard Louis's fiddle last night!" Henry ran toward it, listening, but no music drifted out from inside its old brick walls tonight. "But I heard it so clearly last night."

"I told you there was no guarantee," Ling said. "This is still a dream, remember?"

"But I know the sound of his playing like my own. It was him. Louis! Louis!" Henry felt like he might cry. Having come so close, he couldn't bear this new disappointment. With a grunt, he swung at the building, hitting it with a hard *thwack*.

"Ow!" he cried, shaking out his hand.

Ling's mouth opened in shock. "You... you just touched that. That's impossible." Cautiously, Ling reached out and trailed her fingers across the bumps and grooves in the brick. "Impossible," she said again. "Have you ever been able to touch something while dream walking before?"

"Until yesterday when I grabbed your hand? No. Never."

"Me, either," Ling said.

A piercing scream rang out, sending shivers up Henry's and Ling's spines: *"Murder! Murder! Oh, murder!"*

A ghostly figure broke through the haze, heading straight for Henry and Ling: a veiled woman in an old-fashioned, high-necked gown. She ran as if frightened, as if being chased. As she drew closer, Henry and Ling could see that the front of her dress was red with blood. The woman whooshed past in the space between them, trailing cold in her wake. Then she moved through the facade of the limestone building as if she were made of smoke.

A shimmering hole opened in the wall.

"What was that?" Ling asked, but Henry didn't answer. He stood at the edge of the hole, which was glowing with whatever energy lay inside. The opening wavered uncertainly, as if it might snap shut at any second.

"There are steps leading down. Come on! We have to hurry!" Henry said, nodding toward it.

"Are you a lunatic?"

"Please. I don't think I can find him without you, Ling," Henry pleaded. "It's just a dream, darlin'. If something bad happens, all we have to do is wake up."

"I should've doubled my fee," Ling groused.

And with that, they raced inside and down the steps just as the portal closed behind them.

"Ling?" Henry called in the darkness.

"Here," Ling answered. "Wherever here is."

Dim yellow lights sputtered on and rippled through the black as if someone had flipped a switch, illuminating a long brick corridor that narrowed into darkness farther on. Pipes ran above their heads. There were no other helpful distinguishing features.

A thread of cool wind drifted toward them.

"It's coming from up ahead. So I guess that's the way we go."

They walked quietly for a while, the silence proving every bit as uncomfortable as the dream walk's unnerving strangeness.

"What's it like to speak to the dead?" Henry asked at last, a stab at conversation. "Is it frightening?"

"They don't scare me. They only want to be heard. Sometimes they have messages for the living."

"Like what?"

"'Marry on the eighth day of the eighth month of next year.' 'This is not the time to test your luck—you must wait one month.' 'Tell him I know—I know what you did,'" Ling said, recalling some of the information she'd carried back from the dead.

"You're like the Western Union of ghosts," Henry joked.

Ling shrugged, annoyed. She wasn't in a mood to explain herself to Henry. All day long, she'd been able to think of little other than

George. "Don't you ever worry about this sleeping sickness when you walk?"

Henry raised an eyebrow. "Do you? That is, would it stop you?"

Ling shook her head. "Still, do you think we'd know if we were walking in a sick person's dream?"

Henry had been in all sorts of dreams before. When people were drunk, their dreams were a bit bleary and slow. When people had a fever, their dreams were particularly strange and vivid, and there was always one person in the dream complaining about the heat. Henry had even walked in the dream of a man on his deathbed once. They had been passengers on a ship. The man had been at peace as he looked out at the calm sea and the far horizon. He'd smiled at Henry, saying, *I'm headed over there. But I'm afraid you can't come along.*

"I think we'd know," he said at last.

"So, how did you lose this friend of yours, Louis?"

Henry sobered. "My father didn't approve of our...friendship. He thought Louis was a bad influence."

"Was he?" Ling asked.

"No. Never," Henry said firmly. He wondered just how honest he could be with her. "What would you do if your parents forbade you from seeing your dearest friend?"

"What choice would I have?" Ling said. "They're my parents. I owe them everything."

"You don't owe them everything," Henry said a little defensively.

"Yes, I do. They're my parents," Ling said again, as if that settled the matter. "Besides, the question is academic. I don't have a dearest friend."

"No one?"

The closest Ling had come was George, and they hadn't been close for some time. "Some of us don't need friends."

"Everyone needs friends."

"I don't," Ling said.

"Well, now, that is pos-i-tute-ly the saddest thing I've ever heard. I am compelled as a gentleman to insist that you come to lunch with my friends and me this week. We'll make it a party."

Ling imagined the faces of Henry and his fashionable set as she hobbled toward them in her cumbersome braces. The way their mouths would open in surprise, their discomfort peeking out beneath the sympathetic smiles they'd paste on too quickly. That was never going to happen.

"*Pos-i-tute-ly* isn't a real word," she said.

"Why, it pos-i-tute-ly is! It's in the dictionary, just before *prob-a-lute-ly.*"

"You're doing that simply to annoy me."

"Abso-tive-ly not." Henry's smile was pure innocence.

"Keep listening for your friend's fiddle," Ling said and marched on.

The first time Ling had been visited by the dead, she'd been dream walking down a rainy street among people who were no more than dull splotches against the gray day. Ling was drawn to a pair of beautiful doors painted with the fearsome faces of evil spirit–banishing gods. The doors opened rather suddenly, and standing there beneath a paper parasol was her great-aunt Hui-ying, whom Ling had only known through photographs sent from China. The rain flew upward around her aunt, leaving her untouched. The outlines of her soft body carried a faint shimmer, which Ling would come to know marked the dead from the living. "Daughter: Tell them to break my favorite comb, the ivory one, and bury me with half," her aunt said. "It's in the painted chest, the second drawer down, in a hiding spot at the back behind a false partition."

A day later, her parents received the telegram informing them that Auntie Hui-ying had died on the very night Ling had seen her. The family was frantically searching for Auntie Hui-ying's comb, which they knew was her favorite, but they'd been unable to find it. "It's in the painted chest, the second drawer, behind a false back," Ling had said, parroting her aunt's words.

Later, Ling's father had taken her with him to the farm on Long Island. Under the warm sun, they worked side by side, gathering long beans. Ling's father was a quiet man who tended to keep his thoughts to himself. They were alike in that way. "Ling," he'd said, stopping to smoke a cigarette while Ling ate a peach, savoring the sweetness on her tongue. "How did you know about Auntie's comb?"

Ling had been afraid at first to tell him the truth, in case it was some sort of bad luck she'd brought to their house. There'd been a baby before Ling, a precious son dead at birth, the cord wrapped around his neck. Two years later, Ling had come along. There'd been no other children after her, and both parents doted on Ling. She was their everything, and Ling often felt the burden of carrying her parents' hopes and dreams, of being enough for all that love, of shouldering the obligation alone.

"Whatever it is, you can tell me," her father had promised.

Ling had told him everything. He had listened, smoking his cigarette down to nothing. "Do you think I'm cursed, Baba?" Ling had asked. "Have I done something wrong?"

There had been tenderness in her father's smile. "You've been given a gift. A link between old and new, between the living and the dead. But like all gifts, you must accept this with humility, Ling."

Ling understood what he meant: Don't draw bad luck to you with pride. Outwardly, Ling remained humble, but secretly, she loved walking in dreams and talking to the dead. It made her feel special and powerful. Nearly invincible.

The week before Ling took ill, she'd gone on a picnic outing to Long Island organized by the Chinese Benevolent Association for the students of the Chinese school. It was one of those warm October days that are a parting kiss of summer. Ling and her friends had gone to the water's edge, taken off their stockings, and waded into the chilly Atlantic, reveling in the soft coolness of mud squished between toes that wouldn't see the sun again until June. It had been a perfect day.

That night, her elderly neighbor, Mr. Hsu, died, and Ling saw the old man in a dream, faint and golden, sitting at his favorite table in her family's restaurant. "One last cup of tea before I go," he'd said. At the door, which opened onto a vast canvas of stars, he'd looked back at her with an unreadable expression. "We are made by what we are asked to bear, Ling Chan," he'd said.

Days later, Ling woke tired, with a fever and a terrible headache. Her mother sent her to bed, but the aching and fever got worse. The muscles in her calves stiffened until she couldn't move them without pain. And then she couldn't move them at all. *Infantile paralysis*, the doctors said. *Too much pride*, Ling heard.

In the hospital, nurses held Ling down as the doctor immobilized her legs in heavy plaster casts. "You have to be brave and keep very still, Ling," the doctor scolded as she cried out against the fire of the infection racing along her nerve endings. Holding still was worse than anything.

"She has to learn to be strong," the doctor said.

"She doesn't have to learn to suffer," her mother shot back, shutting him up.

For a month, Ling had endured the agony of the plaster, unable to touch her skin when it burned and itched or massage the brutal spasms of her dying muscles. And when the casts finally came off, she was no better than before.

"You'll need to wear these now," the nurse said, buckling on the ugly metal braces that caged her shriveled legs and bit into the tender skin above and below her knees till there were permanent scars there.

But the worst part was the pain it brought to her parents. Ling could hear them just outside the door, asking the doctors and nurses again and again if there was any new hope of a cure, or at least an improvement.

Stop hoping, she wanted to tell them. *It's easier that way.*

Secretly, she thought: *I deserve this. I brought it on myself*. No matter how much Ling believed in science, in the rational, she couldn't escape the clutches of superstition, of luck—both good and bad—shaping her life. After all, she spoke to ghosts. Deep down, she couldn't help thinking that it was her pride that had brought on her illness. And so, just before Christmas, she'd insisted on working in the restaurant again to help her parents. When the spasms gripped her, she did her best to hide it; she was tired of pity. Every night, she escaped into the dream world, where, for one blessed hour, she could run free. Every morning, she dreaded waking up.

Far above them, Ling and Henry could hear muted hoofbeats and the clatter of omnibuses rumbling down unseen streets. But these sounds came and went, like postcards of sound sent long ago and only now arriving at their destination.

"Well, this is certainly interesting," Henry said.

They'd come to an iron gate, the bars of which had been fashioned with steel roses. The faintest glow seeped through them, warm and golden.

"Do you see that?" Henry whispered. "I've never seen light like that in a dream walk before. It's always . . ."

"Gray," Ling finished.

"Yes," Henry said and smiled. Being with Ling was like traveling in a foreign country and finding the one person who speaks your native language.

Ling tested the bars with her fingertips. "The gate. It's . . . cold," she said, more in astonishment than fear.

"Shall we go inside?" Henry asked.

At Ling's nod, he lifted the latch and pushed open the gate.

Henry had seen many odd things in dreams before—noblemen with owl faces peeking above their ruffled shirts. Trees made entirely of fireflies. Steamer ships resting on mountaintops. But he'd never seen anything quite so realistic or beautiful as the lovely old train station where he and Ling found themselves now. This was nothing like the mundane subway, with its creaking wooden turnstiles and harried New Yorkers rushing and pushing. It was as if they were trespassing in some wealthy, eccentric aristocrat's private underground lair. High above their heads, a herringbone pattern of cream-colored brick fanned out in an undulating plain of cathedral-worthy arches. White-hot gas flickered behind the frosted-glass globes of four brass chandeliers. The light spilled across the smooth surface of a fountain whose water seemed frozen in time. The waiting area boasted a velvet settee, three gooseneck lamps, a colorful Persian rug, and an assortment of fine leather chairs more suited to a library than a train platform. There was even a grand piano with a goldfish bowl resting on its broad back. The entire room had a warm amber glow to it—except for the subway tunnel, which was as dark as funeral bunting.

"Where are we?" Ling asked. She tapped the goldfish bowl and was rewarded with the tiniest quiver of orange.

"I don't know. But it's glorious!" Henry said, grinning. He sat at the piano. "Any requests?"

Ling scoffed. "You must be joking."

"I don't know that one, but if you hum a few bars…" Henry said, noodling around on the keys. "Now this is the elephant's eyebrows. *Elephant's eyebrows* is in the same dictionary as *pos-i-tute-ly*, by the way."

Ling took the gleaming wooden stairs down to the passenger-loading platform and walked to the tunnel's entrance. An arc of gas-jet bulbs, long dead, ringed the brick opening.

"Beach Pneumatic Transit Company," Ling whispered, reading the plaque on the wall.

"I don't suppose the dead are here to tell you which way I should go to find Louis," Henry called from the piano.

"No," Ling said. Her voice carried faintly. "Hello," she said, more forcefully, and it echoed: *Hello, lo, lo.* A thread of wind caressed Ling's face. There was a faint hiss and a pop of blue flame as, all at once, the gaslight bulbs blazed white-hot. A ghost of sound came from inside the tunnel—the whine of metal against metal.

"What's that?" Henry leaped up from the piano and bounded down the stairs to Ling's side.

A bright light pierced the tunnel's darkness. The whine grew louder. A small wooden train car rattled down the dusty tracks, its oracular headlamp bright as noonday sun as it whooshed into the station and squeaked to a stop. The doors sighed open. Henry poked his head in, then turned back to Ling with a grin. "Ling, you've got to see this."

They peered in, gawking at the mahogany paneling and two plush seats, the delicate kerosene lamps resting on end tables.

"Come on," Henry said, climbing inside.

"What are you doing?" Ling cautioned.

"What if this takes us to our mysterious dreamer? What if this is somehow Louis's crazy dream?" Henry's pale, freckled face was so serious. "I've tried everything else. I have to know. Please. We can always wake up, Ling."

"All right," Ling agreed after a pause. "We can always wake up."

The moment they were aboard, the doors slid shut and the train moved backward with a lurch, throwing Henry and Ling onto the seats. Ling closed her eyes and silently reminded herself: *It's only a dream. It's only a dream.* Soon enough, the train came to a gentle stop. The doors opened onto a misty wood marked by skeletal trees. It lacked the detail of the old New York streets and the pretty train station.

Henry gave the air a good sniff. "Smell that? It's gardenia. Makes me think of New Orleans."

"I don't smell anything," Ling said.

Henry's expression had changed from curiosity to something bordering on longing. "There! I hear it. That's Louis's playing. He's here! We found him!" Henry leaped from the train and bolted into the murky expanse of half-formed trees as they bent and folded around him, taking him in.

"Wait!" Ling stumbled after him. "Henry? Henry!" she shouted, her panic rising. She called again and again, but he was nowhere.

It was as if the dream had opened its maw and swallowed him whole.

THE RED RIVER

"Ling? Where are you? Ling!" Henry called, his voice echoing in the fog. He'd thought she was right behind him. But when he turned back, the featureless trees all looked the same to him, and he couldn't tell which way he'd come.

A soft, warm breeze brought the heady perfume of gardenia, along with other notes—moss and river water, the smells of home. Very faintly, he heard the strains of a fiddle sawing away at "Rivière Rouge."

"Louis?" Henry called, the lump in his throat swelling.

Up ahead, the vague trees shifted slightly, revealing a dimly lit path through the middle. The fiddle was stronger now.

"Ling!" Henry tried one last time. He didn't want to abandon her, but he was afraid of losing this vital link to Louis. Perhaps wherever she was, Ling heard the music, too, and would know to come this way. Hoping that was the case, Henry followed the music deeper into the wood.

The sun grew brighter. The fog thinned. The flat trees rounded and grew bark, becoming immense live oaks trailing wispy beards of Spanish moss. Dragonflies pirouetted past Henry's face and darted toward the surface of a sun-brushed river where a blue rowboat, just like the one Henry and Louis had used for their fishing trips, swayed against the bank. Propped up by wooden stilts at the river's edge was a rustic cabin. Smoke curled up from its crooked chimney. The music came from inside. Henry's legs jellied as he approached. What if this was just another cruel trick played on him in a dream? His fist was a weight at his side. He took a deep breath and knocked. The music stopped. Henry put a hand on his stomach to steady himself as the door creaked open.

Louis appeared, as handsome as ever. He blinked—first at the hazy sunlight, then at Henry. "Henri?"

Henry could only nod. He didn't know if it was possible to faint inside a dream, but he thought he was perilously close to finding out. The moment seemed to stretch forever. And then suddenly Louis was smiling wide. "*Mon cher!* Where you been?"

※

As Ling moved through the gray wood calling Henry's name and getting no response, her panic turned to anger. Their agreement had been clear: Ling was to help Henry try to find Louis in the dream world. That agreement did not include entering strange buildings, wandering through an old train station, and getting lost in a creepy, half-finished forest. She should never have consented to help someone from outside Chinatown—ten dollars or not.

"Henry!" Ling called sharply.

"Are you lost?" a sweet, girlish voice answered.

Ling whirled around. "Wh-who's there?"

"You walk in dreams but you're not asleep."

Ling turned in the other direction, looking for the source of the voice.

"You'll make yourself dizzy if you keep turning like that," the voice said, giggling.

"Show yourself!" Ling commanded.

A girl in a wide-sleeved tunic and a long skirt stepped out from behind a tree. She was about Ling's age, small but sturdy with a wide, open face and very straight brows. Her plaited hair was coiled at her neck, secured with two crisscrossed hairpins. "I can walk in dreams, too. Just like you."

135

First Henry, now this girl, too? Soon they'd need to put up traffic signals in the dream world for all the comings and goings. It annoyed Ling. Annoyance was good. Ling preferred it to fear.

"Who are you?" Ling demanded.

"I am Wai-Mae," the girl said, bowing a little. "What is your name?"

"Ling," Ling answered. It always fascinated her that inside a dream walk, there was no language or dialect barrier at all, as if in dreams, they all spoke the same language.

Wai-Mae's brow furrowed. "Just Ling? That's a funny name."

"Where are we? What is this place?" Ling demanded.

"Isn't it beautiful? It's nothing like ordinary dreams!"

"But what is it?" Ling said, more to herself than to Wai-Mae. "How did you get here? Did you come here on the train?"

"The train?" Wai-Mae's eyes crinkled as she smiled. "Oh, yes! The train! Did it also bring you?"

"Yes. But I came with a boy, another dream walker, Henry—"

"There's *another*?" Wai-Mae gasped, delighted. "But where is he?"

"I don't know. That's the trouble," Ling said evenly. She was beginning to think that Wai-Mae wasn't terribly bright. "When we stepped off the train, he ran, and I lost him."

"You lost the dream walker?" Wai-Mae shook her head. "That's very careless, Ling."

Ling glared, but Wai-Mae didn't seem to feel her silent scold. "Can you at least help me look for him?"

Wai-Mae's eyes widened. "Is this other dream walker your *husband*?"

"My...? No! No. He is not my husband," Ling sputtered. "He's... never mind."

"I don't know if it's proper for you to be walking in dreams with a boy who is not your husband, Ling," Wai-Mae tutted. "Very well. I will help you. But you really should be more careful with your friends in the future, Little Warrior. Come. This way."

Ling wasn't sure whom she wanted to kill more for ruining her night's dream walk: Henry or this thoroughly irritating girl. She opened her mouth to say something, then thought better of it, and with a heavy sigh resigned herself to following Wai-Mae through the wood.

But once she found Henry again, she'd have plenty to say to him.

Louis's voice, no longer a memory, unlatched Henry's emotions. He wanted to throw his arms around Louis but was afraid that if he did, Louis would disappear, leaving him in an embrace of smoke.

"Louis, is that really you?"

"You know another Louis looks like me?" Louis said, just as if they were on the *Elysian*, headed up the river on a hot day, as if no time had passed at all. "Where are we? What is this place? Looks like the bayou but it isn't. Not quite."

"It's a dream. We're inside a dream," Henry explained, wiping his eyes with the back of his hand. He was laughing and crying all at once.

Louis let out a long whistle. "Well, then. Got to be the nicest dream I ever had."

Henry couldn't take it another second. He wanted to kiss Louis, to hold him in his arms. He'd never been able to do that in a dream before, but he'd never been in a dream like this one, either. Carefully, he reached out to touch Louis's sleeve, and his heart sank when he couldn't quite make contact. It was as if the thinnest pane of glass separated them. How could it be that he could smell gardenia and feel the grain of the wood but not touch his lover? The logic of dreams was unknowable and cruel.

Sharp barking sounded from the river, and a moment later, a freckled hound came sniffing up to Henry through the grass, its tail wagging.

"Gaspard?" Henry said, amazed. The dog circled him twice before tearing after a mourning dove.

"It's all so real," Henry said, but his wonder soon gave way to anxiety. "Louis, where have you been?"

"What d'you mean, where I been? 'Cept for some trips up the river, I been where I've always been. You're the one who left, not me," he said, and Henry heard the note of recrimination in it.

"Only because I had to. Because of my father," Henry said. He told Louis what had happened the day his father found the letter. "I tried to get word to you, believe me. I've been looking everywhere for you—even in dreams."

"And here I thought you'd gone and forgotten me." Louis played it light, but Henry knew him too well. He was hurt. Maybe even angry.

"Never. I could never forget you, Louis," Henry said, and he wished once more that this weren't a dream and that he could hold Louis.

"I went on over to your house lookin' for you. Thought Flossie might know somethin'."

Henry's heartbeat quickened. "What happened?"

"Found your *maman* sitting in the cemetery talking to the angels. She didn't know nothin'. About 'at time, your daddy come out and found me talkin' to her. He knew who I was, all right. Told me I'd better never come 'round there again or he'd shoot me as a trespasser. Not that that woulda kept me away." Louis's smile was short-lived. "He told me you'd left town and that you didn't want nothin' to do with me no more—you didn't even want to say good-bye." Louis's voice went feathery. "He told me you hated me."

"That bastard," Henry spat. "But what about all those letters I sent you? And two telegrams—one when I reached St. Louis, one from New York. When you didn't write me back, I thought..."

Louis shook his head. "Didn't get no letters. No telegrams, either."

"My father," Henry said. He didn't like to think that anybody at Celeste's would sell them out, but money was money, and his father had a lot of it. It would be just like him to pay someone to intercept Henry's letters and make sure they were thrown out before they could even be delivered. If so, that meant his father had Henry's return address in New York and had done nothing to try to find him. It was a relief to know that his father wouldn't drag him off to military school, but it stung, too, knowing that it was easier for his father to erase his

138

only son's existence than it was for him to tolerate the disappointment of who his son really was.

"But you're here now, *cher*," Louis said. "We're here now."

Louis raised his palm toward Henry's and Henry followed suit, their fingers nearly touching.

※

Wai-Mae's mouth hadn't stopped moving the entire walk through the wood. "Do you know the story of Mu Guiying? She is my favorite of the Dao Ma Dan. When she battles with Yang Zongbao and falls in love with him, saving his life? It's the most beautiful love story," she said, huffing alongside Ling like an excited puppy. There'd still been no sign of Henry. "I think it's my favorite. Except for the Courtesan Yu Tang Chun. Or the Drunken Beauty. Or possibly the Romance of the Three Kingdoms."

"Henry!" Ling called again, more desperately. "Henryyyy!"

"I'm sorry, Ling. Uncle says that I talk too much, and I'm a silly girl and my head is too full of romantic stories to be much good," Wai-Mae said in cheerful apology. "Would you like to know a secret?"

"Not particularl—"

"I am to be married soon!" Wai-Mae exclaimed. "We've never met, but I have heard my husband-to-be is very handsome, with kind eyes and a high forehead. He is a wealthy merchant in America, in New York City, and once I'm there, I'll live very well with servants to wait on me and plenty of money to send back to my family. I'm traveling to San Francisco now on the *Lady Liberty*. I hate the ship. It makes me so sick," Wai-Mae said, putting a hand on her stomach.

"It's very difficult for Chinese women to immigrate to America. How did you manage it?" Ling asked.

"Uncle arranged everything through matchmakers, O'Bannion and Lee. Mr. O'Bannion will greet me in immigration in San Francisco. Then he will take me to my husband in New York City. My future husband is very respected and successful there. I hear you must be careful on the streets, though," Wai-Mae continued, barely stopping to take a breath. "There is all manner of vice and corruption and murder—opium dens and houses of ill repute!—and a lady has to keep her wits sharp, or terrible misfortune could befall her in the Den of Thieves or Murderer's Alley and along Bandit's Roost on Mulberry Bend and—"

"Mulberry *Street*," Ling corrected.

"Mulberry *Bend*," Wai-Mae said again, knowingly. "I have heard the stories, Ling."

And I've only lived there my entire life, Ling thought.

"Of course, I will have a husband to protect me, but..."

Wai-Mae's mouth never stopped. Through her prattling monologue, Ling kept moving, thinking only one thought: *Kill Henry*.

"...it's the love stories I like best, the ones with the happy endings? I would live inside the opera if I could...."

No. Ling would need Henry alive for the tongue-lashing she intended to dole out. Then the murder.

"...I know that women can't perform, but if they could, I would play all the best, most romantic roles, royal consorts, and my gestures would be precise and elegant. And *you* would be the brave Dan. I can already tell you've got a warrior's spirit—"

"Could you be quiet, please? I'm trying to think," Ling snapped.

"I'm sorry." Wai-Mae bowed, embarrassed, and Ling felt like she'd kicked a kitten. "It's only that I've been on the ship for such a long time, and the other women are older and not from my village. They want nothing to do with me. It's nice to talk to someone else. Someone young. With all her teeth."

"How old are you?" Ling asked.

"Seventeen. You?"

"The same."

"You see? We are like sisters already!" Wai-Mae bit her lip hopefully. "And do you like opera?"

"Opera is for old men," Ling said definitively.

Wai-Mae's mouth opened in shocked surprise. "Oh, Ling. How

can you say that? The opera is wonderful! They are our stories we carry with us, just like dreams."

"I don't like fairy tales. I like facts. Science."

Wai-Mae made a face. "Sounds very dull."

"Well, if you're so keen on the opera, you're in luck. My uncle runs the opera house," Ling confessed. "In New York. That's where I live."

Wai-Mae made a high-pitched sound, and it took Ling a second to recognize it as excitement, not distress. "You are the luckiest girl in the world to have such an uncle! Do you go all the time? Do you sit in the balcony and eat pumpkin seeds and imagine yourself living out those scenes? When I come to New York, you and I will go to the opera, and you'll see how wonderful it is! Clearly, fate has brought us together. We shall become the best of friends. And in the meantime, while I am on the ship, we can meet up each night, here in this beautiful dream world."

They'd come to the end of the trees. Ahead, it was only blocks of gray and brown, like a vague sketch waiting for detail. "This seems to be as far as we can go," Ling said.

"Would you like to go farther?"

"But we can't go farther," Ling said, irritated. She really was starting to wonder if Wai-Mae might be a bit simple.

"Then we will change it, make it into whatever we like. Go where we wish."

"You can't change a dream."

"Yes you can."

Ling spoke as if she were a peeved schoolmarm explaining a subject to a confused child. "I've dream walked plenty. It doesn't work that way. You can walk inside an office building. You can take the stairs, which already exist. But you, yourself, cannot turn that building into, say, a schoolhouse or an automobile."

Wai-Mae's expression was quizzical. "What's an automobile?"

Ling shut her eyes, took a deep breath. "Never mind." She started back toward the forest. "Henry! *Henry!*"

"Here we can change things," Wai-Mae said, catching up. "It isn't like other dreams. Here, I'll show you."

Ling stopped and folded her arms across her chest, defiant.

"Think of something you want," Wai-Mae said. "Something small."

I want my legs back, Ling thought. *I want to walk without braces, without people staring at me in pity or fear. I want to wake up without pain.*

Ling swallowed against the sudden lump in her throat. "Fine. Shoes. I want a pair of beautiful shoes."

"Very well," Wai-Mae said, pleased. She reached down and scooped up a rock, and her hand dropped as if the rock had real weight.

"How did—"

"Shhh. Watch." Wai-Mae shut her eyes. Her mouth went tight with concentration. She moved her hands over the rock, skilled as a magician with a well-worn trick, and as Ling watched, astonished, the rock shifted beneath Wai-Mae's hands, no longer solid but something between states, a moment of becoming, observed. Wai-Mae's edges blurred as well, as if she and the rock were joined in this alchemy. The rock wavered for a moment more, and then it was gone. In its place lay a pair of elegant embroidered Chinese slippers.

Ling ran her thumb across the raised thread at the tips of the shoes and felt just the tiniest static, some lingering charge. "How... how did you do that?"

Wai-Mae wiped sweat from her brow. "It's this world. Our dream-walker energy is like magic here."

"Not magic," Ling murmured. Her mind whirred: She knew the dream world was not the real world, and yet, as fantastical as it all was, she'd never been able to change or create anything within it. This seemed unbelievable—as if Wai-Mae had altered the atomic structure of the dream landscape somehow.

"This place makes whatever you dream come true. It makes me very tired, though." Wai-Mae trembled, breathing heavily. For the first time, her mouth wasn't running amok. "Come back tomorrow night, and I will show you how to do it, too."

"But how do I come back?"

"Take the train from the old station, of course. Just as you did tonight," Wai-Mae assured her, grinning. "We will be friends, you and I. I will show you how to change dreams. And you..." Wai-Mae twisted her mouth to the side and looked up to the trees, thinking. "You will tell me stories of your New York City so that I will know it when I get there. So that I will not feel like such a stranger."

Ling couldn't stop staring at the slippers. "Tomorrow night," she said.

The first sharp ring of Ling's alarm clock roared across the dreamscape. Her body grew heavier, a signal that she had begun her ascent into the waking world.

"Till tomorrow, Little Warrior!" Wai-Mae called.

Tomorrow, Ling thought, and like the flapping wings of a dove, the night whitened and twitched, then blurred into a great cottony nothingness.

※

At the first peal of the alarm, Gaspard barked furiously.

"No! Not yet!" Henry yelled. He thrust a hand out toward Louis as if he could grab hold of him and keep his lover from disappearing. But it was no use. Henry gulped in huge lungfuls of air as he woke in his chair at his tiny table in the Bennington. The alarm clock screamed and shook on the floor where it had fallen. Henry lay in the chair, paralyzed, unable to wipe away his tears. From the other room, he could hear Theta yelling. In a minute, she'd come out and growl at him. But Henry didn't care about any of that. He'd seen Louis. He'd talked to Louis.

But would Louis even remember their conversation? People didn't always remember their dreams, and even if they did, even if one crawled under the skin for a little while, it didn't linger for long. Details were forgotten. People brushed them aside, busy with their lives. But Louis didn't have a telephone, and if Henry's father was somehow keeping his letters and telegrams from reaching Louis, then calling for him at Celeste's was useless.

He'd found Louis in a dream, so it was possible to do it again. All he had to do was go back in and give him a suggestion, the way he'd done with Theta when she had a nightmare. That was it! Through the dream world, he could get Louis to come to *him*. But that meant he'd need Ling once more. That was the key—the two of them together. Tomorrow, he'd ask Ling to help him, no matter how much it cost.

"Henry Bartholomew DuBois the Fourth!" Theta marched in, her sleep mask pushed up haphazardly on her forehead so that she resembled a drunken pirate. She slapped off the alarm clock and turned on Henry, furious. "What's our deal, Hen?"

"Now, Theta…"

"Don't you 'Now, Theta' me. What's our deal?"

"No more than—"

"Once a week," Theta finished.

"Theta—"

"This is two nights in a row, and after you promised me today—"

"Theta—

"If you think I'm gonna lose my beauty sleep while you—"

"Theta!" Henry croaked out her name with the last of his strength.

Theta snapped out of her temper. Worried, she fell to her knees beside Henry. "Whatsa matter, Hen? Holy smokes, you okay?"

Henry smiled with chattering teeth. "I'm s-swell. Theta, I f-found him. I f-found Louis," Henry managed to say before he fell, utterly exhausted, into a dreamless sleep.

KEEPING OUT THE DEAD

Adelaide Proctor fished a nitroglycerin tablet from her pillbox, placed it beneath her tongue, and waited for her angina pains to subside. It had been a nightmare that had brought on this spasm—something about an old hand-cranked music box that played a song that had been popular when Adelaide was young. The song's beauty had stirred her longing, promising her everything she'd ever wanted if only she'd follow it deeper and deeper into dreams. Adelaide sensed it calling out to other sleepers, too, like a radio transmission from a far-off station late at night. But then the dream shifted, the song was lost, and she saw Elijah standing silently on the edge of the cornfield, his face painted in deep moon-shadow. "Addie," he'd whispered, beckoning, and her heart began to gallop wildly, a riderless horse, until she woke with a start.

The tablet worked quickly on the tightness in her chest. Once her heartbeat slowed to a steadier rhythm, she forced herself from her bed and staggered to her own music box, atop a small oak cabinet tucked into a corner of the room. When she lifted the box's lid, its tiny Moulin Rouge dancer figurine jerked into motion. With two fingers, Adelaide silenced the dancer's song before it could wake her sister, Lillian. Inside lay a flannel jewelry bag housing a small iron case with the initials EJH. Adelaide opened the case and examined its contents—a lock of dark-gold hair, a tooth, a sliver of finger bone, and a tintype of a young man in a gray uniform. Seeing that everything was secure, she placed the iron case back in its bag and closed it away, locking the doors of the cabinet once more.

Next she gathered a shallow bowl, matches, a candle in its brass holder, a roll of bandaging, bundled sage, and a small crooked silver dagger. These she added to her handbag. She emptied the salt can into each pocket of her robe, grabbed the handbag, and, with the burden of salt weighing her down, shuffled down the hall to wait for the elevator.

The elevator operator rode Miss Adelaide all the way to the very depths of the Bennington without a word; he'd only been there two weeks and had already learned not to question the Proctor sisters. While the lift rumbled down, Miss Addie chanted softly to herself, "*The land is old, the land is vast / He has no future, he has no past / His coat is sown with many woes / He'll wake the dead, the King of Crows.*"

The elevator gates clanged open on the Bennington's underworld. The young man at the elevator's controls peered into the darkness. "Shall I wait for you, Miss Proctor?" he asked uncertainly.

"It's quite all right, dear. I'll ring you shortly. Run along now."

Shaking his head, the young man closed the gate and the elevator groaned back up, leaving Addie alone in the dim basement. Immediately, she took out the candle and lit the wick, waiting for the glow to brighten the gloom. She fed one end of the bundled sage into the flame and waved it through the air, spreading out in wider circles. Next she wiggled up the sleeves of her robe and nightgown. The paper-thin skin of her wrist glowed nearly blue in the dim light from the narrow street-level windows that ran along the park side. Speaking ancient words, she slid the small knife across her thumb, hissing as she dripped blood into the bowl. She pressed her bloody thumb to the basement's eastern corner before marking the room's three other corners. This done, she bandaged her finger, then scooped salt from her pockets, sprinkling frost-thin lines along the windowsills, where she hoped the janitor wouldn't find them. Night pleaded at the windows to be let in. Addie snuffed the candle, gathered her things, and pressed the elevator's call button, watching the golden arrow tick down the floors to the bottom.

When the doors opened, the elevator operator helped Addie onto the lift. "You smell smoke, Miss Proctor?" he asked, alarmed.

"It's only sage. I smudged the basement, you see."

"Beg your pardon, Miss Proctor?"

"I lit a bundle of sage and smoked the room."

Curiosity and suspicion proved too much for the young man at the controls. "Now, Miss Proctor, why'd you want to go and do a thing like that?"

"For protection," Addie said, resolute.

"Protection from what, ma'am?"

"Bad dreams."

"I'm sorry, Miss Proctor. I don't follow."

Miss Adelaide whispered urgently, "I'm keeping out the dead, my dear. For as long as I can."

The elevator operator kept his thoughts to himself, though he'd be sure to mention this to the building management before his shift ended. No doubt they wouldn't want the old woman burning down the whole building. With a small shaking of his head, he yanked the gate shut and turned again to the controls, and the gilded doors closed on the dark of the basement.

DAY EIGHT

A FINE ROMANCE

"Good morning, good morning!" Evie called as she flounced down the halls of WGI wearing a broad smile that masked the hangover from the previous night's party. As promised, Evie had popped out of the cake at midnight. As expected, she'd popped right into a boozy party that went until well into the wee hours. She'd kill for another few hours of sleep. In the hallway, the day's hopefuls clamored to be put on the air. Every morning, there was a line of new talent looking to make a name on the radio.

"I can sing just like Caruso," one fellow explained before launching into an aria so loud Evie was fairly certain it could be heard out in Queens.

"What about me?" another man with a nasal voice piped up. "I can do fourteen different bird whistles!"

"Oh, please don't," Evie muttered, rubbing her temples.

As Evie dropped off her cloche and coat with the coat-check girl, another of Mr. Phillips's many secretaries, Helen, hurried toward her. "Miss O'Neill! I've been looking for you. Mr. Phillips would like to speak with you. Immediately."

Evie's gut roiled as Helen ushered her into Mr. Phillips's private office, an enormous corner room of gleaming cherrywood walls on the tenth floor with a view of Midtown Manhattan. A gold-framed oil painting of a godlike Guglielmo Marconi inventing the wireless took up an entire wall. His painted expression gave no hint as to Evie's fate.

"Wait here. He'll be in shortly," Helen said and closed the door.

Was Mr. Phillips firing her? Had she done something wrong? By the time she heard Mr. Phillips's patrician voice telling his secretary to "hold all calls," she was so anxious she could've climbed the pretty walls.

Mr. Phillips swept into the room with the sort of calm confidence that had helped him make a fortune in the stock market. His suits were tailored in London, and he had an apartment in the city and a house out on Long Island where he hosted legendary parties attended by film and radio stars. But radio was his one true obsession, and WGI was his baby. Talent that Mr. Phillips didn't like had been fired midshow: An emcee or act would be ushered out of the studio during a musical number and immediately replaced with a new act.

"Good morning, Miss O'Neill," he said now, taking the seat opposite her. The sun glinted off his silvery hair. "You're front-page news today, it seems."

He slid a stack of newspapers toward her. The *Daily News*. The *Herald*. The *Star*. Every one of them carried a station-approved glamour shot of Evie, along with a screaming headline:

SWEETHEART SEES HIM AS HER GROOM.

LOVE IS IN THE CARDS FOR DIVINER GAL.

FLAPPER OF FATE IN SECRET ROMANCE.

"Why didn't you tell me about this?" Mr. Phillips asked.

"I...I can explain, Mr. Phillips," Evie said. Under the table, her foot tapped like mad. He would fire her, send her packing, and everything she'd enjoyed the last few months would be gone. When she saw Sam Lloyd again, Evie would need Theta to hold her back to keep her from killing that boy in every way she could imagine—and she had quite an imagination. Evie took a deep, calming breath. *Use your vowels*, she told herself. *Everything sounds better with proper enunciation.* "You see, it isn't quite what it seems...."

"No? I certainly hope it is what it seems, dear girl," Mr. Phillips answered, his eyes brightening. "It's spectacular!"

"It...it is?" Evie squeaked.

"Indeed it is. WGI has been flooded with telephone calls all day. The switchboard operators' fingers are exhausted. People are crazy about your engagement. They can't get enough! They want to know everything about it. Why, it's the biggest thing to hit New York since—well, since you announced you were a Diviner. The 'It Girl' has found her 'It Boy.'"

A tickle nagged the back of Evie's throat. "Oh, gee, well, I wouldn't exactly say Sam is my 'It Boy.'"

Mr. Phillips waved her words away. "The point is, my dear girl, that you and your lucky fellow have made the WGI family very happy. Finally, we've got a leg up on NBC. You and your beau are going to put us over the top. Already, the advertisers are calling. They want to support the station that has the Sweetheart Seer and her fiancé." He smiled. "And when our advertisers are happy, I am happy. You are about to become very famous, my dear."

"I am?"

"Yes. What would you say to being on the air two nights a week? With a small raise, naturally."

Two nights a week? The only other people with that sort of clout were stars like Will Rogers and Fanny Brice. Evie couldn't keep the smile from spreading wide across her face. "That'd be the berries, Mr. Phillips."

"Consider it done. And, of course, we'll want to arrange press for the happy couple."

"Oh. Well, gee, I-I don't know. It's all rather new," Evie said. Her voice had gone high, like she'd been given ether.

"Nonsense." Mr. Phillips glowered, his bushy brows coming to a terrifying, angry V mid-forehead. "We'll arrange it. The public's appetite must be fed. I want you and your fellow"—Mr. Phillips stole a glance at the newspaper story—"Sam out as often as possible. Every night if you can. Now that Scott and Zelda Fitzgerald are in Europe, Americans are hungry for a modern couple to take their place." He lowered a finger at her. "You two are it."

Evie burst into uncontrollable, nervous laughter.

"Is something the matter, Miss O'Neill?"

"Everything's jake," Evie said in a somewhat strangled voice. "Could I make a telephone call, please?"

In the privacy of Mr. Phillips's office, Evie waited for Sam to answer and looked out the tenth-floor windows at tall buildings enveloped by winter fog. Down below, the people hustling along Fifth Avenue seemed rather small. Evie liked being this high; she felt quite powerful, indeed. She'd like to stay up here among the clouds. Evie picked up the day's paper and stared at her name in bold print. Yes, she liked this very much. She just had to get Sam on board.

The operator broke the silence. "I've got that call for you, Miss O'Neill."

Sam's voice crackled over the line, filled with smirk. "Well, if it isn't the future Mrs. Lloyd."

"Daaarling," she trilled. "I've missed you."

There was a brief pause on the other end, then: "Uh-oh."

Through the crack in the door, Evie could see Mr. Phillips and the WGI secretary pool hovering, hanging on her every word. She perched on the gleaming edge of the lacquered desk and laughed like they'd taught her in elocution class, low in her throat, with her head thrown back as if she were catching the wind in her hair. It was supposed to be alluring and high-class, the devil-may-care laugh of a lady of leisure. "Hahahaha. Oh, you! Darling, I simply *must* see you. Shall we say luncheon at noon? The Algonquin?"

Another pause. "Are you feeling okay, Sheba?"

"Now, don't be late, dearest. We have *so much* to discuss, and you know that every moment away from you is like torture. *Adieu!*"

Evie hung up before Sam could say another word.

On her way out, Evie shared the elevator with Sarah Snow. Evie noticed her stockings right away—gray herringbone, very chic. For an evangelist, she was quite fashionable. That was a large part of her appeal. God's flapper, some called her. She gave the subject of Jesus a little hotsy-totsy. A missionary's daughter whose parents had been killed in China when she was only thirteen, Sarah Snow heard the call at the tender age of fifteen. By the time she was twenty, she'd criss-crossed the country twice, holding tent meetings and preaching about the evils of liquor, dancing, and socialism. She'd married at twenty-one and lost her husband to tuberculosis before she'd turned twenty-three. Now, at twenty-five, she was trying to reach her flock on the radio—Moses on the Wireless. That she called for a return to simpler times appealed to plenty of Americans lost in a world turning too fast for them to find their footing. That she was a passionate speaker brought scores to her revival meetings. That she was pretty didn't hurt a thing.

Still, she didn't have nearly the following that Evie did. In fact, the gossip around the station was that the only reason Sarah had managed to hold on to her show was that there was nothing better to slot into that hour, and it would look bad to fire a foot soldier for Jesus.

"Congratulations on your engagement, Evie," the evangelist said, giving one of those saintly, closed-mouth smiles that Evie couldn't have managed if she practiced in a church mirror for a year.

"Thank you, Sarah."

"Is he a Godly sort of fellow?"

Evie suppressed a loud "ha!" "Well, he certainly does know how to make a girl appeal to the Lord."

"I wish you every happiness. I heard they're putting you on two nights a week now. Is...is that true?" Another closed-mouth smile. But Evie sensed the worry behind it. Sarah Snow might have her eyes on the cross, but her heart was full of ambition. It almost made Evie like her more. Almost.

"Yes. It's true," Evie said brightly.

Sarah faced forward again, her eyes on the golden arrow counting down the floors. "I suppose everyone loves a great romance."

Evie's smile faltered. "I suppose so."

Evie blew into the Algonquin and shook the damp from her cloche. The maître d' led her through the packed, oak-paneled dining room. Every head turned as Sam rose to greet Evie.

"Lamb Chop!" Sam clasped her hands and gave a small sigh.

"Makes me sound like dinner," Evie muttered through clenched teeth.

"Does it, my little Venison De Milo?"

Evie glared. "You're enjoying this, aren't you?"

Sam whispered into her ear, "More than you can imagine."

A waiter appeared. "Shall I bring you the Waldorf salad, Miss O'Neill?"

"Yes, thank you. And coffee, please."

"Mr. Lloyd?"

Sam gave a small sigh. "Usually I feast on our love, but since the lady's having something, I'll take a Reuben. Extra horseradish. And an egg cream."

"As you wish, sir," the waiter said. "You two must be very happy."

"Over the moon. Who'd've thought a regular schmoe like me could land a gem like Baby Doll here," Sam said.

Evie had to lock her hands around her knees to keep from kicking Sam under the table. Once the waiter had gone, Evie leaned forward, her voice low. "Laying it on a little thick, aren't you, pal?"

Sam shrugged. "I heard we were in a romance. Thought I'd play along. But if you'd rather not, I'll call the papers right now and tell 'em the truth."

"You'll do no such thing, Sam Lloyd! You got us into this mess. Now we're stuck."

"Is that so? Tell me why I shouldn't fess up to the news boys."

"Do you know how many calls the radio station got today about us? One thousand!"

"A ... thousand?"

"One-oh-oh-oh, brother. And they're still calling! Mr. Phillips wants to put me on two nights a week. This is going to make me famous. More famous." She glared at Sam. "You, too, I suppose."

Sam rubbed his chin, grinning. "I bet I'd be good at being famous."

"How lucky for us all," Evie snapped. "The point is, if you tell them it was just a joke now, I'll look like a joke, too. Nobody wants to back a joke. Makes people grumpy. There's only one solution, I'm afraid. We've got to play out this hand for a bit."

The waiter delivered a plate of rolls and Evie dove for it. Being anxious made her hungry. She could've eaten ten rolls. Sam laced his fingers and leaned his elbows on the table, inching his face closer to Evie's. "Yeah? What do I get out of this deal, Baby Vamp?"

"I agree not to kill you," Evie said around a mouthful of bread. She twirled the butter knife between her fingers.

"Your terms are generous," Sam said. "But I have two conditions of my own."

Evie swallowed her lump of bread. She narrowed her eyes to slits. "I will not pet with you. You can cross that one off the list right now."

Sam smirked. He dabbed a spot of butter from her face with his napkin. "Doll, I have never had to make petting part of a contract. Every girl in my rumble seat has been happy to be there. I had something else in mind."

Evie didn't know whether to be relieved or insulted. "What?" she said, wary.

Sam's smirk vanished. "Project Buffalo."

Project Buffalo. Sam's obsession. According to him, it was some secret government operation during the war, and his mother, Miriam, had been a part of it. She'd left home when Sam was only eight and never returned. The official record said that she'd died of influenza, but two years ago Sam had received a postcard—no return address—with the words *Find me, Little Fox* on the back in Russian. The handwriting was unmistakably his mother's. Sam had run away from home and made it his mission to find her.

"Sam," Evie said as gently as possible, "don't you think maybe it's time to let that go? You say you don't believe in ghosts, but Project Buffalo is a ghost. And you let it haunt you."

"Evie, Project Buffalo took my mother away from me. And I will not rest until I know what happened to her."

Sam's expression was one of grim determination, but Evie could see the hurt there. She knew what it was to lose someone you loved so dearly. If there had been a hope that James was still alive, Evie would've followed every lead until she found him.

"Fair enough," Evie said. "What's the matter? You look like somebody put hot peppers in your Burma Shave."

Sam drummed his fingers on the table. "Evie, did your uncle ever mention Project Buffalo to you?"

"No. Why on earth would you think Will would know anything about that?"

"I got a tip."

Evie raised an eyebrow. "Tips are for cabdrivers and horse races, Sam."

"Hold on. I need to show you something." Sam fished out his wallet and extracted a folded napkin. "There's a fella, used to work for the government. Knows all sorts of secrets, and occasionally, he coughs something up for me. I asked him about my mother and Project Buffalo. He told me it's still going on. And he got me a name of somebody he said knew about it."

Sam slid her the napkin. Evie stared at the name written there: *Will Fitzgerald.*

Evie bit her lip. "When did you say your creepy man gave this to you?"

"He's not a creepy man...."

"Fine, your 'clandestine acquaintance,' then."

"About two months ago."

"Two months ago," Evie repeated.

"Yeah. Two months ago. Why're you making that face?"

Evie shook her head. "Sam, Sam, Sam. I never thought of you as gullible."

"I'm a lot of things, sister, but gullible isn't one of them. And since when did you become an expert on informants?"

"I don't know anything about spying," Evie said, pouring milk into her coffee. "But I do know human nature. Think, Sam: two months ago? The Pentacle Murders?"

"Yeah. I'm familiar."

"Uncle Will's name was all over the papers! And you were working at the museum. How easy would it be to connect the two?" Evie explained. "Face it, Sam—you were taken for a ride. I'm sorry if you don't want to admit it. The con man got conned."

A worm of doubt twisted in Sam's gut. He hadn't taken that into account.

"Sam," Evie said gently, "have you ever considered that maybe that postcard isn't from your mother?"

"That's her writing on the postcard. I know it, Evie. I will find her. I swear I will."

The waiter delivered Sam's Reuben and Evie's Waldorf salad. From the corner of her eye, Evie could see people watching them, gossiping from behind their menus. At the famous round table, Dorothy Parker sat drinking martinis with Robert Benchley and George S. Kaufman, but no one was paying them any mind. Evie and Sam commanded the Algonquin's full attention. Sam was oblivious. He was much more interested in his sandwich, which he was practically inhaling.

"Don't choke. I need you alive. For a while at least," Evie said. "So if I were to help you with Project Buffalo, what would you want me to do?"

"Read whatever I dig up. See if you can get a lead on anything."

"Object reading." Evie sighed. "Going two nights a week on the radio is already taxing me. I'd have to be careful. What's condition number two?"

"You host the museum's Diviners exhibit party at the end of the month."

"Oh, Saaaam," Evie whined. She dropped her head on the table with an Isadora Duncan–worthy sense of drama. "No. I am not helping

Will. Why, it's campaigning for the enemy! I hate that museum, and I hate Will, too."

"You're not helping Will. You're helping me. If the museum goes under, I'm out on the street. By the way, we're being watched." Sam flicked his eyes in the direction of a table full of gawking flappers whispering excitedly to one another.

Evie raised an eyebrow. "No kidding. I didn't just fall off the turnip truck, you know."

"We should give them a little something for their trouble."

"Such as?" Evie said, wary.

Sam leaned forward and took both of Evie's hands in his. He stared into her eyes as if she were the only woman in the world. Like a traitor, Evie's stomach gave a slight hiccup.

"Help me with Project Buffalo and the Diviners exhibit. And I promise I'll sell this romance so hard Valentino couldn't've done better."

From the corner of her eye, Evie could see that more people were taking notice of them. The room buzzed with an energy that made her feel as if she, herself, ran on electric current. She liked that feeling. She liked it very much. Reading a few trinkets and hosting a party—even one for the museum—in exchange for being front-page news and New York City's biggest radio star seemed fair enough.

"You've got yourself a deal, Sam, with one last condition," Evie said.

"I won't take up golf or folk dancing."

Evie narrowed her eyes. "A time limit. Four weeks of the swooniest, swellest romance New York City has ever seen. And then, kaput. Over and out. Off the air."

"Golly, when you say it like that, it sounds as if our love's not real, Lamb Chop."

"There will be a tragic parting. Our love will have burned too brightly to live on." Evie put a hand to her forehead like a doomed opera heroine, then let it flutter into a parting wave. "Toot, Toot, Tootsie! Good-bye."

"Four weeks, huh?" Sam asked, cocking his head.

"Four weeks."

Sam stole a glance at the flappers watching them. They were cute, and probably one of them might jump to date him. So why was he entering into a devil's bargain with Evie? Why did the prospect of a fake romance with her give him the same thrill as thievery?

"Done," Sam said. He stared up at her with big peepers and a lupine grin. "We'll have to make the chumps believe it. Moonlight strolls. Staring into each other's eyes. Sharing the same straw in our egg cream. Dreadful pet names."

"Not Lamb Chop," Evie protested. "That's hideous."

"You got it, Pork Chop."

"I will murder you in your sleep."

Sam grinned. "Does that mean you're sleeping beside me?"

"Not on your life, Lloyd." Evie smirked. "The act's only good when the cameras are flashing."

"Well, then, guess I'd better make this look good now." Sam kissed the back of Evie's hand. The table of flappers let out a collective, swooning *Ohhhh*. The kiss tingled up Evie's arm and gave her insides a soft buzz. *Stop that*, she thought. She'd have to discuss this with her insides later and let them know the score.

The waiter appeared at their table once more. "The meal is on the house, Miss O'Neill, Mr. Lloyd. Thank you for dining with us at the Algonquin today. We do hope you'll come again."

Sam's eyebrows shot up. "I could get used to this." He snugged his fisherman's cap down onto his head.

"Mr. Phillips has arranged an interview for us at WGI today. Four o'clock. We're telling the story of our love. Don't be late."

"Nifty. I'll steal something swell to wear. Whaddaya think—pantaloons?"

He was toying with her. This was the trouble with trusting a fella like Sam Lloyd.

"Sam. Don't make me kill you on a full stomach. I might get a cramp."

Sam smirked. "Nice doing business with you, too, Baby Vamp."

Evie batted her lashes. "Go now before I change my mind."

"Leave separately and disappoint our audience?" Sam nodded toward the other patrons slyly watching from their tables. That wolfish grin was back. But the thread of pure glee was new. Sam slipped his arm through Evie's, parading her through the gaping patrons of the Algonquin. He leaned in to whisper in Evie's ear, and her stomach gave another rebellious flip.

"From now on, Sheba, you won't be able to shake me."

EVERYTHING SEEMED
NEW AND HOPEFUL

Theta and Henry raced down the crowded sidewalk of Forty-second Street, late, as usual, for rehearsal. They squeezed past a preacher and his small flock of parishioners holding a prayer vigil. "This sleeping sickness is God's judgment! Repent!" the preacher thundered, a Bible held high in one hand. "Turn away from loose morals; from those dens of iniquity, the speakeasy; from the devil's music, jazz; and from the untold evils of the bootlegger's liquor!"

"Gee, if I do that, I won't have any hobbies left," Henry quipped.

"If we don't hurry, we're not gonna have any jobs left," Theta said.

A corner newsboy waved a newspaper at Theta. "Paper, Miss?"

"Sorry, kid."

He shrugged and shouted out the day's headlines. "Extra! Sleeping Sickness Spreads, Docs Fear New Plague! Anarchist Bombers Take Out Factory! The Sweetheart Seer Engaged! Extra!"

"What?" Theta stopped short. "Kid, here," she said, tossing over a nickel and practically snatching the *Daily News* from him. "I'll be a monkey's uncle."

"Is this some sort of joke?" Henry asked, reading the front page over Theta's shoulder. "Why wouldn't Evie tell us about this?"

"I don't know what game Evil's playing now, but you can bet I'll find out," Theta said, shoving the crumpled paper into her pocketbook. "If she's marrying Sam Lloyd, I'll eat my hat."

"Gee, that's too bad," Henry said, opening the theater door. "It's an awfully nice hat."

The sharp report of tap shoes competed with the melodic rise and fall of chorines singing scales, announcing that rehearsal was already under way at the New Amsterdam. Wally, the show's long-suffering stage manager, glowered at Henry and Theta as they sauntered down the aisle together, arm in arm. "Well, well, well. If it isn't the Tardy Twins. Congratulations. You're only"—he made a point of checking his watch—"ten minutes late today."

Theta patted Wally's cheek and pursed her lips. "Now, Wally, don't let your ulcer flare up—Hen's got a new song for you. Quiet, everybody!"

"Hey, that's my line," Wally griped. Not to be outdone, he barked, "Quiet, everybody!"

"Go on, Hen," Theta coaxed.

Henry perched at the piano and took a deep breath. "It's a bit rough, mind you. But it goes something like this."

Henry played a lilting melody, singing along in his raspy falsetto:

"Inside a dream I yearned anew
You appeared, like morning dew
My heart leaped up, no longer blue
But only here in Slumberland. . . .

The moon sank low in the morning sky
Why, oh why, must we say good-bye?
I'll see you again, sweet by and by
But only here in Slumberland.

They say that dreams come true, dear,
If you believe their charms
But if my dreams came true, dear,
I'd hold you in my arms.

Sandman come and dust my eyes
Blue moon, won't you start your rise?
Every night, oh, how time flies
When I'm with you in Slumberland . . .
I'll stay with you in Slumberland."

When he finished, Henry turned to Wally. "Well," he asked nervously, "what do you think?"

For once, Wally wasn't cradling his head in his hands and looking like he'd lost the will to live. "You know, kid, that's not half bad."

A voice boomed from the back. "A little slow, isn't it?"

Henry didn't know when Herbert Allen had sneaked in, but his arrival was anything but good news. "It's . . . melancholy. Not much pep. Can you make it zippier, old boy?" Herbie said as he strolled down the center aisle wearing a new plaid suit bought, no doubt, with his latest royalty check.

"Well, the poor fella can't find what he's lost," Henry explained. He tried very hard not to add *you tasteless idiot.* "He's yearning."

"Mmm," Herbie said, wrinkling his nose. "I don't know, Wally. Seems a bit dreary for the Follies."

"I like it," Wally said, to Henry's great surprise. "We could use a wistful number."

Henry enjoyed watching Herbie's unctuous smile vanish.

"Well, I suppose Flo will make the final decision, won't he?" Herbie said.

"Yeah, yeah," Wally said, waving it away. "Take another pass at it, Henry. Rework the bridge and that last chorus, and then we'll show it to Flo. If he likes it, you're in, kid."

"Thanks, Wally!"

"Hallelujah!" Theta said. She jumped up and threw her arms around Henry.

"All right, people, all right. Places for the 'Hocus-Pocus' number. Where are my Diviners girls?"

While Wally barked orders to the performers, Henry daydreamed at the piano. Everything seemed new and hopeful now. It was all because of Louis—he knew it was. He couldn't wait to see him again. And when he did, he'd give Louis a dream suggestion to call the apartment in New York. Somehow, he had to convince Ling to go in with him again tonight. As soon as rehearsal ended, he'd run down to Chinatown and make the arrangements. It was all going to work out.

And the disgruntled expression on Herbert Allen's face was the icing on the cake.

The minute rehearsal was over, Theta rang Mabel, and the two of them barged into Evie's bathroom at the Winthrop Hotel, where they found her soaking in a tub full of bubbles.

"Hey! I'm not decent!" Evie protested.

"If we waited for you to become decent, we'd be waiting for years," Theta said, taking a seat on the commode. She held up the day's newspaper. "Have you lost what's left of your demented mind, Evil?"

"I can't believe you didn't tell me yesterday," Mabel grumbled, perching on the edge of the tub.

"Of all the cockamamie things you've done, this takes the cake— the wedding cake!"

"I'm your best friend," Mabel said, hurt.

Evie wanted to confess everything to Theta and Mabel, but she couldn't risk it. She and Sam had agreed to keep their little arrangement a secret from even their closest friends. If their pals believed they were in love, there was more chance of the public buying it—and less chance they'd be exposed as liars.

Evie scooted lower, into the protection of the bubbly froth. "Gee, it, um, it all happened so fast. I was planning to tell you. Honest."

Theta squinted at Evie. "I thought you hated Sam Lloyd."

"I did hate Sam for a bit. But then I came to see what a truly romantic person he is. How adventurous. And...and sweet!" Evie said, making it up as she went. "Look, can't a girl change her mind about a boy?"

Theta folded her arms across her chest. "Sure she can. We'll wait right here while you change it back. Evie, Sam Lloyd is a con! He could charm the snakes outta Ireland. Sure, he's handsome—"

Mabel made a face. "Do you think so? Well, I suppose he isn't un-handsome—"

"How do you know that drugstore cowboy's not just taking advantage of you now that you're making money?"

"You could at least say congratulations," Evie groused, indignant. She had no right to feel that way. Nevertheless, she did.

"Congratulations," Mabel muttered.

Theta rolled her eyes. "Congratulations. For a wedding present, I'll buy you a matched set of common and sense. Not that you'll ever use it."

"I'll choose to overlook that remark." Evie sniffed.

"Something about this ain't on the level is all I know," Theta said.

In the other room, the telephone rang.

"Oh, no! Could one of you be an absolute daaahling and grab that?" Evie said.

"I do so *lahhve* to be a *daaahling*," Theta mimicked, and marched to the phone on Evie's bedside table with Mabel in tow. "Sweetheart Seer residence. Sorry, but currently the Sweetheart Seer is all wet," Theta said, and Mabel giggled.

"Theta!" Evie howled from the tub. Theta kicked the bathroom door shut.

"Uh-huh...uh-huh...yeah, sure, I'll tell Her Radio Highness. Good-bye," Theta said, hanging up the phone.

"What is it?" Evie asked, tying her robe as she pushed through the bathroom door.

Theta put on a hoity-toity accent. "I am to let Miss O'Neill know that her driver has arrived."

"Driver?" Evie said, eyes wide. The girls rushed to the window. Down on the street, a chauffeur waited beside a shiny green Chrysler.

Mabel gasped. "Holy smokes. It's like you're Gloria Swanson or something. Like you're a movie star."

"A star," Evie repeated, eyes flashing.

"Congratulations, Evil. You've arrived. I guess we'll exit stage left, Mabel."

"If you wait a minute, you can ride with me to the radio show. We could all go together, like real swells!"

"Sorry, Evil. I hafta go back to rehearsal," Theta said.

"Mabesie?"

For the past two months, Mabel had tried to ignore the changes in Evie. The way she now said *eye-ther* instead of *eee-ther*. The way she greeted people she hardly knew with a drawn-out *daaah-ling*. The way she always seemed to have time for parties and dates and her new glamorous pals, but not for Mabel. But this was too much. Weren't she and Evie best friends? Shouldn't a girl share the news of her engagement with her best friend first?

Mabel's conscience told her that she should go and cheer Evie on. But she was angry and deeply hurt, and she didn't think she could tolerate being just one of the faceless crowd again.

"Sorry. I'm not available," Mabel said, turning on her heel. "I'll get the elevator, Theta."

"I'll be right there, kid. I gotta powder my nose first." Theta waited until Mabel was down the hall, then cornered Evie. "Evil, are you really marrying Sam Lloyd?"

"It's in all the papers, isn't it?" Evie said. It wasn't precisely lying.

Theta's eyes searched Evie's for an uncomfortable second. "You break the news to Jericho about your engagement?"

"Why would I?" Evie said, looking away.

"Just a hunch, but I don't think he's gonna take it well."

"I'm sure I don't know what you mean."

Theta patted Evie's face. "Keep telling yourself that."

OUR MOST IMPORTANT WORK

When Jericho opened the day's paper, he had to read the headline four times before it finally sank in: Evie was marrying Sam Lloyd. Sam "A Girl in Every Port" Lloyd. Sam, that grifter who couldn't be counted on, who only looked out for himself. She'd chosen *that jackass* over him. When had it happened? Was that why Evie had avoided him, why she didn't respond to his letters? Was that the reason for her brush-off at the Bennington last night? *Sam Lloyd.* Did girls really go for fellas like that? Did they truly find bad boys more attractive?

Or did they just want to know that a fella was normal, a man, not a machine?

A few months ago, Jericho had been shot. The pain had been a sharp pop of fire in his chest. Reading the article on Sam and Evie's romance hurt even worse. He was glad that Will had already left with Sister Walker so that he could bear the sting of it in private.

Off-key singing sounded in the hall, announcing Sam's arrival, and Jericho cursed his luck.

"Honey, ready my slippers and pipe—I'm home!" Sam shouted as he blew into the library and dropped himself onto the worn brown leather Chesterfield, ruddy-cheeked and smiling. "Freddy, you would not believe the day I've had so far. A real roller coaster. But there's good news: Evie's on board to host the Diviners exhibit opening."

"Congratulations. How'd you manage that?" Jericho said evenly.

Sam stretched his arms across the back of the sofa and smirked.

"Well, I did my best. And my best is pretty irresistible. So what do you think—should we hire a jazz band or an orchestra? See, I think jazz band. But the professor seems like the orchestra type to me—violins and French horns. Frilly-cuff music. Oh, and we could get somebody to cater...."

Jericho dropped the newspaper in Sam's lap. "When were you going to tell me?"

"Gee, Freddy," Sam said quietly, pushing the newspaper aside. "I, uh, didn't want to rub it in."

"Seems exactly like something you'd want to do. And don't call me Freddy." Jericho crossed to the fireplace, poking at the embers till they blazed.

"Did you ever consider that maybe you got me figured all wrong?" Sam said.

Jericho didn't turn away from the fire. "I'm pretty sure I've got you figured exactly right. You're a thief. You steal things. And people."

Usually Sam enjoyed the friendly competition over Evie's affections, but just now, he felt like a real heel. He didn't know exactly what had happened between Jericho and Evie. Maybe they'd kissed. Maybe more than that. But whatever had taken place was a romance of circumstances, he was certain. Surely Jericho had to know he was all wrong for Evie. Jericho spent his nights reading or painting Civil War models. Evie was a bearcat, the life of the party. She'd eat him alive. The more Sam thought about it, the more he came to think that it was better this way. He'd snooped in Jericho's room, looking for clues to Project Buffalo, and he'd found the letters that Jericho had started to Evie and never sent. It bordered on what his old man would call nebbishy. This phony romance would give Jericho time to lick the last of his wounds and move on. In four weeks, he'd be a new man. It would be, "Evie who?" And Sam would help Jericho along. He owed the giant that much. In fact, he'd be doing the big lug a favor.

"Listen, pal, I feel lousy about the way you found out about Evie and me. Let me make it up to you. How's about you and me go out on the town sometime, huh?"

Jericho narrowed his eyes. "You. And me."

"We could go to the fights, or head to the Kentucky Club to hear Duke Ellington play. I could introduce you to some girls. It'd be swell times!" He gave Jericho his most convincing smile.

Jericho didn't return it. "I'm not going to dignify that with a response, especially when we have more important matters to tend to. We've got a museum to save and an exhibit to put together, if you recall."

Sam figured it was best to leave the giant his pride and change the subject. At least they could agree on saving the museum. "What've we got so far?"

Sam followed Jericho to a table that held a paltry assortment of items. "Let's see. We got a gris gris bag. Liberty Anne's diary. A very shriveled mandrake root..." Sam held the grizzled thing up to the light. "Or possibly the world's hairiest potato. And something that looks like chicken bones?"

Jericho swiped the bones into a trash can. "Last night's dinner."

Sam held up a photograph with a gauzy white smear in the background. "Is this a spirit photograph, or is that mayonnaise?"

Jericho snatched the ghostly tintype away. "Spirit photograph."

Sam picked through the rest of the meager collection, his hopes flagging. "This is it? It's not any different from what we already got going on."

"Sam, this entire museum is a Diviners exhibit. I don't see why you haven't grasped this yet."

"This is gonna be a three-legged dog of an exhibit," Sam grumbled. "Buncha spooky knickknacks and haunted doilies. Nobody's gonna line up for this junk!"

"I'll remind you that this was your idea." Jericho spread his arms wide in challenge. "Fine. Why don't *you* curate this exhibit, then? See what you come up with."

Jericho headed to the collections room, and Sam followed, complaining.

"Gimme *something* to work with. A curse. The bloodstained

waistcoat of a murdered aristocrat. A hotsy-totsy medium who, uh, felt the spirits move through her, if you catch my drift—ouch!" Sam said, tripping over a spot on the rug that sent him tumbling into a sideboard.

"Watch it," Jericho said, steadying the sideboard. "These are rare artifacts."

"Thanks for your concern. I'm fine," Sam muttered. He pulled back the rug, exposing the scarred outline of a door with a metal ring attached. "That's the culprit," Sam said, tugging on the ring. "What is this?"

"An old cellar."

"No kidding. What's in it?"

Jericho shrugged.

"Hold on—you've never been down in the cellar?"

"No. Why would I?"

"Freddy, it could be a gold mine down there!" Sam tried the ring again. It wouldn't budge. "I gotta loosen around these boards. Hand me that sword up there, will ya?"

"You mean this antique that's probably worth more than you are?" Jericho shook his head slowly.

"Fine!" Sam flicked open his Swiss Army knife and sawed the blade around the edges of the door as best he could to loosen the thick layers of sticky, packed dust, but the door still wouldn't give.

Jericho sighed. "Here. Move." He grasped the ring with one hand and gave a slight pull, and the door creaked open.

"Holy smokes, Hercules. What are they feeding you?"

Jericho coughed as the dust spiraled up in thick clouds.

"I coulda opened it, you know," Sam added.

"No, you couldn't."

"I was *this close*."

"Wrong." Jericho waved away the last of the dust motes circling in the air. A perilous-looking wooden staircase draped in cobwebs led down into the gloom. "You think those stairs are still any good?"

"Only one way to find out," Sam said. "Let's grab some flashlights."

The wood protested loudly under Sam and Jericho's sudden weight as the two of them made their way down the old steps into the dark hole, their flashlight beams bouncing across the fragile architecture of cobwebs. They jumped to the bottom, landing on a dirt floor in a large room connected to a long, narrow passageway.

Sam whistled. "The bootleggers would kill for this."

He and Jericho walked the passageway, which was scribbled and scratched with names: *James Beardon. Moses Johnson. Maisie Lafayette and children. My name is Osay.* There were several X's instead of names, and a vast mural whose muted colors were ghosts of their former hues. In it, a slave family entered a promised land of bright sun and leafy trees. High above the sun's rays, someone had etched the word *freedom.* The mural had clearly been painted by several different hands over time, each artist adding to the story, but the message was the same.

"Looks like the Transcontinental wasn't the only railroad Cornelius Rathbone built," Jericho said, shining a light around the cavernous space.

Sam's mother used to say that inside everyone was the chance to change the world. It sat like a seed eager to grow into greatness. The professor could have his ghosts. Ordinary people were capable of extraordinary bravery. That was the only magic Sam knew or trusted.

"What are we looking for down here?" Jericho asked.

"Not sure," Sam answered. His light fell upon a closed door nestled in an alcove. "But this might be a good place to start." He tried the knob. "Locked."

From his pocket, Sam again pulled out his Swiss Army knife and stuck the point of it into the keyhole.

"Hold on: Are you breaking in?"

"*Ish,*" Sam said, wobbling his hand in a more-or-less motion.

Jericho leaned against the brick, shaking his head. "You're something else."

"C'mon, Freddy," Sam goaded, still trying to jimmy the lock. "Is your curiosity button on the fritz?"

"No. Neither is my code-of-ethics button. Maybe you can ask Santa to bring you one of those for Christmas."

"What if inside this very room is just what we need to save our Diviners exhibit? You think about that?"

Jericho pondered the point, then exhaled loudly. "Fine."

He pushed off from the wall and turned the doorknob roughly. The door opened easily. "It wasn't even locked. Just needed some strength," he said, stooping to get through the low doorway.

"I coulda done that," Sam said again, following.

Sam and Jericho's flashlight beams bounced around the dank, cramped, cold room, which had been stuffed with all sorts of oddities— oil paintings, broken furniture, a dressmaker's form, and even a sarcophagus, which hung open on a broken hinge. Two stacks of crates had been shoved into a corner against a large mural, aged and worn by moisture in spots. This mural wasn't hopeful like the other ones in the museum; it was a complex nightmare in paint. In a dark, denuded forest of the sort found in fairy tales stood a spindly gray carnival barker of a man wearing a tall hat and a coat of black feathers. His outstretched palm bore a glowing symbol: an eye with a jagged lightning bolt underneath. Behind the gray man lay a long line of frightening specters. They all seemed to be advancing on a young Negro man. The number *144* appeared in the broken sky above.

"What's it say there?" Jericho asked. Beneath the mural, someone had painted words. He stepped closer, squinting to make them out. "'Beware... the King of... Crows.'"

"Cheery," Sam joked, though the disturbing mural gave him the shivers. He thought it might just be the spookiest thing in the entire Creepy Crawly. "Let's see what we got," he said, turning away from it. He lifted a piece of grimy, rusted equipment from one of the crates. His shoulders sagged. "Junk. That's the one thing we're not short on in this place."

All the crates were nailed shut except for one, which had been partially broken. Jericho reached in and pulled out a sheaf of yellowed papers.

"Hey, what's that?" Sam came and stood beside Jericho.

"If I had to guess, I'd say probably none of your business," Jericho said, glancing down at the page.

"That's my favorite kind of business...."

"'The last will and testament of Cornelius Rathbone, recorded this day, the fourth of January, in the year of our Lord, one thousand, nine hundred and seventeen,'" Jericho read aloud. "'I, Cornelius Thaddeus Rathbone, being of sound mind and body, do hereby bequeath my house and all its worldly belongings to William John Fitzgerald, with the proviso that he must continue our most important work....'"

"Old Man Rathbone left this place to the professor?" Sam said, incredulous.

Jericho stared at the document. Years ago, he had asked Will how he'd come to run the museum. Will's story was that he'd bought the dilapidated museum just ahead of the city's wrecking ball. Cornelius Rathbone's last will and testament proved that wasn't true.

But why would Will lie to Jericho about it?

Quickly, Jericho moved on to the second page, a letter.

"What's that one say?" Sam asked.

"It's from Cornelius to Will, dated January thirty-first, 1917. 'Dear William...'" Jericho read aloud.

This letter shall be my last. I fear, for I wait on Death's doorstep, and soon, He shall bade me enter into that house of eternal rest. For these past many years, I could not forgive you the sin of your ambition for leaving me behind to work with the "great minds" of President Roosevelt's ridiculous Department of Paranormal—

"Wait, Teddy Roosevelt?" Sam asked.

"Yes, Sam. Theodore Roosevelt. Large man with a big mustache. Was our president for a bit. May I continue?"

"Go on," Sam grumbled.

It was I, however, who was ridiculous. It is imperative that we put aside our differences and work together in one last endeavor while there is still time. What I previously showed you of Liberty Anne's prophecies was not all. Toward the end of her days, there followed far more disturbing warnings, dire predictions for the nation. At the time, I feared that her fever, which raged so fiercely, had addled her wits. For this reason, I locked away her final prophecy. I see now that I was remiss to have hidden this unholy correspondence from you. I fear we have underestimated the power of the man in the stovepipe hat.

My time grows short. I implore you: Let us bury selfish quarrels before it is too late.

Ever hopeful,
Cornelius

"You know what this is, don't you?" Sam said, waving the letter in the air. "A gold mine! It's the hook we need to make our Diviners exhibit a hot ticket: 'Read the never-before-revealed prophecies of Liberty Anne Rathbone! Hear her dire predictions for the citizens of America before it's too late!' We just gotta hope Liberty Anne's prophecies are somewhere in these boxes."

"Only one way to find out. Let's bring it all upstairs and have a look through everything," Jericho answered, easily hoisting one of the crates onto his shoulder and ducking back through the doorway.

"Yeah. I was afraid you'd say that," Sam said, grunting as he shouldered the heavy load.

☀

"That's all of them," Jericho said as he carried in the last crate.

Sam fell onto the couch, gasping. "I may never use my arms again," he moaned.

"No doubt the girls of New York City sigh in relief," Jericho muttered, trying not to think about Sam's arms around Evie. "Let's see what we've got."

There were six crates in total, and every one had been nailed shut except for the damaged one containing Rathbone's will. Sam reached into it. "Books," he said with a sigh, pulling out musty tomes that released even more filth and dust into the air. "Always with the books." Next was a cache of letters from Will to somebody named Rotke Wasserman in Hopeful Harbor, New York. Sam sneaked one from its weary envelope.

"'My Darling Rotke...I miss you like the flower misses sun...'" Sam read aloud. He whistled long and loud. "Now we're getting somewhere."

"Have some decency, Sam," Jericho growled, snatching the letter away.

Sam put his hands up. "Okay, okay. Don't get hot. Who's this Rotke tomato?"

"She's not a tomato. Rotke was Will's fiancée. She died during the war," Jericho said, tucking the letter back into the crate. "This doesn't feel ethical."

"Ethics don't pay the taxman, Freddy. Listen, we'll just have a look. If we don't find Liberty Anne's unholy correspondence, we'll put the whole mess back in the cellar and forget about it, and nobody'll be the wiser. Deal?"

"Yes. Okay. Fine."

"We're gonna need a crowbar to loosen those others," Sam said, sneezing again. "Don't suppose there's one around here?"

"Somewhere," Jericho said, wiping his hands on his trousers. "I'll be right back. Don't steal anything."

"Who'd wanna steal this bunk?" Sam muttered, rummaging through the books. He opened one and saw Rotke's name scrawled on the inside cover. Pictures had been sandwiched between its pages: one of a younger, blonder Will holding a tennis racket; one of him posing with an old Negro woman above a handwritten note—*Will and Mama Thibault, Diviner, New Orleans, 1906*; a grainy photograph of some fancy estate. Sam flipped the page and came to a few yellowed newspaper clippings of the sort Will liked to collect: articles about small-town mediums or people who could bend spoons with their thoughts; an odd mention of an Indian village that burned to the ground, killing everyone, after a stove blew up.

A paper slipped to the floor and Sam bent to pick it up. It was an aged envelope, slit across the top and emptied of its contents. Rotke's name and a return address were on the back. He flipped over the envelope and stared, dumbfounded, at the addressee:

Miriam Lubovitch
122 Hester Street
New York, New York

"Sam?" Jericho was calling to him, but Sam could barely register it. "Did you get swallowed up?"

"Yeah. Big ghost came and got me. Forward all my mail to the spirit world," Sam said hollowly.

The letter was postmarked September 1914. Sam tore through the book's pages for the envelope's missing contents but found nothing. He took everything out of the crate, but the letter wasn't in there, either. Sam examined the envelope again. Across the front, someone had scrawled *Return to Sender*. He didn't recognize the handwriting. It wasn't his mother's. Who had written it? Whoever it was, Sam needed to find him.

It was time for Evie to make good on her end of their deal.

Jericho appeared on the second-floor landing. "Sam!"

"What?"

"I've been calling you. Did you find something?"

"Nah, just a bunch of dusty books," Sam lied, surreptitiously tucking the envelope into his trousers pocket.

"Well, unless they're haunted, they're not going to help with the exhibit. What's the matter? You look funny."

"Oh. It's, ah, it's just that I should probably go clean myself up," Sam said. His heart was pounding. "I hate to leave you like this, Freddy, but I got a date on the radio."

"Right. Guess you'd better go, then," Jericho said coolly.

"Listen, Freddy, I could come back a little later—"

"No need. I've got it. As usual," Jericho said, disappearing into the stacks. "And don't call me Freddy."

GHOSTS

Ling grimaced against the blustery wind as she made her way to the opera house carrying a knapsack with a basket of dumplings for Uncle Eddie. Steam rose from the slatted bamboo top, and she welcomed both the warmth and the delicious smell of fried pork.

The bustling streets of Chinatown were much quieter than usual—the fear of the sleeping sickness kept most people away. Business in the restaurants and shops was down. The hardworking men and women who came in droves for chop suey on their lunch hours were now heading to Automats and diners far from Doyers, Pell, Mott, and Mulberry Streets. Even the bane of the neighborhood—the white tour guides who brought in buses of "slumming" tourists to hear their lurid, deeply embellished tales of Chinatown's bloody Tong Wars, opium dens, and "slave girls"—were noticeably absent.

The health department had been out testing the water and food; dirt from the streets; dung from the horses, insects, and rodents—anything they thought might give clues as to where the sickness was coming from and how it was transmitted. Ling had even made a special trip to the library to read up on sleeping sicknesses, hoping to find something helpful. She now knew more than she'd wanted to know about parasites, tsetse flies, and encephalitis. None matched what was happening in Chinatown and on the Lower East Side. There were no presenting symptoms, no fevers, aches, or cough.

People simply went to sleep and did not wake up.

The mayor threatened to shut down Chinese New Year festivities, which were only three weeks away. The Chinese Benevolent Association had gone so far as to hire a reporter to take pictures of the "Chinatown Cleaning Crews": men in masks and gloves scrubbing down the sidewalks and kitchens, dropping off linens at the various laundries—anything to keep New Yorkers' fears from escalating into panic and keep the Year of the Rabbit celebration on course.

The tourists weren't the only ones who were worried. Neighbors who'd always been close suddenly became cautious around one another. Before classes at the Chinese school, the teachers made all the students wash their hands, and nurses checked their eyes, mouths, and skin for any hint of infection. The churches and temples were full. The old men and women went by daily to burn incense, make offerings, and ask for their ancestors' blessing. Charms against bad luck had been positioned near windows and doors to ward off evil spirits. A rumor went around—no one knew how it started—that one of the diggers who'd fallen victim to the sleeping sickness had mentioned something about their crew discovering bones in an old subway station, and that he was anxious about having disturbed them.

"Ghosts," the old men whispered in back rooms and over cups of tea.

"Ghosts." The women nodded in the greenmarkets or sitting on benches in Columbus Park.

But Ling's mind wasn't on ghosts or sickness just now. Last night, she'd witnessed an incredible transformation. *Think of something you want*, Wai-Mae had said, as if Ling's emotional state was the necessary force that made the shoes manifest. Was an energy field created by all the thoughts and desires floating through dreams, and, if so, was it more concentrated in that particular part of the dreamscape? Did a person's longing or fear or greed, when applied, bend and shape the universe of the dream somehow? And could you do more than transmute one object into another?

Could you will something into existence through your emotions? Should you?

At the opera house, Uncle Eddie sat on the edge of the stage, putting the finishing touches on a costume.

"That smells good," he called, seeing Ling. "Come. Share with me."

He took the knapsack off Ling's back, opened up the bamboo basket, and offered Ling a dumpling. She bit down, enjoying the squirt of spicy, soupy juice in her mouth as she looked over the traditional headdress for the Dao Ma Dan, the female warrior role. Elaborate beadwork took up the front, and long brown-and-white-striped pheasant feathers curved around each side like whisper-light horns, and Ling admired its beauty. Onstage sat a grouping of red chairs whose various placements, Ling knew, could indicate a seemingly endless variety of meanings, from a bed to a mountain to a mausoleum. Everything about the opera was steeped in symbolism and tradition. From outside in the street came the sound of girls singing jazz slang from a song that was popular on the radio—just some kids stealing a light moment among the dreariness.

"Ah. Modern youth," her uncle said. "They listen to jazz records and stay out half the night. No one cares about the opera anymore. Why aren't you out there with them, terrorizing the streets of Chinatown?"

Ling fingered another sticky dumpling from the basket. "I have more important things to do."

"Eating dumplings with an old man. Very important."

"I might have a new friend," Ling said, and she hoped it didn't sound quite as defensive as it felt. "A, um, a pen pal. She's coming over from China to be married."

Uncle Eddie raised an eyebrow. "That's very difficult."

"She says it's all been arranged," Ling said, putting the dumpling in her mouth.

"Well. It's good, then, that you can help her to become familiar. When I first came to this country, I knew nothing. And I didn't speak a word of English."

He opened his wallet and retrieved a worn photograph of himself as a young man of eighteen, his expression very serious, his long hair braided in the traditional queue.

"Have I ever shown you this picture?" he asked.

Out of respect, Ling shook her head, though her uncle had shown her his picture more than once.

"Well," Uncle Eddie continued, "that's me when I was just about your age. I only planned to be here for two years to make money for my family in China. But then they passed more and more laws. If I left the country, I couldn't come back again. So I stayed. With so few Chinese coming over, it was very hard to run the opera. I worked for my cousin at his restaurant for many years." Her uncle put the picture back in his wallet. "I never saw my mother and father again."

Ling's stomach tightened at the thought of losing her parents. Her mother and father might be overly protective, but they were hers, and she couldn't imagine being without them. Beside her uncle's picture was his resident permit, which all Chinese were required to carry. To be caught without it could mean prison time or deportation. Ling had been born right there in Chinatown. She was considered a citizen. But under the Chinese Exclusion Act, her father never would be. As for her Irish mother, the moment she married an "Asian alien," she'd given up her chance to become an American citizen. Ling lived with the worry that some small mistake could cost them everything, that she could be torn from them as her uncle had been from his own parents.

"She'll be interrogated when she arrives," her uncle said, reaching for another dumpling. "At Angel Island, I was asked nearly six hundred questions."

"Six . . . *hundred?*"

"Oh, yes. Day in, day out, they tried to break me: Who lives in the fourth house on your street in your village? Do you know how to work a clothing press? Are you a laborer? Do you smoke opium? And the medical examinations." He wiped his fingers and shook his head in disgust.

"Why all those questions, Uncle?"

"They hoped to prove that I was only a paper son, who bought his way in with false papers. They wanted to find a reason to keep me out. But…" Her uncle's smile was triumphant and a little rebellious. "Here I am."

Ling fished another dumpling from the basket and breathed in the musty, cozy smell of the old opera house. Most theater was performed at the Bowery Theatre these days, but for the New Year, they were using the old opera house on Doyers Street. Her uncle had been cleaning and pulling things up from the basement for weeks now. Flats of scenery from shadow-puppet shows were leaned up against racks of costumes and rows of masks. "What opera will you do for the New Year?"

"*The Royal Consort of the Emperor Finds Eternal Happiness in Paradise.*"

"I don't know that one."

"It hasn't been performed here in, oh, fifty years or so. It's a love story. And a ghost story, too."

"All your favorites," Ling said, smiling. In his day, Uncle Eddie had been one of the most celebrated Dan of his generation, nearly as good at playing the female roles as the world-famous Mei Lanfang.

"Yes, all my favorites. With luck, we'll see it performed. Luck and an end to this sickness. How is your friend George?"

"The same," Ling said, pushing away the dumplings. Earlier, she'd lit a candle for George at the Church of the Transfiguration, and offered prayers at the temple, too, covering all the bases.

"He's young," her uncle said. "The doctors will find what's causing this sickness very soon. And then they'll find a cure. I'm sure of it."

Ling nodded, grateful for her uncle's reassurance. "Uncle," Ling said, "could the sleeping sickness make it hard for my friend—my pen pal—to come to New York?"

"It could, indeed. I hope that she has friends or relatives in high places to help ease her way. Matchmakers, you say?"

"Yes. O'Bannion and Lee."

"I'm not familiar with that firm. If you're looking for a Lee, you can always ask at the Golden Pearl," Uncle Eddie said. Anyone with the surname Lee could have mail from China sent there for collection, Ling knew. It functioned as a family name–specific post office as well as a store. "Chang Lee would surely know. He's been here longer than I have." Uncle Eddie shook his head. "A girl has to be careful: Some of those matchmakers are not reputable. The girls come thinking they'll marry, and end up as servants instead. Or worse."

"Her uncle arranged everything," Ling said, but now she was worried. What if this O'Bannion and Lee wasn't a reputable firm after all?

"Well. I'm sure it's fine. What is not fine is the state of this opera house," Uncle Eddie said, gesturing to the messy theater. "The Year of the Rabbit will be here soon, and I'm hopeful there will still be a reason to celebrate. I'd best get to work. Thank you for the dumplings."

"You're welcome, Uncle," Ling said, gathering the basket and its top back into her knapsack and reaching for her crutches.

"Ling," her uncle called as she opened the door onto the blustery day once more. "Have the dead told you anything about this sickness?"

Immediately, Ling remembered Mrs. Lin's odd warning in her dream: *It isn't safe.* She'd thought the warning had been about Henry. But could it have been about the sickness, somehow? Had Mrs. Lin known what was causing it—a water source, or meat from diseased farm animals? That was the trouble with dreams; they could have all sorts of meanings.

"No, Uncle," Ling answered.

Uncle Eddie gave a decisive nod. "Well. I suppose if they had something to say, they would tell you first."

"I suppose so," Ling said, but she wasn't comforted by his words. What if the dead were waiting for Ling to act? She could at least try to find some answers on her walks.

On her way back to the restaurant, Ling stopped into the Golden Pearl on Mott Street, where she found Mr. Lee's grandson, Charlie, at the counter, stocking various teas and herbs in the small drawers of a large wooden cabinet.

"I'm sorry, Ling, but my grandfather is in Boston visiting my cousins. He'll be gone for two weeks," Charlie said. "Come back then."

Ling thanked him, then checked the Chinese newspaper for the shipping news. The *Lady Liberty* hadn't docked in San Francisco yet. There was still time to find out about O'Bannion and Lee and make sure that Wai-Mae was safe.

Instead of continuing straight back to the Tea House, Ling took a detour up Mott and down Mulberry, looking for any sign of O'Bannion and Lee. The streets were an odd mix of fear and optimism: Hopeful businessmen went ahead and hung decorations; paper lanterns and red banners with bold calligraphy stretched across Doyers Street from balcony to balcony. But she also saw white-capped nurses and somber-faced health officials marching briskly down sidewalks, knocking on doors. The yellow quarantine sign marred the facade of George Huang's building like a wound.

"Please get well soon, George," Ling whispered.

The door opened suddenly, and two public health nurses bustled out, their words muffled behind the barrier of their surgical masks. They went silent as they looked at Ling and her leg braces and then hurried on their way, picking up their conversation where they'd left off. Ling ducked inside, moving as fast as she could to the dark back of the tenement and George's apartment.

George's sister, Minnie, opened the door. "Ling," she whispered, peering behind Ling. "How did you get in?"

"The nurses just left. No one was watching."

"Come in," Minnie said, ushering Ling inside.

"How is George?"

"The same." Minnie lowered her eyes.

"Can I see him?"

Minnie showed Ling to George's room and Ling sucked in a breath. He was very pale except for the strange red burn marks creeping up his neck. Ling had never seen George so still. But no—he wasn't completely still after all. Beneath the thin skin of his lids, his eyes moved rapidly. George wasn't just sleeping; he was *dreaming.*

"Minnie," Ling said, buoyed by fresh hope, "could I borrow something of George's?"

Minnie's pained face brightened. "Do you think you could find George in dreams?"

"I can try," Ling said.

"They've burned most of his things, in case that's how the sickness spreads."

Ling hadn't thought about that, and it gave her pause. What if dream walking with an object belonging to the sick could make her sick as well? But this was George. She couldn't succumb to fear.

"Wait here." Minnie disappeared into the apartment and then returned a moment later, breathless and secretive.

"Here. I saved this," she whispered, lifting the edges of the handkerchief she carried. Inside was George's prized track medal. He'd been so happy when he'd won it, his parents so proud, and even the announcer telling him he "ran pretty well for a Chinaman" hadn't dimmed his pride completely.

Through the open door of George's room, Ling could hear George's mother weeping softly.

Ling tucked the track medal into her pocket.

"You should go. The doctor will be back soon," Minnie warned. "Please find him, Ling. Please find my brother and tell him to come back to us."

※

By the time Ling returned to the Tea House, her mother was frantic. "Where've you been?"

"My legs hurt. I couldn't walk very fast in the cold," Ling lied, taking some pleasure in the way the lie diffused her mother's anger so quickly.

"I was worried about you. Things are getting worse here," her mother said, looking out the restaurant's front windows at the police and public health officials moving through the dirty patches of snow, knocking on doors. "There's all sorts of people who've been requesting your services. They want you to speak to their dead relatives about this sleeping sickness business, to know what they should do. But I told them you're not doing a bit of that until we know more about how this sickness is spread. You're still getting your strength back."

"I'm fine, Mama," Ling said, George's track medal heavy in her pocket.

Mrs. Chan placed her hands at her hips. "I'm your mother. I'll decide if you're fit enough. Oh!" She broke into a smile. "I almost forgot. You just missed your friend from the science club. The freckled one. Henry."

"Henry was here?"

"Yes. He left you a note." Her mother searched under a stack of receipts. "Is he Irish? Looks Irish. Ah. Here it is."

Mrs. Chan handed over Henry's folded note, which Ling had no doubt her mother had already read. She hoped that he hadn't said anything too revealing. Taped to the letter was a ten-dollar bill.

Dear Miss Chan,

Greetings! I had great success in locating the Louis particle of which we spoke. In the interest of science, let us please repeat our experiment. If this suits you, I suggest that we perform the experiment this evening at precisely the same time and in the same manner as last evening. If you find this agreeable in the name of science, please ring me at the New Amsterdam Theatre, where I am attempting to steer those lost, immoral souls away from a life of sin. The money is a donation for the poor, naturally.

Sincerely,
Henry B. DuBois IV
Secretary and Chief Musical Director
Science Club

Nicely done, you idiot, Ling thought, smiling a bit.

"Who is this young man?" Ling's mother asked. Her expression wavered on the knife's edge between suspicion and hopeful expectation.

"An annoyance," Ling answered, cutting off further inquiry. "I've been tutoring him in his schoolwork. He's a little dumb. May I use the telephone to call him back?"

"Ling!" Mrs. Chan sighed and jerked her head toward the kitchen. "Go on, then, but be quick about it. There's work to be done. And remember: A bit of kindness goes a long way, my girl."

Ling made her way to the telephone in her father's office adjoining the steamy kitchen and put a finger in her ear to tune out the rattle of pans, the hiss of hot oil on the stove, and the rat-a-tat call-and-response of the cooks and waiters—the noisy, sometimes contentious comforts of home. A weary voice answered at the New Amsterdam and announced that Mr. DuBois wasn't yet in.

"I see. Could you deliver a message? Please tell him that Miss Chan has considered his proposal, and her answer is pos-i-tute-ly."

THE "IT" COUPLE

"There she is! It's the Sweetheart Seer! Evie—over here! Evie!" Fans clamored as Evie emerged from her chauffeured Chrysler, waving to them and blowing kisses. Reporters stood ready with their notepads. T. S. Woodhouse tipped his hat. His expression was trouble. Evie acknowledged him with a polite smile.

"There's Sam!" someone shouted as Sam came whistling up the sidewalk, shaking hands and waving genially to the crowd.

"Sam! Sam!" they called, and Evie had to fight to keep her smile fixed in place. Sharing the spotlight with Sam was irritating, but she could make it work for four weeks.

"Pork Chop!" Sam ran to Evie and kissed her hand. In the streets, people cheered.

"Oh, aren't they the dreamiest couple you ever saw?" a woman in the front row said.

"Pouring it on a little thick, aren't you?" Evie whispered in Sam's ear, never losing her smile for the public.

"Nothing succeeds like excess, Baby Vamp," he said, leaning in close. "Besides, when this circus is over in a few minutes, you're gonna do me a big favor."

"Now, wait a minute. I—" Evie's retort was cut short by an electric squawk as Mr. Phillips stepped up to the microphone and the speakers carried his voice out onto Fifth Avenue. "Ladies and gentlemen, WGI is delighted to present New York City's liveliest couple since Scott and

Zelda! Their love has taken the city by storm! And now you can hear Miss O'Neill on this very station two nights a week on the Pears Soap Hour! Without further ado, let me present to you: the Sweetheart Seer, Evie O'Neill, and her very own sweetheart, Sam Lloyd!"

"Hold it!" A cameraman's flash popped. "Thanks."

The reporters shouted for Sam and Evie's attention. But Evie knew who to turn to first.

"Mr. Woodhouse?"

"Why, thank you, Miss O'Neill," Woodhouse purred. "Or should I say the future Mrs. Sam Lloyd?"

Evie's eyes flashed. "Miss O'Neill is just fine for now."

T. S. Woodhouse's pencil hovered over his notepad. "I'm sure we're all dying to know how you two lovebirds first met."

"Well—" Evie started.

"It was a moonlit night," Sam interrupted. "A full moon, as I recall. Just the prettiest September moon you ever saw. I'd lost my dog—"

"Sparky."

"Right. I was calling, 'Here, boy, here, Sparky!'"

"It was the most heartbreaking sound you ever heard," Evie said. "I wanted to cry just hearing it. I still want to cry when I hear Sam's voice."

Sam raised an eyebrow at Evie's jibe. She smiled back. The smile was a challenge.

"Go on, darling," she said, batting her lashes. "Tell them the rest."

"Riiiight," Sam said, suppressing a smirk. "Well now. That was some night. Yes, sir, some night. You see, the glamour girl standing before you was not the dame I first laid eyes on in Penn Station. In fact, at first I thought she was the charwoman. Don't you remember how frightful you looked that night, Honey Pie?" Sam patted Evie's hand. Her strained smile pleased him. "She was sooty and grimy. Had on her mother's dress and those thick woolen stockings that grandmas and war orphans wear. And one of her teeth was missing. Ghastly. But I was smitten."

"Oh, Daddy, you might need a visit to the dentist soon yourself." Evie laughed and tightened her grip on Sam's hand. She hoped it hurt.

"Yes. It had been a long journey from Ohio. Not that Sam minded what I looked like. He was just so surprised to be talking to a real girl. Girls don't usually talk to you, do they, dear? Poor baby just never had a bit of luck with the female species. Why, it was almost as if dames were repulsed by you, weren't they, darling? Didn't you tell me they'd shrink from your touch?"

"But you could see the good deep in my heart, couldn't you, Pork Chop?"

"Yes. I had to look with a magnifying glass, but there it was."

"What does this have to do with a missing dog?" someone shouted.

"Well, despite being covered in filth and smelling like a Bowery ballroom, Pork Chop here offered to read Sparky's leash. Naturally, I assumed she was an escaped lunatic. You can understand, with her looking and smelling the way she did and claiming to have special powers. I figured any minute she'd introduce herself as Marie Antoinette and I'd have to call a cop."

"Hahaha—oh, you, you, you..." Evie pinched Sam's cheek. Hard. "Dear little tiny man. You're just five feet, three inches of pure joy. My own lucky leprechaun."

Sam glowered. "I'm five-foot-ten."

"Are you?" Evie said in astonishment. "Well, now, let's see. I'm five-foot-two...." She swooped a hand across her head to Sam's neck, putting Sam's claim to the test. The crowd roared.

"Five-foot-nine." Sam's smile was strained.

"Love these two. Put them on the radio together. They'd be funnier than Sam 'n' Henry," the reporter said.

"Now, now, only one of us is on the radio. Isn't that right, darling?" Evie said. She cut her eyes at Sam in warning.

"True," Sam said. "Only one of us has enough hot air for two nights a week."

The crowd laughed anew, delighted. Off to the side, Mr. Phillips stood with his arms folded, looking as pleased as if he'd invested in a Thoroughbred expected to win its race. The press took it all down, greasing the wheels of tomorrow's star machine.

"When's the wedding?" someone shouted from the crowd.

"Yeah, when is the big day?" Woodhouse asked, and Evie could swear by his tone that he was on to them. "I wanna make sure I have time to get my suit pressed."

"Um . . . June?" Evie hedged.

"You two lovebirds think you can wait that long?"

"Oh, I think I could wait forever," Evie sniped. "If it meant waiting for dear Sam."

"Mr. Phillips—you gonna broadcast that wedding over the radio?"

"You bet I will!" Mr. Phillips barked.

"Sam! Evie! How's about a picture for tomorrow's papers, huh?"

"Of course!" Evie moved slightly in front of Sam, making sure they could capture the full glory of her new dress.

The photographer waved her back. "Evie, honey, could you step back beside Sam? We want you two crazy kids together."

Sam waggled his eyebrows at her, that annoying smirk firmly in place. "Yes, future Mrs. Lloyd. I'm lonely without you beside me."

"Come on, you two. Show us some of that magic," the photographer shouted. At the crowd's urging, Sam wrapped his arm around Evie's shoulder and pulled her in close.

"Beauuuutiful! Give us a big smile—say 'Cheers.'"

"Cheers!" Sam said, showing his teeth.

"Four weeks," Evie said, gritting hers.

"That was ducky," Mr. Phillips said a few minutes later, pumping Sam's hand after he and Evie had posed for several more pictures with the WGI letters featured prominently above their heads. "Just ducky!"

"Wasn't it, though?" Sam agreed. Behind Mr. Phillips, Evie glared at Sam.

"Go home and rest up before your big date tonight," Mr. Phillips said on his way out. "You lovebirds will be out every night. Oh, and of course you'll be sure to mention WGI."

"Every chance I get," Sam promised.

"Evie, I like this young man of yours," Mr. Phillips said, his parting shot.

Evie gave her boss a bright smile, which faded as soon as he was gone. "'Every chance I get'?"

Sam shrugged. "People are like puppies. You just have to know how to scratch their tummies. Speaking of..."

Evie cut her eyes at him. "You're not getting near my tummy."

"Don't worry. My ticklers are put away. I need to speak to you. Privately."

"Follow me," Evie said with a heavy sigh.

Sam let out a whistle as Evie led him down the gilded halls of WGI. "This is some place."

"Don't get too sentimental about it. You have a limited engagement here." Evie smiled sweetly at the coat-check girl. "Mildred, darling, do you mind if we borrow the shop for a few minutes?"

"Of course not," Mildred said, slipping out through the half door. "Anything for you two lovebirds."

Evie hung the BACK IN FIVE MINUTES sign outside the door and shut both halves. She leaned against the rack of coats with her arms folded across her chest. "You have two minutes, Sam."

"I'll dispense with the charm, then."

"That was charm? Ha!"

"I've brought you a present, future Mrs. Lloyd."

"Future Mrs. Lloyd," Evie scoffed. "Gee, now I kinda hope you brought me cyanide."

"I hear that's the first-anniversary present. Here." He handed Evie the envelope. "Whaddaya make of this?"

She turned it upside down, confused. "It's empty, Sam."

"No kidding. Turn it over. That particular empty envelope is addressed to my mother. Sent by Will's dead lover."

Evie frowned. "Where did you find this?"

"Here's where it gets interesting. I found it in a dusty old crate pulled up from the cellar of your uncle's museum."

"On the level, Sam?"

"My right hand to God."

"Why would Unc—why would Will have this?"

"That was my question. I need your reading services, Sheba."

"Oh, Sam. Now?"

"A deal's a deal, Lamb Chop," Sam said pointedly.

Evie closed her eyes and pressed the envelope between her palms. The envelope was old and hadn't been touched by anyone other than Sam for some time. To dig into its secret past, she'd really need to work at it, and Evie didn't feel like having a throbbing headache for the next hour. "Sorry, Sam. Nothing's coming up."

"Try harder."

"I did try!"

"Don't give me that wad of chewing gum. You barely broke a sweat."

"There's something defective about your objects, Sam. It's just like when I tried to read the postcard in your jacket—" Evie clapped a hand over her mouth as she remembered a second too late that she had never told Sam about that.

"You what?" Sam's eyes narrowed. "First you take my jacket, then you read my postcard? Why, you little—"

"I was curious!"

"That was my private property, sister!"

"YOU STOLE MY TWENTY DOLLARS!" Evie yelled.

The coat-check girl's voice came from the other side of the closed door. "Everything copacetic in there?"

"Just ducky!" Sam shouted back. To Evie, he said, "So you couldn't get a read from my mother's postcard?"

"I just told you that, didn't I?"

The muscles at Sam's jaw tightened. "Look here: I'm gonna ignore the business with the postcard. But you owe me a good read on this one."

"Yes, but Sam—"

"We have a deal, Evie."

Evie narrowed her eyes. "I wouldn't marry you if you were the last man on earth."

"If I were the last man on earth it'd be because you drove the other poor suckers to early graves. *Read.*"

With a grunt at Sam, Evie closed her eyes, breathed deeply, and employed the tricks she'd learned on her radio show over the past two months when an object's history proved elusive. She pressed the flat of her palm against Rotke's handwriting, personal as a thumbprint, hoping it would provide an opening. But no matter how hard she tried, she couldn't get much there—just frustrating blips of memory that wouldn't stay. Undaunted, she concentrated on the scrawled *Return to Sender* message, rubbing her thumb back and forth as if she were reading Braille. A spark of the past flared promisingly, then began to burn down.

"Oh, no, you don't," Evie whispered, kneading harder with the pads of her fingers. The wobbly vision steadied on the front window of a kosher butcher shop hung with thick rations of marbled beef. The door opened and an unfamiliar woman came out. The vision seemed to want to stay with her.

"I've got something," Evie said, a little dreamily. "Does your mother have reddish hair?"

"No. Dark, like me."

Sweat beaded on Evie's forehead as she pressed deeper. The red-haired woman ambled down a crowded street bordered by pushcarts piled high with various wares. Several women draped in sashes reading VOTES FOR WOMEN stood on the sidewalk, and Evie could feel a hint of the red-haired woman's disapproval of the suffragettes, just as she could feel that the disapproval masked a deeper desire to join them. Evie stayed with the woman as she moved past two men unloading a steaming block of ice from the back of a truck with huge tongs.

"I-I can't get a place yet," Evie said, moving her thumb along the envelope. "O-R-C-H... Orchard Street!"

A man in a yarmulke and butcher's apron trundled after the woman, waving a sheath of letters. "There's a man. He's... he's calling to her. 'Anna!' he's saying. 'Anna, you forgot your mail.'"

"Anna..." Sam repeated, trying to place the name.

The red-haired woman stopped to leaf through her mail. Some of it was addressed to Mr. and Mrs. Itzhak Rosenthal.

"Mrs. Rosenthal?" Evie mumbled in her trance.

"I don't know a Mrs. Rosenthal," Sam said.

Evie kept at it. The red-haired woman leafed through the last two letters. One was addressed to someone named Anna Polotnik. The last letter was the one from Rotke to Miriam.

"Got it!" Evie came out of her trance. "Who is Anna... P-o-l-o-t-n-i-k?"

"Anna...Anna..." Sam snapped his fingers as it came to him. "Of course! Anna Polotnik!"

"Of course! Dear old Anna," Evie mocked.

"She was our neighbor when I was a kid," Sam explained. "Came over on the same ship with my parents. Nice lady. When she made borscht, the entire building smelled like cabbage for days. The borscht was good, too. Now I remember—she used to go around with a fella named Rosenthal, Itzhak Rosenthal. She musta married him. Did you see anything else—anything about my mother?"

"No. But Anna didn't look too happy about this letter, Sam. She seemed angry or worried." The aftereffects of going so deep caught up to Evie. Her knees buckled, and Sam helped her to Mildred's chair.

"You okay, Sheba?" Sam took out his handkerchief and blotted at her forehead.

"You'll take all my paint off," Evie said, angling her face away. The dreaded headache had started. "I don't understand why Will had this letter. He told you he didn't know your mother."

"Maybe he didn't," Sam said. "This was in a collection of Rotke's books. Maybe she was the one who knew my mother. I just hope Anna Polotnik can supply the answers. Once I find her." Sam tucked the envelope back into his pocket, along with the handkerchief. "One more thing—now that you've got two nights a week on the radio, it sure would be swell if you could talk up the Diviners exhibit."

"WGI and Pears soap don't pay me to shill for the Creepy Crawly, Sam."

"Just work it into the act: 'All ghosts swear by Pears! The cleanest ghosts in town will be attending the Diviners exhibit at the Museum of American Folklore, Superstition, and the Occult!'"

"Sam, how is it that you can take a perfectly ordinary day and turn it crossways?" Evie asked, rubbing her temples.

Sam grinned and spread his hands wide. "Everybody's got a talent, kid."

Mildred knocked again. "Miss O'Neill? Will you be much longer?"

"That's your cue to leave," Evie said, pushing Sam toward the door. "Don't forget about our date tonight—the party at the Pierre Hotel hosted by some rich Texan who made all his money in oil. He's swimming in it—money, not oil. It's good press."

Sam winked. "Well. As long as it's good press. See you tonight, doll."

"Lucky me," Evie said, and for a second Sam couldn't tell whether she was serious or not.

Sam turned up Fifty-seventh Street toward the Second Avenue El. As he walked, he examined the mysterious envelope again. It was his first big break in some time. Hopefully, Anna Polotnik would know something that would lead Sam to his mother. But first, he had to find Anna.

An open-air touring car draped in advertising bunting for Morton's Miracle Health Elixir advanced slowly. A man stood holding on to the windshield, calling out to people on the street over a bullhorn: "Protect yourself from exotic disease with Morton's Miracle Health Elixir—every bottle made with the goodness of real radium for radiant health! Do not allow your loved ones to fall to the Chinese Sleeping Sickness! Purchase Morton's Miracle Health Elixir today!"

Sam shook his head. Nothing made a man richer than exploiting another man's fears. For a second, Sam considered finding a mark and using his powers to lift the fella's wallet, but he decided against it. Right now, his luck was good. And if there was anything his superstitious mother had taught him, it was not to press your luck.

Feeling hopeful, Sam climbed the stairs to wait for the train.

He'd never noticed the brown sedan that had trailed him for several blocks.

SONS OF LIBERTY

The hush of the Bowery Mission was interrupted only slightly by the occasional whimper from bed number eighteen as Chauncey Miller dreamed of a war that never stopped. Bullets screamed overhead as two medics struggled to carry Chauncey's stretcher across a muddy, smoke-shrouded battlefield. A soldier with a choirboy face lay slumped against barbed wire, staring up at the unforgiving sky, his hands resting prayerlike on the guts spilling from the jagged hole in his stomach.

"Stay with me, old bo—" The medic's words died on his lips as a bullet found its home in his head, and he dropped like a storm-felled sapling. Around Chauncey, the *tat-tat-tat-tat-tat* of machine guns echoed through war-mangled trees while dying men keened for help, for forgiveness, for death.

"Help! Please help me," Chauncey cried out. He couldn't move. When he lifted his head, he could see the bloody, frayed ends of skin and bone where his legs had been. Every night, Chauncey prayed that he'd wake with both legs, back home in Poughkeepsie, and find that the past nine years of his life had been nothing but a terrible dream. Instead, he woke screaming, his face sweaty and his eyes wet with tears.

But not tonight. Just under the cacophonous symphony of gunfire and screaming, Chauncey heard something else—the sad, creaking tune of an old music box. Off to his right, the mission doors appeared between two barren trees. When they opened, the song drifted out from them, erasing the din of war.

Chauncey sat up and swung his legs over the edge of the bed. His legs! With a small cry, Chauncey rested his hands on his knees, then moved them down the sides of his calves, feeling skin and muscle and bone. He flexed his feet, rejoicing in that small victory of motion. He stepped through the doors and plodded down the darkened corridor of the mission, past the beds of lost souls traveling in their own dreams: pushing a plow on the family farm, making love to the girl left behind, diving into a sun-dappled swimming hole in summer. He looked back at his bed, where what was left of his broken body slept on. That was what waited for him when he woke, so he pushed further into his dream until he came to an old subway station.

It was quite beautiful here; an amber glow suffused the entire place, warming the fancy brass sconces and floral oilcloth wall covering, making the tracks gleam. But if Chauncey turned his head just so, the whole picture seemed unstable, as if this lovely, warm scene were trying to write itself across a dark, decaying canvas that peeked through in spots. Chauncey could swear that he heard sounds deep inside the vast dark of the tunnel—sharp clicking noises and thready, low growls made by some nightmare beast he could not name or imagine. But then, just as he had the impulse to turn back, a voice whispered sweetly to him in overlapping waves, *"Dream with me. . . ."*

"Yes," he answered. "All right."

"Promise."

"I promise."

He stepped into the tunnel and found himself outside Le Bon Reve in rural France. He and his mates had gone drinking there one September evening before they'd been lost to the trenches along the Western Front. The saloon's windows were alight. Chauncey put his face to the glass, but he couldn't see anything. Hearty laughter erupted on the other side of the saloon door. And then a chorus of drunken voices took up a song that had been popular during the war. Chauncey could still remember the words.

"Over there! Over there!" came a strong tenor. That was Clem Kutz

singing! He'd know that voice anywhere. Somehow, his old pal Clem was here.

Chauncey pushed through the door and went inside.

Seated around a long, rustic farmhouse table were all the friends Chauncey had lost during the war. Why, there was Teddy Roberts! Poor Teddy, whose mask had sprung a leak and he'd choked on mustard gas, dying with eyes bulged out, a hideous, unnatural grin stretching across his thin face. There was Bertie Skovron from Buffalo, who'd taken a bellyful of shrapnel and bled out, one hand still gripping the field telephone. Medic Roland Carey—funny old Rolly, who'd tell you a right filthy joke as he checked your gums for scurvy or poured stinging alcohol over a nasty cut. The same Rolly, cut down by influenza, was sitting right in front of him. And Joe Weinberger was there, too. Joe, who'd made it back home to Poughkeepsie after the war with a bad case of shell shock. He'd lasted eight months before he went into the barn on a fresh spring morning, threw a rope over a rafter, and hung himself. All of Chauncey's friends were here, alive and young and whole. Brothers. They had their whole lives ahead of them, and the dreams they'd nurtured before the war—to be husbands, fathers, businessmen, heroes worshipped by a grateful nation—were still untouched and waiting to be used.

Clem sang out, "*Johnny get your gun, get your gun, get your gun / Take it on the run, on the run, on the run. . . .*"

The other fellas joined in. "*Hear them calling you and me, every son of Liberty. . . .*"

"*Over there, over there . . . Hoist the flag and let her fly, Yankee Doodle, do or die,*" Chauncey said, though he'd gotten the verse and chorus mixed up. He sniffed back happy tears. "You're here. How are you here?"

His mates welcomed him with smiles. "*Dream with us.*"

Chauncey laughed. "All right, then. All right."

He took a seat at the table, which had been laid out with an enormous feast: boiled eggs and slabs of bread and butter on silver platters, a roast pig surrounded by shiny apples, beer, and cake. Those cold nights when they'd burrowed into trenches in France, their bellies rumbling with hunger and their heads itchy with lice, they'd talked incessantly of the food they'd eat when they returned.

"Who are we fighting this war for?" Teddy had asked once under a cold, starless sky as they passed a lone cigarette among the unit. "What are we doing here?"

"Defending democracy," Chauncey had answered.

Teddy had let the next question out with his smoke. "Whose democracy?"

That had been long ago. They'd died, horribly, all of them. All his friends. But somehow, they were here now, healthy and smiling, as if the war had been a dream and this was truth. Chauncey felt drunk on gratitude and profound relief. Even though just last week the doctors had told him there was something wrong with his liver, and he might want to get his affairs in order—as if he had any affairs to put in order! Well, they were wrong. His liver wasn't failing. He was being granted a second chance at life. Chauncey imagined getting married in the church where his parents had been married, raising a passel of rambunctious kids who liked to fish in the creek. And if anyone asked his future sons to fight a war, he'd tell them to go to hell.

Clem patted his arm and made a funny face. "Sick," he said. "Not much life. Bad dreams."

Chauncey smiled. "Clem, old boy, this is the best dream yet."

The food looked delicious, and even though the past few weeks his appetite had been flagging, Chauncey found that he was eager to eat.

"Bad dreams," Rolly said, and for just a moment, the dream wavered.

"Cheers, boys!" Chauncey said, willing the dream to continue. He spooned potatoes into his mouth and spat them out again just as quickly. The potatoes tasted bitter and dry, like eating a mouthful of sawdust. He looked more closely at the lump. It was moving. Maggots. They were maggots.

"My god," Chauncey said, gagging into his napkin. He wiped furiously at his mouth. "Say, wh-what sort of joke is this, fellas?"

His friends were unbothered. They had abandoned their utensils and scooped up handfuls of food, shoveling it in faster and faster, with desperate strokes, gorging themselves, too fast to chew and swallow. Bertie choked, vomiting up what he'd just eaten, then started in again.

"Slow down there, Bertie," Chauncey warned, but Bertie kept gorging.

Teddy smiled at Chauncey. There was something off about it. Like looking at a picture where another picture is trying to break through, and the image breaking through was of Teddy's mustard-gas rictus grin.

A thread of fear tightened around Chauncey's guts.

Clem cocked his head, listening. His fingers were slick with egg and saliva. "Still hungry," he said in a raw, croaking voice.

The others' heads snapped up. Food scraps hung from their wet mouths. Chauncey's heartbeat accelerated. Around him, the French saloon began to unravel, revealing the dark, cold brick of the tunnel.

"Hungry," they chanted, showing rows of pointed teeth in oily mouths. Soulless eyes stared out of cracked, pallid skin. Chauncey backed away. These were not his brothers. Not Clem or Rolly or Joe and definitely not sweet Teddy. What were these things?

"*Hungry for dreams with us hungry dream with us dream dream hungry dream . . .*" they choruses.

The tunnel crackled with pulses of light that reminded Chauncey of gunfire on the battlefield. There were more of them hiding there in the dark. Dear god. They squeezed out of holes and slithered down the brick, nails *click-click-click*ing in the gloom, beasts waking from slumber. Their hungry growls and screeches echoed in his head, turning his blood cold.

Wake up, he told himself. *Wake up, old boy. Wake now!*

Then, suddenly, there was a train! Chauncey threw himself against its doors. "Open up! Open up! For the love of god, please open!"

The doors hissed apart and Chauncey fell in and pushed the doors shut. Outside, the shining wraiths clawed at the window, mouths snapping. As the train sped away, their angry howls resounded in the tunnel. Chauncey put his hands over his ears. He just wanted to wake up now. Tomorrow, he'd talk to the mission director about a job. Maybe he'd even go home to Poughkeepsie, find a kindhearted girl. He'd give up the drink and then his liver would be all right again. Anything. Anything but this.

Slowly, he became aware that something was on the train with him. An eerie stillness descended. It was like the time during the war when he turned a blind corner in the trench only to come face-to-face with a German soldier. For a second, the two of them had stared, neither knowing what to do. And then Chauncey had pummeled the soldier with his fists, beating and beating until the soldier's head was as pulpy as a dropped melon. Afterward, he'd gone through the boy's pockets with shaking fingers. All he'd found was a picture of the boy with his mother and a sweet-faced dog.

Swallowing down his fear, Chauncey turned his head in the direction of the figure. It wasn't a German soldier or one of those wretched spirits riding with him, but a woman. She wore a high-necked gown of the sort worn once upon a time. A veil covered her face.

"P-please. Please help me," Chauncey said. He barely recognized the voice as his own.

"This world will break your heart. Stay with me, inside the dream."

The woman rose from her seat, and he saw the bloodstains blossoming across the front of her gown. Her mummified hands clasped his face. Her nails were sharp. Through the veil's fine netting, Chauncey could see the woman's dark eyes, set in a leathery face. A skeletal mouth showed double rows of pointed teeth.

"Such a pretty dream we are building. We must all keep it going. There's not much life in you. Still. It will do. We must keep building. The dream needs you."

Chauncey's cry thinned to a quavering whisper. "Please. Please just let me wake up."

"You promised. To break a promise is dishonorable."

"I didn't understand."

"Then I will make you see the world in all its horror."

The train fell away. The battlefield returned—soldiers blown apart, blood-drenched mud flying up, the sky crying tears of terrible light. But this time, Chauncey lay on a table in the middle of it all, his arms and legs gone. And around him, there were men riding into the night with burning crosses. And there were bedazzled people bathing in tubs of Wall Street money while other people dug in the frost-hard ground for sustenance. And there were slaves sold on auction blocks and starving tribes marched away from their homes and witches pressed under the weight of stones. And there was a gray-faced man in a feathered coat and a tall hat who laughed and laughed.

"*Hungry!*" Chauncey's soldier friends dug into his belly with forks as he screamed.

"Enough!" he cried.

The nightmare vanished. Chauncey was back in the train station. The too-bright things waited in the tunnel, watching.

"*This land is so full of dreams. I feel all your longing. So much longing. Dream with me . . .*" the woman said.

"Y-yes," Chauncey managed to say.

She lifted her veil, and her beauty was a terror to behold, a vengeful angel. Her sharp mouth hovered above his face. A glint of metal shimmied through the air. Pain speared Chauncey's chest. Then she put her lips to his, and her dream poured into him, pushing through Chauncey's veins, making his body twitch, robbing his mind of the will to fight. She breathed her dream into his lungs until their dream was the same and it was all he could see, all he would ever see, forever.

"*Not enough,*" the veiled woman said as the station glowed. "*More.*"

⁕

Clipboard in hand, the mission nurse made her nightly rounds. When she came to Chauncey Miller's bed, she drew closer. His sweat-drenched face wore the oddest expression, something between pain and ecstasy, and his eyes moved frantically beneath his closed lids. It made her uneasy to look at him.

"Mr. Miller? Mr. Miller!"

She couldn't wake him. That was when she saw the angry red patches bubbling up on his skin like radiation burns. In the bed beside Chauncey's, an old wino named Joe Wilson moaned. His forehead was slick with sweat and his eyelids twitched with fevered dreaming.

"Mr. Wilson?"

"Dream...with...me..." he gasped.

"Mr. Wilson!" The nurse nudged him, then tugged on his arms, to no avail.

The room filled with whispers uttered in sleep, "Dream with me... dream with me...dream..."

The frantic nurse moved quickly from bedside to bedside. Of the twenty men on the ward, twelve of them would not wake. Her clipboard clattered to the floor as she ran to inform the doctor that they'd better call the health inspector straightaway.

The sleeping sickness had come to the mission.

DAY NINE

A NEW AMERICA

Damp wind gusted against Mabel as she hurried along Central Park West ahead of the rain. She kept one hand on her hat and the other on her nervous stomach as she practiced what she'd say when she knocked at the museum.

"Good afternoon, Jericho! I was just passing by."

"Oh, Jericho, are you hungry? There's a swell diner down on Broadway."

"Jericho! Fancy meeting you here. At the museum. Where you work. Every. Day."

Mabel growled. She was lousy at this sort of coy game-playing. If only she could say what she really wanted to say, flat out.

"Kiss me, you fool!" Mabel exclaimed, lifting her arms skyward. A passing postman tipped his hat and gave her a hopeful smile, and a horrified Mabel shoved her hands deep into her coat and marched up the sidewalk, muttering to herself the whole way.

As Mabel approached the museum, she slowed, noticing the two men in the brown sedan. A life on the front lines of the labor movement had trained Mabel to keep alert for oddities, and something about these men seemed off. They were just sitting, watching the museum. Well, they weren't the only ones who knew how to watch. Mabel stopped beside the driver's-side window and tapped gently on the glass.

The driver rolled down the window, scowling just slightly before correcting his expression with a smile. "Yes, Miss?"

Mabel smiled. "I beg your pardon. Could you tell me the time, please?" She made sure to get a good look at the two of them, as her parents had taught her: Gray suits. Dark hats. Curious matching lapel pins—an eye with a lightning bolt.

"It's just past one, Miss."

"Thank you very much," Mabel said and crossed the street, letting herself into the museum. "Steady, Mabel," she whispered before pasting on a smile and blowing into the museum's grand library with a cheery, "Hello! Anybody home? Jericho?" She dropped her coat and hat on the outstretched paw of the giant stuffed bear.

Jericho's blond head poked up from behind the stacks of dusty boxes cluttering the top of the long library table. "Mabel. What brings you here?"

Mabel's throat felt tight. On the front lines, she had faced hostile union-breakers, men with guns. Why was talking to this one boy so terrifying? "I was just hungry and passing by. Oh! Not that I thought you'd have food here," she said, wincing at her bungle. Quickly, she gestured to the table. "Gee, it's like something vomited paper in here."

Jericho raised an eyebrow. "That's certainly descriptive."

Strike two. "Sorry," Mabel said. "What is all of this?"

"Will's notes from his paranormal-researcher days. We found them in the cellar. I've been going through them for the past hour. Did you know there's mention of Diviners since the dawn of this country?"

Jericho paused, and Mabel wanted to respond with something clever. But being this close to Jericho made her antsy. "Huh-uh."

"John Smith writes about a Powhatan brave—a healer and mystic—who visited Jamestown. A Diviner servant in George Washington's household had a vision that helped Washington narrowly avoid capture by the British. And there's evidence that a few of the witches at Salem were actually Diviners. But this is when it gets really interesting."

Jericho jumped up from the table. From behind a bookcase, he rolled out a large chalkboard. Mabel could just make out the faint remaining chalk lines of Evie's notes from the Pentacle Murders investigation. Quickly, Jericho swiped the eraser across the surface, eradicating the last traces of her presence from the museum. He wrote the date *September 1901* on the chalkboard.

"All right. I'll bite," Mabel prompted. "What happens in September 1901?"

"The assassination of President McKinley?" Jericho chalked *McKinley* beside *1901*.

Mabel blushed. "Oh. Oh, of course."

"It seems that in August 1901, a Diviner, a former slave named Moses Freedman, tried to warn the president about a possible attempt on his life. But no one believed him. In fact, he was taken into custody under suspicion of being an anarchist agitator, and was questioned for months following McKinley's assassination. They held him for nearly a year without charging him."

"But that's illegal!" Mabel protested. "What about habeas corpus?"

"Suspended, under the constitutional provision stating that a person can be held without charge if the public safety might require it."

"That's a slippery slope toward fascism," Mabel grumbled.

"I'm sure Moses Freedman would have agreed with you."

"What happened to him?"

"In early July 1902," Jericho said, adding that date to the board, "he has a vision about a possible mine explosion in Johnstown, Pennsylvania—another warning that goes unheeded—"

"The Rolling Mill Mine Disaster. It was one of the worst mining disasters in American history. It killed more than one hundred men," Mabel blurted.

Jericho raised an eyebrow. "Impressive."

Mabel shrugged away the compliment. "If your parents were union organizers, you'd know these things, too. Some girls are raised on fairy tales; I was raised on mining disasters."

"You had a very interesting childhood." Jericho gave a little half smile, and Mabel felt it deep down.

"So," she said, clearing her throat. "Rolling Mill?"

"Right. Rolling Mill. After that, President Roosevelt sits down with Moses Freedman and determines that he's telling the truth. And that gives him an idea. In 1904"—again, Jericho scribbled with his chalk—"the president creates the U.S. Department of Paranormal to explore the fantastical world. He wants to find and use Diviners to work in the interest of national security. After all, if you've got someone whose supernatural abilities can help them see disaster or danger coming, why not use them?"

"So where does Dr. Fitzgerald fit into all of this?"

Jericho wiped his hands against his trousers, leaving chalk-dust finger streaks. "He was recruited for the U.S. Department of Paranormal. He traveled the country seeking out Diviners, testing them, hearing their stories, and registering them for the government."

Mabel whistled. "You're right. That really would perk up the Diviners exhibit. But won't Dr. Fitzgerald be angry that we're using his private letters and research from that time?"

"Then he shouldn't have left it to us to save his museum," Jericho said bitterly. "We'll only use the letters about Diviners."

"How long did you say you have to put this exhibit together?"

"Ten days."

Mabel shook her head. "That won't be easy." It seemed impossible, in fact. Unless... "Would you like some help?"

Jericho's eyes widened. "Are you volunteering?"

"Reporting for duty."

He gave her another half smile. "That would be swell. Thanks."

"Well, then," Mabel said, feeling on solid ground for the first time. "Let's get to work."

Mabel riffled through one of the files, pulling out a photograph of five people posed in front of an overgrown crepe myrtle. "Is that... Dr. Fitzgerald?"

Jericho nodded.

"He looks so young. Oh, not that he's old now! He just looks... not quite so worried as he usually does."

A handsome, dark-haired man with a bold smile stood beside Will, one arm thrown across Will's shoulder as if they were brothers.

Mabel gasped. "Is that who I think it is?"

"Jake Marlowe. He and Will were friends. Once," Jericho said.

Mabel felt it would be impolite to press Jericho on that point, so she left it alone. Jericho hoisted a strange, dusty contraption from a crate. It was a small wooden box, roughly the size of a cracker tin. A hand crank stuck out from its right side, and in its center was a long glass tube with a pencil-thin, two-pronged filament inside. Just below the filament was a numbered meter that counted in tens from zero to eighty.

Jericho dropped the odd device onto the table. He and Mabel cocked their heads in unison. Mabel tried the rusty crank. It squeaked its displeasure. "I give up. What on earth is that?"

"Not sure yet. I'm hoping one of these letters will give us some clue. Here. You take this crate and I'll take that one. Put aside anything that has to do with Diviners."

For the better part of an hour, Jericho and Mabel sorted through and made stacks of what seemed promising. Plenty of it was just junk— books gone to pulp, water-damaged photographs, a shopping list or postcard with a banal inscription: *The flowers are in bloom. Lovely.* Jericho turned his attention toward a small cache of letters nestled deep inside his crate. Every single one was addressed to Cornelius from Will. There were none from Cornelius back to Will. Jericho pulled the first letter from its envelope.

Hopeful Harbor, New York
February 11, 1906

Dear Cornelius,

Jake is most intrigued by the discovery that these Diviners seem to emit much greater radiation than the average person, similar to the ghost readings we've gotten, and that Diviners have the capacity to disrupt electromagnetic fields. He speculates that these properties could be applied toward any number of advances, from medicine to industry to our nation's defense. Dear Cornelius, believe me when I tell you that these discoveries are as exciting to our merry band of explorers as the sighting of this verdant land must have been to the earliest travelers to these shores. We stand on the precipice of a new world, a new America, and I am certain that Diviners are the key to her extraordinary future.

Fondly,
Will

At the bottom of the page, Will had drawn a sketch of an eye-and-lightning-bolt symbol.

"Hey! I think I may have found the name of our mysterious machine!" Mabel said, waving a piece of aged paper. "It's called the Metaphysickometer."

"That's a mouthful," Jericho said, coming to stand beside Mabel and read over her shoulder.

"Yes. Um. It is. Uh...anyway. Will refers to it in this letter," Mabel said.

New Orleans, Louisiana
February 23, 1906

Dear Cornelius,

This evening, I attended a ritual led by Mama Thibault, sixty-two years of age, born in Haiti, now resident priestess of a voudon shop on Domaine Street. Locals come to her for help with any number of complaints, from physical ailments to spells for true love or the lifting of imagined curses. A hospitable woman with twelve grandchildren to her name, all of whom dote upon her, Mama Thibault said she'd been able to speak to the dead since the age of twelve. "The dead do not frighten me. Takes the living to do that," she claimed. After consulting with the lwas, and extracting a fee of five cents for her services, she allowed us to test Jake's Metaphysickometer during her ritual. As she slipped into her spiritual trance, the needle jumped to forty, then fifty, indicating the increased electromagnetic activity we've come to associate with the presence of ghosts. Interestingly, Mama Thibault herself seemed also to vibrate at a slightly higher frequency, interfering with the operating of much of our machinery. Jake was baffled but intrigued by this finding. Margaret and Rotke have gathered samples.

I hope you are well. Spring shall come soon enough.

Fondly,
Will

Mabel patted the strange box of wires and gears and needles. "Well, hello there, Metaphysickometer! Pleased to meet you. Gee, an early Jake Marlowe invention! Might be valuable. I wonder why he never touts this one like he does everything else?"

"He doesn't like to talk about his failures," Jericho said, stepping over to examine the machine.

Mabel's brows came together in a V. "You don't like him much, do you?"

"I admire what he's accomplished. I respect his achievements. But he's not a man who thinks about the cost of those achievements." Jericho paused. "Or so I've heard."

"Sure would be great if we could include a demonstration of this beauty in the exhibit. I wonder how you make it work."

"Will's letter said it measures some sort of ghostly electromagnetic radiation. So I suppose if there are no Diviners and no ghosts, you get a quiet machine."

"Suppose. Of course, it's been living in the cellar all these years. It might not work at all," Mabel said, thumping the glass. The needle didn't budge. "Oh! I found some photographs, too. Here. This one is of Mama Thibault. Let's put her picture with her letter. Perhaps we can find other pictures and pair them all up. Did you find anything useful?"

"Um...here. This one was promising," Jericho said, grabbing a letter from a stack he'd put aside.

St. Eloysius, Louisiana
June 21, 1906

Dear Cornelius,

I do not know whether or not the fires of hell actually exist, but I can tell you that, if so, the cotton fields of Louisiana on a hot summer's day are good practice for those torments.

"Ha!" Mabel said. "The professor has a sense of humor. Or he did once. Sorry. Go on."

Today we met with a young sharecropper, Guillaume "Big Bill" Johnson, who has the extraordinary ability to hasten a peaceful death for ailing animals. While we watched, he entwined his fingers in the mane of a horse with a broken leg. "Shhh, now. Don't fuss, Clara. Be over soon," he murmured sweetly. The horse trembled mightily for a count of three, and then she slipped into death as if going to sleep. The effort took the wind out of young Guillaume, too. Though barely nineteen, he stands well over six feet and possesses an intimidating strength but a gentle nature. He seemed rather enamored of Margaret and consented to a sample.

I do hope New York's stifling heat hasn't inconvenienced you much.

Fondly,
Will

"Guillaume Johnson...Hmm. No picture of Mr. Johnson, I'm afraid. I'll keep looking. What are these samples he keeps referring to?" Mabel asked, leaning back in her chair by the fire. "It's mentioned in quite a few of Dr. Fitzgerald's letters."

"I noticed that, too," Jericho said, sitting across from her. "Hopefully one of the other letters will make it clear."

Mabel glanced at Jericho shyly. It made him nervous, like he was supposed to do something, but he had no idea what that was.

"Right. Back to it. I'll be upstairs if you need me," he said, carrying his crate up the spiral staircase to the second-floor balcony. From behind the stacks, Jericho watched Mabel at work. Her blue dress was smudged with dust, but she hadn't made a fuss about it. Of course she wouldn't. Mabel Rebecca Rose was too solid for that. Her only crime was being sweet on him. Why couldn't he return her affections in the same way? She was certainly smart and clever. How many girls knew about mining disasters and labor strikes?

The bedeviling thing about Mabel was that she always seemed to do what other people expected of her. She was the very definition of a perfectly decent girl—earnest and helpful, with an unshakable faith in her constructed belief that people were, at heart, good. Jericho wasn't sure he shared that sentiment.

Since the night Evie had ended their brief romance, Jericho had resented Mabel. If not for Mabel, he'd told himself, he and Evie might've had a chance. But now he wondered: Had Mabel just been a convenient excuse? Had it been Sam all along?

Mabel caught him looking. She patted her hair self-consciously. "Did you need something?"

"No," Jericho said, and quickly turned back to Will's letters, coming to one that intrigued him.

October 1, 1907
Hopeful Harbor, New York

Dear Cornelius,

It has been quite a time here. Earlier this week, members of the Founders Club, a private eugenics society, visited as invited guests of Jake's. They were quite interested in our findings about Diviners, and over dinner, there was much spirited debate. The gentlemen of the Founders Club argue that we can create the strongest, most exceptional America through the careful selection of superior traits, as one would with livestock. They believe Diviners are this superior stock. But only white Diviners. No Negroes, Italians, Sioux, Irish, Chinese, or Jews need apply. They argue that these people lack the correct moral, physical, mental, and intellectual properties to advance our nation and make her the shining city on the hill.

I have never seen Margaret so angry before: "We are a democracy, sir, and Diviners are evidence of that democracy and of the proof that all men and women are created equal. For these gifts have been given in equal measure to people of all races and creeds, regardless of sex, whether rich or poor."

The great debate escalated far beyond the polite decorum of a dinner table, and we adjourned before dessert so that a cordial spirit could be maintained. In the privacy of our offices, Rotke made her position quite clear—"I won't be part of it. Not as a scientist. Not as a Jew. Not as an American."

I agreed that their position was nonsense. Margaret was much more frank in her rebuke. I shan't repeat her words here. We were resolute: We would thank the Founders Club for their time and interest and send them on their way. Through it all, Jake remained quiet. At last, he rose from his seat and crossed the floor. Even in this simple action, he demanded our attention.

"Don't you see? We can take their money without telling them what we're really doing. We'll continue to conduct our own research on Diviners. Here and there, we'll trot out a little something to keep the old men happy in their eugenics quest, parade a Diviner or two before them. Simple."

"You're wrong, Jake. They'll come to own us in time," Margaret insisted. "Mark my words."

Jake shook his head and let out a peeved sigh, which did not settle well with Margaret, I can assure you. "Margaret, you're too suspicious," he insisted. "You don't trust anyone."

"If your people came to this country in chains, Mr. Marlowe, you might have the same mistrust," Margaret responded evenly, but her eyes—hard, alight—told the true story of her emotions.

Next, Jake appealed to me, man-to-man. He threw an arm around my shoulders like a brother and squeezed. "William, surely you're on board?"

"Well . . ." I began but said no more. It was cowardly, but my feelings on the matter are quite confusing. I don't care for the Founders Club and their sham science of eugenics. But I don't want to stop our research into those mysteries that lie beyond this world, either. It has become my whole world.

At last, Jake made his way to Rotke and put his hands on her shoulders. "Darling, we need their funding. What we receive from Washington isn't enough, and I've used nearly all of my trust."

"Even if you can see that money comes from a terrible place?" Rotke challenged.

"Just don't look in that direction."

Then Jake took Rotke's face in his hands, the hands that will shape this new America through steel and the atom and whatever we uncover of the supernatural world.

"Trust me," he said as he bent her face toward him so that he could kiss her gently on the forehead.

I heeded Jake's advice and did not look in their direction anymore.

"I'll smooth things over with the old coots. Stay and enjoy the fire," Jake assured us. And with that, our brave son, our golden boy, sailed off with a bottle of his family's best brandy and a fistful of cigars to secure our future. But I fear the damage is done with Margaret. She and Jake will never be friends after this.

As for Rotke, she and Jake are to be engaged, I hear. A better man would be happy for them. After all, Jake has been my closest friend for six years. But I am not a better man, and I am not happy.

This afternoon, Rotke came to me. I could see by her eyes that she had been crying. She asked me to walk with her for a spell. We strolled the woods beyond the manicured hedges of Hopeful Harbor. I begged Rotke to tell me what was troubling her. "It's Jake," she said, wiping away tears. "We quarreled. He doesn't want me to tell anyone I'm Jewish. Not his family, certainly not those eugenics idiots. 'Darling, no one even knows you're Jewish,' he told me. 'They don't have to know. You don't look it.'"

I asked Rotke the question in my heart then. "Does being Jewish matter so much if you don't believe in God?" For as you know, Cornelius, I've never understood this obsession with where we are from that we Americans seem to have. We are from here, are we not? Sometimes I find this clannishness, these ties to old homelands, ancient traditions, and familial bloodlines, to be nothing more than fear—the same fear that keeps us praying to an absent God. If anything, I hope that our research into the great unknown of Diviners and the supernatural world proves that we are all one, joined by the same spark of energy that owes nothing to countries or religion, good and evil, or any other man-made divisions. We create our history as we go.

Rotke sees it differently. "It matters to me, William. It is a part of all that I am. A reminder of my parents and my grandparents. I can't dismiss them and their struggles so easily. If I marry Jake, I'm afraid I shall be erased."

She began to cry again, softly. I didn't know what to do. I am not adept with crying women, especially crying women whom I secretly love. Before I knew it, I was kissing her. Yes, I kissed my closest friend's fiancée. It was not the gentlemanly thing to do, Cornelius. I know you do not approve. I wish that I could say I regret it. I do not.

Rotke broke away from me, pink-cheeked from more than just the cold. Naturally, I apologized profusely until she had recovered enough to say, simply, "I believe we should go back now."

You warned that my passions would get the better of me, Cornelius.

Jake greeted us upon our return. He was in grand spirits, practically boyish. "We have our money," he said, waltzing Rotke around.

I looked away. Once you've learned how, it gets easier to do.

Jake clapped me on the back. "This is the start of everything. And you needn't worry: I'll handle all the affairs. You won't have to engage with the Founders Club at all. I've ordered champagne to be sent up to the drawing room. See if you can find Margaret, and meet me there."

Jake wants money for his experiments and inventions in his quest to build an exceptional, unassailable America. Margaret, the victim of this country's less shining side, wants to prove that all men and women are created equal. Rotke wants to understand the realm beyond this one as well as her own gifts. As for me, my ambitions are great but without form. I don't know what I want, save for the one woman I cannot have.

This is far too immodest a letter, Cornelius. The champagne was a fine vintage, and I am quite drunk. It doesn't matter a whit. You won't respond to this letter, as you've not responded to any of my entreaties. Likely, you won't even read this.

I hear from Lucretia, whom Margaret saw in the market when she visited the city last week, that you've had a troubling cough. I do hope your health improves.

Fondly,
Your prodigal son,
Will

Dumbfounded, Jericho put the letter down. Why had they never talked about any of this? After Jericho's illness crippled him and his parents had abandoned him to the state, it was Will who'd stepped in as guardian. He had sheltered Jericho, fed and clothed him, and taught his ward what he could about running the museum and about Diviners. For that, Jericho supposed he owed him a debt. But Will hadn't given Jericho the parts that mattered most. He hadn't given himself. The two of them had never gone fishing in a cold stream early on a summer's day and shared their thoughts on love and life while they watched the sun draw the curling morning mist from the water. They'd never discussed how to find one's place in the world, never talked of fathers and sons, or what makes someone a man. No. He and Will spoke in newspaper articles about ghosts. They conversed through the careful curation of supernatural knickknacks. And Jericho couldn't help but feel cheated at how little he'd gotten when he'd needed so much more.

Why was there so much silence between men?

"Jericho?" Mabel called, bringing Jericho back to the present. "Sorry, but I have to head home now."

"I'll be right down," Jericho said, pushing the letters to the side. As he did, an odd scrap of paper fluttered to the floor. It was a very brief note in Will's handwriting. There was no date. It read, simply:

Dear Cornelius,

You were right. I was wrong. I am so very sorry.

Sincerely,
Will

"Thanks for your help today," Jericho said, easing Mabel into her coat. "It was a nice change. I'm used to working with Sam. Or rather, working around Sam."

Mabel shifted from one foot to the other and back again. "I could come back and help you some more. If you want me to," she said, agreeable to the end. The way she looked at him just then, with a mixture of curiosity, affection, and admiration, was rather nice. Maybe it would be nice to be adored for once.

"That's okay. I can manage," Jericho said after a pause.

"Oh. Sure," Mabel said, trying to hide her disappointment. "I suppose you've heard the news about Evie and Sam," Mabel said as they walked the long hallway. "I had no idea she and Sam were engaged. She never said a word. Did Sam say anything to you?"

"No," Jericho growled.

Mabel knew she shouldn't have brought up the topic of Evie. But now that she had, it was like a scab she couldn't stop picking. "Well. I suppose we should be happy for them."

"Why?" Jericho asked.

"Because..." Mabel let the rest of the sentence die on the vine.

Outside, the street lamps winked on, trying to do battle against the gentle gray of the late afternoon. A few snowflakes swirled in the blustery air. Mabel shivered as she stood uncertainly on the top step, wondering what she could say to prolong the moment. A Model T shuddered down the street, and Mabel remembered her earlier strange encounter.

"Oh! I nearly forgot to tell you. I noticed something odd on my way in today. There were these two men in a brown car just sitting, watching the museum."

Jericho craned his neck, looking up and down the street. He shrugged. "I don't see anybody now." He crossed his arms, pensive. "I suppose they could be taxmen."

Mabel shook her head. "Those fellows don't sit quietly in cars. They come right up to your door and turn out your pockets. These men reminded me more of Pinkertons, or Bureau of Investigation." Mabel shoved her hands back into her coat pockets. "Well, see you at the Bennington."

"Yeah. See you at the Bennington," Jericho said, watching Mabel walking away in her deliberate fashion.

Why was he still pining for a girl he couldn't have? Evie certainly wasn't sitting around sighing over him. Apparently, she was out every night with Sam, having the time of her life. It was high time he did the same. If he'd learned one thing reading through Will's letters today, it was that there was a whole world out there waiting to be explored, and Jericho was tired of caution.

"Mabel!" Jericho bounded down the steps after her. "Would you like to go to dinner or to the pictures sometime?"

Mabel's face quicksilvered from shock to barely suppressed giddiness. "I'd love to. When?"

"Oh. Um. How's tomorrow?"

Mabel grinned. "Tomorrow's perfect."

"I'll come for you at eight o'clock, if that's agreeable."

"Very, very agreeable."

Back in the quiet of the library, Jericho congratulated himself. "I have a date," he said to the empty room. A date. That was good, wasn't it? It was progress. He gave the Metaphysickometer a gentle thump and set about tidying up the papers nearby.

Under the glass, the needle gave a tiny jump.

DREAMS CAN'T GET YOU

Freshly shaved and smelling of soap, Memphis stood in front of the small mirror over the chest of drawers in the room he shared with Isaiah, buttoning his starched collar onto his crisp white shirt while Isaiah sat in his bed, drawing.

"Memphis, what does 'P-NEU-MA-TIC' mean?" Isaiah asked.

Memphis thought for a second. "You mean *pneumatic?*"

"'At's what I said."

"You don't pronounce the P."

"Still don't know what it means," Isaiah grumbled.

"Here." Memphis handed him the dictionary that had been a present from his parents on his tenth birthday and sat on the bed to lace up his best oxfords. "Look it up."

Isaiah made a face. "Why can't you just tell me? You got all those words in your head already."

"That's right. And you know how they got there? I looked 'em up. Where'd you hear that word? School?"

"Saw it in a dream. Where you going?" Isaiah asked. He sounded like Octavia. Like accusation.

"That's my business."

"You going off with that Theta," Isaiah groused. "Don't like her."

"You don't even know her."

"Why you wanna go with some girl, anyhow?"

"Because someday, I aim to get married and have my own house. With my own wife. No bumpy-headed brothers running around."

Memphis expected Isaiah to protest the *bumpy-head* comment with a righteous "Hey!" He didn't expect to hear sniffling, or to turn and see tears trickling down his brother's face, over trembling lips.

"Ice Man? What's the matter?"

Isaiah wrapped his arms around his knees and drew them to his chest. He wouldn't speak, and Memphis knew he was trying hard not to break down into a full-on cry. He waited him out, and after a minute Isaiah said in a soft, strangled voice, "You gonna go and leave me, too, aren't ya?"

"Aww, Ice Man." Memphis moved to the bed and pulled Isaiah into a hug.

"Everybody's always leaving me behind."

"Shhh, now. That's not true."

Isaiah's head shot up. His teary eyes were equal parts pleading and challenge. "Promise me. Promise me we'll always be together. Like Mama said."

Memphis's heart tightened. There was no question that he loved his brother. But Memphis was nearly eighteen, with dreams of his own. Dreams he kept having to push into smaller drawers inside himself under a label of "tomorrow." He worried that he'd never see any of them realized: never set foot inside A'Lelia Walker's grand town house with the likes of Langston Hughes and Countee Cullen and Zora Neale Hurston, never see a book of his poems in the front window of a bookseller's shop, never see the world outside Harlem. How could he ever get away when there was always some undertow of obligation pulling him back?

"We'll always be together," Memphis said. He held Isaiah a little tighter, as if he could will his love to overcome his resentment. "It's late. You oughta be asleep."

"Not tired."

"That's not what your eyes are telling me."

Isaiah laced his fingers through Memphis's. His anger was gone. He seemed frightened.

"What's the matter, Ice Man?"

"I see things in my dreams."

"What kinds of things?"

"Monsters," Isaiah whispered.

"They're just dreams, Isaiah. Dreams can't get you. Only I can!" Memphis tickled Isaiah, who giggled, crying, "Stop! Stop!" happy as any ten-year-old.

"Ice Man," Memphis asked as he tucked the blanket under Isaiah's chin, "what do you remember from before you had your seizure?"

Isaiah blinked up at the ceiling, remembering. "Mr. Johnson was walking me home. He had a shortcut he wanted to take so I wouldn't be late and get Octavia sore at me." Isaiah paused for a second. "And I remember I was sad about Mama being dead and Daddy being gone to Chicago."

Memphis felt the squeezing in his chest again. He hated knowing that Isaiah was sad. "What else you remember?" Memphis said, more gently.

"Mr. Johnson told me he could take that sad right out of my head if I wanted him to."

"How was he gonna do that?"

"Don't know. He was teasing me, I think."

"Oh."

"And then I had my fit. It was like I was underwater. I saw..."

It was right there on a high shelf of Isaiah's mind, just out of reach. He had a glimpse of a strange man. But then the face became Bill Johnson's, and then it was gone.

Isaiah shook his head. "I can't remember nothing else."

Memphis took a deep breath. He stared at the floor. "And when you were asleep after your fit, did you know I was right by your bedside?"

Could Isaiah remember Memphis's healing hands on his arm?

"Huh-uh."

"But after you woke up, you... you felt all right. Didn't you?"

"What do you mean?"

"You didn't feel sick or anything? Just felt like your old shrimpy self."

"Ain't shrimpy! Gonna be taller'n you!" Isaiah said, play-hitting Memphis. "Sister Walker said I'd prob'ly be taller than Daddy."

"Well, now. Guess we'll have to see on that."

Isaiah's lightness evaporated quickly. "Memphis. I miss going to Sister Walker's house."

"I know."

"I don't think she's bad. She was too nice to be bad."

"Lots of folks can seem nice," Memphis said, but in truth, he'd always liked Sister, too. There was no proof that the work Isaiah had been doing with her, developing his powers, had anything to do with his fit. Otherwise, why wouldn't he have had more of them? It troubled Memphis.

"She made me feel special," Isaiah said. "But I guess I'm not special after all."

"Don't say that. That isn't true," Memphis said, putting his face near his brother's like they used to on Christmas Eve when they'd try to stay up and catch Santa Claus, reasoning that he'd have to come to Harlem first; after all, Harlem even had a St. Nicholas Avenue.

"Memphis? Will you tell me a story? To help me sleep?"

"All right, then," Memphis said quietly. "Once upon a time, there were two brothers, and they were close as close can be. . . ."

Isaiah reached out a hand and placed it on his brother's arm while Memphis cocooned him with words, wrapping him tightly in the magic of a story well told. Just before he fell asleep, Isaiah murmured to Memphis. "I 'member something else from when I was sick. There was a man. A man in a tall hat . . ." Isaiah muttered, trailing off into sleep at last.

Memphis wondered if these nightmares were the toll that not using his gifts was taking on Isaiah—all that energy bottled up till it had to come out somewhere. Octavia might've believed that it was the Devil's business, not the Lord's, but it seemed to Memphis that if there was a God, it would be downright cruel of him to bestow people with certain talents and then expect them not to use those talents. People had to be who they were. And if that was true, why shouldn't Memphis use his healing gift again? Why was he so afraid to explore his own power?

The truth was, Memphis had liked healing. He'd enjoyed the shine it had given him in Harlem, the way the women at church praised him as "God's special angel" and made sure he had the best piece of cake at their after-services suppers. He had basked in the silent approval of the men, who nodded and patted his back and told him he was setting a fine example for other young men, and who welcomed him to say the blessing at their various lodge meetings. When the girls fought to sit near him during Bible study or batted their lashes and asked shyly if they could bring him a cup of water, he'd loved that, too. Sometimes, he'd stood in his bathroom and practiced that winning smile of his, saying to himself in the mirror with all the sincerity he could muster, "Why, thank you, sister. And may God bless you."

It was only Octavia who'd made Memphis doubt, the way she stared at him through narrowed eyes when she would come to sew with his mother some evenings.

"You trying to draw Memphis's face in your mind, sister?" his mother scolded. They were sitting on the front stoop under a summer night filled with stars while a block party took place, all their neighbors dancing and singing and laughing, the good times bathed in the hopeful, buttery light of the brownstones lining 145th Street.

"Just keeping an eye on him," Octavia said.

"He's my angel." Memphis's mother had smiled at him like he was the only boy in the world.

"Sometimes angels fall," Octavia said meaningfully.

Memphis's mother stopped smiling. "God made my boy special, Tavie. You questioning the Lord now?"

Octavia turned her head slowly toward her sister. "Was it God you made a bargain with, Viola? Or somebody else?"

His mother's eyes went mean. "Maybe you need to make your own children so you can quit telling me about mine," she had fired back, slamming the door on her way inside.

"Pride goeth before a fall," Octavia had whispered as she kept her eyes on the impressionistic street carnival to hide the injury Viola's comment had inflicted, a wound Memphis knew that even he couldn't heal.

Memphis had been plenty proud. And his fall, when it came, was as spectacular as the Light Bringer's. From Harlem Healer to numbers runner and bookie. He'd lost his mother, his father, his home, his healing powers, and his faith. And now that his healing power was coming back, for reasons he couldn't begin to understand, he didn't want to make the same mistakes.

"Well, well, well. Smells like somebody got himself a date," Blind Bill Johnson called out from his perch on the couch in the parlor as Memphis entered.

"Evenin', Mr. Johnson."

Memphis wanted to like Blind Bill. The old man was a real help with Isaiah, offering to walk him home from school most days. But the way Bill sat on Octavia's prized couch just now, like he owned it, gave Memphis pause. Looking at Bill, Memphis could almost see the outline of the powerful young man he must've been. Those stooped shoulders had once been broad and thickly muscled, and his veined hands were still plenty big enough to crush an orange to pulp. Bill was fifty-five, maybe even sixty if he was a day. But lately, he seemed stronger, more virile, and Memphis wondered if it was Octavia's attention that gave him a younger man's shine.

Octavia came into the room carrying a plate of meat loaf. She'd done up her hair even though Bill wouldn't see it, and she smelled of Shalimar, which she usually only wore to church. She gave Memphis a pursed-lip appraisal. "Where you going dressed like that?"

Where you think you're going dressed like that? Memphis wanted to say back.

"To the pictures with Alma," he lied.

"Hmph. That Alma gets up to no good," Octavia started, and Memphis sagged, bracing himself for the lecture to come.

"'Scuse me, Miss Octavia," Bill Johnson interrupted. "Nobody in this world could raise these boys better'n you doin'. But, if you'll pardon an old man's opinion, a young man's gotta be about a young man's business. Gotta be a man in the world," Bill said with just enough humility to settle Octavia. He smiled and bowed his head slightly. "I don't mean no disrespect, ma'am. I know I'm not the boy's kin."

Octavia looked over at Memphis with a bit more kindness. "I expect you're right, Mr. Johnson."

"Bill, please."

"Bill," Octavia said, preening. "Go on, then, Memphis. Bill, let me get you some milk to go with that meat loaf."

Octavia turned toward the kitchen but snapped back one last time, a finger pointed at Memphis like an arrow set to fly. "You better live at the foot of the cross and do right, Memphis John."

"Yes, ma'am," Memphis said. He didn't feel like "Yes, ma'am"ing his aunt, but he recognized a reprieve when he heard one and knew it was the wise choice.

"Thank you, Mr. Johnson," he said softly once Octavia had left the room.

Bill's smile was a half-formed thing. "That's all right, son. Old Bill is always happy to do a favor for a friend. After all, a man never knows when he might need to ask for a favor in return," Bill answered, his smile finally unleashed.

WATCHING THE LIGHT

"Memphis, where are you taking me?" Theta gasped as they traipsed through Fort Washington Park, dodging a sudden cascade of late-straggler leaves shaken down by the wind.

"Almost there, baby. I promise!"

They'd spent the evening dancing at the Hotsy Totsy, but Memphis had wanted to be alone, promising Theta that he'd take her straight to the top tonight. The booze had made them a little loose, and they laughed happily as they kicked at the piles of dead leaves, jogging tipsily past amused bystanders and grouchy old-timers clucking that that "wasn't how you do." Finally, they came to the very edge of the park, where it dead-ended at the stripe of gray that was the Hudson River and the small red lighthouse that sat perched at the tip of Manhattan.

"That?" Theta asked, her breath coming out in a chilly puff.

"Didn't I say I'd take you straight to the top? Just so happens I know the password for that joint."

When they reached the lighthouse door, Memphis drew a wrench from his pocket and hit at the lock till it fell open. He grinned. "Told ya I knew the password."

He led Theta up the narrow iron steps, around and around, until they came out in the lighthouse's lantern room. Theta gasped when she saw the water lapping at the bumpy shoreline of Manhattan, the distant, twinkling shore of New Jersey, and the dark river in between, aglow with the occasional sweep of the lighthouse's far reach. It was just a lighthouse, but it felt like the top of the world.

"They say they're gonna build a big bridge right here, going from Manhattan over to New Jersey," Memphis said. "So we oughta enjoy the view while we can."

Memphis stood behind Theta and wrapped his arms around her, resting his head beside hers. "Watch the light now," he said, and they held their breath while the bright beam shone out a welcome into the world, guiding ships confidently up the river. It seemed for a moment as if the light were coming from the two of them, as if they'd already steered themselves to a safe place.

"*A mighty river ribbons through the light / Sing hey to the nightingale, sweet song of night / Sing hey to the tower that shines so bright / Sing hey to the stars and she who mourns their light.*"

"Gee, that's pretty. Who wrote that?"

"I guess I did. I said *light* too many times, though."

"I didn't notice," Theta said.

"I sent some of my poems to the *Crisis* today," Memphis said, handing Theta his flask.

She took a sip, wincing as the alcohol burned her throat, then handed it back to Memphis. "What's the *Crisis*?"

"Just the most important journal in Harlem. It's edited by Mr. W.E.B. Du Bois himself. Lots of people have had their work published there—Langston Hughes, Countee Cullen, Zora Neale Hurston."

"Memphis Campbell," Theta said, grinning.

"Maybe," Memphis said wistfully. "May . . . be."

"You found anything new on that crazy eye symbol?" Theta asked.

"Nothing yet. I swear, I've searched every book I can find about symbols and eyes. I don't know where it comes from, but it's got to have an origin. *Everything comes from somewhere, and somewhere is everywhere. Everything is connected,* my mama used to say," Memphis quoted, imitating the gentle rise and fall of his mother's musical Caribbean accent. "*Gonna take you back to my homeland sometime, and then you'll know. You'll see the thread that stretches across the ocean.*"

"Did she ever take you?" Theta asked.

Memphis stopped smiling. "Naw. But she used to tell Isaiah and me all sorts of tales about Haiti's history and all kinds of African folklore, about our family and where we'd come from and how we got here. Origin stories. I tell you, my mother had a story for everything."

Theta hugged her knees to her chest. "You miss her?"

"Yes," Memphis said, keeping his eyes on the shadowy hills. He drank from the flask. "Yes, I surely do."

"You got a lot of nice stories," Theta said softly. "I don't have that. I don't have an origin story. Just fuzzy memories and this one dream that's like a memory, but I can't really see it, not all the way."

"Tell me what you do see, then." Memphis offered Theta the flask again, but she shook her head.

"It's white, like...like miles of snow. And there are funny red flowers in the snow, spreading everywhere. I hear screaming and horses whinnying and there's smoke and then there's nothing. I wake up." She shrugged. "That's the only story I got."

"We could make our own stories," Memphis said. "You and me."

For a week, Memphis had been rehearsing this speech in the bathroom mirror. But now all his words failed him. So he took Theta's hands in his, watching the light sweep across the room. "Theta..." He cleared his throat, started over. "Theta, I love you."

Theta's smile vanished. She didn't answer.

"That wasn't quite the response I was hoping for," Memphis joked, but his stomach was as tight as piano wire.

"Gee, Poet. I just...I didn't expect that."

"Theta," Memphis said, "I feel I need to warn you: In about five seconds, I'm going to tell you that I love you. There. Now you know to expect it."

Theta still wasn't smiling. "The last fella who told me that...it didn't go so well."

"Well, I'm not the last fella. I'm the right fella."

There are things you don't know about me, Theta wanted to say. *Things that might change how you feel about me.* She didn't think she could bear that disappointment. Theta bit her lip. She ran a finger across the back of Memphis's hand, an idea forming. "When you heal people—"

"Used to. Haven't tried it since Isaiah."

"Sure. But when you used to do it at the church, could you heal anything?"

"Most things, I suppose. I couldn't help my mother," Memphis said, and Theta gave his hand a gentle squeeze.

She looked up into Memphis's face. "Can you take something away with your healing?"

"What do you mean?"

Theta didn't know how to say it without telling Memphis everything. "What if somebody had something about them that wasn't a disease, exactly, more like a..." Theta searched for the right words. "Like a bad Diviner power. The opposite of healing. Something that could harm."

Memphis laughed. "I never met anybody like that at the Miracle Mission."

"No. No, I guess you wouldn't."

"What's all this about, Theta?"

Theta forced a smile. Inside, she could feel herself drifting further away. Who could love somebody like her? "Just curious, Poet. That's all."

She should leave him. That was the noble thing to do. Before he got hurt.

Memphis kissed her on the temple, soft and sweet, and Theta knew she was far from noble, because she didn't have the strength to give him up.

"I love you," he said again.

"I love you, too, Memphis," Theta whispered.

"You just made me the happiest man in Harlem." Memphis grinned. "Now you got more than one story, Princess. This lighthouse, this moment—I reckon it's our origin story."

"Guess so," she said. She hoped everything would be okay.

Memphis kissed her then, and Theta kissed back. Their kiss was warm. It traveled through Theta's body and made her want more. They

236

sank to the floor of the lighthouse. Memphis moved on top of her just slightly. She could feel him against her stomach and it made her go liquid inside. Without warning, Theta's thoughts flashed back to Roy. It was Roy she saw on top of her, holding her down on the bed that last terrible night in Kansas. The uninvited memory raced through her like a swift fever. Heat pooled in her palms. It shot out to her fingers like the survival mechanism of a frightened animal, as if in that moment her body couldn't tell the difference between Memphis and Roy, love and violence.

Terrified, Theta pushed Memphis away and sat up abruptly, breathing heavily. She tucked her hands under her thighs, feeling the warmth begin to subside.

"I do something wrong, Princess?" Memphis asked, confused and concerned.

Theta gulped down air. "No. No, I just ... I just wanna slow down, Poet."

"All right. Okay. We can be slow as you like," Memphis said.

His gentleness made Theta want to cry. "Can we ... can we just lie here?"

"If you like."

They lay side by side on the floor of the lighthouse, and Theta rested her head on Memphis's chest, where she could hear his heart thumping. More than anything, she wanted to keep kissing him. But in her mind, she heard Roy's screams, saw the curls of black smoke rising from under his fingers as he clutched at his face and the room caught fire.

"Everything copacetic, Princess?" Memphis asked.

Just tell him. He's not gonna run. Tell him. Tell him. . . .

"Sure. Everything's jake," she managed to say, and they watched the bright light sweeping back and forth, promising safety.

☼

The moon poured through the flimsy curtains in Isaiah's bedroom as he half woke and rose slowly from his bed, crossing to Memphis's desk. His eyes tipped back in their sockets and his mouth mumbled old words. He grabbed the pencil and began to draw.

In a back room of a smoky gambling hall, Blind Bill bargained with two men who didn't take well to bargains. "Tell Mr. Schultz I'll get him his money. I promise," Bill said.

"Mr. Schultz expects interest. Or he takes his own kind of interest, if you get my meaning," one of the men said, and he kicked at Bill's cane just to make the point clear.

"Yes, sir. Thank you, sir," Bill said. He grumbled a curse at them on his way out. They were bad men. But Bill had met much worse. The sort of men who might pay handsomely for information about truly gifted people, if it came to that.

Jericho yawned as he read over an account from Will's early days investigating Diviners who sensed danger coming and issued warnings that mostly went unheeded. He looked out his window at the neon night and wondered where Evie was now, and if she ever thought of him, and he hated himself for caring.

Elsewhere in the city, the bright young things danced to feverish jazz in the speakeasies while others stumbled home to sleep off the gin. They went to bed humming songs they were sure had been written just for them, songs they believed they would sing that happily for the rest of their lives. They slept and they dreamed: Sweethearts who'd fallen asleep wrapped in each other's arms. Bricklayers and bridge builders whose lives were lived in the shadows of the monuments they built to the greatness of others. Newcomers to America whose tongues still struggled with the texture of English words. Midwestern boys who'd set off for the big city to make their fortunes. Teenage girls in cramped apartments who longed to feel beautiful and adored and seen. They traveled deep into the corridors of sleep, following the music-box song, desperate to join the dream that called to them, a great migration to its promising shores.

They heard a voice whispering, "*Dream with me. . . .*"

Some said no. They drifted into other, less satisfying dreams from which they woke in the morning with a feeling of great loss, as if they'd been offered a fortune of happiness and had squandered it.

Some answered yes. They chased after their elusive desires, ignoring the terrible sounds in the dark, until they realized their mistake. And by then it was too late. There was no leaving now. They would dream until all that remained was the phantom presence of their insatiable desires. Hungry ghosts, still dreaming.

In a basement speakeasy on West Twenty-fourth Street, two flappers slept with their Marcel Wave heads pressed together, lost to dreaming.

At Vesuvio's Bakery on Prince Street, the CLOSED sign hung on the door and the lingering scent of yeast and flour wasn't enough to wake the three young men in baker's aprons who lay sprawled in their wooden chairs, mouths agape, one worker still clutching the broom from last night's sweeping in his hand.

Near the Brooklyn Bridge, in the rumble seat of a car whose windows were fogged with frost, a young couple had stopped their heavy petting. Now it was only their eyes that moved feverishly behind their lids as they dreamed and dreamed and could not stop.

On the top floor of a five-story walk-up, across the street from a rival gambling den, one of Lucky Luciano's hired goons slept beside his Tommy gun while his intended target walked free. Lucky would be furious about the botched job, but it didn't matter to the assassin, because he would never wake again.

Deep below the city, the long metal snakes of the IRT rattled through the dark tunnels, while on the mud-rutted back roads of Connecticut, Sister Walker's car rumbled toward the dark horizon. They'd been driving for miles, following up on leads. Gray strands of stars stretched out above the sleeping towns and quiet farms they passed.

"Here we are. Just like old times," Sister Walker murmured.

The car's headlights bounced off the eyes of a rabbit that sprinted through the winter-dead grass. Will kept a hand on the folder of newspaper clippings in his lap.

"Not quite," he said at last and kept his eyes on the road ahead.

ANOTHER COUNTRY

Just before bed, Ling set her alarm, said her prayers, lit some incense, and slid George's track medal under her pillow, resting her fingers on top in the hope that she'd be able to make contact with him in the dream world. She kept her eyes on the ticking second hand of the clock, letting it lull her into a hypnotic trance. A moment later she woke, gasping, inside the dream world. Henry was there, doubled over, breathing heavily. "Fancy meeting you here."

"Are you all right?" Ling asked.

"Sure . . . just need a minute to catch my breath. I'm . . . not used to doing so much dream walking. Need to get my sea legs under me."

"Don't you carry any jade for protection?" Ling asked.

"I'm plenty jaded all on my own."

Ling rolled her eyes. "You're an idiot. Find some jade. It helps me." While Henry caught his breath, Ling searched for any hint of George, but she didn't see him anywhere.

"George?" she whispered. "George Huang. George, are you here?"

"What are you doing?" Henry asked, coming to her side.

Ling whirled around. "Nothing. I thought I saw a friend, but I was mistaken."

The fog lifted on the streets of the old-fashioned dream-jumble city, and the familiar scene started up like a clockwork show: The fighting men falling out of the saloon doors. The children chasing the rolling hoop, shouting, "Anthony Orange Cross!" The ghostly wagon and driver clopping by—"Beware, beware, Paradise Square!"

"Huh. It's exactly the same scene," Henry said.

"So?"

"Well, it's curious, isn't it? I've had a recurring dream before, but there's always something a bit different each time—the scarecrow in the cornfield has a different hat, or the house that's supposed to be your house has unfamiliar rooms. But this has been the same sequence of events in precisely the same order each time we've come here. If I'm correct, any second now, there should be fireworks right over...there."

Henry pointed, and the night sky exploded with pops of light.

"You see? And now..." Henry gestured like a circus barker. "The man in the vest, please."

Like an old vaudevillian respectful of timing, the man appeared, a glimmering in the haze.

"Ladies and gentlemen! Come one, come all, for a ride on Alfred Beach's pneumatic train. See this marvel for yourselves and be amazed, ladies and gentlemen—the future of travel, beneath these very streets!"

"It's like a loop of dream time that's stuck for some reason," Henry said.

A shriek reverberated throughout the foggy city, and then: "Murder! Murder! Oh, murder!"

Henry and Ling crowded together.

"Here...she...comes," Henry said.

Right on schedule, the ghostly veiled woman in the blood-smeared dress emerged from the fog and ran past them and through the wall of Devlin's Clothing Store. The shimmering portal opened once more.

"C'mon!" Henry said, and he and Ling darted down the steps into the dark underworld of the dream.

※

As they waited in the train station, Henry told Ling about what happened after they'd been separated, how he'd followed the path to the cabin and Louis. "But what happened to you afterward?" Henry asked as he sat at the old Chickering, marveling once more that there was a piano he could play inside a dream.

"I met another dream walker last night. Her name is Wai-Mae," Ling said. "She talks too much. Even more than you do."

Henry smiled at the jibe. "So there are three of us? It's getting mighty crowded in this dream world. Tell me," he said, picking out a melody, "what do you do when you're not talking to the dead or leading wayward musicians into magical train stations, Miss Chan?"

"I help my parents in the restaurant," she said, sitting on the edge of the fountain to watch the goldfish darting about. "But I want to go to college and study science."

"Ah. That stack of books you had with you."

"I remember the first time I read about Jake Marlowe's experiments with the atom. It made me think of dreams."

"Naturally," Henry deadpanned.

Ling trailed her fingers in the cool water of the fountain. "What are these quantized bits of energy we see inside dreams? When I talk to the dead, where do they come from? Where do they go? Can we change the shape of our dreams? I can feel the Qi all around me. If I could understand this energy, this power, perhaps I could turn it into a scientific discovery in the physical world."

"Sometimes I can change what people dream," Henry said.

Ling whirled around. "You can? How? In what way?"

"Well, don't get too excited. I can't change the dream directly. I can only give the dreamer a suggestion."

"Oh. Is that all?" Ling said. She stuck her fingers back into the fountain, smiling as the goldfish nibbled at her fingertips.

"I'm wounded," Henry drawled. "It can be useful, though. If it looks as if the person's having a bad dream, I can help them out. I'll say something like, 'Why don't you dream about something more pleasant—puppies or hot air balloons or top hats—'"

"Top hats? No one wants to dream of top hats."

"How do you know? Perhaps they're very formal dreams," Henry said, smiling. "Anyhow, I give suggestions, and sometimes that's enough to steer the person away from a nightmare." He played around with a new melody. "Were you afraid the first time you walked in a dream?"

"A little. I didn't know what was happening to me. I thought maybe I'd died and woken up in the afterlife."

"And then you were sorry you hadn't worn a top hat."

Ling ignored Henry's joke. "What about your first time?"

"I thought I'd gone mad. Just like my mother."

"Your mother is crazy?"

Henry shrugged. "Oh, you mean to tell me it isn't perfectly normal for mothers to spend all day in the family cemetery talking to statues of saints? Why, don't you know, Miss Chan? The DuBois family is very respectable!"

"Has she always been mad?"

"No. Sometimes she's just peeved."

"It isn't funny."

"Oh, yes, it is. It's terribly, terribly funny," Henry said. He was used to delivering this patter to the jaded theater crowd, who liked to keep things light and entertaining, with no embarrassing sentiment to force them into pretending to care. Over the years, Henry had gotten pretty good at his act: "My parents?" he'd say, perched at the piano. "Tragic, tragic story. They were circus performers eaten by their own tigers just after a rousing performance of 'Blow the Man Down.' Poor Maman and Papa, gone with a roar and a belch and a half-finished chorus."

But he realized how silly it was to pretend with Ling here inside a dream where everything you kept inside could suddenly show itself without warning. Lying about your emotions, putting on a happy face when you didn't feel it, was exhausting.

Henry kept his fingers moving, testing various chord progressions. "My mother tried to kill herself. She sent the servants into town, found my father's straight razor, crawled into the bath, and cut her wrists. But she'd forgotten that I was home. I found her. There was blood everywhere. I slipped and fell in it."

"That's awful," Ling said when she found her voice again.

"It was awful. I loved those pants."

"Your father must have been grateful that you found her."

Henry scowled. "My father has never used my name and *grateful* in the same sentence." He glanced at Ling, ready with another quip. She was looking at him. Really looking. It made him uncomfortable. "I've grown a second head inside this dream, haven't I? Be honest. I can take it."

"Your family has its own cemetery? You must be loaded," Ling said.

Henry laughed. "Oh, yes, darlin'. We are, indeed, loaded." He played a jazzy riff. "We've got a family crypt! Inscribed with nonsense Latin! Generations of the *DuBois bourgeoisie* lined up as a feast for the worms!"

Ling allowed a smile, then went serious again. "Generations. Your family's been here a long time. My parents struggled to get here. I've never even met my grandparents. How did you find the courage to leave home?"

Henry had thought himself a coward for running away. It was strange to hear Ling call it courage. "My father was angry with me over my friendship with Louis."

"Why?"

"He thought it was…" Henry searched for the right word. "Unhealthy." He could sense Ling preparing a follow-up question that he wasn't prepared to answer just yet, so he rushed on. "And he didn't approve of my music. He forbade me to follow my passion. The old man wanted me to become a lawyer. Can you imagine me as a lawyer?"

"You'd make an awful lawyer. Absolutely terrible."

Henry grinned. "Thank you for your confidence in me."

"Terrible," Ling said again.

"Yes, we've covered that sufficiently, I believe. Anyway, when he decided to send me to military school, I packed my suitcase and left. I suppose you think I'm an ungrateful son."

"No," Ling said, considering Henry's reasons. "But I could never leave my parents."

Henry tried to imagine the sort of filial duty Ling felt. If anything, he saw his parents as a burden to be endured. When people talked about "family" as something special, a place where you belonged, a dull anger nipped at Henry, a feeling that he'd been cheated of this basic comfort. Instead, Henry had made his own family with Theta, with his friends in the speakeasies and backstage at the Follies. He imagined that one day he'd hear that his parents were gone and feel only a vague sense of loss. How could you mourn something you'd never really had?

"Well," Henry said wistfully, "it must be nice to be so loved."

"Yes, I suppose it is," Ling said, letting the subject drop. To her surprise, she found that she liked talking with Henry, especially about dreams. Sure, he told too many jokes for her taste. But he was easy and loose, like a gentle stream that carried her along.

For a moment, she considered telling Henry about her plan to look for George tonight. But she decided it was best to keep quiet; that was her mission, not his.

"You asked me if I was afraid the first time I walked in a dream. But what I'm most afraid of is not being able to do it," Ling said quietly. "Here, I'm completely free. I can be myself. I can do anything."

Henry nodded. "I know just what you mean. When I'm here, if someone is having a bad dream, with a word, I can help them have a better dream. I can do something. In the waking world, I can't even get my songs published!"

"Are you sure you're working hard enough?"

Henry raised both eyebrows. "You are quite possibly the rudest person I have ever met. And I work in show business, so that's saying something."

"Fine. I'll be the judge. Play me a song," Ling said.

"Heaven help me," Henry said on a sigh. He played one of his numbers for Ling, a fun little ditty that quite a few of the chorines liked dancing to after hours.

"Well? Did you like it?" he asked.

Ling shrugged. "It's all right. Sounds like every other song."

"Ouch," Henry said.

"You asked."

"It just so happens they're gonna put a song of mine in the Follies."

"Then why do you care what I think?" Ling asked.

"Because..." Henry started. It wasn't really about Ling. There was something about the song that didn't feel right to him, but he couldn't tell what it was anymore. He'd been trying for so long to make other people happy with his music that he'd lost his internal compass.

"Here's one for you. Just wrote it," Henry said. He broke into a big ragtime number. *"I've got a yeaahn to walk with Miss Chan—"*

"Awful."

"Again and agaaain, round the gleaahnn, at half past teaahn—"

"Corny and awful."

"See you theaahn! If you've a keaahn! Dear! Miss! Chaaaannnnnn!"

The lights flickered wildly for a moment. From somewhere came a strange, gurgling, high-pitched whine, like a distant swarm of cicadas. Henry jumped up from the piano.

"I told you that song was bad," Ling said, her heart beating wildly.

But then the train's lamp glowed in the tunnel. It lit up the station as the train came to a stop. The doors opened, and Henry and Ling raced inside.

WE CAN MAKE EVERYTHING BEAUTIFUL

Wai-Mae was waiting for them in the forest. Seeing Ling, she broke into a grin. "You've come back! I knew you would!"

"Wai-Mae, this is Henry, the other dream walker I told you about," Ling said, nodding to Henry. "Henry, this is Wai-Mae."

Henry bowed courteously. "Pleased to meet you, Miss Wai-Mae."

"He is very handsome, Ling. He would make a nice husband," Wai-Mae said in a whisper that was not a whisper at all. Ling's face went hot.

Henry cleared his throat and said, with a formal bow, "Well, if you ladies will kindly excuse me, I'm off to meet a friend. I wish you sweet dreams." He turned and walked down the path until he disappeared into the fog.

"I have a surprise for you," Wai-Mae announced.

"I hate surprises," Ling said.

"You will like this one."

"That's what people always say."

"Come, sister," Wai-Mae said, and Ling stiffened as Wai-Mae linked arms with her, just like the schoolgirls who often passed by the Tea House's front windows, talking and laughing. But Ling had never been terribly girlish or giggly or affectionate. "You're not much for a cuddle, are you, my girl?" her mother would say with a wan smile, and Ling couldn't help feeling that she was letting her mother down by being the sort of daughter who enjoyed atoms and molecules and ideas instead of hugs and hair ribbons. Her mother would probably love Wai-Mae.

Wai-Mae's mouth didn't stop the entire walk. "...and you can be Mu Guiying, who broke the Heavenly Gate Formation. I will be the beautiful, beloved Liang Hongyu, the perfect wife of Han Shizhong, a general. She helped to lead an army against the Jurchens and was buried with the highest honor, a proper funeral befitting the Noble Lady of Yang...."

All of Wai-Mae's stories were romances. *Oh, so you're one of those,* Ling thought, *the girls who see the world as hearts and flowers and noble sacrifice.* Wai-Mae led Ling deeper into the forest, and while Wai-Mae chattered away about opera, Ling noticed that the dreamscape was even more vibrant than it had been the night before. The crude sketches of trees had been filled in with rich detail. Ling ran her palm over scalloped bark. It was rough against her hand, and she couldn't help but touch it again and again, grinning. A sprig of pine needles hung invitingly from a branch. Ling pulled and a handful of needles came away. She brought them to her nose, inhaling, then examined her fingers. *No resin, no smell,* she noted.

"We're almost there!" Wai-Mae chirped. "Close your eyes, Little Warrior," Wai-Mae insisted, and Ling did as she was told. "Now. Open."

Ling gasped. Golden light bled through the breaks in the line of gray trees. Here and there, mutated pink blooms sprang up. Red-capped mushrooms poked their fat heads above the patchy tufts of grass that tumbled down into a verdant meadow rippling with colorful flowers. In the distance, a rolling line of purple mountains brush-stroked with hints of pink rose tall behind an old-fashioned village of Chinese houses whose pitched tile roofs tilted into smiles. So much color! It was the most beautiful thing Ling had ever seen inside a dream—even more beautiful than the train station.

"Where are we? Whose dream is this?" Ling asked.

"It doesn't belong to anyone but us," Wai-Mae said. "It's our private dream world. Our kingdom."

"But it had to come from somewhere."

"Yes." Wai-Mae smiled as she tapped her forehead. "From here. I made it. Just as I did the slippers."

"All of this?" Ling asked. Wai-Mae nodded.

Ling couldn't imagine how much time and energy it must've taken. This was more than transmutation. This was creation.

"There's something magical about this place. We can make new dreams. We can make everything beautiful." Wai-Mae bit her lip. "Would you like to learn how?"

"Show me," Ling said. "Show me everything."

Wai-Mae marched to a puny, half-formed tree at the top of a hill. "Here. Like this. Watch."

Wai-Mae threaded her fingers through the wispy leaves, holding tight. She closed her eyes, concentrating. The bark moved like melting candle wax, and then, with a great groaning, the trunk shot up several feet. Massive branches reached out in every direction, bursting with pinkish-white flowers.

Wai-Mae fell back with a gasp. "There you are," she said, wiping a hand across her brow.

Dogwood blossoms drifted down toward the girls. One landed in Ling's hair. She pulled it free, rubbing the velvety petal between her thumb and forefinger, feeling something primal in its core, some great electrical connection to all living things. If she'd been a true scientist, she would have shouted "Aha!" or "Eureka!" or even "Holy smokes!" But there were no words that she could summon to communicate the magic of the moment.

"Now it is your turn." Wai-Mae twisted her mouth to one side, thinking. "We will need places to sit for our opera. Try changing this rock into a chair."

It was as if Wai-Mae had asked Ling to grab the moon and put it under glass. "But how?"

"Start by putting your hands on the rock."

Ling did as she was told. The rock was cold and dull, like clay awaiting the artist's hands.

"Think only of the chair, not the rock. See it in your mind. Like a dream. Do you see it?"

"Yes," Ling said.

"What does it look like?"

"It's a red-and-gold throne fit for a queen."

"I cannot wait to sit there," Wai-Mae said, excited. "Now see the chair and concentrate."

Ling kept her thoughts on the chair, but the harder she tried, the more it seemed to elude her. *Shift*, she thought, and *Transform* and *Chair*. But the rock remained a rock. Finally, Ling fell back in the grass, exhausted and angry. "I can't do it."

"Yes, you can."

"No, I can't!" She pushed herself up and stalked off toward the forest.

Behind her, Wai-Mae's voice took on a steely resolve. "Little Warrior: You can do this. I believe you can."

"Just because you believe something can change doesn't mean it will," Ling snapped, feeling ashamed of her outburst but helpless to stop it.

Wai-Mae came to her side, offering a moth-eaten dandelion. "Here. Try something smaller. Turn this into a cricket."

Ling glanced from the dandelion to the magnificent flowering dogwood Wai-Mae had managed to create. "This is hopeless," she grumbled, but she took the dandelion from Wai-Mae anyway.

"Concentrate. You are too tight! You want too much control."

"I do not!"

"You do too. Let it become something else. Allow the Qi to move through you like a breath. Think of the dandelion changing from the inside."

"Atoms..." Ling murmured.

Ling took a deep breath and let it out. She did this twice more, and on the third time, she felt a small fluttering at the tips of her fingers that strengthened into a stronger, buzzing current that coursed up her arm and along her neck all the way to the top of her head.

Frightened, Ling dropped the dandelion. But as she watched, the dandelion fluctuated wildly between two states, weed and insect, before settling back to dandelion.

"I almost did it," Ling said, astonished. "It started to change."

Wai-Mae grinned. "You see? Here, we are like Pangu, creating the heavens and earth, but even better, for we can make it as we wish it to be. My powers have gotten stronger each night I've been coming here. Perhaps if you come back tomorrow night and keep coming back as I have, then your power will grow, too."

"Can you bring physical objects into this place?" Ling asked, excited. "Can you take something out of this dream world? Have you noticed anything interesting when the transformation occurs—a smell or a temperature change? Have you experimented?"

"Isn't it enough that this world exists? That we can be everything here that we can't be when we are awake?" Wai-Mae asked.

"No," Ling said. "I want to know how it works."

"I just want to be happy," Wai-Mae said.

Three quick surges of light shot across the sky. Another, smaller spark rippled through the treetops, robbing the leaves there of color. Ling heard that same skin-crawling whine that had frightened her back in the station. The whine devolved into a death-rattle growl, then stopped.

"What was that?" Ling asked.

"Birds, perhaps?" Wai-Mae suggested.

"Didn't sound like birds. Come on. I want to find out where it's coming from."

"Wait! Where are you going, Little Warrior?" Wai-Mae called, scrambling after Ling as she ran through the forest, searching for the source of the light and sound.

At the entrance to the tunnel, Ling stopped. The vast dark crackled with motes of staticky brightness. "It's coming from there."

Ling took a step forward. Wai-Mae grabbed her arm. Her eyes were wide. "You mustn't go in there."

"Why not?"

"That part of the dream isn't safe."

"What do you mean? Not safe how?" Ling asked.

"Can't you feel it?" Wai-Mae backed away, trembling. "*Ghosts.*"

"I've spoken to plenty of ghosts on my walks. There's nothing frightening about them."

"You're wrong." Wai-Mae reached the fingers of one hand toward the tunnel, as if drawn to it. "I can feel this one sometimes in there. She . . . cries."

"Why?"

"A broken promise. A very bad death," Wai-Mae whispered, still staring into the dark. With a shudder, she turned away, hugging herself. "I'm frightened of that wicked place. If we do not trouble her, she won't trouble us."

"But what if I could help?"

Wai-Mae shook her head vehemently. "We must stay away from there. Promise me, Little Warrior. Promise you won't go near it. You must warn Henry, too."

One last bit of light flared like a dying firefly, and then the tunnel was still. Wai-Mae tugged gently on Ling's sleeve, drawing her away. "Come, Little Warrior. Let the ghosts rest."

Once they were back on the path through the forest, Wai-Mae's earlier fear seemed to have gone, and she was her usual garrulous self. But Ling was preoccupied.

"Wai-Mae . . ." Ling started. "Have you heard any talk on the ship about the sleeping sickness in Chinatown?"

Wai-Mae frowned. "No. Is it serious?"

Ling nodded. "People go to sleep and they can't wake up. They're dying from it." Ling took a deep breath. "My friend George Huang is sick from it. His sister let me take his track medal in the hope that I could find him in the dream world tonight."

"Do you think that's wise if he's sick?"

"I had to try. Unfortunately, I didn't have any luck. Whatever dreams he's having are out of my reach. Have you had any walks lately that seemed as if the person dreaming was ill somehow?"

"No. All my dreams have been beautiful. But I will pray for your friend, George Huang." Wai-Mae gave Ling a shy sideways glance. "And you and I are becoming friends, too, aren't we?"

Ling wasn't sure that you could call someone you'd only met inside a dream a true friend. But Wai-Mae was on her way to New York, and for a moment, Ling imagined how fun it would be to parade past Lee Fan and Gracie with Wai-Mae, knowing that they shared an incredible secret all their own, something far beyond Gracie's and Lee Fan's limited comprehension.

"Yes," Ling answered. "I suppose we are."

Wai-Mae smiled. "I am so happy! What would you like to do now, friend?"

Ling took in the wide, sparkling streets of the village, the misty forest, and the purple mountains just beyond it all. It was all there waiting for her to explore, to claim, as if there were no limits. For just a little while, she wanted to be free.

"Let's run," she said.

※

On the path, Henry smelled gardenia and woodsmoke. He heard Gaspard barking, and that was enough to make him run the rest of the way. Splinters of summer-gold sunshine pierced the soft white flesh of the clouds above the bayou, shining down on Louis, who waved from the front porch, a fishing pole hoisted onto his shoulder, Gaspard at his feet.

"Henri!" He grinned. "Hurry up! Fish are bitin'!"

The old blue rowboat bobbed on the water. Another fishing pole leaned against the side, along with a battered metal pail knotted with a length of thick rope. Henry took a seat on one side, and Louis sat opposite him, paddling them down the river. When they came to a shady spot, he and Henry cast their lines and waited.

"Just like old times," Henry said.

The rowboat rocked gently on the current as Henry told Louis about meeting Theta and their life at the Bennington and with the Ziegfeld Follies, the songs Henry was writing and trying to publish, the nightclubs and the parties.

"Maybe you got yourself a fancy New York fella now," Louis said, keeping his eyes on the fishing pole.

There had been other boys, definitely. But none of them was Louis.

"Louis, I want to see you," Henry said. "Come to New York. You'd love it! I'd take you to the Follies and up to Harlem to the jazz clubs. And Louis, there are places for fellows like us. Places where we can be together, where we can hold hands and dance and kiss without hiding. It isn't like Louisiana."

"Always did want to see the big city. It true they got alligators in the sewers?"

"No." Henry laughed. "But the swells have got alligator bags at the parties."

"Well, I surely would like to see that."

Henry's grin was short-lived. "But where should I send the train ticket? If my letters didn't reach you at Celeste's, then there's no guarantee we can trust somebody to deliver it."

Louis rubbed his chin, thinking. "Got a cousin—Johnny Babineaux—works over at the post office in Lafayette Square. You can send it care o' him there."

"I'll buy the ticket tomorrow, first thing!" Tears welled up in Henry's eyes. "I was afraid I'd never see you again."

"Well, I guess you got to pick something else to be afraid of, then," Louis said.

More than anything, Henry wanted to hold Louis. Two years was a very long time. He couldn't stand another minute of separation. He reached for Louis's hand, and this time, nothing stood between them. Louis's fingers, which Henry hadn't felt in far too long, were still wet and cold from the river. Fighting the ache in the back of his throat, Henry ran a finger across Louis's cheeks and nose, resting it against his full lips.

"Kiss me, *cher*," Louis whispered.

Henry leaned forward and kissed him. Louis's lips were warm and soft. Henry had been telling himself, *This is not real. It's only a dream.* But now he stopped telling himself that. It felt real enough. And if dreams could be like this, well, he wasn't sure he wanted to wake up. Henry kissed Louis again, harder this time, and the sky lit up with a strange sort of lightning. The tops of the trees unraveled slightly; the sun flickered like a lamp with a short.

"What was that?" Henry said, breaking away.

"Don't know. You're the dream man," Louis said. But then Louis was pulling Henry down into the bottom of the rowboat, where they lay in each other's arms, lulled into contentment by the sun and the breeze and the gentle lapping of the river.

"I won't ever leave you again, Louis," Henry said.

When the dream walk neared its end, Henry could barely stand to wrench himself away from Louis. "I'll be here every night until you're in New York," he promised.

Gaspard barked happily and trotted up to Henry, his tail wagging like a flyswatter, and poked his wet nose into Henry's hand. Henry rubbed at the dog's floppy ears, enjoying the familiar softness of them. Gaspard's slobbery tongue slicked Henry's cheek.

"Everybody wants to kiss you," Louis said, laughing, and Henry's throat tightened again. It was just like Louis to dream of his dog.

Gaspard tore away, sniffing ahead of them on the path. The hound tensed near a climbing wall of flowering morning glories, growling and barking at the purplish buds.

"Gaspard! C'mon, boy! Come away from there," Louis said sharply.

"What's the matter?" Henry asked.

"I don't want him in those flowers. Don't like 'em."

Henry thought perhaps Louis was joking, but one look at his face said he wasn't.

"They're just flowers," Henry said.

"Gaspard, c'mon, boy!" Louis whistled, and the dog came running. Louis dropped down and nuzzled his face into the dog's fur. "Good boy."

"Are you sure you're okay?" Henry asked.

Louis replaced his frown with a smile. "Fine as morning. Kiss me once for luck, *cher*. And twice for love. And three times means we'll meet again."

Henry kissed him till he lost count.

In her bed, Ling groaned with pain and exhaustion. Her eyes fluttered open long enough for her to feel the terrible ache deep in her bones. She slid her hand under her pillow, her fingers just touching the cold edge of George's track medal as she fell into a deep sleep.

Ling stood in Columbus Park. Clouds roiled overhead in anticipation of some storm.

A heartbeat thrummed in her ears, insistent as a drum.

Every post and tree she saw had the same sign: MISSING. MISSING. MISSING.

George Huang pulsed in the gloom, a ghostly heartbeat. His pale skin was fissured like broken pottery glued back together, and red blisters shone on his neck. When he lifted his threadbare hand, his bones showed through like an X-ray. George spread his arms, and the scene shifted back and forth, as if they were cards being pushed and pulled quickly through a stereoscope. One minute, it was the familiar pathways, trees, and pavilion of the park; the next, the park was gone, and in its place were ominous tenements, shacks with rotting shutters, and filthy streets piled with garbage.

The dream changed. Now Ling found herself in City Hall Park. George floated just above a metal grate beside a drinking fountain. He pointed to a row of buildings behind her. Ling turned back to George, and he fell like rain through the bars of the grate. She crawled onto the grate to look for him and it gave way, plunging her down and down into the darkness.

She was inside the train station. The old sign was there—BEACH PNEUMATIC TRANSIT COMPANY—but rot raced along the walls, the decay taking over, devouring the dream's beauty. Light trembled against the velvety dark of the tunnel like a handful of firecrackers tossed up on Chinese New Year, and in those brief flashes, Ling saw pale blots of form. Eyes. Ravenous mouths. Sharp teeth. There was an ominous insectlike chorus, growing louder.

George's glow was unsteady now, as if he were a Christmas light winking out. He moved his lips as if trying to speak. It seemed to require a tremendous effort. Each time he tried, more sores appeared on his body. Behind him, the dark crackled and crawled with faulty radiance, and the filthy hole filled with animalistic shrieks and growls and broken ends of words, a great roaring wave of terrifying sound curling up into an obliterating crest.

Ling's legs shook with terror. She could not move. In a strobe of light, the veiled woman appeared, her dress dripping with blood as she walked. She was coming up behind George, and Ling wanted to warn him about the things in the dark and the woman, but she could only choke on her fear. George Huang stood his ground even as the sores multiplied, spreading across his chest and up his neck, burning his skin down to the bone in spots. He fought the pain.

And just before the crawling, hungry wave reached him, George choked out his words at last: "Ling Chan—Wake. Up."

Ling woke in her bed. Desperately, she swallowed down air. On the other side of her window, the winter moon was full and bright. The only sound she heard now was her pulse thumping wildly in her head. She was safe. She was fine. It had just been a bad dream.

Only when Ling settled back against the pillow did she realize that she clutched George's prized track medal.

DAY TEN

BEWARE, BEWARE

The crowded bus was standing room only as it lurched down Fifth Avenue across steaming manhole covers, dodging New Yorkers bundled up against the stiff winter wind, but Henry was jolly. He gripped the hand loop and whistled "Rivière Rouge" to the amusement of two young girls giggling in the seats below him, and to the annoyance of the driver, who barked that he could either whistle or walk, his choice.

"I can hum it, if you'd prefer," Henry answered merrily.

"Out!" the driver said, stopping the bus ten blocks shy of Henry's destination.

"You'll be sorry when I'm famous," Henry said. He waved to the still-giggling girls at the window and carried on.

Nothing could dampen his good mood, not even the long wait for the ticket agent at Grand Central Terminal. As he watched the hustle and bustle around him, Henry tried to imagine Louis's expression as he stood for the first time beside the lighted ball of the Grand Central clock, surrounded by more people than he had ever seen on the riverboats. Louis was finally coming to New York. They could be together. That thought buoyed Henry further as he approached the ticket agent's window.

"I need one ticket from New Orleans, Louisiana, to Grand Central Terminal, please," Henry said.

"You want the New York and New Orleans Limited," the ticket agent said.

"*N'awlins Lim'ted, speed my baby down the track, my love won't wait till he . . . she gets back,*" Henry sang softly, making up the words on the spot.

"You want a ticket or a booking agent, kid?"

Henry handed over the collection of crumpled bills he'd taken from Theta's coffee-can piano fund. She'd be pretty sore when she found out he'd dipped into it. But he'd promised Louis a ticket, and besides, Theta would want him to be happy. She'd understand. The piano fund could be rebuilt in a few months' time, and all would be forgiven.

"You need a return ticket?" the agent asked.

Henry smiled. "Not if I'm lucky."

At the post office, Henry packed the train ticket, his letter, and a photograph of him in his best suit standing arm in arm with Theta outside the New Amsterdam Theatre into an envelope. His stomach gave a small flip as the postal clerk stamped the words *Par Avion* on the front of the envelope, inking Henry's hope into it. He couldn't wait until tonight, when he could see Louis again and tell him the good news.

Still whistling "Rivière Rouge," Henry headed home, happier than he'd been in ages. He had a few hours left before Theta's press conference and the surprise the two of them had cooked up. But on his way through the Bennington lobby, Adelaide Proctor came toward him, calling his name somewhat urgently, and his stomach sank.

"Afternoon, Miss Proctor," Henry said, pressing the elevator button. "Please do forgive me. I'm afraid I'm in an awful rush—"

"Oh, but Mr. DuBois, I've been having the most dreadful dreams about you."

"I'm very sorry to hear it, Miss Proctor. But as you can see, I'm just fine."

"No. No, I don't believe you are, young man. Don't you hear the crying? Oh, do be careful, Mr. DuBois!"

"Adelaide!" Miss Lillian called from the other side of the lobby. "We'll be late!"

The elevator arrived and Henry leaped on, eager to make his escape. "Please don't worry on my account, Miss Proctor. Good day to you!" he said, his thoughts already on his music and Louis and dreams that were all good.

"Addie!" Miss Lillian shouted again, impatient.

But Adelaide Proctor still stood in the lobby looking very afraid. And as the elevator gate closed, she called to Henry one last time: "Mr. DuBois: Anthony Orange Cross. Beware, beware, Paradise Square."

A chill prickled along Henry's neck as the elevator carried him up.

Henry got off the elevator with a feeling of unease. How did Adelaide Proctor know about Paradise Square and Anthony Orange Cross? He didn't recall ever walking in her dreams or seeing her in one of his. When he had more time, he'd stop in and ask.

Henry stretched, feeling the tightness in his muscles. They ached a bit, like he'd been exercising all night. In a way, he supposed he had been. Hadn't he and Louis gone fishing? But it was strange to feel it today in his body. In fact, he was exhausted. And no sooner had Henry sprawled into his favorite chair than his eyelids fluttered closed and he was fast asleep.

The dream started in his house back in New Orleans. Henry's father sat at a long table. He wore the powdered wig of a Puritan judge.

"You will never see that boy again," his father said.

Henry turned and ran through the cemetery, which was carpeted in morning glories. His mother's porous saints moved their stone lips in unison: "They never should've done it."

The morning glories climbed up Henry's legs, the vines tightening around his muscles.

"Let me go!" Henry screamed.

All at once, he found himself in a squalid room filled with opium smoke where half-dressed men lay about with glassy-eyed prostitutes. Henry heard the jangling tinkle of an old music box. He followed the sound around the corner and saw the veiled woman sitting on a pallet, turning the crank and crying very softly. She was small and delicate and young, not much older than Henry was. He could feel her anguish, and he wished he could take her out of this terrible place. He drew closer.

"Miss," Henry suggested, "why don't you have a different dream? A happy dream?"

The woman stopped crying. Through the netting, her eyes were dark and hard.

"All my dreams are dead," she growled. "You killed them!" Serpent-quick, she plunged a dagger into Henry's chest.

Henry woke with a start, breathing heavily, one hand over his heart.

"I'm okay. Everything's jake," he said, letting out a long exhale. He glanced at his watch, saw that it was nearly three, and yelped.

"Applesauce!" Henry hissed, reaching for his music and his coat, pulling up his suspenders as he went. "Theta's gonna murder me."

THE DOG AND PONY SHOW

Theta was standing in the wings pacing when Henry blew into the theater so fast he nearly toppled over.

"Sorry, sorry!" he said, kissing her cheek.

Theta's dark eyes flashed. "Cutting it a little close, weren't ya, Hen?"

"But I made it," Henry said. "You look like a million bucks."

"Yeah, but do I look like Russian nobility?"

"I'd buy it."

"Only if I can sell it."

"You'll be the berries, Theta. You always are."

Theta parted the curtain, looking out at the assorted members of the press and the photographer setting up his camera in the aisle, and spied Herbert Allen glad-handing the reporters. His voice drifted up and backstage: "Yes, I've written a swell new song for Miss Knight to sing today...."

Henry peeked over Theta's shoulder and scowled. "That talentless bastard. Shouldn't he be off having another bad suit made?"

"He's not gonna be too happy about what we're doing."

"Huh. Suddenly I'm filled with pep!" Henry joked, but Theta still looked nervous. He held her hand. "Don't worry. We're on our way."

"Promise?"

"Promise. Come on. Now, let us to go and razzle-dazzle ze press-ski."

Theta's eyebrows shot up. "Good thing *you're* not trying to pass yourself off as Russian royalty."

"As we say in my country, I am wounded."

Theta squeezed Henry's hands for luck. "Here goes nothin'."

The reporters quieted as Theta swept onto the stage looking every bit the star in a borrowed chinchilla coat, a long strand of knotted pearls swaying against her green silk dress as she sauntered toward the footlights.

"Holy mackerel," one of the men muttered, captivated.

Florenz Ziegfeld beamed. "Gentlemen, may I present the Ziegfeld Follies' newest star, Miss Theta Knight!" Mr. Ziegfeld said, taking Theta's hand and helping her down the steps and into a front-row seat.

"Sorry I'm late. I had to wait for my stockings to dry," Theta purred and glanced over at Henry.

Don't worry, he mouthed from his seat at the piano.

A reporter tipped his hat. "Miss Knight?"

"That's my name," Theta said, and even that was a lie.

"What do you remember about your life in Russia?"

"It was cold," Theta answered. She dangled her unlit cigarette until a reporter offered a match, and Theta looked up at him with her bedroom eyes. "Even our sables wore sables."

The reporters laughed, and Theta relaxed a little. If you kept them entertained, they didn't get too personal. They asked their questions, and Theta answered each one, making it up as she went along. It seemed to Theta that her entire life had been improvised and reinvented to fit whatever story she needed in order to survive. She knew about lying by omission—how you could leave out parts of yourself to be filled in by other people who only saw in you what worked for their own reinvented lives. Theta rarely corrected them. What was the point? Most of the stars in Hollywood had phony names given to them by agents and studio heads, and backgrounds invented out of thin air and a desire to sell movie tickets. That was part of the dream factory.

Theta stole another glance at Henry. At the piano, he yawned, barely awake. Shadows showed under his eyes, and his face was much paler than usual. Maybe he didn't see it, but Theta did.

"Miss Knight?" a reporter prompted her.

"Huh?" Theta said. "I mean"—she put the husky purr back into her voice, a woman of mystery—"yes?"

"Say something in Russian," a reporter cajoled.

"Twenty-three skidoo-ski," Theta deadpanned.

"What part of Russia is that from?"

"The swell part."

"Now, boys, go easy. Miss Knight was only a little girl when they smuggled her out of a war-torn country in the dead of night, to be delivered to this great country by loyal servants and raised in an orphanage by kindly nuns," Mr. Ziegfeld said. "It was quite traumatic! The poor girl has amnesia and doesn't remember much at all. The doctors don't expect that she ever will."

"That true, Miss Knight?"

Theta blew a plume of smoke in the reporter's direction, enjoying his cough. "If Mr. Ziegfeld says it's true, then it's true." She couldn't wait for this dog and pony show to be over so she could sing and dance. That's the act she was good at, not this one.

"Hey, honey, are you spooked to perform here after what happened to Daisy Goodwin? Murdered right up there on that stage!"

Theta paled. If she told them about that night and the secret power that had helped her to escape from Naughty John, the newspaper boys would have a story to wipe Flo's "Russian princess" invention right off the page.

"I don't spook easy," Theta said, letting her answer out on a plume of cigarette smoke. "If I did, I wouldn't live in Manhattan."

"You worried about this sleeping sickness?"

"Who sleeps? I'm a Follies girl."

"Say, Theta, honey—you wanna give 'em a little song and dance?" Wally nudged.

"It's what I live for." Theta dropped her coat on the chair and walked past Henry. "Look alive," she whispered. "We're on."

Theta's heart beat fast. She avoided looking at Wally. "This is a brand-new song..." Theta started. In his seat, Herbert Allen preened like a man who expected the world to go his way. "...written by the talented Henry DuBois the Fourth."

Theta gestured toward Henry. Out of the corner of her eye, she saw Herbie's face shift from smug to shocked. "It's called 'Slumberland.' Hit it, Hen!"

When Theta finished selling Henry's new song for all she was worth, the news hawks applauded.

"Not bad," one of the reporters mused. "Different."

"Yeah. A real surprise," Herbie said. There was murder in his eyes.

"Gentlemen, I give you the Follies' newest sensation, Miss Theta Knight," Mr. Ziegfeld crowed.

"And her piano player, Henry DuBois the Fourth," Henry mumbled to himself. "Thank you, thank you. Hold your applause, folks."

"Terrific, Miss Knight. Simply terrific," a smiling reporter said. "They're going to love this story in Peoria. Why, you'll be famous everywhere—from New York to Hollywood, Florida to Kansas."

"Kansas?" Theta whispered.

"Yeah. Big state in the middle of the country. Fulla corn, Republicans, and Bible salesmen, and not much else?"

Herbie put his arm around Theta and gave her a squeeze. "Isn't she terrific? Actually, I'm writing new songs for this little lady myself. A whole show's worth. She's my muse!"

"That so? Is this your beau, Miss Knight?" The gossip columnist winked.

"No," Theta said, gently shaking Herbie's hand free.

"Well, you must have somebody—beautiful girl like you."

The skin of Theta's palms crawled with heat like a mess of fire ants. *Calm*, she told herself. *Keep calm.*

"Come on, give us a little juice for the columns," the columnist persisted.

"Uh...sure. I got a fella."

The reporters' pencils were ready to take it all down. "Well, who is he?"

The heat reached her wrists. "Uncle Sam," Theta shot back. "I'm a real patriot. 'Scuse me, I gotta powder my nose."

Quickly, Theta headed for the wings.

"She's something," a reporter said.

"She sure is," Herbie said, looking at Theta as if she were a house he'd bought and was just waiting to move into.

Theta ran into the washroom and yanked off her gloves. Her hands were the color of hot coals. She shoved them under the cold tap, biting her lip as the curls of steam rose up and fogged the mirror. When they felt cool again, she dried her hands, examining them. They looked perfectly normal. But inside her gloves were faint scorch marks.

※

After the press filed out, Henry and Theta went out the stage door into the alley so Theta could get some air.

Henry gave her a big hug. "We did it!"

"Yeah, we sure did."

"If I could only watch one movie for the rest of my life, it would be the look on Herbie Allen's face when you started singing my song."

"That was something, all right."

"Hey, what's the matter? They loved you in there, Czarina Thetakovich!"

"Did you hear that reporter, Hen? Kansas!" Theta said, breaking away and lighting up a cigarette. "What if somebody reads that story and they recognize me? What if they question me about the fire? About Roy?"

"They won't. You're Theta Knight, not Betty Sue Bowers. You don't even look the same. You're safe," Henry said, kissing her forehead. "Okay?"

"Okay," Theta said, feeling a temporary safety with her best friend.

"I've got some news of my own." Henry grinned wide. "Louis is coming to New York. I sent him the train ticket in the mail today."

"Gee. That's great, Hen. So you got through to that noggin of his after all. How'd you do it? Did you tell him our telephone exchange over and over till he finally woke up and called it?"

Henry shoved his hands in his pockets and avoided Theta's gaze. "Not exactly."

"So how did you...oh, Hen." Theta sagged against the side of the theater. "Making plans in a dream? That's no more real than...than me being Russian royalty."

"I thought you'd be happy for me," Henry said, hurt.

"I am, Hen. But I'm worried about you. It's like you live more inside that dream world than you do the regular world these days. You're skinny and beat, and you're miles away even when..." Theta stopped suddenly. Her eyes narrowed. "Hen, where'd you get the kale for the train ticket?"

Henry kept his eyes on the ground. "I'll pay it back."

"Son of a bitch, Henry!" Theta barked. A couple passing by on Forty-second Street gave her a disapproving glare. "Breeze, Mrs. Grundy! This ain't your business," she growled and they hurried on.

"You made that fund for me because you wanted me to be happy. Having Louis in New York will make me happy, Theta." Henry had been excited to share the news with Theta. Now it felt like a mistake.

"Hen, that piano fund is *our* piano fund. It's for *our* future. You and me. A team. At least I always figured it that way."

"I thought you of all people would understand."

"That ain't fair, Hen. You know I'm on your side. Always."

"Yeah. Sure," Henry said, and he and Theta watched the people walking past on Forty-second Street rendered momentarily insubstantial as they stepped through the steam rising from the city's manholes. In the alley, he and Theta stood side by side, but they'd never been farther apart.

TELLING FORTUNES

Between his new role as Evie's pretend fiancé and putting in more hours at the museum now that Will was gone, Sam had found little time to follow up on his Project Buffalo leads. Finally, he managed to slip away and down to his old neighborhood on the Lower East Side. Many businesses were closed due to the sleeping sickness, and Sam had no luck on Orchard Street until a pickle vendor informed him that the Rosenthals had made good and moved to the Bronx.

Now Sam and Evie waited outside the sprawling apartment building on the Grand Concourse, an aspirational Tudor made for Jews who wanted to reinvent themselves once they'd left the crowded tenements of Orchard and Hester Streets—those tenements themselves a remove from the shtetls and ghettos of Russia, Poland, Romania, and Hungary. Every building had its ghosts, it seemed.

"I don't see why I had to come," Evie groused.

Sam put his fingers to his cheeks, making dimples. "Because you're my darling fiancée. Everybody loves the Sweetheart Seer!" he said sarcastically. "Oh, one more thing—if she asks, you're converting to Judaism."

"What? Sam!"

"Don't worry. Everything's jake, Baby Vamp. Just follow my lead."

"If that's supposed to be reassuring, it's not," Evie grumbled.

They took the stairs, dodging a handful of merry children running amok, and knocked at Mrs. Rosenthal's door. Anna Rosenthal was rounder and older than the young woman Evie had seen in her vision. She wore glasses now, and a few threads of gray showed in her dulled red hair, but it was unmistakably the same woman. Mrs. Rosenthal uttered a small cry before crushing Sam into a fierce hug. She stood back, shaking her head affectionately as she assessed him. "Sergei!"

She spoke to Sam in Russian, and he answered in kind, faltering a little. "Sorry, Mrs. Rosenthal, my Russian's a little rusty these days."

"Everyone forgets," she said, and Sam couldn't tell if it was said with sadness or gratitude.

Evie cleared her throat.

"And this," Sam said, hugging her, "is the apple of my eye, my lovely bride-to-be, Evie O'Neill."

"Charmed," Evie said, curtsying.

"Yes, I read all about it in the papers! But I had no idea the famous Sam Lloyd was our Sergei Lubovitch until you telephoned and told me. But, please—come in, come in!"

Mrs. Rosenthal welcomed them into a parlor whose every stick of furniture wore a doily yarmulke. From the kitchen, she brought out a plate of mandelbrodt and a pot of coffee.

"Sergei Lubovitch!" Mrs. Rosenthal exclaimed, pressing her fingers to her lips. "I haven't seen you since you were a baby. And here you are, grown. And so handsome."

"You don't look a day older, Mrs. Rosenthal. Why, I'd know you anywhere," Sam said.

The charm didn't fail to work on Mrs. Rosenthal, who laughed and waved away the compliment. "Tell me of your mother and father."

"My father runs a fur shop in Chicago. My mother, I'm sorry to say, died many years ago."

Mrs. Rosenthal put a hand to her chest and bowed her head. "Such terrible news. Poor Miriam. I remember on the ship coming over, she was so sick with you."

Sam had heard this story quite a few times from his parents. The "We Left Everything Behind and Braved a Treacherous Voyage to a New World in Order to Give You the Best Possible Life" story. Usually it was leverage to get him to do whatever they needed—study the Torah or help his father in the store. He wanted to ask Mrs. Rosenthal about the letter, but he couldn't rush into this and insult her or she'd know this was more than a social call, so he sipped his coffee and waited for an opening.

"The ferries brought us to Ellis Island, and when we see the Statue of Liberty, like an angel in the harbor, we are crying. From joy. From relief. Hope. We had nothing." Mrs. Rosenthal's voice quavered with emotion. "This country took us in."

"God bless America," Sam said. He needed to cut off Anna Rosenthal before she devolved into further sentimentality and, possibly, folk singing, so he reached into his jacket pocket and pulled out the mysterious envelope. "Mrs. Rosenthal, I came across something of my mother's that had me scratching my head, and I wondered if you might know anything about it. It's from someone named Rotke Wasserman."

Mrs. Rosenthal squinted at the writing on the envelope as Sam handed it over. "Yes, yes, I remember. It came after your mother and father were gone. The Wasserman woman sometimes would come to work with Miriam. Because of her gift," Mrs. Rosenthal said matter-of-factly and sipped her coffee.

"Her gift. You mean as a nurse?" Sam asked, confused.

"Nurse." Mrs. Rosenthal made a *tsk* sound, as if the word was an insult. "A nurse, yes. In this country. But before? She was the best fortune-teller in Ukraine. People come from everywhere to ask about marriages, babies, if they should open this business or sell that cow. Even the Mad Monk himself, Rasputin"—Mrs. Rosenthal spat, uttering a curse in Russian—"came to see the great Miriam Lubovitch."

"I thought my mother was a nurse," was all Sam could seem to say.

"On our papers, we had to write occupation. Most write wife, mother, cook, seamstress, maybe. Like that. Your mother puts fortune-teller." Mrs. Rosenthal shook her head. "We're afraid they won't like it. It is not a country for superstition. But that woman, Miss Wasserman, speaks Russian. She says, Miriam, will you take a test for me—"

"What kind of test?" Evie interrupted.

273

Mrs. Rosenthal shrugged. "How should I know? I only know she must do well, because they let us all in. They say, don't worry, don't worry, you are safe here, and they give her something to feel better. Water. Rest. Meat and vitamins for strength. Soon, she is better. And that is why you are here now, Sergei. An American. For a while, your mother, father, and I settled with cousins of mine on Orchard Street before your parents took their own rooms on Hester. Every now and then, Miss Wasserman would come to see you and your mother."

"Why's that?" Sam asked.

Again, the woman shrugged. "To see how you were. She would play games with you. She liked you. Who wouldn't?"

"The letter," Sam said, drawing her attention back to the yellowed envelope. "You didn't send it on to them in Chicago?"

"I should know where they went? For ten years, I hear nothing. I know nothing, till you telephoned," Mrs. Rosenthal said, hurt creeping into her tone.

Sam couldn't imagine why his parents would've been so rude. It wasn't like them at all.

"It was those men, I think," Mrs. Rosenthal said suddenly. "They came and frightened your mother. Your parents were gone the next day, like ghosts."

"What men?"

"Some men in dark suits came to see your mother. I walked them up to your apartment."

"Who were they?" Sam asked. His tapped his fingers frantically. Evie put her hand over his to stop him.

Mrs. Rosenthal shook her head. "They say immigration, which makes us nervous. Some anarchists are Jews. What if they think we are anarchists and throw us out of the country? The men, they want me to go away, but your mother says, 'Anna must stay.' She says my English is better—a lie. I could see she was afraid. They ask her questions: Was she getting along all right? How was the neighborhood? Any trouble to report? Fine, fine, all fine, she told them. It was all fine until they ask about you."

"Me?"

"Sam?" Evie said at the same time.

Mrs. Rosenthal nodded. "How you were, if you were healthy, did you take after your father or were you more like your mother? Were you special?" She made a face. "This is a thing you ask a mother? Is her son special? I think your mother will talk for a week about how special you are. But no." Mrs. Rosenthal worried her napkin in her lap. "This, maybe, I shouldn't say."

Sam had given up on charming Anna Rosenthal. "Please, Mrs. Rosenthal," he pleaded. "I need to know what happened."

After a deep, weary breath, Mrs. Rosenthal continued. "Your mother tells the men, 'That little *pisher* weakling? He is sick and small, a disappointment. Not like me at all.'" Mrs. Rosenthal shook her head. "I was shocked. How could she say such a thing? You were her prince, Sergei. You brought her such *naches*. This was not the Miriam I knew, I can tell you."

From what Sam remembered of his childhood, his mother had always doted on him, taken his side. Protected him.

"The next day, your mother and father left Hester Street for good without so much as a good-bye to anyone—only two weeks before my wedding! I try not to take it personally, but..." Mrs. Rosenthal trailed off, sipped her coffee. She handed the envelope over to Sam. "When that letter came...*psssht*, I was angry. I send it back."

"But you don't know what the letter said?"

"Anna Rosenthal does not snoop in private papers. But there is something. Miriam asked me to keep it. Come."

From a corner closet, Mrs. Rosenthal took a box down from the shelf. "Just after the men visited, your mother gives something to me. 'Anna,' she tells me, 'hide this in your house. I will come later for it.' But she never did."

Mrs. Rosenthal opened the box and retrieved a cookie tin. "It's right that you should have this now."

"I can't thank you enough, Mrs. Rosenthal," Sam said, taking the tin. It was all he could do not to rip off the lid right there. "Gosh, would ya look at the time? Golly, I wish we could stay longer, Mrs. Rosenthal, but we've got to get Lamb Chop here back to the radio station for her show."

"But we'll send you an invitation to the wedding," Evie said cheerily as Sam edged her toward the door.

"You'll come for Shabbos," Mrs. Rosenthal called after them.

"We'll Shabbos as much as possible," Evie said as Sam practically dragged her from the apartment.

☀

"How was I supposed to know Shabbos is the Jewish Sabbath?" Evie said as she and Sam boarded the nearly empty El back to Manhattan. "And it couldn't hurt to invite her to a wedding that'll never happen. Sam, is everything jake? You look like you just got off a roller coaster."

"Evie, I didn't know any of that about my mother," Sam said as he watched the Bronx roll past the train's windows.

Evie shook the tin gently. "I'm guessing it's not cookies."

Evie slid closer to Sam, who pried off the lid. Inside were two items: a file and an old photograph of a woman wearing a long plaid dress and holding a little boy's hand.

"That's my mother," Sam said, staring at the sweet photo. "And that's me."

Evie giggled.

"What's so funny?" Sam asked.

"You in short pants. And those are some chubby cheeks!"

"That's enough of that," Sam said, yanking the photograph away. He lifted the file, which was just a typed sheet. "Looks like a report."

```
U.S. Department of Paranormal
Office B-130
New York, New York
Date: September 8, 1908
Name: Miriam Lubovitch
```

```
Race: Jewish
Age: 20
Country of Origin: Ukraine
Address: 122 Hester Street, New York, New York.
Subject has passed all tests. In good health.
Recommended candidate: Project Buffalo.
```

Across the bottom, the page was stamped: APPROVED.

Sam's insides buzzed. "You know what I'm gonna ask, don't you?"

Evie nodded. "A deal's a deal."

"You know, at times like these, I'd consider making an honest woman of you, future Mrs. Lloyd."

"I said I'd read it. There's no need to torture me, Sam." Evie took the file between her palms and pressed down. But no matter how hard she tried, nothing flared. "Gee, I'm sorry, Sam. I can't get a thing from this report. Honest, I can't," she said, feeling rather put out about it. For her to decide not to read an object was one thing. It was entirely another for a read to feel beyond her capabilities.

"Well, thanks for trying, anyway," Sam said.

Evie examined the file again. "Office B-130. But there's no address. That office could be anywhere."

"I know." Sam sighed. "Every time we get one answer it leaves us with twelve new questions."

"What about your creepy man?"

"Do you mean my contact?"

Evie waved his words away. "Contact, creepy man..."

"Last time I saw him, he told me he thought he was being watched."

"By whom? Gangsters?"

"Don't know. He just told me to stay away. But this is too important. I gotta try."

"Sam, did you ever think of asking a reporter to look into this story?"

"Are you crackers? Bring one of those shiny-suit-wearing newshounds into this?"

"But why not? Put one of those dogs on the scent! They'll find the goods soon enough."

"Nothing doing. I work alone. With occasional company," he acknowledged. "But no reporters. Got it?"

Evie put her hands up. "Forget I mentioned it. Oh," she said, wincing. "What a skull-banger."

She rested her throbbing head against the train window as the El rattled through city canyons. The last rays of sunlight brightened rooftops and glinted off office windows, reluctant to say good-bye. Down below, the afternoon gloom bathed the bustling city streets in deepening shadows of loneliness. Sam laced his fingers through Evie's and held fast. It was a small gesture, but Evie felt it everywhere at once.

"You're the elephant's eyebrows, doll," he said.

Evie's face was suddenly too warm. "Someone has to look after you, Sam Lloyd."

The train rattled to a stop.

"Come on. I'll walk you to the station," Sam said, offering his crooked arm. "Gotta put on a show for the adoring fans."

"Right," Evie said, threading her arm through his. "For the fans."

On their walk to WGI, Sam and Evie were mobbed by New Yorkers who were happy to shake their hands and wish them well. They called Sam's and Evie's names as if the two of them were movie stars or royalty.

"Tell me the truth, Sam—isn't that the best sound you ever heard? I don't think I'll ever get tired of it."

"Gee. You might have to keep me on, then," Sam teased. The truth was, he was enjoying their cooked-up romance a little too much. Whenever Evie looked at him from across whatever room they were working, he got a feeling in his stomach like they were sharing the most delicious secret. It was fun and exciting—the two of them against the world. He dreaded the countdown to the end of it all. Was it too much to hope that he could change her mind along the way?

"Have a swell show, darling," Sam said, playing his part. He kissed Evie's hand and turned to the crowd. "Folks, you have no idea how soft this girl's hand is. Oh, hold on a second—that's her glove. Folks, you have no idea how soft this girl's gloves are!"

Everybody laughed, including Evie, and Sam's hopes rose anew. He gave her a *you liked that?* grin, and he could swear by the way she bit her lip and smiled that she did. He wanted nothing more than to come up with ways to keep her smiling.

"Good-bye, Sam," Evie said, shaking her head.

As she pushed through WGI's front doors, Evie glanced back at the scene on the street. The girls beamed at Sam as he charmed them, his dark hair flopping into his eyes. A twinge of jealousy bit at Evie. She'd had the urge to kiss Sam right there so that everyone would know he was indisputably hers. Except that he wasn't. This was a game. A business arrangement. And falling for Sam Lloyd was the don't-you-dare cherry on top of a worst-idea sundae.

"Stop it, Evie O'Neill," she whispered to herself. "Stop it right this instant."

Evie was startled to see Sarah Snow standing in the deep shadows cast by WGI's grand gilded Art Deco clock.

"You've drawn quite the crowd, Miss O'Neill," Sarah said, her gaze directed out at the throngs of adoring fans, some of them still shouting Evie's name.

"Oh. Well." Evie was suddenly at a loss for words. "You have admirers, too, Miss Snow."

"Not like yours," Sarah said, her eyes still on the crowd. "If I did, Mr. Phillips might not threaten to cancel my radio hour. Apparently, my sponsor doesn't find bringing lost souls to Jesus as entertaining or profitable as reading objects. There's money for Diviners, but not the Divine." For just a moment, Sarah's eyes flashed. But then her placid smile returned. "I must say, I've come to admire your courage, Miss O'Neill."

"My courage?"

"Yes, indeed. It's quite brave of you to handle all those objects belonging to complete strangers. Why, some people would be afraid."

"Afraid of what?" Evie said.

"There's our little radio star!" Mr. Phillips boomed. He marched toward her, brandishing a newspaper, a retinue of secretaries and reporters behind him. "Great showing at the fights last night. You two were more popular than the boxing," he said, holding out the *Daily News*, where the front-page picture showed Sam and Evie sitting ringside. "I tell you, I wish I had twenty of this girl! I hope I'm not interrupting anything?"

"Not at all, Mr. Phillips," Sarah Snow answered calmly. "I was just telling Miss O'Neill how much I admire her courage."

"Whaddaya mean?" a reporter asked.

"Why, the sleeping sickness, of course. After all, we don't know how people take ill. Anyone could have it. Any object could be contaminated."

"Say, that's true," a reporter said, jotting it down. "You ever get spooked about that, Miss O'Neill?"

"Oh. Gee..." Evie said. She'd never thought about it before, but now the worry wormed its way into her thoughts. What did she know about the objects people brought in? About the people? Nothing, really. Not until she was already pressing into their secrets with her hands, and then it was too late.

"Now, now, our Evie isn't afraid of some little old sleeping sickness," Mr. Phillips said, waving the thought away, as he did anything that didn't affect him directly. "It's mostly confined to downtown, isn't it? It's a matter of proper hygiene. Those people don't come to WGI, I can guarantee you."

"Of course, Mr. Phillips. I'm sure it's all perfectly fine. Still, I suppose you never know what you're in for when someone hands you their secrets," Sarah Snow said. Her smile followed two seconds too late.

"These fellas want a picture of us in the studio, Evie," Mr. Phillips said, then escorted Evie and the reporters toward WGI's bank of shining elevators. As the elevator doors closed on the grand marble lobby and the crowd of admirers on the other side of the glass doors, Evie saw that Sarah Snow was still standing in the clock's deep shadows, watching her intently.

It reminded Evie for all the world of a cat watching a mouse.

But then she was on the radio, her voice reaching out to people everywhere. The applause was for her. Afterward, fans lined up around the block to have her sign their autograph books. And Sarah Snow was forgotten.

Evie decided to walk the ten blocks back home to the Winthrop so she could enjoy the admiring looks of people on the street.

"A penny for one who served, Miss?"

A filthy, unshaven man in a wheelchair shook his cup at her. Evie recognized him as the veteran she'd given money to during her first week in New York.

"The time is now. The time is now," he murmured. His anguished eyes searched for something beyond sight.

Evie was angry that this poor man, ruined by war, had been abandoned to a hard life on the streets. If Sarah Snow were here now, Evie would ask her to explain why her God allowed war and poverty and cruelty to happen so often. Sometimes, Evie wished she had an object of God's to read so that she could begin to understand.

"Help," the veteran croaked. "Please."

Evie had three dollars to her name; Prohibition gin wasn't cheap. *To hell with it*, she thought. She was the Sweetheart Seer; she'd get somebody to buy her a drink.

"Here you are, sir," she said and stuffed all three dollars into the soldier's can. Quick as loose mercury, the man grabbed her wrist. His grip was surprisingly strong.

"I hear them screaming," the man whispered urgently through gritted teeth. Spit foamed at the corners of his cracked lips.

"Let go!" Evie cried.

"The eye. Follow the eye," he pleaded.

"Let me go! Please!"

Evie stumbled back and the man banged his head softly against the brick, keening, "Stop, please. Stop screaming. Stop screaming...."

GIFTS

"How come you lied to Sister Walker the other day about where you're from?" Isaiah asked Blind Bill as they walked back from the barbershop toward home. Octavia had to stay late at the school, and Bill had offered to take the boy to Floyd's for a trim so he'd look nice for church on Sunday.

"That woman don't need to know my business," Bill said. "It don't pay to tell folks too much about yourself. You understand me?"

"Yes, sir."

"I want you to tell me about your time with Sister Walker. What she make you do?"

"She didn't make me do anything."

"No, no. I know ain't nobody can make little man do what he don't want to do," Bill said, giving a tight smile. "She do the cards with you, though, right?"

"Yes, sir."

"How many you get right?"

"The last time, I got all of 'em right!" Isaiah crowed.

Bill whistled. "That a fact?"

"Mm-hmm. I was good at it," Isaiah said. "Corner here, Mr. Johnson. Watch out."

"Thank you, son. But you know I ain't Mr. Johnson. You call me Uncle Bill."

"Yes, sir, Uncle Bill," the boy said, and he sounded pleased.

"Seems to me that's a mighty powerful gift you got there. Nothing bad about it," Bill said as Isaiah led him around the corner. Bill could've navigated it himself, but he let the boy do it since it made him feel important.

"That's what *I* said!" Isaiah blurted.

"Well, now, it wouldn't do for me to tell you to go against your aunt. But you know how women do."

"Yes, I surely do," Isaiah said on a sigh. The sound of the little man's voice, going on like he knew about women, made Bill want to laugh. He reached out and ran his hand over the top of Isaiah's head like a pleased father.

"Sometimes men got to have their secrets. Am I right?"

"Right."

"So what we gonna do is, we gonna have a little secret 'tween us men right now, all right? Now, you can't be telling your auntie 'bout none of this. This is men talk!"

"All right," Isaiah said, sounding pleased again.

"Shake on it," Bill said and took the boy's small, soft hand in his own rough, weathered one. "Old Bill thinks you oughta be working on your special gift. Making it stronger. And I'm gonna help you come into your gifts right. What you say to that?"

Isaiah was all balled up. After he'd recovered from his fit, Isaiah had gone to church with Octavia to see Pastor Brown, who had prayed over him, and they'd made Isaiah promise that he'd never use his powers again. But now here was another grown-up, Blind Bill, asking him to open it all back up. Isaiah didn't know what was right or wrong anymore.

"Auntie told me not to," was all he said, as if that could settle the matter.

Bill took a deep breath through his teeth and whistled it out, thinking about just what to say next. "Your auntie is a good woman. A smart woman. I wouldn't never go against her. I just want to make sure whatever Sister Walker done to you is all gone, you see? Want to make sure there's nothing that the pastor and prayer didn't get rid of. Understand?"

"You think something bad could be hiding inside me, left over from Sister Walker?" Isaiah asked, his voice quavery.

"No need to be scared, son. I'll protect you. I'll take it on, as if I was your daddy. Once the bad's gone, you'll have your gifts back, good as new, fresh as Eden. You reckon that's all right, then? If I watch over you and promise to keep you safe like your daddy would do if he were here?"

Isaiah swallowed hard against the ballooning in his throat. Sometimes he couldn't even remember his daddy's face, and when that happened, it was like he was losing a part of himself, like waking from a good dream and trying desperately to go back into sleep and grab the ribbon's end of that other world as it slips away for good. He dug his fingernails into the soft pillowing of flesh at the base of his thumb. "I reckon that'd be okay."

"Good, good. Let's go on up to the graveyard. Ain't far from here."

Isaiah led Bill the few blocks to the cemetery, where they found a mausoleum with an open door and went inside.

"Spooky in here," Isaiah said, his voice echoing a bit in the space.

"Can't have nobody watching us," Bill explained. "Here. Take hold o' my hands, now," Bill said, and the boy laid his own palms, soft and unformed, against the rough calluses of Bill's. "You good, little man?"

Isaiah nodded, then remembered Bill's blindness. "Yes, sir," he answered.

"All right, then. No tickling now. 'Cause I'm real ticklish!" Bill reached out and tickled Isaiah under the chin, making him laugh. The boy sounded happy enough. Good. Bill needed him relaxed. He took the boy's hands again. "Let's start easy. Gonna make a connection with me, now. You tell me if you see a lucky policy number for your old Uncle Bill, and if I win some money, I'll buy you a new baseball. Just close your eyes."

Isaiah took his hands away. "I'm scared."

"Nothing to be scared of. I'ma take care of you."

Isaiah put his hands back.

"Nice and easy now. Just a little taste..."

There was nothing but the sound of leaves skittering across the tombstones. And then, suddenly, a pull on Isaiah's fingers, like the first nibble of a fish on a baited hook. The connection trickled up Bill's arm, warming into a pleasant, electric buzz under the skin. The boy's body stiffened, but his voice had the calm of a sleepwalker. "I see a house and long road. A lot of sky."

"Yeah? You see a number, little man?" Power flowed from Isaiah's body to Bill's. He had to be careful not to drain the boy. He just needed a number.

"A tree." Isaiah jerked. He sounded a little scared. "Tree."

"You ain't scared of no tree, is ya?" Bill said, impatient.

Isaiah twitched twice, yanking on Bill's grip. Dammit. He couldn't stay too much longer or he might hurt the boy. But Dutch needed Bill's money, and that meant Bill needed a number.

"What about a number? What numbers you see?"

Isaiah's whole body trembled. Bill could feel it traveling up his arms.

"One, four, four," the boy said. "One, four, four," he repeated, louder.

That couldn't be right. One, four, four was the number Isaiah had given him the last time, and it had done very nicely for Bill. But odds weren't good that it would be a winner again so soon. "You sure you seeing that right, little man? Look close—"

"One, four, four! One, four, four! Ghosts on the road! Gonna come for us. Ghosts on the road. Ghosts on the road, Ghosts on the road..."

God Almighty, his skin burned! The boy had a grip on him but good. Bill couldn't break it. "I-sai-ah..." he grunted, biting down on his back teeth.

"The snake and the tree and the ghosts on the road. The man, the man, the man in the hat is coming...."

Isaiah's body started to twitch and jerk. Another few seconds and it'd be too much. With a yelp, Bill broke the grip, catching the boy in his arms as he fell.

"Easy now, easy now," Bill said, though Isaiah was beyond hearing. He put a hand on the boy's chest. The rise and fall of his breathing was a relief, and a moment later, Isaiah's voice called out, a little sleepy, "Mr. Johnson?"

"I'm right here, little man. Your Uncle Bill's here. You all right?"

"Mm-hmm. Did I have another fit?" the boy asked, and Bill could hear the fear in his voice as he came around.

"Nah. Weren't no fit. Just...when you see that other world, it's like you go to sleep for a bit. That's all. Just a little sleep. No harm in it. How you feel now?"

"Fine. A little tired, though."

"But you 'member what I told you now, 'bout this being our secret?"

"Yes, sir."

"And you ain't gonna tell nobody that we practicing till you can show 'em all how good you got?"

"No, sir!" The boy sounded light, happy, like a horse that had finally gotten to run wild.

"Not even your brother."

A slight pause. "He's never around, anyway."

"Don't you worry—I'm here now, son. Right by your side."

The boy took his hand as they exited the mausoleum. Bill hugged him close and patted his shoulder just so.

"What say we go get us some ice cream down to Mr. Reggie's, then?"

"Yes, sir!"

"Now. Tell me: Who's somethin' special?"

"I am," Isaiah said quietly.

"You sure about that, now? Don't sound so sure," Bill teased, and this time the boy came back with a resounding "I am! I am!" that startled the birds into squawking flight.

"Lead the way, son."

One, four, four. Bill would play the number again, see if it came up lucky a second time.

"Mr. Johnson?" Isaiah asked as they left the graveyard, hand in hand, walking toward the center of Harlem against a bracing, biting wind.

"Yes, little man?"

"Who is Guillaume?"

BEACH'S PNEUMATIC

On the bus ride to the Seward Park Library, Ling's thoughts were on the previous night's dream walk. She pressed her fingers to the bus windows, feeling the cold glass and thinking of how those same fingers had transformed the dreamscape, shifting its atoms toward something new and full of energy. It had made her aware of the universe she carried inside, of the ways in which she was both wave and particle, always in flux, always changing. It had all been magical, except for that strange moment with the tunnel and Wai-Mae's warning. Surely, there had to be a scientific explanation for the bursts of light and sound coming from that tunnel, some energy source worth exploring? No ghosts Ling had ever spoken to behaved in that manner.

Mrs. Belpre, the librarian, smiled at Ling when she arrived at the library, asking how Ling had liked the books and recommending others. Ling asked if she knew anything about a matchmaking outfit called O'Bannion and Lee, but Mrs. Belpre shook her head.

"And how is your friend George?" she asked in hushed tones.

"The same," Ling said.

"I hope he wakes up soon," Mrs. Belpre said, patting Ling's hand.

Ling vaguely recalled bits of last night's dream she'd had about George. Dreams were symbols. Puzzle pieces. For the life of her, she couldn't quite put this one together yet. There had been something about George in the train station.

The train station. That was curious.

When Ling dream walked, she could read words quite clearly. In actual dreaming, though, she never really could. The words blurred or her mind drifted elsewhere. But last night—yes, she remembered now!—she had been able to read perfectly: BEACH PNEUMATIC TRANSIT COMPANY. On impulse, Ling made her way to the card catalog, flipping through until she came to an entry that excited her. There it was on the card, in black and white: *Beach Pneumatic Transit Company*.

It was real. Or it had been.

Ling put aside her science books and combed through old newspapers, reading about a place she thought she and Henry had invented, a place that existed only in dreams.

Rew York Tribune

FEBRUARY 26, 1870

ASTONISHING ACCOMPLISHMENT! MR. A. E. BEACH AT LAST UNVEILS PNEUMATIC UNDERGROUND RAILWAY WITH OPULENT RECEPTION!

Pledges to Extend Line to Central Park

A marvel of modern transport was unveiled this morning deep below the hustle and bustle of New York's crowded city streets. The Beach Pneumatic Transit Company, constructed by teams of men working day and night and with great secrecy until recently, was introduced to a curious public by its inventor and architect, Mr. Alfred Ely Beach, editor of *Scientific American*.

For a year, the corner of Warren Street and Broadway, occupied by Devlin's Clothing

Store at Number 260 Broadway, has been the subject of much speculation. Passersby have remarked on the shaking ground, the tunneling equipment, and the piles of dirt left behind the store each night. As of today, the entire thrilling enterprise is speculation no more.

"Ladies and gentlemen! Today we unveil the future of travel beneath these very streets—the Beach Pneumatic Transit Company. See this wonder for yourselves and be amazed," Mr. Beach crowed to a handsomely furnished waiting room filled with reporters, dignitaries, and city politicians eager for a ride on his underground marvel, which runs the length of Broadway, originating at Warren Street beneath Devlin's Clothing Store and terminating at Murray Street, traveling a distance of three hundred feet by means of forced air generated by a large fan, though Mr. Beach proposes to build longer tunnels.

Ling read the newspaper again: Beach Pneumatic Transit Company; Devlin's Clothing Store; 260 Broadway; corner of Broadway and Warren. Accompanying the article was an artist's illustration of the station as it had looked on opening day: the elevated waiting area, the chandeliers and fountain, and even the piano. It was clearly the same station from their dream walks. Furiously, she read through the other clippings until she came upon a second article:

BEACH'S PNEUMATIC DREAM RUNS OUT OF AIR

City to Close First Underground Station Today

Ling quickly read the article through. Mr. Beach had a hard go of making his experimental dream come true. And just as it looked hopeful, an economic panic gripped New York and the rest of the country in 1873. There was no money to advance an idea of an underground train system. Mr. Beach's subway prototype was closed for good in 1873, becoming a shooting gallery for a while. In 1875, its beautiful fixtures were sealed behind rock.

Future articles only briefly mentioned the Beach Pneumatic Transit Company. The city moved on. Devlin's Clothing Store became Rogers, Peet & Co., which burned to the ground. Another building went up in its place. In 1904, the first subway station, City Hall, opened near the site of the old pneumatic train. Tunnels were dug. New subways were built, though Mr. Beach would never live to see them. His pneumatic transit dream was long gone, nothing but an obscure footnote in New York City history.

So why was it showing up in Ling's and Henry's dreams now?

A commotion up front drew Ling's attention. Police officers had arrived and were asking patrons to pack up and leave. Mrs. Belpre argued in hushed tones with the health inspector, who pestered her for the names of everyone she knew who had visited the library in the past two weeks. "To investigate further," he said. "After all, it's a matter of public health."

Mrs. Belpre remained firm. "No. It's a matter of privacy."

"What's the matter?" Ling whispered to a mother gathering her children.

"They're closing the library because of the sleeping sickness," the mother answered in Cantonese. "They're afraid the library might be contaminated. They're calling it a public health emergency. Just this morning, they closed the elementary school and boarded up the temple and the public bath."

A police officer came to Ling's table. "Everyone has to leave, Miss," he said and seemed apologetic. Ling stacked the articles and books neatly on the table and made her way to the door.

On her way out of the library, Ling passed a man poised on the front steps with a bucket of glue and a brush. He pasted a bill to the library's front doors: CLOSED UNTIL FURTHER NOTICE BY ORDER OF NEW YORK CITY DEPARTMENT OF HEALTH.

As Ling waited for the bus back to Chinatown, her mind raced. The Beach Pneumatic Transit Company had existed. It had been built underneath Devlin's Clothing Store. And every night, Ling and Henry saw both in their dream walks. The bus arrived but Ling didn't get on it. Instead, she boarded the Broadway trolley, stepping off at City Hall Park.

In her dream, George had led her to a drinking fountain, so Ling set off in that direction until she found it. She took a sip and watched governesses pushing baby carriages down the tree-lined path. What, precisely, was she hoping to discover here? Beside the fountain was the grate. Ling stood over it, looking down through the old metal bars into the underground, feeling the breeze coming from below.

"Spare a penny, young lady?" a vagrant asked from a park bench.

He reeked of urine. Ling moved just slightly upwind. She stared out at the symphony of movement on Broadway—cars and trolleys and people rushing everywhere without stopping. Last night in the dream, as Ling stood in this very spot, George had been pointing to something behind her. What had he wanted her to see? Ling scrutinized the row of office buildings until she realized that this was the very corner she and Henry saw each night in that strange, repeated dream loop at the beginning of their walk—just from an earlier era. It was as if she and Henry were being visited by a ghost city lost to the pages of history.

"Hard on the streets in the cold, Miss," the vagrant said, and this time, Ling dropped a penny into his palm.

"Thanks, Miss. Yes, cold, cold, cold. Used to sleep down there, in the tunnels," he said, nodding at the grate. "But I don't go down below no more. Bad dreams there. You can hear it calling you. Bad dreams was what got Sal and Moses and Ralph. And I ain't seen hide nor hair of old Patrick and his wife, Maudie, neither." His eyes widened and he dropped his voice to an urgent whisper. "Somethin's down there, Miss. Ghosts," he said, looking up at the spectral spires of the foggy skyline.

Then he leaped up from the bench and toddled off, palm outstretched, toward a passing couple, calling, "'Scuse me, kind sir, dear miss, spare a penny?"

The air smelled of coming rain, so Ling left City Hall Park and took the bus back to Chinatown. On the edge of Mulberry Street, people crowded into Columbus Park, where a man with a bullhorn who was accompanied by a Chinese translator explained that there would be mandatory health screenings starting immediately.

"All residents must report with documentation," the man barked.

There was outrage in the crowd.

"You can't treat us this way! We have rights!" Thomas Chung called. He was twenty-eight, a lawyer who'd graduated from Princeton. Watching him there in the park beside his mother and father, Ling thought he looked as much a hero as Jake Marlowe.

"*Citizens* have rights," the man with the bullhorn shouted back.

"I was born here. I am a citizen. But we have rights as human beings," Thomas said. Others joined his protest—not just people from Chinatown, but neighbors she recognized from over on Orchard and Ludlow Streets and Little Italy, too. The man with the bullhorn was shouting, "If you do not comply, we will be forced to put you all in quarantine camps!"

"Ling!"

Ling turned and saw Gracie Leung squeezing through the crowd.

"Ling! Did you hear? Isn't it awful?" she said once she'd reached her.

"Hear what, Gracie?" Ling asked, irritated. She hated the way Gracie drew out her gossip in breathless fashion.

"It's George!"

Ling went cold. "What about George?"

Gracie burst into tears. "Oh, Ling. He *died*!"

Everything in the park narrowed to a point. Ling could scarcely breathe.

"That's why they're here now," Gracie said, pointing toward the man with the bullhorn. She wiped away her tears. "His mother found him this morning. His entire body was covered in blisters, like he'd been eaten up from the inside, and there was nothing left. And when they went to move him, his bones…" Gracie choked back a sob. "His bones crumbled like ash."

Ling remembered the very end of her dream. Something terrifying had been closing in on George, and he already looked dead, like a man who knows his executioner waits. *Ling Chan—Wake. Up*, he'd said, a command.

A warning.

EYES ON THE SKY

"You're awfully quiet tonight, Miss Chan," Henry said from his perch at the piano as he and Ling waited for the train into the dream world. Down below, Ling sat on the edge of the fountain, her fingers trailing absently through the water.

"My friend George died today," Ling said numbly. "He had the sleeping sickness."

She watched the goldfish zipping through the water, an agitation of orange.

"Oh, Ling. I'm awfully sorry to hear it," Henry said, coming to sit beside her.

"Thank you," Ling mumbled. "I dreamed about him. Last night."

Henry was quiet for a moment. "Maybe he was saying good-bye."

"Maybe," Ling said. But the dream hadn't been peaceful in any way. George's death had hit Ling hard. Somehow, all along, she had believed he would beat it. He was young and strong. But she understood that illness was capricious and unfair. After all, Ling had been young and strong, too. And it hadn't made a bit of difference to her legs.

The train whooshed into the station. Without a word, Henry offered his arm, and Ling did not refuse it.

"What's the matter, Little Warrior?" Wai-Mae said the moment Ling got off the train in the forest.

"She lost her friend George to the sleeping sickness today," Henry said, and the three of them stood listening to the soft chirrup of birds, not knowing what to say or do next.

"We should give his spirit rest," Wai-Mae said at last.

"What do you mean?" Henry asked.

"It is very important to honor the dead. To make certain they can be happy in the afterlife, especially if it has been a very hard death," Wai-Mae said. "Otherwise, the spirit can't rest."

Henry thought of his mother sitting in the cemetery working her rosary beads, all those painted saints giving her comfort. He thought, too, of burying Gaspard with a soup bone. Rituals were important. "I'll get Louis," he said, patting Ling's shoulder. "We'll do this right, Chinatown–New Orleans style."

Henry, Louis, Wai-Mae, and Ling gathered on the hill above the golden village. Louis played a slow tune on his fiddle and Henry sang a hymn he'd learned as a boy. Wai-Mae plucked a twig from a nearby tree and transformed it into incense, which she lit with a candle made from a stalk of grass. Its sweet, smoky fragrance joined the pine and gardenia.

"How did you do that?" Henry asked, astonished.

But already Wai-Mae had gathered a handful of pebbles and was squeezing them in her fist, a look of fierce concentration on her face. When she opened her hand, it held a cup of tea.

"For your friend," she said, and Ling left the offering on a bed of wildflowers.

"I don't have a picture of George," Ling said to Wai-Mae. "We should have one."

Wai-Mae handed her a stick. "Draw."

Ling did as she was told, dragging the stick through the dirt to make a simple representation of a face—a circle, two slashes for eyes, a line for a nose, and another for a mouth. Ling looked to Wai-Mae.

"You know what to do," Wai-Mae said, guiding Ling's hands to the image in the dirt.

Ling shook her head. "I don't think I can do it."

"Yes, you can," Wai-Mae assured her.

Ling pictured George's face in her mind, but all she could see was the ghostly George from her dream. She took a deep breath, and then she saw him as she had known him in life—skinny, hare-quick, mouth in a half smile, brows raised as if he were constantly surprised. That stupid snort. His hopeful eyes darting toward the Tea House door each time it opened, as if someone might walk through with his beautiful future cradled in her hands.

The buzzing sparked across the tips of her fingers. It coursed along her skin everywhere and shot straight up her neck, making her head balloon-light. And then the vibrations resonated deep inside, as if some part of her had joined this dream world, all her molecules shifting toward something yet to be written. Cracks formed in the earth.

Ling opened her eyes, feeling a bit woozy. Where the crude dirt drawing had been, a sapling, yellow-green with new life, now reached toward the sun. Tiny red buds struggled out of white casings. As she watched the light sparking along its fresh tendrils, it struck Ling as both funny and yet so perfect. This was the essence of George: something always on the verge of being born. Something not ready to die. She turned her head away so that the others couldn't see her tears.

"I did it," she whispered. And Ling didn't know if the tears sliding down her cheeks were for her dead friend or the guilty joy she felt at discovering this new power.

Brief lightning fluttered through the dreamscape. The tops of the trees lost all shape and color, as if they'd been erased by an angry child. The whining insect chorus pierced the quiet for just a moment. Wai-Mae said a prayer over George's symbolic grave. Ling scooped up a handful of dogwood blossoms and placed them near the sapling.

"For George. May all his dreams be happy now."

Henry nodded at Louis, and the two of them took up with a good-times song, as if they were joining a funeral procession on Bourbon Street, sadness giving way to celebration of the life lived. Far above, the dream sky settled into its rich golden hue.

"When I die, I hope someone will remember me so kindly," Wai-Mae said.

Nearby, a small flock of egrets took flight, crying into the shining pink clouds.

Wai-Mae took Ling's hand. "Look, his soul is free."

Ling kept her eyes on the sky, and she did not turn around to look at the pulsing light in the tunnel, nor did she listen to the screeching, growling chorus rising in the deep dark.

DREAMS WERE EVERYWHERE

The dreams were everywhere.

From the moment the people took their first breaths, they exhaled want until the air was thick with yearning.

Jericho dreamed of Evie. Firecrackers exploded in the sky above her. The ragged light gave her face an angel's glow and framed the outline of her body beneath her flimsy chemise. Her lips were an invitation, and Jericho moaned her name in his sleep.

Sam dreamed that he was a child walking with his mother, his hand in hers, safe and loved. But they were separated by sudden crowds of soldiers filling the street. Sam was lost. And then his mother's voice drifted out from a radio in a store window: "Find me, Little Fox."

In Mabel's dream, she climbed a tall platform and towered above a crowd of people who chanted her name. They were there to see her and no one else.

Isaiah dreamed of the boy in the boater hat and the girl with the green eyes, happy as can be, and Isaiah was afraid for them, as if he could see the storm bearing down on their idyll. He screamed and screamed that they were in danger, but no sound came out.

Drunk on gin, Evie would not remember her dreams come morning.

Theta dreamed of Memphis, and Memphis of Theta, and in both dreams, they were happy, and the world was kind.

But dreams can't be contained for long. Their natural trajectory is forward. Out. Up. Away. Past all barriers and borders. Into the world.

This is true of nightmares, too.

In the gloomy tunnel, the pale, hungry creatures crawled down the walls and into the old station. They tested the rusted gate. When it opened, they sniffed at the damp air, breathing in the intoxicating fumes from so much want, tasting it on their tongues, pushing out farther, crawling into the city's sewers and into the miles of subway tunnels, hiding in the archways when the trains rumbled past. They loitered in the shadows on the edges of the stations, where they could watch the bright lights of the people so full of yearning.

"*Dreams*," they murmured, ravenous.

In Substation Number Eleven beneath Park Row, the rotary converters shuddered to a halt, flummoxing the two men on duty. They thumped the dials on their control panels but the dials did not respond. "I'll go, Willard," said the more junior of the two, whose name was Stan. He grabbed a wrench from the tool board and, flashlight in hand, made his way along a futuristic corridor of humming pipes and tubes, taking the staircase down into the rotary converter room, that marvel of modern engineering, now dark and silent. Flipping the switches on the wall did nothing. Stan's flashlight beam swept over the hulking converters; in the dark, they were like the rounded backs of sleeping metal giants. On the far side of the room, light pulsed behind one of them—a downed wire, perhaps, or a small electrical fire trying to spark. Stan approached cautiously. He stopped when he heard the sound—a syrupy growl made deep in the throat. The growl shifted into a quick, low-pitched shriek that chilled Stan to the bone.

"Who's there?" he barked, gripping the wrench tight.

It was quiet for a moment, so quiet that Stan could hear only his own breathing, which was amplified by the cavernous room. And then, without warning, the scream exploded like a storm front. It sounded as if it were being torn note by note from the throats of a hundred damned souls. It filled the room so completely that Stan couldn't tell where it was coming from.

Behind the converter, the light crackled anew—one, two, three—projecting macabre shadows onto the substation's high white-tiled wall.

And then the thing stepped out. It appeared to have been a man once. Now it was something else entirely, something not human: pasty skin as cracked as dry earth and blighted by red patches and sores, hair thinned to spindly tufts. Opaque blue soulless eyes stared from its chalky, skeletal face. The glare of the flashlight caught the razor-sharp edges of small, yellowed teeth inside a rotted mouth that hung partially open.

"Help me..." Stan whispered like a frightened child. Because this was the stuff of nightmares left behind in the nursery.

The thing saw Stan. It cocked its head, sniffing. From deep down, the growl started, like a dog giving warning over its food. Black drool dribbled down from the sides of its mouth, and then its jaw unhinged, wider than humanly possible. It shrieked again, and Stan didn't care that he'd wet his pants or that he was blubbering as he stumbled backward toward the door. He was running now, but it was no use. Because there were more. Quick as beetles, they scuttled around the room. And there was nothing—no wrench, no flashlight, no reason—that could save him as the bright things closed in.

Back in the control room, Willard sat in his chair whistling to himself until Stan's scream echoing up from the substation's bowels stopped him cold.

"Jesus," he said on a sharp intake of breath. "Stan?" he called. And again, "Stan, that you?"

There was no answer.

"Stan?"

Nothing.

Willard knew he should get up. He should grab the lantern and go see what was what. One foot in front of the other and down the stairs. Easy.

He didn't move.

"Stan? You okay?" he called again, a little quieter this time.

He'd count to five. If Stan didn't come back by then, he'd go see. Under his breath, Willard counted softly: "One...two...three..." He took a shaking breath. "...Four..." And another. "...Fi—"

A shriek answered him. Up and down the corridor outside the control room, the lights flickered wildly. And then they winked out one by one, as if the electricity were being sucked up through an invisible straw. Still, Willard could not make himself go in the direction of the sound, even as he heard the guttural growls and eerie, breathy screeches crawling closer.

So the nightmares came to him.

And like the people and their dreams, they were hungry for more.

SMALL'S PARADISE

At half past midnight, Memphis paced in front of the Hotsy Totsy, nervously jangling the change in the trousers pocket of his borrowed tuxedo. His stiff shirt collar felt as tight as a tourniquet. He read over the poem he'd written that day, folded the paper again and tucked it back inside his suit jacket, then resumed pacing and occasionally peering down the street.

"Lord, Memphis, you're about to wear a hole through that pavement," the doorman, Clarence, said. "Somebody after you?"

"More like I'm after somebody," Memphis said.

A taxi pulled to the curb. Memphis heard a familiar husky voice calling, "Keep the change," and turned to see Theta stepping out of the backseat in a black beaded dress and white fox stole. She'd ringed her dark eyes in heavy kohl pencil so that they shone like two dark pearls. Her black bob was sleek and sharp. A smile tugged at the corners of her crimson mouth as she moved toward Memphis like a vision.

"Good evening, Princess," he said when he found his voice.

"You clean up nice, Poet," Theta said.

"You are..." He searched for the right word. "Incandescent."

Theta arched a thin brow. "Remind me to pack my dictionary next time."

Memphis smiled big. "Next time. I like the sound of that."

Clarence shot Memphis a look and opened the door, but Memphis waved him off.

"Aren't we going in?" Theta asked.

"Not here. It's a surprise, remember?"

Memphis escorted Theta over to Seventh Avenue and 134th Street. A cop walking his beat approached and Memphis hung back, keeping a careful distance from Theta. The cop tipped his hat to her, and Theta managed a tepid smile in response. When the cop moved on, Memphis fell into step with Theta again.

"Next corner," he said.

"So what's this big secret you got planned?"

"You're about to find out. Close your eyes," he said. "Now. Take three giant steps. Aaand…open."

Theta blinked up at the bright marquee. "Small's Paradise? Is this a joke?"

Memphis hooked his thumbs under his lapels. "Do I look like I'm kidding in this getup?"

"Okay, I give: What's the occasion?"

Memphis grinned. "It's the eighteenth anniversary of our very first date."

"This joint is swank. Where'd you get the cabbage for this, Poet?" Theta whispered as a white-gloved doorman ushered them inside with a cool "Good evening."

"Oh, sold some stock. Made a fortune on Canadian whiskey. Found out I'm actually a Rockefeller. You know how it goes," Memphis said. In truth, he'd been saving his money for weeks.

Memphis tipped the headwaiter five hard-earned dollars, and they were shown to a decent table—not as nice as the ones occupied by the really rich folks who could afford to tip a lot more than five dollars or the famous folks who could just waltz right in and have a table put down for them beside the dance floor, but it would do. The rule in the nightclub was that you could bring in your own flask, but Memphis wanted to buy bootleg from the waiters. It was expensive, but it kept the money here in Harlem, and it made Memphis feel like a real swell to do it in front of his girl. He wanted Theta to see him not as a strug-gling poet sharing a bedroom with his little brother in his aunt's house while running numbers for a Harlem banker, a fella trying to figure himself out as he moved along, but as man in the know. A somebody. Like the kind of crowd she ran with on the regular.

The house band—Charlie Johnson's Paradise Orchestra—kept the jazz percolating for a throng of dancers packed in so tightly it was a miracle anybody could move at all. Tuxedo-clad waiters twirled and danced between tables, keeping their heavy trays hoisted high above their heads without spilling a drop. There was even one enterprising waiter on roller skates. The whole atmosphere was one of a glamorous, anything-goes circus.

"When this band gets tired, the other band'll take over," Memphis said over the noise. "You never have to stop dancing. They'll still be going strong come sunup. We can stomp all night long."

"Let's hope there's no raid this time!" Theta shouted back.

"If it weren't for that raid, we never would've met."

"That's true. But one escape is enough, don'tcha think?" Theta said.

A waiter swooped down and delivered their cocktails, disguised in teacups. "Here you are, Miss. Sir," the waiter said, and Memphis could hear the subtle judgment lurking just under the courtesy: *What're you doing here with a white woman?*

"Thank you," Memphis said, making a point to be extra polite, even though it made him mad to do it. Like he was apologizing for some crime he hadn't committed. Even now, as he sneaked a look around, he could see disapproval in the faces of some folks. But maybe if he became a great man, a respected poet, it would be enough to let them bend the rules. And Memphis was writing every day now. Already he'd filled a notebook with new poems. Like the one in his pocket he'd written especially for Theta.

Memphis kept stealing glances at her now as she watched the dancers, hoping she was impressed. The last time they'd been together at the lighthouse, Theta had said that everything was fine, but Memphis could tell it wasn't. He was worried that it was him, that he wasn't enough. It was part of the reason he'd wanted to make tonight special.

"Everything copacetic, Princess?"

"Everything's swell," Theta answered, but beneath the silk of her gloves, Theta's skin prickled with a soft heat, and she tried not to panic. *It's nothing,* she told herself and kept her eyes on the dance floor, and after several deep breaths, the prickling went away. But she'd been feeling it more and more—ever since that night in the theater when she'd been running for her life from the Pentacle Killer. Once it had even happened in her sleep. She woke from a nightmare about screaming horses running wild in the snow around a burning village to find that her palms were as warm as freshly lit coals. She'd had to shove them under the tap for a few seconds to return them to normal.

"Well, then. I guess I should give you this." Memphis took the folded paper from his pocket and laid it on the table beside Theta's glass.

"What's this?"

"Anniversary present," Memphis said. "Been working on it for a week now."

Theta toyed with the edge of the paper. "Should I read it now or later?"

Memphis shrugged. "Whatever suits you."

Fresh heat licked up Theta's fingers. Her heart beat wildly. "I . . . I think I'm gonna save it for later, like a present," Theta said, slipping the note under her beaded handbag. She felt like crying, but she was afraid that if she did, her hands would really start acting up again. So she kept her eyes trained on the people dancing until they were a pretty blur of color.

Memphis tugged at his collar. His special anniversary date seemed to be going off the rails, fast. He watched as a group of white fellas escorted their dates to the floor, laughing and carefree. Every night, they came up by the carload to catch the action, then took it back with them downtown, where it was reborn in Broadway shows, swank clubs, and hotels that catered to whites only. It burned Memphis up that they could come here to *his* neighborhood, to *his* clubs with their dates, and it was no trouble at all. They expected to be able to do it, no questions asked. But Memphis had to be careful with his own girl in his own home.

Under the table, out of sight, Memphis laced his fingers with Theta's, enjoying the silky softness of her glove. Just to stroke her palm was a thrill. A couple of tables away, a group of Harlem high-hats stared with disapproval. Well, damn them. Damn the white fellas making the rules and the good people of Harlem for playing by them.

Memphis grasped Theta's fingers more solidly. Theta gasped.

"Trust me," Memphis said, and he brought their clasped knot of fingers out of hiding, resting them on the smooth sea of tablecloth. He stared back at his own people a few tables over, challenging them. Finally, they looked away, and Memphis enjoyed the thrill of winning: *Don't tell me how to live.* The orchestra launched into another dance number. More dancers swarmed toward the already crowded floor. A white couple passed by, their hands joined like Theta's and Memphis's. The girl, a blond in a sparkling rhinestone headband, looked from Theta to Memphis and back again. The girl might've taken a lot of care to dress the part of a sophisticate, but her expression was the truest thing she wore, and it was one of naked contempt. She paused for just a second to let her judgment settle on them.

Theta stared back. She didn't look happy. Memphis held Theta's hand firmly, letting her know that everything was jake. He was with her. Her hand was warm in his, very warm, and suddenly, Theta's expression changed from challenge to fear. Rabbit-quick, she yanked her hand away. The blond's smile was smug as she and her fella ran to join the happy dancers. Memphis felt it all like a stab to his gut.

Theta jumped up quickly, bracing herself on the table and nearly knocking over her drink as she did. She grabbed her purse. "I'm sorry. I'm not feeling so good, Poet. I-I gotta go home," she said and ran from the club.

"Theta! Theta!" Memphis shouted. He started after her but was stopped by the waiter.

"Your bill, sir."

"I'll be right back, I swear!"

"I've heard that one before," the waiter said, unmoved, and Memphis felt doubly humiliated by Theta's abrupt departure and this man's suspicion. Nobody was stopping white patrons at the door. Everybody was watching as Memphis reached into his wallet and dropped some bills on the silver tray.

"Happy?" he said.

The special night hung in tatters. To top things off, Theta had left the poem he'd worked so hard on. Angrily, Memphis grabbed the paper and stalked away, never noticing the faint outline of two singed handprints on the edge of the white tablecloth.

※

Harlem streets that had been bathed in neon hope taunted Memphis as he walked toward home. A cluster of young, drunk downtowners pushed out of the whites-only Cotton Club and stumbled down Lenox Avenue singing "Everything Is Hotsy Totsy Now" at the top of their lungs. They took up most of the sidewalk, and Memphis wanted to knock into them, pushing them into the street. Instead, he shoved his hands deep into the pockets of the suit he wore, his fingers still clutching the crumpled poem.

"Hey, Romeo! What happened to your big date?" Clarence called, laughing, from the front door of the Hotsy Totsy as Memphis passed by. "Aw, now, don't worry none, Memphis. Plenty of girls inside."

Not the one I'm in love with, Memphis thought. At the edge of the neighborhood, on a derelict street far from the excitement of Lenox Avenue, a man sprawled across a sidewalk, reeking of liquor. Memphis recognized him as one of the local drunks—Noble Bishop. He didn't have a coat. A man could freeze to death out here.

Memphis shifted from foot to foot. "Hey. Hey there, Mr. Bishop. You all right?"

The drunkard swore at him.

Fine. Lie there, Memphis thought. He knew what Octavia would say: "You can't help a person who doesn't want to be helped."

But the man was a wreck. His shirt was ripped, and there was a nasty wound on his arm that looked bad. Memphis stood in the cold, torn.

"Looks like you could use a doctor," Memphis tried.

Noble Bishop gaped up with red eyes and an expression devoid of hope. His voice wasn't much more than a frayed thread of sound. "Why? He gonna make me free?" And then he laid his head down on the cold sidewalk and cried.

Memphis was no doctor and he was no saint. He couldn't make either of them free. But he might be able to do something about Noble's festering cut if he was brave enough to try. Or would he fail at that, too?

"Mr. Bishop, I better take a look at that cut on your arm," Memphis said, drawing closer. His heart thumped in his chest. The whole night was a disaster, and here he was flirting with the possibility of even more trouble.

The drunk kicked at him halfheartedly. "Don't need no help from you! Git!"

"You need help from somebody. Just let me have a look. That's all."

Reluctantly, Noble offered his arm, an expression of barely checked violence in his eyes. He smelled not just of booze but of piss, too. Fighting back his revulsion, Memphis gripped the man's arm at the wrist and just below the elbow and closed his eyes, trying to draw on that healing place deep within. But nothing caught. No spark. And suddenly, the night veered from awful to hopeless.

"It's gone," Memphis said to himself. He felt frantic. "I lost it again."

"Let me go!" The man smacked Memphis on the shoulder and cuffed him once on the ear.

"Ow! Quit it, you old drunk!" Memphis said, dodging Noble's blows.

"Let go! Let go!" Swearing to beat the band, Noble landed a punch that caught Memphis in the thigh, and the whole lousy night swelled up inside Memphis like a wave. He didn't want to heal Noble Bishop; he wanted to hit him and keep hitting him. He wanted to strike back at the world. Gritting his teeth, he grabbed the man's arm and held on tight.

"You want this arm to rot off, you damn fool? Stop it, 'fore I hit you back! Stop—"

The connection surged through Memphis quick and hard, like an electrical current. His body jerked twice. The back of his tongue tasted of iron. The street beyond blurred, grayed, then filled with light. The last thing Memphis saw was the drunk's eyes going round as coins as he tried, but failed, to speak.

Memphis felt as if he were falling, and all around him was a sound like rushing water. His body settled, and he stood once more in that other, healing place that lay between this world and the next. He felt the press of spirits beside him. Their hands welcomed him back first, and then he saw them standing all around: vague shapes of ancestors draped in layers upon layers of cloth, reaching across oceans and generations, unknown yet so familiar. There was the soft, distant rhythm of drums and subdued singing. A warm breeze brought the smell of salt and heat-baked sand.

When their hands fell away, the shapes parted, and Memphis saw his mother in a coat of shiny blue-black feathers, waving at him through amber fields of sun-ripened wheat.

"Memphis. Son..." Her voice was raspy, her words slow, as if it took great effort to speak. "We h-haven't much t-time." She clutched her stomach as she gagged, vomiting up a small, feathery tuft. A thin stream of oily drool dripped from her lips. Her voice thinned to a croak. "Follow. The. Eye. Heal. The. Breach."

Dark, roiling clouds massed on the horizon, blocking out the sun. Angry light crackled against the churning sky and pitchforked down into the earth. Ghosts appeared in those brief flashes; they swayed in the wheat like shimmering scarecrows. These dead bore no resemblance to the shadowy spirits who'd welcomed Memphis into the healing space. There was nothing benevolent or ancestral about these wraiths. Instead, there was something terrible and hungry about them, as if they could eat and eat and never be filled.

Another storm of lightning lit up the sky, and Memphis could see that it swirled around the man in the stovepipe hat. It balled in his palm. He seemed delighted by this. His laugh was everywhere at once. He extended a hand toward Memphis, and though he was far away, his face loomed large and close. "Mine," the gray man said in a voice as old as time. He strode through the field toward Memphis, and the dead moved with him.

Memphis's mother coughed and spasmed with some violent change. Her eyes widened as she fought to whisper one last word: "Run."

Before Memphis's eyes, his mother was swallowed up in a whirl of blue-black feathers and desperate cawing as she transformed into a crow and flitted up, crying into the angry sky. She dove down and tugged at Memphis's collar with her beak, as if trying to pull him away from that place, but the man in the stovepipe hat and his retinue of dead were like a magnet, drawing him in. Memphis could hear his heartbeat pulsing in his ears. His eyes fluttered. He felt as if he could fall and never stop falling.

The shock of feathers across his cheek like a slap startled him. The crow cawed in his face, and Memphis jolted out of his healing trance, sweating and confused. His hands still gripped Noble Bishop's arm, but Noble himself lay on the ground, still as death.

"Mr. Bishop, you gotta get up now," Memphis pleaded, panicking as he shook the motionless old drunk. "Mister, please, please wake up. Please!"

Terror curled inside Memphis. He was close to crying. High above, the sky pulsed with lightning. Wind kicked up, sending dead leaves skittering down the street. A pounding rain started. Lightning struck a tree across the street and a branch fell off, burned and smoking. Memphis dragged the old man into the alley, where he could be protected.

"Sweet Jesus," Memphis said, looking down at Noble's still body. "I've killed him."

A couple of policemen walking their beat came down the street. Memphis knew these particular cops were dirty for Dutch Schultz, and they'd love nothing better than to take one of Papa Charles's runners in for any offense they could think up. Murder would be a hell of a charge.

"Mr. Noble, please, please wake up," Memphis pleaded.

Bishop Noble coughed and breathed. And then he settled into a light snore that was the best sound Memphis had ever heard.

"I did it," he said, grinning in astonishment at his hands. "I did it," he said again, almost reverently. The cops were nearly there.

"Hey! There's a sick man here!" Memphis shouted from behind the protection of the wall. Once he saw the cops heading toward the alley, he turned and ran away, climbing up and over the fence toward home.

PART TWO

A CITY OF SIX MILLION DREAMS

The gloom of January weighed on New Yorkers. The days were short and the nights were very long for people who'd grown to fear sleep. Mothers kept close watch by their children's beds. The rich asked their servants to sit nearby and wake them every few hours. The bootleggers' business was booming. The city was wary and afraid and close to violence.

But for Ling and Henry, it was the nights they lived for. Dreams provided an escape from the worries of the real world, a refuge of hope and possibility. While they waited in the beautiful old train station, Henry would play the piano, trying out new songs, looking to Ling for approval or boredom. If she wrinkled her nose as if something smelled bad, he abandoned it. But if she cocked her head to the side and nodded slowly, he knew he was on the right path.

"Anytime you want to come to the Follies, just say the word, and I'll get you the best seat in the house," Henry promised.

"Why would I do that? I can listen to you here."

"It's not just me, you know. There are grand dance numbers and singers, big stars. It's very glamorous, don'tcha know?"

"It sounds long and tedious."

"Most people love the Follies."

"I'm not most people."

"Darlin', truer words were ne'er spoken," Henry said and laughed.

Wai-Mae was always there to greet their train when it arrived in the forest. She'd beam at Ling and take her hands like a sister, then glance shyly at Henry.

"Miss Wai-Mae, you look radiant this evening," Henry would say with exaggerated courtesy, and Wai-Mae would giggle behind the cover of her hand. Sometimes, Ling and Wai-Mae would join Louis and Henry for a picnic on the grass bordering the river behind Louis's cabin, where music echoed across the forest—the bright syncopation of Dixieland threaded with the high notes of the erhu.

"Here, I'll show you how to dance the Charleston," Ling said, hopping up and taking Wai-Mae's hand in hers.

But when she showed her, Wai-Mae begged off. "What a terrible dance! So ungraceful! Not like the opera."

"Show us how it's done," Henry teased, and Wai-Mae moved with serpentine grace through the grass, rippling the sleeves of her gown as if she were spring coming to life.

"That's beautiful," Louis said. "I never seen anything like it. Not even at the balls in the Quarter."

"If only women could perform," Wai-Mae said, coming to sit beside Ling again.

"Women can't perform in Chinese opera?" Henry asked.

"Oh, no! It's only for men."

"Even the female roles?"

"Yes."

Louis grinned. "Hmm. Sounds like you got yourselves a drag ball."

Henry laughed and looked away.

"What is a drag ball?" Wai-Mae asked.

"Nothing," Henry said quickly, nudging Louis gently with his elbow. "Show us some more, Miss Wai-Mae, if you wouldn't mind."

Wai-Mae danced and Ling curled her toes in the dewy grass, enjoying the slick cool of it. She and Henry had come to accept this as ordinary. The old dream walking, which had once seemed strange and thrilling, bored them now. Here, they could write their own dreams, and every night, the dreams became that much more real.

Louis proved to be kind and funny, and Ling could see why Henry liked him so much. When she looked up at him, the golden sky at his back, Louis shimmered as if he were carved of sunshine. Ling liked the way he talked, as if his words had been dunked in warmed honey.

"Perhaps you should marry Louis," Wai-Mae said as she and Ling walked back to their spot in the forest on the edge of the village. "He'd make a fine husband. He is very handsome. Almost as handsome as my husband-to-be. But not quite."

Ling resisted the urge to roll her eyes. There was nothing Wai-Mae couldn't turn into a penny-novel romance. "I'm not ready for a husband."

"You're seventeen!" Wai-Mae tutted.

"Exactly," Ling said.

Wai-Mae's sigh was weary. She patted Ling's hand like a worried auntie. "Don't fret, Ling. I'm certain your parents will find someone for you," she said so earnestly that Ling could only take it in stride and not be insulted.

Wai-Mae's patience did not extend to Ling's scientific experimentation. "When will you be finished?" she complained as Ling stared at a house in the village that they had altered earlier, waiting to see if it changed in any way while she observed it. "Science is so dull!"

"Science is anything but dull," Ling said. "And I need to test things."

"These atoms you talk about. What are they?"

"They're building blocks of energy. Everything in the world, all matter, is made of atoms," Ling explained. "Even us."

"What about dreams? What are they made of?" Wai-Mae asked.

"They're born of people's thoughts, I suppose. Their emotions. Endlessly renewing, endlessly creating," Ling said. But she wondered: Could an energy field be generated from all the thoughts, desires, and memories inside dreams? Was that how the dead were conjured? And what happened when you put a few dream walkers inside that landscape? Could their interactions transform dream into reality?

Each night, toward the end of her dream walks, Ling conducted her experiments. First she marked her hands with ash from a fire.

When she woke, she examined her hands for the marks, but there were none. The next night, she slipped a few pebbles into her pocket to see if she could bring them out of the dream, but it didn't work. She'd even tried to bring a pheasant feather into the dream world for Wai-Mae, but when she stuck her hand into her pocket, there was nothing there at all.

"Perhaps some things are beyond testing," Wai-Mae mused as she watched a sparrow hopping from branch to branch before it flew off toward the shimmering rooftops of the village and disappeared altogether. "Perhaps there are things that exist only because we make them so, because we must."

Henry and Louis spent hours fishing the river or playing music on the cabin's front porch, Louis on fiddle and Henry on harmonica. Other times, they'd go for long walks with Gaspard, and Henry would tell Louis all about New York and his friends there. "I'll take you to Evie's radio show and we'll cut a rug at the Hotsy Totsy with Memphis and Theta—you'll love it there. You get that train ticket yet?" Henry asked.

"Not yet, *cher*. But I'll walk over to the Lafayette PO in the morning and see if it's there."

"Louis, do you ever remember your dreams in the morning after you've woken up?" Henry asked, worried. If Louis didn't remember, then how would he know to go pick up the ticket?

"I reckon I must. Who could forget this?" Louis said, nuzzling Henry's throat.

"Just in case, I want to try something. Louis: When you wake up, you'll remember. You'll remember everything."

"Everything," Louis whispered, and he kissed Henry, taking his tongue sweetly into his mouth.

There was only one uneasy moment in the dreams for Henry, and it was the thicket of morning glories. Every time they passed the purple-blue blooms, Louis would pull Henry away. He wouldn't go anywhere near the thicket. In fact, he seemed downright afraid of it.

"What those flowers ever do to you?" Henry joked on one such occasion.

Louis didn't laugh. "Don't know. Just gives me a bad feeling," he said, rubbing his head. "Smell gives me a headache."

But the moment they were away from the morning glories, Louis's mood lightened once more. He broke into an easy grin, yanked his shirt off over his head, and tossed it at Henry. "Gonna get to that rope swing first!" he shouted, running toward the sparkling river.

"Wait!" Henry called. Laughing, he dropped his own clothes on the grass and ran after Louis.

Sometimes, a part of the dream world lost its color or winked out, like a lightbulb that needed changing. When this happened, Ling and Wai-Mae would concentrate, pushing their energy into the dead portion, and the dreamscape would shift under their hands, warming and blooming.

"My, but that is something," Louis would say, and if he was envious that he and Henry couldn't seem to perform this alchemy, too, he never said it.

Above their heads, a steady stream of ones and zeros trickled down like rain, which made Henry think about music theory and song structure and Ling of the Bagua of the I Ching. Whole dream worlds were born of this numerical rain: The ghostly jazz bands of New Orleans' West End inked themselves into existence against the filmy sky. A swooping Coney Island roller coaster skated a constant figure eight, a memory from Ling's childhood. A Chinese puppet show appeared, the sticks operated by unseen hands.

It was as if all time and space were unfolding at once around them, a river without end. The borders of their selves vanished; they flowed through time, and it through them, till they didn't know if these things they saw had already been or would come to pass. Henry had never experienced such a profound sense of happiness, of being right in his self and in the world.

"To us," he said, raising a glass.

"To us," the others echoed, and they watched the sky give birth to new dreams.

If the nights were magical, the days were less so. For the first time in their friendship, Henry and Theta were bickering. The dream walking exhausted Henry so much that he didn't wake before three or four in the afternoon. He'd missed three rehearsals in a row.

"I can't keep inventing stories to save you, Hen," Theta warned. "And Herbie's up to something. I think he's trying to get his song in over yours. You better show up today, if you know what's good for you, Hen."

"I'm not worried about Herbie," Henry said, reaching for one of Theta's cigarettes.

"You should be. And since when do you smoke?"

Henry smirked. "I just need a little pep." He wiggled his fingers like a jazz baby.

Theta swiped the cigarette out of his mouth. "Then get some sleep. Real sleep."

But Henry didn't listen. He couldn't listen. There were only Louis and dreams, and Henry would do whatever he could to have both. Already he and Ling were pushing the limits of what they could tolerate. Each night, they set their alarms for later and later.

But here in the dream world, Ling was on to something. She could feel the energy coiled beneath her fingers when she transformed a featureless rock into sunflowers whose petals were repeating spirals of pattern, the Qi moving strongly through them both, all those atoms shifting, changing, whole universes being born. No—made. She and Wai-Mae were making them. *We did that*, Ling would think. Like gods. It was magic and it was science, a blend, like her, and it was more beautiful than anything.

One night, as the girls lay back in the dewy grass watching pink clouds drifting lazily across the perpetual sunset, Wai-Mae turned on her side to face Ling.

"What happened to your legs, Little Warrior?"

Ling sat up quickly. On impulse, she tugged her skirt hem down. "Nothing," she said.

"No. I see the way you are with them, always hiding. You're holding something back. Some secret." Wai-Mae's expression was resolute. "If we are to be friends, you must tell me everything."

Ling hugged her knees to her chest—a simple action in the dream world, impossible when she was awake. "A few months ago, I got very sick. When it was over, the muscles in my legs and feet had stopped working. I need leg braces and crutches to walk now. But sometimes, just before I'm fully awake, there's a moment when I'm still holding on to the dream. And I forget. I forget what happened to me. I forget about the sickness and my legs. For those few seconds, I think that the infection was a bad dream, and I'll get up and walk out of my room and run down the stairs as if nothing ever happened. But then the truth creeps in. The only place I'm free is in dreams."

"Dreams are the only place any of us is free," Wai-Mae said, turning Ling's face toward hers with just a finger. Wai-Mae's hands smelled earthy, like moss on the hillside. "There was a boy in my village like you. Every day, they massaged his legs to help with the pain. You have to work fire back into the muscles, Little Warrior."

Gently, Wai-Mae lifted the hem of Ling's skirt and trailed her fingers down Ling's shins. Then she began to work the muscles, kneading with surprisingly strong fingers. Ling suppressed a gasp. In the hospital following the infection, the doctors had immobilized her legs in plaster, then splints, then braces. Her legs felt separate. A caged exhibition. No one touched them. Even Ling touched her own body as little as possible.

"Do that every day," Wai-Mae commanded. She leaned her head back, toward the sun, gazing out at the golden hills. "I, too, want to stay here always. In dreams. No pain, no strife." Her face settled into sadness. "I will tell you a secret of my own. I don't like Mr. O'Bannion. He is not a good man, I don't think. He lies."

"What do you mean?"

"I heard gossip today on the ship about one of the other girls he brought over. They say that when she arrived in America, there was no husband to greet her, no marriage. She had been tricked. Instead of a husband, the girl was forced to work *in a brothel*," Wai-Mae whispered. "They say she is broken now. She cries all the time. Oh, sister, I must trust the judgment of my uncle, but still, I'm afraid."

Ling wondered whether she should tell Wai-Mae about her own misgivings. But she didn't want to worry her unnecessarily. She'd wait until she could speak to Mr. Lee. And she would redouble her efforts to find this Mr. O'Bannion. If necessary, she'd have Uncle Eddie speak to the Association so that they could make sure a similar fate wouldn't befall Wai-Mae.

"Don't worry. I'll look after you," Ling said.

Wai-Mae smiled at Ling. "I am so grateful that I have you."

Ling looked into Wai-Mae's endless brown eyes, and she felt the dream stirring inside her, shifting her molecules, rearranging her atoms, transforming her into something new and beautiful. It made her dizzy.

"What is it, sister?" Wai-Mae asked.

"Nothing," Ling said, catching her breath. "Nothing."

"Soon I will be in New York," Wai-Mae said, a smile lighting up her face. "We will go to your uncle's opera, or perhaps even Booth's Theatre. And on Sundays, we can promenade like fine ladies in our very best bonnets. Oh, such fun we'll have, Ling!"

"No one wears a bonnet," Ling said, trying not to giggle.

"My village is very small," Wai-Mae said, embarrassed. "You will show me what's fashionable."

"If I'm showing you what's fashionable, you're in trouble," Ling said, feeling chastened for teasing Wai-Mae.

"We will be like sisters," Wai-Mae said.

"Yes," Ling murmured. But what she wanted to say as the pearl-white flowers shook down from the low branch of a blooming dogwood tree was *No. We will be friends. True friends. Best friends.*

"Come, dear Ling," Wai-Mae said, jumping up and offering her hand.

And they passed the hours dancing under skies so shimmery blue it hurt to look up.

☀

In the city of six million dreams, Evie and Sam were the dreamiest. New York couldn't get enough of the newest gossip sensation. Everywhere they went, they were mobbed: Sitting ringside at the fights. Posed beside a millionaire's champion horse at a Long Island stable. Dining in the elegant Cascades Room of the Biltmore Hotel beside an orderly row of potted cherry trees. Watching *Bye, Bye, Bonnie* at the Ritz Theatre. Stepping out of Texas Guinan's infamous 300 Club with confetti in their hair or skating on the frozen pond in Central Park. Fans clustered outside the radio station and the Winthrop Hotel and even the museum hoping for a glimpse of New York's latest golden couple. Nightclubs vied for their patronage. Gifts small and large arrived by messenger in boxes thick with tissue paper—*"A token of our 'divine' affection!"*—and inside would be a brooch or cuff links and a promise of the establishment's best table on any night Sam 'n' Evie would care to grace them with their presence and, oh, perhaps the Sweetheart Seer would be kind enough to mention their establishment fondly on the radio or in the papers?

Letters poured in by the thousands. The *Daily News* posted a picture of the adorable sweethearts in Mr. Phillips's majestic office, buried up to their necks in fan mail. *Radio Star* listed Evie's "Tips for Savvy Shebas," which included "Never leave the house without rouging your knees" and "Keep your enemies close, and your flask closer." Thanks to the two of them, WGI was fast becoming the number one radio station in the nation. A line stretched around the block from WGI to get in to Evie's show.

She loved every minute of it.

"And don't forget, darlings," she reminded listeners. "Sam and I will be hosting the opening-night party for the Diviners exhibit at the Museum of American Folklore, Superstition, and the Occult next week. If you buy a raffle ticket, you can win a free object reading performed by yours truly."

※

On the West Side of Manhattan lay a congested strip of real estate called Radio Row where an enterprising sort could purchase radio parts of all kinds, from the commonplace to the hard-to-find. What Sam sought now was very hard to find, indeed. It was all he thought about as he walked up Cortlandt Street, past stores blaring music and competing sidewalk salesmen trying to entice passersby with the siren's call of the newest, most expensive models: "Brand-new crystal set!" "Westinghouse—it's all electric!" "Radiola means quality!" "Trust Cunningham tubes—they're insured!" "Sound so clear you could go next door and not miss a note through the wall!"

Sam stepped inside a dark showroom, past the boring suburban mom-and-pops admiring the showroom wares, carefully avoiding eye contact with overeager salesmen readying their smooth pitches. He kept his head down on his way to the sales counter, hoping he wouldn't be recognized. At the counter, a mustachioed man with slicked-back hair finished writing up a sales slip and smiled at Sam. "Could I interest you in a new radio today, sir? We've the newest models in stock—six-, eight-, and ten-tube circuits."

"What I really need is a Buffalo tube. But so far, I haven't had much luck finding it. I understand Mr. Arnold carries them?" Sam said, sliding over a folded note attached to a five-dollar bill he'd lifted from a wallet on the way over.

The man's smile vanished. "Mr. Arnold, you say?"

"Yes. Ben Arnold. That's the fella."

"Excuse me for a moment, won't you?" The man disappeared behind a heavy drape at the back of the store. A few minutes later, he returned. "It seems that we don't have that part right now, sir. It has been ordered." The man returned Sam's note minus the five dollars. "This is your receipt of purchase. But I'm afraid this is the last time Mr. Arnold can order this part for you, sir. Your particular model is very...popular at present. A bit too popular, if you take my meaning."

Sam grimaced. *Sam 'n' Evie*. The spotlight from their cooked-up romance was throwing a little too much glare on Sam's private life.

"Pal, I hear you like a crystal set," Sam said.

Out on the street, he opened the note. A key had been taped to the inside. There was no accompanying information. A salesman waved Sam over. "Could I interest you in a Zenith six-tube model with superior musical tone? It's fully electric!"

"Thanks, pal. So am I," Sam shouted. He shoved the note and key in his pocket, walking away from the cacophony of Radio Row toward the rumble of the Ninth Avenue El.

Down the street, the men in the brown sedan watched it all.

☀

Every day, the newspapers carried bold warnings about the sleeping sickness.

New York's health commissioner encouraged citizens to wash their hands frequently, to clean homes daily, and to avoid large crowds, especially open-air markets, protests, and workers' rallies. Citizens needed to keep clear of buildings plastered with yellow quarantine posters. For the time being, they advised people not to travel to Chinatown or "foreign neighborhoods." Some parents petitioned to have Chinese students barred from the classroom. Letters to the editor blamed the scourge on immigrants, jazz, loose morals, the flouting of Prohibition, bobbed hair, the automobile, and anarchists. Lawmakers argued about whether to add yet another brick in the ever-rising legislative wall of the Chinese Exclusion Act. They called for a return to traditional American morals and old-time religion. On the radio, Sarah Snow exhorted her followers to turn away from jazz babies and give themselves over to Jesus. Afterward, an announcer assured listeners that

"Pears soap is the one to keep your family safe and healthy and free from exotic disease."

In Chinatown, a large rock painted with a message—CHINESE GO HOME!—shattered the front window of Chong & Sons, Jewelers. An arsonist's fire gutted the Wing Sing restaurant overnight; Mr. Wing stood in the softly falling wisps of soot-flecked snow, his sober face backlit by the orange glow as he watched everything he'd built burn to the ground. Police broke up social club meetings and even a banquet celebrating the birth of Yuen Hong's first son. The mayor refused to allow the Chinese New Year celebrations to go on out of fears for public health. In protest, the Chinese Benevolent Association organized a march down Centre Street to City Hall, where the protestors were ordered to disperse or face arrest and possible deportation. The streets smelled of pork and winter, ash from the burnings and incense from the prayers offered to ancestors they hoped would look favorably upon them in this hour. On every street, red plaques appeared outside buildings to guide the dead back home. Talcum powder dusted the thresholds; entrances were watched for signs of ghosts.

Fear was everywhere.

At a eugenics conference in the elegant ballroom of the Waldorf-Astoria Hotel, genteel men in genteel suits spoke of "the mongrel problem—the ruin of the white race." They pointed to drawings and diagrams that proved most disease could be traced to inferior breeding stock. They called this science. They called it fact. They called it patriotism.

People drank their coffee and nodded in agreement.

☀

As Memphis Campbell made his runner rounds, his thoughts were elsewhere. He and Theta hadn't spoken since their disastrous night at Small's Paradise. Memphis didn't understand how you could tell a fella you loved him and then run out like that. He missed her terribly, but he had too much pride to call. Theta would need to come to him first.

"Memphis, you listening to me, son?" Bill Johnson asked. "You get that number right?"

"Yes, sir, Mr. Johnson. One, four, four," Memphis said. "I'll put it in for you, just like I did yesterday and the day before that. Don't know why you keep playing it if you're not winning."

"Call it a hunch," Bill said, but he sounded angry. The bluesman cocked his head, angling it toward the sound of Memphis's voice. "Heard a peculiar story this morning over to Floyd's. You know that ol' drunk, Noble Bishop?"

"I know him some," Memphis said. His stomach had gone to butterflies.

"Never known him when he's not stone-cold drunk or shaking like a old dog from the lack of it. But this morning, he showed up to Floyd's sober as a deacon and asking could he work around the shop sweeping up. Said he had a visitation from an angel. A miracle." Bill paused a moment to let his next words sink in. "A healing."

"Is that so?" Memphis said, trying to keep his voice even.

"It is." Bill's lips twisted into a sneer. "Seem like a waste of a miracle, you ask me. What's that old no-account drunk gonna do with a gift like that? He prob'ly be back in the gutter by next Tuesday," Bill spat out. "The Lord sure works in mysterious ways."

"That's what they say," Memphis said and smiled.

"That is, in fact, what they say," Bill said, and did not smile.

When Memphis got home, there was a telegram waiting for him.

DEAR POET, SORRY FOR THE DISAPPEARING ACT. FEELING MUCH BETTER NOW. P.S. HOTSY TOTSY TONIGHT? YOURS, PRINCESS.

"Who sent you a telegram?" Isaiah asked, wide-eyed. "Somebody die?"

"Nope. Everybody and everything is very much alive," Memphis said, feeling like there had been two miracles.

☀

That night, Henry and Ling set their alarms for their longest dream walk yet—a full five hours. The next day, Henry woke to Theta sitting at the foot of his bed, glaring at him through a cigarette haze. Light seeped under the roller shades.

"What time is it?" Henry asked. His mouth was dry.

"Half past three. In the afternoon," Theta said tersely. "You look like hell."

"Why, thank you, Miss Knight."

"I'm not kidding. How long before you can get up outta that bed?"

Henry's muscles ached like he'd been moving furniture all night long. He ran his tongue across chapped lips. "I'm right as rain. Just got a little cold, that's all."

"No, you're not okay." Theta slapped down a piece of paper. It was an advertisement cut from the newspaper for a lecture by "Dr. Carl Jung, renowned psychoanalyst" at the New York Society for Ethical Culture. "This egghead fella, Jung—he knows all about dreams. Maybe he knows about dream walking. Maybe he could help you, Hen."

"I'm fine."

"I think we should go."

"You go."

"You could at least hear what he has to say—"

"I said I'm fine!" Henry snapped.

Theta flinched. "Don't yell," she whispered.

"Sorry. Sorry, darlin'," Henry said, feeling guilty and angry at the same time. His teeth chattered and his stomach hurt. "Come sit next to me. It's so cold."

For a second, it looked like Theta might give in and lie down next to him with her head on his chest, like old times. Instead, she swiped back the newspaper advertisement and headed for the bedroom door without looking back. "I gotta bathe. Rehearsal's in an hour. In case you care."

At rehearsal, Henry was so exhausted he could barely concentrate.

"Henry! That was your cue!" Wally barked from the front row.

Henry looked up to see the dancers glaring at him.

"Sorry, folks," Henry drawled, snapping back to the present. For a second, his eyes caught Theta's. He saw the worry there just before it edged into anger. He tried to make her laugh with a silly face, but she wasn't having it.

"If there's anything I hate, it's having my time wasted. Let's get this show on the road," she announced to no one in particular, though Henry understood the comment was meant for his ears.

☀

Other stories appeared here and there: A couple of subway workers vanished underground. Their lanterns were found still glowing in the tunnel they'd been hollowing out for the extension of the IRT. A pocketbook belonging to a Miss Rose Brock mysteriously ended up on the tracks near the Fourteenth Street station. Despondent over a failed love affair, she'd gone to a speakeasy on the West Side with friends and disappeared. Suicide was feared. A token booth clerk was suspended on suspicion of drinking when he swore he saw a faintly glowing ghost down at the dark end of the tracks. One minute, the pale thing was crouched on its haunches, he claimed, and the next, it skittered up the walls and out of sight. Some riders reported seeing odd flickers of greenish light from subway train windows. Diggers working on the construction of the new Holland Tunnel refused to go below. Down in the depths, they'd heard the terrifying swarming sounds of some unnameable infestation. A Diviner had been called in to give his blessing; he insisted it was all clear, but the workers knew he'd been paid to say it, and now they would only go down in groups and wearing every one of their charms against bad luck. The vagrant population was down; all the unfortunates known to frequent subway platforms, sewers, and train tunnels for warmth in the winter had seemingly disappeared in a matter of days.

On the West Side, two boys had been playing near a storm drain when one was suddenly swept away. Police searched the area below the grate, shining flashlights in sewer lines. They found nothing except for the poor boy's baseball and one of his shoes. But the surviving child insisted that it wasn't the water to blame, for he'd seen an unearthly pale hand reach up from below and yank his friend down by his ankle, quick as a rabbit snatched by the strong jaws of a trap.

People disappeared. That wasn't unusual in a city where ruthless gangsters like Meyer Lansky, Dutch Schultz, and Al Capone were as famous as movie stars. But the missing weren't gangsters "disappeared" after a disagreement or turf war. Handmade signs appeared on lampposts and outside subway entrances, desperate pleas from frantic loved ones: VANISHED: PRESTON DILLON, FULTON STREET SUBWAY STATION. MISSING: COLLEEN MURPHY, SCHOOLTEACHER, AUBURN HAIR, BLUE EYES, TWENTY YEARS OF AGE. DO YOU KNOW: TOMAS HERNANDEZ, BELOVED SON? LAST SEEN ENTERING CITY HALL SUBWAY STATION. LAST SEEN IN THE VICINITY OF PARK ROW. LAST SEEN LEAVING FOR WORK. LAST SEEN. LAST SEEN. LAST SEEN . . .

But these were insignificant stories in a city full of them. These random accounts were pushed to the newspapers' back pages, past flashy reports about Babe Ruth driving his new Pierce-Arrow touring car to Yankee Stadium or a shining picture of Jake Marlowe surveying the marshy ground of Queens for his Future of America Exhibition or exhaustive reports on what the Sweetheart Seer wore to a party with her beau, the dashing Sam Lloyd.

For the newspapers, it seemed, were typeset with dreams of their own.

"You write a lot of love songs. Have you ever been in love?" Ling asked Henry on the eighth night as they waited for the train.

"Yes," Henry said and did not elaborate. "How about you?"

330

Ling remembered looking into Wai-Mae's eyes.

"No," she said.

"Smart girl. Love is hell," Henry joked. He sat down at the piano and played something new.

"What is this song?" Ling asked. It sounded different from the other songs Henry had been playing. Those were forgettable. But the piece taking shape now was strange and lovely and haunting. It had weight.

"I don't know yet. Just something I'm playing around with," Henry said. He seemed embarrassed, like he'd been caught telling his deepest secrets.

"I like it," Ling said, listening intently. "It's a sad sort of beautiful. Like all the best songs."

"Is...is that a compliment?" Henry put a hand to his chest in a mock-faint.

Ling rolled her eyes. "Don't get cute."

※

Sister Walker had been driving for twelve hours straight, so while she napped in her room back at the motel, Will kept a grip on his coffee cup and stared out the window of the Hopeful Harbor diner. Crepuscular light veiled the tops of the snow-dusted hills. The sky was a distant bruise. A bronze plaque in front of the courthouse across the street commemorated a spot where George Washington had once tasted victory. Quite a few Revolutionary War battles had been fought in this part of the country, Will knew, battles that turned the tide of the war and helped decide the fate of a new country, taking it from an exciting idea of self-governance to possibility and then reality. A government by the people, for the people.

America had invented itself. It continued to invent itself as it went along. Sometimes its virtues made it the envy of the world. Sometimes it betrayed the very heart of its ideals. Sometimes the people dispensed with what was difficult or inconvenient to acknowledge. So the good people maintained the illusion of democracy and wrote another hymn to America. They sang loud enough to drown out dissent. They sang loud enough to overpower their own doubts. There were no plaques to commemorate mistakes. But the past didn't forget. History was haunted by the ghosts of buried crimes, which required periodic exorcisms of truth. Actions had consequences.

Will knew this, too.

"More coffee?" the waitress asked Will and poured him a fresh cup anyway. "Shame you're here at such a miserable time of year. The road up into the mountains is awful treacherous just now."

"Yes," Will said. "I remember."

"Oh, so you've been here before?"

"Once. It was a long time ago."

"Gee, what you ought to do is come back in the spring, drive on up there to the old Marlowe estate. Beautiful grounds. It's closed now, but they open it up in the spring."

Will fished out a quarter and left it on the table beside the full, untouched cup of coffee.

"Thank you. I'll do that," he said.

Back in the motel, by the weak light of a bedside lamp, Will read through his stack of clippings gathered from newspapers around the country:

THE BOSTON GLOBE

"...I was walking in old Salem, up near the hill where they used to hang the witches, you see, when Buster, my dog, barked up a storm, and a terrible feeling come over me. I saw them silhouetted by the mist in their black dresses, some with heads wobbling on broken necks and eyes dark with hate...."

THE CEDAR RAPIDS EVENING GAZETTE

Mr. and Mrs. Samuel Stuart of Altoona have asked for any assistance in locating their daughter, Alice Kathleen, who disappeared on her way home from a territory band dance. The orchestra in question, the Travelers, has also disappeared, and curiously, no other territory bands can remember much about them at all, though there are many accounts of people who've gone missing once the band has come through town....

THE NEWPORT MERCURY

...Passing by the site of a former slave auction block, the ship's captain, John Thatcher, claimed to hear terrible cries and swore that he saw, for a moment, stretched out along the port, the ghosts of whole families in chains, their eyes on him in accusation, inciting in him a feeling "as if a day of reckoning were at hand..."

THE DOYLESTOWN DAILY INTELLIGENCER

...Mrs. Coelina Booth will not enter the woods beyond her home anymore, for she believes they are haunted by malevolent spirits. "1 noticed the birds had stopped singing in our trees. Then I got a chill for no good reason, and I heard giggling. That's when I saw them—two phantom girls in pinafores with teeth sharp as razors and all around them the bones of the birds...."

...The longtime groundskeeper reported graves desecrated and one tomb left open....

...Graves disturbed...cattle mutilated...

...Sudden fog rising up on the road late at night near the old church cemetery...

...The farmer discovered his faithful horse,
Justice, by the drinking pond, "torn apart
and covered in flies...."

...Claimed to see a gray man in a long coat
and a tall black hat out in the field during a
lightning storm...

...Claimed to see a man in a tall hat standing in the graveyard under a yellow moon...

...Claimed to see a man in a tall hat leading a band of ghosts into the dark woods...

As the last of his convenient illusions tore away, Will turned off
the light and slipped into bed.

But sleep did not come for a very long time.

DAY SEVENTEEN

A RETURN ADDRESS

Sam and Evie stood in line at the main branch of the New York City post office, watching the large wall clock's filigreed hand tick off precious minutes. The post office was surprisingly busy. Long lines, and it wasn't even Christmas. At window number six, a statuesque redhead grew exasperated with the addled clerk, who couldn't seem to locate her package. "Could you look again, please?" the woman asked in a clipped, slightly British accent. "It was sent parcel post two weeks ago from Miss Felicity Worthington and addressed to Mrs. Rao, Mrs. Gemma Doyle Rao."

"Excuse me, but aren't you Sam and Evie?"

Evie turned around. A young woman in a flowered hat beamed at her, excited.

"Guilty!" Evie said, preening.

The woman gasped. "I adore your show! Oh, do you think I could get an autograph for my mother? It would make her so happy, and—"

"Sorry, sis, we're not in the Sam 'n' Evie business just now," Sam said, shutting her up.

"That was rude," Evie whispered to him through clenched teeth.

"We don't need the attention right now, Sheba. This is why it's good not to be famous."

Evie's eyebrows shot up. "That is the stupidest thing I've ever heard come out of your lips, Sam Lloyd. And you say a lot of stupid."

"Next," the clerk called, waving Sam and Evie over.

"How ya doin', Pops?" Sam said. "We need some help with an address."

"No kidding," the clerk deadpanned without looking up. "Where to?"

"Oh, no, we're not mailing anything," Evie said. "We're curious about an office here in this very building."

The clerk glared over the top of his glasses. "Two years away from a watch and a pension," he said with a sigh. "What office is that?"

Sam handed over his mother's mysterious file. The clerk frowned. He disappeared into the mystical recesses of the post office. A few minutes later, he returned. "Sorry. I can't help you with that unless you're with the United States government."

"What do you mean?" Evie asked.

"That office is restricted. Belongs to the feds. Or it did once. It's not in use anymore. Sorry." He handed back the file. "Next!"

"How're we gonna get back there?" Evie asked as she and Sam walked away from the window.

Sam thought for a minute. "What we need is a distraction. Something that'll get us a big crowd in here."

"You want a big crowd?" Evie repeated.

"That's what I said."

"I just wanted to be sure. Sometimes you mumble. Here. Sign this." Evie handed Sam a scrap of paper and a pencil. She signed her name beside his. "Leave it to me."

Evie pranced past the line of impatient people, swinging her beaded handbag on her arm. The young woman who'd recognized them was at the clerk's gated window now.

"I am terribly sorry to interrupt," Evie said, smiling at the woman. "Here's your autograph, darling." To the clerk, she said, "I've already forgotten—which stamp do we need for the marriage license again?"

The clerk only looked confused, but the girl gasped, then bit her lip.

"On second thought, never mind. I'm sure I'll find it. Can't keep the justice of the peace waiting," she said, winking at the girl.

Humming, Evie tottered away, then hid herself in a spot with a view of the telephone booth.

"Any second now..." Evie said to herself, watching through the fronds of a potted palm.

Their young fan skittered toward the telephone booth, not even bothering to shut its folding door all the way.

"*New York Daily Mirror*, please," the young woman shouted into the receiver. "Yes, is this the *Daily Mirror*? Well! Hold on to your hat, because I've got a scoop for you. I'm at the post office, the big one on Eighth Avenue? The Sweetheart Seer and Sam Lloyd are here. They were collecting a marriage license, and I heard them saying something about a justice of the peace. They must be planning to elope!" She paused. "Well, I have no idea why they'd be procuring a marriage license at the post office, but they're here, and you'd better hurry before they get away!" The girl clicked her finger down on the disconnect bar, then placed another call. "Yes, the *Daily News*, please..."

Satisfied, Evie sneaked back to Sam under the stairs to wait.

"What did you do, future Mrs. Lloyd?"

Evie grinned. "Good things come to those who wait."

Sam gave her that lupine grin. "That a promise?" he said, and Evie's stomach went flippy-floppy again.

They didn't have to wait long. Within ten minutes, a crew of competing reporters rushed the building. On the street, people took note, and soon the post office was mobbed by New Yorkers excited by the prospect of catching the famous couple trying to elope. Sam peeked out to see police arriving to hold back the sudden swarm of fans. It all had the feel of a friendly riot.

"Is this enough of a distraction for you?" Evie asked.

"Sheba, this is a first-rate confluey."

The last of the day's sun streamed in through the high windows and fell across Evie's face, lighting it up—lips quirked into a smile of amusement, dark blue eyes gone to squinting because she probably needed a pair of cheaters but was far too vain ever to wear them. She was grinning now, really enjoying the spectacle. Sam had spent time traveling with a circus, but being with Evie was its own circus, a real trapeze act. He wanted to do something grand and ridiculous to prove himself to her—like go to Belmont and bet all his money on a horse. Hell, he wanted to buy her the damned horse and name it for her. It was stupid to let a girl get under his skin this way. But he didn't feel like stopping it.

"What is it?" Evie said, patting at her hair. "Is there something on my face?"

"Yeah. There's a face on your face."

Evie rolled her eyes.

"It just so happens to be a really nice face," he said, and he could swear that he saw Evie blush.

"Over there!" someone in the crowd shouted, but they were looking the wrong way, toward a man and woman walking a small terrier on a leash. The cops shouted and blew their whistles as the crowd broke free, surging toward the other side of the post office and the hapless wrong couple about to be swept up in their frenzy.

"Let's ankle, Baby Vamp!" Sam reached for Evie's hand. She clasped her fingers around his, and Sam reveled in the sureness of it as they sneaked down the stairs into the basement, enjoying the sounds of chaos from above. They passed through a large main room where sorting machines hummed and hammered, creating a constant, mechanized thunder. Letters shot down clear tubes and into waiting trolleys to be sorted by postal workers too busy to notice Sam and Evie as they passed through. At last they came to another portion of the post office, which splintered off into a vast warren of drab hallways. The search was starting to feel fruitless when, finally, they came to a set of stairs that led down one more level to a long, cheerless line of office doors.

"B-118, B-120," Evie called as they walked. They passed several more, and a men's room. "B-130!" The dark, pebbled window of B-130's door still bore the ghostly traces of former lettering that read, simply, STATISTICS. "That's a good way to keep people out—make it sound like a flat tire of a place."

Sam jangled the doorknob. "Locked."

"What now?" Evie asked.

"Wait a minute." Sam fished in his pocket for the key he'd gotten from his contact. He tried it in the lock but it wouldn't fit. He groaned.

"We could break the glass," Evie said.

"Last resort. We don't want anybody to know we were here." Sam pressed his face to the glass, cupping the sides of his eyes to block the hallway's glare. He could just make out a shaft of light coming from up high on the right by the lavatory. "Hold on. I've got an idea," Sam said, heading to the men's room.

"I do not believe that answering the call of nature qualifies as an 'idea.'"

"Just hold on to your hat for a second," he said, disappearing inside. A moment later, the men's room door opened again. Sam leaned out and crooked a finger at Evie.

Evie folded her arms. "You want me to go in there?"

Sam waggled his eyebrows. "Don't you just love a cozy spot for two, Baby Vamp?"

"There's nothing more romantic than a row of urinals, Sam, but what's your plan?" Evie said, following him inside.

"That." Sam pointed to a small hinged window near the ceiling. "It leads right into office B-130." Sam laced his fingers together, palms up. "Come on. Upsy-daisy. I'll give you a boost."

Evie's eyebrows shot up. "You're joking."

"I used to do this in the circus all the time. Piece of cake."

"Why do I think that piece of cake is going to be Pineapple Evie-Upside-Down Cake?" Evie grumbled.

"Those shoes look dangerous. Better take 'em off first."

"I love these shoes more than you, Sam."

"We'll come back for them."

"They're from Bloomie's. I'm not leaving them." Evie slipped off her satin Mary Janes and bit down on the leather straps, letting the shoes dangle from her mouth.

"So that's what it takes to shut you up!" Sam joked.

"Ah will draaahhph dese on your heeaad. Ah schwearrr Ah weeeal," Evie managed to say as she stepped onto Sam's finger bridge and he hoisted her up. Evie grabbed hold of the window as her stockinged feet scrabbled for a hold on the slick white-tiled wall. "Saaam!"

"Hold on!" Sam stepped up into a urinal and wedged his shoulder under Evie for extra leverage.

"Naaah eenufff!" she called, slipping.

"Okay. Then I'm apologizing for this in advance," Sam said. He placed his hands firmly on her backside, boosting her up. He was glad Evie couldn't see his grin. "Take your time. I'm good."

"Saaam, Ah'd kick you if Ahh were'n afraaay you drophh me."

With a grunt, Evie scrambled through the window and landed with an audible thud on the other side.

"Evie! You jake?" Sam called.

"Yes. Fortunately, there's a desk by the wall. Sam?"

"Yes, Mutton Chop?"

"Remind me to kick you later."

"Will do," Sam said. "Just don't forget to unlock the door."

Sam ran around front as Evie opened the door, arms spread wide in a welcoming gesture. "How nice of you to stop by. I think you're going to love what I've done with the place."

It took a few seconds for Sam's eyes to adjust to the gloom. He wished he'd brought along a flashlight. "The dust is a nice touch."

"Isn't it, though? I had a decorator come in. I said, 'I'd like something a bit Fall of the House of Usher, but less cheery.' Honestly, where are we, Sam?"

Not much remained of whatever the U.S. Department of Paranormal had once been. Three desks. A few chairs. An oak file cabinet. Bookcase lined with begrimed volumes of large, rather dull-looking books. An American Eagle Fire Insurance calendar hung from a rusted nail on the wall, left open to April 1917. Beside it was a map of the United States dotted with thumbtacks pressed into towns in every state. Each thumbtack had been assigned a different number: 63, 12, 144, 48, 97.

"What am I looking for?" Evie called, opening and closing desk drawers, where she found nothing but dust balls.

"Anything with the words *Project Buffalo* on it," Sam said, marching to the file cabinet. It was locked. "Got a hairpin?"

Evie rummaged in her purse and came up with one, and Sam slipped it into the lock and yanked open the drawer. It was empty. They were all empty.

"Dammit!" Sam punched the side of the cabinet. "Ow," he said, shaking out his hand.

"What now? There's nothing here," Evie said. She and Sam stood at loose ends in the middle of the office.

"I really thought we'd found it," Sam said quietly, and Evie could tell how disappointed he was. It meant so much to him, and this was the best clue they'd had so far. She looked around for something, anything, that might prove useful.

"Sam . . . ?" Evie said, an idea taking shape.

"Yeah?"

"Didn't you say you found that letter from Rotke in a book?" Evie nodded at the bookcase.

A flicker of hope quirked Sam's lips. "Baby Vamp, you're a genius."

"Oh, Sam, you're just saying that because it's true."

They dove for the large leather-bound books. Evie swept away a layer of dust. "Ugh. That's the end of these gloves. 'The Declaration of Independence.' Say, I've heard of that," she said. When she opened the book, she found that it had been hollowed out, the pages cut into a ragged box that held two slim glass bottles. Whatever liquid the bottles had contained had long since evaporated, but a crusted blue film remained inside.

"Booze? Perfume?" Evie opened and sniffed one, shaking her head. "Definitely not either."

"Let's see what's inside *The Federalist Papers*," Sam said, coughing as the dust spiraled up into his face.

"Looks like an ordinary book," Evie said. "Not hollow. Any hidden messages?"

On a hunch, Sam turned the book upside down and shook it. Several pieces of paper fluttered to the floor. Sam picked one up. It was a rectangular card with a series of patterned holes punched into it. The other cards were the same except for the typed headings: *Subject #12. Subject #48. Subject #77. Subject #12. Subject #63. Subject #144.*

"Sam, what are these?" Evie said, turning one of the cards over. "Why are there all these little holes?"

"It's code."

"Honestly, Sam, how can this be code? They're just holes."

"The holes are the code. Listen, one Christmas, I worked at Macy's—"

"As an elf?"

"Yeah. I put you down for two lumps of coal," Sam shot back. "As a punch card operator. We kept information on sales in code. That's what these cards are—coded files. All these little holes? Information."

"So how do we get to see that information?"

"They hafta be read by a special machine."

"You see one of those special machines around here?"

Sam peered into the gloom. "No."

Evie flipped through the cards again, reading aloud. "Subject number twelve. Subject number forty-eight. Subject number seventy-seven...Wait a minute." She ran back to the wall, looking from the cards to the map. "These subject numbers correspond to different towns! Why, look—they're all over the country. Subject number seventy-seven is in..." She searched the map. "Here! South Dakota. And Subject number one forty-four is..." Evie traced a finger to another thumbtack. "Bountiful, Nebraska."

"Subject number twenty-seven, New Orleans. Subject number twelve, Baltimore..." Sam said.

"How many of these are there?" Evie said, stepping back a bit to take in the whole of the map.

"Don't know. The highest number we've got is one hundred forty-four."

Evie frowned at the wall. There was a thumbtack stuck into Zenith, Ohio, beside a number. Subject zero.

Footsteps sounded in the hall, coming closer.

"Sam!" she whispered urgently.

"Here. Grab some of these," Sam whispered back, stuffing some of the punch cards into his vest. "Put 'em in your purse."

"That's the first place someone would look." Evie lifted her skirt and shoved the punch cards into her stocking, under the garter, beside her silver flask. She smoothed her skirt back down. "Were you staring at my legs, Sam Lloyd?"

"Your flask, actually. I'm a sucker for silver," Sam said, moving to the door.

Evie came up behind him. "What if we get in trouble?" she whispered. "This isn't like breaking into a pawnshop. We're trespassing in a government office!"

Sam's wolf grin was back. "I like it when the stakes are high."

He opened the door a crack. At the far end of the corridor were two men in gray suits. Their gait was calm but deliberate, and something about it unnerved Sam, though he couldn't say why. The men seemed out of place—not like postal workers. More like security of some sort. If pressed, Sam could use his skills to disorient the men long enough to get away, but that was an absolute last resort. He liked keeping his divining talent—if that's what it was—a secret. Secrets were protection.

Evie peered over his shoulder. "Who is that? Police?" she whispered, confirming his gut reaction.

"Don't know, but they don't look friendly. Come on. We can't get out that way," Sam said, shutting the door. "We'll have to go out the way we came in."

"Sam. There's nothing to catch us on the other side. We could break an ankle. What if those men hear us? What if they want to use the lavatory?"

The footsteps were very close now.

"Maybe they don't even want this office," Evie whispered.

"Maybe," Sam said, but he flipped the latch on the door anyway. The footsteps echoed louder, coming closer, then stopped just outside the office. Sam grabbed Evie's hand, and they dove under the desk and squeezed in together. The space was tight. Evie could only curl up against Sam. His hand rested on her arm and his mouth was against her neck.

The doorknob rattled, then fell silent. It was followed a few seconds later by the click of a key in the lock. Evie took in a sharp breath.

"Easy, Sheba," Sam whispered, his breath warm on her skin.

Hallway light spilled across the office floor, then receded as the door was shut again. From their hiding spot under the desk, Evie and Sam could see the gray trouser legs and black shoes of the two men as they moved silently around the abandoned office. File drawers were opened and shut. One of the men stood in front of the desk, very close, and Evie's heart hammered so hard in her ears, she feared it could be heard plainly. Sam rubbed his thumb in small circles against the inside of her wrist. It was meant as a reassuring gesture, but it sent shivers up her arm and made her head buzzy.

One of the men spoke. His voice was bland, almost soothing. "See anything that looks like a prophecy?"

"Not unless it's written in dust," the other man said. His voice was quieter and raspy, like a broken whisper.

Both pairs of shoes faced the wall with the map. "So many chickens to round up."

The men stood in the gloom a moment longer. The door opened to hallway light, then closed again. The key turned in the lock. The footsteps moved away. Evie turned her head, and Sam's mouth was a breath away from hers. There was a feeling inside her like bees.

"That was close," she whispered. Her head was light.

"Yeah. Yeah, it was," Sam said. Neither of them moved. His hand still cupped her wrist gently.

"I-I suppose we can go now," Evie said.

"Suppose so," Sam answered.

"Well," Evie said, then she crawled out from under the desk and stretched. Sam followed, but he turned away and leaned against the wall for a moment.

"You jake?" Evie asked.

"Sure. Just, um, gimme a minute," Sam said. He sounded winded. In a second, he turned to her, looking a little flushed, as if he were newly drunk. "I, ah, guess we'd better breeze while we can."

They started down the long hallway. Sam could still smell a bit of Evie's perfume on his collar. He gave her a sideways glance just as she looked his way, grinning, clearly invigorated by their shared adventure. And Sam's heart felt suddenly too big for the cage of his chest.

A janitor came around the corner with his mop and pail, and Evie let out a yelp of surprise. The janitor startled, then narrowed his eyes. "Hey! You're not supposed to be down here. Who let you in?"

"Gee. We're awfully sorry, Pops. We were looking for the dead letter office so we could pay our respects," Sam said, and Evie let out a little snort of laughter, which she covered with a cough. "Guess this isn't it. Excuse us, won'tcha?"

They sidled past the janitor, holding fast to each other's hands. Evie's giggles bubbled up, and that was all it took to make Sam lose his composure.

"You're not supposed to be down here!" the janitor yelled after them as they broke into a run, both of them laughing hysterically.

✳

By the time Sam and Evie arrived at the Waldorf, the *Radio Star* people were waiting.

"I'm gonna see if I can scare up one of those punch card–reading machines," Sam said, smoothing back his thick dark hair and securing his Greek fisherman's cap in place once more.

"Who do you think those gray-trousered men were?" Evie asked.

"Don't know. But I got a feeling they weren't looking for dead letters."

"Oh! Don't forget about tomorrow night! Pears soap is very excited that you're coming on the show with me."

"Do I hafta?"

"Yes. You do. It'll only be a few minutes, Sam. Just enough to sell soap and make the advertisers happy, which will make Mr. Phillips happy, which will make me happy."

"That's a long chain of happy. Okay, Sheba. I'll see you at nine."

"Nothin' doing. Show's at nine. You'll see me at half past eight."

On the other side of the windows, Mr. Phillips's secretary waved impatiently to Evie and nodded toward the magazine people.

"I suppose I'd better get in there," Evie said. She could still feel the lingering ghost of Sam's touch on her arm.

"Suppose you'd better," Sam said, without moving.

"Well," she said.

"Yeah," Sam said.

"So long, my lovely leprechaun," Evie called as she backed away.

Sam doffed his hat to her. "So long, Mutton Chop."

Sam watched through the hotel's tall front windows as, inside, the photographer had Evie pose with a tennis racket, as if she were pretending to reach for a serve. It was just a photograph, but Evie's expression was one of fierce concentration, as if she meant to hit that ball out to the stars. Sam knew he should be moving on, but he couldn't seem to go.

On the road to New York, Sam had spent a wild couple of months with daredevil aviator, Barnstormin' Belle. He'd liked her plenty, but in the end, he'd left her to chase after Project Buffalo.

"Always thought it would be a plane that'd bring me down someday. Never figured it would be a boy like you," she'd told him. "Someday, a girl's gonna break your heart. Let me know when it happens. I'd like to send her a thank-you note," she'd said, slapping a pair of aviator goggles over eyes glistening with tears. "Scram, Flyboy. I got a show to do."

Sam had a skill that often let him take what he needed. But you couldn't do that with love. It had to be given. Shared.

Through the window, Evie saw him. She made a funny face—a silly gesture—and Sam felt it deep inside.

"Don't get soft, Sergei," he muttered to himself.

The uniformed doorman approached Sam. "May I help you, sir?" he said, letting Sam know he'd worn out his sidewalk welcome.

"Pal," Sam said, giving Evie one last, longing look, "I really wish you could."

FUNNY FEELINGS

At a noisy Horn & Hardart Automat on Broadway, Evie hunkered down in a corner and kept an eye out for T. S. Woodhouse, who pushed through the door at last with his usual louche swagger.

"I was surprised to get your call, Sheba," he said, taking a seat and helping himself to a forkful of her apple pie. "Why, these days, you're busier than Babe Ruth's bat."

Evie tucked a dollar beside his hat. Woody glanced at it, then took another bite of pie. "Aren't you getting enough press these days, Sweetheart Seer?"

"It isn't about me this time," Evie whispered.

Woody grinned. "I have never heard those words from your lips."

Evie ignored the jibe. "Woody, I need you to put that feverish brain of yours to work on something that requires real investigation for once."

"I do love the way you ask for favors, Sheba. Full of humility and grace."

"You want humility and grace, head to a nunnery. This is important."

"I'm all ears."

Evie wasn't entirely certain she should trust Woody, but he was all she had. She looked around to make certain they weren't overheard. "You ever hear of something called Project Buffalo?"

The reporter raised an eyebrow. "Is this a charity that takes kiddies to zoos?"

"No. It was a government project during the war, maybe even before that."

Woody wiped his mouth, keeping his eyes on Evie. Then he took out his pencil and wrote *Project Buffalo* on his notepad. "Go on."

"I-I don't really know much about it, except that it might have had something to do with Diviners."

"How's that?"

"As I said, I don't know. I only know that Sam's mother went to work on it—"

"Doing what?"

"She was a nurse," Evie said, keeping her face blank. Woody didn't need to know everything. "That's the whole crop."

"I guess I'll have to ask Sam if I want to know more. . . ."

"No!" Evie said, placing a hand on Woody's arm. "You mustn't tell Sam. He'd have a conniption fit if he knew I was talking to you. This is strictly confidential, Woody. I only want to help him find out what happened to his mother."

Woody's slow smile alarmed Evie. "Ah, young love. Okay. What was Mrs. Lloyd's first name?"

"Miriam. Miriam Lubovitch. They changed their name to Lloyd somewhere along the line."

Woody kept his chin down but flicked his gaze up at Evie. "Sam's Jewish, then?"

Evie held his stare. "So's Al Jolson."

Woody shrugged. "I've got nothing against Jews. But some folks do. Your Mr. Phillips, for one. Just a friendly tip. Okay, I'll see what I can dig up. But it's gonna require a great deal of digging." He cleared his throat, glanced meaningfully at the dollar, and waited.

"That's what rats do, don't they? Dig?" Evie shot back. She rummaged in her purse and handed him another dollar. "That's all I can spare."

"My bookie thanks you, Miss O'Neill. One more thing: What happened up at Knowles' End with Hobbes?"

"I told the papers all about it then. It's old news," Evie said, pushing the rest of her apple pie around on her plate with her fork.

Woody smirked. "The truth, the partial truth, and nothing but. See, I got a funny feeling something happened up there that you're not talking about."

"Such as?"

"Such as maybe John Hobbes wasn't human."

Already, Evie was regretting her decision. If you gave a fella like T. S. Woodhouse half an inch, he'd bulldoze his way in for more. "We all get funny feelings sometimes, Woody. Have a milk shake and forget about it. Sorry to cut this short, but I have to perform for a ladies' supper club before the show."

"You gonna get a read on the chicken salad?" Woody teased. Then he turned serious. "I'm gonna find out the truth about what happened, Sheba. No matter how long it takes," he said and gobbled the last bite of pie.

FAVORS AND MIRACLES

"Memphis! Memphis!"

Outside Floyd's Barbershop, Memphis turned to see Rene, one of Papa Charles's runners, waving him down. "Memphis! Papa Charles wants you."

"What for?" Memphis said, his heart racing a little at the thought. Papa Charles didn't just send for people without reason.

"Didn't say. Just said to come get you and bring you to the Hotsy Totsy. Now."

A crow cawed from the top of the lamppost.

"What're you squawking at me for? Why don't you make yourself useful and tell me what Papa Charles wants?"

The crow squawked again and fell silent.

"Thanks for nothing, bird," Memphis said, hugging himself against the cold.

At the Hotsy Totsy, Memphis entered Papa Charles's well-appointed office, nodding at Jules and Emmanuel, Papa's bodyguards, who sat outside his door, Tommy guns resting on their laps.

"Memphis, come in," Papa Charles called from behind his big desk. "Have a seat, son."

Memphis perched on the edge of the chair. He tried to lick his lips but his mouth was dry. The heavy smoke from Papa Charles's cigar made his eyes burn. Papa Charles folded his hands on his desk and looked at Memphis.

"Memphis, I've known you for a long time. Knew your daddy well. Your mama, too."

"Yes, sir."

"And I've always looked after your family, haven't I? I made certain that Isaiah had a new baseball glove, or I sent one of my boys over to fix Octavia's icebox when it wasn't working?"

"Yes, sir," Memphis said, his unease growing. Was he in some sort of trouble?

"And when you got arrested a few months ago, who got you out of jail?"

"Those cops framed me. They were dirty for Dutch Schultz and trying to send you a message," Memphis protested. If he hadn't been working for Papa Charles in the first place, he wouldn't have gotten pinched, so it seemed unfair of his boss to bring it up now.

Papa Charles made a *We all know how it works* gesture. "Still," he said, blowing out circles of smoke. "I have done you favors, yes? The time has come I need a favor from you."

Memphis swallowed hard. "What sort of favor?"

"You know Mr. Carrington, owns the big store on One Hundred Twenty-fifth?"

Carrington's was a department store where mostly white people shopped. Memphis had been inside once, but when one of the store detectives seemed to go everywhere Memphis did, he'd left in a hurry.

"Yes, sir. I know it," Memphis said tightly.

"Mr. Carrington has been a good friend to us. And he needs a favor. I heard this morning that his wife has the sleeping sickness." Papa Charles tapped his cigar against the side of a silver ashtray. "Part of my job is to look out for Harlem, for what is in our best interests. We don't need the trouble people are having down in Chinatown. Don't want the health department up here shutting down our businesses and restaurants and clubs. It would be very bad for all of us if this got out."

"So why doesn't Mr. Carrington get a doctor? He can afford one."

"Doctors haven't been able to cure the sleeping sickness. Mr. Carrington remembers you, remembers your work at the Miracle Mission."

Papa Charles picked a stray thread from his spotless wool trousers. "If we do a good turn for Mr. Carrington, he'll do a good turn for us. Like help to keep Dutch Schultz's men from causing us trouble."

The whole mess of the situation was dawning on Memphis. "Papa Charles, you know I don't do that anymore. Not since my mother."

"Memphis," Papa Charles said on a sigh, and then he gave Memphis the sort of stare that got things done in Harlem. His words were quiet and deliberate. "You think I was born yesterday? I knew the minute Bishop Noble came into Floyd's talking about a heavenly healing that it was you. Do you deny it?"

Memphis looked down at his hands.

"Do. You. *Deny*. It?"

"No, sir," Memphis said, his voice nearly a whisper. "But I've only done it that one time," Memphis lied. "I don't know if I can do it again."

"Then I guess now's as good a time as any to find out." Papa Charles stubbed out his cigar. "Grab your hat and come with me."

Out in front of the Carringtons' apartment building on 127th Street, a handful of schoolgirls skipped rope and sang a clapping song. They giggled as Memphis walked up the stoop and Papa Charles rang the bell, but Memphis was too uneasy to play along with them and they picked up their clapping song again: "Miss Mary Mack, Mack, Mack, all dressed in black, black, black..." they sang, and a shiver crawled up Memphis's spine.

"Afternoon, Bessie. We're here to see Mr. Carrington. I believe he's expecting us," Papa Charles said, handing over his hat.

"Yes, sir, Mr. Charles," Bessie answered, taking their coats, too. She smiled shyly at Memphis. "Hey, Memphis."

"Hey, Bessie," Memphis said.

"Lord, I hope you know what you're doing," she said in hushed tones as she led them upstairs. "I'm scared to even change the bedsheets."

They followed Bessie down the hall to a closed door, where she knocked gingerly. "Mr. Carrington? Mr. Charles and Mr. Campbell are here to see you, sir," she said.

"Show them in," came a muffled voice.

Bessie opened the door wide, stepping aside so that Memphis and Papa Charles could enter the sick woman's room, then closed the door quickly behind her as she left.

The bedroom was still and gloomy. The drapes had been drawn. Mrs. Carrington lay in the four-poster bed with her mouth partially open. Her lips quivered just slightly, as if she were about to speak, and her fingers twitched where they lay against the covers. Under the lids, her eyes moved back and forth. A cluster of red marks showed on the pale map of her neck. Memphis tried not to stare at the marks, but he couldn't help it.

"Thank you for coming," Mr. Carrington said. He smelled of liquor. "Do you need anything before you, um...?"

Papa Charles placed his hands on Memphis's shoulders. "He'll be just fine. Won't you, Memphis?"

"Yes, sir," Memphis croaked, and he hoped that was true.

"Would you all kindly bow your heads?" Memphis asked Mr. Carrington and Papa Charles. It wasn't that he wanted them to pray; he just didn't like being watched. It made him nervous. Once the men complied, Memphis approached the bed and placed his hands lightly on Mrs. Carrington's arm. *Whatever is good in this world, be with me now*, he thought and shut his eyes.

The connection came faster this time, the current of it traveling up Memphis's arms. Under the warm yellow sun, the hands of ancestor spirits welcomed him. But no sooner had Memphis joined to Mrs. Carrington than he sensed that something was wrong. Every time the healing began to take hold, it was quickly undone. Something was fighting him.

His mother's voice came to him. "Memphis, stop!"

His mother was there in the tall reeds, and she looked scared.

"Mama?" Memphis said.

The spirits of his ancestors faded into mist. Angry clouds moved across the sun. It grew colder.

"Memphis!" His mother choked and coughed. A tuft of feathers

356

tumbled from her lips. Her eyes were huge; her voice rasped toward a squawk. "Memphis, get out *now!*"

But it was too late. His body twitched and jerked as he was pulled under a great wave, and when he surfaced again, it was as if he were awake inside Mrs. Carrington's dream. He was on a blue bicycle, riding through a bright green field of freshly mown grass that smelled of high summer. Mrs. Carrington's laughter echoed in his ears. She was young and free and happy. The happiness affected Memphis like a drug. His body relaxed. It was nice here in Mrs. Carrington's dream, and Memphis struggled to remember his purpose.

He was supposed to heal this woman. To wake her up.

As he renewed his concentration, a shrieking voice broke through. *"Who dares disturb my dream? I will make you live in nightmares. . . ."*

The warmth vanished. Cold flooded through his veins. Memphis wanted to break the connection, but he couldn't. Something had him, strong as an undertow. He struggled against its pull, but it was no use. The bicycle, the field, the sun—all of it went away. It was dark now, and he couldn't move. Where was he? Far away, through a dot of light, lay a train station. One minute, the station was beautiful; the next, it was nothing more than a rotted, filthy ruin.

Memphis had been trying to heal Mrs. Carrington, and still, they were joined. He felt what she felt. Her mind desperately wanted to drift back to the happy time in the grass and the blue bicycle. Her yearning was a gnawing hunger clawing at Memphis's guts, as if its craving would never be satisfied. But Memphis sensed, too, that the dream was draining Mrs. Carrington's life force. In order to heal her, Memphis would first need to stop her dreaming. But how?

Wake up, Mrs. Carrington, he thought. *There are people who want you to come back. Wake up.*

A threatening growl interrupted Memphis. He lost his concentration. What was that sound? The dark sparked with flashes of green. A figure approached. She wore a long dress and a veil. Mrs. Carrington's heartbeat sped up; so did Memphis's. The tunnel was loud with an awful din. The ghostly figure came closer. Memphis could sense great rage and sorrow in her, something beyond his healing.

"Who intrudes on my dreams?" the woman shrieked. And then her eyes widened with recognition and a strange joy. "So much life in you! More than all the others. You could feed these dreams for a long, long time. *Dream with me.*"

Her mouth was on his, sucking the life from him even as her kiss promised him everything he ever wanted. Flocks of hopes fluttered past Memphis's eyes: Memphis and Theta sitting beneath a lemon tree under a warm sun, a typewriter on his lap. Isaiah laughing as a little dog jumped for a ball. Their mother hanging wash on the line, smiling over at her boys while his father smoked his pipe and read his newspaper. But when Memphis struggled against this dreaming, nightmares intruded: Soldiers blown apart. His mother wasting away to nothing on her deathbed. A fearsome wood and the man in the stovepipe hat holding out his palm, emblazoned with the eye and lightning bolt. "You. And I. Are joined."

These terrible things turned him back toward the beautiful dreaming.

His eyes blinked open to buttery sun shining down on a grand town house. The door opened, and a butler welcomed Memphis inside. "Evening, Mr. Campbell. Take your coat, sir? Everybody is awfully excited to hear you tonight."

The butler handed Memphis a program: *Miss A'Lelia Walker presents new poetry by Memphis John Campbell.*

"Just like Langston Hughes, Mr. Campbell. You've made it, sir." The butler paused outside a second door and smiled wide. "Would you like to go inside, sir?"

The last of Memphis's resistance gave way. All he wanted was to have that door opened for him and to walk right through. "Yes. Yes, I would. Thank you."

The second door opened into a grand parlor filled with elegant people who greeted Memphis's arrival with applause. The applause grew, and Memphis never wanted it to stop. He was losing himself to the room and the joy and the want. Theta blew him a kiss from the front row. The great A'Lelia Walker, patron of Harlem poets, writers, and artists, drew back a curtain, and behind it was a table holding a stack of books with Memphis's name on the spine.

"My book," Memphis murmured, a half smile on his lips.

From high atop a shelf, the crow squawked something fierce.

"Go away, bird," Memphis said. "This is *my* night."

When he looked toward the table again, he saw that it sat inside a long, dark tunnel.

"You don't want to keep them waiting, do you, Mr. Campbell?" A'Lelia Walker asked. Her hand threatened to snap the curtain closed, shutting him out.

"No, ma'am," Memphis said.

The growling was back. It was thicker now, almost a hornet's nest buzz. The smiling audience crowded around Memphis. "*Dream with us...*" they whispered, and urged him forward toward the table of books and the hungry dark waiting behind it.

With a great flapping of feathers, the bird caromed about the room. In the mirror, Memphis saw the warm sands and his ancestors. One of those ancestors, a man with a tall staff, spoke to him in a language Memphis did not know but which resonated deep inside him, urging caution. *Look closely now*, it seemed to say.

The muscles of Memphis's neck tensed against some unseen threat and his heartbeat doubled. He turned his head. Mrs. Carrington stood in the corner, her face pale and her mouth struggling to speak.

"Don't. Promise," she wheezed. "It's. A. Trap."

Memphis opened one of the books that carried his name, riffling through the pages.

Blank. Every single page, blank.

Look closely now.

"Where are my words?" he asked.

"*Words don't matter. Dream with us.*"

But Memphis knew that words did matter. *Look closely now.*

"Where are my words? Why have you taken my stories?" he asked.

359

As soon as he said it, the curtain to his dream slammed shut. A'Lelia Walker vanished, and the edges of her shining parlor peeled away. He was back in the long dark tunnel now, with those strange greenish lights winking on, raining down. The crow left its perch. It pecked at Memphis's cheek. He gasped and put a hand to his wound. Blood pooled on his fingertips. Quickly, Memphis grabbed hold of Mrs. Carrington's wrist. In his head, he heard the distant drums of his ancestors, and, acting on some primal instinct, he smeared her with his blood. Memphis cried out as a great roaring rushed through him, like a dammed ocean unleashing its power at last.

In the next second, Memphis fell on the floor beside Mrs. Carrington's bed. His arms shook and he gagged as if he might vomit. He felt as if he'd run full-out for miles. Muffled voices became clearer.

"Memphis! Memphis, sit up now, son. Come on." Papa Charles's hands were on him, helping him off the floor.

In her bed, Mrs. Carrington sat straight up. Her dark eyes were wide and blinking. Her fingers clawed at the air. Her mouth opened and closed as if she had been drowning and was now trying to choke the last of the water from her lungs.

"Emmaline!" Mr. Carrington cried as he rushed to his wife's side. "Emmaline!"

With a shuddering gasp, she inhaled.

And then she was screaming.

✺

MIRACLE ON 125TH STREET! DEPARTMENT STORE KING'S WIFE WAKES FROM SLEEPING SICKNESS! screamed the front page of the late-edition extra.

Eager New Yorkers swarmed around the newsies, whose fingers could barely keep up as they peeled off the freshly printed newspapers, which told of Mrs. Carrington's miraculous awakening. From her sickbed, Mrs. Carrington reported that she could remember nothing from her time asleep except for a happy dream about riding a blue bicycle and a music-box song. Mr. Carrington claimed that his wife's sudden recovery was due to "the great healing power of the Almighty himself." Sarah Snow came round to take a picture, a fresh orchid pinned to her very fashionable dress as she sat at Mrs. Carrington's bedside. The Carringtons made no mention of Diviners or of Memphis.

But as Blind Bill Johnson sat in the Lenox Drugstore sipping his coffee and listening to Reggie read the story aloud to an eager group of patrons, he knew who had done the healing.

The time for patience was over.

A PERFECTLY DECENT GIRL

On the evening of what should have been Mabel's first date with Jericho, she had come down with a terrible cold. Now that the rescheduled evening had rolled around at last, Jericho was second-guessing every choice he'd made. He'd gotten a reservation at the Kiev, a tearoom in the West Fifties where patrons could drink tea, eat blintzes, and dance to the orchestra between courses if they liked. He didn't know why he'd chosen that place. He wasn't a dancer, and taking a girl to a restaurant with dancing announced your intention to do just that. The whole evening had begun to seem like a bad idea, but it was too late to back out now.

"Hey, Freddy!" Sam said as he blew through the front door. "Listen, I gotta step out—holy smokes! Is that a...are you wearing a tie?" Sam leaned against the wall and watched Jericho as he struggled and failed for a third time to make the proper knot.

"I have a date," Jericho said, unraveling it once more. "Why are you covered in dust? Never mind. I'm pretty sure I don't want to know."

"You're right. You don't want to know. And I hope that date is with an antiques dealer, because that thing around your neck is a genuine artifact. Did you find it in the museum or on a dead clown?"

"Go away, Sam."

"And leave you in a time of crisis? Huh-uh. You need me. More than you know. Wait right here," Sam called as he raced toward his room. Jericho heard drawers opening, and a moment later Sam returned with a very fashionable gray-striped necktie. "Here. Borrow one of mine."

Jericho regarded it dubiously. "Who'd you steal this from?"

"Fine," Sam said, holding it out of reach. "Go out in your grandpa's tie. See if I care."

"Wait!" Jericho swiped the gray-striped number from Sam. "Thank you."

"You're welcome. So, ah, who's the lucky girl?" Sam asked, waggling his eyebrows suggestively. When Jericho ignored him, Sam grabbed one of Jericho's Civil War soldier figurines and held it up to his mouth. "Oh, Jericho," he said in a high-pitched voice. "Take me in your arms, you big he-man, you!"

"Please put General Meade back in Gettysburg. You're changing the course of the war. And it's just a date."

"With girls, it's never just a date. First lesson, Freddy," Sam said.

"As always, I'm grateful for your sage advice," Jericho said, finishing the knot.

Sam nodded approvingly. "You clean up nice, Freddy. Don't do anything I wouldn't do." Sam grinned as he dropped into Will's chair.

"Such as behave like a decent human being?" Jericho said, reaching for his hat and scarf from the hall coatrack.

"Who just gave you a proper tie?"

"Get out of Will's chair."

"You're welcome!" Sam shouted as the door closed.

"I'm sorry about my mother and father and all those questions they asked," Mabel said as she and Jericho sat in a leather booth inside the Kiev. "For radicals, they're practically Republicans about my suitors."

"It's all right," Jericho said, watching couples old enough to be their grandparents glide across the worn parquet floors to the tepid strains of a second-rate orchestra. It was a far cry from the sort of nightclubs Evie and Sam attended every night. He hoped Mabel wasn't too disappointed with this choice.

"Nice place," Mabel said, just like the good sport she was.

"Mmm," Jericho said around a mouthful of gooey pastry.

"It's nice that they have dancing."

"Yes. Dancing is…um, nice," Jericho said. He felt like a horse's ass. And Sam's necktie pinched.

Mabel sipped her spicy tea, her stomach churning with nerves as she tried to think of a conversation starter that would turn the evening around, and fast. "Say, I've got a fun game!" she said, finally. "If you were a Diviner, what power would you want to have?"

"I'm not a Diviner," Jericho answered.

"Neither am I. That's why it's a game."

"I'm not good at these sorts of games." Jericho ate another bite of blintz.

I've noticed, Mabel thought, and stirred her tea for the twentieth time.

"Fine. What sort of power would *you* have?" Jericho asked.

"Oh. Anything would do, I suppose. It would just be nice not to be so hideously ordinary." Mabel laughed and waited for Jericho to disagree with her: *Why, don't be silly, Mabel—you're anything but ordinary. Why, you're extraordinary all on your own!*

"There's no such thing as hideously ordinary. If something is hideous, it's automatically extraordinary. In a hideous way."

"Never mind. Let's change the subject," Mabel grumbled.

"I told you I wasn't good at this game," Jericho said. "Besides, the more I read about Diviners, the more I think it's a curse as well as a gift."

"What do you mean?"

"Diviners are truth-tellers. But people rarely want the truth. We say that we want it when, really, we like being lied to. We prefer the ether of hope."

"But hope is necessary! You have to give people hope," Mabel insisted.

"Why?"

"Why what?"

Jericho folded his arms across his chest. "In an amoral, violent world, isn't it unconscionable to keep offering hope? It's like advertising for soap that never gets you clean."

"Now you're just being cynical."

"Am I? What about war? We keep grappling for power, killing for it. Enslaving. Oppressing. We create ourselves. We destroy ourselves. Over and over. Forever. If the cycle repeats, why bother with hope?"

"But we also overcome. I've seen people fight against that sort of oppression and win. What you're talking about is nihilism. And frankly," Mabel said, taking a steadying breath, "frankly, that bores me." Nothing emboldened her quite as much as someone claiming the good fight couldn't be won.

"How is it nihilism to embrace the cycle and let go—of attachments and morality and, yes, the opiate futility of hope?" Jericho fired back. Mabel's naiveté annoyed him. She might think she'd seen the world, but, really, she saw only a particular slice of the world, neatly bordered by hedgerows trimmed daily by her parents' idealism. "All right," he pressed. "If you believe in hope, what about true evil? Do you believe there is such a thing?"

Mabel felt as if the question were a test, one she might easily fail. "I believe real evil is brought about by a system that is unjust or by people acting selfishly. By greed." She'd never really articulated her thoughts on the matter before, and it satisfied her to say them aloud.

"That's the do-gooder answer."

Mabel bristled. "I don't go for the bogeyman. There's plenty of evil to fight in life without having to make up devils and demons and ghosts. If you believe that there is Evil in the world, capital *E*, doesn't that take away your belief in free will? I still maintain that people have choices. To do right. To have hope. To *give* hope," Mabel said pointedly.

Jericho was very quiet, and Mabel feared she'd insulted him. But then he looked her in the eyes in a way that was unnerving.

365

"Have you ever had a moment that forced you to question what you believe?" he asked. "Something that forced you to reexamine your ideas of morality, of good and evil?"

"I…" Mabel stopped. "I suppose not. Have you?"

"Once." Jericho was very still. "I helped a friend end his life. Does that shock you?"

Mabel was stunned into silence for a moment. She wasn't sure she liked knowing this about Jericho. "Yes. A little."

"He was very sick and suffering, and he asked me to do it. I had to weigh that choice: Was it murder, or was it mercy? Was it immoral or was it, given the circumstances, the moral choice? I'd thought I'd made my peace with it. But now I'm not so sure."

Mabel didn't know what to say. She had constructed an entire idea of Jericho as smart and good and noble, and this sudden confession did not fit neatly into that architecture. Her own life had been built upon a foundation of "doing good." She'd not had much opportunity to challenge what that meant.

"I'm sorry," she said. It seemed the flimsiest of comforts, but it was all she could offer.

Jericho pushed his plate away. "No. I'm sorry. That probably wasn't the sort of thing you say on a date. This evening isn't going very well, is it?"

"Well, it isn't as bad as the time I accidentally stepped into a latrine at a labor camp, but I'd wager you're correct."

Jericho gave a small *Ha!* and Mabel had her first genuine smile of the night. "Why, Jericho. You just laughed. Will Nietzsche be mad at you?"

Jericho felt like a heel. He'd picked a fight for no reason at all. Mabel's only sin was not being Evie. She at least deserved a fair shake as herself. If nothing sparked after that, well, so be it. At the very least, he should try to salvage the evening and end the date on a happier note.

He folded his napkin and stood with his hand out. "Mabel, would you like to dance?"

366

"Well, I certainly don't want any more tea," she said, joining him.

"I'm not much of a dancer," he said apologetically. "And by that I mean that I don't dance at all."

"That's all right. I'm not much of a dancer, either. But we're the only people under the age of seventy in here, so I suppose that's something, isn't it?"

Jericho winced. "It's pretty dreadful, isn't it?"

Mabel wrinkled her nose in agreement. "But the blintzes are good."

Jericho escorted Mabel to the dance floor, where they stood facing each other, awkward and uncertain. The orchestra struck up a tune whose notes were laced with old-country drama—blood feuds and doomed romance, survival and reinvention.

"May I?" Jericho asked nervously.

Mabel nodded. Jericho placed his hand at the small of her back and she jumped just slightly.

"Sorry. Did I . . . ?"

"No! It's . . . it's fine. I'm just . . . it's good." Her cheeks were bright red.

Jericho rested his hand on her back once more, and this time Mabel put her left hand on his shoulder and raised her right hand to meet his, trying to ignore the heat suffusing her cheeks. Slowly, they moved around the dance floor—one, two-three, one, two-three—the older folks looking on approvingly, shouting encouragement in Russian and English. They managed several passes around the floor without incident. At the end, the old folks applauded, and Mabel was both proud and embarrassed.

"We should quit while we're ahead, I think," Jericho whispered.

"Agreed."

On the walk home, the conversation was all about the Diviners exhibit and the brilliance of Charlie Chaplin. By the time they returned to the Bennington, fifteen minutes ahead of Mabel's curfew, they'd made plans to go to the Strand to see a Buster Keaton picture.

"There might be people younger than sixty there," Jericho said, and Mabel laughed.

Mabel strangled the strap of her pocketbook as her stomach fluttered. "Well, good night, Jericho."

"Good night, Mabel," Jericho said. He wasn't precisely sure about the protocol of ending a mostly-but-not-entirely-disastrous first date. A handshake seemed too formal. Kissing a girl's hand seemed like something only swashbuckler matinee idols could get away with and not feel like a complete fool. And so, rather impulsively, Jericho kissed Mabel sweetly and briefly on the lips and then took the stairs up to his own flat.

Mabel slumped back against the wall feeling summer-light. And even the sight of Miss Addie roaming the halls, trailing salt from her dressing-gown pockets and mumbling about the dead coming through the breach, couldn't dampen her spirits.

The moment Mabel went inside, she bolted for the telephone, ignoring her mother's pleas for information. She grinned as Evie's voice came over the line.

"Sweetheart Seer residence. How may I direct your call?"

"Evie, it's me."

"Mabesie! How do you like my secretary voice? Do you think it gives me an air of mystery?"

"I knew it was you."

"Oh. How disappointing. But you sound out of breath! Are you running from wolves? Do tell."

"You won't believe it. I don't believe it!"

"What is it?"

"I . . . I'm still pinching myself."

"Mabel Rose! If you don't stop torturing me and tell me this instant, I'll . . . I'll . . . well, I'll do whatever clever threat I can't think of just now."

"Are you sitting down?"

"Pos-i-tute-ly prone and ready to hear this story already!"

"Jericho kissed me."

There was such a profound silence on the other end that Mabel was afraid she'd lost the connection. "Hello? Evie? Operator?"

368

"I'm here," Evie said quietly. "Jeepers. That's swell news, honey. How...how did it happen?"

"It was after our date this evening and—"

"Wait a minute—you had a date? Why didn't you tell me?"

"Well, Evie, you're awfully hard to catch these days," Mabel said, hoping Evie caught her drift: *You've been too busy for even your best pal.*

"Tell me about the kiss. Did he kiss you a lot?"

"No. Just the once. What happened was—"

"Did he say anything to you first?"

"Not...well, he—"

"What was his expression? Could you read anything in his face?"

"Evie! Will you please let me tell the story?" Mabel pleaded into the receiver.

"Sorry, Mabesie."

Mabel continued. "We went to the Kiev Tearoom—"

"Ugh. They have such sad little blintzes. If blintzes could frown, those would."

"And in the beginning," Mabel said, without stopping for Evie, "it wasn't going terribly well, to be frank. But then, then he asked me to dance, and, oh, Evie. It was so romantic. Well, to be perfectly honest, it was terrible until we got the gist of it. Why, oh, why didn't I let you to teach me how to dance?"

"One of the great mysteries of our time. And the kiss?" Evie asked, biting her lip.

"I'm getting there. He walked me to my door. He was very quiet and—"

"Regular quiet or brooding quiet?"

"Evie, please."

"Sorry, sorry. Go on."

"He said, 'Good night, Mabel,' and then he...just...kissed me." Mabel gave a little squeal.

Evie closed her eyes and pictured Jericho's face in the first light of morning.

"I can't stop playing it over in my mind like the best Valentino picture ever, except that I'm Agnes Ayres, and Jericho is Rudy."

"Well, he's no Rudy," Evie grumbled, "but I get the gist."

Mabel was telling her something else, but Evie didn't want to talk about it anymore. She'd done the right thing by Mabel and, most likely, by Jericho. She'd thrown him over. Why did doing the right thing feel so awful? Did that mean it wasn't the right thing, or did right things always feel awful, which would in fact be a terrible deterrent to doing right?

"Evie?"

"Hmm?"

"Did you hear what I said?"

"Oh. Sorry, Mabel. There was a, um, a spider. On the floor. Dreadful!"

"Eek! You'd think such a fancy hotel wouldn't have spiders."

"Yes, I'll . . . uh . . . I'll just call down for a bellhop. Sorry, Mabesie."

"Wait! What do you think I should do?"

"I wouldn't rush into anything. Boys like girls who seem to have other beaus. They're fickle that way." Evie sniffed. After all, she'd been pretty easily forgotten.

"Jericho isn't that sort of fellow," Mabel insisted.

"Trust me, they're all that way." She was mad at Jericho. She had no right to be, but she was anyway.

"Gee, Evie, you really don't seem very happy for me."

"Oh, Pie Face, I'm sorry. I am excited for you. Why, I'm pos-i-tute-ly throwing a party for you here," Evie said brightly, feeling guilty. "I think you should go to the pictures with him and just be your charming self."

"But I'm not charming. That's the trouble."

"Then . . . this will be good practice?"

Mabel laughed. "You're the worst friend ever, Evie O'Neill!"

"Yes, I know," Evie said.

THE TIPPING POINT

The land has a memory.

Every stream and river runs with a confession of sorts, history whispered over rocks, lifted in the beaks of birds at a stream, carried out to the sea. Buffalo thunder across plains whose soil was watered with the blood of battles long since relegated to musty books on forgotten shelves. Fields once strewn with blue and gray now flower with uneasy buds. The slave master snaps the lash, and generations later, the ancestral scars remain.

Under it all, the dead lie, remembering.

Adelaide Proctor had been on this earth for eighty-one years. She, too, had a history. She was a distant relation of John Proctor, hanged during the Salem witch trials. Witchcraft was her birthright, and as a young girl, Addie had read the accounts with great interest. There *had* been witchcraft, of course—the simple provenance of cunning folk, midwives, and herbalists: Superstitions practiced in the interest of safety. Curses muttered or occasionally offered with a bound lock of hair and cast into an evening fire to be regretted in the morning or not regretted, depending. But none of it had anything at all to do with the Devil and everything to do with the frailties of the human heart. Here were spells for healing loneliness. Curing the sick. Ensuring good fortune. Assuring safe passage on rough seas. Delivering babies into the world with a boon upon their brows. These tales comforted Addie, for she needed comforting.

Sometimes she'd fall into a dreamy trance. Then she could see into another world of spirits or read messages in the remains of the tea leaves in a cup as clearly as words in a book. She dared not tell anyone these secrets, though she was a little in love with her ability. It made her feel special—almost as special as Elijah Crockett made her feel.

A fine boy was he, her Elijah, with eyes the gray-brown of a river rock. "I'll take you to wife, Adelaide Proctor," he'd said, slipping a daisy chain on her head. He kissed her sweetly and marched off to fight in a war of brother against brother.

She could hear the cannon fire and the screams from Harris Farm. The battle raged for two weeks. In the end, thirty thousand casualties littered Virginia's farmland. A chain of dead boys lay side by side across the field. The boy she loved most lay among them. In his shirt pocket was her last letter to him, caked in blood.

Heartsick with grief, Addie believed that her longing was strong enough to fashion a spell. She wrote her pledge, sealed it with a sprig of laurel and her thumbprint inked in blood, and left it in the hollow of an old elm as she'd read one should do to seek favor of the spirit world. All she asked was to see and speak to her Elijah once more.

This she did and waited.

The war brought other miseries. The men who moved the dead from the battlefields brought typhus back to the Virginia country-side. Whole households fell. On a hot summer morning, pain gripped Addie's belly, and by evening she was wild with fever. The room wobbled and narrowed, and then she was somewhere else—a colorless world where she could feel the press of spirits about her. There was a lone chair like a throne, and in it sat a tall gray man in a coat weighted with shiny blue-black feathers. His nose was long and hawklike, his lips thin. He had eyes as black as the depths of a country well.

"Adelaide Keziah Proctor. You seek an audience with me."

Addie hadn't sought an audience with anyone other than her Elijah, and she told the man so.

"You must speak with me first. Long before your ancestors colonized this land, I was here. The North Star shone its light upon my face. From its people, I draw my power. This nation feeds upon itself. Such dreams! Such ambition! I, too, have dreams. Ambitions. I can taste your desires upon my tongue. Walk with me, child."

Addie walked with the man in the stovepipe hat through woods where crows perched in trees like sentient leaves. Where he walked, the grass yellowed and curled up onto itself, brittle and dry. They came to the old graveyard on the hill. Elijah's grave was not more than three months made. Addie's latest bouquet wilted upon it.

"What would you give to see Elijah again?" the gray man asked.

"Anything."

"Every choice has consequences. Balance must be maintained. For what is given, something else is taken. Think well upon your motives, Adelaide Proctor."

Addie had thought upon her motives every night as she cried softly into her blanket so that her sister, Lillian, sleeping peacefully beside her, would not hear. At sixteen, Adelaide had lost the love of her life. The boy who should've been her husband and the father of her children lay six feet under the mocking sweetness of summer clover. She did not waver in her choice.

"Anything," she said again, and the man in the hat smiled. "May I see him, sir? Oh, bring him to me, please!"

"You shall have your Elijah in time," the man said. "Sleep. For you are young; your days are many. But know this: You belong to me now, Adelaide Keziah Proctor. When the time comes, I shall call upon the promise you make this day. For your patriotism to me."

He pressed his thumb to her forehead and she tumbled backward through the grave, unable to stop herself from falling.

Addie woke to a great thirst and sweaty bedsheets. Her fever had broken. The moon was a faded wax seal against the pale gold parchment of dawn. But where was Elijah? The man had promised. For days and days, he did not come, and Addie began to believe her promise was nothing more than a fever dream.

Then came the signs.

She would find her diary open to a page about her love for Elijah.

Warm winds blew through open windows, and with them came the sweet sunshine smell of him. On a moonlit night, she was sure she heard music coming from the tall grass of the field. It was the faintest whisper of a song Elijah used to sing to her. And the daisies: She'd find them on her side of the bed, lying across her hope chest, or beside her music box. Once, when she took her apron down from the hook, she reached a hand into the pocket and came up with a coating of waxy white petals. Only Elijah knew that daisies were her favorite. Her mother accused her of trying to call attention to herself, but Addie knew these small favors belonged to Elijah. Even in death, he remembered her. Her joy was boundless.

Fever visited the Proctor household once more, this time with a vengeance. When it finally took its leave a week later, it had claimed Addie's father and younger brother, two servants, and the foreman's wife and baby daughter.

Balance.

Addie attended their funerals mute and pale, fearful of what she'd done, of what might still come. That night, she heard her name whispered so sweetly that she woke with a fresh tear upon her cheek. Beyond her window, the moon bled bright behind passing clouds. A nightingale chirruped a warning.

Her name came again, soft as moonlight. "Adelaide, my love. I am here."

Awash in silvery moonlight, Elijah stood at the edge of the field. He'd returned to her, as the man had promised. Addie rushed out after him, following the firefly glimmer of him through the woods, into the old churchyard, past tombstones, until she came to his grave marker. Whispers sounded around them in the September dark. It was cold here, so cold. Elijah shone like a coin in a pond. He was her beautiful love, but there was something of the grave about him now. Weeds wove into his thinning hair. Shadows ringed his eyes and made gaunt his cheekbones. His shirt wept blood where the bullet had done its work.

"You've summoned me, my love."

"Yes," Addie said, eyes brimming with tears. "I've paid the price for you, too."

"Don't you know that every soul you give him increases his power? That it binds you to him forever?"

Addie didn't understand. Why wasn't Elijah happy? "I did it so that we could be together always."

"And so we shall. For I cannot rest until you do. I am bound to love you till you die."

His mouth opened in a scream then. From it fell beetles and maggots and all manner of death. In the trees, the crows cawed, and it sounded like cruel laughter. This creature before her was not Elijah, not the Elijah she'd kissed under the sun. He was something else entirely, and she wanted no part of him. Adelaide ran. She ran past the tombstones and the scarecrows, all the way back to the safety of her bed, which was no safety at all.

In the morning, when she threw back the blanket, she screamed loud enough to wake her sister. There in the covers was a dead mouse with its eyes missing and its entrails ripped out. It lay on a blanket of browned daisy petals.

Addie read the books. She learned the spells. At midnight, she went to Elijah's grave and dug up what was left of him, breaking off a sliver of finger bone, prying out a tooth, cutting off a lock of his hair, scooping up a handful of graveyard dirt. These she placed in an iron box, and then she performed the ritual to bind Elijah's spirit so that he could not come to her anymore. He could not harm her.

But what of the King of Crows, the man in the stovepipe hat?

Addie had given him power when she asked to see Elijah once more. She'd tied herself to him by an invisible thread that she could not sever. She had entered into a bargain blindly. No, not blindly. She'd made the choice. She'd pledged her allegiance to that man in the hat. In the years since, she'd had time to reflect. To question the vow hastily made for love, fashioned from grief, from a need to believe in something grander than herself.

Adelaide Proctor was old now. She had watched them bury the

boy she loved in the muddy soil of Virginia, and she had buried her family soon after. On a day in April, she read about the president, assassinated by John Wilkes Booth, and of the assassin's death, too. When President McKinley also fell to an assassin's bullet, she was there. She'd seen the birth of the automobile and the aeroplane. The steam trains crossed the country, the gleaming tracks clumsy sutures across wounded miles of stolen land. In New York Harbor, the ships sailed in with their precious, hopeful cargo gaping at Liberty's torch. The towns spread and grew; the factories, too, belching smoke and ambition into the air. The wars continued. Hymns were raised to the glory of the nation. The people were good and fine and strong and fair, hardworking and hopeful; also, vain and grasping, greedy and covetous, willfully ignorant and dangerously forgetful.

Addie Proctor had seen much in her eighty-one years in this magnificent, turbulent country impossible with possibility, and so she knew to be afraid now, for they'd reached a tipping point. There were ghosts everywhere in the country, and no one seemed to notice. People danced while the dead watched them through the windows. And all the while, the man in the stovepipe hat gained power. He was coming.

Though she had been warned against it, Addie went to the basement, where she drew the marks upon the floor in chalk and muttered the prayers, performing the small ministrations of salt and blood, rituals to keep the dead away.

She hoped it would be enough.

EUREKA

"Henry!" Ling called as she walked the familiar path past the giant Spanish elms of the bayou. Henry and Louis, bathed in sunshine, sat on the weathered dock. Henry responded with a wave. "Hurry! Before our alarms go off," Ling said.

"Be right there!" Henry called back.

"'Evenin', Miss Ling!" Louis shouted and waved to her. The sun shone brightly down on him, and Ling got a funny feeling in her stomach, some warning she couldn't yet name.

"All good dreams must come to an end," Henry said, joining her, flushed and happy as they walked the forest path. "What's that mark on your dress?"

"Dirt," Ling said, snapping back to the moment. She brushed at the stubborn stain.

"I thought it was another experiment. Like the ash."

"No, but I do need your help. I want to see if I can wake you from inside the dream."

Henry shrugged. "All right. I'm game. What do you want me to do?"

"You only need to stand still."

"Sounds like my music career so far."

"And stop making jokes," Ling chided. "Ready?"

"Ready."

"Here goes: Henry. It's time to wake up," Ling said. Nothing happened. "Wake up, Henry!" Ling said again, louder this time.

"Try shaking me awake," Henry suggested.

Ling grabbed Henry by the shoulders and shook him, softly at first, then more violently.

"Whoa there! Don't want to scramble my brains!"

"Huh." Ling reached over and pinched Henry's arm.

"Ow! Is this science or just an excuse for you to beat me up?"

"Sorry," Ling said sheepishly. She stood back, thinking. "There's got to be a way...."

"Maybe *I* should try to wake *you* up," Henry said.

Ling scoffed. "I am not very suggestible."

"No?"

"No."

"Is that a challenge?"

"No," Ling said. "Just a fact."

Henry arched an eyebrow. "Care to put that to the test? For science?"

"It will be a waste of your time, but be my guest."

"All right, then." Henry raised his hand like a sorcerer. "Oh, Ling Chan, Madame Curie of the dream world," he intoned dramatically, barely keeping a straight face. "Sleep hath released thee! Now is the time thou must waketh!"

Ling rolled her eyes. "You're an idiot."

"Fine. I will be pos-i-tute-ly serious." He cleared his throat and stared at Ling. "Wake up, Ling."

After several long seconds, Ling smirked. "I told you so," she said, breaking off a sprig of pine from a nearby tree and inhaling its fragrance.

Henry had been kidding before, but now he wanted to rise to the challenge. If there was a way for them to wake themselves inside the dream, there'd be no need for alarms. Theta wouldn't be angry with him, because she wouldn't know he was dream walking. He thought about it for a minute. How had he helped Theta change her nightmares?

Henry turned to Ling once more. "Darlin', you're tired and you need your sleep. You'd really like to wake up now, back home in your bed, so why don't you?"

Ling's mouth went slack, and her face settled into a peaceful expression. And then, with the briefest sigh, she vanished from the dream world. For a moment, Henry was too stunned to move.

"Ling?" He swiped a hand through the air where Ling had stood. "Huh. Well, what do you know 'bout that?" he said, feeling quite pleased with himself. He couldn't wait to lord it over Ling tomorrow.

Just then, crackling light appeared inside the tunnel like fireflies on a hot July night, and then the bayou began to darken, the gray sky eating up the last of the shining color as if shutting down for the night. The edges of the dream world wavered and curled up like someone had pulled the thread, unraveling the fabric of it till the cabin, the trees, and the flowers lost their rich detail.

Henry heard soft crying inside the tunnel.

"Hello?" Henry said, approaching.

A song drifted out, and Henry recognized it as one his mother used to play on their piano in New Orleans, back when she could do such things. He'd always sort of liked the old tune.

"*Beautiful Dreamer, come unto me . . .*" he sang softly, a calming habit, because he was uneasy. Just under the music was that unsettling growl he and Ling had heard once in the station.

"Hello?" he said again.

A gust of wind blew from the tunnel, and with it, a thick whisper that surrounded Henry: "*Dream with me. . . .*"

The whisper made Henry feel warm and loose, as if he'd had a strong drink. He drew closer to the tunnel. Something was moving in the dark. Briefly illuminated by the short bursts of light was a girl.

"Wai-Mae?" Henry called.

There was another pop of light and Henry saw the outline of a veil. He blinked, and in the afterimage, he saw disquieting things that made him wish that he weren't there alone, for the figure in the tunnel was coming slowly toward him.

In the next second, his alarm rang. And then Henry was waking, his body immobile as he lay in his bed at the Bennington.

✳

When Ling woke from her dream walk, her body ached and the back of her mouth tasted of iron. She wiped away blood from where she'd bitten her lip on the way back. But it didn't matter, because Henry had done it. He'd woken her up, and Ling smiled despite the split lip.

"Eureka," she murmured, exultant but also exhausted, just before she fell into a true, deep sleep in which she was only a mortal, not a god. Come the morning, she would barely remember her dreams of George Huang, his pale, glowing skin cracking open in fissures as if he were rotting from the inside, as he lurched through the subway tunnel with fast, jerking, puppetlike movements, hands reaching and clutching, as he approached the sleeping vagrant taking shelter between the concrete archways. Nor would she remember the unholy shriek torn from George's throat as he descended upon the screaming man and the underground was filled with the lightning-flash phosphorescence of the hungry, broken spirits answering George's call.

DAY EIGHTEEN

THE TINY UNIVERSE

"I don't know if we should allow Ling to go to the pictures with Gracie and Lee Fan, what with things being the way they are," Mrs. Chan fretted as she parted the lace curtains of their second-floor window and peered out at the police burning the contents of yet another store where two victims of the sleeping sickness had worked.

"Let her go with her friends," Mr. Chan said. "We'll manage for a few hours. It's good for her to be away from all this."

"But you be careful, Ling," Mrs. Chan said. "I heard from Louella that they've begun stopping Chinese on the streets and checking them for the sleeping sickness. And there's been worse. Charlie Lao and his son, John, were harassed outside their shop on Thirty-fifth Street. John has a black eye to show for it. I'll be glad when this is over."

"It will never be over," Uncle Eddie said, and Ling knew he didn't mean the sleeping sickness.

☀

The moment they reached Times Square, Lee Fan and Gracie went shopping, while Ling went to the pictures, as they'd discussed before-hand, agreeing to meet up later. Now a giddy excitement took hold of Ling as the words *Pathé News* flickered across the slowly opening curtains. Two distinguished-looking men strolled along a snowy path, hands behind their backs. And then there were white words on black screens:

Niels Bohr and Albert Einstein,
two giants of science,
explore the tiny universe of the atom.

The atom. Smaller than the human eye can see.
Yet with the power to transform our world!
Just as the farmer harvests wheat from the land,
we may harvest energy from the atom.

The image shifted, and a dark-haired man, handsome as a matinee idol, waved to crowds from his open-air touring car. Ling smiled, her face bathed in the movie's glow.

Jake Marlowe announces
Future of America Exhibition
in New York City.

On-screen, the great Jake Marlowe's lips moved silently as he spoke into a microphone before a large crowd gathered downtown. The scene shifted to black again:

"Once, great men sailed uncertain seas
in search of what was possible.
We know what is possible.
We have built what many said was impossible.
It is called America.
And we are the stewards of her brave future—
a future of vision, of democracy, and of
the exceptional."

For a moment, Ling allowed herself to imagine another newsreel that might play someday, in which she was one of those giants of science shaking hands with great men like Jake Marlowe while her parents looked on, proud. And she was starting to think that her dream walking just might hold the key to the scientific discovery that would make her imaginings reality. For if she and Henry could travel to another dimension of dreams and create within that nebulous world, perhaps time and space and, yes, even matter itself were nothing more than constructs of the human mind. Perhaps there was no limit to what they could do or where they could go once they'd learned to see differently.

The organist launched into a zippy tune, signaling the start of *The Kid Brother*. Ling placed her gray hat securely over her ears, grabbed her coat and crutches, and sidled up the aisle past the surprised usher.

"But, Miss, the picture's just starting," he said.

"I know," Ling said. "I only wanted to see the newsreel."

Out on Forty-second Street, the air had grown colder. Tiny flecks of snow danced in the wind. Ling's breath came out in a puff, and even this was thrilling. Energy. Atoms. Qi. A newsie hawked the day's headlines—"Chinese Sleeping Sickness Spreads! Mayor Vows: Not Another Spanish Influenza Epidemic in Our Lifetime! Threatens Full Quarantine in Chinatown!"—and just like ice crystals, dreams, and movie images of Jake Marlowe, Ling's happiness vanished. She looked down at the sidewalk, keeping her face hidden, and walked on. A crush of people blocked the city sidewalk and overflowed into the street, upsetting the taxi drivers, who honked their displeasure. Ling couldn't go through and she couldn't get around. She wanted to ask someone what was happening but she didn't want to call attention to herself. A heavy, military-style drumroll echoed in the streets. It sounded like a parade, and Ling pushed deeper into the crowd, searching for a better vantage point.

And then she saw: The drum-and-fife company preceded orderly rows of men in white hoods and robes marching in lockstep down Broadway waving American flags and hoisting banners proudly proclaiming KEEP AMERICA WHITE AND YOU KEEP AMERICA SAFE and THE

WATCHER NEVER WEARIES. Around Ling, many in the crowd applauded and whistled, cheering on the Knights of the Ku Klux Klan.

"Excuse me, excuse me," Ling said, turning against the tide of people, desperate to get back to Forty-second Street and the bus home. A young man sneered at her as she pushed through: "There goes one of them dirty Chinese now."

Everything in Ling's body went tight with fear. She wished she hadn't been so eager to get rid of Lee Fan and Gracie. *Just get to the bus stop*, she told herself and kept walking. The man and his friends followed, taunting.

"Hey, you—girl!" The young man's voice had shifted from sneering to something-to-prove. "Where you going? I'm talking to you!"

Ling's heart pounded. She didn't dare look back. The men were close, though, and the bus still too far. Three months ago, she could've broken into a run to get away. Now the jangle of her leg braces was loud in her head as she struggled on, and her arms shook from trying to move her crutches so fast. She was afraid she'd put a foot wrong, lose her balance, and fall in the street. Some people watched what was happening with expressions of vague discomfort, one man even giving a meek "Hey, now! Leave her be." Others barely noticed before moving on. No one stepped in to stop the bullying, though. Ling's head was down but her eyes were up, searching the streets wildly for a place to duck into for help. A restaurant window's neon sign boasted BEST ROAST BEEF IN NEW YORK! just above a new, hand-lettered sign that read, simply, NO CHINESE ALLOWED.

"You're a long way from home, aren't you, girl?" the man called. "Do you even speak English?"

He was right behind her. She could smell his aftershave lotion. To her right, the giant marquee of the New Amsterdam Theatre beckoned. Ling changed course, heading toward its doors. Her crutch came down hard in a pothole, jarring her entire body. She was close to tears. And then Henry stepped out of the theater's alleyway, blowing on his hands in the cold.

"Henry!" Ling shrieked. "Henry!" she screamed again.

He saw her, went for an automatic wave, and froze.

"Help m—" Ling cried as a clod of muddy ice hit her, hard, knocking her off-balance. Her purse dropped and the clasp broke, scattering the contents as she fell.

"Dirty Chinese! Go home!" the young man shouted as he ran past with his friends, laughing. *I am home*, Ling wanted to say, but the words were stuck in her throat as she sat sprawled in the wet muck of Forty-second Street.

"Cowards!" Henry shouted. He was suddenly beside her, helping her to her feet, fetching her crutches, gathering her things off the street and putting them back into her purse. "Ling! Are you all right?"

"I'm f-fine," she mumbled. Her eyes brimmed with tears. "I just, just need to go home."

"All right. I'll take you." Gently, Henry brushed the dirt from her coat. As he did, his gaze traveled to Ling's braces, her crutches, and the ugly black shoes, and for just a second, his bright smile dimmed. He recovered quickly, his smile too polite, the way people looked when they didn't want to upset you. And the tears Ling had kept at bay streamed down her face, hot and shameful.

"Oh, hey. Hey, darlin'," Henry put an arm around Ling, and she stiffened at his touch.

"I'm sorry," he said, releasing her. "You're pretty shaken up. How about a cup of hot cocoa first? You like cocoa, don'tcha?"

"I'm fine. Just...point me toward the bus."

"Well, now, you see, I have a firm policy that I never drink hot cocoa by myself. It's against my religion."

"You have a religion?" Ling sniffled.

"Well, no. Not really. But if I did, that would be the first commandment."

Ling wiped her eyes with the back of her hand and chanced a sideways glance at Henry. He was standing there in his tweed coat, his slim shoulders hunched up toward his ears and a thick plaid scarf wound around his neck, as if he were an overly wrapped Christmas present, her purse dangling from his elegant fingers. He looked ridiculous, and she wished she could laugh, but instead, she was crying.

Earlier, her heart had been full of wonder as she watched the newsreel, thinking about a world of atoms and change and possibility. Now the moment had shifted into something else, and she didn't like it. The snow salted down, coating them both in wet flakes.

"One hot cocoa," Ling said, taking back her purse. She nodded toward the restaurant window's NO CHINESE ALLOWED sign. "If you can find somewhere that'll let me in."

"Don't worry. I know just the place," Henry said and offered his arm.

✺

"Sorry it's only tea," Henry said across the small marble-topped table from Ling. "But at least it's hot."

They were in a basement speakeasy located on a narrow Greenwich Village street. Ling blew on her steaming tea and looked around warily at the flocked red wallpaper, better suited to a bordello; the women with closely cropped hair and mannish suits; the men sitting close together.

"What sort of place is this?" Ling whispered after an uncomfortable silence.

"A safe one," Henry answered, stirring milk into his tea. "Why didn't you tell me the truth before?"

"I didn't want you to feel sorry for me. I get enough of people staring at me in horror. Or pity." She took a sip of her tea. It was still too hot. "It's just...in the dream world, I'm the way I used to be. I can run and dance. I'm strong. Not like here. I didn't want you to see me this way—weak."

"Darlin', you may be a lot of things, but weak isn't one of them. How long have you been..." Henry trailed off.

"Crippled? If we're going to have this conversation, there's no point in being precious," Ling shot back. "Not long. Since October."

"And will you always...?"

"It was infantile paralysis," she said firmly.

Henry nodded. "I'm sorry," he said after a pause.

388

"Why? You didn't cause it."

"No. But I'm sorry nonetheless. It's terribly unfair."

"Nobody promised life would be fair. That's why I love dream walking so much. It's the one place where I feel like myself. Where I'm free."

"Well, I'll drink to that." Henry raised his teacup and took a sip. "To the place where we can be free."

Two men from the corner table got up to dance, hands joined, cheeks pressed close together, and Ling tried not to stare. She hoped her discomfort wasn't too evident.

"Speaking of free," Henry said. He took a deep breath. "As long as we're being honest, I should...I want to tell you the truth about Louis."

Henry's heart beat quickly. Why was being himself with another human being more terrifying than anything he could imagine in a dream?

"When I said that Louis was my friend, that wasn't entirely true. He's more than just a friend. He's the only boy I've ever loved. He's...he's my lover." Henry sat back and folded his arms across his chest. His expression was a dare. "So. Go ahead, Miss Chan. What do you have to say to that?"

Henry. And Louis. Lovers. It was a bit shocking, but it also explained so much that hadn't made sense, something Ling had felt deep down. Years before, Ling had overheard a bit of gossip about Uncle Eddie and the real reason he'd never taken a wife. It was because of his friend Fuhua. The two of them were said to be closer than brothers. They went everywhere together. One day, Fuhua was arrested for gambling. During the interrogation, it was discovered that he had entered the country illegally by pretending to be someone else—that he was a "paper son." There was nothing to be done. Within a week, Fuhua was deported to China and forbidden to enter the country ever again, breaking her uncle's heart. Or so the gossip went.

"Is it true?" Ling had asked her mother later. In those days, she shared everything with her mother.

Her mother had gotten very upset. "That's a terrible thing to say about your uncle, Ling!"

"Why?" Ling had asked, her cheeks hot with a shame she didn't understand.

"Because it's . . . unnatural, two men together. It's a sin. Ask Father Thomas. He'll tell you," her mother said. "You mustn't ever say that about your uncle again, Ling."

Ling hadn't cared if the story about Uncle Eddie was true or not; she'd been upset to think of her beloved uncle unhappy. After her mother's explanation, though, the idea had taken root in her: This was wrong and sinful. It was an idea she'd never had to challenge until now. But Henry wasn't wrong. He sometimes made jokes when he should be serious, but he was kind. She might not fully understand his life, or he hers, but she realized that in the dream world, they'd been telling each other truths all along. She liked Henry. She liked Louis, too. Ling had spoken to the dead plenty, and not one of them had ever said a word about love being a sin. Until the priests could satisfactorily prove their hypothesis, she would take the word of the dead over the priests'.

"Very well," Ling said at last.

Henry's eyebrows shot up. "That's it? Just 'very well.'"

Ling warmed her hands on the sides of her cup. "Yes."

"You are a strange one, Ling Chan," Henry said, shaking his head, the relief apparent on his face.

"I've never had a friend like your Louis. I've never really had friends."

"Their loss," Henry answered.

Ling turned on him. "Are you saying that just because you've been trained to be polite? Or do you mean it?" Ling put up a hand. "Don't answer out of habit. Be truthful."

"You really aren't much for social niceties, are you?"

"Why should I lie? What good does that do?"

When she had lain in the hospital after the infection with her legs paralyzed, the nurses had smiled politely and told her not to worry. But she knew from their eyes there was reason to worry, and being told otherwise only made her fear greater. It was her uncle Eddie who had been honest with her.

"Will my legs get better, Uncle?" she'd asked him. "Will they be like before?"

"No, they will not," he'd said, his face and voice resolute so that she wouldn't have false hope. "This is how it is now. There is strength in acceptance, Ling. Your legs have been taken from you. But how you choose to live with that has not."

"I prefer the truth," Ling now said to Henry, a little less bitterly.

Henry hadn't been trained in honesty, only avoidance. Back in New Orleans, he'd been raised with the sort of southern manners that meant never really saying what you thought. He'd learned to smile and nod and go along, to call something "interesting" instead of "hogwash." To be a good southern gentleman meant prizing politeness and pleasantry above all else. Being honest was a strange sensation, like using a long-neglected muscle.

"I think being friends with you will be challenging," he said at last.

" 'Will be challenging'?"

Henry shrugged. "I suppose you're stuck with me now, Miss Chan. I apologize in advance."

Ling's smile was big and goofy.

Henry whistled. "That smile of yours is a real beauty."

Ling shook her head, letting her hair cover her face. "It's stupid."

"Right. What I meant to say is, that stupid smile of yours is a real beauty."

This time, Ling actually giggled.

"The creature laughs!" Henry said.

"I'm not such a killjoy!"

"Actually, you are. A bit. Hey! I'm giving that honesty you asked for a twirl. How do you like it?" Henry said.

"You're awful."

"Oh, you say the sweetest things. I think you're awful, too, darlin'," Henry said, and Ling couldn't fight her grin.

"Thank you for saving me today," she said.

"Thanks for saving me, too."

The little jazz band in the corner picked up the beat. Boys led their partners onto the floor, moving them gracefully around and around. Ling watched the dancers wistfully, tapping her fingers softly against the table. Henry saw it all.

"Would you care to dance?"

Ling's face clouded. "This isn't the dream world."

"I know." Henry stood and offered his hand. "One dance."

Ling stared at Henry's fingers, and then she grasped his hand and let him lead her to the floor. Mostly, they shuffled in place slowly, but it didn't matter to Ling. She was dancing. It was almost as good as dream walking.

As they emerged onto snowy Barrow Street, Henry looked at Ling and asked, "Why do you do that?"

"Do what?" Ling asked.

"Yank your skirt hem down over your braces when somebody looks at you."

"They're ugly. People are bothered by them."

"They're not bothering me," Henry said, and Ling unfurled another of her rare smiles.

"So you really don't like girls?"

"I like girls very much. Just…not in the marrying way, if you follow."

Ling nodded.

"More important, I like you, Miss Chan. Friends?"

"I suppose so."

Henry smirked. "That was a very Ling Chan answer. If you ever give me a compliment, I might fall over dead. What's the matter now? You're frowning again."

"Henry, could I show you something?"

"As long as you promise it doesn't involve small children or yodeling."

"Neither. But I do need you to come with me downtown. Unless you're afraid?"

"Darlin', I'm only afraid of bad reviews," Henry said and flagged down a taxi.

UNFINISHED BUSINESS

On the ride downtown, Ling told Henry of her haunting dream about George Huang, and about her curious finding in the library on the Beach Pneumatic Transit Company.

"It was a real place—the first New York City subway. It opened in 1870, they stopped using it in 1873, and then it was sealed for good in 1875," Ling said. "And Henry, the drawings of the station were remarkably close to what you and I see each night in the dream world."

"The fountain? The piano?" Henry asked, and Ling nodded. "The goldfish?"

"Even the goldfish. And it was built beneath Devlin's Clothing Store! So why is an old train station showing up each night in our dream walks?"

"You know how dreamscapes are— they're a jumble of symbols, odd bits of mental string collected from our daily lives, and other people's as well."

"Yes, and like a river, they change constantly. But you asked the question first: Why do you and I keep returning to the same place, where the same sequence of events plays out in the same order, each night, like some sort of loop?"

"I did say that, didn't I?" Henry mused, rubbing his chin. "That was very smart. I feel much better about my standing as a member of the imaginary science club now. All right—why? And what does it have to do with George, and with us?"

"That's what I want to find out."

The taxi stopped at City Hall Park. Henry paid the driver, and Ling showed Henry the grate by the water fountain. "This is where George took me that night. He led me here, very deliberately. And then he pointed to those buildings across the street. Do they seem familiar?"

Henry cocked his head and squinted at the block of Broadway between Murray and Warren. "If I'm not mistaken, it looks a bit like the street where we start our dream walk each night."

"I believe it is." Ling eased onto the park bench and loosened the straps on her braces, rubbing the soreness from the spots where the leather chafed. "That building on the corner of Warren and Broadway was where Devlin's stood before it burned down."

Henry sat beside her on the bench and stared at the new building occupying the corner now. It bore no resemblance to the one in their dreams. "So this spot is somehow connected to our dream each night, but we have no idea why, and George wants us to know ... something about it."

A whistling park custodian cleared soggy missing-persons signs from the lampposts. Ling waited until he'd moved on.

"Remember when I told you that the dead appear when they have a message to deliver? And that they almost always choose a dream scene that reminds them of a favorite place—like my auntie standing in a garden she loved, or Mr. Hsu in the Tea House, where he ate every single day?" Ling took a deep breath. "Well, sometimes the dead come back instead to a place where they have unfinished business. They can't leave until it's resolved."

"You think there's some unfinished business George has to take care of here in City Hall Park?" Henry said, gesturing to the pigeons strutting across the stones.

"Not George. The woman in the veil." Ling gave Henry a sideways glance. "What if I told you the people in my neighborhood think that this sleeping sickness in the city isn't a sickness at all, but a haunting? They say it's the work of a restless spirit."

"Do you believe that?"

"I know it sounds ridiculous, but I'm starting to wonder if it might be true."

"I thought you were a scientist."

"Just because I believe in science doesn't mean I ignore superstition. Sometimes there's a basis for those superstitions. And anyway, I'm not the only one who's wondered. You did. And Wai-Mae warned us about the tunnel. She said she could *feel* the ghost, and that the ghost frightened her—'She cries' is what she told me."

"The Crying Woman comes," Henry intoned. "Well, hold on to your hat; here's where it gets even more interesting: Last night, after I woke you up from inside the dream...by the way, I had planned to hold that impressive skill over your head, but now I fear it's not appropriate."

"Just tell me what happened," Ling growled.

"The moment you left, the dream world went dark."

"What do you mean?"

"Like a theater whose show is finished for the night. It's hard to explain, but it's almost as if once you were gone, or once we weren't there together, there was no need to keep up the whole shebang. And a few seconds later, I heard a woman crying inside the tunnel."

Ling breathed in sharply. "You didn't go in, did you?"

"A *woman was crying*, Ling! Despite my misgivings about my parents, they did raise me with proper manners. I can't ignore a damsel in distress."

"No. I suppose you can't. What happened next?"

"The dark glowed with greenish light. I heard that growling again, and then—I can't swear to this—I thought I saw someone moving inside."

"Her?"

"Possibly. And then my alarm woke me."

"Wai-Mae mentioned that there was a bad death," Ling said. "Every night when we see that woman run past us, she's clearly in distress. And there's the blood on her dress."

"Yes. Bloody clothing is often a clue that something has gone

395

awry," Henry said. "But why would our mystery woman have anything to do with this sleeping sickness, if you truly think that's the case?"

"I don't know. I'm working from a theory. It might not be the correct one. I can't help but think that George wants me to know something about her, that he's trying to lead me to clues."

Henry clamped his hands under his armpits to fight the cold. "Right now, the only clues we have lie in that dreamscape. We'll have to piece it together from that, I suppose."

"Agreed. So," Ling said, counting off on her fingers, "there's the Beach Pneumatic Transit Company. The fireworks. Someone named Anthony Orange Cross. Devlin's Clothing Store."

"Haunted trousers. It always comes back to the haunted trousers."

Ling gave Henry a withering glare.

Henry nodded. "Fair enough. No haunted trousers."

A gray storm cloud drifted over the top of City Hall for a moment, obscuring its cupola. Ling watched the cloud dissipate, transforming into a less ominous version of itself. "'Murder! Murder! Oh, murder,'" Ling murmured. "Maybe the veiled woman was murdered, and she… needs us to find her killer so she can rest?"

"I'll bet it was the wagon driver—'Argh, Miss, 'tis the horses that drove me to murder!' Get it? *Drove* me to murder? Thanks, folks. Two shows daily!" Henry wiggled his fingers, then dropped them again. "Sorry. What if this Anthony Orange Cross was the killer?"

"And he chased her and killed her in Paradise Square—'Beware, beware, Paradise Square!'" Ling added.

"Wait a minute!" Henry sat up very straight. "Adelaide Proctor!"

"If this is another joke, I'll skin you alive."

"There's an old woman who lives in my building, Miss Adelaide Proctor. Likes to wander the halls in her nightgown and season the carpets with salt and talk about murder and mayhem and other unsavory spooky things. She's a bit…odd."

"You mean crazy," Ling said.

"I'd say eccentric."

"That's a nice way of saying *crazy*."

396

"As I was saying, the other day, she looked right at me as I was getting on the elevator and said, 'Anthony Orange Cross. Beware, beware, Paradise Square.'"

Ling threw her hands up in exasperation. "Why didn't you tell me this before?"

"It didn't come up in conversation! Besides, I'm in the *theater*, darlin'. I meet an awful lot of strange people. It's an occupational hazard."

"How did she know that exact phrase?" Ling pressed. "Is she a dream walker, too?"

"Not that I know of. At least, I've never seen her wandering the dreamscape on her broomstick. She asked me if I could hear the crying." He paused, his eyes on Ling. "You're making that frowning face again. Not the usual Ling-Chan-contempt-for-most-of-humanity expression, but something more akin to dread."

"I don't like this, Henry," Ling said. "Something isn't right. Can you speak to the crazy lady and ask her what she knows?"

"Yes, for the sake of our mystery, I will endure an afternoon with the mad Proctor sisters," Henry said.

A distant clock tolled five. Ling gasped.

"Now you're really starting to scare me," Henry said. "What's the matter?"

Ling gathered her crutches. "I was supposed to be home a half hour ago."

"Oh, is that all? I thought you'd seen the ghost of Anthony Orange Cross."

Ling's expression was grim. "I'm not afraid of ghosts. But I am afraid of my mother."

⁂

The moment Henry and Ling entered the Tea House, Mrs. Chan marched toward them, drying her hands on a towel, her eyes flashing. "Ling Chan! Where have you been? I have been worried sick! Lee Fan and Gracie have been back since half past three. I nearly had half the neighborhood out looking for you!"

For the first time since Henry had known her, Ling appeared truly cowed.

"I-I...um..."

"I beg your pardon, ma'am," Henry jumped in, pouring on the southern charm. "I don't know if you remember me—Henry DuBois the Fourth, from the science club? Gee, I feel awful. This is entirely my fault. You see, Ling was separated from her friends, and I just happened to come along. Naturally, I wanted to be certain she was safe. But then I was so utterly entranced by our discussion of Einstein's relative theory..."

"Relativity," Ling corrected quickly under her breath.

"...that I completely lost track of the time."

"Funny," Ling whispered.

"What?" Henry said.

"Lost track of..." Ling shook her head. "Never mind."

"Please accept my humblest apology, Mrs. Chan. I can assure you that I have been looking after Ling as if she were my very own sister." Henry kept such a straight face that he doubted Theta's acting skills could match his.

Ling's mother softened. "Well. 'Ta, then, for bringing Ling home safely, Henry. Could we fix you a plate before you're set on leaving us?"

"Oh, no, ma'am. I have to get to the Foll—to Mass," Henry said. Out of the corner of his eye, he saw Ling's mouth hanging open.

But Ling's mother was smiling. "I can't thank you enough, Henry. You're a good soul. Why, you must come along on our outing tomorrow to see Jake Marlowe break ground for his new fair."

"How I wish I could, but I—"

"I won't be taking no for an answer," Ling's mother said, hands at her waist. "You deserve a proper thank-you for your kindness today. We'll see you here at noon." And with that, she went back to work.

"So very early," Henry whimpered quietly.

Ling showed Henry out. "Thank you," she said.

"You're welcome. Mothers love me."

"I meant for today. Earlier."

"Oh. Well. That's what friends do. From now on, no more secrets. For either of us."

"No more secrets," Ling agreed.

"I'm going to see if I can speak with Miss Proctor. See you tonight, the usual place?"

Ling nodded. "And tomorrow, too."

"Yes. At noon," Henry said, grimacing. He glanced over Ling's head at Mrs. Chan, who was bustling about the restaurant like a general inspecting troops. "Your mother is truly terrifying, by the way."

"You don't know the half of it," Ling said.

"When Louis arrives, I'm bringing him straight here for dumplings. He'll love them," Henry said. "And I can't wait to get my lucky hat back from you. Louis gave it to me the first night we met. Took it right off his head and plopped it on mine. If you like, I'll ask him to bring two more from New Orleans, one for you and one for Wai-Mae. Then we can become the dream world's first barbershop quartet. 'Constipation, constipation, constipation, constipationnnn!'" Henry sang out.

"You are the strangest person I've ever met."

"There you go with that sweet talk again."

Something nagged at Ling, something she felt she should tell Henry. It was just a feeling, though, and she didn't yet know how to put it into words.

"Ling! Come out of the cold this instant!" Mrs. Chan called, her voice muffled on the other side of the glass.

"Your mother bellows, fair Juliet," Henry said, bowing with a hammy Shakespearean-actor flourish. "Away with me! Fie! Fie! Ham on Fie!" he said, yanking on his own collar and stumbling backward.

Ling shook her head as she watched him go. "Definitely the strangest person," she said, and she was surprised at how much she missed Henry already.

OBJECTS DON'T LIE

When Sam had worked for the circus, he'd managed to walk away with a very nice tuxedo tailored for him by a Russian tattoo artist who also had great skill with a needle and thread. The tuxedo had always managed to elicit attention; Ruth, the Bearded Lady, and Johnny, the Wolf Boy, had both given him an appreciative up-and-down appraisal whenever he'd stepped into the ring wearing "The Tux." He hoped it might work some magic on Evie tonight.

Just before Sam left the museum for WGI, a note had been delivered to his door: *If you want to know more about that part for your radio, come to the shop tonight. Nine o'clock.* He knew Evie would be spitting mad that he'd missed her show. Hell, he couldn't blame her. But his contact was not a fella who gave second chances. He hoped Evie did.

The Winthrop Hotel's ballroom was wall-to-wall with swells. Sam worried he wouldn't find Evie in the crush. But all he had to do was follow the sound of laughter and applause. There was Evie, sitting on the back of a stuffed alligator.

"...He asked me to read his wristwatch, and when I did, I saw him in his altogether...one of those nudists. Well, I couldn't very well say that on the radio...."

Sam pushed his way to the front, past the crowd of admirers. Evie looked so beautiful in her marabou feather–trimmed midnight-blue dress, a sparkling band of rhinestones resting across her forehead, that for a moment, it squeezed the breath out of him.

"Well, if it isn't my beloved," Evie snarled, eyes flashing, and Sam knew that no tuxedo was magical enough to save him from the rough evening to come.

"Hiya, Lamb Chop. Could I borrow you for a minute?"

Evie gave him a sideways look. "Sorry. I was available at nine."

"I know. I'd love to tell you all about that." He glanced meaningfully at the others.

"Do carry on. I won't be a moment, darlings," Evie said with a bow to the appreciative audience of swells. "You were supposed to meet me at the show, Sam!" Evie hissed to Sam under her breath while keeping her smile toothpaste-ad bright for the party guests who applauded as she and Sam walked through the crowded ballroom. "I've spent the last two hours worried that you were bleeding to death in a ditch," Evie continued. "Now that I know you're okay, I just want you to be bleeding to death in a ditch."

"Aww, Lamb Chop, you missed me."

"That's what you just heard?"

"What can I say? I'm an optimist."

"The world is full of dead optimists. Sam, Sam, Sam!" Evie's head swished like windshield wipers with each utterance of his name. The drink in her hand was nearly gone.

"That's me. Say, how much of that coffin varnish have you had, Sheba?"

Evie closed one eye and looked up at the hotel's coffered ceiling, bright with chandeliers, her lips moving as she counted. "This is three. At four, we can play martini bridge." She giggled.

"Holy smokes," Sam whistled.

"Wait a minute: Are you waiting for me to get ossified so you can take liberties with me, Sam Lloyd?"

"No. I like my girls fully conscious when I kiss 'em. I'm funny that way," Sam said. He grabbed her glass and downed the rest of it, eating the olive.

"Hey! What's the big idea?" Evie protested.

"I'm saving you from yourself."

"I don't need any saving," Evie grumbled. "What I needed was that drink. You didn't even save me the olive."

Sam put up his hands in a gesture of apology. "Okay. That's fair. Abso-tive-ly fair. Let's say the tables were turned. If I were about to walk off a cliff, what would you do?"

Evie pursed her lips. "Push?"

"I don't believe that."

"You would on the way down. So what was so important that you missed the show? And it had better be good, Sam. Appendectomy-scar good."

"Not here."

A party guest set his teacup on a side table and turned to applaud the orchestra. Evie swiped the cup, sniffed it, smiled, downed the secret booze in one gulp, and put the empty cup back. Quickly, she motioned Sam away from the scene of the crime and into a room marked PRIVATE. Inside the small office were a fainting couch and a desk with a telephone and a rolling chair. Evie lay back on the couch, propped her feet up, and rubbed her temples.

"Rough night?" Sam asked, perching on the edge of the desk.

"And how. Some fella brought in his wife's handkerchief. He said he was worried that she was spending too much money shopping, but he was really worried that she was having an affair. He was right, by the way. The handkerchief came from her lover," Evie said.

"Gee, what'd you tell him?"

"I told him she was spending a little too much money and that perhaps they should go out for dinner and dancing more often." Evie let out a long exhale. "You wouldn't believe the awful stuff I find out about people."

"Why don't you tell them the truth?" Sam asked.

"The truth doesn't sell soap. Keep it light and happy and entertaining. Give 'em hope, kid!" Evie said, imitating Mr. Phillips's booming baritone.

"But that makes you no better than those phony con men on

Forty-second Street," Sam said. "You're the real McCoy, Sheba. You don't need to fake it."

Evie sat up, glaring. "I did not come to this party to hear a lecture from you, Sam Lloyd. You steal people's wallets. Don't act like you're better than I am."

"Me? Sure, I'm a thief and a con. But not you, kid. Unfortunately, you care. I know you."

"No, you don't," Evie said, lying back again. "You just think you do because you're my pretend fiancé. But nobody really knows anybody. We're all just a bunch of Pears soap ads walking around clean and neat, ready to wash away to slivers."

"What's real, then?"

"I dunno anymore, Sam. I really don't. I just…don't wanna think about it."

Sam felt the air going out of the evening. "Well, before you get completely blotto, I need your services."

Evie laughed and applauded slowly. "I should've guessed. Well, nothin' doin'. You didn't come through for me tonight, so I am under no obligation to help you. *And you still haven't told me what happened!*"

"Sorry, doll. Honest, I am. At the last minute, I got a message from my canary."

"Your what?"

"My—what'd you call him? Creepy man?"

"Oh. Him," Evie said, blowing a wayward curl off her forehead.

"He almost never gets in touch. I'm the one who puts out the word for him. But he slipped a note under my door telling me to meet him at the radio shop at nine."

"I hope the shop was at least playing my show," Evie grumbled. "Well? What'd you find out?"

"That's the funny thing: He never showed."

"There's quite a bit of that going around," Evie said pointedly.

"When I got there, the place was dark and all locked up. I woulda picked the lock, but if I got pinched, I was afraid it wouldn't look too good for your fiancé to be a jailbird," Sam said. "But I don't like it. Something smells."

"You just have an overactive imagination, Sam."

"Doll, when my imagination's overactive, it usually involves activities polite society doesn't allow me to talk about. I thought you'd be on my side here."

Evie softened. "Gee, Sam, I'm sorry. I didn't mean to upset you."

"I have to find the truth." Sam Lloyd did not ask for favors. Whatever he needed, he paid for or took—no strings, no debts. So it took everything he had to offer Evie the file again. "Please?" he asked, the word unfamiliar. "Could you please try one more time?"

The soft pleading of Sam's tone stirred Evie's sympathy. "All right, Sam. I'll see what I can do." She sat up and patted the seat of the divan. "Here. I won't bite. Unless you start to sing."

Sam bounded over and sat beside her. Evie took the file and put everything she had into it, but no matter how hard she tried, she couldn't get a read. She broke away, woozy and angry.

"Thanks anyway, kid," Sam said, taking the file back.

"I refuse to be beaten!" Evie groused, reaching for it again.

Sam tucked it inside his jacket pocket. "Nah, it's jake, doll. I'll . . . I'll take you back to the party—"

"Sam!" Evie said, jumping up from the divan and knocking over a tableside bust of a stern-looking Roman general. "Stay!" she said, righting the bust at the last second. "Good boy."

Sam's eyebrows shot up.

"Listen, Sam: Do you still have that photograph from Anna Polot . . . Pala . . . Anna Anna?"

Sam took out his wallet and fished out the photo he now kept inside its folds. "It's just a picture of me with my mother."

"I know. But it's worth a try, isn't it?"

Sam grinned. "That's my girl."

"I am not your girl," Evie said, fighting a smile.

At first, the photo was also cold. But Evie wasn't about to lose again. She concentrated until there was a momentary spark, and then she reached into that spark of memory, teasing it into flame. She saw a woman with brown hair pinned at the back of her neck and dark, full brows and knew at a glance that she was Sam's mother. In Miriam's hands was the very photograph Evie held now.

"I see her," Evie said dreamily.

"You do?" Sam's voice was so hopeful.

"She's lovely, Sam. Truly."

Evie breathed in and out, letting herself go under by degrees, getting more of a picture. The first memory was small and simple: A very young Sam sat beside his mother as she stroked a hand across his hair. There were few things more powerful than a mother's love, and that's what Evie felt here: No matter what Miriam Lubovitch had told those men, she loved her son very much. As much as Evie's mother had loved James, which was infinitely more than she'd ever loved Evie. It wasn't true that parents didn't have favorite children. They did, and Evie had not been it. The pain of that memory reached through the booze and squeezed a fist around Evie's heart, threatening to derail the reading. In defiance, she pushed deeper into the photo's secret history.

Now she saw a beautiful room with marble floors, heavy crystal chandeliers throwing off prisms of light, and walls hung with expensive-looking portraits of expensive-looking people. There were children in the room. Some sat at tables drawing pictures or answering questions. Some fussed with their collars. One little girl played with her doll.

But where was Sam? Was he here?

And then she saw young Sam seated at a table in a corner, his mother standing just behind his chair, looking nervous. Across from Sam sat Will's long-dead fiancée, Rotke Wasserman. She drew a card from a deck, hiding its face. "Let's try one more time. Sam, can you tell what card I'm holding?"

"Um, Five of…Clubs?"

"Why don't you try again," Rotke urged.

"King of Hearts?" little Sam lisped from a mouth with a front tooth missing. "Jack of Diamonds!"

Rotke smiled at Sam but shook her head at his mother.

"Am I in trouble?" Sam asked.

"*Nyet, bubbeleh*," his mother said, kissing him on the cheek. "Go out and play."

The memory blurred around the edges, and Evie leaned into it. Children played on the grass on a stretch of perfectly manicured lawn. It was a beautiful spring day, and their joy was infectious. But one child was crying. Evie followed the sound to the girl with the doll.

"What's the matter, Maria?" Rotke asked, crouching before the child.

The girl began to answer in Italian.

"In English, please."

"The boat is on fire. It's sinking," the little girl cried. And as she did, other children seemed to become agitated as well, as if they had all seen the same dream.

"Rotke! Rotke!" A man ran out of the house and onto the lawn, and Evie's mind swam. Fair hair. Spectacles. Younger, yes, but it was most definitely Will. Evie was so surprised that she could barely concentrate on what her uncle was saying.

"...Message over the wireless...the Germans have torpedoed the RMS *Lusitania*. They've killed Americans."

The past buzzed like a staticky radio seeking a signal. And then it landed tenuously on some other bit of its history briefly recalled:

"Miriam, the government has asked us to recruit Diviners. Project Buffalo. We need your help."

Sam's mother, frightened: "I don't like the plan."

"It will be fine. There are precautions."

"What you want to do—it's dangerous. It will draw bad spirits."

"We're going to win. Come to the Harbor, Miriam. I'm asking. They won't."

Evie lost her footing in the reading. Images came too fast, like a film sped up—so much memory and emotion she felt sure she'd be lost inside them if she didn't let go. She collapsed against Sam as she took her hands from the photograph. He put his arms around her, holding her close. "I got you. It's okay."

Evie rested her cheek against his warm chest and listened to the rhythmic comfort of Sam's heartbeat as she waited for the dizziness and trembling to subside. She liked the weight of his chin atop her head and the smell of shaving cream clinging to his neck. She should sit up, she knew, but she didn't want to.

"Did you get anything, doll?"

Should she tell Sam she'd seen Will? What would he do if he found out that Will knew his mother and had been lying all this time?

"You were at a table, and Rotke was asking if you could guess at the cards in her hand. But you couldn't. I don't understand: Why was she testing you?"

"Beats me, Sheba. I don't remember any of this stuff," Sam said, frowning. He rubbed at his forehead, as if that motion could shake loose the memories. "How come I can't remember?"

"Your mother loved you so much, Sam," Evie said, and she felt Sam's arm tighten around her. "Objects don't lie. I could tell."

"Thanks," Sam muttered. "Anything else?"

"I-I couldn't see everything," Evie lied. "But someone was asking your mother to help the government with Project Buffalo in some way. But she thought what they wanted was too dangerous, that it would draw bad spirits, whatever that means. And I heard something about 'Come to the Harbor.' Do you know what that means?"

Sam shook his head. "Plenty of harbors around, though."

"Do you know anything about where this picture was taken?" Evie asked.

Sam stared at the photograph. He shook his head. "I don't recognize it. Why?"

"I couldn't tell precisely, but it looked a bit like a castle."

"A castle castle?"

"No, Sam. A sand castle," Evie retorted. "Yes, of course, a castle

castle. But here's the strange part: I've seen this particular castle before, in my dreams."

Sam raised an eyebrow. "And were you married to a handsome prince in that dream? Was there a scepter and a throne?"

"Ha, ha." Evie rolled her eyes. "Haaaa. But I have seen it in my dreams. At least, I think I have. Or one like it."

"Someday, I'm gonna buy you a castle, future Mrs. Lloyd," Sam said. He liked the feel of Evie leaning into him, his arm around her.

"I don't know what to think when you're not horrible. It's very confusing," Evie slurred. Impulsively, she kissed Sam, then laid her head on his shoulder again.

Over the past few months, when he wasn't picking pockets, searching the museum for clues to his mother's whereabouts, betting on the fights, or sweet-talking chorus girls into passionate encounters in speakeasy cloakrooms, Sam had had the occasion to imagine kissing Evie. At first, these imagined scenarios had been full of hot air and Sam's ego: Evie saying, *Oh, my darling. I never knew it could be like this. Kiss me, you fool!* before going limp in his arms due to Sam's manly demonstrations of love. These fantasies were never quite satisfying, though, as if even Sam's fevered imagination knew that was a load of bunk.

What he'd never imagined was a day like they'd had—breaking into an office in a federal building, finding secret coded cards, and narrowly escaping from cops, Evie's hand in his and a smile on her dusty face because she enjoyed the hunt as much as he did and they were in it together.

"The room's gone fuzzy. Does it look fuzzy to you, Sam?" Evie mumbled.

"I think one of us is drunk, Lamb Chop."

"Must be the room," Evie sighed.

"It's not the room."

"Well, it's not me. I can hold my liquor like a sailor," Evie slurred, her words getting very messy. A few seconds later, she was snoring.

With a sigh, Sam maneuvered the pos-i-tute-ly dead-to-the-world

Evie into the rolling chair and then pushed her into the elevator and up to her room, where he dropped her onto the bed.

"I'd imagined this evening going a whole lot differently," Sam grunted as he tucked Evie in. Her mouth was open and tiny snores escaped. "You are not a delicate sleeper, kid."

Sam planted a kiss on the top of Evie's messy head. "Sweet dreams, Sheba."

AND DO THEY DREAM?

The city is composed of islands crisscrossed by avenues and streets, tunnels and trolley lines—a grid of connections waiting to be made. Majestic bridges span the rivers in steel-spoked splendor, while the ferries carry their loads safely to shore.

The bridges, the tunnels, the ferries and streets. And do they dream?

The ferries dock in the terminal. They open their metal mouths to sing out the people who march forward, unseeing, heads like battering rams as they grimace at the blustery cold and sometimes forget to sing, sometimes forget that they were made for singing. The playful wind takes exception to this, and a hat skitters across a sidewalk, chased by a businessman in gray, which brings a chuckle to the audience of news agents and shoeshine boys, the telephone girls hurrying to work in shoes that pinch, the bricklayers, the street sweepers, the sidewalk vendors whose carts teem with whatever the citizens think they might need.

High above it all, the window washers hoist themselves up by the miracle of rope and hover in midair on small planks to clean away the grit of so many dreams discarded. They wipe with their cloths until the lives on the other side of the glass become clearer. Every now and then, faces appear at these windows. Eyes meet for a second, maybe two, the observed and the observer each surprised to find the other exists. Then they look quickly away, the connection unmade, islands once more.

The wind whistles down into the skyscraper-bound canyons, across the broad expanses of the avenues and the narrow confines of the streets, where lives unfold in secret, day in, day out:

Sometimes a man sighs for want of love.

Sometimes a child cries for the dropped lollipop, its sweetness barely tasted.

Sometimes the girl gasps as the train screams into the station, shaken by how close she'd allowed herself to wander to the edge.

Sometimes the drunk raises weary eyes to the rows of buildings rendered beautiful by a brief play of sunlight. "Lord?" he whispers into the held breath between taxi horns. The light catches on a city spire, fracturing for a second into glorious rays before the clouds move in again. The drunk lowers his eyes. "Lord, Lord..." he sobs, as if answering his own broken prayer.

The cars drive on. The people hurry to and fro. They sigh and want and cry and dream. Taken together, their symphonic *whyohwhy* might reach the heavens and make the angels weep. Alone, they are no match for the noise of industry. The jackhammers. The cranes. The streetcars, subways, and aeroplanes. The constant whirring machinery of the dream factories. And do these things dream of more?

Another day closes. The sun sinks low on the horizon. It slips below the Hudson, smearing the West Side of Manhattan in a slick of gold. Night arrives for its watchful shift. The neon city bursts its daytime seams, and the great carnival of dreams begins again.

Evie woke in the middle of the night with a throbbing headache. With tremendous effort, her eyes struggled open. The room wobbled, then settled into focus. She had a vague memory of kissing Sam. In a woozy panic, she looked down, relieved to see that she was still in her party dress and alone. A wave of boozy nausea washed over her and she stumbled to the bathroom, where she splashed water over her puffy face. It was early, before dawn. Plenty of time to sleep, and to figure out a way to let Sam down easy. Evie angled her head to drink straight from the bathroom tap. Then she crawled back to bed to sleep it off.

It was the light that woke her.

Evie blinked, her eyes adjusting to the buttery morning sun bathing her room in a hazy glow. But this wasn't her room at the Winthrop. This was her room on Poplar Street, back in Zenith. Slowly, she took it in: the dresser with her silver hand mirror, the painting of a Victorian girl selling flowers, the star-pattern quilt sewn by her grandmother when she was born. She was home.

Hurriedly, she dressed and went downstairs, passing through the living room, where the Philco had been left on and a familiar voice burbled out of the radio cabinet's speakers: "Now, dear Mr. Forman, you must let me concentrate! The spirits are throwing a real lulu of a party...."

How could her voice be coming from the radio if she was here in her parents' living room in Ohio? She vaguely remembered standing on the platform in a pretty subway station and boarding the sweetest little train. She must've fallen asleep. This was a dream. That she knew this was a dream didn't lessen her excitement. Quite the contrary; she felt everything even more, as if she were one step ahead of the moment and desperate to hold on to it. As if she would do anything to make it stay.

The smell of bacon wafted out from the back of the house. Evie followed it through the dining room and into the familiar blue-and-white kitchen with the big window over the sink that looked out on a neat row of black-eyed Susans lining the gravel driveway.

"Good morning, dear." Her mother smiled as she settled flapjacks onto a plate. "Breakfast is nearly ready. Don't play too long."

"I won't," Evie said, her voice quiet and even, as if she were afraid that to speak any louder would break the spell and end the magic of this dream.

Her father strode into the room and kissed her mother on the cheek before sitting at the table with his newspaper. He looked up at Evie and smiled. "Don't you look pretty as a picture today!"

"Thank you, Papa."

Still at the stove, her mother called over one shoulder, "Evie, be a dear and call your brother in to breakfast, won't you?"

Evie's heartbeat quickened. James. James was here.

Light poured through the screen door, so bright she couldn't see what lay beyond. She pushed through and saw that it was all as she remembered it—the rope swing tied to the enormous oak tree, the summer garden with its ripe tomatoes, her father's Buick parked by the toolshed. The hazy sun bathed it all in ephemeral beauty. Birds tweeted at the feeder. Cicadas buzzed pleasantly in the sweet, feathery grass.

Someone was singing. *"Pack up your troubles in your old kit bag and smile, smile, smile. . . ."*

Through the hedges, Evie spied a flash of arm, a dangling leg, and her calm fell away as she ran toward the figure sprawled on the weather-beaten bench.

"James?" Evie whispered so faintly she wasn't sure he'd heard. But then he sat up, smiling wide at her. With the sun behind him, he glowed.

"Well, if it isn't my brave sister, Artemis, come to us from the hunt! Pray, what news from Olympus?"

Every night, James would read to her from tales of Greek myth. They often spoke to each other in code that way—she was Artemis, he Apollo. Papa was Zeus. Mama was Hera. It was how they made it through insufferable social gatherings: "But soft! See how yon harpies descend upon the buffet," James would whisper as a group of church ladies took the best treats at a luncheon. "Release Cerberus," Evie would whisper back, giggling.

She was supposed to tell him something for her mother, but her heart ached so much that she couldn't remember what it was. "I . . . I just missed you. That's all."

"Well, I'm right here."

Evie's throat tightened. He was there—golden and sweet, her brother-protector, her best friend. A thought intruded, a terrible thought. Evie tried to push it away, but it buzzed at the edges of her consciousness, a bee in the garden.

"No. You're dead," she whispered. It felt strange to her that even in dreams, she knew this. Even in dreams, she wasn't safe from pain. She lost her battle with the tears. And then she felt the shock as his fingers wiped them from her cheeks.

"Now, now, old girl. Don't you know brave Artemis doesn't cry? Here." He plucked a black-eyed Susan and handed it to her. "Hold on." From the bench, he retrieved a book of poetry—Wordsworth, his favorite. He nodded to the open page. "Here. Put it here."

Evie laid the flower in the book's crease, and James read the poem beneath it: "Though nothing can bring back the hour / of splendour in the grass, of glory in the flower; / We will grieve not, rather find / Strength in what remains behind." Smiling, he slammed the book shut. "There. Preserved for all time."

Mama's voice drifted to them from the back porch. "James! Evangeline! Your breakfast will get cold!"

"Yon Hera beckons us to Olympus."

Evie wanted to grab the edges of the dream like a blanket and wrap it around her, safe and happy. The sun warmed her face. The cicadas grew louder. Across the lawn, her mother and father waved from the back porch, happy and bright. But something wasn't quite right. The house flickered just slightly. For a brief few seconds, it seemed almost like the entrance to a tunnel rather than a house, and something about the dark inside made Evie very afraid.

"James?" she said, panicked. "James!"

She saw him at the gate, dressed in his army khakis, a rifle slung across his back. The dream was turning. Evie was desperate to grab it back before it was too late.

"James, don't go," Evie warned as fog rolled in, rendering her brother a ghost. "You won't come back. And we'll be lost without you. We'll be broken forever. James! Come back!" She was crying now, calling his name over and over, a lament. Her parents and the house were gone. In their place were the tunnel and a woman in a veil. "You can have him back. *Dream with me. . . .*"

"I can . . ." Evie murmured. All she had to do was say yes. And then James would stay with them forever. The dream made her believe it. Why, it couldn't be simpler!

"I—"

"Brave Artemis!" James said. He stood at the top of the hill in the misty forest of that other dream she hated. "Time to wake up now."

"No!" Evie screamed as the explosions started.

She woke in her bed, her stomach roiling. She barely made it to the toilet before she vomited up the night's booze. And then she lay on the cold tile floor, crying.

※

Across town, Nathan Rosborough stumbled from an all-night poker game quite a bit poorer than when the evening had started. Drunk on Scotch and desperate to be accepted by the other, more important, stockbrokers, he'd played down to the skin of his wallet. He hadn't wanted them to think he was some kind of quitter. But now, as he sobered a bit, he was worried. He'd be lucky to scrape together enough to eat in the coming week. This thought weighed heavily on Nathan as he stared out at the skyline, the colossus unfurled, and felt a longing so powerful it bordered on obscenity. Then he fished his last nickel from his pocket and stumbled down the steps of the Fulton Street subway station to wait for the train.

The platform was deserted at this hour. A newspaper story about a missing heiress had been taped to the wall beside an advertisement for a dandruff cure: Nora Hodkin, age eighteen. She had been seen four days ago heading to the downtown IRT wearing a blue dress and a brown hat. The grainy newspaper photograph of Nora Hodkin showed a pretty, wide-eyed girl astride a horse. Her distraught parents offered a five-hundred-dollar reward to anyone who found her.

Five hundred dollars! Nathan loosened his tie and sprawled out on a bench, thinking about what he could do with a reward like that. Why, he could move out of his cramped room in his boardinghouse and into a nice little place of his own farther uptown with a view of the East River. Come summer, he might even have enough for a week's rental out on Long Island Sound. He liked the idea of coming back to Wall Street tanned and salt-kissed, with tales of decadent parties where the girls shed their clothes to dance on tables and white-gloved waiters passed around caviar served on little silver spoons. Nathan could practically feel the warmth of the beach sun on his back, and soon, his head bobbed on his neck as he fought sleep.

A strange noise snapped him back to attention. His skin had bubbled up into gooseflesh for some damned reason.

"Hello?" he called out sleepily. "Is somebody there?"

Nathan hurried to the edge of the platform, cupped a hand over his eyes and peered down the long, curving stretch of tracks. By golly, there was someone on the tracks—a girl!

"Hey—hey you, there!" he called to her. "Miss, you'd better come up from there. You'll be hit."

Nathan looked around for help, but there was no one else waiting with him at this late hour. Since they'd gone to the new coin-operated turnstiles, there were no longer any ticket choppers sitting nearby. He was utterly alone—except for the motionless girl in the tunnel. Some trick of shadow and high, stark subway light bathed her in phosphorescence. She glowed, this girl. *Like an angel*, Nathan thought. And she wore a blue dress.

"Miss Hodkin? Nora?" Nathan tried.

The girl's head jerked up as if she registered the name.

It must be her—had to be! And suddenly, this lost, shining girl waiting for rescue seemed like the answer to Nathan's desires. She was pretty. Her parents were rich. There was a reward. And when the boys back at the Exchange heard about his heroics, they'd clap him on the back, stick a cigar in his mouth, and say *Attaboy!* He'd be made—a man in full.

All of this buzzed through Nathan's brain in a matter of seconds as the girl swayed precariously in the gloom. Then she turned and stumbled around the curve, out of sight.

"Miss Hodkin! Wait!" Nathan called to no avail. "Doggone it!"

Nathan was still a little woozy from the Scotch, but the booze also made him brave as he hopped onto the tracks and jogged down the center of the subway tunnel after his damsel in distress, the bright light of the station receding behind him. According to the appeal from her parents, Nora Hodkin had been missing for four days. She had to be weak from hunger, Nathan figured. Yet she was surprisingly quick. His lungs ached from trying to keep up. He was deep into the tunnel now and uneasy. The only light came from two weak work lights set up high, and Nathan slowed, mindful of the electrified third rail. Steel support beams flanked the tracks. In the eerie gloom, they loomed like giants' legs. It sounded funny down here, too. He heard a high, tight whine— almost like train wheels, but not quite—and here and there, animalistic growling. What *was* that? It was enough to make him want to go back.

Just then, he spied the bright back of the girl's blue dress as she lumbered across the tracks ahead.

"Miss Hodkin!" he called, closing the distance between them.

To the relief of Nathan's aching legs and lungs, the girl finally slowed, and as she did, he noticed for the first time that Nora Hodkin didn't move quite right. Her gait was uneven, and her arms twitched in a strange, quicksilver way, her fingers clutching at air.

She's drunk or faint. That was his brain talking. But his gut disagreed. The girl's movement was purposeful, not drunk; she moved as if driven by strong need. There was something not quite human about her. And just as this thought took form in Nathan's Scotch-hazed mind, she stopped and turned.

Nora Hodkin might've been pretty at one time. But the thing facing him now had a gaunt, bleached face as fissured as a broken vase. Milky-blue eyes fixed on him. Nostrils flared as she sniffed, once, twice. Cracked lips peeled back from sharp, yellowed teeth. Black ooze dripped from the corners of her new smile. And Nathan understood at last what drove her: hunger. She was hunting. Leading him into a trap, like prey.

She reached out her talonlike fingers. *"Dream . . . ?"* she pleaded in a hair-raising growl. *"Dream!"*

If Nathan Rosborough had been able to scream, it would've rung through the underground and rattled the windows of the trains passing through. Instead, it was Nora Hodkin whose mouth unhinged in an unholy screech.

"Jesus . . . oh, Jesus," Nathan whispered, backing away.

The glowing girl in the blue dress dropped into a crouch, knees wide as she scuttled toward him, brushfire-fast. Nathan turned and ran as fast as he could toward the Fulton Street station. His earlier hopes deserted him. His one overwhelming desire was simply to survive.

Behind him, the thing that had once been Nora Hodkin loosed a second screech that bounced off the walls. Nathan was sober now, his mind sharpened by animal fear. Greenish lights pulsed between concrete subway columns.

A train?

In the dark, there were hungry growls and high-pitched, demonic cries that nearly brought him to his knees.

No. Not a train. More of *them*.

He heard the rapid *click-click-clack* of what sounded like many claws scraping across brick. She'd called them. Dear God! They were gaining on him. Nathan could smell their stench. Suddenly, Nora Hodkin leaped down, cutting off his escape. She was trying to talk. Her voice was a broken gargle, a fire consuming the last of its fuel. *"Must dream . . ."*

The distant lights of the subway train shone far down the tracks, too far to be of any help to Nathan. The night came alive with more like her—sickly, glowing, used-up things crawling from the depths, creeping along the walls and ceiling of the underground, hungry. The demonic drone escalated into a shrieking din as they dropped down like radium-painted rain.

Nora smiled at Nathan and opened wide.

DAY NINETEEN

PROMETHEUS

The land of Flushing, Queens, was flat and favorable, with nothing to stand in the way of grasping aspiration. Already, steam shovels hovered on the edge of the proposed fairgrounds, ready to clear the way for Jake Marlowe's vision of tomorrow. In the center of the field stood a makeshift wooden platform, which held the mayor and the city council, who eagerly awaited Jake Marlowe's arrival. A huge crowd had turned out to watch their hero break ground on what would become the Future of America Exhibition of 1927. They stood holding small American flags on sticks under a sky so brilliantly blue it seemed wet with paint.

"Is he here yet?" Ling asked as she strained to see around the tall people in front of her.

"Would you like to get closer?" Henry asked.

"Yes, please," Ling said.

"Mr. and Mrs. Chan," Henry asked politely, "may I escort Ling closer to the stage?"

"Why, that would be lovely, Henry," Mrs. Chan said, beaming.

As Henry parted the crowd for Ling, she looked back at her parents. Her father smiled, and her mother waved her flag. "I think my mother is already planning our wedding."

"Well, if it gets you out of the house more often, I'll try to look besotted. Prepare yourself, woman!" He stared, moony-eyed, at Ling, then flared his nostrils like a matinee idol in the throes of passion.

Ling curled her lip in disgust. "You look like you have gas."

"It's my secret love glance. I call it 'From the Very Bowels of Love.'"

"Henry?"

"Yes, *mein Liebchen?*"

"Take me to Jake Marlowe."

"That cad! I'll see him on the field at dawn!" Henry made a gun of his thumb and index finger, pointing it skyward as if ready to shoot.

"Hurry up. I don't want to miss this," Ling said.

Henry let his hand drop. "Very well. I suppose I'll let him live. This way, m'lady."

"Did you speak to the crazy woman?"

"Not yet. I was afraid if I went this morning, I'd be stuck there through the afternoon as a special guest at a kitty-cat birthday party or an ancient mummification tutorial and miss this," Henry said, just as he and Ling made it to the front. He grinned. "And I knew you wouldn't have wanted to miss this."

Mayor Jimmy Walker stepped to the microphone, his voice booming out in a long preamble that ended with the heart-quickening words, "A man who needs no introduction, Mr. . . . Jake . . . Marlowe!"

The crowd responded with cheers and a waving of flags. The air fluttered with red, white, and blue. With the sun shining behind him, Jake Marlowe stepped onto the platform, removed his hat, ran a swift hand across his slick black hair, and raised the hat to the assembled, a hero's gesture. Applause erupted. The crowd loved the very idea of him.

"Isn't this the berries?" Henry asked Ling, but her shining eyes said it all.

The microphone squawked with Marlowe's first word. He put a hand to his chest in apology and humility, and the crowd laughed and loved this, too. And then his words echoed across the promised land of Queens, as if cast toward the future. "Ladies and gentlemen . . . men . . . en . . . I am pleased to announce . . . ounce . . . ounce . . . a marvelous step forward for American . . . can . . . greatness. A celebration of our heritage . . . age . . . age . . . and our great prospects for prosperity . . .

perity...and progress...gress. The Marlowe Industries Future...ture...of America...ca...ca Exhibition and Fair...fair...fair!"

The winter sun gathered what small warmth there was in her cold light and tithed it to Jake Marlowe's shining, smiling face. Fresh cheering erupted as Jake Marlowe exited the stage and made his way to a clearing, where he peeled off his coat, rolled up his shirtsleeves, and posed with a shovel atop a weedy mound. "Gentlemen, we are like Prometheus, creating a legacy from the clay of the earth."

His shovel bit into the soft, wet ground and the flashbulbs popped, immortalizing the moment. Balloons were released; they floated up to the sky as if claiming it. The band took up a rousing rendition of "The Stars and Stripes Forever" while Jake Marlowe strode through the crowd, shaking hands and tousling the hair of children as the reporters tried to keep up, their shoes sinking into the grasping mud of Queens.

"Will the fair really open in only three months?" a reporter asked.

"You may bank on it."

"But that's awfully fast, Mr. Marlowe. Even for you."

Marlowe grinned as he offered a peppermint to a ringleted, blue-eyed child nestled in her father's arms. "*Can't be done.* My three favorite words—to disprove. We have a thousand Marlowe Industries employees, models of modern efficiency, working to make certain that it does. The American business model is the best model."

"Only a man as rich and ambitious as you would break ground in the dead of winter."

"I'm not afraid of the weather, only of not going after what I want."

"Speaking of that, what do you think about the unions and this business out at the Hibernia mines?"

Marlowe kept walking, working the crowd as he answered. "The notion of the union is fundamentally un-American. At Marlowe Industries, we believe in a fair wage for fair work among fair men."

"Catchy. That your new business slogan?"

Marlowe winked. "It might be."

"When are you going to get married?"

"When I find the right girl."

"I got a sister—in the right light, she's a beauty!"

Everyone laughed. They were buoyant with good times and hopeful possibility. T. S. Woodhouse pushed his way through, pad and pencil in hand, and sidled up to the great man. "How do, Mr. Marlowe. T. S. Woodhouse of the *Daily News*." Woodhouse sneezed twice into his handkerchief. "Sorry. Caught a nuisance of a cold."

"You should be taking Marlowe VitaHealth Tonic. Good for what ails you," Marlowe advised.

"I've been taking Irish whiskey for what ails me. Just one question for you: Will Diviners be included in your Future of America Exhibition?"

Marlowe's smile wavered. "No."

"Why not? Aren't they evidence of the unlimited American future?"

"They're evidence of something, all right—chicanery. In the greatest nation on earth, we have no need for flimflam or hocus-pocus. We believe in opportunity and the power of the self-made man."

Fresh cheers went up. T. S. Woodhouse waited for them to subside. "Sure, sure, who doesn't love a Horatio Alger story? But you're not a self-made man, are you, Mr. Marlowe? You came from old money."

"Leave him alone!" a thick-necked man in a Shriners fez growled.

"What're you, one of those Bolsheviks?" someone else cried and gave Woodhouse a small shove.

Marlowe put out a calming hand. "Now, now," he admonished. But as he turned to Woodhouse, his anger was evident. "I made my own way. My family money didn't create those inventions. Nor did they test-fly all those new aeroplanes or run trials on lifesaving medicines. I did."

"But your family's money helped finance them," Woodhouse said, sneezing.

"My family's fortune was lost during the war, as you well know.

Every last cent of it. I was the one who rebuilt it. In fact, I surpassed it. That's the American way."

"For some Americans."

"Mr. Woodhouse, that may not be a cold you have. You may be allergic to the notion of hard work and success."

The crowd responded with a round of laughter, applause, and shouts of "Hear, hear!" With the sun streaming down on him like a William Blake painting, Jake Marlowe strode through the pressing masses, shaking hands with the people now calling his name like a wish.

"Hold on!" Henry yelled to Ling as Marlowe moved closer to them. Henry waved wildly. "Mr. Marlowe! Mr. Marlowe! Please, sir!" he shouted. "This is one of your biggest admirers, Miss Ling Chan! She's a scientist, like you!"

"Henry!" Ling whispered, embarrassed.

"Is that so?" Mr. Marlowe said.

Ling's heart beat quickly as the spectators cleared the way and Jake Marlowe came closer. Unlike other people, his gaze didn't go automatically to her braces and crutches. He looked her straight in the eyes as he bowed.

"Well, then. I am pleased to meet you, Miss Chan. Will you be coming to the fair, then?" Marlowe asked.

"I . . . I hope so. Sir."

Marlowe laughed. "You don't sound too sure about it. Here. Let me make it easier." He reached into his pocket and wrote something on a sheet of paper, then handed it to her.

"Excuse me, can we get a picture for the papers?" T. S. Woodhouse asked and gestured to the news photographer in the clearing.

"Hold it!" the photographer shouted from behind the curtain of his camera. The flash erupted with a puff of gray smoke, immortalizing Henry, Ling, and her hero in silver gelatin. "Thank you."

"See you in the spring, Miss Chan," Mr. Marlowe said and moved on.

"What's it say? What's it say?" Henry asked, angling for a better look at the paper in Ling's hands.

"'IOU Miss Ling Chan—two free tickets to the Future of America Exhibition,'" Ling read. At the bottom was Marlowe's signature. She now had Jake Marlowe's autograph.

Ling looked ready to faint or vomit. "I talked to Jake Marlowe," she said, incredulous. "This is his signature."

"Well, it was nothing, really," Henry said. "No, please! No more gratitude! Your happiness is thanks enough."

"Thank you, Henry," Ling said.

"Shucks. 'Tweren't nothing."

Ling beamed, holding the piece of paper like a sacred object. "Jake Marlowe touched this!" she said, and it was as close to a squeal as she'd ever come.

"Why, Miss Chan," Henry drawled. "I believe you are pos-i-tute-ly smitten."

* * *

T. S. Woodhouse turned and squeezed his way through the throngs of smiling, optimistic people happy to have something to be happy about.

On the way across the muddy field, he was surprised to see Dr. Fitzgerald's assistant, Jericho Jones. He vaguely remembered hearing some scuttlebutt that Will Fitzgerald and the inventor had been friends at one point, past tense. If he'd sent Jericho to mend fences, Marlowe's comments about Diviners surely wouldn't do anything to help.

At the edge of the park, white-capped nurses in starched uniforms passed out flyers to the people coming to hear Jake Marlowe paint a bright future for them. "Examinations today in the Fitter Family tent," they called. "Free of charge." A Negro couple walked in, but no one handed them a flyer. In fact, the nurse pretended not to see them at all, passing one to the white family behind them instead.

Woodhouse sneezed into his handkerchief again.

"Gesundheit," said a pretty nurse.

Woodhouse smiled at her. "Gee, thanks. I feel cured already."

"Here. Have one." The nurse handed him a pamphlet:

Could you be an exceptional American? Do you exhibit unusual gifts? Have you ever had unexplained dreams of the future or the past? Have you or anyone in your family had a visitation from spirits from beyond? The Eugenics Society administers tests to likely candidates free of charge.

There was an address at the bottom.

Woodhouse knew he was anything but exceptional, unless there was a test for cleverness. Or survival.

"I'll pass this along to any likely candidates," he said, tipping his hat. He passed through the Fitter Family tent, smiling at a couple of siblings squawking over who got to go first until they saw the nurse holding the syringe, and then they fell quiet. He peeked through the crack of a curtain at a table where a pretty nurse asked a woman and her teenage daughter a series of questions. "...I see. And have you ever seen in your dreams an otherworldly being, a tall man in a stovepipe hat, perhaps accompanied by a host of crows?"

Woodhouse wrote it down on his pad, sneezed again, and moved out into the crowd. He bumped hard into a young man, knocking off his cap.

"Apologies," Woodhouse said, brushing dirt from the brim as he handed it back.

"No trouble," Arthur Brown said as he donned his cap once more. He leaned against the hot dog stand, watching Jake Marlowe move through the crowd clean as a newly made promise. His eyes scanned the whole of the fairgrounds, taking in everything.

"This exhibition's gonna be the biggest thing to hit this city in a long time," Woodhouse said, nodding briefly toward the adoring crowds before scribbling more notes on his pad. "Gonna make a big bang."

Arthur nodded, then tipped his head and looked up at the wide, blue, American sky, where not a cloud could be seen. "It surely will," he said.

THE GOLDEN BOY

At the appointed hour, Jericho waited for Jake Marlowe in his private tent bordering the fairgrounds, which were already bustling with industry, the air a symphony of hammering, shouting men—proof that the great Jake Marlowe intended to make good on his promise to erect the fair quickly. The inside of the tent had the feel of an officer's quarters, as if the two of them had come to plot the next battle surge. A long table housing a diorama took up the center of the room. Jericho walked around the table, admiring the clean-lined perfection of the model's buildings as he read the title cards beneath each one: HALL OF PROSPERITY. HALL OF AVIATION AND ROCKETRY. STANDARD OIL PAVILION. ATOMIC ENERGY PAVILION. EUGENICS EXHIBITION TENT. RADIO. MACHINES. MEDICINE. AGRICULTURE.

"Impressive, isn't it?" Marlowe entered the tent, wiping the dirt from his hands. "You're getting a first look at what we're building—the greatest exhibition of its kind dedicated to the advancement of American business, ingenuity, and ideals. A utopian vision of an American tomorrow."

"Sounds like an advertisement."

"I suppose it is," Marlowe agreed, laughing. "But why not take pride in this country? It's the envy of the world. A place where any man can realize his dream. We, the dreamers, built this nation."

"The Indians and the slaves might disagree," Jericho shot back.

"Did you come to lecture me about American history, Jericho? Or did you need this?" Marlowe held up a vial of blue serum.

If there was anything Jericho hated, it was this. He hated being at the mercy of a man he both admired and hated, someone who'd saved his life and enslaved it.

"Now, now, no need to look embarrassed. I'm glad you're here. I was very pleased to get your letter. Here. Take a seat." Marlowe offered Jericho a chair, settling into the one opposite him. Casually, he poured coffee from a silver pot and handed the cup to Jericho, who was grateful for the warm drink. "I heard about what happened to you up in Brethren."

"How?"

Marlowe stirred two cubes of sugar into his own coffee. "You don't get to be top dog without knowing how to get the information you need. That was reckless of Will. And to think he dragged his niece into it, as well. This foolish obsession of his is going to get people hurt." Marlowe's expression went somber. "So is this Diviner business."

Jericho wished he could tell Marlowe about what they had done, how they had stopped a maniacal demon from manifesting in New York City. What they had done wasn't reckless; it was desperate. They had saved lives, and the public would never know.

"Believe me, Evie can't be dragged into anything she doesn't want to do," Jericho said.

"The Sweetheart Seer. She is quite something," Marlowe mused. "Isn't she engaged to that Sam Lloyd character? Well, she could certainly do better. A good man like you, perhaps."

Jericho looked down at his shoes, and it was all the confirmation Marlowe needed.

Marlowe was still watching him closely.

"What is it?" Jericho asked, annoyed.

"And have you had any strong feelings of aggression or agitation?" Marlowe asked.

Strong feelings of aggression and agitation pretty much sum up being eighteen, Jericho thought. "When I was shot, but otherwise, nothing out of the ordinary."

"Good. Very good." Marlowe gulped down his coffee and put the cup and saucer aside. "I'm glad you brought up the subject, Jericho. You know, I've been thinking—what if you were to come out to California and work with us at Marlowe Industries?"

"What could I offer you that you don't already have?"

"You're my crowning achievement." Marlowe leaned forward, resting his forearms on his thighs. That face the press lionized was no less impressive up close. "If we could study you, find out why you've survived against the odds, well, think of the good that could be done for America, for mankind. And for you, Jericho." The great man looked Jericho in the eyes. His gaze was powerful. Inescapable. Jericho could feel the idealism pushing out from Marlowe like rays of sun on the first day of spring. "I'd like to make you the star of the Future of America Exhibition."

Jericho's brow furrowed. "Me? Why?"

"It's time people knew. Jericho, you *are* the future of America. You are the next evolution of our species. A vision of all our hopes and dreams: Stronger. Faster. Smarter. Heroic. Tell me: When was the last time you were sick?"

"I...I can't recall."

Marlowe leaned back against his chair, smiling. "There you are! How fast did you recover from the gunshot wound?"

"A week, give or take."

"A week! A week and you were good as new—better than new!" Jake Marlowe laughed. "Remarkable. Jericho Jones. A true native son. Our golden boy."

It was true that Jericho had survived against all the odds. But the way Marlowe talked about it made him seem like a product rather than a human being. Wasn't it some alchemical, mysterious connection between science, Marlowe's genius, and whatever it was that made Jericho unique that had resulted in this advancement? Marlowe had made the parts and invented the serum. But he couldn't claim credit for it all. He couldn't claim credit for who Jericho was.

Choices. That's what made a man. Wasn't it?

Marlowe strolled over to the model and busied himself with perfecting the alignment of the buildings. "In the laboratory, we could study you. Study your blood. Run you through a conditioning program and a battery of tests."

"And what would I get out of it?"

Marlowe frowned at a Winged Victory statue that was seemingly out of place. He picked it up and the angel hovered over the model fairgrounds as its creator searched for a spot to place it. "We'll fine-tune to make sure that you don't ever suffer the same fate as the others in the Daedalus program. You won't end up like your friend Sergeant Lester."

"Leonard. Sergeant Leonard."

"Right," Marlowe said. "Of course. Sergeant Leonard."

"But so far, I've done fine with just the serum."

"Indeed. You've done just fine. But what if you could do more than fine, Jericho? What if you had the chance to be extraordinary? Exceptional. The sort of extraordinary, exceptional man Miss O'Neill couldn't resist." Marlowe's eyes gleamed. "I assumed when you mentioned her there was a reason."

Jericho didn't answer.

"When you stand on the stage at the exhibition and demonstrate how superior you are, there won't be a girl in this world you can't have. That's the law of the animal kingdom: The stronger beast wins out," Marlowe said, placing the Victory statue in the center of the model.

Jericho glowered. "I'm not a beast."

"Now, now, don't get sore. I mean it as a compliment."

"I don't want to be your exhibit. I only want to have a normal life."

"Normal!" Marlowe thundered. He loomed over the table. "No man worth his salt wants to be 'normal,' Jericho. Be remarkable! Aim high. After all, do you honestly believe that your young lady wants a normal, ordinary life? Not from what I've seen. How funny that she's Will's niece. They're as different as chalk and cheese."

"Like you and me," Jericho snapped.

"Am I really so repugnant to you?" Marlowe said quietly.

He was hurt, Jericho realized with a mixture of pride and shame.

"It's...it's not that I'm not grateful for what you've done for me. Sir."

"It's not your gratitude I want, Jericho," Marlowe said. "I remember the first time I saw you, lying on that bed in the hospital. You didn't cry, and you didn't complain. They told me you were smart and that you liked to read, particularly about philosophy and machines—you'd gained an interest in helping your father fix things around the farm. And I asked you a question to start us off. Do you remember?"

Jericho did remember. It was the morning that he'd truly realized the full, intractable horror of his situation. For an hour, he'd stared at the ceiling, fighting desperately to hold on to his thinning hope in miracles. But as he listened to the moans and cries of those around him, he understood that hope was not a construct of faith meant to bring man closer to God but one of denial and delusion meant to keep him from accepting that God did not exist. He wondered if he stopped eating, if he let himself slip away, if that could be considered suicide, which he'd been taught was a sin.

But was it a sin if there was no God?

He'd heard the *tap-tap* of shoes coming closer. He could have turned his head to see, but he continued staring at the ceiling. Suddenly, the smiling nurse was standing beside his paralyzed body, saying, "There's someone here to see you, Jericho." Jake Marlowe's face loomed above his, blocking the light.

"Hello, Jericho," Jake Marlowe had said.

Jericho hadn't answered.

"Now, Jericho, where are your manners? Mr. Marlowe has come all the way from Washington to see you," the nurse *tsk*ed, and Jericho imagined her falling off a cliff.

He still didn't say hello.

"I'm sorry, Mr. Marlowe," the nurse said. "He's not usually so disagreeable."

"That's all right, Miss Portman. Could you leave us for a moment?"

"Certainly."

Marlowe stood next to Jericho's bed, examining the metal cage that kept Jericho breathing. "I invented this, you know. It's no substitute for good lungs, but I'm working on that. I understand you like mechanical things as well."

Jericho did not answer.

"So. Tell me," Marlowe tried gamely, "what do you think is man's greatest invention?"

Jericho turned his head just slightly toward Marlowe, looking him straight in the eye. "God."

He waited for Marlowe to be shocked or horrified. He waited for a lecture. Instead, Marlowe had put a hand on Jericho's head like a father, saying quietly but firmly, "I'm going to help you, Jericho. You're going to get up from this bed. You're going to walk and run again. I will not stop until you can, I promise you."

And just like that, the snare of hope trapped Jericho again.

Marlowe made good on his promise. But like all deals with the Devil, there were drawbacks. In the past ten years, his relationship with Marlowe had gone from idolatry to rebellion and resentment.

Fathers and sons.

"What if I don't want to be your experiment or exhibition any longer?" Jericho said. "What if I want to be my own man?"

Marlowe's eyes flashed. Jericho knew that look well. The great man did not have much patience for insubordination.

"You want to be your own man? Be your own man. Without this." Marlowe held up the precious vial of serum and stuffed it into his pocket.

Jericho squirmed a bit. What game was Marlowe playing now? "You wouldn't do that," he challenged. "You care about your experiment too much."

"I could start over with somebody else."

"If you could do that, you would have already. And that golden boy or girl would be standing on the stage with you."

"Fine. Go without the serum, then," Jake said evenly.

As far as Jericho knew, Marlowe's little blue miracle powered the machinery of his body. It kept his heart beating, his lungs breathing, his blood pumping. And it kept his mind from devolving into madness. Marlowe was bluffing. Had to be.

Jericho was scared, but he refused to let Marlowe win. "All right. Maybe I will."

"I wouldn't advise it."

"Why not? What will happen if I do?"

Marlowe didn't respond.

"I deserve an answer," Jericho said, raising his voice. He banged his fist on the table, toppling some of the buildings on Marlowe's artfully arranged Future of America model.

"Careful," Marlowe cautioned, and Jericho wasn't sure if he meant the model or Jericho himself.

"I honestly don't know what will happen. Because you're the only one who's come this far. Just you." Once more, Marlowe leaned forward, his face grimly determined. "Jericho, let me help you. You'll get your girl. You can have everything you want. Together, we will be part of greatness."

Just like on that spring morning ten years before, Jericho could feel hope's snare around his ankle. If he submitted to Marlowe's grand plan, became part of his experiment, could he have a better chance at happiness? Would he be considered not a freak but a golden son—a prototype for the new, exceptional American? Could he have everything he wanted?

Could he have Evie?

Choices.

Already Marlowe had restored order to the toppled model, everything in its place.

"I'll think about it," Jericho said, enjoying the irritation flitting across Marlowe's face. The great Jake Marlowe couldn't control everything, after all.

"As you wish," Marlowe said.

He went to his left pocket, fished out the small vial there, and placed it in Jericho's palm.

Jericho stared at it, confused. "Where are the others?"

"You earn them. That is one month's supply. I'm giving you thirty days to make up your mind. After that, you're on your own."

ONCE UPON A TIME

"Isaiah!" Memphis shouted. "Did you do this?"

He showed Isaiah his defaced poetry book.

Eyes wide, Isaiah nodded.

Three of the pages were covered in disturbing drawings. Isaiah's pencil had gouged the paper.

"You're acting like you're two instead of ten," Memphis griped. "I know you're mad at the whole world right now, Isaiah, but you can't be doing this. You can't ruin a man's personal property."

"I didn't mean to. I was asleep," Isaiah protested.

Memphis didn't know whether to believe Isaiah or not. The way he'd acted lately, he could've done it out of spite. Now the poem he'd worked so hard on was a shambles. Memphis wasn't even sure he could recover any of it.

"I was having another nightmare," Isaiah said. "Those are the monsters in the subways."

"Monsters. In the subways." Memphis's laugh was short and bitter. "They pay full fare?"

"I saw them!" Isaiah yelled. "She made them. They're down there. They're hungry."

"Isaiah! I swear." Memphis threw his hands in the air and let them fall to his sides again. He held up the book. "You owe me."

"What's all this fuss about?" Bill Johnson said, tapping into the room.

"Nothing, Mr. Johnson," Memphis grumbled. He pointed a finger at Isaiah. The finger was a warning. "But I'm not leaving anything of mine around you anymore."

Memphis tucked the book inside his coat.

＊

Isaiah trudged alongside Blind Bill as they walked through St. Nicholas Park, his baseball glove under his arm, the ball cupped in his other hand, and a scowl on his face.

"Now, what you got to do next time," Bill instructed, his blind man's cane tapping out ahead of him on the path, "is you got to put a li'l spit in your palm—just a li'l bit, now. Not too much. That'll make that old ball fly like it has an angel's wings."

Isaiah was quiet. Bill didn't need to see the boy to know that he was angry. He could hear it in the way Isaiah kept kicking up dirt as he walked. Memphis was supposed to take his little brother to play ball, but he was so angry about Isaiah drawing in his book that he'd refused. Bill knew he was a poor substitute. Just like he knew Memphis Campbell had healed Noble Bishop and lied about it. It still made Bill furious to think about the healer using his gift on that old drunk and not doing a goddamn thing to help Bill. Seemed like he and Isaiah had something in common: They were both mad at Memphis.

"Little man!" Bill said brightly, hoping to cajole the boy out of his mood. "Why'nt you tell me one of your funny stories you got, 'bout frogs or what-have-you?"

"My mama and daddy used to tell me stories," Isaiah said. "Memphis, too. Before he went and got a girl."

"That so?" Bill could infer Isaiah's shrug in the silence. "You want me to tell you a story, then? That it?"

Sniffling. Then: "Don't care."

"Mm-hmm. Tell you a story, tell you a story," Bill said, nodding and thinking. "All right. There was this fella—"

"That ain't the way you start a story!" Isaiah interrupted.

437

"Say, now! Who's telling it?"

Isaiah missed stories. His mama used to tell good ones, all about a rabbit in Mr. McGregor's garden and a warrior named François Mackandal who ran down from the hills to chase the bad men away. Sometimes, Isaiah would get the stories confused and François Mackandal would be a farmer chasing a rabbit down the hill. His daddy liked funny stories. And Memphis told the best stories of all. He missed when it was just the two of them together in the back room watching the night lights of the city climbing up the wall while they waited for sleep to come, back before all this nonsense with that girl, Theta. He missed the way it had been once upon a time. Isaiah felt like crying again. He turned it into anger at Bill for not knowing the right way to tell a proper story.

"You gotta start with 'Once upon a time,'" Isaiah insisted.

"Well, well, well, all right, then," Bill teased. "Once. Upon. A time. That better? You happy now? Once upon a time, in a faraway land, there was a race of proud people. Kings and queens. Like the pharaohs of old."

"Is this a Bible story?"

"You never gonna know you keep running your mouth."

Isaiah kept quiet.

"And the land these people lived in?" Bill continued. "It was something. Fulla magic, and the people was fulla magic. And there was lions and fruit trees and everything you could want."

"Everything?"

"Didn't I say everything? Everything still mean everything, don't it?" Bill started again. "But the people of that land was betrayed. Men come and stole 'em away from their kingdom—had to put chains on 'em to keep the magic down. Then they put 'em on ships and brought 'em to a new land. A hard land where they worked all day and all night long. And they suffered. They suffered. And then, a long time later in that new land, along come a prince."

"Like in 'Cinderella'?"

"Naaww," Bill said, affronted. "This fella look like you and me. Big and strong and black as night. They said he was so strong he could grab the straps of a plow with both hands and pull that old plow better'n any horse. This prince had a powerful magic. He could suck the life right outta things. Could put an old dog down if its time had come or take the boll weevil sickness off the cotton. Yes, sir. That prince was mighty powerful. And that made some folks nervous, you understand? Too. Much. Power." Bill spat out the words on a fierce whisper. "Soon, ever'body was talking 'bout the prince and sayin' he killed people."

"Did he?"

"No. No, little man, he didn't," Bill said softly.

"What happened?"

Bill took in a deep breath. The air smelled good, like chimney smoke and sunshine on snow. "One day, some men come and they took the prince to see the king's castle and ask him to show off that power of his. First, they brought in a chicken. Old squawking chicken, and the first thing that prince thought was, *There's dinner.*"

Isaiah laughed. "I ate four drumsticks last night!"

"You got a good appetite." Bill reached out and patted the boy's head. Once upon a time, he might've had himself a son like Isaiah Campbell, a boy who liked baseball and frogs and tall tales. If things had been different.

"What happened next?"

"Well, sir, the prince took that old chicken, but lord, did it fight him, all flutterin' feathers and pecking—such a big fuss for a li'l old bird. Soon enough, the chicken stopped fighting. And then it lay cold and still in the prince's hands."

"He...killed it?"

"Quick and easy, like. So it didn't suffer none," Bill said quietly.

"And they ate it, right?"

"Right. Right," Bill said. "Well, the king and his court were mighty impressed by this. That night, some men come to talk to the prince. Shadow Men."

"What's a Shadow Man?"

"Nobody you want to be messin' with. Like the bogeyman made real. They heard 'bout what the prince could do with the chicken. They

439

brought in something else for him. A man. They said he was a bad man, an enemy, and they asked the prince to use his magic like he done with the chicken. But the prince had never done that on no man before, no matter what the people in the town said 'bout him. And he was afraid."

"Afraid of what?"

"Afraid it would curse him forever."

"But if that man was a bad man, how could it?" Isaiah asked.

Bill took another breath, let it out slowly. "Ain't that simple, little man. Ain't that simple to know what the truth of somethin' is. Just 'cause somebody tell you 'This the way it is' don't mean you oughta believe it. You gotta make sure for yourself."

"I don't understand."

"Supposin' a couple people told ever'body you stole bread from the bakery."

"They'd be liars! I wouldn't steal nothing!"

"I know you wouldn't. But some folks might believe 'em. 'Fore you know it, they telling ever'body you're bad. Other folks hear it and they believe it, too. Don't bother to check into the story 'cause they'd rather just believe that than find out for themselves."

"Why?"

"Looking for truth makes a man hafta look at himself along the way."

Cold wind eddied around Bill's trouser legs and he felt it in his bones. Isaiah took Bill's hand. The soft trust of the boy's fingers was a surprise.

"Did the prince kill that man?"

"Yes," Bill said after a pause. "Yes, son, he did."

"And was he cursed?"

"Yes, he was."

"How? Did it turn him into a monster?"

Bill was still for a moment, listening to a winter wren trilling from a nearby perch. "I expect it did," he said, feeling suddenly tired, more tired than he could remember feeling in a very long time. "Come on now. Let's go home."

Isaiah let go. "That ain't the end of the story!" He sounded angry.

And scared. Like somebody had told him the monsters under the bed were real. "Tell me the real end!"

Why shouldn't the child know the way of things? Still—killing a man was one thing. Killing hope in somebody so young was another. Once upon a time, Bill knew this. Once upon a time, he'd had the same hope. He had believed in goodness. If he wanted to believe in goodness now, all he had to do was walk the boy home to his aunt and a warm supper.

"Okay. But first, you tell me something. What do you remember 'bout the time when Memphis was a healer?"

"I'm not supposed to talk about that."

"It's just us. Man talk. Nobody needs to know."

"He fixed my broken arm," Isaiah said.

"How's that?"

"I fell outta the tree after church and Memphis put his hands on me and then I had a dream that we were in a bright, peaceful place and I could hear drums. When I woke up, Reverend Brown and Mama and everybody was crowded around and my arm wasn't broken no—any—more."

Bill tipped his face toward the sky, letting the weary winter sun warm his cheeks. He remembered the way sunlight looked peeking through clouds after a rain. He'd like to see that again.

"The prince broke the curse. He married the princess and took her away, back to his homeland. He freed his people, and they lived happily ever after. The end," Bill said. "Ain't that how fairy tales go?"

"I suppose so," Isaiah said, but he didn't sound convinced. "Mr. Johnson?"

"Whatcha want? Got no more stories for you."

"You all right?"

"'Course I'm all right. Why wouldn't I be?"

"Your eyes are all wet," Isaiah said.

"No, they ain't, neither," Bill whispered. He could taste the salt. "Come here, little man." Bill held out his trembling hand, and the boy, trusting as a lamb, came right to him, and Bill swallowed hard as he laced his big fingers with Isaiah's small ones and pulled the child close, hating himself all the while.

Later, after he'd carried the boy home and put him on the bed, after Dr. Wilson had been sent for and come and Octavia's prayer circle had gathered in the parlor to pray for the boy, Bill sat on Octavia's couch sipping coffee, letting people tap his shoulder and praise him for saving the boy again, thanking Jesus that Bill had been there when Isaiah had suffered another of his fits, or who knows what might have happened?

Bill listened to their whispers—"Look at that, crying for him just like Isaiah was his own son"; "That sure warms the heart on a cold day." Around him, these people were dim shades in a perpetually gray world.

His hand shook on his cup. He had no stomach for the coffee.

"I just hope the little fella's all right," Bill said, and even he wasn't sure if it was a lie.

Later, he perched at the end of Isaiah's bed and listened and waited for the older Campbell boy to come home and heal his brother. And once he did, Bill could siphon away some of that healing energy for himself. If Memphis wouldn't heal Bill's sight directly, well, he'd get it however he could.

"Mr. Johnson?"

Blind Bill startled at the sound of Isaiah's voice. "Little man? That you?"

"How come I'm in bed? 'S not the nighttime."

"You had yourself a fit," Bill said, moving toward the boy, hands at the ready.

"Isaiah? Is he awake?" Octavia burst into the room and Bill pulled back, shoving his hands into his pockets.

"Isaiah? Oh, thank you, Jesus."

"I'm all right. Why's ever'body making a fuss?" Isaiah said sleepily.

"I'll let you be," Bill said. With his cane, he tapped his way down the hall and out the front door, where he heard a robin singing. Bill snatched the bird up, and in a moment, its song was stilled.

THE COLLECTIVE UNCONSCIOUS

Theta knocked firmly on Evie's door in the Winthrop Hotel. "Open up, Evil. I know you're in there. I'll just keep knocking until—"

The door swung open to reveal a very rumpled Evie, a velvet sleep mask pushed up on top of her tangled curls. She regarded Theta with a look bordering on murder. "What's the big idea, waking a girl before it's decent, Theta?"

Theta pushed past Evie. She eyed the empty bottles and glasses littering the filthy room. "Big night?"

"The biggest." Evie yawned, falling back onto the bed. "Before the party proper, we had a little merry here in my room. I met this maaarvelous burlesque queen from Poughkeepsie, some darling stock-brokers, and a very entertaining fellow who could bounce a quarter off the end of the dresser and have it land in a glass of gin on the night-stand and... aaaah! Are you trying to kill me, Theta?"

Late-afternoon sun pierced the hotel gloom through the window where Theta had yanked the drapes aside.

"Depends."

"Depends on what?"

"Whether or not you keep using that phony accent around me."

Evie rubbed her forehead. "Oh, applesauce. Theta, will you have a talk with my head, please? Tell it to stop playing the marimba across my skull."

Theta sniffed the nearby glasses, finally finding one that didn't smell of gin. "Hold on." She disappeared into the bathroom, returning a moment later with a glass of water and two aspirin. "Down the hatch. Doctor's orders."

"What's the rumble? What're you doing here?" Evie managed to say between gulps.

Theta had been trying to figure out how to talk about this with Evie for weeks. She narrowed her eyes. "If you breathe a word of what I'm about to say, I swear I'll hunt you for sport and wear your skin as a coat."

Evie opened one eye. "It would have a satin lining, though. Promise me it would."

"Evil..."

"All right. I'm shutting up." Evie mimed locking her lips and throwing away the key.

One of Theta's eyebrows shot up. "Boy, do I wish that really worked," she muttered. "Okay. Listen: All these Diviners running around—"

"Not this again..."

"What happened to shutting up?" Theta barked and Evie quieted. "These Diviners. Any of 'em dream walkers that you know about?"

Evie rolled onto her side, her brow furrowed. "What do you mean?"

"I mean, are any of 'em able to walk around inside a dream just like they were walking around Times Square. Sleeping, but fully awake at the same time."

"Inside people's dreams?" Evie asked, confused.

Theta threw up her hands and rolled her eyes. "Do I need elocution lessons? That's what I said."

Evie scoffed. "That is pos-i-tute-ly impossible."

"It's not."

"Pull the other leg!"

"Henry can do it."

Evie propped herself up on her elbows. "You're telling me that Henry, our Henry, can walk...in dreams?"

"That's exactly what I'm saying. Henry's a Diviner." Theta tore into her handbag and pulled out her silver cigarette case. "Evil, you gotta let me smoke or I'm gonna chew all my fingernails off."

Evie made a face before waving her approval, and Theta slipped a cigarette free and tapped the end of it against the case's hard shell. "You remember at Christmas, when Henry asked you to read his hat because he was trying to find Louis?"

"Yes. I wasn't much help, though."

"Well, Henry finally found Louis in the dream world," Theta said, lighting up and taking a drag deep into her lungs. "That ain't all. He's met another dream walker. A girl named Ling, lives in Chinatown. Every night, they've been meeting inside dreams and walking around. He thinks I don't know, but I do."

"Gee, sounds like a swell talent. So what's got you all balled up about it?"

"You know how you get sick if you read too much? It's the same with Henry and dreams. We had a deal—no more than one hour a week. Evil, he's walking every night now, and I don't even know how long he's under. He's missed rehearsals, and even when he shows up, he isn't really there. His mind's on dreams," Theta said on a stream of cigarette smoke. "He's the only family I got."

"What can we do? You want me to come with you and we'll sit Henry down?"

"Lecturing Hen won't help. But this lecture might." Theta pulled out a newspaper advertisement and shoved it into Evie's hands.

"'The Society for Ethical Culture presents World-Renowned Psychoanalyst Carl Jung: Symposium on Dreams and the Collective Unconscious,'" Evie read. "Gee, say that three times fast."

"We got a dream question, we go to the dream expert."

"'Eight o'clock in the evening on January...'" Evie stopped reading. "Theta, that's tonight!"

"Yeah. So you'd better get moving. It's gonna be a full house. I'll meet you there on the front steps of the Ethi-Whatchamacallit at seven thirty."

445

"Theta, I can't. Sam and I are going to the pictures tonight—the theater owners asked for us in particular. They've got a special projector that can play sound on film! Isn't that the elephant's eyebrows?"

"Yeah. Terrific. Listen, tell Lover Boy there's been a change of plans. If he's gonna be married to you, he'll have to get used to that." Theta squinted hard at Evie. "Whatsa matter? You're making a face like you got caught stealing cookies from an orphanage."

"No, I'm not."

"That proves it. You're definitely guilty of something. Spill." Theta folded her arms and waited.

"Oh, all right." Evie sighed. "I need to confess to somebody before I go mad. This romance with Sam? It's a publicity stunt."

Theta slapped her hand on the bed. "I knew it! I smelled something as phony as your new accent!"

"Hey!"

"I know you're crackers, Evil, but I'm glad to see you're not *that* crackers. So was I right about you and Jericho?"

Evie hung her head. "It was just the one time. Oh, Theta. I'm such a terrible friend. I am the worst friend ever!"

"Don't get fulla yourself. I'm not crowning you for it," Theta grumbled. She drew hard on her cigarette. "If you're really goofy for Jericho, you should tell Mabel. If he's not dizzy for her, well, she can't be sore at you about it."

"Oh, yes, she can! You don't know Mabel. Beneath that bleeding heart lies a grudge factory."

"Well, she can't stay sore at you forever—especially if you've spared her months of batting her peepers at a boy she can't have."

"But what if I don't really like Jericho enough, not in the way he likes me or the way that Mabel likes him? Then I've led him on. Toyed with his affections and broken Mabel's heart for a selfish whim." Evie pulled the blanket up to her chin. "And then there's Sam."

Theta narrowed her eyes. "What about Sam?"

"Sometimes when Sam's pretending to be in love with me, my stomach does funny things."

"Well, get some milk of magnesia and stop it. Listen, the best thing you can do about Sam is play your part and forget about it. I know that type. He'll have another tomato on his arm in twenty minutes."

Evie frowned. "I'm not a tomato."

Theta stubbed out her cigarette in a glass. "Evil, I know you—you'll sort out this boy trouble. Frankly, it's the least interesting thing about you. And right now, we got bigger problems."

"Right," Evie said, straightening up. "Henry. To the rescue we go."

"I'll see you at the egghead lecture at seven thirty. And seven thirty means seven thirty, kid. Eastern standard time. Not Evil-O'Neill-anything-but-on-time time."

"You're one to talk," Evie groused. "You never make it to the theater when you're supposed to."

Theta tucked her clutch under her arm and held the hotel room's door open with her foot as she yanked her gloves back on. "I like to give Wally the vapors, I'll admit. But I'm always on time for my friends."

"Yeah? Well . . . well," Evie sputtered. "Well, at least I don't smoke!"

Theta posed in the doorway. "You sure about that? Let's set you on fire and find out."

Evie hurled her pillow at Theta, who was quicker. The pillow hit the door and bounced onto the floor with the rest of the garbage.

At fifteen minutes past eight o'clock, Evie leaped from a cab on the corner of Sixty-fourth Street and Central Park West and rushed up the steps of the New York Society for Ethical Culture. A murderous-looking Theta glared down at her from just outside the closed doors.

"I said seven thirty," Theta barked, grabbing Evie by the arm and steering her into the foyer. "Maybe instead of elocution lessons they should give you telling-time lessons."

"Sorry, but at the last minute Mr. Phillips asked me to read something for his wife's cousin. I couldn't very well say no to the boss," Evie huffed out as they pushed through the doors into the foyer, where Mabel waited. It was Evie's second glare of the evening, although Mabel's was more exasperated than murderous.

"Oh. Hi, Pie Face. I didn't know you were coming," Evie said.

"I happened to run into Theta on her way out, and since I'd planned to attend the lecture, I suggested we come together. She said she wants to know about dreams and the unconscious for her acting," Mabel said.

"Yes. For her acting," Evie said evenly and did her best not to look at Theta.

"The lecture's already begun, though, and the usher told me absolutely no one can go in," Mabel said.

"Oh, don't you worry. I'll take care of it." Evie flounced over to the man at the door. "How do you do? I'm Evie O'Neill. The Sweetheart Seer? Gee, I'm awfully sorry we're late—I was visiting a children's hospital, you see, and—"

"I'm sorry. No one is admitted." The man stood like an iceberg.

"But I'm the Sweetheart Seer!" Evie said brightly. When the man seemed unimpressed, she added, "I read objects with help from beyond? WGI? I'm a Diviner."

"Then you should be able to read the time," the man said, pointing to the advertisement for the lecture. "I'm afraid what you are is late, Miss. No admittance."

Back outside, Theta marched down the steps, puffing madly on a cigarette. She whirled around to face Evie. "I told you seven thirty."

"Yes, I believe we've established that," Evie huffed. She stared back at the closed doors, dumbfounded. "That man has never heard of my show."

"What're we gonna do now?" Theta said, more to the sky than to anyone else.

"You really need to ask him some questions for your acting?" Mabel asked.

"Yeah," Theta said after a pause. "I really do."

"Then bundle up and follow me," Mabel said, walking toward Central Park.

"Where are we going?" Theta asked, grinding her cigarette under her heel.

"The Kensington House. Apparently, Dr. Jung stays there when he's in New York."

"How do you know that?" Evie asked.

"An old friend of my mother's once hosted a fancy luncheon for him in Geneva," Mabel answered as they crossed the street and headed into the park.

Sometimes Evie forgot that Mabel's mother had been a Newell, one of New York's great society families, before she married Mabel's father and was disowned. She wondered what it must be like for Mabel to know that an entire side of her family lived with maids and butlers and chauffeurs to take care of their every need while Mabel shared a two-bedroom flat with parents who actively campaigned against that sort of wealth and privilege.

"Do you ever see your mother's family, Mabesie?"

"Once a year," Mabel said. "On my grandmother's birthday. Mama sends me out on the train and a driver picks me up in a Rolls-Royce."

"Your mother gave all that up for love?" Theta asked.

"Yes," Mabel said. "And because she wanted to be her own person, with a different sort of life."

"That's a lot to walk away from." Evie whistled.

The grainy halos of the park lamps lit up the barren branches of the stately winter trees flanking the cobbled path inside Central Park. The glassy surface of the frozen pond reflected the waxing moon, making it seem attainable. The tops of Fifth Avenue's tony apartment buildings shone in the distance as the girls' shoes crunched through the remnants of old snow.

"How are things with Jericho?" Evie asked Mabel, keeping her voice light, as if she were asking about the weather. "Has he tried to kiss you again?"

"Evie!" Mabel sputtered at the same moment Theta said, "Jericho kissed you?"

"Gee, I might as well tell the *Daily Mirror* as tell you," Mabel complained.

"I'm sorry, Pie Face, really, I am. But it's just Theta, and she's thrilled for you. Aren't you, Theta?"

"Sure I am." Theta flicked a glance Evie's way. The glance said, *What are you doing? Why are you torturing yourself?* Evie fluttered her lashes in response: *I do not know what you are insinuating. I am above your petty insult.*

"No, he hasn't," Mabel said, unaware of Evie and Theta's little exchange. "But we've been very busy putting the exhibit together." Mabel cast a suspicious glance at Evie. "You *are* coming, aren't you, Evie? You won't let some radio nonsense keep you?"

"I said I'd be there and I will be there." Evie sniffed. "Oh, look! It's started snowing. Isn't it beautiful?"

The girls stopped at the top of an archway and watched the glistening flakes flutter down over the pathway and rolling lawn. The night held its breath for a moment. In the hush, they could hear jazz and merriment coming from the nearby Central Park Casino, whose lights shone through the gaps in the trees, making Theta think of the lighthouse and Memphis. She'd tried calling his house that afternoon, but hung up with a "Sorry, wrong number" when his aunt answered the phone. Snow melted on the backs of her gloves, and she felt that strange stirring in her gut. In the dream, it was always snowing. Snow everywhere. Henry said dreams were clues, but for the life of her, she couldn't figure out what her dream wanted her to know.

"Say, Mabel, you find out anything interesting for this Diviners falderal?" Theta asked.

"Oh, all sorts of things. It's in the exhibit," Mabel said without elaborating further. It was her private experience with Jericho, and she didn't want to share it. Especially if Evie was going to blab all of Mabel's personal information without a second thought.

"The full creepy crawly, huh?" Theta pressed. "People who can talk to ghosts. People who can see the future and read objects, like Evil here. People who could, I don't know, burn things, set them on fire."

"Set things on fire?" Mabel scrunched up her face. "Goodness, no! Nothing like that."

"Honestly, Theta, and you call me Evil," Evie said with a laugh. "Where'd you come up with that one?"

The slightest tingle rippled along Theta's fingertips. "Just making conversation. It's freezing," she said and walked faster through the falling snow.

※

In the quaint lobby of the small, traditional Kensington House, the girls waited, until at last a very tall, white-haired man wearing wire spectacles and a tweed jacket strolled inside. He puffed on a pipe.

Mabel poked Evie and Theta. "That's him! Come on!" she whispered urgently.

"Dr. Jung?" Mabel said, rushing to greet him. Evie and Theta followed.

"Yes. I am Dr. Jung."

"Thank heavens! We've been waiting for you."

"Have you?" Dr. Jung's brows formed a V atop his spectacles. "Forgive me. Did we have an appointment?"

"No, but we're desperate to talk to you. It's a matter of some urgency."

The psychiatrist blew out a puff of smoke, considering. He allowed a polite smile. "Well, then, I suppose you had best come this way."

After they introduced themselves, Dr. Jung ushered Theta, Mabel, and Evie into a cozy, handsomely furnished office lined with shelves of important-looking books and bade them sit before settling into a chair himself.

"Now, how may I be of help to you?"

"Doctor, what do you know about Diviners?" Theta asked.

"I thought you wanted to know about acting," Mabel whispered.

Dr. Jung waited for the girls to settle. "Ah. I have heard of them," he said, his Swiss accent neatly clipping the ends of his words. "So. Am I to understand that you are interested in psychic phenomena and the paranormal?"

Theta cut her eyes at Mabel. When Theta had invited Mabel along to the lecture, she'd had no idea they'd end up talking to Jung himself. There was no way around it. She'd have to let Mabel in on the truth. "I suppose so. See, I have a pal, a Diviner, who can walk in dreams. I mean really walk around inside them, like he's awake, seeing everything."

Mabel's eyes widened. "Who is it?"

"Who do you think?" Theta said.

"It's Henry," Evie confirmed.

"Wait a minute—how do you know this?" Mabel swiveled from Evie to Theta. "Why does Evie know?" She swiveled back to Evie. "So you can keep *some* secrets, just not others."

"Honestly, Mabesie, are you going to make me wear the crown of thorns for long?" Evie said through gritted teeth. "I'm *sorry!*"

Dr. Jung cleared his throat, and the girls quieted. "Lucid dreaming, you say? That is quite a power, indeed. Please. Continue."

"Lately, my pal Henry and this other dream walker, Ling—"

Dr. Jung's eyes widened. "There are two?"

"That was going to be my next question," Mabel said, giving Evie a wary glance.

I don't know this one, Evie mouthed to Mabel.

"It's a long story," Theta said. "The point is, they've been meeting up in the dream world in the same place every night—a train station. And from there, they go to some magical-sounding place where they can touch things and smell flowers and . . . well, from what Henry tells me, it's all very real. Look here, Doc, I know it sounds like we're lunatics, but it's true."

Dr. Jung rubbed his eyeglasses clean with a handkerchief. "Your friend and his compatriot walk freely through the unconscious realm. They are at play inside the psyches of many people, as well as engaging with the experiences and memories of all humanity—the collective unconscious."

"Sorry, Doc, you lost me," Theta said. "What's this collective unconscious?"

The psychiatrist hooked his spectacles over his ears again. "Think of it as a symbolic library that has always existed, which houses all our personal and our ancestral experiences and memories, shared knowledge that each individual seems to understand on an innate level, like an inheritance. Religion. Myths. Fairy tales. All of it gains its power from the collective unconscious. And dreams are like a library card, if you will, that provides access to this great archive of shared symbols, memories, and experiences."

"Can it hurt you, though? If you get hurt inside a dream, you wake up. But what about if you're living inside that dream, like my friend Henry? Could something bad happen to him or to Ling?"

"An interesting question. Have you ever heard of the shadow self?"

Evie and Theta shook their heads.

"It's a dark side, isn't it? Like Dr. Jekyll and Mr. Hyde, if I'm not mistaken," Mabel said, and she took some satisfaction in knowing this.

"Yes. That is so." Dr. Jung blew out puffs of spicy tobacco. "Every one of us has a conscious self. This is the face that we present to the world every day. But there is another self, which remains hidden even from our own minds. It contains our most primitive emotions and all that we cannot abide in ourselves, all that we repress. This is the shadow."

The psychiatrist relit his pipe. At the strike of the match, Theta's hands began to prickle.

"Is this shadow self evil?" Evie asked, and for a moment, her mind flashed on John Hobbes and his terrible secret room.

"It depends on how fiercely one guards against the shadow self and to what lengths he would go to protect himself from that knowledge. Such a person doesn't even know he is doing evil. Think again of your Dr. Jekyll and Mr. Hyde. The goodly Dr. Jekyll is, one might say, possessed by his shadow self, Mr. Hyde, who does unspeakable things. Dr. Jekyll projects—that is, assigns—his intolerable qualities onto the split self, Mr. Hyde. That is an extreme example, of course, but it does occur. That is the shadow's greatest power over us—that we do not see it. Once we are conscious of our shadow, we can become enlightened."

"I think my pal Henry has a shadow side—"

"Everyone has a shadow side," Dr. Jung corrected gently.

"How do we get him to stop and wake up?"

"The only way to correct the shadow is to become conscious of it. To accept it and to integrate it into the whole person. Perhaps your friend will find this solution on his own by exploring his dreams, for our dreams wish to wake us to some deeper meaning. All that is hidden eventually reveals itself, no matter how fervently we fight to keep it locked away."

Theta thought about her dreams, of the snow and the horses, the burning village. And Roy. Always Roy. How hard she worked to keep her past in the past, where it couldn't harm her. But now the head doctor was saying she couldn't keep a lid on it forever. The uncomfortable itching in her palms had progressed to a burning sensation.

"Are you feeling well, Miss Knight?" Dr. Jung said, his brow furrowed. "You seem anxious."

"It's, um, awfully stuffy in here is all."

"Actually, it's a bit chilly," Mabel said.

"I-I just need some air. We've already taken up too much of your time, Doctor. Thanks. You've been swell."

Panicked, Theta sprang from her seat. As she did, a book fell from a shelf behind the psychiatrist, knocking over a candle. The flame lit a section of Dr. Jung's coat sleeve, but the psychiatrist snuffed it out before it could truly catch.

"Gee, I'm awful sorry," Theta said, horrified. "I shouldn't've jumped up so quick." She tried to conjure cool thoughts—ice cream, winter wind, snow. No. Not snow.

"All fine," Dr. Jung said, examining his scorched sleeve. He retrieved the book from the spot on the rug where it had landed, spine up, pages fanned, and examined the page. "Hmm. Curious, indeed. Didn't you say you felt too warm, Miss Knight?"

"Yes," Theta whispered.

"What is it?" Evie asked.

"A meaningful coincidence. A powerful symbol from the collective unconscious." Dr. Jung held the book open for them to a drawing of a grand bird consumed by fire. "The Phoenix rising from the flames."

The book was open to page number one hundred forty-four.

THE GREEN LIGHT

Far below the surface of the city, Vernon "Big Vern" Bishop and his men tried to keep warm while they waited for the bootlegger who'd hired them to store a shipment of hooch. The job was simple: Canadian whiskey came in by boat. Before the boat docked, Vernon and his men rowed out, picked up the barrels, rowed back, and hauled the booze into the cavernous old stone tunnels that snaked below the Brooklyn Bridge. For his crew, Vernon had chosen Leon, a big Jamaican who did a little amateur boxing now and then, and a Cuban named Tony whose English was limited, but Vernon got on with the Cubans okay because his wife had come from Puerto Rico and spoke Spanish. From her, Vernon had picked up words and phrases here and there, enough to make small talk.

It was very dark here. The only light came from the lamp on Vernon's digger's helmet, Leon's lantern, and the flashlight Tony gripped tightly.

"¿Cuánto tiempo más?" Tony asked, pacing to keep warm.

Vernon shrugged. "Till the boss man comes."

"Don't like it here," Leon grumbled, his breath coming out in smoky puffs that evaporated in the lantern light.

Vernon was comfortable in the tunnels. As a sandhog, he'd built some of them. That was dangerous work—deep underground, where a man could only dig a certain number of hours a day or else the pressure could get him. But he took pride in knowing that he was responsible for digging out to make way for the city's future—the subways, bridges, and tunnels of tomorrow.

"Telling you, it doesn't feel right," Leon said.

"Don't be bringing that island superstition into it," Vernon chided, borrowing a phrase from his cousin Clyde.

Clyde had served in the all-black 92nd Division during the big war. After it was over, he walked into Harlem decorated and proud, despite the fact that he'd lost a leg to a bullet wound gone to rot. They'd smoked cigars and rolled craps in the back of Junior Jackson's grocery till the wee hours, laughing and drinking whiskey, listening to two fellas cutting each other on stride piano. But Clyde looked haunted. Later, under the yellow-tinged moon, he'd said, "I saw things in that war that a man shouldn't ever have to see. Things that make you forget we're human and not just a bunch of beasts crawling out of the sludge somewhere. And the damnedest part of it all is, I couldn't for the life of me remember what we were fighting for in the first place. After a while, fighting just got to be habit."

Five months later, Clyde had gone down to Georgia to visit relatives. He'd walked into town for a cold drink. The local folks hadn't taken too kindly to Clyde wearing his uniform with its shiny medals and told him to strip it off. Clyde refused. "I fought for this country in this uniform. Lost a leg doing it, too. Got a right to wear it."

The good folks of Georgia disagreed. They dragged him through town tied to the back of a truck, set him alight, then strung him up from the tallest tree. Somebody said you could hear his screams clear over to the next town. His family never even got his medals back.

Funny that Vernon remembered Clyde just now. For the past few nights, he'd dreamed about his long-gone cousin. In the dream, Clyde had no crutch, and his uniform was crisp and clean. He'd waved to Vernon from the front porch of a house with a garden in front and a fine peach tree in the yard, the very sort of place Vernon had dreamed of running himself. Beside Clyde was a pretty girl in an old-fashioned bridal gown and veil. *"Dream with me . . ."* she'd whispered in Vernon's head.

He'd taken it as a sign that everything was going right, that this job for the bootlegger and the extra money might mean a piece of the pie for Vernon at last. But now something about the dream crawled under Big Vern's skin like an itch he couldn't scratch. He couldn't say why.

Down the long cannon of tunnel, he heard a sound. The men jumped up, alert.

"That them?" Leon whispered.

Vernon held up a hand for quiet and stared into the dark, waiting. "No signal."

The bootlegger always shined his flashlight in code: three short blasts. But whoever lurked down in the tunnel wasn't doing that. Vern's muscles went tight. It could be cops. Or rival bootleggers with guns drawn in an ambush.

Vernon strained, listening. What he heard was faint but persistent— a whine like bees trapped inside a house and trying to get out. But deeper. Almost human. It made his skin prickle into gooseflesh. Instinctively, he stepped back.

"What is that?" Leon asked. He raised the lantern. His eyes were huge.

"Shhh, quiet now," Vernon whispered.

They waited.

"You hear it still?" Vernon whispered.

"No," Leon whispered back, but just then, it came again, a little louder. "Told you I don't like this. Let's get out of here."

Vernon gripped Leon's arm. "Can't go till the boss say go."

"Hang the boss! He's not down here with whatever that is."

"You don't just walk off the job with these Sicilian fellas," Vernon warned. "We wait with the booze."

A loud screech reverberated in the tunnel. The men felt it in their teeth.

"Dios mío," Tony whispered.

"Boss or no boss, I'm gone," Leon said.

Tony nodded.

"We go," Vernon agreed.

The men ran. The lantern's wobbly light threw their shadows up the old brick walls in looming, macabre waves. Suddenly, the lantern went out, plunging them into near darkness. There were only Vern's miner's hat lamp and Tony's flashlight now, and they weren't enough. Their frantic breathing was loud in their ears. Vern knew he should calm down, slow his breaths so that he didn't faint. They all knew this. It didn't matter. Whatever lurked in that corridor had them panting like trapped dogs.

"You hear that?" Leon asked, panicked.

The sound was moving closer. They could pick up the individual guttural growls buried inside the collective clamor. What was it? How many?

"It's coming from behind us," Vern said. "Where's the lantern? Leon, get it lit!"

Another screech.

"Leon!"

"Trying, aren't I?"

A screech came from their right and the men went still. It was very close.

"Thought you said it was behind us," Leon whispered urgently.

Vernon swallowed hard. "It was."

"Let's go back!" Leon said and took off running back toward the vault under the bridge.

"Leon! Wait!" Vern called seconds before Leon's scream rang out, then stopped abruptly.

Vernon had always wondered what his cousin Clyde had seen in the war that was too terrible to mention. Just now, he thought he might find out.

"Dios mío," Tony said again. He dropped the flashlight and slid down the wall, putting his hands around his neck. "Ayúdame, Santa María!"

Vernon grabbed the flashlight. "Get up, Tony! We're moving." He hauled the terrified Tony to his feet, half dragging him down a set of darkened stairs leading deeper into the underground. A series of twists and turns later, they came out in an abandoned, partially flooded subway station. High above them, once-magnificent brick ceilings arched down into columns striated with years' worth of water marks. The water was up to Vernon's waist, but he was well over six feet; Tony, on the other hand, was only five and a half feet tall. The water reached his chest as he prayed fervently.

"Not far now," Vernon said. He had no idea how far it was, but he needed Tony beside him.

The water rippled from below. In the distance, a splash bubbled up.

"¿Qué es eso?" Tony whispered, his voice filled with terror.

With a shaking hand, Vernon swept the flashlight's insufficient glow across the wide expanse of the flooded station: The illuminated walls slimed with years of mold and neglect. An abandoned ticket booth sitting like a small mausoleum. Vernon had been in a lot of subway stations, and he knew there had to be stairs leading up and out.

He swung the flashlight beam to the right of the old ticket booth.

A wall.

To the left.

There it was—a corridor!

"Tony!" Vernon whispered. He showed him the corridor in the grainy white light. "Ahí."

Tony nodded. "Sí."

The flashlight winked out. Vernon smacked it against his hand, but it was no use.

The sound was back and no longer confined to the distance. It was all around them.

"Move!" Vernon shouted. "¡Vámonos!"

It was hard to run with the weight of water pressing against their bodies and only Vernon's headlamp to show the way. Vernon bumped into the wall. He gritted his teeth to hold back his scream and plunged his hands under the murky water, searching for the ladder he knew had to be there. His fingers were rewarded with the feel of metal rungs.

"It's here," Vern assured Tony. "Ladder."

The water rippled again with a long and powerful swoosh. Trembling, Vernon swung his head in the direction of the movement, out where the old tracks had been, where only a skeletal fretwork of steel beams now stood.

Just last week, Vernon had celebrated his birthday—twenty-one—in a little joint under the stairs of a brownstone on the West Side. He very much hoped to do the same for his twenty-second. Or maybe he'd gather his small family—his wife and their new baby—and find another place, a better place. Move out to New Jersey or down to Baltimore, where his sister was a teacher. There was a lot of country; he didn't have to spend his years breathing in dirt and gas, hauling whiskey, gasping for air when he got topside, so thirsty he could never get his fill of water. Yes, they'd go—out like the pioneers, questing for their stake, for what the land had been holding in trust for them.

Clack-clack-clack-clack. The terrible sound echoed in the watery chamber as the glowing green things streamed out of the tunnel and down the walls, burning against the dark. Pointed teeth glinted from the mouths that opened to emit those terrible sounds.

Behind him, Vernon heard Tony's screams.

"Tony!" he called, whipping his light around. "Tony!"

But Tony was gone. Only Vernon remained—Vernon and those things in the dark, getting closer. With a shout, Vern was up the ladder and onto the platform, and then he was running. Running like the settlers on the prairie racing to pound their stake into the hard, fertile ground of the heartland, securing their place and their children's places, the generations springing up under the blue sky. Vernon ran toward the faulty light of his headlamp as it bounced across the darkness.

The corridor curved up and to the left. Vernon followed the bend, the terrible guttural screeching filling his ears. Vernon remembered what it was in the dream that had unsettled him. In the dream, Clyde had stood under a lightning storm.

"It's coming," he'd said, and looked off in the direction of a skinny gray man in a tall hat, who laughed and laughed.

Vern's headlamp shook as it illuminated the corridor and what waited for him there. He'd staked his claim in the wrong spot.

"Sweet Jesus," he whispered as the corridor was filled with an angry green light from which there was no escape.

DAY TWENTY

ANTHONY ORANGE CROSS

Henry sat in the Proctor sisters' overstuffed living room drinking bitter, smoky tea with Miss Addie and Miss Lillian while a herd of cats mewled and purred and rubbed up against his trouser cuffs. He made small talk for as long as was socially acceptable, listening to the Proctor sisters' tales of various ailments, discord within the Bennington, and one story about an animal trainer mauled by a circus bear that was particularly gruesome and put Henry off the circus for the foreseeable future. At last, there was a blessed lull in the conversation, and Henry seized his opportunity.

"I was curious about something you mentioned the other day, Miss Adelaide," Henry said. "As I was getting on the elevator, you said, 'Beware, beware, Paradise Square' and 'Anthony Orange Cross....'"

Miss Lillian's cup stopped on the way to her lips. "Oh, Addie, honestly. Why would you bring up such unpleasantness?"

After the carnivorous bear story, Henry couldn't imagine what Lillian Proctor would consider unpleasant, but his heart beat a bit quicker at her words. "Was this Anthony Orange Cross fellow known to you, Miss Lillian? Was he wicked?"

"Anthony Orange Cross isn't a person," Miss Lillian said. She sipped her tea. "They're streets. Or they were, once upon a time. Those names are gone now to the dustbin of history."

"Streets? You're certain?" Henry said, deflating.

"Anthony is now Worth Street. Orange became Baxter. Cross had been renamed Park Street well before we arrived, though most people in the Points still called it Cross."

"We have lived here a very long time. We've seen many things come and go," Miss Adelaide said.

"Near Chinatown, then?" Henry asked.

"Indeed. The intersection of Anthony, Orange, and Cross Streets once formed a little triangle called Paradise Square, down near Chinatown. And it *was* wicked. It was the foul heart of Five Points."

"I'm sorry. I'm not familiar with Five Points," Henry said.

"It was the most wretched slum on earth at one time! A place of thieves and cutthroats, bandits, and women of ill repute. Opium dens and people crowded into stinking, rat-infested rooms to sleep on top of one another. Oh, it was filth and degradation the likes of which civilized people cannot imagine. The mission could only do so much." Miss Lillian tutted, shaking her head.

"The Methodist Mission and the House of Industry," Miss Addie said and put her milky teacup on the floor for the cats. "It provided care and work for the less fortunate. Lil and I volunteered there for a brief spell, helping to rescue fallen women."

Anthony Orange Cross was a forgotten intersection, not a killer. Paradise Square had been a slum. What did any of it have to do with the veiled woman? Henry wasn't entirely sure that she was a ghost. Perhaps she was just a feature of their nightly walks, no more substantial than the fireworks or the children playing with stick and hoop? A message in a bottle delivered long after the writer is gone.

"Do you recall a murder that might've happened while you were with the mission?" Henry asked, a last-gasp attempt. "In Paradise Square, perhaps?"

"Young man, there were murders nightly," Miss Lillian said. "You'd need to be more specific."

"I don't have a name, unfortunately. It's a woman I've seen in my dreams," he said, looking hopefully to Miss Adelaide, who stared into her cup. "She wears an old-fashioned dress and a veil." Henry was losing steam and hope. "She might've had a little music box that plays an old tune. *'Beautiful dreamer, wake unto me . . .'*" he sang.

"*Starlight and dewdrops are waiting for thee. . . .*" Miss Addie sang in a whispery rasp. Her head snapped up. "The one who cries. I've heard her in my dreams, too."

"Now, Addie, you mustn't become agitated. You remember what the doctor said, don't you?" Miss Lillian scolded. "Mr. DuBois, my sister has a weak heart. You mustn't upset her."

"Yes, ma'am," Henry said. He didn't want to exhaust Miss Adelaide, but he needed more information. "I only wondered if the woman in my dreams has a name?"

"The music box! That's it. Yes. Yes, I remember. She came to us at the mission. Only for a few days. Don't you recall, Lillian?"

"No. And I don't wish to. Now, Addie—" Miss Lillian started, but Adelaide would not be stopped.

"I'd been trying to remember. It was there, but I couldn't quite . . ." Miss Addie made a motion as if she were trying to grab something and bring it close. "She didn't speak much English."

"We had a lot of immigrants—they were easily preyed upon," Miss Lillian said.

"She loved music so. Singing as if she were on the stage. Such a sweet voice," Miss Addie said. "Yes, music. And that was how that terrible man reeled her back in."

"What man?" Henry pressed, hoping Miss Lillian wouldn't throw him out for it.

"That Irishman who ran the brothel," Miss Lillian snapped. "I remember it now. He came for her one morning, talking sweetly. He gave her a little music box as a gift. He promised her a husband if she'd agree to go back." Miss Lillian sighed. "That was that. She went away with him. I saw her only once after that. She was sick with opium and riddled with pox all along her pretty face. Syphilis," Miss Lillian hissed. "It had rotted her nose right off, so she wore the veil to hide it. She still had the music box."

"That's it! It's her," Miss Addie said, agitated. "Oh, we are not safe."

"Now, Addie, it was a long time ago," Miss Lillian soothed. "That time is past."

"The past is never past. You know that, Lillian," Miss Addie whispered.

"We are safe. Everything put away in the box," Miss Lillian said calmly, and Henry didn't know what she meant.

"What happened to her?" he asked.

"I haven't any idea." Miss Lillian sighed and brought an orange tabby up onto her lap, scratching him lovingly behind the ears. "But I imagine it was a bad end."

"She's connected to him," Miss Addie muttered. "They all are. I know it."

"Now, Addie..."

"Connected to whom, ma'am?" Henry asked.

Addie looked at Henry with wide eyes. "The man in the hat. The King of Crows."

"Addie, you're entirely too riled. I'm afraid we must say good-bye to you, Mr. DuBois."

Miss Lillian rose, signaling the end of the visit. Henry thanked the Proctor sisters for their time and the tea. Miss Addie reached for his china cup, frowning at the contents. "I don't like the pattern of those leaves, Mr. DuBois. Some terrible day of truth is at hand. For you or someone you love. Careful," she whispered. "Careful."

Henry was still thinking about the Proctor sisters' odd tale as he raced into rehearsal. It was the sort of story he'd usually share with Theta—"You won't believe what the Jolly Vampire Sisters just told me!"—if they weren't on the outs. To top it all off, he was twenty minutes late, thanks to an all-too-brief nap he'd fallen into, unable to fend off sleep. In the dream, Louis had waved to him from the *Elysian* as it churned up the Mississippi. Henry tried desperately to reach the boat, but the morning glories were so thick they blocked his path. And then the vines climbed up his body, wrapping around his neck until he woke, feeling choked.

At the loud bang of the theater doors, Wally's head turned on his thick neck. "Well, well, well," he said, glancing up the aisle. "If it isn't Henry. DuBois. The Fourth. All hail."

"S-sorry, Wally, I...I felt sick, and I guess I fell asleep."

Wally sighed. "You been sick a lot lately."

"Sorry. I'm jake now, though," Henry said, slipping into his spot at the piano. He wiped a hand across his clammy forehead. Sweat dampened his armpits and the front of his shirt. Onstage, the rest of the cast and crew were crowded around Theta, congratulating her on the day's splashy newspaper article heralding ZIEGFELD GIRL RUSSIAN ROYALTY.

"Now that we're *all* here," Wally said pointedly, "let's take the Slumberland number from the top!"

Dancers scampered into position onstage, tugging at bloomers and securing tap shoes. Henry's earlier fear faded, replaced by exuberance as he opened the score. Finally, one of his songs had made it into the show. He put fingers to the keys, playing along, his excitement vanishing quickly as the tap-dancing chorus girls sang along:

> "Don't you worry, don't be blue
> Everything you dream comes true
> Sing vodee-oh-doh, Yankee-Doodle-Doo
> And shuffle off to Slum-ber-laaand!"

Henry's breathing went tight, as if he'd been punched. The song was awful. His song. They'd ruined it. And they'd done it behind his back. Henry stopped playing.

"What's the matter? You lose your place?" Wally asked. "You feeling sick again?"

469

Henry gestured to the piano score. "These aren't my words. Where's the song I wrote?"

"Well, uh, Herbie smoothed it over a bit," Wally said.

"It wasn't quite polished. I just gave it some zip and pep," Herbie Allen said from the back row, as if he were Mr. Ziegfeld himself.

Onstage, everything had come to a standstill.

"What's the big idea? Are we running the number or aren't we?" one of the girls asked.

Wally wagged a finger. "Henry, play the song."

"No," Henry said. It was a word he used so infrequently that he was startled by the feel of it on his tongue. "I want to play *my* song."

Whispers of gossip rippled down the chorus line.

"Everybody needs help now and then. Don't take it personally, old boy," Herbie said. Henry wasn't a violent fellow, but right then, he had the urge to punch Herbert in his smug mouth.

"How else would I take it, Herbert, when you massacre my song?"

"Now, see here, old boy—"

"I am not your boy," Henry growled.

The entire cast was silent as they looked from Henry to Wally to Herbert and back again. Suddenly, Mr. Ziegfeld's voice boomed out from the very back row.

"Mr. DuBois, you are a rehearsal accompanist. I do not pay you for your musical interpretation." The impresario marched down the aisle and stood in the middle like the commander of a mutinying ship.

"No, Mr. Ziegfeld, I'm not. I'm a songwriter. My songs are a damn sight better than this garbage."

One of the midwestern chorus girls gasped.

"Forgive my language," Henry added.

Mr. Ziegfeld gave Henry a flinty stare. "Your time will come, if you behave, Mr. DuBois. Now. Let's get back to the number. We have a show to rehearse."

The great Ziegfeld turned on his heel. The dancers shuffled quickly into formation. Just like that, Henry had been dismissed, no discussion. In his head, he heard his father's voice: *You will go to law*

school. You will uphold the family name. You will never see that boy again.
A dam gave way inside Henry.

"Mr. Ziegfeld!" Henry called, rising from the bench. "You keep saying we'll add more of my songs, but it seems like I never can get that chance. It always goes to some other fella."

"Henry..." Theta warned, but Henry was beyond warnings.

"I'm out of waiting, sir. If you don't want my song, well, I guess you don't need me. I'll pack up and go."

The great Ziegfeld didn't even rise from his seat. "I wish you luck. But you'll get no recommendation from me."

In her tap shoes, Theta *clip-clop*ped to the front of the stage and cupped a hand over her eyes to cut the glare of the lights. "He's just tired, Flo. He doesn't mean it."

"Don't talk for me, Theta. I mean every word."

"You're free to go, Mr. DuBois. Herbie, could you play for us, please? Wally—from the top."

As the horrible number started up again, Henry marched down the aisle and pushed through the theater doors onto noisy Forty-second Street. The enormous marquee loomed over his head. Foot-high black letters promised AN ALL-NEW REVUE!

"All new!" Henry shouted to passersby, who looked at him as if he were crazy. "That's right, folks! Step right up. We know you bore easily. Your shiny playthings lose their luster. Even now, you're asking yourselves: What's next? What am I missing? Will this make me important?"

It was all a machine that required constant feeding—Henry hated the machine, and he hated himself for wanting the sort of admiration it promised, as if he had no worth unless someone was there to applaud it.

"Hen!" Theta raced after him in her skimpy dancing costume and no coat. "Hen! Whatsa matter with you? Are you crazy? You just lost your job!"

"I am acutely aware of that fact, dear girl." Henry tried for humor, but his words were as brittle as damp chalk.

"You gotta apologize to Flo. Tell him you haven't been sleeping and you lost your head. He'll take you back."

Henry's anger was a live thing, a snake in his hands. How many times had he been forced to choke down how he felt in order to make someone else happy? How many times did he put away his own needs to accommodate somebody else's? Well, he wouldn't do it anymore. Not this time. Not over something as important as his music. "Is that what I should do, Theta? Walk in there with my hat in my hand, beg for scraps, pretend I'm nothing, be grateful for what I get? Should I spend my hours swallowing it down every time Herbie's awful songs get into the show instead of mine? Should I be polite when Wally lets that idiot ruin my song without even asking me what I think?"

"It's just a matter of time—"

"I. Am tired. Of pretending." Henry bent his head back. The marquee letters blurred with each blink of his eyes. "They're never gonna let me in, Theta!" Henry shouted. He was unused to shouting. A lifetime with his father had taught him to hold everything in. But now it tumbled out like the contents of an overstuffed closet. "Don't you get it? I don't fit. The songs I want to write aren't the songs they want to hear. All this time, I've been trying to figure out what they want and give it to them. I don't want to do that anymore, Theta. I want to figure out what I want and write those songs. Songs I care about. And if I'm the only one singing 'em, so be it." Henry wiped his eyes quickly with the heel of his hand. He tucked his hands under his armpits and turned away from Theta.

"Hen, nobody believes in you more than me. But right now, you gotta have a job. I'm just being honest."

It was direct, like Theta usually was. That was one of the qualities he had always loved about her. But right now, it infuriated him.

"If that's true, if we're just being honest here," he said, giving *honest* a bit of snarl, "why don't you go in and tell Flo all about Memphis? In fact, why don't you call up the papers and give 'em an exclusive: 'Fake Russian Royalty in Love with Harlem Poet.'"

For a moment, Theta's mouth opened just slightly. He'd struck a blow. Wounded her with her own weapon. But then the practiced cool slid down her features like a gate over a closed shop. "We don't all get to live in dreams, Hen. Some of us gotta live in this world. No matter how unfair."

With that, she stormed back into the theater, slamming the door behind her.

"Goddamn it," Henry muttered.

The train started with a jolt, and then it was snaking through the dark miles underground. Henry leaned his head against the window. Had he just walked out on the Follies? He had. Every muscle in his body ached. The taste of blood soured his lips, and he ran a tongue over a chapped mouth. When had he gotten so run-down? He needed more sleep was all. The gentle rocking of the train, the darkness, and the exhaustion made Henry's eyelids flutter.

His head snapped up. A spot of drool cooled against his chin. He wiped it away, and the matron next to him smiled. "You should get more sleep, young man," she said kindly.

"I suppose you're right, ma'am."

The train stopped suddenly between stations, and Henry sighed as they waited for whatever the trouble was to be cleared. The droning hum of the train crawled up Henry's spine. It was an odd sound—not really mechanical. More...animal, like a swarm far off in the tunnel. A flicker of movement drew his eye to the train window. The lights inside the train bleached the darkness outside so that, at first, Henry saw only his reflection. He pressed his face against the glass. There was a girl on the other set of tracks. She was crouched down, knees to the sides, arms resting on the tops of her bent legs as if she was ready to spring. In the dim work light, she was nearly gray.

Henry looked around, but no one else on the train seemed to

notice the girl outside the window. He turned back to the window, cupping his hands on either side of his face to cut the glare. The girl's head snapped up. She saw him, and her jaws opened and shut, her rotted needle-teeth coming together each time in a fierce bite.

The droning hum he'd heard earlier had increased to a fast war cry.

"D-do you see that?" Henry asked the other passengers.

"See what, Henry?" the matron asked.

"That girl on the ..." Henry's heart thundered in his chest. "H-how do you know my name?"

The matron transformed into the veiled woman.

"*Dream with me ...*" she growled.

In the dark of the subway, the wraithlike girl's mouth unhinged, and from deep in her throat came an inhuman shriek as she sprang toward the train.

"Get away from me!" Henry shouted, jumping from his seat.

A businessman backed away, hands up. "You were having a bad dream. I tried to wake you."

Quickly, Henry reached out and grabbed the man's sleeve, testing it.

"Now, see here!" the man said, yanking his arm back. "That's quite enough, young man."

"You're not a dream. You're real," Henry said and laughed, relieved. His shirt was sweated through.

The other passengers stared. A mother pulled her son closer.

"... Must be drunk ..."

"... Or he might be sick ..."

The train hissed into the Fulton Street station, and Henry realized he'd slept through his stop. But he couldn't stay on the train another minute. When the doors opened, he bolted and ran up the steps to the streets, welcoming the cold blast of air that greeted him, hoping the entire time that he was awake.

"Extra! Extra!" a newsie shouted. "Park Avenue Princess Catches Sleeping Sickness! Mayor Orders Crackdown!"

Henry tossed a nickel at the newsie. "Hey, give me a little punch to the gut, will you?"

The newsie blinked. "You tryin' a get outta work or somethin', Mister?"

"Just land one, will you?"

The newsie buried his fist in Henry's gut and Henry reeled, coughing. "Yep. Definitely awake. Thanks, kid. I owe you."

The newsie shook his head. "If you say so."

☀

By the time Henry made it to the Tea House, he was trembling.

"What happened to you?" Ling said, pouring him tea.

"Bad dreams," Henry said, warming his hands on the hot cup. "I found out about our mystery woman, though."

Henry told Ling about his revelatory afternoon with the Proctor sisters.

"Anthony, Orange, and Cross were streets," Ling said in wonder. "George led me to that intersection, too."

"Very well. I'm all ears. What does it mean, Mademoiselle Chan?"

Ling tapped her spoon absently against the side of her cup. "Wai-Mae's ship docks in San Francisco tomorrow. I think George has been trying to warn me that she's in danger of suffering the same fate. That she needs my help to avoid it."

"What should we do?"

"I have to tell Wai-Mae. Tonight. She needs to know."

"I don't envy you that task," Henry said, slipping back into his coat.

"She'll be heartbroken," Ling said.

"Somehow, I think she's not the only one," Henry said gently, and Ling felt near tears. She had grown very close to Wai-Mae and hadn't realized how much she'd been looking forward to having her as a friend in New York. Now it was all in jeopardy.

475

At the door, Henry stopped. "I still don't understand what the Beach Pneumatic Transit Company has to do with all of this, though. An old train station? Doesn't make sense."

Ling shook her head. "I can't know everything."

Henry grinned. "That's a relief."

"Henry..." Ling started. She had a terrible feeling of misfortune that she couldn't place.

"Yes, darlin'?"

She shook her head. "Nothing. Same time tonight?"

"Pos-i-tute-ly," Henry said, enjoying Ling's pursed-lip annoyance.

ENOUGH TO SAVE US

In the dream that finally found her, Adelaide was a girl of seventeen, with hair gilded by summer sun. There was the big house and the well and the wagon Papa would use to drive them into town on Sundays. It was all just as she remembered it, when she allowed herself the luxury of remembering. Nostalgia, like morphine, was best in small doses. Drifting through the dream was the sweetest girlish singing she'd ever heard, something exotic to her ears. It was exquisite pain, this song, as if the string of notes had crawled inside her like a long vine, twining itself to her longing. Addie's heart was full of want. She could burst from it.

"Elijah," Addie said, naming the desire.

And then, like magic, he was there, shadowed on the edge of the cornfield with the old church steeple rising in the distance.

"Free me, Addie," he whispered.

There was a reason Addie couldn't do this before, but she couldn't think of it now, not with her lover so close and her need so strong.

"Will you do that for me, Addie? Will you?"

"Yes," Addie whispered. Her face was wet in the moonlight. "Anything. Anything."

In her sleep, Adelaide Proctor rose from her bed and walked to her dressing table. She opened the cabinet and took out her music box. She wound the key at the back and smiled as the tiny French dancing girl twirled round and round to the sweetly tinkling bells of a song that had been popular before the Civil War. Addie remembered her last dance with Elijah, when he took her hand and promenaded her down the center. Oh, how handsome he was, smiling across the aisle at her as they waited for the other couples to take their turn at the reel. How impatiently she waited for the excuse to hold his hand once more.

Addie passed into the night-shadowed parlor. The man in the stovepipe hat sat in the Morris chair. His broken, dirt-caked fingernails clicked against the chair's wooden arms, one, two, three, one, two, three. He nodded at Adelaide.

In her head, she heard Elijah: *"Free me, my love."*

A sleepwalking Adelaide Proctor left her apartment carrying the box in her arms. The hall lights flickered as she passed. At the end of the hall was a garbage chute, which led down into the incinerator. She tugged down the handle. Its metal maw gaped open, hungry. Adelaide removed the iron box's lid. One by one, she tossed in the contents— first the finger bone, then the tooth and the lock of hair. She rubbed her thumb across the tintype of Elijah, reluctant to part with it even in sleep. Finally, she threw it in, listening as it clattered down the chute.

Humming the music-box tune, Adelaide slipped back into her moon-drenched apartment, stumbling past the mewling cats circling her ankles anxiously and into her bed, where she could embrace that perfect world she'd been promised on the other side of sleep. And then she was dreaming of soldiers and of light streaming through the trees like electric rain, and the man in the stovepipe hat was laughing as they screamed, and everywhere, everywhere was death.

DIVINER AND DIVINER

New York is a city short on patience, cleanliness, clement weather, and citizens who hold faint opinions. It is not a city short of people trying to make a career of being famous, no matter what the opportunity. The ribbon-cutting ceremony exists for just this sort of thing. Mr. Ziegfeld had recruited New York City's most famous Diviner and her beau to cut the ribbon on his dazzling new Ziegfeld Theatre, trumpeting the Follies' new revue, *Diviners Fever*. Mayor Jimmy Walker was on hand, as well as some of the Follies' biggest stars. So was a smug-looking T. S. Woodhouse.

"Hiya, Sam," he said, sauntering up. He licked the tip of his pencil. "Beautiful day for a ribbon cutting. Why the long face? Say, you and your fianceé aren't on the outs, are you?"

"Why would we be?" Sam said. He didn't trust T. S. Woodhouse a bit.

"Oh, I don't know. Young love is restless love." Woodhouse smiled. It was not a warm smile. "Say, how'd a fella like you end up with a dame like Evie O'Neill?"

"Whaddaya mean by that?" Sam said. He matched Woody's smile, but his eyes were hard.

"I figured her for riding in cars with pretty boys from Harvard or oil barons from Texas with a lotta money and only a little sense."

Sam shoved his hands in his pockets and glared. "Guess Lamb Chop doesn't go for that after all."

Woodhouse held Sam's gaze. "I suppose you're right. Say, there's a pretty interesting rumor going around about you and your Lamb Chop," he said.

"Yeah? What's that?"

"That the whole romance was cooked up by WGI's publicity hounds."

Sam had had enough. "Get lost, Woody. If you were anybody worth knowing, you'd be higher up on the masthead and wouldn't have to make chump change writing gossip about Sheiks and Shebas for the *Daily*. Radio's gonna put you news boys ten feet under soon enough, anyway. You might wanna hustle yourself a new job."

Woodhouse's self-congratulatory smile turned cold. "That so? What do you think I should be writing about instead? Bootleggers and bookies? Or maybe secret government programs, like Project Buffalo?"

Sam felt squeezed of air. "Whaddaya know about Project Buffalo?"

"Ah, gee, sport. What would I know, a bum like me?"

"Where'd you hear about Project Buffalo?" Sam pressed.

"What are you two talking about over here?" Evie said.

T. S. Woodhouse's gaze flicked from Sam to Evie and back again. He smiled. "I was just wondering which headline would be more interesting tomorrow: 'Sam 'n' Evie: Still Sparking' . . . or 'Splitsville'?"

Sam glared at Evie. "You told him about Project Buffalo?"

"I-I . . . it isn't what you think, Sam."

"Oops. Looks like I've sparked a lover's quarrel," Woody said, triumphant. He took out his pencil. "Anything you'd like to say for the late edition?"

Sam took Evie's hand, pulling her over to a corner of the dais. "How could you do that? I told you: no reporters. You promised to keep it a secret between you and me, Evie. I trusted you," Sam said, his words quiet but angry.

"Sam, could we talk about this later?" Evie matched his tone. "I'll explain everything, but . . ." She nodded toward the large crowd. "People are watching."

"Oh, sure. I see. Wouldn't want to disappoint your adoring public,"

480

Sam said, hurt joining the anger. He didn't trust many people, but he'd trusted her. "Well, I don't care anymore, Evie. I've had enough. You know what? Maybe I'll just blow this whole thing wide open. Tell you the truth, I'm tired of going to parties every night, anyway. I'm tired of playing your pretend fiancé. Tired of you. Just tired."

A secretary gestured for them. "Miss O'Neill? Mr. Lloyd? You're needed."

"Sam . . . please." Evie reached for Sam, but he shoved his hands in his pockets.

"Come on. Let's get this over with," he said and walked away.

The Ziegfeld girls danced their way through a Diviners-inspired musical number. Theta was giving it her all, but even her talent couldn't save the lousy song, and Sam hoped Henry hadn't written it. Out of the corner of his eye, he saw Evie glancing over at him nervously. She looked miserable. Maybe he shouldn't be so hard on her, but he couldn't help it. He was furious with Evie. Project Buffalo was his life, not hers. She knew what it meant to him. How could she be so cavalier about it?

The dancers cleared off. Mr. Ziegfeld spoke a few words, and then Sam and Evie were on.

"Gee, that was swell, Mr. Ziegfeld," Evie chirped into the WGI microphone. "It doesn't take a Diviner to see that this show will be the elephant's eyebrows!"

"Isn't she terrific, folks? And how about a hand for that lucky fella of hers, Sam Lloyd?" Mr. Ziegfeld gestured to Sam, who gave a half-hearted wave. He came and stood next to Evie, but they were miles apart.

"Evie! Sam! Evie!" the reporters called. T. S. Woodhouse raised a finger again and again. Evie answered the other reporters' questions but refused to call on him.

"Gee, Miss O'Neill, I've got the distinct impression you're ignoring me, and I'm all balled up about it," Woodhouse shouted, garnering chuckles from the crowd.

"Why, Woody, I couldn't ignore you if I tried," Evie said pointedly.

"It's about this silly rumor I heard floating around town that maybe this romance is a buncha hooey. *Daily News* readers want to know: You two lovebirds on the level, or is this some kinda scheme cooked up by WGI to keep the ink wet on headlines and make the radio station money?"

There was murmuring in the crowd.

"I wouldn't expect you to understand about true love, Mr. Wood-house. You manage to cheapen everything," Evie spat back, defiant, but Sam could hear the panic in it. "Sam and I happen to be mad for each other."

"Yeah?" Woodhouse sneered. "I guess that's why you're standing so close together."

As if on command, Evie's hand shot out for Sam's. Sam didn't return the gesture.

"Ah, yes. True love," Woodhouse said, just like W. C. Fields. The remark had done its work, though.

"When's the wedding?" a man in the crowd shouted, a challenge.

"Yeah, when's the wedding?" a reporter chimed in. "You never say. Or maybe there's not gonna be a wedding?"

"Sam, are you excited about the big day?" another reporter asked.

For the first time, Sam looked over at Evie. Her eyes were wide and she clutched a handkerchief tightly in one fist. This charade meant everything to her, he knew. She bit her lip, and he knew she was plead-ing with him silently: *Please don't spoil it with the truth.* He'd gone into this phony romance scheme with his eyes open. But somewhere along the way, his feelings had changed. He'd wanted more. He'd let his guard down. And now she'd gone and sold him out. He could do the same to her right this minute. He could tell everyone the truth about their cooked-up romance. It would serve her right.

"Sam?" the reporter prompted. "I said, are you excited about the wedding?"

"What fella wouldn't be?" Sam said, looking away.

They played their parts, waving to the crowds shouting their names and pressing themselves against the police barricades hoping for a closer look, hands reaching, needing that reflected glory.

"Miss O'Neill, I certainly hope you can't read anything bad in these," Mayor Walker joked as he handed Evie the ribbon-cutting scissors for the new Ziegfeld Theatre.

"Here goes!" Evie said. She snipped through the bow and the ribbon fell away. The onlookers cheered.

Down in the throngs of people, a haunted, hollow-eyed man in a tattered soldier's uniform pushed his wheelchair toward the platform, muttering to himself. People stepped back as he knocked into them.

"Watch it, buddy," a man growled, but the broken soldier didn't hear him.

"The time is now," the soldier said, over and over.

Onstage, Evie moved to the right and accepted a bouquet of flowers from a fan.

"The time...the time is now," the soldier whispered fervently as he reached into his pocket for the revolver. All eyes were on Evie, who lifted her arm in a wave, blowing kisses to the crowd.

The soldier raised the gun. It shook in his hand. "The time is now," he moaned.

Evie's smile was still bright as she turned in the soldier's direction. Her eyes saw the gun in his hand but couldn't quite make sense of it, as if he might be holding a fish or an albatross. Sam was quicker. Time slowed and sharpened at once. Blood thrummed in his ears, blocking out the gasps of the stunned crowd. These people receded in Sam's mind. There was only Evie, the man, and the gun. Sam wasn't close enough to tackle the man before he could get a shot off. There was no time to think it through. Sam pushed Evie aside and thrust his hand toward the man with the gun. "Don't see me," he growled. He poured every ounce of will into that one movement. Sam felt as if he'd been struck by a tuning fork. His body trembled from the effort. His knees buckled, but Sam held on.

"Don't. See. Me."

The soldier's haunted eyes emptied of all consciousness, like a sleepwalker's. Sam lunged forward and pried the revolver from the man's grime-coated fingers. Several people closest to the man with the gun had also gone slack, heads cocked toward the sky, lost in some private reverie.

But the rest of the sizable crowd watched it all.

Police raced to the stage and surrounded the still-dazed soldier. In the mass of onlookers and reporters, incomprehension gave way to astonishment—had they really seen what they thought they had? Murmurs became shouts. People raced forward from everywhere at once.

"What's happening? What is it?"

"Sam Lloyd is what happened! He saved Evie O'Neill's life!"

The story passed from one person to the next with breathless excitement, drawing still more people. They overflowed the banks of the sidewalks, snarling traffic. Taxi drivers honked their horns and shook their fists through their open windows while the cops tried to contain the swelling crowd before things got completely out of hand.

"Did I just see what I think I saw?" one reporter asked

"He put a hex on that fella, like hypnotizing him!" another answered.

"He's a Diviner, too!" a lady shouted from the back.

"He's a Diviner! A Diviner! A Diviner!" They were all shouting questions now, pressing closer, cheering, clapping, calling Sam's name. A flashbulb popped, and then another. Evie put up a hand to keep the light from hurting her eyes. T. S. Woodhouse's sneer had been replaced by an expression of surprise.

"Evie, did you know? Did you know your fella was a Diviner, too?" a society reporter asked.

A teary Evie stared at Sam. "I . . ."

"She's had a shock—give her some air!" somebody shouted.

"She didn't know," T. S. Woodhouse said, loud and firm. He moved his hand through the air as if he were blocking out tomorrow's big headline. "'Seer Didn't See This Coming for Sweetheart'!"

"'Their Love is Diviner and Diviner!'" another reporter yelled.

The flash again. Knifepoints of white.

"Come on, Sam, put your arm around her!"

Evie had never seen Sam like this. Bewildered. Frightened. A little lost. His shirt was sweated through, and he looked ill and possibly ready to faint. She was still reeling from all the excitement, but she understood this much: Sam had done it for her. He'd risked his life to save hers. Evie slipped her arm through his, anchoring him. No one could see her gently easing the tension from his fist. No one else could see her fingers gripping his, keeping him close. The crowd swelled onto Sixth Avenue, causing a traffic jam. The policemen had given up and were redirecting traffic to the side streets. The mayor had his hands up, reassuring people, asking for calm.

Beside Evie, Sam trembled.

"I've got you," Evie said. She reached over and wrapped his arm around her waist, letting him hold on to her as if she were a buoy. This pleased the people, who cheered and clapped and whistled. She could feel Sam's pulse thumping.

"He was going to shoot you," he whispered, dazed. "I had to stop him."

A reporter got up in Sam's face. "Hey, big hero! Look this way!"

Evie gave the shutterbug a push. "Leave him alone!" she growled.

"C'mon, Evie. Your fella is big news."

"He's not your story right now!" Evie tried to protect Sam, but there were too many people surging forward, and she lost her grasp on his fingers.

"Sam!" Evie shouted, reaching out, but the celebrating crowd had him. Strong men lifted Sam up in the air on display, moving down Sixth Avenue like a saint's procession on feast day.

The broken soldier had come to as the police dragged him away through the streams of people, who booed and hissed and spat at him.

"They never should've done it," the soldier cried over and over.

"Evie! Evie! Hey, outta my way—that's my pal over there!"

Evie turned to see Theta running toward her, frantic. "Oh, Evil, you okay, kid?"

And with that, Evie burst into tears and let Theta hold her.

※

All afternoon, Evie searched for Sam. She even stopped by the museum, where she was surprised when Mabel answered the door.

"Hi, Pie Face. Is Sam here?"

"No. Do you want to wait for him?"

Over Mabel's head, Evie spied Jericho lurking in the hallway. He saw her and walked back into the library without so much as a hello.

"No. Thank you. If you see Sam, will you tell him I'm looking for him and to call me either at the Winthrop or WGI?"

"Sure. Say, is everything all right?"

"I certainly hope so," Evie said.

Evie made one last appeal via the radio at the end of the show. "This is the Sweetheart Seer with a message for Sergei—I'm sorry. Please come home. And by home, I mean the Knickerbocker."

WGI was so ecstatic about the news that Sam was a Diviner that they insisted on hosting a party that evening at the Knickerbocker Hotel. The telephone operators and secretaries had spent the entire afternoon burning up the telephone lines, inviting every swell in town, as well as any reporter with more than an inch of column space. By eleven thirty, the hotel's ballroom was packed, but Sam was nowhere to be found, and Evie's heart sank.

As she stood listening to a portly man in a tuxedo drone on about the stock market—"Safest place in the world to put your money. Put it all in today. Every last cent!"—a bellhop delivered a note on a silver tray. "A message for you from Miss Anna Polotnik?"

Evie tore open the envelope. The note read, simply, "*Roof. Now.*"

"Won't you excuse me?" Evie said sweetly. She sauntered gracefully from the room, then hiked up her dress and ran for the stairs.

"There you are," Evie said, huffing and puffing as she came out onto the hotel's roof. "I've been looking everywhere."

"Congratulations. You found me." Sam leaned forward, resting his forearms on the wide stone ledge. "How's the party?"

"Oh, you know. Lots of hot air and silver gravy boats. Aren't you cold?"

"Yes."

"Do you want to go inside?"

"No."

"Are you all right?"

"Sure."

"Are you lying?"

Sam shrugged and stared out at the jagged city. It was clear he wasn't coming down, so Evie propped open the door with her purse and went to stand beside him. Searchlights had been positioned down below, compliments of WGI. White-hot, they swept back and forth, bouncing off anything with shine.

"That time we went to the Tombs to see Jacob Call," Evie said softly. "That policeman looked right at us. You put up your hand, and it was like he couldn't see us. Like we were cloaked in some way."

Sam didn't answer.

"How long?"

Sam shrugged. "I never know. Depends on how suggestible the person is. I've had folks who last twenty seconds and some who come around quick—I've been caught with my hand in the cookie jar, so to speak. Usually, it's about ten to twelve seconds. Long enough to grab the goods if you're fast. And I am."

"I meant how long have you been able to do this *don't see me* routine?"

"Since I was a kid, maybe eleven, twelve? We'd moved to a tough part of Chicago. These older boys used to bully me, knock me around for being a Jew and for being scrawny and little. There was no way I could take 'em all on. But once I learned that I could do that," he said, putting out his hand, "it was like hiding in plain sight. It made me feel like I wasn't this small, sick kid at their mercy. For the first time, I felt powerful."

"Why didn't you tell me before, when you knew about me?" Evie asked.

Sam let out a long exhale. "I needed it to be a secret until I found my mother."

"But now it's not a secret any longer."

"No. I reckon it's not."

"Why did you do that today?"

"You're honestly asking me that?" Sam looked at Evie, and suddenly, she knew. *Don't see me* was more than Sam's Diviner power; it was his entire worldview. It was how he'd gotten along in life, keeping hidden, only letting people see what he wanted them to see. His whole life was a sleight of hand. And he'd risked it all. For her.

"I...thank you for saving my life," Evie said quietly. Her face was hot and her head buzzed. She was too afraid to face Sam, so she stood beside him, and side by side, they stared out at the twinkling city. "I'm so sorry about what I said to Woody. I promise I thought I was helping you, Sam."

Sam let out a long sigh. "I know. Who knows? Maybe that rat can find something useful after all. I suppose that soldier fella was right out of his mind. Shell shock."

"I suppose so," Evie said. "The funny thing is, I know that soldier. At least, I've met him before."

Sam turned his face sharply toward Evie. "What? When?"

"My first week in New York. And then again after my radio show the other night. I tried to put money in his cup and he grabbed my wrist—"

"Doll, you shoulda told me."

"It was nothing—"

"That's not nothing. Especially now."

Evie turned and leaned her elbows against the roof's stone ledge, lifting her eyes to the night sky. Smoke and steam from unseen sources blew past in great billowing hiccups. Vague impressions of stars hid in New York's perpetual neon haze.

"What happened after he grabbed your wrist?" Sam asked.

"He said, 'I hear them screaming. Follow the eye.'"

"Follow the eye..." Sam said, thinking. "You think he meant that eye symbol we saw on my mother's file?"

"Why would he know anything about that?"

"I don't know. But it seems like a pretty big coincidence him saying that, then coming after you with a gun."

A door opened somewhere inside the hotel and the sounds of the party drifted up from below: a woman's braying laughter; the high, fast tempo of the orchestra. The door closed again, leaving only the everpresent hum of the sleepless city.

"You and Jericho..." Sam started, then he shook his head. "Nah. Forget it."

He'd been about to ask if she still carried a torch for Jericho, Evie knew, and she was glad he'd stopped himself. She still had feelings for Jericho. But she had feelings for Sam as well. It was confusing and, yes—if she was perfectly honest—more than a little exciting to have two handsome fellas interested in her. But she wasn't sure she wanted the responsibility of loving anyone right now. The truth was, she was afraid that when she fell hard for a boy, she'd lose herself along the way. She'd seen it happen to lots of girls. They'd go from drinking gin, driving fast cars, and boldly shimmying in speakeasies to these passive creatures who couldn't make a move without asking their beaus if it would be okay. Evie had no intention of fading behind any man. She didn't want to slide into ordinary and wake up to find that she'd become a housewife in Ohio with a bitter face and an embalmed spirit. Besides, things you loved deeply could be lost in a second, and then there was no filling the hole left inside you. So she lived in the moment, as if her life were one long party that never had to stop as long as she kept the good times going.

But right now, in this moment, she felt a strong connection to

Sam, as if they were the only two people in the world. She wanted to hold on to both him and the beautiful moment and not let go.

"Sam," Evie said.

He turned his face to her. His mouth—why had she never noticed how perfect his mouth was? Impulsively, she kissed him once on those perfect lips and stood back, waiting. His expression was unreadable, and Evie's stomach fluttered.

He shook his head. "Evie. Don't."

Evie's cheeks went hot. For months, he'd been toying with her. And now that she'd put herself out there, he wasn't interested. "Why not? Because girls shouldn't kiss first?" She didn't mean for it to sound so angry, but she was hurt and embarrassed. "Am I supposed to look up at you through fluttering lashes, all phony innocence, and wait for you to feel moved? I burned that rule book a while ago, Sam."

"I don't care about that," Sam said. "Just...please don't kiss me if you don't mean it."

All of Evie's old fears bubbled up. She wanted to kiss Sam, but she was afraid of what that meant. What was right? Why was it so hard to know? "I mean it right now," she said.

Sam kicked at a bit of gravel on the roof's floor. "That's always your answer, isn't it? Don't think about tomorrow."

A melancholy undertow threatened. In a minute, it would drag away any hope of momentary happiness. "Now is the only thing you can count on, Sam. It's all we really get," she said quietly, and felt that it was the truest thing she'd said in a long time.

For a second, the searchlights fell across their scared faces. Then the bright, restless columns moved again. They reached into the heavens and disappeared, unanswered prayers.

Evie reached for Sam. She was interrupted by the arrival of the *New York Herald*'s society reporter. "There you are! We've been looking for you two lovebirds all over. Gracious, it's freezing up here! Come down to the ballroom. Everyone's waiting."

Evie still wasn't sure if Sam wanted to keep up the charade they'd started.

"Guess we'd better go make nice," Sam said, offering his arm, and Evie took it, grateful.

"Guess we'd better," she said.

Dutifully, Sam and Evie marched into the ballroom to applause. Beside her, Sam was skittish as a colt. Evie squeezed his hand and he squeezed back. "Just another con game," she whispered, and the smirk he put on was just for her, she knew. People crowded around, patting Sam's back, telling him he was a hero. Then the white-haired emcee quieted everyone.

"I know we've already had New Year's. But let's usher in the New Year…of the Diviners!" the man barked while people raised their glasses and cheered. "Ready? Here we go: Ten…nine…eight…"

Their counting became a swelling chorus of everything that was good, everything that was hoped for. All Sam and Evie could see was each other.

"Four…three…two…one!"

Confetti and streamers rained down from the ceiling. Horns and blowers bleated their tinny congratulations. The air was giddy with celebration. The little orchestra took up with "Auld Lang Syne," everyone warbling along drunkenly to the familiar tune, looking sharp and smug, as if it were all so clever, because they were celebrating a new New Year they'd just invented. As if they believed they could rewrite time itself whenever it pleased them, in the same way they revised whatever truth dared to inconvenience them.

"We'll take a cup of kindness yet for auld lang syne. . . ."

"Happy Diviner New Year, I guess," Evie said, a little breathless.

"To hell with it," Sam said and wrapped Evie in his arms, kissing her fiercely.

WAKING UP

Ling and Wai-Mae sat among the soft flowers in the meadow. The sun was bright and warm. The hills glowed, a constant gold. But for the first time in many nights, Ling couldn't enjoy it fully. As Wai-Mae talked happily of her impending arrival in New York and her wedding day, Ling's misery increased. She needed to tell Wai-Mae what she suspected about O'Bannion and Lee, but she couldn't bring herself to say it. She didn't want it to be true—for Wai-Mae's sake and, selfishly, for her own.

Waiting for her courage to find her, Ling kept her eyes trained on the village below, basking in the beauty of the sun glinting on the red tile roofs. "It's pretty. Is it your village back home?"

"No. It is a place I saw once and remembered. A place I loved." Wai-Mae blinked up at the canopy of leaves. "They had the most beautiful opera there. It was so magical! I had been very sad and homesick, but I sat in the balcony watching the opera, and for a while, I was not sad anymore. I escape to it in my mind whenever I need to." As Wai-Mae poured cups of tea for them, she flicked a glance at Ling. "Perhaps you need an escape. What's troubling you, Little Warrior?"

"I…" Ling's mouth had gone dry. Looking into Wai-Mae's guileless face, all of Ling's usual honesty deserted her. Wai-Mae would be heartbroken.

"It's about this sleeping sickness, isn't it?" Wai-Mae said, and Ling didn't correct her. Wai-Mae waved the thought away with a gesture. "You worry too much, sister. For now, leave your troubles behind."

"I can't leave them behind."

"Of course you can! Troubles have no business here in our perfect world. If we don't like something here, we will simply change it."

Ling's sadness edged into annoyance. "You don't understand. People have died. These are my neighbors. This is my neighborhood. It's making trouble for us."

A tiny centipede crawled across Wai-Mae's leg. "They hate the Chinese. They have always hated us. Calling us names. The men, so full of hate, until the night when they come for you," she said bitterly, crushing the bug with her thumb and wiping her hand in the grass.

"What do you mean?"

Wai-Mae looked up. For a moment, her expression was stormy, but then she blinked, and her smile returned. "Oh, dear Ling, I don't like to hear about such things, to know that they are upsetting you."

"Sometimes we have to hear upsetting things."

"No. Not here. Never here." Wai-Mae smiled, letting the sun warm her face.

"Yes. Even here. Especially here, away from the noise." Ling took a deep breath. She'd put the truth off long enough. "Wai-Mae, I went looking for your matchmakers, O'Bannion and Lee. I've asked my uncle and at the library. There is no such firm. They don't exist."

Wai-Mae's brow furrowed. "What do you mean?"

"I believe there are some bad men bringing you over not to marry, but to..." Ling's tongue couldn't form the words. "To work."

"Don't be silly! My uncle arranged everything. Mr. O'Bannion will meet me at immigration," Wai-Mae said decisively. "I will have a husband and a new life in New York."

"I don't think so. Wai-Mae, they mean to trick you. You'll be a servant." Ling swallowed hard. "Or worse."

"Why are you saying these terrible things to me?"

"Because I don't want you to be hurt! They'll make you a..." Ling struggled with the word. "...a prostitute, Wai-Mae. You'll never be married. You...you shouldn't get off the ship."

Two silent tears rolled down Wai-Mae's cheeks. Her lips trembled. "It can't be true. My passage is paid. My uncle arranged it."

"I'm sorry," Ling said.

"I won't hear any more!"

"I'm trying to protect you!"

"I won't hear it!" Wai-Mae stood up. She backed away, shaking her head. "No. You are wrong. I will be a wife to a merchant in America. A good man! A respected man!"

"Wai-Mae—"

Wai-Mae spun around, her mouth tight, her eyes hard. "You had no right to do that. To spy on me like an immigration official, questioning everything! I thought we were friends."

"We are," Ling said. She reached out for Wai-Mae's hand, but Wai-Mae yanked it away.

"You will not take my dream from me!" Wai-Mae growled deep and low, her face hardening with anger, a transformation as startling as any they'd made themselves inside the dream. In the cup, the tea boiled over, splashing onto Ling's hand. She gasped and dropped the cup as the liquid scalded her. An angry red welt rose up across the length of Ling's thumb.

She'd been hurt inside a dream.

And Wai-Mae had done it.

Cradling her hand, Ling leaped up and marched toward the wood.

"Where are you going?" Wai-Mae asked, fearful.

Ling didn't answer.

"But it isn't time for you to wake yet! Let's play opera. Or . . . or we can do more of your science, if you like!"

Ling did not turn around.

"Everything will be fine, sister! I know it will," Wai-Mae said, trotting after Ling. "Please, don't worry. Here—we can make something wonderful."

Ling didn't want to make anything else. The dream had turned sour. She kept walking.

"Come back, please!" Wai-Mae called. "You promised! You promised!"

Ling ran down the hill and through the forest, calling Henry's name.

❄

Henry and Louis lay side by side on the dock with their feet in the cool river, enjoying their last night on the bayou. His train was scheduled to arrive in New York tomorrow, and there'd be no need for these nightly visits anymore. Tomorrow couldn't come fast enough for Henry.

"Henri, there's somethin' I need to tell you 'bout," he said, suddenly serious, and Henry's stomach tightened, like sensing the first drops of rain at a long-planned picnic.

"Sounds like an awfully serious talk to have without your shirt on," Henry joked.

Louis sat up. "I shoulda told you 'bout it before. Concerns you."

"Are you trying to tell me you're not coming to New York after all?" Henry propped himself up on his elbows and stared out at the sun patches dotting the river. "You got the ticket, didn't you?"

"That ain't it," Louis said, and Henry was relieved.

Louis took a deep breath. He twirled a fallen leaf between his fingers, making it dance like a ballerina. "Just before you left town, your daddy tried to get me to go away. He sent a man over to Celeste's with a fat envelope fulla money and said it was all mine if I'd agree to leave town on the next boat up the river and never see you again."

"Bastard," Henry muttered. His father ruined everything. He didn't want to be related to a man like that. How did you learn to be a man if the one who raised you was a bully who wasn't worth your respect? "How much money?"

"A thousand dollars," Louis said.

A sinuous fear wrapped itself around Henry's heart. "I suppose a fella could live pretty well on that, if he had a mind to."

"I reckon he could."

Henry pulled up a handful of grass. "Did you take it?" He gave Louis a sideways glance and saw the hurt on his face.

"That what you think of me?"

"I'm sorry, Louis. I didn't mean it. I didn't really think you'd do that," Henry said, cursing himself. He wished he could take it back.

Louis let out a long sigh and blinked up to the sky.

"Please, Louis. I'm sorry."

Louis shook his head. "You know I can't stay mad at you, *cher.*" He kissed Henry on the cheek, but it was halfhearted, Henry could tell. Louis was still nursing the wound.

Gaspard's bark sounded up on the path. "What manner of trouble that dog got himself into now?" Louis said, hopping up.

Henry followed, but all he really wanted to do was pull Louis back down on the dock and kiss him. He felt lousy that they'd fought, and he wished he could take back what he'd said.

Gaspard dug furiously at the morning glories, barking and growling as if he'd cornered an animal.

"Gaspard!" Louis shouted. "Get away from there right now!"

"He's just being a dog," Henry said. "Probably got a bone there somewhere. After all, it's his dream, too."

"He shouldn't be digging in there. Gaspard!" Louis whistled, but the dog wouldn't budge.

Louis took a step forward onto the morning glories and stumbled. He put a hand to his head, hissing.

"Louis!" Henry righted him.

Louis stepped back. "I'm...I'm all right, Henri. Gaspard!"

Henry marched through the blanket of purple flowers and shooed Gaspard away. The dog bounded over to Louis. The spot where he'd been digging was dirt and nothing more.

"Henry!" Ling called from the path.

"Ling, what's the matter?" he asked as she reached him. "Is Wai-Mae with you? Say, what happened to your hand?"

Ling's voice shook. "I want to go back, Henry. I want to wake up."

"You want me to wake you up, like last time?"

"No. Together. We need to go together."

Henry looked over at Louis with regret.

"Go on, *cher.* I'll see you soon enough," Louis said. "You can't refuse a lady."

"Just one more day," Henry said, hoping he hadn't ruined everything.

"One more day," Louis said.

"You need to wake Louis up," Ling said, and from her expression, Henry knew not to argue.

"Louis," Henry said, "it's time for you to go on back to the cabin now. And then, in a few minutes, you'll wake up, and when you do, you can watch the sunrise and have some chicory coffee before you catch your train to New York."

Louis laughed. "All right, then, Henri. All right." He climbed the steps to the cabin with Gaspard wagging along behind. From inside, Louis's fiddle picked up the strains of "Rivière Rouge," right where he'd left off, and then it went quiet.

"What's got you so spooked?" Henry asked Ling.

"Not here. I'll explain later. But I don't want to be here anymore," she whispered.

"But we didn't set our alarms, darlin'. We're stuck till we wake up on our own."

"Then let's see if we can find a different dream somewhere else," Ling said. "Even if we go back to the streets where we come in. If we enter through Devlin's, maybe we can reverse it."

"Sounds reasonable. We just reverse our steps. Which way is the station from here?" Henry asked, looking around.

Through a gap in the trees, he spied the dark mouth of the tunnel.

Ling followed his gaze. "We're not supposed to go in there."

"Seems like it's either through the tunnel or we wait until we wake up."

"But one of us could wake up first, stranding the other one here," Ling said, shivering. A question had been lurking in the depths of her. Only now could it surface. "Henry, what happens if you die in a dream?"

Henry shrugged. "You wake up."

"Even here? Even here, where everything's real?" she said, feeling the heat from her burn.

Light pulsed against the velvety dark of the tunnel.

"It's happening again," Henry said.

The edges of the trees unraveled, as if there was some sort of energy surge.

"What is that?" Henry said.

"I don't know," Ling whispered, fear stealing most of her breath. Wai-Mae's words swam back to her: *I'm frightened of that wicked place. If we do not trouble her, she won't trouble us.*

The lights were dimming, as if the dream itself were going to sleep for the night. The hideous growling had returned, though. It made Ling shiver.

"I want to know what's inside. I need to know," she said, despite her apprehension.

"We're just reversing our steps," Henry agreed. He offered his hand, and Ling took it, and together they stepped across the threshold into the dark.

"Why is it so cold?" Ling whispered, shivering as her breath came out in wispy puffs.

"Don't know," Henry said, his teeth chattering slightly. There was something tomblike about the tunnel, as if he and Ling were trespassing on a private crypt, and Henry was relieved to see the station glowing up ahead. "Not too far." Henry pointed to the distant circle of golden light. "See? 'Second star to the right, and straight on till morning.'"

"What nonsense are you talking now?" Ling *tsk*ed.

"*Peter Pan*," Henry said.

"Just keep walking," Ling said.

Ling stumbled over something in the dark, and when she crouched down to see, the old bricks on the sides of the tunnel flickered, then steadied into a greenish glow, like a mercury-vapor lamp warming up.

"Ling!" Henry whispered urgently, and Ling left whatever lay in the dirt to join him. They drew closer to the wall and the glowing bricks. Something was happening inside the stones, like watching a little show on a nickelodeon screen.

"Is there a film projector?" Henry said, looking around, but it was clearly coming from the wall itself. There were all sorts of stories playing out inside the glowing bricks: A little girl having a tea party with her parents. A soldier laughing around a table with his mates. A man waving to an adoring crowd.

"What is this?" Ling said.

Henry walked from one brick to another and then another, studying the images. "I think...I think these are other people's dreams," Henry whispered.

Henry stepped back to take in the whole of the wall. It stretched up and up, glowing screens of dreams as far as he could see. From where he stood, the images reminded him of the circuitry in a vast machine, as if the snippets of lives they watched there were powering the entire dream world—the station; the train; the bayou, forest, and village where Ling and Henry played to their hearts' content each night. But here and there, a brick would fade out, too, as if all the energy had been drained from it. As if those dreams had died and needed to be replaced by other dreams—more circuitry for the machine.

Something caught Ling's eye, and she put her face close to the brick to get a better look. Wide-eyed, she turned to Henry, motioning him over. "Do you see it?"

"What am I looking for?"

"Her," Ling whispered on a puff of cold breath.

Henry got right up on the tunnel wall. In the corner of the flickering image was the veiled woman, watching the dream. She walked from brick to brick, from dream to dream, like a night watchman making sure the factory was safe. The surface of one of the bricks wobbled, as if there were a snag in the film. And in those shards of dark, Ling and Henry saw the nightmare twin of the man's good dream. In it, he ran from a pack of inhuman creatures through the subway tunnels.

"Hungry ghosts," Ling said, looking at Henry with frightened eyes.

Suddenly, all the bricks lit up, showing the same image: the veiled woman running into the tunnel, terrified, the bloody knife in her hand, as she crawled into the silent train car. And then there was nothing but darkness.

A shrill, bestial scream echoed the length of tunnel.

"What was…" Ling couldn't finish. For down at the spot where they'd entered, a figure now appeared, a dark silhouette in a dress, drawing closer.

"Henry…" Ling whispered.

He nodded. "Start walking. We're just reversing our steps."

Hand in hand, they walked toward the ring of light and the promise of the station at the end of it. But no matter how fast they walked, the station stayed just out of reach.

"It keeps getting farther away," Ling said. "Like it wants to keep us here."

Behind them, there was snarling and scratching in the dark.

"I can wake you up. You know I can."

"Don't you dare! We go together or not at all," Ling said.

"All right. I'm going to give you a suggestion, then. Let's see if you can imagine us someplace else, in a different dream. Ling, why don't you dream about…about…" His mind was blank. "Dream about the New Year! Dream about the lion dancers and moon cakes and fireworks."

Ling shut her eyes tight, but she was too frightened. Her mind couldn't think of anything but those terrible sounds. It was like a swarm approaching. But a swarm of what?

Henry cried out.

"Henry?" Ling opened her eyes. Henry was nowhere to be seen. "Henry!"

Ling was alone with whatever lurked in the dark.

☀

Henry came to on the floor of his room in the Bennington, the sheets tangled around his ankles, his heart pounding. He'd fallen out of bed, and it had been enough to wake him. Ling was still there in that terrible place. From where he lay, he could see the telephone on the side table in the hall, but the post-dream paralysis kept him anchored to the floor, counting down the seconds until he could move again.

☀

The swarm in the dark grew louder.

Ling tried to run but stumbled, putting a hand to the wall to steady herself. The picture inside the stone was disrupted. One by one, the bricks showed the same image of the veiled woman's face. Serrated teeth glinted beneath the netting. But it was the ghost's dark eyes that unsettled her most—they were fixed on Ling's.

A soft ringing sounded in the tunnel, but it was drowned out by the hideous guttural whine. Glowing fingers pushed through the walls as if the tunnel were giving birth to a dozen nightmares at once.

"Who dares disturb my dream?" The veiled woman drew closer. In her hand, a knife shone.

Ling shook. She wanted to close her eyes, but she couldn't tear them away from the things slithering out of the tunnel walls, and the queen leading them.

Wake up, Ling thought. *Please let me wake up.*

The soft ringing was mingled with the bestial noise. And then it rose above the din, becoming a brash, insistent alarm that surrounded

Ling, capturing her full attention. Her body went heavy as the dream faded into a gray blankness.

"Ohhh," Ling moaned in her bed. Her body ached horribly, but she didn't care. She had never before been so grateful to be awake.

Through her closed bedroom door, she heard her mother complaining angrily. "A wrong number. I'd like to see whoever that was have *his* sleep ruined. . . ."

Ling managed a weak smile. The telephone. That's what had brought her back. Henry. Henry hadn't left her.

She looked down at her hand.

The angry burn was still there.

THE SHADOW MEN

The sedan carrying the two men crept steadily along rain-drenched roads. Both men were of roughly the same height, neither too tall nor too short, too fat nor too slim. They were dressed in the same dark suits, pressed white shirts with starched collars, and deep gray fedoras pulled down snugly on heads of closely cropped hair that fell on the color spectrum somewhere between dun and dirt. They were unremarkable in appearance, men meant to disappear into their surroundings, leaving no trace of their ever having been. When they stepped into a store or a roadside cafe, the owners of these establishments would be hard-pressed to remember any details about them. The men were courteous. Kept to themselves. Paid the tab, left a tip, and did not make a mess. For the men were well acquainted with messes and the cleaning thereof.

The men drove. Sometimes their drives took them to small towns in the middle of the country, to houses where anxious mothers listened to their questions and patted the hems of aprons gone gray with the years and from a lack of coins in the cookie tin.

We're simply following up on this article in the local paper about your neighbor's son, the Diviner? When did he first exhibit these Diviner talents, as you say?

Did you or anyone else see these ghosts?

Have you ever heard him make mention of seeing a funny gray man in a stovepipe hat?

No, I'm sure you're not in any danger, but such people should be watched. You needn't worry. We'll take care of that. Just go on and live your normal life.

But remain alert.

Report anything suspicious.

The windows of a roadside cafe smiled a golden welcome into the night.

"Pie sounds good, Mr. Adams," the driver said, angling off the road.

"I do like pie, Mr. Jefferson," the passenger replied.

Inside, it was warm. A few locals bent their heads over plates of eggs and sandwiches, just a few islands of humanity, together in their aloneness. The men took their seats and blended in. The waitress poured two cups of hot black coffee and brought out plates of apple pie, and the men finished both. The cafe had a radio. A program burbled from the speakers, some girl preacher leading sinners to Jesus: "Let the Holy Ghost be your senator and your congressman...."

"You fellas from around here?" the waitress asked, clearing the empty plates and leaving the bill.

"Not far."

"What line of work you in?"

"We're salesmen..." Mr. Adams glanced at the waitress's name tag. "Hazel."

"Oh? Whatcha selling?"

He smiled. "America."

"Would you fellas like more coffee for the road?" Hazel the waitress asked.

Mr. Adams gave an apologetic smile. "I expect we should be moving on," he said, taking on the vocal inflections of the locals in the cafe. Even speech patterns could give one away. "Thanks for the pie."

He paid the bill, tipped a dime, and stepped out into the brisk air with his partner. Dusk hung gnarled garlands of winter clouds over the rolling hills.

"Telephoned Mr. Hamilton. He'll confer with the Oracle," Mr. Jefferson announced. He worked at his teeth with a toothpick.

"Nifty. Let's tend to that other business."

They drove the sedan to a less friendly part of town, down into a ravine where the long fingers of neon barely reached. The driver opened the trunk and hauled out the hog-tied girl, forcing her to her knees in the dirt. He removed her hood, and she took in shaky gulps of air, blinking at the unfamiliar surroundings. Her face was snot- and tear-streaked.

"Wh-where are we?" she asked.

Mr. Adams leaned against the back of the sedan. "We're going to ask you again: Have you ever spoken to a creature of immense power, a gray-faced man in a stovepipe hat?"

The girl shook her head. Fresh tears slid down both cheeks. "P-please, Mister. I was just playing at that card-reading business. I'm not a Diviner. I d-don't know n-nothin' about that." She sniffled, unable to wipe her nose, and the snot ran free. "I just wanted some-body to pay attention to me."

Mr. Adams smiled. "And here we are. Attentive."

The girl started to sob. Sobs were an annoyance.

"You're absolutely certain you're telling us the truth now?"

The girl nodded violently.

Mr. Adams let out a long, weary sigh. "Pity."

In the blinking white light of the roadside arrow—THIS WAY TO PARADISE!—the Shadow Man was rendered nearly gray, a shadow's shadow, as he pulled on his leather gloves. He opened his case and selected a length of wire.

"What are you doing?" the girl asked. Fear had taken her tears from her.

Mr. Adams wrapped the ends of the wire around his gloved hands, pulling it taut. "Defending democracy."

Later, the Shadow Men stood in a field under an empty night sky pierced by the false hope of winking light, the delayed SOS of dying stars. Mr. Adams finished taking a piss. He zipped up and wiped his hands on the girl's scarf, then set it alight, watching as the flames crawled up the length of fabric like a flock of orange birds swirling toward the sky. His face was mottled by smoke. The burning scarf grew too hot to hold, and he dropped it in the dirt.

"That's done, then," Mr. Adams said. "What's next?"

Mr. Jefferson folded back the newspaper to the small article circled in black. Another Diviner in another nameless town.

Mr. Adams opened the passenger door. "And miles to go before we sleep."

The long road cut through night-hushed land, over hills and down into rain-swollen valleys, past moldering scarecrows and graveyards and telephone poles with timber arms outstretched like Toltec gods. It wound around sleeping towns, the silent factory whistles and the quiet school bells. It pressed against the straining borders of the prairies and showed up in the dreams of the nation's people as a symbol; the pursuit of happiness needs endless thoroughfares. On the edges, the ghosts peeked through spaces between the trees, remembering, attracted to the restless yearning of the people, to the pull of a country built on dreams.

The driver sang a tune about a girl named Mamie who loved her way to hell, loved the Devil and loved him well. The passenger read the day's newspaper, licking his finger to turn the pages. The story was about another teacher fined and jailed for teaching evolution. A lawyer had mounted a defense. Some people protested at the courthouse with Bible scripture painted on signs.

"Do you think it's true?" Mr. Jefferson said, breaking the silence.

"What's that?"

"That we came down from the trees? Just a bunch of apes in suits."

"Makes as much sense as the other theory," Mr. Adams said.

Mr. Jefferson chuckled quietly and took up his song again. Far off, a dark mass of clouds roiled on the horizon. The road purred beneath the sedan's wheels as they turned their unceasing revolutions.

THE LAST DAY

MULBERRY BEND

All morning, Ling had been able to think of nothing but last night's unsettling dream walk and what she and Henry had discovered inside the tunnel. The burn still hurt. As soon as she had a moment at the restaurant, she'd telephoned Henry, catching him on his way out the door.

"I'm just on my way to Grand Central to meet Louis's train now," he said. "I promise to bring him straight to the Tea House. We can talk about it then," he promised and hung up.

At lunch, Charlie Lee stopped by the Tea House to let Ling know that his grandfather had returned from Boston, and as soon as she'd finished cleaning the tables, Ling took advantage of the afternoon lull to visit Chang Lee at the Golden Pearl, bringing him an offering of oranges for the coming New Year. Chang Lee was nearly eighty, but his mind was as sharp as ever, and Ling held out hope that he might know something helpful to put her own mind at ease about Wai-Mae.

"I understand from my grandson that you had a question about the neighborhood—some matchmakers, was it?"

"Yes, Uncle. A firm called O'Bannion and Lee," Ling said eagerly. "Do you know it?"

"Yes," Mr. Lee answered and said nothing more. But she could read the judgment in his silence, and her earlier hope that they might turn out to be reputable matchmakers after all waned. "They had an office here once," Mr. Lee said at last. "It was in the Bend."

"The Bend?"

"Mulberry Bend."

Mulberry Bend. Wai-Mae had been correct about that after all.

"O'Bannion and Lee," Mr. Lee continued. "Not matchmakers. *Procurers.* They promise girls passage to America from China to marry wealthy husbands. And once the girls are here in America..." Mr. Lee shook his head sorrowfully. "The girls are sold. Prostitutes forced to work to pay back the debt of their passage here. The girls are poor, alone in a new country, with no laws to protect them. What can they do? They are trapped."

"Why hasn't anyone stopped them?"

"Someone did," Mr. Lee said. "They were murdered. Right down the street."

"I-I never heard about a murder."

"I imagine not. O'Bannion and Lee were murdered in *1875*."

"In 1875?" Ling repeated.

"Yes. Murdered by one of the poor girls they'd ruined. She plunged her dagger into each man's heart." He shook his head. "They were bad men. I remember seeing her sometimes. An opium addict. She played a little music box."

A buzzing began in Ling's belly. "Did she wear a veil?"

"Yes. She did. How did you know that?"

The buzzing raced up Ling's neck to her scalp. She felt dizzy. "Where is Mulberry Bend, Uncle? I'd like to see it."

"You see it every day."

"I'm sorry. I don't understand."

"It's called Columbus Park." Mr. Lee spread his hands wide. "Mulberry Bend was razed in 1897, and the park was built in its place. Mulberry Bend has been gone for decades. And so have your O'Bannion and Lee." He blew on his fingers, as if scattering dandelion fluff to the wind. "Ghosts."

THE THREE-TEN FROM
NEW ORLEANS

Henry paced the platform of track ten on the lower level of Grand Central, watching down the tracks as if it were his future arriving in billowing clouds of steam. A fresh red carnation poked up from his lapel. At last, a mournful whistle-moan announced the approach of the train. Henry's pulse beat in rhythm to the wheels, *chugga-chugga-chugga-chugga*. The metal beast slid past. Henry craned his neck to check each window, but the faces at the glass were blurs. The train stopped in a long, sighing hiss. A uniformed man shouted, "Now arriving—the three-ten New York and New Or-leeeans Limited!"

Doors opened. Happy passengers trundled off and into the arms of waiting family and friends. Henry trotted up and down the platform, his heart leaping each time a handsome dark-haired young man came down the steps, but none was Louis. Porters loaded suitcases and trunks onto trolleys and wheeled them away. The teeming platform emptied of people until only Henry and the porters remained. Had he somehow missed Louis in the crowd?

"Excuse me," Henry called up to a porter stepping back onto the train. "I'm looking for a friend who was on the three-ten. Are there still passengers on board?"

The porter shook his head. "No, sir. Nobody left on the train. They're all off now."

"Are you sure?"

"Yes, sir. Not a soul left."

He must've missed him. Louis was probably upstairs now in the wide lobby, suitcase in hand, his head tilted back, his mouth hanging open as he took in the grandeur of the big-city station. Henry raced up the stairs and into the main waiting room, walking briskly between the long wooden pews, where people sat reading newspapers or fussing with children. He thought he saw Louis walking toward a telephone booth, so he hurried after him, calling Louis's name.

"Can I help you?" the man said, turning around. He was easily ten years older than Louis.

"Beg your pardon. I thought you were someone else," Henry said and went back to walking the length and breadth of Grand Central. Henry's excitement had now turned to fear. He remembered how hurt Louis had been when he asked him about the bribe. For all his good nature, Louis could be thin-skinned about a slight. What if he was so hurt by Henry's careless remark that he'd decided not to come after all?

Then again, what if Louis had simply missed the train?

Hope restored, Henry hurried to the ticket window. "Pardon me, when is the next train in from New Orleans?"

"Half past six this evening," the clerk answered.

Henry sat on a bench and waited. He was still waiting at half past six. And still at eight o'clock, when all the other passengers had gone off with their families. By nine o'clock, as the janitors pushed brooms across the wide marble sea of Grand Central's main waiting room, and the tracks had gone mostly quiet, it was clear that Louis wasn't coming at all.

Henry pushed out into a bright-lights city that had lost its luster and made his way down to a club he knew on Barrow Street in the Village. He'd wanted to show Louis everything, but now he just wanted to get drunk or punch somebody. Maybe both.

"Whiskey," Henry said to the bartender. He slapped down the money he'd earmarked for his night out with Louis. It didn't matter now. Henry gulped it down, enjoying the burn, then threw down twenty dollars and opened his flask, offering it to the bartender.

"Would you like to make a contribution to the Feeling Sorry for Myself Fund? It's a very worthy charity, I assure you," Henry said.

With a shrug, the bartender filled the flask to the top.

Henry was well on his way to being drunk when he stumbled to the speakeasy's telephone booth and dialed his number at the Bennington. He rested his head against the folding glass door and listened to the tinny ringing coming through the receiver while he drank from his flask.

On the fifth ring, Theta picked up. "Nobody's home," she said, her usual greeting, and Henry wished he were sitting next to her at their messy kitchen table.

"Is this Czarina Thetakovich of the Orpheum Circuit?" Henry slurred. "Collect call from that cad, Henry DuBois the Fourth."

There was a slight pause.

"Please don't hang up," Henry whispered.

"Hen? Where are you? Whatsa matter?"

Henry stared at the phone booth's wooden ceiling. Tears streamed down his face. *You can stop your sniffling, Hal. Men don't cry.* That was what his father had always said. Well, Henry was a man, and he had a lot to cry about.

"Louis never showed up. I spent the piano-fund money and made you mad, and all for nothin', Theta. I'm sorry. I'm sorry."

"Ah, Hen," Theta sighed. "Just come home."

Henry wiped his nose on his sleeve. "Yeah?"

"Yeah."

"You still my best girl?"

"You can't get rid of me that easy. We're family. Come home."

"Okay. I will," Henry said and hung up.

But first, there was something he needed to do.

Henry barreled down the streets of Lower Manhattan, past quarantine plasters and dark, closed businesses with signs in their windows reading THIS ESTABLISHMENT CLOSED BY ORDER OF NEW YORK CITY DEPARTMENT OF HEALTH. He was still drunk when he reached the quiet borders of Chinatown. The streets were nearly deserted, and eerie in their quiet. The Tea House was mostly empty, but Henry could see Ling inside. He waved to her and gestured to the alley, and a moment later, she joined him there.

"Imaginary science club member Henry DuBois the Fourth reporting for duty," he slurred. He tried to salute, lost his balance, and banged into a garbage can. "Shhh," Henry said, settling the top on it.

"Are you drunk?" Ling whispered.

"As usual, your powers of observation are acute, ma'moiselle."

"What's happened? Where's Louis? I thought you were meeting his train."

"Ah. Now we come to the heart of the matter. Or the lack of heart. One of us, it seems, lacks heart. He never showed. Ling, I need you to go in with me. I need answers."

"I don't think that's a good idea."

"Really? I think it's a spiffing idea."

"You're drunk."

"You're observant. Say! Have you considered becoming a scientist?"

"And you're a bad drunk. Henry, listen to me: The dream world isn't safe."

"I know. Ghosts. Monsters. Things in tunnels." Henry slumped against the wall. "And that's precisely my point: What if something happened to Louis last night? What? You're making a funny face."

Ling took a shaky breath. "I found out about O'Bannion and Lee. They died in 1875. They were *murdered*, Henry. By one of the girls they tricked. A girl who wore a veil and listened to a music box. I don't think we should go back in, Henry. Not tonight."

"One hour in the dream world. That's all I'm asking. I can't get to the bayou without you. It takes both of us. You know that."

"You need sleep. Real sleep, Henry. We both do. Let's talk tomorrow."

Henry looked up at the cold, dead stars.

"I don't believe in tomorrow much anymore," he said.

When Henry returned to the Bennington, he found that Theta had left a note: *"Meeting Memphis. Back soon. Welcome home, Piano Man."* A crisp five-dollar bill peeked up from the top of the piano-fund jar. A piece of masking tape had been affixed to the front. PIANO FUND—DO NOT TOUCH, it read.

Henry fumbled with the metronome. Vaguely, he was aware that he was drunk and angry and hurt, and that was a bad way to go into a dream walk. But he didn't care. He needed to see Louis. He needed answers. And if Ling refused to go with him, he'd go it alone, see if he could get there on his own steam. The metronome's steady tick worked its magic, and Henry was out in seconds, the heaviness of the alcohol pulling him more deeply under.

When he woke inside the dream world, he wasn't on the streets of old New York. Instead, he stood on the platform of the train station, which glowed with an extra polish tonight. Everything appeared washed in a golden haze. Henry smiled. He'd done it. He didn't even question how he'd done it.

"I've tumbled into Slumberlaaaand," he sang as he stumbled toward the dark tunnel, impatient for the train.

Henry thought about the night before and all they'd seen there. He wavered at the tunnel's threshold for another few seconds. But then all he could think about was Louis.

"Awww, to hell with it," Henry said and stepped inside.

THE ACE OF SPADES

While the Sweetheart Singers warbled her theme song and Mr. Forman purred the show's introduction into his microphone, Evie dabbed at her face with a handkerchief and looked out at the audience, where people waited hungrily with their objects. Her mind was on Sam. Theirs was supposed to be a pretend romance, nothing more. But then Sam had saved her life, and she'd kissed him. She'd wanted to kiss him—that much was clear. His kisses had been passionate and tender and dizzying; Evie hadn't wanted to stop. When the party broke up at last, and Evie headed home, she glanced through the taxi's rear window to see him standing there in the middle of the busy street watching her leave, his hands shoved into his pockets, a sweet grin on his face as the cars and taxicabs zoomed around him, horns honking angrily. The deal with Sam was supposed to make Evie's life easier. Instead, she was more confused than ever.

"And don't forget that the Sweetheart Seer will be the special guest of the Museum of American Folklore, Superstition, and the Occult at tonight's grand Diviners exhibit opening, beginning at the *spoooooky stroke* of deepest midnight! That sounds rather *crrreepy-crrrrawly*, Miss O'Neill," Mr. Forman prompted.

"Yes. Rah-ther," Evie said tightly. Through the glass of the engineer's room, she could see Mr. Phillips, who did not look pleased to have his radio used in such an unscripted fashion. "Shall we bring up our first guest, Mr. Forman?"

Mr. Forman took the hint. "Ladies and gentlemen, please welcome to the Pears Soap Hour stage—Mr. Bob Bateman!"

To polite applause, a handsome man came forward. He seemed sweetly nervous. "How do you do, Miss O'Neill?"

"I'm doing much better now that you're here," Evie shot back, enjoying the audience's laughter. "How can I be of help to you today, Mr. Bateman?"

"It's awfully nice to meet you. You're such a swell girl and all."

"Gee, Mr. Bateman, that's awfully sweet of you to say," Evie said. "Oh, you brought me a comb. Golly, I hope this doesn't mean that my bob looks a fright!"

More laughter. It was a great audience, a great show—one of her best. She hoped Mr. Phillips was paying attention.

"Oh, no, Miss O'Neill. You look beautiful," he said, and Evie actually blushed.

"Careful there. This young lady's engaged to a Diviner," Mr. Forman interjected, to the crowd's delight.

"He's a lucky fella," Mr. Bateman said, and Evie's smile wobbled just a bit. She no longer knew what game she and Sam were playing.

"This comb belonged to my best pal, Ralphie," Mr. Bateman said, and Evie snapped back to the moment.

"Oh. Uh-huh," she said.

"He died during the war."

There were clucks of sympathy from the audience.

"Gee, I'm sorry," Evie said. "My brother was a war hero, you know."

"Yes. I've heard that. I figured you might be sympathetic to an old Army man like me. The thing of it is, when he was over there, Ralphie married a French girl on the quick, but I don't know her name and, well, the family has been trying to find her all these years. I'm sure you understand. I thought maybe you could get a name for us?"

"Of course," Evie said quietly. She put her hand on Mr. Bateman's. "I'll do whatever I can."

Mr. Bateman put the comb in her hands. It was just an old tortoise comb, something you could get at any drugstore. Nothing special.

Evie closed her eyes. She rubbed her thumb over the tips of the teeth. Then, when she was ready, she held it between her palms, pressing gently, and waited for information.

But the comb didn't seem to want to yield its treasures to her. To get at its memories, she'd need to go deeper. That was unpredictable on the radio. But Bob Bateman was a war hero, and everyone was waiting. Evie would not send him away with nothing. Gritting her teeth, she dove further under, concentrating so hard that she could feel sweat prickling along her upper lip and trickling down her spine. Evie forgot caution. She cared only about getting a read, no matter what it took.

Her head jerked back as the vision flared. The sensation was a dizzying one. She was running. No. Something was moving. The scenery. Trees. Rocks. More Trees. Seen through a window. Ah! She was on a train. Evie breathed through, searching for her footing in the memory, and was rewarded with a steadier picture. Yes, she was in a train compartment crowded with soldiers. A card game was in play on the small tray table. A skinny, dark-haired boy sprawled across his seat, writing in his dairy. There was no girl in sight. Perhaps she was elsewhere on the train. Evie would find her.

"Anybody know where we're headed?" the diary writer asked. He seemed nervous. His eyes. There was something familiar about his eyes. Brown. Sad.

"They never tell us nothin'," the card dealer answered around the cigarette in his teeth.

"Just seems funny they didn't tell us."

"We'll find out soon enough," the dealer said. "Who's in?"

The longer Evie stayed under, the more she felt that there was something strangely recognizable about all the men, something she couldn't quite place. Stay light. Don't go too deep. That was the name of the game on the radio. But Evie was in deep already. She needed to know.

Outside the windows, the land rolled on. Trees. Hills. Light snow fell.

The dealer flattened a card against his forehead, facedown. "What am I holding, huh? What is it? Who can call it? Joe? Cal?"

"It's the Ace of Spades," came a new voice, so shocking in its familiarity that Evie could scarcely breathe.

With a grin and a head shake, the dealer threw the card on the table, faceup. Ace of Spades.

"Son of a bitch," a freckle-faced soldier said. "Right again."

"That's our Jim," the diary writer said. Evie went cold inside. She'd placed his face. The soldier with the gun. The one who'd tried to shoot her on Forty-second Street. Her arms shook and her legs trembled. Nausea crept up into her throat. It was too much. She needed to quit, but she couldn't—not yet. She had to see the soldier's face. The one who'd guessed the card. She had to know who...

And then he was there. Right there. Smiling and bright-eyed and so young. Just the way she remembered him.

"All right," her brother said, grinning. "Which one of you wise guys took my comb?"

In the next moment, Evie slipped to the stage floor. She was vaguely aware of a commotion around her, voices that sounded as if they came from underwater.

"Miss O'Neill? Miss O'Neill!" cried Bob Bateman.

"Please, stay calm!" said Mr. Forman.

Excited murmurs from the audience. Anxious voices: "Make her stop!" "How?" "Do something!"

And then someone pried the comb from her stiff fingers, severing the connection. Evie came to with a great, heaving inhalation, as if her lungs had stopped working for a moment and were now desperate for air. Her head lolled from side to side. The bright white lights hurt her eyes. Evie's knees buckled as she tried to stand. The studio audience gasped. One of the Sweetheart Singers rushed over to prop her up. The back of Evie's tongue tasted of blood. The inside of her cheek was raw where she must've bitten it. Mr. Forman provided a glass of water, and Evie gulped it down greedily, not caring that she spilled it down the front of her dress. Pushing off from the Sweetheart Singer's embrace, she lunged toward Bateman on unsteady legs.

"Where...where did you get this?" Evie choked out when she could speak again. The studio lights were daggers. Her eyes watered and her nose ran. She was afraid she might vomit.

"I told you, it was my buddy Ralphie's...."

"That's not true!" Evie half yelled, half cried.

The audience was uncomfortable with this unseemly display. They'd come for a good time and answers about lost pets or family treasures whose secret histories might connect them to royalty or millionaires. Mr. Forman tried to intervene, but Evie's voice rose over his. "Where did you get my brother's comb?"

"Say, now—I came on for a little help," Bateman snapped, but he seemed more unsettled than angry. "I don't have to stand here and listen to this."

In the booth, the engineer gestured wildly to Mr. Forman, who practically shoved the Sweetheart Singers up to the microphone, where they launched into an upbeat tune to drown out the drama unfolding in front of them. Bob Bateman grabbed the comb from Mr. Forman and started down the middle aisle toward the doors in the back even though the ON AIR sign glowed red. Evie stumbled after him, eliciting further murmurs of disapproval and shock from the audience, but she didn't stop, careening like a rolled marble down the hallway of the radio station after Bob Bateman.

"Mr. Bateman! Mr. Bateman!"

The man hurried his steps. She burst through the doors and out into the madness of the street. Cold rain fell in fat drops that stuck to her eyelashes. Bob Bateman was halfway down the street. Evie chased after him and grabbed hold of his arm.

"Where did you get that comb?" she demanded through clenched teeth.

"Look, I already told you—"

"You're lying. You're lying, you're lying!" She was crying now. Big hiccuping gulps. Making a scene right there on Broadway, with everyone looking on. But she was beyond caring. She only wanted the truth. "How did you know my brother?"

"What?"

"My brother, James! He was on that train. The vision—I saw him!"

Bob Bateman's face showed panic. He gave the street a quick glance and leaned in close to Evie, lowering his voice. "Listen, sweetheart, it's not even my comb."

"What?"

"It's not mine, okay?"

"B-but you s-said—"

"They paid me to say that. It's not even my comb," he said again.

"Who? Who paid you?"

"I don't know. Some fellas in dark suits...Adams! His partner called him Mr. Adams."

"Why would they do that?"

"How should I know?"

"Take me to them."

"You're crazy," the man said. Evie latched on to his arm with both hands. "Let go!"

"Not until you take me to them." Evie dug her nails into the man's arm to keep him there.

"Ow! I said let go!" The man stepped down on Evie's instep. She howled more in shock and anger than in real pain, and he yanked his arm free. A crowd had gathered to watch the spectacle.

"Crazy," Bob Bateman groused to everyone watching. "She's crazy! Those Diviners are all crazy!" he yelled and ran off.

By the time the wet, bedraggled Evie returned to the radio station, the Pears Soap Hour had ended. She hid behind the thick, fanned leaves of a potted plant, watching a group of men smoking in the lobby, and listened to Mr. Forman's voice piped through the loudspeakers as he explained to the audience sitting by their radios that "Miss O'Neill has taken ill, overcome by the spirits from beyond."

"Overcome by spirits, all right," one of the smoking men quipped.

Mr. Forman reminded listeners that Sarah Snow's Mission Hour was coming up next. The Wireless Wonders Orchestra played the Sweetheart Singers on, and they sang an inoffensive tune to make housewives happy.

Evie waited in the ladies' lounge until her audience had cleared out and a new one came in. Sarah Snow's soothing voice reverberated in the Art Deco fortress of WGI.

"Evie, there you are." It was Helen, Mr. Phillips's secretary. She looked a bit stricken, like someone delivering a bad telegram. "Honey, Mr. Phillips wants to see you."

"Oh. Pos-i-tute-ly," Evie said without fizz. "Let me just freshen up."

Helen patted her arm. "I'll let him know."

In the mirror, Evie dabbed at her face and hair with a towel. She wiped away the spidery mascara beneath her eyes and put on a fresh coat of red lipstick. She trudged down the forever hallway, her heels clacking across the gleaming marble floors. She reached Mr. Phillips's office and kept walking, all the way to the back door. Then she broke into a run.

THE WOLF AMONG US

ANNOUNCER

Good evening, ladies and gentlemen of our listening audience. This is Reginald Lockhart, coming to you from the WGI studios in New York City. Wherever you are, the Black Hills of South Dakota or the rugged plains of the Heartland, whether you are a weary worker building the great towering monoliths of our cities or a businessman who has built an empire...all can find comfort and salvation through Miss Sarah Snow, God's messenger on the wireless.

(Organ music plays out. Smiling grandly, Sarah Snow, in a dress and cape, a spray of white orchids pinned to her left shoulder, steps to the microphone and opens her arms wide, as if to embrace her audience.)

SARAH SNOW

Thank you, Mr. Lockhart. Welcome, brothers and sisters! Now, I know that it has been a rather unsettling evening. But there is nothing that the power of prayer cannot soothe.

I know you will join me in praying for Miss O'Neill. Worry not—for the Lord is with thee. Brothers and sisters, as you know, there is no greater country than ours. "America, America, God shed his grace on thee / And crowned thy good with Brotherhood, from sea to shining sea...."

Yes, from sea to shining sea, we are an example to nations. The bright torch of liberty in a dark and troubled world. God has tasked us to be the gatekeepers, and each and every one of us is a steward of Americanism.

(A lone man shouts "Amen." This is followed by ripples of embarrassed laughter at the man's impulsive exclamation. Sarah Snow smiles good-naturedly.)

SARAH SNOW

Oh, hallelujah, amen! That's right, brother—don't be shy about showing that the Holy Spirit moves in you. Don't hide your light under a bushel! Rejoice and sing! Hallelujah!

(Silence.)

SARAH SNOW

I said, "Hallelujah!"

(Isolated calls of "Hallelujah!" ring out.)

SARAH SNOW

Yes, yes, hallelujah, indeed, friends. (Pause) What does it mean to be a steward of Americanism? What does God ask of us here in this most blessed of nations? God says, "Be shepherds to the flock of freedom! Turn back that old, crafty Mr. Wolf and keep my precious flock safe!" And what do we answer? Do we answer, "Gee, Lord, that wolf doesn't seem like such a bad fellow? He might take a sheep now and then; that's what wolves do. I'm busy over here with my own concerns. Let someone else tend to the flock."

(Sarah Snow looks into the audience, allowing her gaze to travel across the room slowly. A woman answers, "No.")

SARAH SNOW

Oh, amen, sister, amen! We answer, "Yes, Lord! We will be your shepherds of freedom! We will watch over your flock and see it grow, see it spread into every land! We will defend the borders of that freedom from all threats, by whatever means we must."

SARAH SNOW

But sometimes, brothers and sisters, sometimes we don't know what the wolf looks like. Sometimes that wolf creeps in wearing sheep's clothing, with false papers or an anarchist's heart, or with the ability to read your deepest secrets from your personal property. Sometimes the wolf smiles a friendly smile and says, "Why, I love these sheep, I love freedom," and waits for you to turn your back.

We have to keep vigilant against these threats to our flock. We must be suspicious of the wolf among us. We have to strike at the wolf, to turn him out like Jesus turned the moneylenders from the temple!

(Calls of "Amen!")

SARAH SNOW

Now, I hear some people say, "But Sarah, if we do that, aren't we giving up our freedoms? Aren't we betraying the very ideals we claim to be defending?"

Freedom demands sacrifices, brothers and sisters.

Do you allow your children to do whatever they like? Of course not. You want to keep them safe. And so you say to them, "You may not play in that yard. Stay away from those children down the block; they aren't the sort you want to associate with." And what do you do when your children disobey? You punish them. You do it out of love and a desire to keep them safe. But you have to do it; you

have to do it if you love your children.

Well, we love America. And just like our precious children, we want to shepherd America.

To keep her safe.

But there are the wrong sort of children down the street, brothers and sisters. Anarchists who hate our freedoms and want to destroy it with bombs and bloodshed and unions. Bootleggers and gamblers who pollute our morals with sin. And so-called soothsayers who claim they can do what only God Almighty Himself can do, who put themselves above democracy, above God. Listen now to the word of the

Lord!

(She holds up a Bible, opening it to the page she needs, reading aloud.)

SARAH SNOW

"There shall not be found among you anyone who...practices divination or tells fortunes

527

or interprets omens, or a sorcerer or a charmer or a medium or a necromancer or one who inquires of the dead, for whoever does these things is an abomination to the Lord. And because of these abominations the Lord your God is driving them out before you."

(Sarah Snow closes the Bible and clutches it to her chest with her left hand, raising her right hand high.)

SARAH SNOW

Therefore, brothers and sisters, let us be the Lord's faithful shepherd and drive the wolf out before us! Drive him out! Expose him for what he is—a wolf who would eat us from within. Only then can we be safe and sound. Only then can America shine a light on the rest of the world like a true shepherd of democracy, like a missionary of Manifest Destiny. Hallelujah!

(This time, the radio audience erupts into a rousing, full chorus of "Hallelujah!" without prompting. Sarah Snow smiles, then raises a hand to quiet the people.)

SARAH SNOW

God bless you, God bless all true Americans, and God bless the United States of America.

Now please join me in singing "Christian,
Dost Thou See Them?"

(An organ hums. The choir takes up the hymn.)

SARAH SNOW

Christian! dost thou see them
on the holy ground,
How the powers of darkness
Rage thy steps around?
Christian, up and smite them,
Counting gain but loss,
Smite them by the merit
of the Holy Cross!

The radio played in the parlors of the Foursquares in Minneapolis and in the kitchens on the South Side of Chicago. The sermon reached the ears of senators and congressmen, of preachers tending congregations and reformers attending meetings on Prohibition. It crackled along wires strung through the ether and was reborn in the office of the boss overseeing the migrant workers, the farmer worrying about a crop in the frost, and the factory foreman preparing his production quotas for the next morning's shift.

The hymn's marchlike strains played in the small home in Lake George, New York, where Will spoke with a little girl who'd seen from her attic window one cold night a dozen flickering wraiths coming across the winter-frozen lake as the sky churned and flashed above them. Will sat perfectly still as the little girl told him how these ragged spirits seemed to be heading somewhere, drawn by some invisible thread, but that when they came upon a fawn, they surrounded it and fell upon it, feasting with such a frightening ferocity that the poor animal scarcely had time to cry out, and the girl sank down to her floor away from the window, well out of sight, afraid they'd come next for her.

In the studio, the hymn ended.

Sarah Snow pronounced her balm of a benediction, soothing the weary hearts of a skittish nation on the verge of change.

It was followed by a cheery appeal for Arrow shirts, the shirt that makes the man.

NOT SAFE ANYWHERE

A terrible uneasiness weighed on Ling as she made her way to see Uncle Eddie at the opera house. She shouldn't have let Henry go like that. She should've made him stay and drink some tea until he'd sobered up a bit. Maybe if he'd stayed, they could've talked about what was really happening inside that dream world and what they needed to do to stop the veiled woman before it was too late.

"Where are you going?" a policeman said, putting up his hand. "Nobody leaves the neighborhood tonight, Miss. Mayor's orders."

"I'm just on my way to see my uncle down the street."

The policeman noted her crutches. He nodded her on. "All right, Miss."

The opera house was noisy with the banging of hammers. Two of Uncle Eddie's apprentices pounded the edges of a painted canvas to a wooden frame. The doors of the large wardrobe were open, and Uncle Eddie brushed lint from the colorful costumes inside. Ling ran a finger down the curving pheasant feather of the Da Dao Man's headpiece. "Uncle, how do you get rid of a ghost?"

Uncle Eddie stopped, mid-brush. "That is a very odd question."

"Hypothetically," Ling added quickly.

"Hypothetically? For the sake of science?" Uncle Eddie said, not missing a beat. Ling kept her expression neutral, and after a moment her uncle went back to brushing the costume clean. "Is your ghost Chinese or American?"

"I don't know," Ling said.

"Well, for us, we say you have to give a proper burial. In Chinese soil. You must perform the proper rituals and say the prayers to give the spirit rest."

"What if that isn't possible?"

"You put a pearl in the corpse's mouth. For an American ghost..." Uncle Eddie's eyes twinkled. "Tell it there's no money in haunting and it will go away. Careful!"

Uncle Eddie's attention was diverted to the stage, where the two stagehands struggled with the large canvas flat. It wobbled and threatened to fall over.

"Ling, do you want to see something special?"

She nodded and followed her uncle to the edge of the stage. The men had averted disaster, but the canvas flat faced backward now.

"Everyone needs training." Uncle Eddie sighed. "Turn it around, please! This way!"

The two men turned very slowly, positioning the flat against the stage wall, painted side out.

"Beautiful, isn't it?" Uncle Eddie said. "It's the original canvas from the last time the opera was performed. They wanted to have an American audience, so they made it more like an American play, with scenery."

The room seemed to come to a point on the stage. Ling's chest squeezed tight, as if someone were wringing the air from her lungs. She stared at the painted scene, barely comprehending what she saw: Golden hills. A meadow of colorful flowers. Bright sunshine. The red roofs of a Chinese village and a mist-shrouded forest.

Just as Ling had seen them every night in her dream with Wai-Mae.

They had the most beautiful opera there. I escape to it in my mind whenever I need to.

All of Ling's uneasy questions shifted into chilling answers: Wai-Mae was waiting for them when they arrived each night. She was never in the station or up above on the streets outside Devlin's, as Ling and Henry were. When Ling had asked about the dreamscape, what had Wai-Mae said? *I made it.* She'd talked about Mulberry Bend and Bandit's Roost, which were nothing more than blighted memories of Five Points, a slum wiped away and replaced by the greenery of Columbus Park. And then there were O'Bannion and Lee. The matchmakers who Wai-Mae insisted were bringing her over had been dead and gone for fifty years. Murdered in 1875. *Murder! Murder! Oh, murder!* They'd been murdered by the girl in the veil.

The clues had been there for them all along. George had tried to make her see them. In the tunnel, he'd told her to wake up. He'd wanted her to know about the ghost, to see who it really was.

And who had warned them against going inside the tunnel? Wai-Mae. Wai-Mae was the ghost.

But what if some part of Wai-Mae didn't know that? What if the dream was her way of fighting that knowledge? Ling needed to talk to Henry, desperately. She wished he weren't drunk. He'd been so upset about Louis... because Louis never showed up.

Louis, too, never appeared aboveground, Ling realized. Like Wai-Mae, he was always waiting for them in the dream world, shimmering in the sun. Shimmering. Ling's head went light as she realized at last what had been poking at her these past few days. It was Henry's comment about the hat. She'd thought it was his. But it had been Louis's first.

She'd told Henry from the start. She could only find the dead.

A chorus of police whistles shrilled in the streets. They were answered by loud sirens. Through the windows, Ling saw a herd of police marching up Doyers Street.

"What's happening?" Ling asked.

"Shhh." Uncle Eddie turned off the lights and they kept watch at the windows. Across the way, the police battered down the door of an apartment building. There was shouting as people were forced outside and into police wagons. A truck with a searchlight mounted on its back slunk around the narrow curve. Its white-hot sweep illuminated frightened faces peeking out from behind curtained windows. Two men attempted to escape from an apartment window onto a second-floor balcony. They were met on the fire escape by policemen with clubs at the ready. Police were everywhere in the streets, whistles blowing, as they rounded up the citizens of Chinatown. Many weren't going willingly, some shouting, "You cannot treat us this way. We are human beings!" A man's voice came over a megaphone in English telling everyone not to move, that this was a raid.

Ling spied Lucky moving in the shadows. He was making a run for the opera house through the chaos on the streets. Uncle Eddie spirited him inside, and he and Ling waited for the Tea House waiter to catch his breath.

"The mayor has issued a full quarantine," Lucky managed to tell them. "They're taking us to a detainment camp."

"Where are my parents?" Ling pleaded.

"Your father told me to go quickly out the back and come to you. I barely escaped."

"Is Baba all right?" Ling begged.

Lucky hung his head. "I am sorry, Ling. They took your father. He couldn't find his papers."

"I will go to the Association and see what I can find out from the lawyers," Uncle Eddie said, racing for his coat and hat.

"They'll take you, too, Uncle," Lucky said.

"So be it. I won't wait like a dog."

Lucky nodded at Ling. "Mr. Chan wanted to make sure they didn't get Ling."

Ling was torn. She wanted to go with Uncle Eddie, to be with her mother and father. But she also needed to get to Henry and tell him what she'd come to realize about the dream world.

"Uncle?" she said. Her eyes brimmed with tears.

"You must wait here," Uncle Eddie said, opening the costume wardrobe. "I'll come back for you once I've spoken to the Association." He helped Ling climb inside. She sat on the floor of the closet, cradling her crutches, hidden under a mound of heavy costumes. "You'll be safe in here," her uncle said and shut the door.

But Ling knew she wasn't safe anywhere. Not when people could hate the very idea of you. Not when there were ghosts in your dreams. Ling shut her eyes and listened to the sounds of her neighbors being taken away in the night. She held her breath as the police broke into the darkened opera house and searched it. They opened the wardrobe but, seeing nothing but a rack of costumes, closed it again and left. For what seemed like an eternity, Ling lay on the floor of the wardrobe, feeling the cramps in her legs. When it was quiet, she let herself out. For a moment she stood, not knowing what to do or where to go. Then, quite decisively, she yanked a pearl and a pheasant feather from the headpiece of the Dao Ma Dan, hoping her uncle would forgive her for it, and shoved both objects deep into her pocket. She peeked through a crack in the opera-house doors and, seeing no one, let herself out, watching for police as she walked the eerily empty streets of Chinatown, which reminded her once more of her dream. Stifling a sob, Ling sneaked into the Tea House, stepping over broken dishes on her way to the telephone directory, where she found the address for the Bennington. She grabbed Henry's hat, placing it on her head.

Then, keeping to the shadows, she made her way to the El for the long ride uptown.

THE PARTY GOES ON

The wind had picked up in advance of the predicted nor'easter. It whipped at the hand-painted banner Mabel and Jericho had hung above the museum's front doors so that it appeared to spell out TIGHT! DIVERS BIT! Inside, Jericho and Mabel put the finishing touches on the Diviners exhibit. Mabel arranged the small triangles of watercress sandwiches she'd made on silver trays she'd borrowed from the Bennington's dining room while Jericho put the last of the exhibit's cards in place.

"Looks nice," Mabel said, coming to stand beside him.

"It does at that," Jericho agreed. "I couldn't have done it without your help, Mabel. Thank you."

You're right, she thought. "You're welcome," she said.

Sam arrived, shaking the damp from his coat. "Getting ugly out there."

"I hope it doesn't keep people away," Mabel fretted. "You look swell, Sam."

"Thanks, Mabel. So do you. Where's Evie?"

"I thought she was coming with you!" Mabel said.

Sam was half out of his coat. With a sigh, he shrugged it back on and buttoned up. He swiped a sandwich triangle from a tray and stuffed it into his mouth. "Keep the exhibit on ice. I'll be back with the guest of honor."

"You know where she is?" Mabel asked, rearranging the hole left by Sam's sandwich grab.

"I got a pretty good idea."

A short while later, Sam burst into the speakeasy beneath the Winthrop, threading quickly through the crowd. A knot of soused revelers bent over a fountain where someone had dropped a small hammerhead shark into the water. It lurked in the shallows, lost, as the partiers pointed and laughed. Evie held court at a table full of fashionable swells, men and women of facile smiles and fickle allegiances who seemed to be eating up every elocution-perfected word out of her mouth. The man sitting too close to her interrupted, spinning out a story that Sam was certain was a bore. He marched over and tapped Evie on the shoulder.

"Why, hello, Sam," Evie said too brightly, and Sam knew she was halfway to drunk already.

"Evie, can I have a word?"

"See here, old boy, can't this wait?" an older man with a thin mustache broke in. "Bertie was just telling us the most amusing story about—"

"I'm sure it's a real knee-slapper, pal. I might need to go make out a will in the event I die of laughter. Evie, a word?"

"Well, I *never*," one of the girls tutted.

"Doubtful," Sam shot back.

Sensing trouble, Evie hopped up with a blithe "Keep my seat warm and my drink cold, darlings!" and followed Sam to a corner. Her beaded dress had come unstrung and she trailed tiny glass beads like an exotic, molting bird. "What's the big idea, Sam? Why were you so rude to my friends?"

"Those are not your friends. Your *real* friends are wondering where you are. Did you forget?"

Evie's blank expression told him that she had.

"The Diviners exhibit party at the museum. It's tonight. You're the guest of honor."

Evie bit her lip and rubbed at her forehead. "Honestly, Sam. I can't tonight."

"Why? You sick?"

Sam pressed his lips to Evie's forehead, and Evie's stomach fluttered.

"No. But I . . . it was a bad show, Sam. Very bad."

"You'll have a better show next time."

"No. You don't understand," Evie mumbled.

"I understand that you promised, Evie."

"I know. I know I did. And I'm sorry. Truly, I am. But I—I can't."

Sam crossed his arms. "Why not?"

"I just can't. That's all. Oh, excuse me!" Evie called, flagging down a passing waiter. "Could you be an absolute darling and get me another Juice of the Venus de Milo?"

"Certainly, Miss O'Neill."

"Do you know why they call it that? Because after two, you can't feel your arms," Evie said, trying for a smile though her head ached and her soul was weary. And now she was letting everybody down. Well, they'd get past it. It would all go fine without her. She couldn't face all those people at the museum, not after tonight's show. She could barely face Sam. He was staring at her with something bordering on contempt that pierced through the alcoholic fog she'd been sinking herself into for the past few hours.

"Is this all you want?" Sam asked bitterly. "A good time?"

"You're one to talk!"

"I like a good time. But not all the time." He held her gaze.

Evie blushed. "If you came here just to get a rise out of me, mission accomplished. You can scram."

"Your friends are counting on you."

"Their mistake," Evie whispered. "You want me to go back to that museum? To talk about ghosts? You weren't there in that house with that . . . that thing. You don't know how it was!" Her eyes brimmed with tears as she spat out the words. "Ask Jericho. He knows. He understands what it was like."

538

She wanted to wound now, and Sam's flinch registered as one more sin she'd hate herself for come morning, but now that her tongue was loose, she couldn't stop the words from tumbling out.

"I can see those…hideous beasts coming out of the burning walls. I hear Naughty John telling me—warning me—about my own brother! He knew about James, Sam. When I stand still, I see all of it. So I don't stand still, and I certainly don't go looking for more. And every night before bed, I pray for those pictures to go out of my head. When the prayers don't work, I ask the gin to do it."

Evie could feel a headache threatening. She'd let Sam lead her to this. That was her mistake.

"I'm sorry I'm not Jericho," Sam said coolly.

"I'm sorry for everything," Evie mumbled.

"That include last night?"

Evie didn't answer.

"Evie, my dear!" a mustachioed gentleman called to Evie from the periphery. "You're missing all the fun!"

"Don't you dare start without me!" she shouted, wiping away tears with her knuckles.

With her smudged eyes and her dainty red Cupid's bow lips, Evie reminded Sam of a sparkling party favor on the cusp of New Year's, just this side of discarded. The comment about Jericho had hurt. Badly. He tried to swallow it down. "Evie," he said, taking gentle hold of her hand. "The party can't go on forever."

Evie looked up at Sam, defiant but slightly pleading, too. Her voice was nearly a whisper. "Why not?"

She pulled her hand free of Sam's grasp, and he let her go, watching as she ran headlong toward the hedonistic throng.

FORGET

As Henry stepped into the tunnel, he was aware of vague shapes in the dark above, and he knew these creatures traveled between worlds—supernatural and natural, dream and reality. Glowing eyes watched his every step. Those same shapes sniffed the air around him, taking in his scent, but for some reason they didn't follow, and Henry stepped out into the forest and made his way to the bayou, calling Louis's name. But when he got to the cabin, everything was gray and dull. No sunlight on the river. No smoke coming from the chimney. No sweet music to greet him. He peeked into the cabin's windows, but it was too dark to see. When he tried to open the door, his hand moved through it like water. A thread of panic wove itself into Henry's heart.

"Louis Rene Bernard—you better answer me, dammit!" Henry kicked at a tree, but it was like kicking at air. He slumped down on the still-solid ground and let himself cry angry tears.

"Henry?"

At the sound of Wai-Mae's voice, Henry startled. She stood just inside the mouth of the tunnel. Her dress wavered between states, shifting from an old-fashioned gown to her usual plain tunic. Everything about her seemed ephemeral.

"Is Ling with you?" Wai-Mae asked.

"No. I came by myself. I needed…I need to find Louis. To ask him why he didn't come to the station today. I waited all day. He never showed."

Wai-Mae stepped over the threshold into the dead grass. Her cheeks were pale, but her eyes sparkled. "Poor Henry. You want to be with him very much, don't you?"

"Yes. It's all I want."

Wai-Mae put her hands on the lifeless Spanish elm. Where she touched the tree, it blossomed. "It takes so much energy to make dreams."

She ran a hand through the grass. It sparked with color and spread all the way to the river, a rippling carpet of green. "To make things the way you wish." Wai-Mae exhaled—three short, fierce breaths—and the air filled with birdsong and dragonflies and blue sky. Slowly, the bayou dreamscape came to life, like a carousel starting up. "To keep the hurt out."

Wai-Mae stared back at the tunnel, frowning. "Sometimes, I— *she*—remembers. She remembers that they promised her everything— a husband, a home, a new life in a new country—only to break her heart. But they can't stop her dream now. She wants to help you, Henry. Yes," Wai-Mae said, blinking, as if she'd just remembered something very important that had been lost for some time. "She wants *me* to help you be with Louis. Do you want to see him?"

Henry felt woozy. The dream blurred around the edges. "Yes," he said.

From inside her dress, Wai-Mae took out a music box. "What would you give to see him again? To have your dream?"

Dreams. That was what Henry had been living on for most of his life. Never really here, always somewhere in his mind. He was as much of a dream walker awake as he was asleep. He didn't want to think anymore.

"Anything," he said.

"Promise?"

"Yes."

"*Then dream with me*," Wai-Mae said, offering the music box.

Henry turned the little crank of the music box. The tinny song drifted out and Henry whisper-sang along. "*Beautiful dreamer, wake unto me. Starlight and dewdrops are waiting . . . f-for thee. . . .*"

The alcohol and the exhaustion took hold. As the song played, Henry thought of all he had lost: The loving, strong parents he'd longed for but knew were nothing more than a child's wish. The easy way things used to be with Theta. The music inside him that he'd never finish, never put out into the world as his story. He cried for poor, sweet Gaspard and those summer-still nights at Celeste's, the boys with their arms flung carelessly over each other's slender shoulders. Most of all, Henry cried for Louis. How could Louis have left him like that? How were you supposed to go on if you knew love was that fragile?

"Forget." Wai-Mae kissed Henry's cheek. "Forget," she said, and kissed the other. She raised the dagger high. "Forget."

Sweetly, she kissed his lips, and then she plunged the slim blade into Henry's chest, just above his heart. Henry gasped from pain, and she breathed her dream into his open mouth. It flowed into Henry, siphoning away his memory and cares and will, along with his life. For a moment Henry thought about fighting back, but it all seemed inevitable, like finally giving in to drowning after a fruitless, exhausting swim. Already the iciness was spreading through his veins, weighting his limbs, filling him with an aching hunger that could only be fed by more dreams. Henry felt as if he were falling into a deep, deep well. The music-box song came to him, distorted and slow. As his eyes fluttered, he could see glimpses of those radium-bright, broken creatures watching him from the dark.

They opened their mouths—*"dreamwithusdreamdreamdream"*— and their din swelled as it joined the song, a discordant lullaby.

The fight left Henry. The dream army advanced. Henry closed his eyes and fell deep.

☀

A dog's insistent barking woke him. Henry opened his eyes to blue skies sponged with shimmering pink-white clouds. He felt as if he'd been sleeping for ages. The prickly points of grass blades scratched against his arms and neck where he lay; his surroundings smelled of warm earth and river, sweet clover and Spanish moss. Another bark caused him to turn his head to the right. In the tall green grass, an excited, puppyish Gaspard snuffled closer. He smeared Henry's cheek with his slobbery tongue.

"Gaspard. Hey, boy." Henry sat up and buried his face in the dog's velvety fur. Down the dirt path, smoke puffed from the cabin's chimney. Henry could smell it now. Woodsy and sweet, it burned the back of his throat just right. A pot of jambalaya was on. Henry could almost taste the spicy roux.

He heard Louis's fiddle sawing away on "Rivière Rouge." Gaspard ran toward the cabin and Henry followed. Dragonflies floated on the feathered edges of sunflowers. Birds chirruped their June song, for it was high summer. It would always be summer here, Henry knew. The old hickory steps creaked beneath the weight of his feet. He was back. He was home. The door opened in welcome.

There was a bed against the wall, and a small table with two chairs and a stool, where Louis sat, handsome as ever, the fiddle nestled under his stubbly chin. Shafts of sunlight poured through the windows, bathing Louis in a golden shimmer. He smiled at Henry. "*Mon cher!* Where you been?"

"I've been..." Henry started to answer but found he couldn't quite remember where he'd been or what that other life was like, if it had been important or lonely, wonderful or awful. He had a vague feeling that he was angry with Louis. For the life of him, he couldn't think why. It no longer mattered. All of it floated away the moment Louis crossed the sun-drenched floor to kiss him. It was the sweetest kiss Henry could recall, and it made him want another and another. Henry pulled Louis down onto the bed and snaked a hand up his shirt, marveling at the warmth of his lover's skin.

"I will never leave you again," Henry said.

Outside, the morning glories bloomed fat and purple and spread across the ground in a widening bruise.

KNOWING

"Did you find Evie?" Mabel asked as Sam stormed into the library, tossed his coat on the bear's paw, and threw himself on the sofa.

"Yeah. Sorry, kid. We have to do this without her."

"She's not coming?" Jericho asked. He removed Sam's coat from the bear and held it out to him, waiting patiently until Sam rose from the sofa, took the coat, and hung it properly in the closet.

"Remind me to give Evie a piece of my mind," Mabel fumed.

"Save it," Sam advised. "She doesn't deserve any piece of you."

There was a knock at the door, followed by a series of progressively more urgent knocks.

"I knew she'd come!" Mabel hurried down the hall and opened the door not to Evie but to a bedraggled Ling.

"Oh. If you're here for the party, I'm afraid you're early," Mabel explained.

"I'm looking for Henry DuBois. I'm a friend of his. I tried his apartment, but he wasn't answering. Then I remembered that the Diviners exhibit was opening tonight, and I hoped . . . Please, may I come in? It's urgent—"

A taxi screeched to a halt at the curb and Theta jumped out, still in her stage makeup and costume. She tossed money at the cabdriver through the passenger window and shouted, "Keep the change!"

Memphis crawled out from the backseat, holding Henry in his arms.

"What's the matter?" Mabel asked as they reached the steps.

"It-it's Henry." Theta sputtered, wild-eyed. "I came home and the metronome was going. He's dream walking. But look—" Theta pointed to the faint red blisters forming on Henry's neck. "I can't wake him up. I think he's got the sleeping sickness."

Henry's lips were parted; his eyelids twitched. Another mark bloomed on his skin.

"Should I call a doctor? Should I call my parents?" Mabel asked.

"A doctor won't help. Neither will your parents," Ling said. "It's her. She's got him. You'd better let me in."

* * *

The angry wind howled at the windows and across the roof of the museum as Ling sat in the library among strangers while the dreaming Henry lay on the couch, precious minutes ticking by.

"My name is Ling Chan," she started. "I'm a dream walker."

"The other Diviner," Mabel said.

Ling briefed everyone about her walks with Henry and all they'd seen and experienced there, from the Beach Pneumatic Transit Company to the strange loop they'd seen each time with the veiled woman. She told them, too, about the Proctor sisters' revelations to Henry, and what she'd learned about the veiled woman haunting the site of her past and the dream machine she'd been building brick by brick, ghost by ghost, a grand architecture of illusion meant to keep painful memory at bay. "Henry is in trouble. He needs help. *Our* help."

"I'm confused," Mabel said. "Your friend Wai-Mae is actually a ghost, the veiled woman—they're one and the same?"

Ling nodded.

"So she doesn't even know she's a ghost," Mabel said, mulling it over. She looked to Theta. "It's like what Dr. Jung talked about—the shadow self."

Sam whistled. "That's some shadow. Mine just makes me look taller."

"She doesn't really know what she's doing," Ling said.

"Horsefeathers!" Theta's eyes glimmered. "That lie's been around since Adam. She knows. Somewhere, deep down, she knows. I want her dead."

"She's already dead," Sam said.

Theta glared.

Sam put up his hands in surrender. "Just making a point."

"You said the station was for Beach's pneumatic train? You're sure?" Memphis asked.

"Yes," Ling said.

"That mean something to you, Poet?"

Memphis reached into his coat for his poetry book. "Isaiah asked me about it. In fact, he even drew a picture of it. Isaiah's my brother," he explained to the others as he opened the book to Isaiah's drawing of Beach's pneumatic train and the glowing wraiths crawling out of the tunnel.

"That's it," Ling whispered. "That's where we go each night. How did your brother...?"

"Isaiah's got this gift. He can see glimpses of the future, like a radio picking up signals," Memphis said, echoing Sister Walker's words to him in her kitchen months before. Hadn't she said she needed to talk to Memphis before she left? How he wished he'd taken her up on that offer. They'd certainly have plenty to talk about when she got back, and Octavia couldn't stop him this time. "There's something else I should tell you. You know that lady who survived the sleeping sickness, Mrs. Carrington?"

Sam shrugged. "Yeah. Sure. Was in all the papers. She took a picture with Sarah Snow."

Memphis took a deep breath. "I'm the one who really healed her."

Ling looked up at Memphis. "You can heal?"

"Sometimes," Memphis said gently. "But I'd never had a healing trance like that one. It was more like a dream than a trance. I couldn't tell what was real and what wasn't. And...I think I saw her. All I can say is that she had me sucked right in, so I believe you about her power."

Sam sat up. "I'm trying to understand all this—"

"Don't strain," Jericho muttered.

"This ghost, Wai-Mae, or the veiled woman, or whoever she is, she can trap people inside dreams?" Sam finished.

"I think so," Ling said. "From what Henry and I saw inside that tunnel, it seems that she gives them their best dreams, and as long as they don't struggle, they stay there. If they fight it, their best dream turns into their worst nightmare."

"But *why* does she do it?" Jericho asked.

"She needs their dreams. She feeds off them. They're like batteries fueling her dream world. That's why the sleeping sickness victims burn up from the inside. Because it's too much. The constant dreaming destroys them."

"What happens to those dreamers when they die?" Memphis asked, and the room fell silent.

"They can't stop wanting the dream," Ling said at last. "They're insatiable. Hungry ghosts."

"Monsters in the subways," Memphis murmured.

Sam frowned at Memphis. "I don't like where that's headed. 'Monsters in the Subways' is not the title of a big, happy dance number."

"Shut up, Sam," Theta said. "Memphis, what is it?"

Memphis paced the same section of carpet. "Isaiah kept telling me about this bad dream he was having. About a lady making monsters in the tunnels. About 'monsters in the subways.' I thought he was making up a story so he wouldn't get in trouble for drawing in my book. But I got a bad feeling he was telling the truth."

"The disappearances," Jericho said. "Missing people. It's been in all the papers."

"You think it's all connected?" Mabel asked.

"I know it is," Ling said.

Lightning flashed at the windows. A rumble of thunder followed.

"It's been all around us. We just haven't been paying attention," Jericho said.

"Because it wasn't happening to you," Ling snapped.

"Yeah? You and Henry were happy to ignore it when it suited you," Theta said coolly.

"You're right," Ling said. "Now that I know, I have to stop her."

"Yeah? How you gonna do that?" Sam asked. "Ask her pretty please to stop killing people because it's not nice? Somehow I don't think she's gonna be copacetic with that."

Ling stared at her hands. "I don't know, but I have to try. I'm going back into the dream world. I'm going to find Henry, and then I'll face Wai-Mae."

"What about those things in the tunnel—if they really exist, if Isaiah is right about that—your hungry ghosts?" Memphis asked. "How do we get rid of them?"

"At Knowles' End, once Evie banished John Hobbes's spirit, the ghosts of the Brethren disappeared, too," Jericho said, breaking his silence on that topic. "Like they were an extension of him." The room fell silent for a moment.

"You know for sure that's the case here?" Sam asked at last.

"No," Jericho admitted.

"Swell. Isn't there some kinda ghost primer in this joint: Reading, Writing, 'Rithmetic, Ridding Yourself of Soul-Stealing Demons for Fun and Profit? Why isn't there ever anything useful around here?"

Mabel handed Sam a watercress sandwich.

"Thanks, Mabes."

"Bad death," Ling murmured.

"What? Wha' bad deaph?" Sam said around a mouthful of sandwich. "Don't like the sound of that, either."

"Wai-Mae said the ghost had a bad death. But we don't know how she died. All we know is that our dream walk starts the same way each night: Wai-Mae runs past us toward Devlin's Clothing Store. Beach's pneumatic train station was built under Devlin's Clothing Store on Broadway and Warren, near the City Hall station. There's got to be something down there that's important to her. But I don't know what."

On the Chesterfield, Henry's fingers stiffened as he was caught in the net of dreaming. Two new burn marks appeared on his neck.

"Whatever you're gonna do, let's get started," Theta said. "Please."

Memphis put a hand on Henry's arm. "I could try to heal him."

Theta reached over and slipped her hand into Memphis's. "She almost killed you last time."

"But this time I won't fall for her tricks."

"No," Ling said sharply. "You can't protect yourself once you're inside a dream. Anything can happen. You'll be caught, just like Henry. It has to be me. I'm awake inside the dream. It's different. I'll go after Henry."

"And what if that doesn't work?" Jericho asked.

"It has to work."

"But what if it doesn't?" Jericho persisted.

Ling looked over at Henry. "We go into the tunnels. Find what's so important to Wai-Mae that it keeps her here."

Loud, haphazard pounding reverberated through the museum, as if someone was knocking and kicking the front door at the same time. And then a muffled voice yelled, "Hey! Lemme in! 'S freezing out here!"

"Evie!" Mabel said.

They opened the front door to see Evie leaning against the door-jamb. Her mascara was smudged and she reeked of gin.

"As promised, I should like to offer my services to the cause of this swell creepy-crawly party," she said and gave a flourish of a bow, smacking her head. "Ow! Whennid you put in that wall?"

"Evil, are you blotto?" Theta demanded.

"Cerrrtainly not," Evie mumbled. She blew out a gust of boozy air, lifting a curl from her forehead. "Well. Perhaps a *soooo-sahn*. That's French. I know some French . . . *avous*."

"Holy smokes," Theta said, throwing her hands in the air. "Just what we need."

Evie barged in, knocking a tray of poppet dolls from a side table onto the floor. "Uh-oh. Your poppets are pooped," she said, giggling.

"Go home, Evie. We got enough trouble here," Sam said, directing her back toward the door.

Evie wobbled around him. "Unhand me, fiancé!"

"I am not your fiancé. It was a publicity stunt, remember?"

"Right," Evie said, nearly swallowing the word.

"Your engagement isn't real?" Jericho said.

Evie peered up at Jericho and quickly averted her eyes. "I can assure you that the feelings Sam Sergei Lloyd Lubovitch has for any girl are nothin' but an act."

Evie stumbled a bit, and Jericho caught her. He kept his arm around her shoulders. "I've got you."

Mabel took it all in, a weight in her stomach. "I'll make coffee," she said dully and walked the long hall back to the kitchen.

"I have not missed this joint," Evie announced as she tottered down the hall toward the library. She swilled from her flask, dribbling gin down her chin and onto the front of her dress. "Oops. The Sweetheart Seer did not see that coming."

Sam replaced her flask with a cup. "Drink this."

Evie turned doleful eyes to him. "Why you do this? What'd I ever do to you?" She took a sip and grimaced. "Tastes like water."

"It is water."

"You know what the trouble with this water is? There's no gin in it," she said, shoving the cup back at him. "Say, I thought this was a party! Where is everybody?" Evie said, twirling around unsteadily. She stopped when she saw Ling. "How do you do," she said, moving toward Ling, her hand outstretched. "I'm Evangeline O'Neill."

"I know who you are," Ling said.

"Evie, this is Henry's friend Ling Chan, the other dream walker I told you about," Theta said.

"Right. Dream walker." Evie slapped the chair. "Ever'body an' his uncle's a Diviner! 'S gettin' crowded."

"Pipe down, Evil, or I swear I'll deck you," Theta said.

"We have to do it tonight. At once," Ling warned them, steering them back to the crisis at hand.

"Tonight?" Mabel said.

"We can't wait," Ling said. "It has to be now, before she draws him in any deeper."

"What's goin' on?" Evie asked. "'S this a party game?"

"We got ghost trouble," Sam said. "That sleeping sickness? It's caused by a ghost."

Evie shook her head vehemently. "No. Not again. Can I tell you a secret? I don't like ghosts very much. They are terrible people."

Memphis let out a low whistle, shaking his head.

Theta's eyes brimmed with tears. "It's got Henry, Evil."

For the first time, Evie noticed Henry lying on the Chesterfield, still and pale. "Henry. Sweet Henry."

"We'd better get started, Freddy," Sam said.

Jericho ripped a piece of bedsheet from part of the exhibit and painted a sign in thick letters—CANCELED—then hung it across the museum's front doors. "Getting awfully windy out there," he said.

"Ling, how long should I set the alarm for?" Theta asked, adjusting the clock's arm.

"Two hours. I don't think it's wise to be under longer than that. And I'll need Henry's hat," Ling said.

Theta put Henry's weathered boater in Ling's hand, then sat down beside Henry, stroking his forehead. "We're coming for you, Hen."

Ling began removing her braces so that she could be comfortable. She noticed Jericho watching her intently, and her cheeks flamed. "I would appreciate it if you wouldn't stare."

Jericho blanched. "It's not what you think."

"Infantile paralysis," Ling said brusquely. "Since you seem so curious."

"I know," Jericho said, so low and quiet he could barely be heard above the thunder. He draped a blanket over Ling. "Comfortable?"

"Yes," she said.

"Go get our boy, Ling. Bring him back safe," Theta said.

Ling nodded. Mabel put the clock on the table, and Ling listened to its steady *tick-tock*, wishing it were a comfort. She cradled Henry's hat to her chest. With her other hand, she gripped the feather, a reminder of the battle to be fought. Then she inhaled deeply, closed her eyes, and waited for the most important dream walk of her life.

THE FOLLY OF DREAMS

Ling woke on the now familiar streets of old New York. But this part of the dream no longer had the same energy and color as before. When the wagon clopped past, it was little more than a suggestion of a man and a horse. Alfred Ely Beach's voice ebbed in the fog: "Come . . . marvel . . . be amazed . . . the future . . ."

The entire scene was like a worn memory fading away to nothing. For a moment, Ling worried that she wouldn't be able to reach Henry at all. There was a muffled cry—"Murder!"—and a few seconds later, the veiled woman sprinted past, her presence so minimal it opened just the slightest wobbling space in the wall. Ling dove in quickly after her, praying it wouldn't close as she attempted her pass. Without Henry at her side, the walk through the ghostly underground was dark and lonely and frightening. But Ling couldn't waver now. At last, she reached the train station. It was aglow and welcoming, as if expecting her, but Ling took no comfort from it now that she knew the source of its making. Ling plinked a key on the piano.

"Henry?" she called. "Henry? It's Ling. I'm coming for you."

The train's lamp blazed in the dark, announcing its arrival, and then Ling was on board, alone, traveling back to the private dream world and Wai-Mae.

When Ling arrived in the meadow, she found Wai-Mae sitting in the grass near the dogwood tree they'd made, singing happily to herself, and for just a moment, Ling's resolve ebbed. Wai-Mae wore the jeweled headpiece of a royal concubine, like one of her beloved romantic opera heroines. Seeing Ling, she smiled. "Hello, sister! How do you like it?" she said, turning her head left and right to show off the headpiece with pride.

A day ago, Ling would've found it sweetly charming.

"It must've taken a lot of energy to make that," Ling said coolly.

"But worth the effort," Wai-Mae said, smiling, and Ling felt a bit sick. "I'm glad you came back. Will you take some tea with me?" Wai-Mae poured a cup and held it out to Ling.

Ling didn't take it. "I can't stay long. I've come to talk."

Wai-Mae swept her hand through the air as if she were clearing the last tendrils of smoke from a room. "About last night?"

"Yes. And other matters."

"That's all forgotten, sister. I've forgiven you for what you did. I know you meant well. But I don't want to talk about such unhappy things anymore. Here. Sit with me and I will tell you all about tonight's opera, and you will play whatever role you wish—except for the role I play, naturally."

Ling didn't move. "Wai-Mae, where's Henry?"

"Henry? He's with Louis, of course."

"Wai-Mae. You need to let him go."

"I don't know what you're talking about. He is happy with Louis in their dream."

"No. He's trapped inside a dream. You can't stay here, Wai-Mae. None of us can live inside a dream. You're...hurting people. You're hurting Henry."

"I would never hurt Henry."

"All of this"—Ling gestured wide—"is draining him of his Qi. He'll die, Wai-Mae. And then he'll become one of those burned-up, discarded things, those hungry ghosts, loose in our world."

Wai-Mae put her hands over her ears. "Nothing you say makes sense! Go away if you only want to trouble me."

Ling needed to find a way to break through Wai-Mae's clouded mind and make her see. She offered her hand. "I want to show you something. It's important. Will you walk with me...sister?"

At the word *sister*, Wai-Mae smiled. "Is this a new game?"

"It's an experiment," Ling said.

"Science again." Wai-Mae sighed. "Very well, Little Warrior. But then we must make our opera."

Ling led the way through the forest. For once, Wai-Mae wasn't chattering, and Ling could sense her wariness.

"Where are you taking me?" Wai-Mae asked.

"Just a little farther now."

As they broke through the line of trees, the entrance to the tunnel loomed.

Wai-Mae stepped back, scowling. "Why have you brought me to this cursed place?"

"Why don't you want to go inside?"

"I've told you! Something terrible happened there. She lives there now."

"The veiled woman. The one who cries."

"Yes, yes. I've told you all of this before," Wai-Mae said, looking away.

"How do you know this?"

"I-I just do! I can...feel her."

"Why is it that you can feel her emotions but Henry and I can't?"

"How should I know?" Wai-Mae snapped. She folded her arms across her chest. "I don't want to stay here. Let's go back."

"You know what happened in there, don't you? You've always known. Who is she?"

"Stop it!"

"Remember, Wai-Mae. I know you don't want to, but you must. You must remember what happened."

"I won't have my dreams ruined."

Ling didn't move. "Wai-Mae, a terrible injustice was done to you, and for that, I'm sorry. I am so sorry for all the pain. But you can be at peace now. You can be at rest. I can help you."

Wai-Mae looked baffled. "I'm already at peace. Here. In dreams."

"Just come inside with me. That's all I'm asking," Ling said, taking a step backward toward the tunnel. The skin of her neck prickled into gooseflesh. "Walk through the tunnel with me this one time, and I promise I'll never mention it ever again."

Ling took another step backward and Wai-Mae's mouth parted in horror. "Sister! You mustn't go in—it isn't safe!"

"Why? What will she do to me?"

Ling took another step, and Wai-Mae balled her fists at her mouth. Her eyes were huge. "She'll . . . she'll . . . don't."

"In science, we need proof. Prove me wrong. Come after me."

And with that, Ling stepped inside the tunnel.

"Ling! Please!"

Wai-Mae's cry echoed around Ling. She kept her eyes on Wai-Mae, standing in the sunshine, but she could feel the darkness at her back. Her skin buzzed with fear.

Wai-Mae came closer. Her breathing was shallow, her voice desperate. "Please, Ling."

Heart hammering, Ling took another step backward, and another. Behind her, the dark sighed, like a long gust of wind through dry leaves, and it took all of Ling's will not to run back toward the light.

Wai-Mae hesitated for another moment, and then, carefully, she stepped into the darkness, glancing around fearfully at the earthen tomb. Nothing happened, and Ling wondered if perhaps she'd gotten it wrong after all.

"Sister? Where are you?"

"I'm here," Ling said, her voice hoarse. "Come to me."

As Wai-Mae moved through the dark, light crackled along the walls, making her jump.

"Please. Let's go back, Ling."

"Just a little closer," Ling said.

The bricks sputtered to life, glowing with so many dreams. Like a curious child, Wai-Mae drew closer to the wall. She put her hand to first one, then another, then another, staring at the image of the veiled woman as she ran toward Devlin's.

Wai-Mae sang, soft as a lullaby. *"La-la-la-la-la . . . wake unto me. Starlight . . . sweet dreams . . ."* Her song became a whisper. *"Are waiting. Waiting for . . . for . . . me."*

A phosphorescent aura softened the outline of Wai-Mae, like something raised from the deep, and then she fell into the dirt, her face in her hands. The howl torn from her nearly broke Ling's heart.

"Why?" Wai-Mae sobbed.

"I'm sorry," Ling said, fighting tears. "So sorry."

"How could you do this to me?" Wai-Mae said, shaking.

"Let me help you, Wai-Mae."

Wai-Mae's eyes flashed. Her teeth lengthened, sharpening to points. "You are dishonorable! Like the man who tricked me here."

Behind Ling, the dark felt alive. Nails clicked on stone. Scratching. And Ling didn't know what was more terrifying—the thought of what might lie in the vast dark behind her or the creature transforming before her. Wai-Mae rose from the dirt, walking slowly toward Ling. As she did, her modest tunic shifted into the long white dress. Bloodstains seeped through and stretched across the fabric in flowering wounds. The headpiece dissolved, and Wai-Mae's neatly coiled dark hair came undone. It fell loose across her shoulders, snarled and broken. Her sharp teeth gleamed. Purple pockmarks painted themselves upon the pale ribbon of Wai-Mae's throat. Her waspish voice stung the air: "I will show you the terror of your desires. I will show you the folly of dreams. I will show you how the world tears you apart. Here is your dream turned to dust."

The veil descended. In her hand was the dagger. Wai-Mae lunged, grabbing the back of Ling's neck. *"Dream with me, sister,"* she growled, plunging the dagger in. She parted her lips and pressed her dream into Ling's mouth.

Ling fought back until she no longer could. Her arms hung at her sides, loose and long, as if she'd put down a heavy burden at last.

And then she was tumbling down.

※

Mabel shut off the alarm, but Henry and Ling slept on.

Jericho's face was grave. "I can't wake her."

Theta shook Henry. "Wake up! Come on, Hen! Please."

In the eerie silence that followed, Theta stood and faced everyone. "Well, I'm not sitting here while that witch kills my best friend. I say we go into the tunnels and find that train station and whatever is so damned important down there. I say we burn it if we gotta. Whaddaya got around this Creepy Crawly to help us out?"

Mabel rifled through drawers, pulling out all manner of things—ceremonial knives, protective charms, a wooden stake, stones, and a wooden box.

"Any of these things work?" Theta asked, examining a woven wheel with feathers attached.

"Possibly," Jericho said. "The trouble is, we don't know how they work. And Will has always said that each culture has its specific beliefs about ghosts. You can't guarantee that a gris gris bag will keep you safe from a Chinese ghost, for instance. You'd need to know more about what you're up against."

"How can we find that out?" Theta asked. "The two people who know the most about our ghost are out cold."

"Maybe if we had somebody who could get a read on the situation once we're down there?" Sam said and looked over at Evie, slumped in her chair.

"I don't think Evil could read the directions on a can of beans right now," Theta said.

"I am perfectly capable, I can assure you," Evie sniffed.

"Swell. Somebody get the Great Blotto some coffee." Sam opened the weapons cabinet. "And a few of these knives couldn't hurt."

"Agreed. These flashlights will also come in handy," Memphis said, testing the batteries in each one.

"Jericho, you and Mabel stay here and keep trying to wake them up," Sam said as he grabbed for his jacket.

"I should come with you," Jericho protested. "I'm bigger."

"Yeah, I know. I got eyes," Sam sniped. "But if something goes really south with Ling and Henry, we need somebody who could drag them off to the showers. Or fight whatever comes in here."

"I don't like it," Jericho said.

"I don't like any of this, pal!" Sam yelled. "If you got a better idea, let me know."

Jericho didn't have a better idea, but he resented being stuck at the museum instead of where the action was. That was always his role, and he was tired of it. "Fine," he grumbled.

"Theta, I'd feel a whole lot better if you stayed here," Memphis said.

"Nothing doing. Henry's my best friend, my only family. He's all I got."

"You've got me," Memphis said softly.

"Poet, I didn't mean it that way...."

"Mabel shouldn't go. Theta shouldn't go. Why is no one being chival...chivaroos...how come none of you bums is looking out for me?" Evie pouted as she sprawled across her chair.

"I am," Theta said. She yanked Evie to a sitting position, put a cup of coffee to her lips, and practically poured it down her throat.

A TERRIBLE WAY TO DIE

By the time Theta, Memphis, Evie, and Sam reached City Hall Park, the rain was coming down steadily. Gutters ran with leaf-clogged, muddy rivers, all of it pouring down into the sewers and drains. From here, they could see the police lights still shining on Chinatown, but the park was empty.

"Remember, people have been disappearing in these tunnels," Memphis said. "Keep your wits about you."

"If that's supposed to make me feel better, you better find another line of work," Sam said.

"Then here's something else to cheer you," Memphis said. He held the lapels of his coat close to his neck and looked up at the stormy gray clouds in the night sky. "We better hope those tunnels don't fill up."

"Let's ankle. I want this over with and Henry safe," Theta said, shivering in the cold rain.

"I'd say our best bet is to try getting there through the City Hall station," Memphis said.

"We really gotta go through those tunnels?" Theta asked.

Memphis offered an apologetic shrug. "I don't see any other way."

They hurried down the steps of the City Hall station and pushed through the turnstiles. The platform was deserted.

"Gee. Like a library in here. Hello!" Evie called, letting her voice echo down the tracks.

"Can it, Evil!" Theta snapped. "If those...things...are down here, you really want 'em sniffing after us?"

Evie bowed her head, cowed. "I just like how my voice sounds."

Theta rolled her eyes. "Ain't that the truth."

"This way," Memphis whispered, and they followed him to the end of the platform, peering over the railing to the tracks below.

Theta stared down at the drop. "You gotta be kidding me."

Memphis held her hand. "I'll help you, Princess. Just stick with me."

"Poet, I'm gonna stick so close to you you'll think you gained a hundred and two pounds."

Memphis climbed over and jumped down first. He caught Theta, enjoying the weight of her in his arms. "Piece of cake," he said, smiling. "Come on down, Evie."

Evie attempted to clear the railing, but her heel caught. She took a flying leap, nearly flattening Memphis as she tumbled. "Careful, there," he said, catching her.

"Which way?" Sam asked, jumping down and wiping his hands on his trousers.

"Ling said Beach's pneumatic train station was near Broadway and Warren Streets, so that way." Memphis pointed straight ahead to the long curve of tunnel, lit only by a series of work lights high on the walls. It was dark and filthy and dangerous—no ledge, just wall and track. If a train were to come now, they'd be trapped. The third rail thrummed with electricity they could feel in the air and on the backs of their teeth.

"Watch out for that. That's the one with all the juice," Sam warned.

"It's freezing down here," Evie grumbled, the edges of her words still a bit messy. The coffee and the bitter cold had managed to take her from very drunk to less drunk with shades of irritable and belligerent.

"You'll live," Sam said. "Unless those hungry wraiths get us, in which case you won't, but you also won't have to worry about being cold anymore. So all in all, it's a grand night in Manhattan. Hip, hip, hooray."

"You're in a very funny mood," Evie said.

"I'm a funny guy," Sam grumbled and kept his flashlight trained on the path ahead. "Just keep walking."

Memphis lifted his eyes, taking in the grimy grandeur of the underground. "It's sort of beautiful, though, isn't it? Like a city below the city."

"If you say so, Poet. How much farther?" Theta asked, keeping her eyes on the edge of the ties; she didn't want her shoes getting caught between them.

Memphis bounced his flashlight beam across the concrete archways. "If Ling's right about the location of Beach's station, maybe a hundred feet?"

A rat scuttled quickly along the tracks, making Theta gasp. Memphis put his arm around her. "It's more scared of us than we are of it."

"It must be pretty scared, then," Theta said.

The passageway took on water as they walked. It smelled of sulfur and rot. They covered their noses, breathing through their mouths.

"Sam," Evie said a moment later, "I don't know what's happening."

"How drunk are you?"

"No. I mean . . . I mean 'bout any of this. About the dead and John Hobbes. Will. Rotke. Those cards we found. Project Buffalo," she said, the last word tripping off her booze-thickened tongue. "I need to tell you something, Sam. It's about tonight and what happened at the show."

Sam gestured to the dark underground, his flashlight beam bouncing off the metal and earth. "You want to have this conversation now? Here?"

"Shhh, listen. This fella brought a comb for me to read. Sam, it was James's comb," Evie said, keeping one hand on his back to steady herself.

"What are you talking about?"

"The comb. He said it belonged to his pal, but he was lying. That comb belonged to my brother. When I was under? I saw James."

Sam kept the flashlight trained on the path ahead as he took in what Evie was saying. "Did you know this fella?"

"Not from Adam. I swear."

"So how'd this Abe Stranger get your brother's comb?"

"He told me these men paid him to bring it to me. Men in dark suits."

"You think they're the same guys who busted in while we were in the post office?"

"I don't know, Sam. I don't know anything anymore." Evie swallowed. "Like you and me, for instance."

"There is no you and me. You made that pretty clear tonight," Sam muttered. "Listen, you asked me to play a part, and I did. From now on, I travel solo."

"Now who's lying? You forget. I read your personal effects. I know you."

"You know bupkes."

But the gin had loosened the last of Evie's restraint. "I've seen you. The true you. I've held your secrets in my hands. You're scared, Sam. You pretend you're not, but you are. Just like the rest of us."

Sam whirled around. "All you know about are parties, good times, and telling people what they wanna hear on the radio. And breaking hearts."

Sam pushed on, shining his flashlight ahead of them in the darkness. He hated that Evie had unsettled him like this. That was the trouble with letting people in—once you'd taken off the armor, it was hard to put it back on.

Evie stumbled after him. "Right! I forgot. I'm just a girl on the radio. Well, I only read what people choose to give me, Sam. You steal whatever you like and never think about what it costs anyone," Evie said, eyes brimming with tears.

"Don't cry," Sam said. He was all balled up inside. "Please don't cry. I got no defenses against girl tears."

"You can't have my tears, Sam Lloyd. I revoke them," Evie said through chattering teeth. "But don't go tellin' me what I know. 'Cause you don't know."

"I don't even know what we're arguing about anymore."

"Let's just put the ghost to bed. I want a bath. I want twelve baths. And then, tomorrow, we can announce the tragic end of our engagement. You wanna be alone? Be alone," Evie said, and she and Sam walked on in silence.

The water was now shin-deep. It sluiced up the sides of the tunnel as they walked and splashed up onto their clothes, chilling them through. Evie glanced through the arched steel supports of the subway tunnel toward the other side of the tracks and the platform heading in the opposite direction. The dark lit up for a second, revealing the bleached form of a man wearing a miner's hat. But there was something not quite right about him. He fell into a squat, his mouth opening and closing, opening and closing.

Evie gasped.

"What's the matter now?" Sam asked.

"Did—did you see that?" Evie whispered.

"See what?"

Evie pointed through the archway to an empty space. "Nothing," she said. "Nothing."

"Hey! I think I found it!" Memphis called. He stood in front of an old gate adorned with gilded flowers, markers of an age long past. The rust couldn't obscure how beautiful it had once been. Memphis and Sam tugged the gate open against the tide of water, the hinges protesting the sudden use after so many years asleep.

"We're in," Memphis said.

The flashlights weren't much help in the deep, velvet darkness of underground, but eventually everyone's eyes adjusted to the gloom. Memphis swept his flashlight beam around the forgotten station, briefly illuminating its decayed beauty.

"Holy smokes," Sam said, angling his head back to take in the high, arched ceilings. The stained-glass window was caked in decades of dust. A tarnished chandelier dangled precariously from its broken chain. Sam cleared cobwebs from the chipped piano keys. He plinked one, but it made no sound. It was like being inside a shipwreck on land. Down below lay the rotting remains of New York City's very first subway train.

"Careful on the stairs," Memphis cautioned as they stepped down to the lower platform. He stuck his head inside the car. "Nothing here but a bunch of dust."

Memphis's flashlight beam fell across the broken bulbs ringing the station's entrance and the etched lettering of the plaque there: BEACH PNEUMATIC TRANSIT COMPANY.

"Just like Isaiah's drawing," Memphis murmured.

"I don't like the feel of this place," Theta said.

"Why can't ghosts ever haunt some place swell, like the 21 Club?" Evie sneaked a drink from the secret flask she kept hidden in her garter.

"Evil!" Theta wrestled the flask from Evie's grip. "I'm gonna murder you."

"Oh, please, Theta! It's awful down here."

"Mine," Theta growled. She took a quick belt and handed it over to Memphis. "Don't let her have that back."

"I. Had. A very bad daaaay!" Evie yelled, and it bounced off the walls of the station.

"Shhh!" Theta whispered. "You wanna get us killed?"

Sam marched over to Evie. "You're on the air, Sweetheart Seer. Time to find something to read so we can find out what gets rid of these ghosts, save our friends, and get out of here."

Evie's face twisted into an expression of disgust. "I'm an object reader, not a compass. You can't just point me north."

Theta glared. "I'd love to point my foot right up your—"

"Can't she just read one of these lamps, or a piece of brick?" Memphis interrupted.

"I could. But it would be too much. It's not particular to any one person," Evie said, her mouth having to work hard to pronounce *particular*. "No one appreciates the artistry."

"If it's all the same to you, I don't wanna be here any longer than I have to be. The quicker we find something that looks like it belongs to our ghost, the better," Memphis said.

While Theta and Evie stood nearby, Theta moving her flashlight around the empty station, Sam kept his flashlight trained on Memphis as he poked into crumbling crevices of brick, looking for any object that might be helpful.

"Nothing," Memphis said after a while, and wiped his hands on his trousers. "Let's look down below."

The four of them walked the dusty tracks, shining their lights along the rocks piled there, kicking at mounds of dirt and watching the bugs scatter.

"There's nothing here, Memphis," Sam said.

"Only one place left," Memphis said, nodding toward the tunnel. "I suppose we'd better go in there."

"I was afraid you'd say that," Theta said.

The dark was oppressive. The flashlights did very little to cut the gloom. Theta kept one hand out in front of her for guidance.

"You would not believe the secrets I have to hold back on the radio," Evie said, as if the booze had unlocked the cabinet that held all her thoughts and they just kept tumbling out. "People are so lonely so much of the time. Mostly, that's what I feel, lurking under everything they put in my hands: how utterly, terribly alone people think they are when all they have to do is just reach out and touch someone..."

Evie's fingers grazed Theta's shoulder. Theta screamed, and Evie scrambled backward.

Memphis whirled around, knife at the ready. "What is it?"

Theta rested a hand on her heart. "Evil! You wanna give me a heart attack?"

"I was...I was just..." Evie panted. "Making a point."

"Well, don't."

"It's like that time I read your bracelet," Evie said. "I didn't want to tell you what I saw, because what if it upset you? Some people never think about that," Evie said too loudly, with a hard glare at Sam. "About the stuff I carry around with me all the time."

"What did you see when you read Theta's bracelet?" Memphis asked.

"She didn't see anything, Poet. Shut up, Evil!" Theta growled, but she sounded more frightened than angry.

"I did see! I was scared for you, Theta," Evie said. "All that fire."

"What's she bumping her gums about now?" Sam asked.

"She's drunk. But she's shutting up now, right, Evil?" Theta said.

"Aye, aye, Captain." Evie saluted. She turned and tripped, falling onto her backside in the dirt. "Ow."

Memphis helped Evie stand. His fingers grazed something solid in the spot where Evie had been sitting. "Sam, would you kindly shine that light over here?"

The beam of light caught the gleam of polished gray in the dirt. Memphis crouched down and brushed away the years of dust. "I think we might've found what we're after."

"Congratulations, Evil," Theta said, shuddering. "Seems like your can is a compass after all."

Evie stared at the mummified remains—the sunken eyes and the exposed, rotted teeth and the tattered, bloodstained dress. "I don't want to touch a thing on that….that…" she said, wagging a finger generally in the corpse's direction. "That."

"Evil, we gotta know."

"Okay," Evie said after a pause. "For Henry, okay." She struggled to take her gloves off. The half-empty sheaths flapped at the ends of her fingers. "These have stopped working."

"Oh, for Pete's sake." Theta tugged the gloves free.

Evie's mouth twisted into a pained grimace, the scream perched behind her teeth, as her fingers landed on the skeleton. "Why couldn't I have been a dream walker?" she squeaked. "Why'd it have to be object reading?"

"Come on, Sheba. You can do this." Sam nudged her.

Evie grasped the dead thing's wrist, breathing in and out as she tried to relax. The vision began as a tingle that spread up her arms, tightening the muscles of her neck. And then she was under, the vision playing out like a movie across a bright screen.

"A ship. I'm on a ship," Evie said. She gagged. "Seasick."

"You okay?" Sam's voice.

"You care," Evie murmured.

"What?" Sam said.

"Nothing," Evie mumbled. She allowed herself to ease back a bit until she felt better. "There's a ship unloading passengers," she said in a detached voice. "And a sign . . . Port of . . . San Francisco."

Guards funneled passengers toward a building for processing. Evie felt unmoored. She could feel the girl's fear pressing against her, making her heart race, so she tried to distance herself by concentrating on the paper in the girl's hand. It was printed in both Chinese and English: "*O'Bannion and Lee, Matchmakers.*" Two men entered the stuffy building. One was a big, burly white man with muttonchop sideburns and a handlebar mustache. The other was a Chinese man in a Western-style suit who smiled without showing his teeth. They paid the immigration official fifty dollars to look the other way, and took the girl and two others with them. The reading threatened to slip away.

Evie gripped the bony wrist tighter and a squalid New York City slum came into view: Streets thick with mud and horse dung. Filthy ragamuffins begging for scraps. A toothless, grime-coated woman talking sweetly to a rag-enrobed baby at her bare breast. Flies swarmed her.

"Shhh, that's a good boy," the woman said, and Evie could see that the baby was dead.

A drunk hoisted his tankard and, in a thick Irish brogue, shouted, "Welcome to Five Points, hell's backyard."

From atop a soapbox, a man harangued the crowd. ". . . close our borders to the wretched Chinese, whose loose women pollute our young men, destroy our families, take the white man's job . . ."

"Sheba? Anything?" Sam's voice floated to Evie from far away.

Evie's vision settled on a disheveled woman lying on a cot, clutching a music box. She had the glassy eyes of an opium addict. But it was the same girl. Evie sensed it.

"I think I found her," Evie murmured.

She could feel the opium in her veins, making her woozy and sick. Distance. She needed distance.

The man with the muttonchops pushed back the curtain. "Put aside your dreams. It's time to get to work, Wai-Mae."

A man waited with his coat off. Evie knew why he was there and what Wai-Mae was expected to do for this man. She couldn't stay in this vision any longer. She tried to break the connection, but it seemed the vision had something else to show her.

With a small grunt, she bit down on her back teeth as she traveled further under.

The filthy streets again. The muttonchop man dressed in a fine suit. Wai-Mae's hand on the knife. Wai-Mae racing toward him, plunging the dagger into his chest again and again. The man's blue eyes, surprised, shocked. The blood spreading across his white shirt, pulsing through his fingers. The man falling to the street. Police whistles. Shouts.

"Murder, murder," Evie mumbled.

Evie could feel her own heart beating with the girl's as she ran from the mob and down the steps into the basement of Devlin's, into Beach's pneumatic train station. She hid inside the stilled train car, beneath a velvet sofa, where she slept, and in her dream, there was the sound of men working. Wai-Mae opened her eyes only once, to see the light dimming down to nothing, but she was too weak to do anything but sleep.

Waking now. The gnawing hunger for opium. Evie gagged as Wai-Mae retched up bile and shivered. She staggered out of the car to find the tunnel bricked over. The dark was everywhere. Wai-Mae banged her hands against the brick, desperate. She slid down the wall. Evie felt the air thinning, making her head tight. Out. That was what Wai-Mae wanted. Out. Out of this terrible tomb. And the only way she'd been able to escape was through dreams.

Evie broke the connection and fell onto her knees in the dirt, gasping.

"Evil, you okay?" Theta gave Evie's back a couple of hard thwacks.

"Ow! Quit it!" Evie said, scrambling away.

"I thought you were choking!"

"I'm...tryin' a...breathe." Evie gulped down a few lungfuls of air. "She came down here to hide," Evie said, breathing heavily still. "But it was the day they closed up the station. While she slept there in that car, they bricked it all up. They buried her alive."

"What a terrible way to die. All alone," Sam said.

They fell silent as the horror and sadness of Wai-Mei's death hit them.

"Did you get anything about how we get rid of this dame or her Ziegfeld Ghost Follies?" Theta asked at last.

Evie kept a hand at her neck to calm her racing pulse. "I can't say for certain, but there was a feeling when I was under. This terrible place...I-I think it's keeping her here. She can't rest. We need to carry her bones out of here. She needs to be cared for."

"A proper burial," Memphis said.

"Fine. We'll have a funeral. Where?" Sam asked.

"Trinity Church isn't far from here. There's a graveyard. It's hallowed ground," Memphis said.

"You think that'll work?" Theta asked. "Jericho said each culture has its own beliefs."

"Beats me. I'm a rookie at this ghost game," Sam said with a shrug.

"We can't leave her in this terrible place," Evie said. "That much is clear."

"Well, I for one am all for getting out of here. Memphis, help a fella out?" Sam said.

Carefully, they lifted Wai-Mae's skeleton. Some of the bones fell into dust, but others remained intact.

"We can't put these in our pockets," Sam said.

Memphis took off his coat. "Here."

Sam laid the bones inside, and Memphis carefully wrapped them into a bundle.

"Here," Sam said, handing Evie the skull. "You can carry that. Merry Christmas."

Evie's mouth twisted in revulsion. "You've ruined the joy of the season for me forever."

"For Pete's sake, let's breeze," Theta said, gathering the blood-stained dress into a ball and marching back into the decrepit, abandoned station. "Shame," she said, looking up at the former grandeur gone to rot. But she was thinking, too, of Wai-Mei's tragic life.

As they cleared the tunnel, a sound came from behind them: soft but steady, like heavy rain dropping down from the ceiling—one, two, three, *fourfivesix*, more and more. Theta chanced a glance behind her and saw the thing that was so like a man squatting in the dark, his mouth open to emit a syrupy howl. Lights winked in the long darkness. In the glow, she saw only flashes: A sharklike tooth. Pale, cracked skin. Unseeing eyes.

"Memphis," Theta whispered.

The flashlight shook in his hand. He started to raise it, but Theta pushed his hand back down, shaking her head.

"Keep walking," Sam said. "Up and out."

"I hate g-ghosts," Evie whispered. "I really, really do."

The aged wood of the steps leading up to the passenger waiting platform creaked loudly under the weight of all four of them. Thick whispers filled the station. Above them, the mottled ceiling crawled.

Theta's voice was whisper-thin. "What do we do now?"

Memphis grabbed her hand. "I think we run."

MORNING GLORIES

Henry opened his eyes to sun. He was lying in the bottom of the row-boat, bobbing on the current. He didn't know how long he'd been floating there; he only knew that Louis wasn't beside him.

"Louis?" he called, sitting up. "Louis!"

He spotted Louis sitting under a weeping willow in the wide field of morning glories up on the hill.

"There you are," Henry said, coming to sit beside him. "Been look-ing all over for you."

"Looks like you found me," Louis said, and his voice sounded hollow.

"What should we do—go out in the boat? Take Gaspard for a walk? Fish?"

"I want to tell you about the morning glories, Henri. I remembered about them. Why I don't like them," Louis said quietly, and Henry felt a warning deep in his gut that the dream was turning.

"It doesn't matter," Henry said. He didn't want to have this con-versation. All he wanted to do was float down the river, just the two of them under a portion of sun that was all theirs. "Come on. Fish are biting."

He offered his hand, but Louis didn't take it. "I have to tell you now, while I'm brave enough to do it."

Henry saw that Louis wouldn't be moved, so he sat and waited.

Louis's words were slow, as if each one cost him. "'Member when

I told you I stopped by Bonne Chance that one night, askin' after you? Your daddy sent some men to see me. They told me to let you go. But I couldn't do that. So they roughed me up some. It's not like I hadn't taken plenty o' blows before, for bein' different." Louis scooped up handfuls of dirt, rubbing the grit of it between the pads of his fingertips. "But one of 'em, he hit my head mighty hard. Always thought I had a hard head, but..." Louis offered a ghost of a smile for his joke. It flickered on his lips for a second and then vanished. He looked up to the cruel blue of the sky. "I remember now, I remember..." he said, and it was with equal parts wonder and sorrow.

Inside Henry, some truth was descending like an avenging angel.

"I don't want to be here. Let's go down to the river, baby." Henry pulled desperately on Louis's arm, but Louis resisted.

"I need to tell you, *cher*. And you need to hear it. My head hurt something fierce. A real *mal de tête*. So I lay down right there on the ground to rest." Louis plucked a purple blossom from the lush patch of flowers and twirled it in his fingers. "It was a bleed on the brain. Nothin' to be done about it. The men come back and they found me on the ground, cold and still. And they buried me right there, under the morning glories. And that's where I am still, *cher*. Where I been since you left New Orleans, a long time gone."

"That can't be true."

"It is true, *cher*."

"You're here! You're right here."

"Where is here, Henri?" Louis insisted. "Remember, Henri. Remember."

Henry closed his eyes and shut out the world. It was astonishingly simple to do, a birthright, passed down to him from parents who never wanted to see the truth of anything, including their son. But just because someone refused to see the truth didn't mean it ceased to exist. Henry didn't want to remember, but it was too late. Already, he was surfacing.

"I waited for you. At Grand Central. But you never got off the train. Just like you never got my letters or my telegrams."

He remembered. The piano fund. Theta. When he opened his eyes, the tops of the trees were losing color. Dull pain throbbed in his body. His face was wet. "I want to stay with you."

"Can't, *cher*. You got all those songs to write."

Henry shook his head. "No. No."

"I don't know how I got here, or why I got to have this last time with you. I'm mighty grateful for it. But it's time for me to go now. You, too. You gotta wake up, Henry."

Henry looked at Louis. His lover was achingly beautiful. In Henry's memories, Louis would look like this always: young and full of possibility, shimmering around the edges. Something about that triggered other memories. Who had told him about the dead shimmering? He could see a girl with bright green eyes trained on him, weighing.

Ling. Brusque, honest Ling.

She'd told him from the beginning: She could only find the dead.

Ling. And Theta. Evie and Sam.

With each stroke of waking, the pain sharpened. Gaspard whimpered and licked Henry's hand. The hound looked up at him as if waiting for an answer to a question. Henry leaned his head back and blinked up at the indistinct leaves of an elm until he could find his words.

"I know. I know," Henry said. He cried out as the pain sliced through him.

"Gonna need some strength," Louis said. "Kiss me, *cher*."

Louis put his lips to Henry's, kissing the last of his strength into Henry. And when they pulled away, Louis was fading, like a sliver of moon late in the morning sky.

"Gaspard. Come on, boy. Time to go home." Louis whistled and the dog bounded toward him. The setting sun warmed the river to a shimmering golden-orange. "I'm headed over there. But you can't come along. Not yet."

Louis waved from the riverbank, and he was a bright thing, a portion of borrowed sun.

"Write me a good song, Henri," he called.

Henry's throat tightened as he waved back. "Sweet dreams."

Louis mounted the steps to the cabin, fading to gray as he went, and then Henry heard the faint, aching cry of a fiddle. The notes lingered on the wind for a moment more, and then even that was gone.

But some other memory was coming to him—a sense that there was somewhere he was needed, like a twin missing the other.

"Ling," Henry said as it came to him, and he set off running toward the forest.

THE OPIATE FUTILITY
OF HOPE

On the long Chesterfield, Henry and Ling lay perfectly still, dreaming, while Mabel and Jericho kept watch silently. Mabel took one of the soggy watercress sandwiches from the stack wilting on the fancy plate. Already she'd turned away several angry partygoers at the door. It spelled doom for the museum, though that seemed a moot point now.

"What do you suppose they're dreaming?" she asked, nibbling a corner of sandwich.

"I don't know."

"I hope they're all right down there."

"I shouldn't be here. I should be with them," Jericho said, and some dam gave way inside Mabel.

"So you could look after Evie?" she asked, looking up at Jericho.

Jericho turned back to watching their sleeping friends. "I didn't say that."

"You didn't need to. Was it after Knowles' End or before?"

Jericho kept silent, but the muscle at his jaw tightened.

"I suppose it doesn't really matter," Mabel said, pushing the rest of her sandwich aside. Black spots danced before her eyes as she fought back stinging tears. "Why did you kiss me, then, if you prefer her?"

"It isn't as simple as that," Jericho said.

Lightning flashed at the windows. Harsh light streaked across Mabel's fists. She could see every freckle on her skin. He'd chosen Evie. It didn't matter that Evie was liable to break his heart, that she could never care for Jericho the way Mabel did, or that Mabel had volunteered her time to help with the exhibit. It didn't matter that Evie could have any boy she wanted, and would. *He'd chosen her.* The realization sucked the air from Mabel's lungs. Every day, Mabel Rose worked to make the world a little fairer. But the hard truth was that there was some unfairness you couldn't do anything about. You couldn't make a boy like you just because you liked him so very much. And tonight, as she'd watched Jericho with Evie, she knew the truth: Jericho was in love with Evie. Did Evie know? Had she known all along, even as she had encouraged Mabel and given her advice?

God, she was such an idiot.

And she hated this dress. Evie had been wrong—it didn't suit her disposition at all. That was just the way Evie wanted to see her. The way everyone wanted to see her: Good old Mabel. Reliable, predictable Mabel. Chipper Mabel.

When she got home, she was going to burn this dress.

Jericho indulged in his odd habit of making a fist and releasing it. Mabel had found it eccentric but charming before. Now it grated on her.

"Would you like some coffee?" Jericho asked.

It was a peace offering, Mabel knew, but she wasn't going to give him the satisfaction. She shook her head.

Jericho crossed the room and poured himself a cup of coffee he didn't want or need. The truth was that Jericho wanted Evie but wasn't sure that he could have her. He could have Mabel but wasn't sure that he wanted her. Neither scenario made him feel very good about himself. More than ever, he wished he had someone to explain his emotions and girls to him, to help him figure out how you knew when it was right.

"I kissed you because I wanted to," Jericho answered after a while.

"Are you just being kind?"

"No. That's the truth."

"If you want to kiss me again, you can," Mabel said. "But only if you really want to. I'm not Evie. I never will be."

Jericho reached over and took her hand, and her stomach knotted. What did that mean? Was it brotherly affection, or some deeper passion? It was not a kiss; that much was clear. *It's over*, her mind whispered. *There's still hope*, her heart insisted. What was it Jericho had called it—the opiate futility of hope? Well, right now, Mabel wanted to be drunk on it.

On the couch, Ling sucked in a thin thread of air. Her fingers stiffened, then softened again.

"Is she all right?" Mabel asked mechanically.

"I think so. We should probably keep close watch," Jericho said, breaking away.

"Of course," Mabel said, hating that he was right, hating that she was all wrong.

TERRIBLE ANGELS
COME TO EARTH

In the ruin of Beach's pneumatic train station, the growling whine was everywhere. The strange, bright things uncoiled and dropped to the dusty tracks. The way they moved—twitching and lurching, followed by lightning-quick bursts of adrenaline—was like watching wounded animals determined to survive.

"*Dreamdreamhungryhungrydream . . .*" they chorused.

They seeped out of the cracks in the walls like cockroaches. Memphis counted five, ten, a dozen at least. It was ten feet to the gate. Memphis held tightly to Wai-Mae's bones. With the other hand, he laced his fingers through Theta's.

"Run," he said, and the four of them bolted across the dusty platform and burst through the gate. Behind them, the wraiths growled their displeasure.

"Which way back to the station?" Theta screamed.

"This way." Memphis swung his light to the left and stopped short. He thrust his arm out to hold back the others, then carefully shone the beam forward again. A ghostly woman in a blue dress was caught in the hazy light. Her head whipped in their direction. She sniffed. Her upper lip curled, revealing jagged teeth.

"Don't move," Memphis whispered. "Be . . . perfectly . . . still."

The girl in the blue dress took one stumbling step forward, sniffing again. She swayed unsteadily. And then her mouth opened with a shriek. Other shrieks answered, the roar of an unholy army.

Sam flicked his flashlight to the right. The long corridor appeared empty. "Other way," he yelled, and they ran deeper into the underground.

"I don't want to say I told you so," Evie said, her voice bumping with the movement. "But I did, in point of fact, tell you so."

"Save your breath," Sam panted. "You're gonna need it."

Memphis glanced over his shoulder at the greenish wisps flickering between the underground arches. A pack of them was weaving toward them, jerking and twisting. Their terrible barking grunts rang down the tracks. A warning. Or a call for reinforcements.

"Watch it!" Memphis called, yanking Sam back just before his boot went under the wooden covering of the third rail.

"Thanks, pal," a shaky Sam managed. "I coulda been cooked."

"Don't thank me yet. There's miles of tunnels down here. Plenty of places for those things to hide."

"Keep moving," Theta insisted. "I can see a station up ahead. Gotta be Brooklyn Bridge."

The bright lights of the station bounced before their eyes as they ran. They were close. A sound like claws clicking across a tile floor made the hair on Sam's neck tickle. He looked up. Nothing. But just to his right, about three steps ahead, some movement caught his eye. He flashed his beam to the space between arches. Up high, a wraith hissed and scurried down the subway wall in a backbend, like a giant spider, its fingernails clacking against the tile, loud as tap shoes. It hissed again as it dropped to the tracks in front of them. A stuffed rabbit dangled from its ghostly hand.

"What. Is. That?" Theta said, stopping completely.

"It's a kid," Memphis said. "It's just a kid."

"Was a kid," Sam corrected, backing away. "Some kind of... demon now."

"All children are demons," Evie said, breathing heavily. "This is precisely why I always refused to babysit."

"Shut up, Evil," Theta said in a terrified whisper.

The night was alive with shrieks and growls and deep-throated calls, a demonic chorus drawing nearer. In front of them, the little girl unhinged her mouth. Blood dark as midnight coursed down the deep cracks lining either side of her mouth; she was like a hungry animal sensing prey.

"Oh, that is uncalled for," Evie whispered in terror.

The ghostly little girl lunged, jaws snapping, but her coordination was off. She tumbled, face-first, onto the tracks. In that split second, Memphis yanked Evie out of the way, tugging her toward the Brooklyn Bridge station. From the tracks, the thing that had been a little girl turned her head toward them, sniffing. Shrieking, she chased after Memphis and Evie. The other things were visible in the tunnel, flickering against the darkness, cutting off any chance for Sam and Theta to follow.

"Come on," Sam said, leading Theta across the tracks and through the pillars to a connecting tunnel.

"But Memphis—"

"We can't go that way. Theta!" Sam insisted. "It's this way or we're dead."

Reluctantly, Theta watched them go and raced alongside Sam as they headed into the tunnels, away from Memphis and Evie.

❉

Memphis and Evie climbed onto the platform at Brooklyn Bridge station, pushing through the new coin-operated turnstiles, past the relic of a wooden ticket chopper, and headed straight for the empty ticket booth. Memphis wrenched open the door and pushed Evie inside, following on her heels. He slammed the door and locked it. The glowing wraith was nowhere to be seen. But in a moment, her small hands crept over the edge of the platform as she pulled herself up, crawling forward quickly, like a bug.

"I had a friend back home, Dottie, who was double-jointed, and I thought it was the berries. But that is truly hideous," Evie whispered.

"Shhh," Memphis cautioned.

The wraith child sniffed twice, then threw herself at the iron grating of the ticket booth. With a shout, Evie and Memphis fell back against the wall of the tiny space. The wraith's arm pushed through the tiny cut-out at the bottom where change was made daily. And then it squeezed itself through like a snake.

"I. Hate. Ghosts!" Evie screamed. She yanked open the door and pulled Memphis after her as they ran up the steps toward the street. The first staircase ended in a corridor that branched left and right.

"Which way? Which way?" Evie cried.

It didn't matter. At both ends, the wraiths were coming. And from below, the little girl had begun her ascent.

"Get behind me," Memphis said, sweeping Evie back with his arm.

"I want to tell you not to be noble, but I'm terrified," Evie said.

"Me, too."

Instead, Evie came around and stood beside Memphis, holding his hand.

"I really wanted to be somebody," Evie said, her voice catching.

The wraiths were closing in. The little girl had reached the top of the steps. She was a foot away. Evie could smell the rot on her and see the deep, dark gashes in her glowing skin. She wanted to shut her eyes but was too afraid. Memphis squeezed her hand.

The thing that had once been a little girl stepped very close to Memphis and inhaled deeply. She shrank back, hissing. She let loose a spine-chilling howl. The others answered. Memphis and Evie stood perfectly still. The girl slunk back down the steps, down into the dark, sniffing for other prey.

"Why did it do that?" Evie whispered.

"I don't know," Memphis whispered back. He glanced down the corridor, left and right. "They're not moving. Let's run while we can," Memphis said, and Evie didn't have to be asked twice. They kept alert as they inched up the next set of steps, not making a sound until they broke out onto the rain-soaked streets, and then, as the pounding rain washed over them, they let loose the screams they'd held back. People passing by under the cover of umbrellas stared at them as if they were lunatics. One woman covered her mouth with a gloved hand. "Dear me," she said, and it was only then that Evie realized she still held Wai-Mae's skull in the crook of her arm.

"We're performing *Hamlet*," Evie said, tucking the skull inside her coat. "Every evening at eight, and a matinee on Sunday."

"Do you see Theta?" Memphis asked, whipping around in circles.

"Perhaps they got out first, and they're already on their way to the graveyard," Evie answered.

"I don't want to leave without Theta."

"I'm not going back down there," Evie said. "We said we were going to Trinity Church. They'll know to meet us there. The sooner we bury these bones, the safer we'll all be."

Rain coursed over Memphis's worried face. "You certain about that?"

"I'm not certain about anything anymore, Memphis."

Memphis gave the underground one last, woeful glance. He held the bones tightly to his chest. "It's about six blocks to Trinity. We'd better hurry."

"Time for your second act, Yorick," Evie said, holding fast to the skull as she trotted after Memphis in the rain.

✳

Sam and Theta had run north, coming out in a tunnel under construction, and the way ahead was a dead end, blocked by debris, steel and wood scraps, pipes, giant drills, and digging equipment. Sewer water and runoff from the storm streamed into the tunnel via a pipe. Already the water was up to their knees.

"Sam, stop!" Theta called, doubled over. "Where are Memphis and Evie?"

"I-I don't know," Sam gasped, holding a hand to his side where it ached. "But we gotta get outta here."

"How? It's a dead end, and those things are behind us!" Theta said. Her eyes searched the claustrophobic space for a weapon, and she decided on a section of pipe, which she wielded like a bat.

Sam pushed through the fetid water to a set of rungs jutting out from the concrete wall. He peered up. "I think this ladder leads to a manhole and the street!"

Theta pushed against the water, moving toward the wall. She stopped suddenly.

"Theta, hurry!"

Theta shook her head. She gripped the pipe tightly. "Something moved. Under the water."

Sam held perfectly still. He swept his flashlight beam across the murky brown water. "Nothing. It's okay. Just keep moving."

Theta took another step and stopped again. The water's surface buckled; a glow came up from underneath, rippling out in waves. And then the wraith broke through, rising up in front of Theta, blocking any hope she had of reaching Sam and the ladder. It was big, well over six feet, and broad, with the build of a bricklayer or ironworker. Its eyes were milky, as if it had not seen light for a very long time, but its teeth were needle-sharp, and that mouth...that mouth opened with an unnatural elasticity, dark, viscous drool coursing down over a chalky jaw. And that sound—as if all the demons of hell were singing.

Theta's throat constricted, forcing her breath out in short, shallow puffs. Fear tightened its grip on her, and a sense memory arose—nights spent listening for Roy's boots banging up the steps, Theta staring at the turning doorknob, stiffening her body in anticipation of the blows.

"Theta," Sam shouted. "Hold on!"

But Theta couldn't really hear Sam. It was as if she were in danger of floating away, out of her body, away from fear and pain, the way she used to do with Roy, like a child crooking a finger inside her and showing her the way to a hiding closet. She was vaguely aware of Sam lunging, swinging the knife at the wraith's broad back, vaguely aware of the knife sticking fast but having no effect. Her body shook as Sam thrust out a hand, screaming, "Don't see me," but the broken thing lurched toward Theta, undaunted.

"*Dreamdreamhungrydream* . . ." it said in that garbled, satanic voice.

The lamp on the front of the thing's digger's helmet flickered in Theta's eyes, hypnotic keystrokes of light.

Roy's voice rang in her head:

Where's my dinner, Betty Sue? Were you flirting with that boy, Betty Sue? I saw you. Don't lie to me. You know how I feel about lies.

The wraith latched on to her arm. It smelled of spoiled meat and curdled milk. Theta turned her head and shut her eyes. She thought of Roy coming for her with his fists and his taunts and his belt.

"*Dreamhungrydreamhungry . . .*" the thing growled. Unthinking. Unfeeling.

Its foul breath was on her neck, filling her nostrils.

Roy. Roy smelling of beer. Drunk on anger and disappointment and violence.

The trembling in Theta's body had progressed to shaking. Her palms itched. Tears ran down her face, but she could not make a sound.

Don't you cry or I'll give you something to cry about.

The undead's stinking, dangerous mouth was close.

On the bed. Him on top. Her mouth bloody. Blood in her nose. Close to choking.

With a cry, Theta put up a hand, a barrier between herself and the thing that wanted only to infect her with the shared dream, to stay alive any way it could, to break her as it was broken. Its skin was soft and oily against the thin cotton of her glove, like rotting fruit. Theta gagged, vomiting a little in her mouth. The itching under her skin caught, like gas finding flame at a stove burner. The temperature inside Theta rose. Rivulets of sweat poured down her body. The heat raced along her nerve endings, shooting out to her hand. The thing screeched as Theta burned it. It lashed and shook as it burned down to bone.

"Theta!" Sam said sharply. And then, more gently, "Theta, let go."

She opened her eyes and saw Sam. The fabric of her glove had burned away, and in some places, it was embedded in her flesh. She gripped a scrap of the thing's shirt. Sam pried it loose and dropped it, leaving it to float on the water. He examined her hands. They were red and blistered.

"Gonna need to see to those," Sam said. "You hurting?"

"Not yet," Theta said.

"We have to get up to the street, Theta."

The water. It was up to Theta's chest. She nodded, shivering. The earlier heat had gone, and now she felt as if she would never be warm again. "Sam? Please. Don't...don't tell Memphis."

Sam glanced down at the digger's hat bobbing in the sewer's water current. He looked back at Theta. "I didn't see nothing."

The way they'd come crackled with light like a dozen gangsters firing Tommy guns from a moving car at night. Shrieks bounced off the walls. More were coming.

"Time to go," Sam said.

Theta waded through the filthy water and climbed up the ladder, wincing as the pain bit at her burned palms. And then she and Sam were sliding the manhole cover off, pulling themselves up onto the neon-painted puddles of Broadway and running for the graveyard.

***

Ling found herself on the barren streets of Chinatown. Fog clung to the rippling New Year's banners and the zigzag fire escapes. There were no lights at the windows, and the businesses were shuttered. Big yellow quarantine notices had been stuck to every door. The windows of the Tea House were dark. The rest of the city loomed as a distant silhouette, shadowy and unreachable.

Where is everyone? Ling didn't know if she'd thought that or said it aloud. Her mind was as cloudy as the streets. But her body was tense, alert, ready for some impending battle.

A ship's horn blasted a farewell, and through a clearing in the fog, Ling could see to the harbor and the great big steamer sailing away, her parents and Uncle Eddie at the stern, crowded in among Ling's neighbors, all of them waving good-bye. Her sorrowful mother fluttered her handkerchief. Her father's mouth moved, but Ling couldn't hear what he was saying as the fog swallowed them up.

"Baba! Mama!" Ling cried, and it echoed in the empty streets.

The high shimmer of a gong rattled the windowpanes. Zhangu

drums beat out a steady warning of war. The heavy pounding matched the furious rhythm of Ling's heartbeat. And just under the drums, rising, was a high-pitched, insectlike whine that made Ling's skin crawl.

Glowing faces appeared at the windows and receded. Ling whirled around. At the bottom of the street, George Huang waited. He seemed carved of chalk. Lips as colorless as new corn twitched around a diseased mouth. Deep fissures erupted on his face, neck, and hands, his skin cracking open as if he were rotting from the inside. George's mouth opened in a shriek. For a moment, Ling couldn't think. She could only stare at the pale figure of George Huang, that thing between life and death, as his fingers reached toward her, clutching and straightening like a puppet's. Then he dropped to a crouch and skittered up the side of the building like a fast-moving beetle.

Run, a voice inside her said faintly. *Run*. How to run? Why had her body forgotten this simple movement? *Run*. When she looked down, the street was a river of pitch. Slick hands emerged from the sticky ooze. They grabbed at her ankles. Ling gasped as the braces appeared on her legs, the buckles tightening and tightening. She cried out, and suddenly the dream shifted and Ling lay on a hospital bed, her back arching with pain as spasms ate away at her legs, the muscles dying.

Two neat lines of beds flanked the room, stretching as far as Ling could see, all of them occupied by dreamers. They sat up and turned their rotting faces to her, chorusing, *"Dream with us dream with us dream forever dream with us dream dream forever dream."*

Uncle Eddie was beside her, his expression grim as he read her medical chart. "They never should've done it," he said, placing the chart on the bed. The words swam: *Subject #28. New York, New York.*

Another spasm gripped Ling and she cried out in agony. A nurse swept the curtain around them. She bent her face close to Ling's. "Would you like the pain to end?"

"Y-yes," Ling begged.

"Then *dream with us.*"

Through a parting in the curtain, George appeared, and Ling's mouth tried to form the words to warn the nurse, to say *look, look, ohpleaselook behind you*, but the words could only bounce around inside her head.

The hospital lights arced. In the flashes of light, George's eyes shone bright as a demon's.

"George. I'm sorry. Please. Please," Ling whispered.

He looked at her for just a second as if he knew her. Then his mouth spread wide, the muscles of his neck straining as if he were trying to birth something from his throat. His fingers, wrinkled as funeral crepe, reached toward her, lighting first on her medical chart.

Don't look, Ling told herself. *Don't look and it won't be real.* The insect drone was so loud Ling thought she'd lose her mind. And then there was silence. When Ling opened her eyes again, George was gone.

Words had been scrawled on her medical chart: *"Don't promise. Pearl."*

Ling heard her name being called. It sounded as if it were coming from another room, an adjacent dream.

"Ling! Ling Chan, where are you?"

"Henry!" Ling called.

Henry swept the curtain aside. He clutched the fabric as if it were the only thing holding him up.

"Henry? Are you really here?"

Henry managed a half smile. "It would seem so," he said, and even his voice was weak.

"How did you find me?"

"If I were guessing, I'd say you came after me." Henry took several shallow breaths. "I'd say you're somewhere right now, sleeping with my hat in your hands."

"Yes," Ling said, remembering. "Yes."

Henry stumbled to the bed. Red marks dotted his neck. "Ling. It's time for a different dream now."

"I can't. I can't. The pain."

"You're not feeling any pain, darlin'. That's just a bad dream. You can wake up in your bed anytime you like."

"No. We have to go back. Back to the tunnel. Wai-Mae. We have to end it."

"All right, then." Henry took Ling's hand. "Why don't you dream about the tunnel, Ling? You know the one I mean. And you and I are both there. We are *both there*."

Henry's words swirled through Ling's head. She relaxed, and the hospital dream fell away. Ling was back inside the tunnel. The bricks glowed brightly with dreams trapped in service to the great machine of forgetting. Henry lay on the ground, weak and pale.

"Henry?" Ling whispered.

Bells. The lilting notes of a tinny music-box song. The rustle of blood-stiffened skirts. She was coming.

"Do it," Henry said.

Ling's body still ached. She hadn't much strength. If she was going to defeat Wai-Mae, she needed to get on top of the pain and change the dream as she had learned to do under Wai-Mae's tutelage.

Breathe deeply.

Concentrate.

One thing at a time.

Wai-Mae blazed in the dark. "What are you doing, Little Warrior?"

Ling didn't answer. She directed every bit of her mental energy to changing her legs back. But it wasn't working.

"Do you think it was you who changed the dream all those times? No. That was my power, not yours."

"No. I did it. I felt it."

"I only allowed you to think it was your doing. So you would be happy. So you would come back to me."

The courage Ling had carried into the dreamscape ebbed. It was like the day she learned she would never run again, never walk without those ugly braces. Once again, her choices had been taken from her without her consent. She felt the unfairness of it like a punch.

"You can choose to be happy." Wai-Mae moved a hand across the entrance to the tunnel, and the surface came alive with new wonders: Ling in a beaded gown, dancing the Charleston on strong, sturdy legs.

Ling standing before a mesmerized crowd at Jake Marlowe's Future of America Exhibition as he demonstrated her advance in atomic science. Ling shaking hands with Jake Marlowe himself while her parents looked on, so proud—all of it so close Ling felt she could reach out and grab these dreams in her fist.

"Or you can choose to be unhappy." The surface clouded. The image disappeared. In its place was a new picture, of Ling struggling to walk over New York's bumpy streets while people stared. Ling sitting at the back of her father's restaurant behind the teak screen, alone.

"Turn away from the world, sister," Wai-Mae said gently. "Stay and dream with me. If we take that one"—she nodded toward Henry—"we will have so much power. Enough for many, many dreams. Soon, the other world will open for us. The King of Crows is coming. He will—"

A loud *thwack* reverberated in the tunnel as Henry smashed a rock against one of the brick screens. His whole body trembled, but he reached down deep, and with a cry, he smacked the rock against the wall again, cracking the screen. The energy inside it swooshed out on a tail of light that swirled around, then dispersed into the dark. Wai-Mae faltered a bit. Henry went to smash another, but he could barely lift his arm.

"You have no honor!" Wai-Mae grasped Henry's head between her palms. "I will make you suffer as I suffered."

"Wai-Mae, stop! Stop and…and I will dream with you," Ling promised.

Wai-Mae released Henry, and he again fell to the ground. Sick and hurting, he made a feeble swipe at Wai-Mae's ankle, but she stepped easily out of the way.

"*Will you dream with me?*" Wai-Mae trailed fingertips lightly down Ling's arm, and in the gesture were both terror and desire, a coin twirled on a bargaining table the moment before coming to rest in judgment. "*Will you promise?*"

Don't promise. Pearl.

Ling reached into her pocket. Nothing.

Pearl, she thought. *Pearl*. A spark flared at her fingertips. It tripped up her hand. She could feel the pearl taking shape, round and hard and real.

"*Will you dream with me?*" Wai-Mae asked, more insistent. "*Will you promise?*"

"Ling…" Henry warned. "Don't."

Ling brought her hands to her mouth as if in prayer. Then she motioned Wai-Mae closer with a finger. Wai-Mae dropped down; her face hovered near Ling's.

"I. Will." Ling brought her mouth to Wai-Mae's. "Not!"

Quickly, Ling pressed her lips to Wai-Mae's. She loosed the pearl she'd just slipped beneath her tongue. Wai-Mae's eyes widened in surprise. Her fingers fanned at her throat.

"Take…it…out," Wai-Mae growled.

Ling shook her head. Henry crawled to Ling's side. The tunnel wobbled, erasing itself. As it did, the dream world also began unraveling. Pine needles browned and fell. The forest thinned to sticks. The flowers of the meadow sank back into grass that flattened to nothing. For a moment, they were aboveground, on the streets of Five Points. Firecrackers exploded in the sky, brief pops of hope above the sagging rooftops.

"No," Wai-Mae croaked, trembling. She struggled to breathe. Two tears streaked down her cheeks. "This…will all die with me. No more. Without dreams is to die twice."

They were back in the old train station. Light crackled up the walls and along the expanse of ceiling like shorted electrical wires. And then the station began to curl in on itself, a dream unwritten, something to be forgotten by the banal blur of morning.

"Please…" Wai-Mae begged.

For a moment, Ling's courage wavered. She looked to Henry. "Can't we save her?"

"We are saving her," he reminded her.

Wai-Mae glowed, a star brightening before death. Bright rays fractured her body, a violent birth, an inevitable collapse. And then there was an explosion of white light, shooting out across the dreamscape.

Henry and Ling shielded each other and shut their eyes against its brilliance.

☀

In the graveyard of Trinity Church, Memphis and Evie dug at the muddy earth to make a shallow grave. She swiped a filthy, wet arm across her equally sopping brow.

"Where are they?" she called over the rain.

"I'm sure they'll be here any second," Memphis answered, but he sounded nervous. "Best thing we can do is to keep digging."

"I was afraid you'd say that," Evie groused.

"Memphis!" Theta came tearing around the corner of New York's oldest church with Sam right behind her.

Memphis leaped up and embraced her. "I was so worried about you."

"We ran into a little trouble with a fella who wouldn't take no for an answer," Sam said.

"One of those things had you cornered?" Memphis said.

Theta nodded.

"How'd you get away?" Memphis reached for Theta's hands and she cried out. Memphis saw the weeping flesh there. "Theta! How'd you get these burns?"

"I-I..."

"It was a steam pipe," Sam said with a quick glance at Theta. "Let's just get these bones into hallowed ground and give 'em a proper burial."

Sam, Evie, and Memphis dug furiously until they'd managed a decent hole.

"Good enough, you think, Memphis?" Sam asked.

"I say it's good enough," Evie insisted.

"Then here goes nothing," Sam said, rocking back on his heels and breathing heavily.

Memphis and Theta lowered Wai-Mae's skull and remaining bones into the shallow grave, then Memphis packed the dirt over it with hands made cold by the wet and the chill in the air.

"I don't know about Chinese rituals. But it seems as if we oughta say a prayer of some kind," Memphis said.

"What kinda prayer do you say to get rid of a ghost?" Theta asked.

"I surely don't know. But I expect a prayer of any kind is better than none."

All of them bowed their heads except for Sam.

"Sam?" Evie nudged him with an elbow.

"Trust me: If God exists, he'll know I'm faking it."

Memphis kneeled in the mud. He placed one hand on the grave. "Be at peace, restless spirit," he whispered. He felt the tiniest jolt, a fraction of connection, and then it was gone.

"Is that it? Did we do it?" Theta asked.

Sam shrugged. "Don't look at me. I'm not the ghost expert. Is anything trying to kill us?"

Under the shadow of Trinity Church's great gothic spire, they huddled together in the rain, listening for the hungry wraiths and hearing nothing but the drops and the sudden comfort of the city's horns and irritable shouts and constant hum of noise.

"I think we did it," Memphis said with both relief and awe.

"Let's go back to the museum," Theta said, teeth chattering. "I want to know if Henry's all right."

"Let me see those hands first," Memphis said.

"Poet..."

"Theta."

Reluctantly, Theta held out her raw palms. Memphis took them in his own hands.

Theta winced.

"Sorry," Memphis said. "Do you trust me?"

"Yes," she whispered.

"It'll be okay. I promise."

Memphis shut his eyes. The spark when it caught was gentle, like being sweetly cradled in the healing trance. He heard drums and the joyful noise of ancestor spirits singing, and up above was blue, blue sky forever. His body warmed. He heard Theta's voice calling, "Memphis?"

Theta stood in front of him, grinning like somebody seeing happiness for the first time. "I can feel you," she said without actually speaking aloud. "And I'm not afraid."

Her head dipped back and her eyes closed. A rush came over Memphis; he felt made of light. The singing was everywhere, and for just a moment the two of them were joined, one body, one soul, as if they'd jumped a broom and landed on the other side in a place of sunshine.

Memphis's eyes fluttered open. Theta's eyes were wide, and she was crying.

"Did I hurt you?"

She laughed through tears. "You could never hurt me."

Her hands lay in Memphis's, the last of the burns fading to nothing.

In the rain-swollen tunnels, the wraiths vanished with a long sigh. The subways scattered the last of their essence as they rattled through, carrying sleepy passengers eager for bed, ready for sleep. Tonight, their dreams would be safe.

In the dreamscape, the shining lair had begun its final unwinding. Henry and Ling watched it go, its memories lost to whatever archive held such passions.

"Louis?" Ling asked after a moment. The lights were winking out, one by one.

Henry shook his head.

"I'm sorry, Henry."

Henry looked up at the ceiling, where the herringbone pattern lost its glorious detail. "I think it's time we woke up, don't you?"

"Yes. I'm ready."

"You know what to do?"

"Don't worry," Ling assured him.

"I'm not," Henry said. "Ling, darlin', it's been a long night. You've done well. You can wake up now, anytime you like. Wake up, Ling Chan."

Ling's face went slack. Her eyelids fluttered. And then she was gone from the dream world, leaving only the vaguest sense she'd ever been there at all, just another shifting of atoms. And just before she woke, she thought she saw George, shimmering and golden, smiling at her from the bend in Doyers Street on a New Year's Day, fireworks exploding with color high above his head, a moon cake in his hand, as if he had all the time in the world to enjoy it.

While Henry waited for Ling to wake him back in the real world, he sat one last time at the Chickering before it, too, was gone. He rested his fingers on the keys, and then he began to play. He was still playing when he heard the alarm begin to scream, and the last remnants of the dream station blurred into feathery whiteness and disappeared forever.

It was Theta's mud-spattered, worried face Henry saw first through the narrow slits of his heavy eyes when he awoke back in the museum.

"Henry?" she pleaded. She was soaked through and smelled like a garbage dump, but she was by his side.

"Theta," he croaked.

"Henry!" Theta hugged him. Henry gagged. "Whatsa matter? You sick?"

"No." Henry coughed. "You smell bad."

Theta was laughing and crying at the same time.

"How's my best girl?" Henry asked.

"Everything's jake," Theta said, holding tightly to him.

Memphis stood back, leaving them be. After all, didn't he have a brother, too?

"Ling," Henry said, reaching for her. Theta went to pull Ling into the circle, even though she looked uncomfortable.

"I don't hug," Ling said, sandwiched between the two of them.

"Sam!" Sam said, hugging himself. "You're welcome. Don't mention it."

Evie wasn't right. Her eyes were glassy and she seemed unsteady on her feet.

"Evil?" Theta asked, concerned.

"Did one of those things get her?" Ling asked.

594

"Evie," Sam said. "Hey. You okay?"

Evie turned and threw up.

❋

It was nearly dawn. Filthy and famished, Theta, Memphis, and Sam crowded around the long table, wolfing down the limp watercress sandwiches. Theta offered Henry half of hers. Jericho handed Ling a cup of broth.

"It's not fancy, but it's warm," he said, and she thanked him with a nod. "Could I use your telephone, please?"

Jericho brought her the phone as well, and a moment later, he could hear Ling speaking Chinese in hushed tones to someone.

Across the room, Mabel poked the dying fire into flames to chase away the chill. Evie sprawled in a chair, nursing a cup of coffee. She looked rough. The remnants of the scuttled Diviners exhibit were still everywhere.

Theta took out a cigarette.

"There's no smoking in the museum," Jericho said.

Theta glared up at him as she struck a match. "There is now. Hand me that ashtray, will ya, Mabesie?"

"I thought I was the only one who called you Mabesie," Evie said.

Theta shrugged and kept smoking. Mabel folded her arms across her chest and looked away.

Ling hung up the telephone and took a sip of her broth.

"Everything copacetic with your parents?" Sam asked.

"There was a protest. People surrounded the mayor's office, and he gave the order to bring everyone back to Chinatown. But I wouldn't say everything is copacetic. It's only one battle."

"Amen," Memphis said, locking eyes with Ling, an unspoken understanding passing between them.

"As we're all present and accounted for, I call this meeting to order." Jericho paced the room, just as Will so often did. "It should be patently clear by now that something is going on in this country. First

John Hobbes. Then this business with Wai-Mae and those wraiths in the tunnels. There are ghosts and demons among us. Every day, there are more reports. And it seems like we're the only ones who can do something about it."

"You mean we have to work together," Mabel said coolly, looking from Evie to Jericho.

Sam raised an eyebrow. "You trying to unionize us, Mabel?"

"No. Even the Wobblies are easier to organize," she said.

Evie's eyes were still closed. "I hate ghosts."

"All these powers and we know bupkes about 'em," Sam said. "It's like having the keys to a brand-new roadster and not knowing how to drive it."

For a moment, there was nothing but the steady percussion of the rain and the crackle of the fire. With a sigh, Evie sat up and opened her bloodshot eyes. "Sam, I think we should tell them about what we've found."

"Nothing doing," Sam said.

"Either you do it or I will."

"This is twice you've done this to me. Remind me never to tell you a secret again."

"It's not your secret anymore."

"Fine," Sam grumbled. He placed a coded punch card on the table. It was a little worse for the wear, thanks to the evening's activities, but it was still intact.

"What's this?" Memphis asked, picking it up.

"Evie and I found these files in a basement office in the post office. Used to belong to the U.S. Department of Paranormal."

"The what?" Ling asked.

"It was a secret government division started by President Roosevelt to investigate supernatural phenomena and recruit Diviners to aid in the interests of national security," Jericho explained.

"Teddy Roosevelt? On the level?" Theta said, impressed.

"Hey. How'd you know that, Freddy?" Sam asked.

"It's all here in Will's letters to Cornelius Rathbone. Diviners have been around since the dawn of the country," Jericho explained, gesturing to the useless Diviners exhibit. "You'd know that if you'd been around. Sam, Evie, Memphis, Ling, Henry—every one of you is a Diviner in some way."

Mabel put a hand on Theta's shoulder. "Some of us are just hideously ordinary, I suppose. Or does that make us extraordinary?" Mabel said, digging at Jericho just a bit.

Sam and Theta exchanged a furtive glance, but Evie caught it.

"What was that look about?" Evie asked.

"Nothing. Just stretching my eyes," Sam said quickly. "So what now? Do we start a speakeasy? A ghosty quilting bee? Does *everybody* want a radio show?"

"We find out why," Ling said. "Why do we all have these powers? Where do they come from? Why now? Why us?"

"It used to be that I could only get a few seconds' worth of secrets," Evie said. "And it was patchy—like watching a movie shown through a broken projector. But in the past six months, it's grown much stronger."

Memphis said, "I couldn't heal since...for a long while. But now it's coming back, and yes, it's much stronger."

"Same for me," Sam said. "When I took that soldier down, he was really gone."

"Ling and I—our powers were stronger when we were together," Henry said.

"It seems that we're all connected," Ling agreed. "Like atoms coming together to make a new molecule."

"But why?" Theta said. "What for?"

"It must mean something," Memphis said. "Was it Henry and Ling battling Wai-Mae in the dream world that got rid of those wraiths? Was it Evie reading those bones and us burying Wai-Mae's remains in the Trinity Church cemetery so she could be at peace that ended the haunting? We don't know."

"You buried her where?" Ling said, eyebrows drawn to a tight V.

"Trinity...cemetery?" Sam said.

Ling threw her hands up. "You can't bury someone in the city! That's bad luck."

"I'm *sorry*," Sam said. "I didn't stop to read up on it."

Memphis continued. "All we know for sure is that it took all of us to stop it for good."

"Has it?" Evie said quietly.

"Has it what?" Memphis asked.

"Has it stopped for good?"

And with that, the conversation broke down into shouting and squabbling. Jericho tried in vain to restore order. He brought the gavel down hard, cracking the table. Sharp static burbled from the Metaphysickometer, silencing everyone. The needle jumped erratically.

"What's that?" Sam said. "Why's it doing that?"

"I don't know," Mabel whispered.

The front door to the museum banged open and shut, the slam echoing through the old mansion.

"Quiet!" Jericho whispered. Everyone crowded together around the table. Jericho lifted the fireplace poker from its holder and held it like Babe Ruth, ready to swing. The clack of shoes echoed in the hallway. The door swung open.

Framed in the doorway, Will stopped short, his gaze traveling from person to person. "Are you starting an orchestra?"

"Will, I—" Sister Walker came up behind Will. "Oh. I didn't know you had company."

"Neither did I," Will said.

Memphis squinted. "Sister Walker?"

"Hello, Memphis. I'm happy to see you here. I've been wanting to talk to you for a long time now."

Will acknowledged Evie with a terse nod. "Hello, Evangeline."

Evie folded her arms across her chest. "Uncle Will," she said coldly.

"Well, Will. Looks as if they're all here at last," Sister Walker said. She took off her hat and shut the door.

A NEW START

On the streets of Chinatown, drums thundered and firecrackers siz-
zled, exploding into pops of light. The Year of the Rabbit had begun.
Neighbors crowded onto second-floor balconies. Children watched
from fire escapes, eager to see the action below. The crowd was smaller
this year; some people still feared the sleeping sickness, even though
there'd been no new cases reported. Still, Mr. Levi had come with his
grandchildren, who thrilled at the sight of the undulating lion dancers. And Mr. and Mrs. Russo, who ran the pastry shop on Mulberry,
had also arrived with several cousins in tow. Everyone clapped and
cheered, delighted by the spectacle and the food and the hope of
the celebration—a new start was always welcome. Couples handed
out red envelopes filled with money, eager for good luck to bless them.
Ling tucked hers into her pocket. Later, she'd add it to her college
fund. But now there was a banquet to serve. The Tea House was filled
with hungry people eager to feast, and the smells of meat and fish, soup
and noodles—the best of her father's kitchen—made Ling's stomach
growl.

Behind the teak screen, Ling poured tea and placed two plates of
oranges and a moon cake on the table: one to honor George, the other
Wai-Mae.

"Happy New Year," she whispered.

Jericho dripped with sweat as he drove himself through his daily physical regimen. He collapsed on the floor. Three hundred push-ups. Two hundred pull-ups. His arms didn't even shake. He made a fist. It was no trouble at all. Silently, he slid open the drawer and took out the leather pouch stashed there beneath his undershirts. The ten empty vials clinked as he unwrapped the strings. Carefully, he removed the stopper in the smaller vial Marlowe had given him, drinking down an ounce of blue serum, enough for the week. Three ounces left. He dropped to the floor and started again.

Evie stepped from a taxi and rushed toward the monolithic WGI building. Her hand was on the door when she heard, from behind, "Look! It's her!" A trio of excited girls huddled together, pointing and whispering.

Here we go, Evie thought. She braced herself as the girls surged forward, then grew befuddled as they ran right past her. She stepped out onto the street to see where they'd gone. The girls had stopped halfway down the block, where they surrounded Sarah Snow.

"We just adore you, Miss Snow," one of the girls chirped.

Sarah beamed. "Bless you all," she said and signed their autograph books.

Henry walked into the Huffstadler Publishing Company wearing a new jacket and holding tightly to the sliver of jade Ling had given him with a curt "Don't lose this."

Behind his desk, David Cohn greeted Henry with a raised eyebrow. "Back for more abuse?"

"I hope not. I wanted to leave my card in case you hear of somebody looking for a rehearsal pianist. I quit the Follies."

"That was either very brave or very dumb. Let's go with brave," David said.

From behind Huffstadler's closed office door, they could hear the publisher berating the Amazing Reynaldo—"What kind of two-bit Diviner can't even let a man with a mistress know that his wife is on the way up?"

Henry and David both grinned.

"Well, thank you," Henry said, tipping his boater.

"Say, Mr. DuBois. I know of a place that sometimes needs piano players. It's a club down in the Village, the Dandy Gentleman." David gave Henry a meaningful look. "You know it?"

Henry nodded. "I do. Swell place for a certain kind of fella."

"Are you a certain kind of fella?"

"Depends who's asking."

"A certain kind of fella. There's a show there tonight, starting around eleven thirty."

"What a coincidence." Henry smiled. "It's possible I might be there around eleven thirty tonight."

As Henry bounded down the steps, the first few bars of a song began to take shape in his head. "A *certain kind of fella . . .*" he sang, and flicked the jade like a coin, catching it cleanly again and again, feeling like a man whose luck was turning for the good.

☀

Sam grabbed the day's mail at the museum, grimacing at the scary-looking notice from the New York State Office of Taxation. He stopped when he came to the envelope addressed to Sam Lloyd—no return address, no name, no stamp. Sam found a letter opener and slit through the envelope's top. An article from the morning's paper fluttered out. It was a brief notice about a man who'd been found under a small hill of powdery coal waste out at the Corona Ash Dump along the Flushing River. The man, who had been strangled, had nothing on him except for a receipt from a radio shop on Cortlandt Street and a motor vehicle operator's license for one Mr. Ben Arnold.

✳

Mabel found herself without an umbrella as the rain came down, so she ducked into a basement bookseller's on Bleecker Street and shook the rain from her arms just as someone else barreled through the front door, hitting her in the back with the doorknob.

"Gee, I'm awfully sorry if I... why, if it isn't Mabel Rose!" The man removed his cap and stuck out his hand, pumping hers in a firm hand-shake. "Remember me? Arthur Brown? Golly, but you're soaked. Heya, Mr. Jenkins!" Arthur called to a small, portly man in a vest reading a book behind the cash register. "Any chance of a towel for my friend?"

Mr. Jenkins offered Mabel a thin dishtowel and she blotted it against her face and hair, trying to preserve what was left of the wash-and-set she'd gotten at the beauty parlor the day before. It was a lost cause, but she had been trained to take on lost causes.

"The others are upstairs, Arthur," Mr. Jenkins said, taking back the towel. "I let them in." Mr. Jenkins suddenly looked nervous. "I hope that was all right."

Arthur nodded. "It's jake. I'm late."

"Late for what?" Mabel asked.

Arthur seemed to be weighing his response, and Mabel was afraid she'd been rude. Arthur glanced toward the drapes at the rear of the shop and back to Mabel. He offered his arm. "Would you like to find out?"

✳

As Memphis rounded the corner of Lenox and 135th Street, the crow found him, keeping pace as it fluttered from newel post to street lamp. Memphis sighed. "Good to see you again, Berenice."

602

"That bird's got something to say to you." Madame Seraphina, the second-most powerful banker in Harlem and the most powerful mambo, stood in the doorway of her Obeah shop, tucked under the stoop of a brownstone. "Birds are messengers from the land of the dead."

"That's what my mother used to say."

Seraphina pointed a long, graceful finger. "There's a weight on you. I can see it. Come. Let me help you."

"No weight on me, ma'am. I don't wear worry," Memphis said, tipping his hat and turning away.

"Stay your feet!" Seraphina commanded. *"Kijan ou rele?"*

"Pardon?"

"What is your name?" she said slowly.

Unease twisted in Memphis's gut. He'd heard mambos could fashion a curse using any bit of personal information, even something as innocent as a name.

"It's Memphis," he answered after a pause. "Memphis Campbell."

"Yes. I already know who you are, Mr. Campbell." Madame Seraphina raised her chin, appraising him. "The Harlem Healer. The Boy Wonder. Not a boy anymore. You Haitian?"

"On my mother's side."

"But you don't speak Creole?"

"Not much."

"It's important to know where you come from, Young Oungan," she clucked. "Come. Let me talk to the *lwas* for you."

"I'm late to meet Papa Charles," Memphis lied.

Madame Seraphina's lips curled into an easy smile that didn't match the flintiness of her eyes. "Papa Charles is sleepy. If he doesn't wake soon, the white man will come in and take all that he has built. Rabbits in the garden," she said, and Memphis didn't know what she meant.

"I just run the numbers."

"You just run the numbers," she mocked and took a sucking breath in through her teeth. "You grew up handsome, I see," she said, laughing

603

at Memphis's embarrassment. Then: "I bet you miss your *manman*. She came to see me once before she passed."

Memphis's head shot up. He'd have to be crazy to take on a real Haitian mambo, but he'd had enough taunting. "Don't talk about my mother. You didn't know her."

Madame Seraphina's shoulders moved just slightly, as if she could barely be bothered to shrug. "There *is* a weight on your soul. I know. I can see." Her smile was gone. "Come and let me help you while I can."

But Memphis was already backing away.

"You'll come to me one day," Madame Seraphina called after Memphis as the crow squawked and squawked.

※

The New Amsterdam Theatre dressing room was a delightful chaos of feathers, sequins, and half-dressed Follies girls pressed close to the mirrors, mouths open in awkward positions as they glued an eyelash into place or lined their peepers with kohl.

When Theta arrived, she found a single red rose on her dressing table. Smiling, she inhaled its spicy sweetness. "Is this for me?"

"Yeah. Special delivery. Oh, you owe me fifty cents. I tipped the boy for you."

"Thanks, Gloria," Theta said, handing over the change. Had Memphis sent it? "Where's the card?"

"Huh. There was one," Gloria said. "There it is! It fell on the floor."

Theta spied the small envelope under the makeup table. She picked it up. *Miss Theta Knight*, it read in neat, curlicued script.

"Who's your fancy man?" Sally Mae teased. There was a stripe of mean in it.

"Your boyfriend," Theta shot back, making the other girls laugh.

Theta bit her lip to try to hide her smile as she slid the small card from its cream-colored envelope. In the next second, she uttered a cry.

"Theta? Whatsa matter, honey?" Gloria asked. They were all looking at her.

604

"Who left this?" Theta whispered.

"I told you, a delivery boy. Kid barely out of short pants. Why?"

Theta didn't hear the end of it. Nearly upending a stagehand wheeling a rack of Follies finery, she bolted down the hall and burst through the stage door, where her breath escaped in staccato puffs in the icy cold. To her left, cars ambled down the street. To her right was the empty alley. No sign of a delivery boy. The buildings dwarfed her but offered no protection. She felt small and alone. Her hands grew hot. She plunged them into the puddle of rainwater atop a garbage can, melting a bit of the metal.

There had been only four words on the card.

Four words that could tear it all down.

Four words that terrified her.

For Betty—found you.

THE HOME OF THE FREE
AND THE BRAVE

The country awakens with the dawn.

The citizens rise and wash, shave and brush. They don stockings and dresses, pants, shirts, and suspenders. They button up their need. Affix their aspirations. Tuck histories neatly inside drawers, creating themselves as they go, a rhapsody of reinvention.

In the West, mountains rise like myths. Morning breezes rustle the frost-stiff edges of grass and wheat across the prairies. Cows huff clouds of steam from flaring nostrils and wait for the relief of the farmer's pail. Rivers bubble with the occasional surprise of a surfacing fish.

Shadow-painted hills play warden to the miners as they trudge toward the shaft's yawning maw, metal pails clanking against their protective charms—the small cross, the rabbit's foot, the lock of hair given by a wife—nestled beside company scrip deep in coverall pockets. Lamps stretch on bands around their heads, an illuminated third eye to calm their fears. They load the platform like sailors setting out for a new world, the breaker boys in front, already coughing in anticipation of the dust that fills their small lungs eight hours a day, six days a week. Wives and mothers, their faces sober in the first pink of morning, wave to them with kerchiefs, prayers on their lips in case the charms don't work, while company guards patrol with clubs to prod the workers and guns to keep the union men at a distance.

From its perch in an iron cage, the canary watches, wary.

The machinery lurches into motion, sending the weary cage of men and boys down to the hidden darkness deep in the heart of the country.

For its heart is rich in dark treasures.

In the scab-tough oil fields of Oklahoma, giant iron derricks peck wounds into the ground. Oil gushes from the broken land like a promise, a baptism in crude hope, fuel for the engines of the nation's desires. The roughnecks bathe in the sudden shower, and though they will never see its riches, never reap the harvest of its black gold, they celebrate as if it could be theirs at any time—a birthright promised to them, the right to life, liberty, and the pursuit of happiness, a race run in perpetuity.

The afternoon sun rises into the wide sky, high and hopeful as a stock market arrow. Frost wears away from the patchy soil, no match for the day's warm optimism. A few hearty buds poke through on the trees. Already they yearn for spring, a constant striving.

In a clapboard one-room church nestled beneath the barren branches of a magnolia tree, a revival reaches its peak. Faithful arms beseech the sky. Bodies rock forward and back, spines bent into question marks, souls waiting for deliverance from doubt and uncertainty, waiting for a reason to fall to their knees in the sawdust with tear-stained cheeks and sin-purged hearts.

The immigrants pour into the cities, and the edges of the neighborhoods fray, then braid themselves into new American patterns. These new Americans push out into this country one step ahead of ancestors touching spectral fingers to the generations of the diaspora. *Go*, they whisper, *but do not forget us.*

Outside a redbrick prison, protestors set up for another day of placards and marches, cries for justice that go unheard by the two Italian anarchists inside—a fishmonger and a shoemaker, seekers of the American dream now appealing their fate in its court while the electric chair bides its time.

The lady in the harbor hoists her torch.

The Gold Mountain twinkles in the early-morning fog hugging the shoreline of California, a pretty mirage.

The atoms vibrate, always on the verge of some new shift.

Shift and the electrons lean toward particle or wave.

Shift and the action requires a reaction.

Shift and the stroke of a typewriter elevates *i* to *I*, changes *God* to *god*.

Shift and the beast acquires a thumb; the thumb, a weapon.

Shift and rights become wrongs; the wrongs, justification.

It's all in the perspective.

Dusk approaches now, stealthy.

Their prayers done, the faithful collapse in an exhausted heap. The preacher's white shirt has gone transparent with sweat. The cicadas raise their collective hymn. Pressed by wind and the weight of unanswered prayers, the trees bend their arms low, brushing the first hope of spring across heads weary with belief.

In another part of town bordering the cotton fields, where three small girls sleep cheek to jowl on a cot at the back of a sharecropper's shack, a fleet of Model Ts and trucks creep forward with headlights off. Men in hooded white robes unfold themselves from these silent vehicles and lumber forward, lugging their own cross and a can of kerosene. Fathers and brothers, uncles and cousins are dragged from the shacks and down the front steps while the women scream—for mercy, for hope, for naught. The rope is hoisted. The kerosene poured. The match is struck against the cross, setting the night on fire, a false light in the dark, and the screams pitch into keening.

Through the radios of the nation, a lady preacher calls out to the lonely: "Are you washed in the blood of the lamb?"

In a tent at a winter's fair, smiling nurses ask questions and gather information from volunteering families. They ask, *Have you ever demonstrated special abilities? Have you ever seen in your dreams a funny man wearing a stovepipe hat? Would you care to have a simple blood test? No, it won't hurt—just a small stick, we promise.* At the end, after the tears and blood, they bandage the children's tiny wounds and deliver to the proud parents a bronze medal: Yea, I have a goodly heritage. Something to crow to the neighbors about.

Another boastful crop in the land of plenty.

The dusty road cuts through sleeping fields, which wave golden with corn in the summer. An old farmhouse sits not far from a weathered barn and a lone, gnarled tree. The tractor and plow are idle. Though it is late, the mailman's truck rattles down the bumpy, mud-swollen road. He parks beside the mailbox, digs inside his pouch, retrieves the letter. After a last check of the address to be sure—number 144—he pushes it inside the mailbox, shuts the door, and lowers the small metal flag.

Night falls on the white-picket fences and red barns. On the Burma Shave signs and billboards for Marlowe Industries reassuring sleepy roadside travelers that all is as it should be. On the searchers, the seekers, the strivers, the dreamers—indefatigable adherents of a can-do spirit. On the unremarkable sedan of the Shadow Men folding into the seams of a night already unfurling its blanket of forgetting across the country as it ushers them into dreams.

The ghosts watch these ministrations. They remember and yearn; some remember and regret. But they remember. They wish they could tell the citizens the secrets they know about the past, about mistakes, about love and desire, hope and choice, about what is important and what is not.

They wish, too, that they could warn them about the gray man in the stovepipe hat, about the King of Crows.

For not all ghosts remember, and the citizens have need of warning.

❋

The Shadow Man walked through the echoing corridor and stopped before the thick steel door bearing the symbol of a radiant eye shedding a lightning-bolt tear. He adjusted his tie, unlocked the door, and entered. The room was simple, rustic in its comforts: A single cot. A nightstand. A toilet and washbasin. The only light came from a ceiling fixture, which was regulated by a man at a switchboard each evening and a different man in the mornings. The right side of the cell was anchored by a simple wooden table and the type of large upholstered chair one might find in any American sitting room. It was the one thing of comfort in the dank room, and the woman sat in it, her eyes closed. The woman was of average height but too thin, and this lack of substance made her nearly into a ghost.

Tonight's dinner sat untouched on its tray. "Mmm, Salisbury steak. My favorite," said the man, whose name was either Hamilton or Washington, or, possibly, Madison.

The woman didn't answer.

"Mashed potatoes. And peas and carrots. Delicious." He slid the fork through the potatoes and circled the utensil near her face. "Open wide."

The woman didn't move. The man dropped the fork back on the tray. "Now, Miriam, if you don't eat, we'll be forced to give you a feeding. You remember how unpleasant that was, don't you?"

The woman's skin twitched along her jawline, assuring the Shadow Man that she did, in fact, remember.

"What, no smile for me?"

Her expression did not change.

"Wouldn't you like to see your family again?"

"I have no family," she whispered.

"All you have to do is find the others and give us the names. Tell us where they are."

The man moved about the room as if accustomed to its contours. He ran a finger along the desk, examining the layer of dust there before rubbing it away. "Afterward, you'll take a nice walk in the woods. You'll like that, won't you, yes? To smell the fresh air? Does it remind you of the birch trees bordering Moscow? Does it smell of home?"

Her reply was feathery light. "This is my home."

"Then it should be no trouble." The Shadow Man placed a hand on the woman's shoulder and she flinched. "Tell us: Where are the Diviners, Miriam? Where are our little chicks who should come home to roost?"

"I don't know. I can't see."

"Would you like to go under the water again?"

The woman's eyes widened in fear but she did not answer. Instead, she closed her eyes and breathed in and out, faster and faster. She meant to run away inside her mind, far from their methods. The Shadow Man meant to stop her.

"Your son is out there, Miriam. Your Sergei."

Her eyelids fluttered. Good. He was getting through.

"We know you managed to send a postcard to him."

"He has no power. It didn't work."

The man whispered directly into her ear, making her skin crawl. "We've seen his power, Miriam. We know you're lying."

The Shadow Man unfolded the newspaper and placed it in front of her. Her eyes darted to the picture. She scooped it up in eager, shaking hands.

DIVINER AND DIVINER!

**Sam Lloyd Saves His Sweetheart Seer from
Crazed Gunman in Times Square, Reveals
Diviner Power to Amazed Crowd**

"He looks an awful lot like you, your Sergei. Same caginess around the eyes. It would be a shame if something were to happen to him. Wouldn't you agree, Miriam?"

"That is not my son. It is someone else," she said at last. Her voice trembled.

"Let's not kid ourselves, shall we? We're far beyond that now. It's him. And he's in danger. They're all in danger, Miriam." The Shadow Man's shoes made a soft, hollow sound as he circled her chair. "Wouldn't it be nice to see him again?"

Again, she refused to answer.

"Miriam, we face threats to our freedom from within and without.

Security is our priority. This is the home of the free and the brave, and it must remain so. But if we don't know where they are, we can't protect them."

He stopped in front of her, forcing her to look up.

"Let's try again."

With a last glance at the front page of the New York *Daily News*, the woman closed her eyes and allowed her mind to wander toward the other world.

"What do you see?"

"Their energy draws him," Miriam said, her voice faraway. Her body shuddered slightly with her efforts.

"Who?"

"The man in the stovepipe hat. The King of Crows."

"Good. What else?"

The woman's shuddering had progressed to shaking as her mind flooded with terror.

"No! You can't let it happen. You mustn't. Not again." With a cry, she broke off and fell against her bed, sweating and crying.

"You must tell us where they are, Miriam."

"N-no."

The Shadow Man sighed. "Very well. We'll try again tomorrow."

The woman wept into her palms. "We never should have done it."

"What's done is done," the Shadow Man said. "You have the thanks of a grateful nation."

Fear showed in the woman's eyes, followed quickly by hate, and then she spat in the Shadow Man's face. The man removed a neat pocket square and calmly wiped the insult from his cheeks. With the same air of calm, he pulled a wrench from his pocket. The woman fell onto her cot, backing into a corner, hands up. The man walked to the other side of the room. He arced the wrench around the knob to the radiator, cutting off the heat.

"It gets rather chilly at night here, I'm afraid," he said, yanking the blanket from her bed. "When you're ready to cooperate fully, Miriam, do let us know."

The man closed the steel door behind him. The lock slid into place. A moment later, the loud babble of a radio flooded the quiet of the small room, growing louder and louder until the woman curled up into a ball and cupped her hands over her ears. But more than the radio, it was what she had seen in her trance that would make sleep impossible tonight.

The Shadow Man had left the newspaper. Miriam smoothed out the front page and placed a hand on the picture of her son and Evie O'Neill.

"Find me, Little Fox," she whispered. "Before it's too late. For all of us."

Author's Note

While *Lair of Dreams* is steeped in actual history, it is also a work of fiction and, as such, some liberties have been taken for dramatic license. ("Stand back, everyone! She's got a license for fictional drama!") The Museum of American Folklore, Superstition, and the Occult is a creation from my imagination, just in case you tried to find it on TripAdvisor. And as far as I know, there are no carnivorous ghosts haunting the subway tunnels of New York City. I'm pretty sure. Well, mostly sure. Okay, not at all sure. You know what? Ride at your own risk.

The Beach Pneumatic Transit Co. really did exist—though, sadly, the little fan-powered train only ran for a few years. Alfred Ely Beach's subway prototype was long gone by 1927, but with plenty of abandoned tunnels and stations in New York City's underground, it's fun to imagine that some ghostly vestige of that old subway station could have existed for our Diviners. If you'd like to know more about Beach Pneumatic, I recommend reading Joseph Brennan's excellent publication on the topic at columbia.edu/~brennan/beach.

Sadly, the Chinese Exclusion Act was all too real. Passed in 1882, it sharply restricted immigration to the United States from China. Even more restrictive legislation followed, and these discriminatory, xenophobic laws stayed on the books for decades. If you'd like to read more about the Chinese Exclusion Act and its impact, I highly recommend Erika Lee's *At America's Gates: Chinese Immigration during the Exclusion Era, 1882–1943* (Chapel Hill: University of North Carolina Press, 2003). If you'd like to read a personal family history of Chinatown, I also recommend Bruce Edward Hall's *Tea That Burns: A Family Memoir of Chinatown* (New York: Simon & Schuster, 1998). And if you find yourself in New York City, please do visit the wonderful Museum of Chinese in America (mocanyc.org).

The story of America is one that is still being written. Many of the ideological battles we like to think we've tucked neatly into a folder called "the past"—issues of race, class, gender, sexual identity, civil rights, justice, and just what makes us "American"—are very much alive today. For what we do not study and reflect upon, we are in danger of dismissing or forgetting. What we forget, we are often doomed to repeat. Our ghosts, it seems, are always with us, whispering that attention must be paid.

Acknowledgments

This was a Busby Berkeley production of a book, and over the past few years, quite a few folks have seen me through it all. (Thanks for the kaleidoscopic legwork, y'all.) I owe a debt of gratitude, a fruit basket, and a One Direction lunch box to the following lovely people:

The incredibly talented, wise, and patient Alvina Ling, editor extraordinaire, and the also talented and wonderful Bethany Strout and Nikki Garcia. You are the Charlie's Angels of Editorial. Boo-ya.

The hardworking LBYR team: Megan Tingley, Andrew Smith, Melanie Chang, Lisa Moraleda, Hallie Patterson, Victoria Stapleton, Jenny Choy, Emilie Polster, Stefanie Hoffman, Adrian Palacios, Tina McIntyre, and Barbara Bakowski. "And ya don't stop."

Wizard designer Maggie Edkins for the spooky, atmospheric book jacket.

The incredible, laser-eyed copyediting/proofreading/fact-checking team: JoAnna Kremer, Christine Ma, and Norma Jean Garriton, respectively. They probably all have PTSD now.

Agent Barry Goldblatt, who deserves some kind of medal for patience and bravery at this point in our long collaboration. Josh Goldblatt—thanks for the manga and anime breaks and for explaining to people, "My mom's not crazy; she's just on deadline."

Heroic assistant Tricia Ready for keeping the ship upright and for the research help, read-throughs, and reminders to grab my keys on the way out. Researcher Lisa Gold, who is true to her name and who doesn't flinch at my midnight e-mails. Bill Zeffiro, for the music info and the quick wit.

The Lovely & Amazing Writing Group—the Spanx of good friends (total support): Pam Carden, Brenda Cowan, Anna Funder, Michelle Hodkin, Cheryl Levine, David Levithan, Emily Lockhart, Dan Poblocki, Nova Ren Suma, Robin Wasserman, and Justin Weinberger. I love you guys. And Laurie Allee and Gayle Forman for all of that, plus saving me many times over. xo

The Brooklyn Tuesday Night Writing Workshop: Emma Bailey, Michelle Hodkin, Ben Jones, Kim Liggett, Julia Morris, Susanna Schrobsdorff, Nova Ren Suma, and Aaron Zimmerman.

The "Away" Team: Holly Black, Cassandra Clare, Jo Knowles, and Kelly Link. And the Fourth of July BBQ Brainstorm Trust: Theo

Black, Elka Cloke, Chris Cotter, Eric Churchill, Holly Rowland, Jeffrey Rowland, Emily Seville Lauer, and Josh Lewis. And Kat Howard, for her critiquing service above and beyond.

The Superhero Librarians Club ("Can we find it? Yes, we can!"): Karyn Silverman, Jennifer Hubert Swan, and Sara Ryan.

This book was written in many NYC & Brooklyn cafés: Thanks to the delightful staff at Think Coffee, Four & Twenty Blackbirds, Southside Coffee, and the late, great Red Horse Café, RIP. Thanks, too, to the Brooklyn Writers Space.

Finally, this book could not have been written without the many wonderful, knowledgeable people who kindly gave of their time and expertise. Their guidance was invaluable, and any mistakes, inaccuracies, or willful jazz riffs on factual information are strictly the fault of the author. Thank you a thousandfold to the Museum of Chinese in America, New York City, and to Yue Ma, associate director of collections; Samantha Chin-Wolner, collections assistant; and Kevin Chu, collections and digital archives assistant, at the MOCA archives. Thank you, Professor Shirley J. Yee, Gender, Women & Sexuality Studies (specializing in the late nineteenth and early twentieth centuries), the University of Washington. Thank you, Zhen Wang Luo and Gabe Law, for the information on Chinese funeral customs. Thank you, Bryan Berlanger, director, National Capital Radio and Television Museum, Bowie, Maryland. Thank you, Carey Stumm and Brett Dion at the New York Transit Authority Archives. Thank you to the Schomburg Center for Research in Black Culture of the New York Public Library. Thank you, Steve Duncan, badass urban explorer and historian, for gleefully detailing the various ways one could be maimed, killed, or arrested running around in NYC's miles of rat-infested subway tunnels. Yeah, I'm good topside, thanks.